COMMAND AUTHORITY

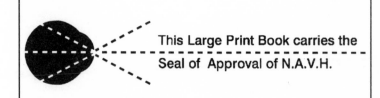

This Large Print Book carries the
Seal of Approval of N.A.V.H.

COMMAND AUTHORITY

TOM CLANCY
WITH MARK GREANEY

THORNDIKE PRESS

A part of Gale, Cengage Learning

GALE
CENGAGE Learning

Detroit • New York • San Francisco • New Haven, Conn • Waterville, Maine • London

LIBRARY OF CONGRESS CATALOGING-IN-PUBLICATION DATA

Clancy, Tom, 1947-2013
    Command authority / by Tom Clancy with Mark Greaney. — Large print edition.
        pages cm — (Thorndike Press large print basic)
    ISBN 978-1-4104-6497-2 (hardcover) — ISBN 1-4104-6497-0 (hardcover)
    1. Ryan, Jack, Sr. (Fictitious character)—Fiction. 2. Ryan, Jack, Jr. (Fictitious character)—Fiction. 3. Large type books. 4. Political fiction. I. Greaney, Mark. II. Title.
    PS3553.L245C66 2013b
    813'.54—dc23   2013042128

Published in 2013 by arrangement with G. P. Putnam's Sons, a member of Penguin Group (USA) LLC, a Penguin Random House Company

PRINCIPAL CHARACTERS

United States Government
John Patrick "Jack" Ryan: President of the United States
Dan Murray: attorney general of the United States
Arnold Van Damm: President's chief of staff
Robert Burgess: secretary of defense
Scott Adler: secretary of state
Mary Patricia Foley: director of the Office of National Intelligence
Jay Canfield: director of the Central Intelligence Agency
Admiral James Greer: director of intelligence, Central Intelligence Agency
Judge Arthur Moore: director of the Central Intelligence Agency
Keith Bixby: chief of station, Kiev, Ukraine, Central Intelligence Agency

The U.S. Armed Forces
Admiral Mark Jorgensen: chairman of the Joint Chiefs of Staff
Eric Conway: Chief Warrant Officer Two, United States Army, OH-58D Kiowa Warrior pilot
Andre "Dre" Page: Chief Warrant Officer Two,

United States Army, OH-58D Kiowa Warrior copilot

Barry "Midas" Jankowski: lieutenant colonel, United States Army, 1st Special Forces Operational Detachment Delta

Harris "Grungy" Cole: captain, United States Air Force, F-16 pilot

The Campus / Hendley Associates

Gerry Hendley: director of The Campus / Hendley Associates

John Clark: director of operations

Domingo "Ding" Chavez: operations officer

Sam Driscoll: operations officer

Dominic "Dom" Caruso: operations officer

Jack Ryan, Jr.: operations officer / intelligence analyst

Gavin Biery: director of information technology

Adara Sherman: director of transportation

The British

Sir Basil Charleston: director general of Secret Intelligence Service (MI6)

Anthony Haldane: international financier, ex–Foreign Office

Victor Oxley aka Bedrock: 22nd Special Air Service Regiment — Officer, British Security Service (MI5)

David Penright: officer, SIS (MI6)

Nicholas Eastling: SIS officer, Counterintelligence Section

Hugh Castor: managing director, Castor and Boyle Risk Analytics Ltd

Sandy Lamont: senior business analyst, Castor and Boyle Risk Analytics Ltd

The Russians / The Ukrainians

Valeri Volodin: president of the Russian Federation

Roman Talanov: director of the Federal Security Service (FSB) of the Russian Federation

Stanislav Biryukov: director of the Foreign Intelligence Service (SVR) of the Russian Federation

Sergey Golovko: ex-director of the Foreign Intelligence Service (SVR) of the Russian Federation

Oksana Zueva: leader of the Ukrainian Regional Unity Party

Tatiana Molchanova: television newscaster, Novaya Rossiya (New Russia)

Dmitri Nesterov, aka Gleb the Scar: *vory v zakonye* ("thief-in-law"), operative of the Seven Strong Men criminal organization

Pavel Lechkov: Seven Strong Men operative

Other Characters

Caroline "Cathy" Ryan: First Lady of the United States

Edward Foley: husband of Mary Pat Foley, former director of the Central Intelligence Agency

Dino Kadić: Croatian assassin

Felicia Rodríguez: Venezuelan university student

Marta Scheuring: "urban guerrilla" of the Red Army Faction

Malcolm Galbraith: owner of Galbraith Rossiya Energy Holdings, Scottish entrepreneur

PROLOGUE

The flag of the Union of Soviet Socialist Republics flew high above the Kremlin in a rain shower, a red-and-gold banner waving under a gray sky. The young captain took in the imagery from the backseat of the taxi as it rolled through Red Square.

The sight of the flag over the seat of power of the largest country in the world jolted the captain with pride, although Moscow would never feel like home to him. He was Russian, but he'd spent the past several years fighting in Afghanistan, and the only Soviet flags he'd seen there had been on the uniforms of the men around him.

His taxi let him out just two blocks from the square, on the north side of the massive GUM department store. He double-checked the address on the drab office building in front of him, paid his fare, and then stepped out into the afternoon rain.

The building's lobby was small and plain; a lone security man eyed him as he tucked his hat under his arm and climbed a narrow staircase that led to an unmarked door on the first floor.

Here the captain paused, brushed wrinkles out of his uniform, and ran his hand over his rows of medals to make certain they were perfectly straight.

Only when he was ready did he knock on the door.

"*Vkhodi!*" Come in!

The young captain entered the small office and shut the door behind him. With his hat in his hand, he stepped in front of the one desk in the room, and he snapped to attention.

"Captain Roman Romanovich Talanov, reporting as ordered."

The man behind the desk looked like he was still in his twenties, which greatly surprised Captain Talanov. He was here to meet a senior officer in the KGB, and he certainly did not expect someone his own age. The man wore a suit and tie, he was small and thin and not particularly fit, and he looked, to the Russian soldier, like he had never spent a day of his life in military service.

Talanov showed no hint of it, of course, but he was disappointed. For him, like every military man, officers in the KGB were divided into two classes. *Sapogi* and *pidzhaki.* Jackboots and jackets. This young man before him might have been a high-ranking state security official, but to the soldier, he was just a civilian. A jacket.

The man stood, walked around the desk, and then sat down on its edge. His slight slouch contrasted with the ramrod-straight posture of the officer standing in front of him.

The KGB man did not give his name. He said, "You just returned from Afghanistan."

"Yes, comrade."

"I won't ask you how it was, because I would not understand, and that would probably just piss you off."

The captain stood still as stone.

The jacket said, "You are GRU Spetsnaz. Special Forces. You've been operating behind the lines in Afghanistan. Even over the border in Pakistan."

It was not a question, so the captain did not reply.

With a smile, the man slouched on the desk said, "Even as a member of the most elite special operations unit in military intelligence, you stand out above the rest. Intelligence, resilience, initiative." He winked at Talanov. "Loyalty."

Talanov's blue eyes were locked on a point on the wall behind the desk, so he missed the wink. With a powerful voice, he replied with a well-practiced mantra: "I serve the Soviet Union."

The jacket half rolled his eyes, but again Talanov missed it. "Relax, Captain. Look at me, not the wall. I am not your commanding officer. I am just a comrade who wishes to have a conversation with another comrade, not a fucking robot."

Talanov did *not* relax, but his eyes did shift to the KGB man.

"You were born in Ukraine. In Kherson, to Russian parents."

"Yes, comrade."

"I am from Saint Petersburg myself, but I spent my summers with my grandmother in Odessa, not far from where you grew up."

"Yes, comrade."

The jacket blew out a sigh, frustrated at the continued formality of the Spetsnaz man. He asked, "Are you proud of those medals on your chest?"

Talanov's face gave away his first emotion now.

11

It was indecision. "I . . . they are . . . I serve the
—"

"You serve the Soviet Union. *Da,* Captain, duly
noted. But what if I told you I wanted you to take
off those medals and never put them back on?"

"I do not understand, comrade."

"We have followed your career, especially the
operations you have conducted behind the lines.
And we have researched every aspect of your
private life, what little there is of it. From this we
have come to the conclusion that you are less
interested in the good of the Communist Party,
and more interested in the work itself. You, dear
Captain, have a slavish desire to excel. But we do
not detect in you any particular passion for the
joys of the collective or any unique wonderment
at the command economy."

Talanov remained silent. Was this a test of his
loyalty to the party?

The jacket continued. "Chairman Chernenko
will be dead in months. Perhaps weeks."

Captain Talanov blinked. *What madness is this
talk?* If someone said such a thing in front of a
KGB man on base back in Afghanistan, they
would be shuffled away, never to be seen again.

The jacket said, "It's true. They hide him from
the public because he's in a wheelchair, and he
spends most of the time up in Kuntsevo at the
Kremlin Clinic. Heart, lungs, liver: Nothing on
that old bastard is working anymore. Gorbachev
will succeed him as general secretary — surely
you've heard he's next in line. Even out in some
cave in Afghanistan, that *must* be common knowledge by now."

The young officer gave up nothing.

"You are wondering how I know this?"

12

Slowly, Talanov said, "*Da,* comrade. I *am* wondering that."

"I know this because I have been told by people who are worried. Worried about the future, worried about where Gorbachev will take the Union. Worried about where Reagan is taking the West. Worried everything might come crashing down on top of us."

There were a few seconds of complete silence in the room, and then the KGB suit said, "Seems impossible, I know. But I am assured there is reason for concern."

Talanov couldn't take it anymore. He needed to know what was going on. "I was ordered to come here today by General Zolotov. He told me I was being considered for recruitment into a special project for the KGB."

"Misha Zolotov knew what he was doing when he sent you to me."

"You *do* work for the KGB, yes?"

"I do, indeed. But more specifically, I work for a group of survivors. Men in KGB and GRU, men who know that the continued existence of our organizations *is* the survival of the nation, the survival of the people. The Kremlin does not run this nation. A certain building in Dzerzhinsky Square runs this nation."

"The KGB building?"

"*Da.* And I have been tasked with protecting this building, not the Communist Party."

"And General Zolotov?"

The jacket smiled. "Is in the club. As I said, a few in GRU are on board."

The man in the suit came very close now, his face inches from the chiseled cheekbones of Roman Talanov. In a voice barely above a whisper he said, "If I were you I would be saying to myself, 'What the fuck is going on? I thought I was being recruited into the KGB, but instead I've just met a crazy man talking about the impending death of the general secretary and the possibility of the fall of the Union.' "

Talanov turned to face him and squared his shoulders. "Every word you've said here, comrade, is treasonous."

"That is true, but as there are no recording devices in this room, it would take you to stand up as a witness against me. That would not be wise, Captain Talanov, as those survivors that I mentioned are at the very top, and they would protect me. What they would do to you, I can only imagine."

Talanov looked back to the wall. "So . . . I am being asked to join the KGB, but not to do the work of the KGB. I will, instead, do the work of this group of leaders."

"That's it, exactly, Roman Romanovich."

"What will I be doing specifically?"

"The same sort of things you have been doing in Kabul and Peshawar and Kandahar and Islamabad."

"Wet work?"

"Yes. You will help ensure the security of the operation, despite what changes the Soviet Union undergoes in the next few years. In return, you will be protected no matter what might happen in the future regarding the Union."

"I . . . I still do not understand what you think will happen in the future."

"Are you listening to me? It's not what *I* think. How the fuck should *I* know? It's like this, Talanov. The USSR is a large boat, you and I are

14

two of the passengers. We are sitting on the deck, thinking everything is just perfect, but then" — the KGB man moved around the room dramatically, as though he was acting out a scene — "wait . . . what's this? Some of the boat's best officers are preparing to abandon ship!"

He moved back in front of Talanov. "I might not see the iceberg in our path, but when those in charge are looking for the *fucking* lifeboat, I'm smart enough to pay attention.

"Now . . . I have been asked to tend to the lifeboat, a great responsibility entrusted to me by the officers." The jacket grinned. "Will you help me with the lifeboat?"

Captain Talanov was a straightforward man. The metaphors were starting to piss him off. "The lifeboat. What *is* it?"

The jacket shrugged his narrow shoulders. "It's money. It's just fucking money. A series of black funds will be established and maintained around the world. I will do it, and you will help me keep the funds secure from threats both inside and outside the Union. It will be a simple assignment, a few years in duration, I should think, but it will require the best efforts of us both."

The man in the suit walked to a small refrigerator that sat against the wall between two bookshelves. He pulled out a bottle of vodka, and then he grabbed two stemmed shot glasses from a shelf. He came back to the desk and filled them both.

While he did all this, Captain Roman Talanov just looked on.

"Let's have a drink to celebrate."

Talanov cocked his head. "Celebrate? I haven't agreed to anything, comrade."

"No. You haven't." The man in the suit smiled

15

and passed over one of the glasses to the bewildered military man. "Not yet. But you will come around soon enough, because you and I are the same."

"The same?"

The jacket raised his glass to Talanov. "Yes. Just like the men at the top who came up with this scheme, you and I are both survivors."

1

The black Bronco shot through the storm, its tires kicking up mud and water and grit as it raced along the gravel road, and rain pelted the windshield faster than the wipers could clear it.

As the truck charged along at sixty miles an hour, the back doors opened and two armed men climbed out and into the rain, one on each side. The men stood on the running boards and held on to the door frame with gloved hands. Their eyes were protected from the mud and flying rocks and water by large goggles, but their black Nomex suits and the submachine guns around their necks were wet and mud-splattered in moments along with the rest of their gear: helmets with integrated headsets, ballistic protection on their chests and backs, knee and elbow pads, and magazine pouches. Everything was soaked and caked with mud by the time the Bronco closed on a cabin in the center of a rain-swept pasture.

The vehicle decelerated quickly, skidding to a stop just twenty feet from the front door. The two men on the running boards leapt off and raced toward the building, their weapons scanning the trees all around, searching for any targets. The driver of the Bronco joined soon after; just like the others, he carried an H&K submachine gun with a fat silencer on the end of the barrel.

The three operators formed in a tight stack near the entrance, and the man in front reached forward and tried the door latch.

It was locked.

The man in the back of the stack — the driver — stepped forward now, without a word. He let his H&K drop free on his chest, and he reached behind his back and pulled a pistol-grip shotgun from his pack. The weapon was loaded with Disintegrator breaching rounds: three-inch magnum shells with fifty-gram projectiles made of a steel powder bound by plastic.

The operator placed the barrel of the shotgun six inches from the top hinge of the door, and he fired a Disintegrator directly into the hinge. With an enormous boom and a wide blast of flame, the steel powder load slammed into the wood, blowing the hinge from the door frame.

He fired a second round into the lower hinge, then kicked the door, which fell into the room beyond.

The shotgunner stepped to the side and the two men holding automatic weapons rushed into the dark room, guns up and weapon lights burning arcs in the black. The driver restowed his shotgun, grabbed his H&K, and joined up with the others in the room.

Each man had a sector to clear and did so quickly and efficiently. In three seconds they began moving toward a hallway that led to the rear of the cabin.

Two open doorways were in front of them now, one on each side of the hall, with a closed door down at the end. The first and second men in the train peeled away; number one went left through the doorway, and number two went into the room on the right. Both men found targets and fired; suppressed rounds thumped loudly in the confined space of the cabin.

While the first two men were engaging in the rooms, the lone man still in the hallway kept his weapon trained on the door ahead, knowing full well he would be exposed from behind if anyone entered the cabin from the outside.

Quickly the two men returned to the hallway and aimed their guns forward, and the man at the rear turned around to check behind them. A second later they moved on to the closed door. They stacked up again, and the first man quietly checked the latch.

It was unlocked, so he paused only long enough to lower his body a few inches while his mates did the same. Then the three men moved in as a team, and the lights under the three guns swept their sectors.

They found their precious cargo in the center of the unlit space. John Clark sat in a chair, his hands in his lap, squinting straight into the bright lights. Inches from him on both his left and his right, the tactical lights illuminated two figures standing, and a partial face of a third man was just visible behind Clark's own head.

The three gunmen in the doorway — Domingo Chavez, Sam Driscoll, and Dominic Caruso — all fired simultaneously. Short bursts from their weapons cracked in the room, flashes erupted from their muzzles, and the scent of gun smoke replaced the dank smell of mold in the cabin.

John Clark did not move, did not even blink, as

the bullets slammed into the three figures around him.

Holes appeared in the foreheads of the targets, but the figures did not fall. They were wooden stands, upon which photorealistic images of armed men had been attached.

Quickly the tactical lights scanned the rest of the room independently, and one of them centered on fourth and fifth figures, positioned next to each other in a far corner. The wooden target on the left was the image of a man with a detonator in his hand.

Ding Chavez double-tapped this target in the forehead.

A second light swept to the corner and il-luminated the image of a beautiful young woman holding an infant in her right arm. In her left hand, low and partially hidden behind her leg, she held a long kitchen knife.

Without a moment's hesitation, Dom Caruso shot the female target in the forehead.

Seconds later a call came from across the room. "Clear," Driscoll said.

"Clear," Caruso repeated.

"We're clear," Ding confirmed.

John Clark stood up from his chair in the center of the room, rubbing his eyes after catching the full intensity of three 200-lumen tactical lights. "Make your weapons safe."

Each of the three operators thumbed the safety of his MP5 on and let his weapon hang freely from his chest.

Together the four men surveyed the holes in the five targets and then headed outside the room and checked the targets in the rooms off the hall. They stepped outside of the dark cabin, where they stood together on the porch to stay out of the rain.

"Thoughts, Ding?" Clark asked.

Chavez said, "It was fair. It slowed things down when I had to catch up to the guys so we could stack up at the door. But any way we roll this, if we want to breach with at least three operators, we're going to have to wait on the driver."

Clark conceded the point. "That's true. What else?"

Caruso said, "When Ding and Sam engaged in the rooms off the hall, I was on my own. I covered the space we hadn't cleared yet, which was the doorway at the end of the hall, but I couldn't help thinking it would have been nice to have one more man to check six. Any hostiles who entered from the outside would have had an open shot at the back of my head. I kept my head on a swivel, but it's not the same as having another gun in the fight."

Clark nodded. "We are a small force."

"Smaller now without Jack Junior," Dom Caruso added.

Driscoll said, "We might want to think about bringing someone new into the unit."

"Jack will be back," Chavez replied. "You know as well as I do that as soon as we reactivate he won't be able to stay away."

"Maybe so," said Dom. "But who knows when that will happen."

Clark said, "Be patient, kid," but it was clear to the others on the porch that Clark himself was champing at the bit to do something more impactful with his time. He was a warrior, he'd been in the middle of most every conflict the United States had been involved in for more than forty years, and although he'd retired from active operations with The Campus, he was clearly ready to do more than train.

Clark looked out off the porch at the Bronco now; its doors were wide open, and the storm had only increased in intensity. By now the floorboards would have an inch of standing water, and the torn fabric upholstery would be waterlogged. "Glad I told you to use the farm truck."

Ding said, "It needed a good interior detailing."

The men laughed.

"All right. Back to work," Clark said. "You guys head back up the road, wait twenty minutes, and then try again. That will give me time to rehang the front door and move the configuration around. Dom, your grouping on the second target in the bedroom could have been a little tighter."

"Roger that," Dom said. He'd fired his MP5 three times at target two, and all three rounds had struck the target's head within two and a half inches of one another, but he wasn't going to argue the point with Clark. Especially since all of Driscoll's and Chavez's targets had sub-two-inch groupings.

"And Sam," Clark said. "I'd like to see you breach the door a little lower. If you can get your head down another three inches as you enter, it could mean the difference between catching a round to the forehead and just getting a haircut."

"Will do, Mr. C."

Dom started to head off the porch, but he looked out at the weather. "No chance we are going to wait for the rain to stop before trying this again?"

Ding walked straight out into the mud and stood under the heavy downpour. "I had a drill instructor back at Fort Ord, an Alabama redneck but a hell of a DI, who liked to say, 'If it ain't rainin', you ain't trainin'.' "

Clark and Dom laughed, and even Sam Driscoll, the quietest of the bunch, cracked a smile.

EASTERN EUROPE

© 2013 Jeffrey L. Ward

2

The Russian Federation invaded its sovereign neighbor on the first moonless night of spring. By dawn their tanks ground westward along highways and back roads as if the countryside belonged to them, as if the quarter-century thaw from the Cold War had been a dream.

This was not supposed to happen here. This was Estonia, after all, and Estonia was a NATO member state. The politicians in Tallinn had promised their people that Russia would never attack them now that they had joined the alliance.

But so far, NATO was a no-show in this war.

The Russian ground invasion was led by T-90s — fully modernized fifty-ton tanks with a 125-millimeter main gun and two heavy machine guns, explosive-reactive armor, and a state-of-the-art automated countermeasure system that detected inbound missiles and then launched missiles of its own to kill them in midair. And behind the T-90 warhorses, BTR-80 armored transporters carried troops in their bellies, disgorging them when necessary to provide cover for the tanks, and then retrieving them when all threats had been neutralized.

So far, the land war was proceeding nominally

for the Russian Federation.

But it was a different story in the air.

Estonia had a good missile defense system, and Russia's attack on their early-warning systems and SAM sites had been only marginally successful. Many SAM batteries were still operational, and they had shot down more than a dozen Russian aircraft and kept dozens of others from executing their missions over the nation.

The Russians did not yet own the skies, but this had not slowed down their land advance at all.

In the first four hours of the war, villages were flattened, towns lay in rubble, and many of the tanks had yet to fire their main guns. It was a rout in the making, and anyone who knew anything about military science could have seen it coming, because the tiny nation of Estonia had focused on diplomacy, not on its physical defense.

Edgar Nõlvak had seen it coming, not because he was a soldier or a politician — he was a schoolteacher — but he had seen it coming because he watched television. Now as he lay in a ditch, bloody and cold, wet and shaking from fear, his ears half destroyed from the sustained crashing of detonating shells fired from the Russian tanks poking out of the tree line on the far side of the field, he retained the presence of mind to wish like hell his country's leaders had not wasted time with diplomacy in Brussels, and had instead spent their time constructing a *fucking* wall to keep the *fucking* Russians out of his *fucking* village.

There had been talk of an invasion for weeks, and then, days earlier, a bomb exploded over the border in Russia, killing eighteen civilians. On the television the Russians blamed the Estonian Internal Security Service, a preposterous claim given credence by Russia's slick and state-sponsored media. They showed their manufactured proof and then the Russian president said he had no choice but to order a security operation into Estonia to protect the Russian people.

Edgar Nõlvak lived in Põlva; it was forty kilometers from the border, and he'd spent his youth in the seventies and eighties fearing that someday tanks would appear in that very tree line and shell his home. But over the past twenty-three years that fear had been all but forgotten.

Now the tanks were here, they'd killed scores of his fellow townspeople, and they would surely kill him with barely a pause on their way west.

Edgar had gotten a call two hours earlier from a friend who lived in Võuküla, several kilometers to the east. His friend was hiding in the woods, and in a voice flat and detached from shock he told Edgar the Russian tanks had rolled on past his village after firing only a few shells, as there was nothing in Võuküla except for some farmhouses and a gas station. But behind the tanks and the soldiers in the armored personnel carriers, just minutes behind them, in fact, a force of irregulars came in pickup trucks, and they were now systematically burning and pillaging the town.

At that moment Edgar and the other men with him here sent their families away, and then, bravely or foolishly, they'd taken their rifles into the ditch to wait for the armor to pass and for the irregulars to appear. They could do nothing to stop the tanks, but they would not let their village be burned to the ground by Russian *civilians*.

This plan evaporated the instant a half-dozen tanks broke off the main force moving up the highway, formed a picket line in the trees, and

27

then began pounding Põlva with high-explosive rounds.

This was Edgar's childhood nightmare come to life.

Edgar and the men with him had vowed to fight to the death. But then the tanks came; this was no fight.

This was just death.

The schoolteacher had been wounded almost immediately. As he moved from one position to another he'd been caught in the open as a round hit the high school's parking lot. Shrapnel from an exploding station wagon had sliced through his legs, and now he lay in the mud on his rifle, waiting for the end.

Edgar Nõlvak did not know much about military things, but he was sure that at the pace they were moving, the Russians would be in the city of Tartu, to the north of his village, by midafternoon.

A sound like paper tearing filled the air. He'd been listening to this sound for an hour, and he knew it meant incoming fire. He pressed his face back into the cold mud.

Boom!

Behind him, a direct hit on the gymnasium of the high school. The aluminum-and-cinder-block walls blew out ahead of a billowing cloud; the wood flooring of the basketball court rained down in splinters over Edgar.

He looked again over the edge of the ditch. The tanks were only a thousand meters to the east.

"Where the *fuck* is NATO?"

One thousand meters away, Captain Arkady Lapranov stood in the open hatch of his tank, Storm

Zero One, and shouted, "Where the *fuck* is my air cover?"

It was a rhetorical question; the commanders of the five other tanks he controlled heard it but did not respond, and the two men in his vehicle, the driver and the gunner, waited silently for orders. They knew there were helicopter gunships they could call forward if any air threats appeared, but so far they'd seen no sign of Estonian aircraft, nor had the Russian airborne warning and control system detected any aircraft in the area on radar.

The skies were clear.

This was a good day. A tanker's dream.

A thousand meters away the cloud of dust and smoke over the gymnasium settled enough so that Lapranov could see behind it. Into his mike he said, "I want more rounds in that building beyond the previous target. HE-FRAG. Without proper air support I am not moving forward on that road until I can see what's to the right of the intersection."

"Yes, sir!" Lapranov's gunner shouted from below.

The gunner pressed a button, and the autoloader computer chose a high-explosive-fragmentation round from the magazine, and its mechanical arm chambered it. The gunner used his video-viewing device to find the building, then put his forehead against the rubber pad on the sight panel and aimed his crosshairs on target. He pushed the fire button on the control panel, and then, with a violent lurch, the 125-millimeter smoothbore gun launched a shell through the blue sky, across the fallow field in front of them, and directly into the building.

"Hit," said the gunner.

They had been proceeding like this all morning. So far they had moved through four villages, shelling big targets with their 125-millimeter gun and raking small targets with their coaxial machine guns.

Lapranov had expected more resistance, but he was starting to allow for the fact that Russia's president, Valeri Volodin, had been right. Volodin had told his nation NATO would have no stomach to fight for Estonia.

In his headset, Lapranov heard a transmission from one of the tanks under his command.

"Storm Zero Four to Storm Zero One."

"Go, Zero Four."

"Captain, I have movement in a ditch in front of the last target. Range one thousand. I see multiple dismounts."

Lapranov looked through his binoculars, scanning slowly across the ditch.

There. Heads popped up out of the mud, then disappeared again. "I see them. Small-arms position. Don't waste a one-twenty-five. We'll clean them up with the coax when we get closer."

"Roger."

Another salvo was fired into the buildings on a low hill beyond the intersection, and Lapranov scanned through his optics. The town was deathly quiet; there was virtually no resistance.

"Keep firing," he ordered, then he knelt back down into his commander's station to get a pack of cigarettes and a lighter. "Wipe this place off the map."

Seconds later, another transmission came through his headset: "Storm Zero Two to Storm Zero One."

"Go," Lapranov said as he lit his smoke.

"Movement to the south of the hospital. I . . . I think it is a vehicle."

Lapranov dropped his lighter back inside and looked through his binoculars. It took a moment to find the area; the hospital was a few kilometers beyond the high school, on a small hill. But he scanned to the south of the building and finally he saw the movement on the road in the shadows.

At first he thought he was looking at a jeep, or maybe an SUV.

Another T-90 called in. "Storm Three to Storm One. I think it's a helicopter."

"Nyet," said Lapranov, but he looked closer. The dark vehicle seemed to stop at an intersection, then began moving laterally into a parking lot.

"What the *fuck*?" Lapranov said. "Maybe it is a helo. Gunner, can you ID it through your Catherine?" The Catherine long-range fire-control thermal imager built into each tank allowed the gunner to see distant targets on a video screen. Lapranov himself had access to a Catherine screen, but he'd have to sit down inside the turret for that, and he was having too much fun up here.

The gunner came over Storm Zero One's intercom. "Confirmed light helicopter. Single rotor. Can't make out markings — he is behind a truck in the shade. Shit, he is low. His skids must be just a meter aboveground."

"Armament?" Lapranov asked. He squinted into his binoculars to get a better view himself.

"Um . . . wait. He has twin pylons with machine guns. No missiles." The gunner chuckled. "This guy wants to come out and play against us with his pop guns?"

Lapranov heard a commander of one of the other tanks on the net laughing.

But the captain did not laugh. He took a long drag on his cigarette. "Designate it as a target."

"Roger. Designated as a target."

"Range to target?"

"Four thousand two hundred fifty meters."

"Shit," Lapranov said.

The effective range of the 9M119 Refleks missile system, used against tanks as well as low and slow aircraft like helicopters, was four thousand meters. This small helo hovered just out of range.

"Where is my air support? They should have seen this fucker on radar."

"They won't see his signature. He's moving between the buildings. Too low to the ground. He must have flown over the hill through the entire town like that to stay off radar. Whatever the hell he's doing, he's a good pilot."

"Well, I don't like him. I want him dead. Call in some support. Pass on his coordinates."

"*Da,* Captain."

"All Storm units, load HE-FRAG and resume the attack."

"*Da!*"

Within seconds, all six tanks fired 125-millimeter main gun rounds into the buildings at the center of Põlva, killing four and injuring nineteen with this single salvo.

BATTLE FOR PÕLVA

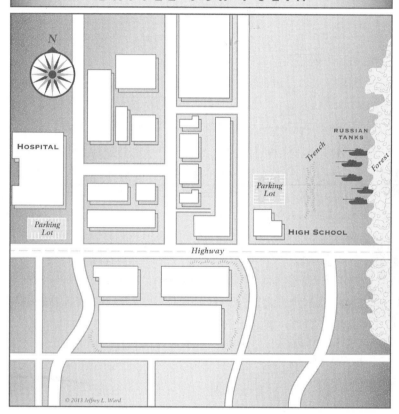

© 2013 Jeffrey L. Ward

3

Edgar Nõlvak heard the shells tear through the sky overhead, and he looked back over his shoulder in time to see them impact against the city hall and the bus station. When the smoke cleared, he noticed a vehicle moving along a road, higher on the hillside. At first he thought it was a black or green SUV; it even seemed to stop in a parking lot. It was difficult to see because it was shaded by the big hospital building next to it, but eventually Edgar realized what it was.

It was a black helicopter. Its skids were no more than one or two meters above the ground.

The man lying next to him in the mud grabbed Edgar by the arm. He pointed at the helicopter and shouted hysterically. "They are behind us! They are attacking from the west!"

Edgar stared at the helicopter, unsure. Finally he said, "It's not Russian. I think it is a news helicopter."

"They are *filming* this? They are just going to watch us die?"

Edgar looked back to the tanks as another shell came crashing down, hitting just sixty meters from the ditch where he lay. Mud rained down on him and the others. "They are going to die themselves if they don't get the hell out of here."

Lapranov was enjoying his cigarette. As he took a long drag, a transmission came through on the net. "Storm Zero Four to Storm Zero One."

"Go, Four."

"Sir, looking at that helo again on the Catherine . . . there seems to be some sort of a pod above the main rotor."

"A what?"

"A pod, sir."

Upon hearing the last transmission, Lapranov dropped down into the commander's compartment and looked at his own Catherine long-range monitor. He could see the helo better now. Yes. There was a round device on top of the main rotor shaft of the little aircraft.

"What the hell is —"

The cigarette fell from his mouth.

Oh, shit.

Lapranov had studied the silhouette of every aircraft flown by every NATO force. Softly, he said, "That's . . . that's an OH-58."

The driver in Storm Zero One came over the net. "Negative, sir. The Estonians don't have —"

Lapranov shouted into his mike now as he launched upward, frantically grabbing at the hatch handle so he could pull his turret hatch shut. "It's the *fucking* Americans!"

Chief Warrant Officer Two, Eric Conway, U.S. Army, Bravo Troop, 2nd Squad, 17th Cavalry Regiment of the 101st Airborne Division, glanced down at his multifunction display and looked at the thermal image of Russian tanks in the trees more than two miles away. Then he returned his attention to his blades above. The tips of the four main rotor blades of the OH-58D Kiowa Warrior spun perilously close to the walls of buildings on either side of the street. If he did not hold his cyclic perfectly steady he would strike one of the buildings and send his helo spinning and crashing, and his own poor flying would kill him and his copilot even before the Russian tanks got their chance.

Satisfied he was steady, he blew out a long breath to calm himself, then spoke through his intercom. "You ready, dude?"

His copilot, CW2 Andre Page, replied calmly, " 'Bout as ready as I'm gonna get."

Conway nodded, then said, "Lase target."

"Roger. Spot on."

Quickly Conway keyed his mike to broadcast on the fires net. "Blue Max Six Six, Black Wolf Two Six. Target lased."

Four full miles beyond the OH-58D Kiowa Warrior, hidden behind the relative safety of a forested hill, two massive Apache Longbow attack helicopters hovered low over a pasture just north of the village of Aarna. The flight leader, Blue Max Six Six, received the transmission from the scout helo at the same time his copilot/gunner, seated in front of and below him, saw the laser spot tracker on his multifunction display indicating a laser fix on the first target, several miles away.

"Roger, Black Wolf Two Six. Good laser. Stand by for remote Hellfire mission."

The Kiowa Warrior scout helo hovering over the town of Põlva was not heavily armed. But its power was not in its onboard stores; rather, its power came from its ability to find and fix targets for the big Apache gunships behind it. This was VCAS, very close air support, and CW2 Conway and his copilot had taxed their skills to the limit by, essentially, driving their helo through the village to stay off enemy radar so they could get into position to scout for the Apaches.

"Roger, Blue Max Six Six. We're gonna need to hurry this up. We are out in the open."

In the tree line, the commander of the tank on the northern flank of Lapranov's squadron shouted into his microphone: "Storm Zero One, this is Storm Zero Six. Laser warning!"

"Shit!" Lapranov muttered into his headset. The little helicopter in the distance may not have been armed with missiles of its own, but it was, apparently, designating targets for some unseen aircraft.

"Arena systems on!" he commanded.

The T-90's Arena countermeasure system used Doppler radar to detect an inbound threat to the tank. As soon as the attacking projectile was within range, the Arena-equipped tank would fire a defensive rocket designed to close to within two meters of the missile before exploding, destroying the threat.

Lapranov next said, "This helo is spotting for Apaches or jets. Where is my air cover?"

The commander of Storm Zero Five answered back: "Inbound in ten minutes."

Lapranov slammed his fist into the wall of his commander's console. "All tankers, load Refleks."

The 9M119 Refleks guided missile round was designed to fire from the main gun, then "grow" fins and race toward its target. It would take the six gunners upward of thirty seconds to unload the high-explosive shell already chambered in the main gun and then have the autoloader replace it with a Refleks.

Storm Zero Two said, "Target is beyond effective range, sir."

Lapranov shouted, "Just do it, damn you!" He hoped like hell firing all six missiles at the little Kiowa Warrior on the hill would force the American chopper to break its laser targeting sequence long enough for the Storm tanks to get back into the cover of the forest.

Four miles due west, hovering north of the village of Aarna, the two Apache Longbows each carried eight Hellfire missiles. On command from the flight lead, both gunners launched. As the Hellfires flashed through the blue sky toward an unseen target in the east, the Apache lead transmitted to the scout helo in Põlva.

"Be advised, Black Wolf Two Six. Multiple Hellfires off the rails and inbound, target Alpha."

In Storm Zero One, Captain Arkady Lapranov saw the streaking blip on his Catherine. He knew it was heading to Zero Six, as that was the tank whose laser indicator alarm had sounded.

The first Hellfire missile appeared above the hill as a tiny quivering spark of light. On the backdrop of blue sky, there was no perspective to show it was approaching for several seconds, but then it angled down toward the tree line.

Storm Zero Six's automatic Arena system saw the incoming Hellfire missile, and it launched a rocket to defend itself from it. Fifty meters from impacting the tank, the Hellfire exploded, sending metallic shrapnel all through the trees.

The Arena worked once, but the second inbound Hellfire came too quickly behind, before the Arena could reset and reacquire the new target. The missile slammed into Storm Zero Six's turret before the system could launch another defensive rocket.

Lapranov was inside the commander's station of his tank with his hatch closed, and Zero Six was one hundred twenty meters to the north of him, but still the explosion sent pieces of metal pinging off the hull of his tank.

A second tank, Storm Zero Two, fired two Arena defensive rounds a moment later, and it managed to survive two inbound Hellfires. As the second missile was destroyed in front of Zero Two, Storm Zero Five announced it was now being painted by a laser beam.

Zero Five disintegrated a moment later.

Lapranov gave up on the Refleks missiles; the four remaining tanks' autoloaders were still in the process of selecting the right projectile from the magazine.

Lapranov shouted, "Fire smoke and disengage!" to all Storm units, and then in his own intercom, "Driver, get us out of here! Back! Back! Back!"

"*Da,* Captain!"

In the Kiowa Warrior hovering four feet above the ground in Põlva, Eric Conway and Andre Page watched while the four remaining tanks began pulling back away from the town, trying to get into the cover of the trees. A dozen huge bursts of white smoke all around them shrouded them in a puffy cloud.

Page said, "They're popping smoke and bugging out."

Conway spoke calmly into his mike: "Change

39

polarity."

"Roger," answered Page, and he switched his thermal imaging system from white hot to black hot.

On the screen in front of them, the four tanks hiding in the wide cloud suddenly appeared as plain as day.

In Conway's headset he heard, "Black Wolf Two Six, be advised, two more missiles away."

"Keep sending 'em," Conway said.

While Page pointed his laser on the fourth tank from his left, Conway moved his attention back to his rotor blades. He'd come left a little; the tips were only six feet from impacting the second floor of the hospital. He checked the right side quickly, saw he had a little more clearance over there, so he smoothly rocked the cyclic to his right and re-centered his helicopter in the parking lot.

In the trees one of the T-90s' countermeasure systems fired, and small explosions flashed on the TIS image. They were nothing, however, compared with the massive detonation of the fifty-ton tank that happened a second later when the trailing Hellfire slammed into its turret from above.

"Good hit, Blue Max. Target destroyed. New target lased."

"Roger, Black Wolf Two Six. Firing . . . missiles off the rails and inbound."

Lapranov's Storm Zero One was twenty-five meters back in the trees when the tank's laser warning indicator sounded. He screamed for the driver to get them deeper in the woods, and the T-90 shredded a path through the pines as it tried to retreat.

Moments later, Zero One's own automatic

countermeasure system fired. The captain could do nothing but grab on to the handholds above him and shut his eyes.

The moment of panic and sheer terror experienced by Arkady Lapranov did not translate to any empathy for the men and women in the homes he had blown apart throughout the morning. He cowered in his commander's control center and hoped like hell the Arena would save him.

His countermeasures saved him twice, but a third missile broke through, slammed into the Kontakt-5 explosive-reactive armor, triggering a detonation on the skin designed to blunt the incoming round's power, but the Hellfire tore into the steel of the fifty-ton tank like a bullet through flesh. The three men inside died microseconds after the Hellfire warhead's detonation, the turret of the T-90 fired one hundred fifty feet straight up, and the vehicle itself was knocked back like a plastic toy slammed on a concrete driveway. It exploded, pieces of armor ripped through the forest, and secondary explosives sent flames and black smoke billowing into the cold sky.

A minute later CW2 Eric Conway transmitted his battle damage assessment over the fires net. "Blue Max Six Six, Black Wolf Two Six. Good hit. I see no further targets."

From behind him, the Apache Longbow lead said, "Roger, we are RTB."

Conway held his gloved fist high, and Page bumped it with his own fist, and then Black Wolf Two Six banked to the north and began both climbing and rotating at the same time. It picked up horizontal speed and shot over the four-story

41

hospital on its way back to base.

In the ditch a kilometer or so to the east, Edgar Nõlvak had risen to a sitting position so he could get a better look at the six smoldering tanks in the tree line.

There was no cheering or celebration in the mud. The men here only half understood what had just happened, and they had no way of knowing if the next wave of Russian war machines was even now rolling through the forest. Still, they took advantage of the end of the attack. Some ran to their cars to bring them closer, while others dragged the injured out of the ditch and toward the parking lot so they could be transported to the hospital in the civilian vehicles.

Rough, unsure hands grabbed Edgar Nõlvak and pulled him along. He slid through the mud, wincing with the pain in his legs that was only now becoming apparent, and he said a silent prayer for his village, for his country, and for the world, because he had the feeling he was witness today to the beginning of something very bad.

The battle of Põlva was recorded as the first engagement between NATO and Russia, but by late afternoon a dozen such incidents had taken place throughout eastern Estonia.

Russia's war plan had hinged on NATO remaining unwilling or unable to support its member state. Russia's gamble had failed, and it withdrew from Estonia the next day, claiming the entire exercise as a success: The country's only intention had been to root out terrorists in some villages along the border, and this had been achieved.

Everyone in the West knew, however, that Russia

had wanted to drive all the way to Tallinn, and its failure to do so was nothing less than a total defeat for Valeri Volodin. It was clear to all, probably even to Volodin himself, that he had underestimated the resolve of NATO in general, and the USA in particular.

But while the celebrations in the West erupted with the Russian withdrawal, officials in the Kremlin were already moving on past this setback and working on a new plan to move its power to the West.

And this plan would be sure to take into account the danger posed by the United States.

4

Two attractive twenty-somethings sat at a table in the center of the pub. This was like most Wednesday nights for Emily and Yalda; they drank their ales and they complained about their jobs at the Bank of England. It was nearly eleven p.m., and the bulk of the after-work crowd was long gone, but the two women always worked late on Wednesdays, putting together reports that were both tedious and stressful. To reward themselves for their efforts, they had developed the habit of popping in here at the Counting House pub for dinner, drinks, and gossip, before heading to the Tube and their flats in the East End.

They'd been keeping up this ritual for a year, and by now they knew all the regulars at the Counting House, if not by name, at least by sight.

This was The City of London, London's financial center. Virtually all of the men and women who frequented the establishment were regulars who came from the trading houses, banks, investment firms, and the stock exchange, all located in this section of town. Of course, there were strangers in and out each Wednesday, but rarely anyone who generated much interest.

Tonight, however, there was a new face in the

crowd, and Emily and Yalda's work talk trailed off quickly as soon as they saw him walk through the door.

He was a tall man in his late twenties or early thirties, in a stylish gray suit that said money and class, and even the conservative cut of his jacket could not hide the physicality of his body underneath.

He was alone, and he found a booth in the corner of the bar area, unscrewed the tiny tealight bulb on the table, and sat down in the low light. When the waitress came by a moment later he ordered, and soon a pint of lager was delivered to him. He looked at his beer while he drank it, checked his phone a couple of times, but otherwise he seemed lost in deep thought.

His disinterest and brooding appearance only increased his stock with Emily and Yalda, who watched him from across the room.

By the time he started on his second pint, the two women from the Bank of England were halfway through their third. They were no shrinking violets; usually they were up off their chairs immediately when they saw a good-looking chap in the pub unencumbered by either a date or a wedding ring, but neither Emily, a redhead from Fulham, nor Yalda, a brunette of Pakistani descent who had been born and raised in Ipswich, moved in the direction of the tall man in the corner. Though he did not look angry or cruel, there were no cues in his body language that gave any indication of approachability.

As the evening wore on it became something of a challenge between the two of them; they giggled as each tried to cajole the other into making a move. Finally Emily ordered a shot of Jägermeister for liquid courage and drank it down in one long gulp. After giving the liquor only a few seconds to kick in, she stood up and made her way across the room.

Jack Ryan, Jr., saw the redhead coming from twenty paces. *Shit,* he mumbled to himself. *I'm not in the mood.*

He looked into the golden lager in front of him, willing the woman to lose her nerve before she arrived at his table.

"Hello there."

Jack was greatly disappointed in his powers of psychic suggestion.

She said, "I thought I'd come and check on ya. You fancy a fresh drink? Or how 'bout a fresh lightbulb?"

Jack looked up at her without making much eye contact. He smiled a little, doing his best to be polite without appearing overly friendly. "How are you tonight?"

Emily's eyes widened. "An American? I knew I hadn't seen you before. My friend and I were trying to guess your story."

Jack looked back to his beer. He knew he should feel flattered, but he did not. "Not much of a story, really. I'm here working in The City for a few months."

She extended a hand. "Emily. Pleased to meet you."

Jack looked into her eyes for a quick moment, and determined her to be not quite inebriated, but not terribly far from it.

He shook her hand. "I'm John."

Emily brushed her hair back over her shoulder. "I love America. Went over last year with my ex.

46

Not ex-husband, no, nothing like that, just a bloke I dated for a while, before I realized what a narcissistic sod he was. A right bastard. Anyway, got a holiday out of him, at least, so he was good for something."

"That's nice."

"Which one of the states do you call home?"

"Maryland," he said.

She looked deeply into his eyes while she talked. Jack saw immediately that she registered a faint sense of recognition, and she was confused by this. She recovered and said, "That's East Coast, right? Near Washington, D.C. Haven't been to the East Coast. Me and my ex did the West Coast, quite loved San Francisco, but the traffic down in L.A. was bloody awful. Never did quite get used to driving on the right side of the —"

Emily's eyes widened suddenly, and she stopped talking.

Shit, Jack said to himself. *Here we go.*

"Oh . . . my . . . *God.*"

"Please," said Jack, softly.

"You're Junior Jack Ryan."

As far as Jack knew, he had never been called this by anyone in his life. He thought the girl might have been a little tongue-tied. He said, "That's me. Junior Jack."

"I don't believe it!" Emily spoke louder this time, just below a shout. She started to turn back to her friend across the room, but Jack reached out and gently took hold of her forearm.

"Emily. *Please.* I'd appreciate you not making a big deal out of it."

The redhead looked around the room quickly, then at Yalda, who was looking their way. Emily turned back to Jack and, with a conspiratorial nod, she said, "Right. I understand. No problem. Your secret's safe with me."

"Thanks." *Not in the mood,* Jack said to himself again, but he smiled.

Emily slipped into the booth, across from him. *Damn.*

They talked for a few minutes; she asked him a dozen rapid-fire questions about his life and what he was doing here and how it was that he was all by himself without any protection. He responded with short answers; again, he wasn't rude, he was simply trying to politely exude lack of interest from every pore of his body.

Emily had conspicuously not invited her friend to join them, but Jack saw a pair of men had ambled over to the olive-complexioned beauty sitting alone, and she was now in conversation herself.

He turned his attention back to Emily just as she said, "Jack . . . would it be forward of me to ask you if you'd like to go somewhere else where we can talk?"

Jack stifled yet another sigh. "Do you want an honest answer?"

"Well . . . sure."

"Then . . . yeah. That *would* be pretty forward."

The young woman was taken aback, not sure what to make of the American's response. Before she could speak, Jack said, "I'm sorry. I've got a really early morning tomorrow."

Emily said she understood, then told Jack to stay right where he was. She rushed back over to her table, grabbed her purse, and came back. She pulled out a business card and a pen, and began writing a number down.

Ryan took a sip of his lager and watched her.

"I hope you'll give me a call when you aren't busy. I'd love to show you around town. I was born and raised here, so you could do worse for a tour guide."

"I'm sure."

She handed Jack her card in an overt fashion that he knew was designed to show off for her friend, who was now sitting alone again. He took it with a forced smile, playing along for her benefit. She had, after all, played along with his ruse and not announced to the room he was the son of the President of the United States.

"Lovely to meet you, Jack."

"Likewise."

Emily reluctantly headed back to her table, and Jack worked on finishing his beer. He slipped her card into his coat; he would get home and then he would toss it onto a shelf with nearly a dozen other cards, napkins, and torn bits of envelopes, each one with the phone number of a female he'd met in similar circumstances in just two weeks here in the UK.

As he drank, Jack did not look toward Emily's table, but a few seconds later the redhead's friend shouted loud enough to be heard throughout the entire establishment, "No bleedin' way!"

Jack reached inside his coat for his wallet.

5

Two minutes later he was out on the sidewalk —
they called it a pavement over here, which Jack
found to be one of the more logical of all the
discrepancies between British English and American English.

He walked alone through the night to the Bank
underground station, oppressed by the feeling that
he was being watched. It was just his nerves — he
had no reason to suspect he was really being followed — but each time he was recognized by
someone he didn't know his concerns grew that,
despite his best intentions, he was continuing to
expose those he cared about to danger.

He had come to the UK thinking he would slip
into the fabric of the city unnoticed, but in his
two weeks here at least a half-dozen people — in
pubs, in the Tube station, or standing in line to
buy fish and chips — had made it clear they knew
exactly who he was.

Jack Ryan, Jr., was the same height as his world-
famous father, and he possessed the same strong
jaw and piercing blue eyes. He'd been on television
when he was younger, but even though he'd done
what he could to stay out of the public eye as
much as possible in the past several years, he still

looked enough like his younger self that he couldn't go anywhere without harboring concerns.

A few months earlier he had been working for The Campus when he learned Chinese intelligence knew something about who he was and what he really did for a living. This knowledge by the enemy compromised not only Ryan but also his friends and coworkers, and it also had the potential to compromise his father's administration.

So far the Chinese had not been a problem; Jack hoped his father's air strike on China had blown the hell out of anyone who could link him with intelligence work, but he suspected the real reason had more to do with the fact that the new leaders in Beijing were doing their best to make amends with the United States. That their motivations were economically based and not due to any new altruism on the part of the Chicoms did not diminish the fact that — for now, at least — the Chinese were playing nice.

And Jack knew his breakup with Melanie Kraft, his girlfriend of one year, had also contributed to his feeling of mistrust and unease. He'd met several women in the UK (the single females here didn't seem to have the shyness gene more common in U.S. women) and he'd been on a few dates, but he hadn't put enough distance between himself and Melanie yet to consider anything serious.

At times he wondered if a series of no-strings-attached one-night stands might cure him of his current malaise, but when push came to shove, he recognized that he wasn't really that type of guy. His parents must have raised him better, he surmised, and the thought of some asshole treat-

51

ing one of his sisters like a consumable product off the shelf made him ball his fists up in anger.

He'd come to face the fact that although he'd never had trouble attracting members of the opposite sex, he really wasn't cut out to be much of a Casanova.

Jack had come over here to the United Kingdom in the first place to put some distance between himself and The Campus after the leak. He expressed to the director of The Campus, Gerry Hendley, that he'd like to take a few months to hone the analytical side of his work. He couldn't very well knock on the door at CIA or NSA without proper clearances, something Jack Ryan, Jr., would never be able to obtain, considering his clandestine work of the past few years. But Gerry knew how to think outside the box. He immediately suggested Jack delve into international business analytics, promising young Ryan that if he joined up with the right firm he would be thrown neck-deep into the world of government corruption, organized crime, drug cartels, and international terrorism.

That sounded just fine to Jack.

Gerry offered to make some introductions on Ryan's behalf, but Jack wanted to make his own way. He did some research into companies involved in business analysis, and he learned one of the biggest and best out there was a UK firm called Castor and Boyle Risk Analytics Ltd. From everything Ryan had read, C&B seemed to have its fingers in virtually every nook and cranny of the world of international finance.

Within a week of Ryan reaching out to Castor and Boyle, he was in London interviewing for a six-month contract position as a business analytics specialist.

Ryan made it clear in that first meeting with the co-owner of the firm, Colin Boyle, that he wanted no leg up due to his lineage. Moreover, he said if he was hired, he would do everything he could to downplay his identity, and he would ask the firm to respect his privacy and do the same.

Old boys' networks and college-chum nepotism were virtually the coin of the realm here in The City, so Boyle was both stunned and intrigued to discover that the son of the President of the United States sought to be nothing more than just another hardworking young analyst with a cubicle and a computer.

Boyle wanted to hire the lad on the spot for his laudable ethics, but he heeded young Ryan's wishes and had him sit for a daylong barrage of tests. Accounting, research methods, a personality questionnaire, and an in-depth survey of his knowledge of politics, current events, and geography. Ryan passed them all, he was offered the contract, and he returned to Baltimore only to shutter his condo and pack his bags.

Ten days later, Ryan reported for duty at Castor and Boyle.

He'd been on the job for two weeks now, and he had to admit he found his work here fascinating. Although he was a financial analyst, and not an intelligence analyst, he saw the work as two sides of the same coin, not two separate disciplines.

Castor and Boyle worked in a surprisingly cut-throat and fast-paced industry. While Colin Boyle was the better-known face of the company and the man who appeared in the media regarding C&B's work, the real operational force of the firm was led by Hugh Castor. Castor himself had served as a spymaster for UK domestic intelligence, MI5, during the Cold War, and he made the successful transition into the field of corporate security and business intelligence after leaving the government.

Others in the firm specialized in forensic accounting and the auditing of business ledgers, but at this early point in his assignment at Castor and Boyle, Ryan was more of a generalist.

This wasn't exactly the same as the analytical work he had done for The Campus. He wasn't digging through top-secret sensitive compartmented intelligence files to discern patterns in the movements of a terrorist, he was instead digging into the convoluted business relationships of shadowy front companies, trying to master the shell game of international business so that Castor and Boyle's clients could make informed decisions in the marketplace.

And he wasn't assassinating spies in Istanbul or targeting America's enemies in Pakistan, but nevertheless, he felt his work mattered, if only to the bottom line of his firm's clients.

Jack's short-term plan was to work very hard here in London, to learn everything he could about financial crime and forensic business analytics, and to stay away from Hendley Associates so as not to expose The Campus any more than he already had.

But again, that was in the short term. In the long term? In the long term, Jack wasn't really sure what he was doing. Where he would go. He wanted to return to The Campus when it was up and running again, but he didn't know when that would be.

When his father was Jack's age he had already

served his country in the Marines, married, earned his doctorate, made a ton of money in the markets, written a book, and fathered a child.

Jack was proud of the things he had done for The Campus, but being the son of President Jack Ryan meant he would always have some incredibly large shoes to fill.

Ryan climbed out of the Tube at the Earl's Court station at 11:50 p.m. and made his way up to street level with the few other travelers out tonight. A steady rain had begun to fall, and as was often the case, Ryan had left his umbrella at the office. He grabbed a free newspaper from a rack at the station's exit and used it to cover his head as he crossed the street and entered the residential neighborhood.

Ryan strolled alone down the rainy street. On Hogarth Road he slowed, then turned and looked back over his shoulder. It was a habit he'd picked up working overseas with The Campus. He wouldn't perform an SDR, a surveillance-detection run; that would entail an hour or more of backtracking, changing his route, and using various forms of transportation. But he was, at least, keeping an eye out for any followers.

Jack had the presence of mind to alter his daily routine when possible. He made it a point to go to a different pub every evening after work, and with so many choices both in The City, where he worked, and here in Kensington, where he lived, he knew he could be here in town for months before he had trouble finding a new place.

As well as varying his nightspots, he also did what he could to change up the route he followed each night. The warren of streets in Kensington meant there were several ways he could get to and from his flat without always approaching from the same direction.

But even with these countermeasures, Jack couldn't shake the feeling he was being watched. He was unable to put his finger on it, and he had no evidence at all to confirm his suspicions, but some mornings on his predawn jog or during his commute from Kensington to The City, some afternoons out to lunch with his colleagues, and most evenings when he headed home on his own, he felt a prickly sensation and an almost palpable sense of eyes on him.

Was it the Chinese? Had they followed him here to London? Could it be British intelligence, just keeping an eye on him informally? Or might they have picked up a whiff of his former activities?

Could it even be the U.S. Secret Service, watching over him, making sure he was safe? Jack was the first child of a sitting U.S. President to refuse his Secret Service protection, a fact that had troubled many, and while they would have no mandate to protect him, he could not completely dismiss the possibility out of hand.

The more he wondered about the reasons for his sense he was being followed, the more he told himself it was nothing more than paranoia on his part.

He looked back over his shoulder again on Cromwell Road. Just like every other time he'd "checked his six," there was nothing there.

A few minutes later Jack turned onto Lexham Gardens, glanced at his watch, and saw it was past midnight. He'd have to fall right to sleep in order to get five full hours before rising for his morning run.

He entered his building, stopping in the doorway once more to see if he was being followed. As before, he saw no one.

It was just his imagination.

Perfect, Jack. When your dad was your age he was saving British royalty from IRA gunmen and commandeering Russian submarines. You can't even go out to a pub for a pint without getting the heebie-jeebies.

Shit, man. Get hold of yourself.

He'd taken some measures to keep a low profile since joining The Campus, but as he climbed the stairs to his flat, he realized his goal should be complete anonymity. He was far from home and alone, and the potential to redesign his physical presence was both possible and necessary.

He decided then and there he would grow a beard and mustache, he would cut his hair short, he would change the style of his clothing, he would even get back into the gym and bulk up to some degree.

His transformation would not happen overnight, he knew this, but he had to make it happen before he could truly relax and get on with his life.

6

Two months later

Dino Kadić sat behind the wheel of his Lada sedan, eyeing the row of luxury sport-utility vehicles parked on the far side of the square. A half-dozen BMWs, Land Cruisers, and Mercedeses idled nose to tail, and just beyond them, one of the city's most chic restaurants glowed in neon.

They were nice trucks, and it was a nice restaurant. But Kadić wasn't impressed.

He'd still blow the place to hell.

If he were anywhere else on earth the motorcade would have tipped him off that some serious VIP was having a late meal in that restaurant, but this was Moscow; around here, any self-respecting mob goon or reasonably well-connected businessman commanded his own fleet of high-dollar vehicles and crew of security men. The half-dozen fancy cars and the steel-eyed entourage protecting them did not prove to Kadić anyone of particular importance was dining inside; he figured it was probably just a local tough guy or a corrupt tax official.

His target tonight had arrived on foot; he was just some foreign businessman — important somewhere, perhaps, but not important here. He was not an underworld personality or a politician. He was English, a high-flying emerging-markets fund manager named Tony Haldane. Kadić had gotten close visual confirmation of Haldane as he entered Vanil restaurant alone just after seven p.m., and then Kadić repositioned here, under a row of trees on the far side of the street. He parked his Lada at a meter on Gogolevskiy Boulevard and sat behind the wheel, waiting with his phone in his lap and his eyes on the restaurant's front doors.

The cell phone resting on his leg was set to send a signal to the detonator in the shoebox-sized improvised explosive device under the leafy foliage in one of the planters sitting outside the front door of the restaurant.

Kadić watched from his position one hundred twenty meters away as the security men and drivers stood around the planter unaware, clueless to the danger.

He doubted any of those guys would survive the blast. And he could not possibly care less.

He drummed his fingers on the steering wheel — from nerves, not from boredom — and felt his heartbeat increase as the minutes ticked off. Despite how long Dino had been doing this sort of thing, each time brought the adrenaline rush anew. The battle of wits that came along with devising and orchestrating and executing an assassination, the anticipation of the explosion, the smell of burning accelerant and plastic and, yes, even flesh.

Kadić first felt the thrill twenty years earlier when he was a young Croatian paramilitary fighting in the war in the Balkans. When Croatia signed its truce with Serbia, Kadić realized he was having too much fun with the war, and he wasn't ready to stop fighting, so he organized a mercenary para unit that conducted raids into Bosnia, targeting Serbian Army patrols for the Bosnian government. The CIA took interest in the group, and they gave Kadić and his men training and equipment.

It did not take long for the Agency to realize they had made a huge mistake. Kadić's Croatian paramilitary force was implicated in atrocities against Serbian civilians living in Bosnia, and the CIA broke ties with Dino Kadić and his men.

After the war ended, Kadić began plying his trade as a contract killer. He worked in the Balkans and in the Middle East, and then, around the turn of the millennium, he moved to Russia, where he became a killer-for-hire for any underworld entity that would employ him.

He did well for himself in the industry for a few years and then bought property back in Croatia, where he settled into semiretirement, living mostly off the money he'd made in Russia over the past decade, although from time to time a contract came his way that he could not refuse.

Like this Haldane hit. The contractor, a Russian underworld personality, had offered a princely sum for what Kadić determined to be a low-risk operation. The Russian had been very specific as to the time and the place of the hit, and he'd told Kadić he wanted to make a big and bold statement.

Nyet problem, Dino had told the man at the time. He could do big and bold.

He calmed himself with a slow breath, told himself to relax.

A phrase, in English, had been taught to him by

the Americans a long time ago, and he said it aloud now.

"Stay frosty."

It had become a ritual in those quiet moments before the noise of a mission, and it made him feel good to say it. He hated the Americans now; they had turned on him, deemed him unreliable, but they could not take back the training they had given him.

And he was about to put this training to use.

Dino glanced at his watch and then squinted across the dark square toward the target area. He did not use binoculars; there was too great a chance someone walking past his parked car or even looking out a window in one of the nearby apartments or shops would notice the man in the car with the binos pointed precisely at the location where the bomb would soon detonate. Any description at all of his car to investigators after the blast would cause the Interior Ministry to search hours of security-camera footage of the area, and soon enough he would be identified.

That would not do. Dino aimed to get out of this op clean, and this meant he'd have to eyeball it from distance. The people who hired him for this job ordered him to make an angry statement with his explosive, so the bomb was constructed with overkill in mind. For this reason Dino had positioned himself back a little farther from his target than he would have liked.

From this distance he would have to ID his target from the color of his camel coat as he left the building, and, Dino decided, that would do just fine.

He checked his watch yet again.

"Stay frosty," he said again in English, and then

he switched to his native Serbo-Croatian. *"Požuriti, prokletniĉe!"* Hurry up, damn it!

Inside Vanil, a cordon of four bodyguards in black suits stood in front of a red curtain separating the private banquet area from the dining room, and although the locals in the restaurant were accustomed to plainclothes security men all over this most insecure city, a cursory look at this protection detail would indicate these were top-of-the-line bodyguards, not the much more common cheap "rent-a-thug" variety.

Behind the armed guards and behind the curtain, two middle-aged men sipped brandies at a table in the center of the large, otherwise empty room.

One of the men wore a Burberry suit in gray flannel. The knot of his blue tie was as tight and proper now as it had been at eight that morning. In English, but with a thick Russian accent, the man said, "Moscow has always been a dangerous place. In the past few months I'm afraid it has only become exponentially more so."

Across the table, British subject Anthony Haldane was as nicely dressed as the Russian. His Bond Street blue pin-striped suit was fresh and pressed, and his camel coat hung from a rack nearby. He smiled, surprised by the comment. "These are troubling words coming from the nation's security chief."

Instead of giving a quick response, Stanislav Biryukov sipped his *chacha,* a Georgian brandy made from distilled grape skins. After wiping his mouth with the corner of his napkin, he said, "SVR is Russia's *foreign* security service. Things are going relatively well in foreign environs at the moment. The FSB, internal security, is the organization presiding over the current catastrophe, both in Russia and in the nations adjacent to Russia."

Haldane said, "You'll excuse me for not making the immediate distinction between FSB and SVR. To an old hand like me, it is all still the KGB."

Biryukov smiled. "And to an older hand, we would all be Chekists."

Haldane chuckled. "Quite so, but that one is even before my time, old boy."

Biryukov held his glass up to the candlelight; he regarded the deep golden color of the liquid before carefully choosing his next words. "As a foreigner you might not know it, but FSB has authority not just over Russia but also over the other nations in the Commonwealth of Independent States, even though our neighbors are sovereign nations. We refer to the border nations as 'the near abroad.' "

Haldane cocked his head. He pretended not to know it, and Biryukov pretended he believed Haldane's lie. The Russian added, "It can get a bit confusing, I will allow."

Haldane said, "There is something off about Russian internal security operating in its former republics. Almost as if someone forgot to tell the spies that the Soviet Union is no more."

Biryukov did not reply.

Haldane knew the SVR director had some objective by inviting him out for drinks tonight, but for now the Russian was playing his cards close to his vest. Every comment was calculated. The Englishman tried to draw him out. "Does it feel like they are operating on your turf?"

Biryukov laughed aloud. "FSB is welcome to

those nations. My work in Paris and Tokyo and Toronto is a delight compared to what they have to do in Grozny and Almaty and Minsk. These are ugly days for our sister service."

"Might I infer that is what you wanted to talk to me about?"

Biryukov answered the question with a question of his own: "How long have we known each other, Tony?"

"Since the late eighties. You were stationed at the Soviet embassy in London, as a cultural attaché, and I was with the Foreign Office."

Biryukov corrected him on both counts. "I was KGB and you were British intelligence."

Haldane looked like he was going to protest, but only for a moment. "Would there be any point in me denying it?"

The Russian said, "We were children back then, weren't we?"

"Indeed we were, old chap."

Biryukov leaned in a little closer. "I mean to cause you no consternation, my friend, but I know you retain a relationship with your government."

"I am one of Her Majesty's loyal subjects, if that is what you mean to say."

"*Nyet.* That is *not* what I mean to say."

Haldane's eyebrows rose. "Is the director of Russian foreign intelligence accusing me of being a foreign spy in the capital of Russia?"

Biryukov leaned back from the table. "No need to be dramatic. It is quite natural that you have kept up old friendships in MI6. A little back-and-forth between a well-connected businessman like yourself and your nation's spy shop is nothing at all but smart business practice for both parties."

So that *is the game,* Haldane thought, with some

relief. Stan wanted to reach out to British intelligence using his old friend as a cutout.

It makes sense, Haldane thought, as he drained his glass. It would not do for the head of SVR to pop around to the British embassy for a chat.

Haldane said, "I have some friends well positioned within MI6, yes, but please, don't give me too much credit. I have been out of the service for a long time. I can pass along any message you want me to convey, but the clearer you can make things for me, the less chance I will have of mucking the whole thing up."

Biryukov poured both men another snifter of *chacha.* "Very well. I will make things very clear. I am here tonight to inform you, to inform the United Kingdom, that there is a push by our president to reunite our two intelligence services, to reestablish an umbrella organization above both foreign and domestic security." He added, "I think this is a very bad idea."

The Englishman nearly spit out his brandy. "He wants to reboot the KGB?"

"I find it hard to believe the Kremlin, even the Kremlin of President Valeri Volodin, would be so brazen as to call the new organization by the title Komitet Gosudarstvennoĭ Bezopasnosti, but the role of the new organization will be virtually that of the old. One organization in charge of all intelligence matters, both foreign and domestic."

Haldane mumbled, almost to himself, "Bloody hell."

Biryukov nodded somberly. "It will serve no positive function."

This seemed, to Haldane, to be a gross understatement.

"Then why do it?"

"There is a quickening of events, both domestically in Russia and in the former republics. Since the unsuccessful attack on Estonia a couple of months ago, President Volodin and his people are increasing Russia's sphere of influence on all fronts. He wants more power and control in the former satellite nations. If he can't take power and control with tanks, he will take it with spies."

Haldane knew this because it was all over the news. In the past year the nations of Belarus, Chechnya, Kazakhstan, and Moldova had all elected staunchly pro-Russian and anti-Western governments. In each and every case Russia had been accused of meddling in the elections, either politically or by using their intelligence services or those in the criminal underworld to affect the outcomes to Moscow's advantage.

Discord, in large part fueled by Moscow, was the order of the day in several other bordering nations; the invasion of Estonia was unsuccessful, but there remained the threat of invasion in Ukraine. In addition to this, a near–civil war in Georgia, bitterly disputed presidential campaigns in Latvia and Lithuania, riots and protests in other nearby countries.

Biryukov continued, "Roman Talanov, my counterpart in the FSB, is leading this charge. I suppose with complete control over Russian intelligence activity abroad, he can expand his influence and begin destabilizing nations beyond the near abroad. Russia will invade Ukraine, probably within the next few weeks. They will annex the Crimea. From there, if they meet no resistance from the West, they will take more of the country, all the way to the Dnieper River. Once this is achieved, I believe Volodin will set his eyes on

66

making beneficial alliances from a position of power, both in the other border countries and in the former nations of the Warsaw Pact. He believes he can return the entire region to the central control of the Kremlin. Poland, Czech Republic, Hungary, Bulgaria, Romania. They will be the next dominoes to fall."

Biryukov drank, but Haldane's mouth had gone dry. This was talk of a new Cold War at the very least, and it certainly could lead to a new hot war. But the Englishman had known the Russian long enough to know the man was not prone to exaggeration.

Haldane asked, "If Talanov takes over SVR's responsibilities, what will they do with you, Stan?"

"I am concerned about our fragile democracy. I am worried about the freedom of the Russian people. I am worried about a dangerous overreach that could lead to a broad war with the West." He smiled with a shrug. "I am not worried about my future employment prospects."

He added, "I will have more information for you soon. You and I have both developed sources before. It takes time."

Haldane laughed in surprise. "You want to be *my* agent?"

The director of the SVR leaned over the table. "I come cheaper than most. I want nothing in return except comfort in the fact the West will do anything it can, politically speaking, of course, to thwart the FSB's attempt to increase their hold on my nation's foreign security service. If you publicize this internationally, it might have a cooling effect on Talanov and Volodin's plans."

Haldane caught himself wondering about the impact this news would have on his investments in Europe. He was, after all, a businessman first and foremost. But he cleared his head of business and did his best to remember his past life in the intelligence field.

He found this hard to do; he had not worked as an employee of MI6 in nearly two decades. He put his hands up in the air in a show of surrender. "I . . . I really am out of the game, my friend. Of course I can return to London straightaway and talk to some old acquaintances, and then they will find someone more appropriate to serve as a conduit for your information in the future."

"*You,* Tony. I will only talk to you."

Haldane nodded slowly. "I understand." He thought for a moment. "I have business here, next week. Can we meet again?"

"Yes, but after that we will need to automate the flow of information."

"Quite. I don't suppose it would do for us to have a regular date night."

Stanislav smiled. "I will warn you now. My wife is every bit as dangerous as FSB director Roman Talanov."

"I rather doubt *that,* old boy."

7

President of the United States Jack Ryan stood outside the White House's South Portico with his wife, Cathy, by his side and his Secret Service contingent flanking them both. It was a crisp spring afternoon in D.C., with bright blue skies and temperatures in the low forties, and as Ryan watched a black Ford Expedition roll up the driveway he could not help thinking this great weather would make for a nice photo op here with his guest on the South Lawn.

But there would be no photos today, nor would the meeting go in the visitor log kept by the White House. The President's official schedule, put online for all the world to see, for reasons Ryan could not fathom, was cryptic regarding Ryan's activities today. It said only, "Private Lunch — Residence. 1:00 p.m. to 2:30 p.m."

And if Scott Adler, the secretary of state, had his way, this meeting would not be happening at all.

But Ryan was President of the United States, and, on this, POTUS got his way. His visitor today was his friend, he was in town, and Ryan saw no reason why he shouldn't have him over for lunch.

As they waited for the Expedition to come to a

stop, Cathy Ryan leaned closer to her husband. "This guy pointed a gun at you once, didn't he?"

There was *that,* Ryan conceded to himself.

With a sly smile he replied, "I'm sorry, hon. That's classified. Anyway, you know Sergey. He's a friend."

Cathy pinched her husband's arm playfully, and her next comment was delivered in jest. "They've searched him, right?"

"Cathy." Ryan said it in a mock scolding voice, and then he joked, "Hell . . . I hope so."

Ryan's lead personal protection agent, Andrea Price-O'Day, was standing close enough to hear the exchange. "If it comes down to it, Mr. President, I think you could take him."

The Expedition parked in front of them, and one of the Secret Service agents opened the back door.

Seconds later, Sergey Golovko, former officer in the KGB and former director of Russia's foreign intelligence service, climbed slowly out of the vehicle.

"Sergey!" Ryan said, his smile warm and his hand outstretched.

"Mr. President," Golovko replied with a smile of his own.

Cathy came forward and accepted a kiss; she'd met Sergey before and thought him to be a kind and gentle man, despite whatever had happened between him and Jack a long time ago.

As they turned to head back into the White House, Ryan could not help noticing that Sergey seemed noticeably older than he had the last time the two had met. Though he smiled, he moved slowly and sluggishly, and his shoulders hung slumped inside his blue suit.

Ryan told himself this should not come as a great surprise. Statistically, the life expectancy of a Russian male was around sixty, and Sergey was over seventy. On top of this, Golovko had been traveling on a grueling speaking tour here in the United States for the past two weeks. Why shouldn't the man look a little the worse for wear?

Face it, Jack, he thought, *we're all getting old.*

As the entourage walked through the Diplomatic Reception Room on its way to the staircase to the second floor, Jack put his hand on the back of the smaller Russian. "How are you, my friend?"

"I'm well," Sergey answered as he walked. And then he added with a shrug, "I woke up this morning a bit under the weather. Last night in Lawrence, Kansas, I ate something called a barbecue brisket. Apparently, even my iron Russian stomach was not prepared for this."

Ryan chuckled, put his arm around his old friend. "I'm sorry to hear that. We have a great physician on staff here. I can have her come up and talk to you before lunch if you would like."

Sergey shook his head politely. "*Nyet.* I will be okay. Thank you, Ivan Emmetovich." He caught himself quickly, "I mean, Mr. President."

"Ivan Emmetovich is fine, Sergey Nikolayevich. I appreciate the honorific of my father."

Anthony Haldane and Stanislav Biryukov stood in the lobby of Vanil restaurant chatting while donning their coats. As they prepared to leave, the SVR director's principal protection agent radioed to the street to have Biryukov's Land Rover pulled up to the door.

The men shook hands. "Until next week, Anthony Arturovich."

71

"*Da svidaniya,* Stan."

Tony Haldane exited the doors along with one of Biryukov's security men, who headed out in advance of his principal to check the street. Stanislav himself stood in the doorway, surrounded by three bodyguards, waiting for the all-clear.

As Haldane stepped to the curb behind the row of SUVs to hail a taxi, Biryukov was ushered out the door, twenty-five feet behind the Englishman. He had just stepped between the two planters bracing Vanil's doorway when a flash of light enveloped the entire scene.

In microseconds a thunderclap of sound and pressure rocked the neighborhood.

The explosion threw security men like debris into the street, the armored Range Rovers jolted or rolled over like Matchbox cars, and projectiles from the explosion shattered window glass and injured passersby one hundred meters away. Dozens of car alarms erupted in bleats and wails, drowning out all but the loudest moans of pain and screams of shock.

On the far side of the park, Dino Kadić sat back up in his Lada. He had knelt down, almost to the floorboard, to press the send button on his phone while out of the direct line of any shrapnel, though his sedan was mostly shielded by the corner of a bank building.

Before the last bit of debris from the blast had rained back to earth, Kadić started his car and pulled out into light evening traffic. He drove off slowly and calmly, without a look back at the devastation, although he did roll his window down slightly as he left the scene, taking in a deep breath of the smoke already hanging in the air.

■ ■ ■ ■

President Jack Ryan and First Lady Cathy Ryan sat down with their guest for lunch in the Family Residence dining room on the second floor of the White House, just across the West Sitting Hall from the master bedroom. Joining them for lunch was the director of national intelligence, Mary Pat Foley, and her husband, former director of the CIA, Ed Foley.

Having the former head of Russia's security services over for lunch in the White House's private dining room was somewhat surreal to the small group of those who both knew about today's luncheon and remembered the Cold War, but times had changed in many ways.

Golovko was no longer a member of Russia's intelligence service — in fact, he was much the opposite. He was a private citizen now, and proving to be a thorn in the side of the current occupant of the Kremlin. The State Department had warned President Ryan it would be perceived as provocative by the Russians if they knew Golovko was coming to the White House for lunch. Jack acquiesced reluctantly, and only partially; he ordered the event to remain informal and to be kept below the radar.

Sergey Golovko had retired from intelligence work three years earlier, and almost immediately he made headlines in Russia because he, unlike most intelligence chiefs, did not go into politics or business. To the contrary, Golovko took his small pension and began speaking out against the *silo-viki* — a Russian term used to denote members of the intelligence community and the military who became high-ranking and powerful political leaders. The Kremlin had become filled to capacity with ex-spies and ex–military officers, and they worked together as a tightly knit coalition in order to gain and hold power, using the skills they learned controlling the security services to now control every aspect of public and private life.

The new man in charge at the Kremlin, sixty-year-old Valeri Volodin, was himself a member of the *siloviki,* having worked for years in the FSB and, previous to this, as a young officer in the KGB. Most current members of the executive and legislative bodies were former members of either the internal or foreign intelligence service, or military intelligence (the GRU).

As Golovko began publicly airing his displeasure with the policies and practices of the Volodin administration, Volodin did not take kindly to the ex–SVR man's comments, especially those critical of the rollback of democratic institutions by the new regime. As a fervent opponent of the *siloviki,* Golovko knew it was just a matter of time before his own safety was at risk. Old colleagues of Golovko's still in the SVR warned the ex–spy chief it would be in his best interest to leave Russia and not look back.

With a heavy heart, the former SVR head exiled himself from his motherland and moved to London, where, for the past year, he'd lived modestly enough, though he continued to criticize Volodin and his ministers. His speaking tours took him all over the globe, and he could be seen on television somewhere on the planet almost every week, appearing in interviews and roundtable discussions.

Ryan looked across the table at Golovko now

and could not help wondering how someone who looked so frail could keep up a schedule nearly as arduous as his own.

Golovko saw the look, and he smiled at Ryan. "Ivan Emmetovich, tell me, how are your children?"

"Everyone is fine. Katie and Kyle are at school here in D.C. Sally is at Johns Hopkins, finishing up her residency."

"Three doctors in the family. Very impressive," Sergey said, tipping his wineglass to both Ryans.

Jack chuckled. "Three docs, but only two physicians. As a doctor of history, I've noticed my specialty is not as useful as an M.D. in a house full of kids."

"And what is Junior up to these days?" Sergey asked.

"Actually, Jack Junior is over in your neck of the woods. He moved to London just two months ago."

"Is that so?" Golovko said with mild surprise. "What is he doing there?"

"He is working in the business analytics field for a private firm. Spending his days evaluating corporate buyouts and international finance deals."

"Ah, he's in The City, then."

"He is, but he's living in Earl's Court."

With a smile, Sergey said, "He got his father's brains. He should have become an intelligence officer."

The President took a bite of his salad, careful to give nothing away.

Cathy Ryan interjected, "One spook in the family is enough, don't you think?"

Sergey held his water glass up to her. "Of

course. It is a difficult career. Difficult for the family, as well. I am sure having young Jack work in a safe and secure profession is a great comfort to you."

Cathy sipped her iced tea. "Very much so."

Jack thought his wife's poker face was much better than his own.

Sergey added, "I'd love to see him. I live not far from Earl's Court, in Notting Hill. Perhaps young Ivan Ivanovich could find time to have dinner with me some evening."

"I'm sure he would like that," Ryan replied.

"Don't worry. I will not tell him too many old war stories."

"My son wouldn't believe you, anyway."

The room erupted in laughter. Of those present, only Ed and Mary Pat knew the full history between the two men. Cathy was having a hard time imagining the aged Russian ever having been a threat to her husband.

The talk turned to Ed and Mary Pat, and their time in Moscow in the eighties. They talked about their fondness for the country, the people, and the customs.

Ryan ate his lunch, his eyes still across the table on Sergey. He imagined his old friend would probably much rather be drinking vodka instead of sipping iced tea, and eating borscht instead of pork tenderloin. Although his fork had poked and prodded his plate, Jack didn't think he'd eaten a bite.

Cathy asked Sergey about his speaking tour, and this seemed to perk him up considerably. He'd been to nearly a dozen cities across the United States in the past two weeks, and he had something nice to say about every one. He'd been speaking about what he saw as the corrupt administration of Valeri Volodin, mostly at universities, and he also had a book in the works to pound the message home even further.

On that subject, Ed Foley said, "Sergey, we're a year into Valeri Volodin's first term. Just yesterday Volodin signed a new decree whereby he is allowed to handpick the governors throughout Russia's eighty-three regions. It looks, to an old hand like me, as if the rollback of democracy is picking up steam."

Golovko replied, "From Volodin's point of view, it makes sense for him to do this."

"How so?"

"Regional elections are coming up later in the year. There was always the chance, small though it may be, that the population would elect someone whose loyalty to the central government was in question. It is Volodin's goal to control everything from Moscow. Putting his own people in charge in the eighty-three regions will help him do that."

Mary Pat asked, "Where do you see democracy in Russia at the end of Volodin's first term?"

Golovko took a long sip of ice water. He said, "President Volodin explains away his iron fist by saying, 'Russia has a *special democracy.*' This is his reference to the fact he controls most of the media, handpicks governors, and throws businessmen in jail who he feels don't keep the interests of the Kremlin in mind with every business decision they make." Golovko shook his head slowly in disgust. Ryan saw a sheen of perspiration glisten through his thin white hair. "A *special democracy.* Russia's special democracy is more commonly known around the world by another name. Dictatorship."

There were nods of agreement all around.

"What is happening in Russia is not about government. It is about crime. Volodin and his cronies have billions of dollars of interests in Gazprom, the government natural-gas concern, and Rosneft, the oil concern, as well as minority ownership and total control over banks and shipping and timber concerns. They are raping the country of its wealth and natural resources, and they are using the power of the Kremlin to do it. After three more years of Volodin and his *siloviki* in power, I am afraid what is left of Russia's democracy will only be a memory. This is no exaggeration on my part. Central power is a snowball that picks up snow as it rolls downhill. It will get bigger and bigger, and it will move faster and faster. In a few years there will be no one able to stop it."

"Why do the people stand for it?" Cathy asked.

"The social contract in Russia is very simple. The population is willing to give up liberty and turn a blind eye to government corruption in exchange for security and prosperity. This worked as long as there was security and prosperity, but it is failing now.

"I was there, in 1990. A pensioner who normally took a hundred rubles to the market for groceries suddenly learned he would need one-point-six million rubles to buy the same amount of goods. Shopkeepers basically had the job of telling people they were going to starve to death.

"The Russians are happy those days are gone. Volodin is a dictator, but most see him as a protector. Having said that, the economy is turning and the demographics in Russia are changing, and not in his favor. Birthrate amongst the Slavs in all nations has been in the negative level for nearly two decades. As the iron fist squeezes harder, and the transfer of Russia's resources leaves Russia and bankrupts the nation, more and more people will start to notice its pressure."

Sergey Golovko began coughing for a moment, but it subsided and he wiped his mouth with his napkin before saying, "The failure of the existing social contract in Russia will not lead to a new social contract, it will only lead to Volodin removing more and more freedoms."

Jack Ryan said, "Benjamin Franklin put it like this: 'Those who would give up essential liberty to purchase a little temporary safety deserve neither liberty nor safety.' "

Golovko regarded the quote for a moment. "If this man said this in Moscow he would be hauled into Lefortovo and questioned by the FSB."

Jack smiled. Either Golovko did not know who Benjamin Franklin was, or else he'd just forgotten. He said, "Franklin made that comment two hundred fifty years ago, when our republic was going through a trying time."

Mary Pat said, "My concerns about Volodin are not just on the domestic front. Recent events in the former republics have the Kremlin's fingerprints all over them."

"Roman Talanov's intelligence services and Valeri Volodin's strong-arm tactics have created a vast region of client states."

Ryan said, "The Commonwealth of Independent States aren't so independent anymore."

Golovko nodded animatedly at this, took another long sip of water, and used his napkin again, this time to dab sweat off his brow. "Very true. They have meddled in elections, bought and threatened leaders and influential people, undermined opposition groups.

"Belarus, Georgia, Moldova . . . they are effectively satellites once again. Uzbekistan and Tajikistan never left the fold. Others are teetering. We saw what happened in Estonia when one of Russia's neighbors did not do what Moscow wanted it to do. If it had not been for you, Ivan Emmetovich, Estonia would be a vassal state, and Lithuania and Latvia would fall as well."

Ryan corrected him politely: "Not me, Sergey. NATO."

Golovko shook his head. "You led the way. Europe did not want to fight, but you convinced them."

That had been a sore subject around the White House. Ryan just gave a slight nod and sipped his tea.

Mary Pat asked, "What are your thoughts on the conflict in Ukraine?"

"Ukraine is a special case, partially due to its size. Ten times as large as Georgia, and it has a huge population of citizens who align their family history with Russia, not with Ukraine. It is a Slavic nation as well. It is forgotten by many in the West that the Slavic nations of Ukraine, Belarus, and Russia share a common heritage. Volodin clearly wants to unite them as one for historical reasons, and he wants to control the other former republics as a buffer from the West."

Ed Foley said, "When Ukraine started talking about joining NATO there were grumblings from Russia, of course, but only when Volodin came to power last year did the real threats begin."

Sergey began coughing again. When he stopped, he tried to laugh off the coughing fit. "Excuse me.

I get excited when the topic is Valeri Volodin."

Most in the room chuckled politely. Dr. Cathy Ryan, on the other hand, wasn't laughing. She'd been noting Golovko's pale skin and increasing perspiration. "Sergey, we have a doctor on staff here. If you like I can have Maura come up after lunch and take a look at you, just to make sure you are okay." She spoke in the same polite but professional manner in which she addressed the parents of her patients. She had her point of view on the matter, and she wanted to get it across, but she did not push.

"Thank you very much for the offer, Cathy, but I'll return to the UK tonight and visit my physician in London tomorrow if the stomach pains continue." He smiled weakly, obviously in some discomfort. "I am sure I will feel much better by the morning."

Cathy let it go with a look that indicated she was not satisfied. Jack noticed the look, and he knew this would not be the end of the discussion.

Poor Sergey, he thought.

But Golovko was more concerned about the subject under discussion than his own health. "Yes, Edward. The Russians are afraid of a Ukrainian pivot back to the West and away from their sphere of influence. Volodin was furious that the nationalists retook control of the country. He fears they will join NATO, and he knows that once that happens, the West will have to fight to protect them."

Golovko added, "Volodin has his eyes on the Crimea, in southern Ukraine, and he knows once Ukraine joins NATO, that will be difficult for him to achieve. The way he sees it, he has to move soon."

Ryan said, "He is right that there is no treaty between Ukraine and NATO. And if he does invade, getting Europe on board to fight for the Crimea is a nonstarter."

Golovko waved a hand in the air. "Europe wants their oil and their natural gas, and Russia supplies it. They have been kowtowing to Moscow for a long time."

"To be fair," Ryan countered, "they *need* their oil and their natural gas. I might not like it, but keeping Russia happy is in their interests."

"That may well be, but as Russia moves closer and closer to them by installing puppet after puppet in Eastern and Central European nations, the NATO states will have less mobility on the issue than before. They should exert their leverage against Moscow while they still have a little left."

Ryan agreed with Sergey, but this problem had been growing for years, and he knew it would not be settled over lunch.

After a dessert of assorted sorbets that Sergey did not touch, Mary Pat and Ed said their good-byes, and Jack and Cathy invited the Russian across the hall to the Yellow Oval Room, a formal parlor Cathy liked to use for private receptions.

On the way, Golovko excused himself to go to the restroom, and Jack led him to the bathroom off the living room. As soon as he stepped back into the hall, Cathy approached him.

Softly, she said, "He is ill."

"Yeah, he said he ate something that didn't agree with him."

Cathy made a face. "It looks worse than that. I don't know how you are going to do it, but I want you to talk him into letting Maura take a look at him before he goes to the airport."

"Not sure how —"

"I am confident you can charm him. I'm really worried, Jack. I think he's really sick."

"What do you think is wrong?" Jack was taken aback.

"I don't know, but he needs to get checked out. Today, not tomorrow."

"I'll try to persuade him, but he always was a tough son of a bitch."

"There's tough, and then there's foolish. I need you to remind him he is a smart guy."

Ryan nodded, acquiescing to his wife. He was President of the United States, but he was also a dutiful husband, and as much as anything, he didn't want Cathy haranguing *him* about Sergey for the rest of the afternoon.

8

Dino Kadić made it back to his rented room thirty minutes after the bombing, pulled a beer from his refrigerator, and flipped on the television. He needed to pack, but it could wait for the length of time it would take him to have a dark Yarpivo. He would leave Moscow by train first thing in the morning, but for now he would take a few minutes to enjoy himself a little and watch the news coverage of his operation.

He did not have to wait long. After only a few sips he saw the first images from the scene: shattered glass and fires burning at the front of the restaurant. The camera moved to the left and panned past several SUVs scattered and tossed on the street; beyond them was the domed Cathedral of Christ the Savior, the flashing lights of emergency vehicles reflecting off the windows.

Kadić leaned back on the sofa, enraptured by the beauty of the chaos he created.

An attractive female reporter, just on the scene, seemed utterly shocked by the carnage around her. She lifted her microphone to her mouth and struggled to find words.

Kadić smiled while she went into the few details of the bombing available to her. Mostly she just stammered and detailed the devastation with poorly chosen adjectives.

After a minute of this, though, she brought her hand up to her ear and stopped talking suddenly, as she listened to a producer on her earpiece.

And then her eyes went wide.

"Is this confirmed? Can I say this on air?" She waited for a reply in her earpiece, and Kadić wondered what was going on. With a quick nod, the reporter said, "We have just been told that the director of the Foreign Intelligence Service, Stanislav Arkadyevich Biryukov, was leaving the restaurant at the exact moment of the explosion, and has been injured. His condition is presently unknown."

Kadić lowered the beer bottle slowly and stared at the screen. A less cynical man might have taken the first news reports about the Vanil bombing as some sort of error. *Surely* she was mistaken. Incorrect information from stand-up reporting in the first minutes on a scene like this was the rule, not the exception.

But decades of work with intelligence agencies and mafia groups had made Dino Kadić nothing if not cynical. As soon as he heard Biryukov had been on the sidewalk at the moment the bomb detonated, he took the report as accurate, and he knew it was no coincidence.

He'd been set up. The contractor of the Haldane hit had instructed him on the time and location of the bombing, and had demanded more explosive be used to increase the blast radius. Whoever had done this had orchestrated Kadić's operation to take out the real target, the head of the SVR.

"Picku matirinu!" It was Serbo-Croatian, akin to "Oh, fuck," but even more profane.

And Dino Kadić knew something else. The people who set him up like this wouldn't think twice about sending someone to silence him, so he could take the fall without being able to bring anyone else down with him.

As he sat there on the little sofa in his rented flat, he was sure.

It wasn't *if* they would come for him . . . It was *when.*

And Kadić, being the cynic that he was, didn't give himself much time. He would pack in sixty seconds and be down in his car in one hundred twenty seconds.

"Stay frosty." He threw the beer bottle at the TV and leapt to his feet, began collecting his most important belongings and throwing them into a rolling duffel.

As a pair of dark green ZiL-130 truck-buses pulled up to the entrance of an apartment building on Gruzinskiy Val Street, the back door of each vehicle opened. In a matter of seconds, twenty-four members of the 604th Red Banner Special Purpose Center leapt to the pavement. They were Interior Ministry troops, some of the best trained and most elite in the Russian police force. To those walking by on the sidewalk on Gruzinskiy Val, the men looked like futuristic robots in their black body armor, black Nomex balaclavas, and smoked Plexiglas visors.

Eight men remained at ground level, while two teams of eight took the two stairwells up to the fourth floor. As they ascended, they held their AK-74 rifles against their shoulders and pointed them just offset of the man in front of them in the stack.

On the fourth floor they left the stairwells. A few apartment owners opened their doors in the hallway and found themselves staring down teams of masked and visored men with assault rifles. The residents quickly shut their doors, and several turned up the volume on their televisions to shield themselves from any knowledge of whatever the hell was going on.

The Red Banner men converged outside room 409, and the team leader moved up the train, positioning himself just behind the breacher.

"Time to go," Kadić said, sixty seconds exactly after leaping from the couch. He zipped his duffel closed and reached to pull it off the bed.

Behind him, the apartment door burst open, breaking from the hinges and flying into the room. Kadić spun to the movement and then threw his hands into the air, dropping the duffel. He had no choice but to attempt to surrender, though he understood almost instantly what was going on.

He was, after all, a cynic. There was no way in the world these men could have made it here so fast unless they were tipped off.

Unless he had been set up.

He croaked out one word in Russian.

"Pozhalusta!" Please!

The leader of the Red Banner unit paused, but only for an instant. Then he opened fire. His team followed suit, guns erupted, and the Croatian assassin jerked and spasmed as round after round ripped into his chest.

He toppled back onto the bed, his arms outstretched.

The team leader ordered his men to go through his belongings, while he began searching the body himself. They turned up a handgun — it had been stowed in his case — and the officer who found it took it by the barrel with his gloved hand and passed it grip-first to his leader. The team leader slipped it into the hand of the dead Croatian, closed the man's bloody fingers around it, and then let it drop onto the floor.

A minute later he said, "We're clear." He pinched the transmit button on the side of his shoulder microphone. "Clear. One subject down."

The team leader had his orders. Someone on high wanted this man dead, and a nice neat package of justifiable force had been easy enough to arrange.

Red Banner did what the Kremlin told them to do.

9

Jack, Cathy, and Sergey entered the Yellow Oval Room. Coffee was laid out for them, but Sergey did not touch his, so Jack and Cathy ignored theirs as well.

Golovko said, "I apologize for my passion at lunch."

"Not at all," said Jack.

"My wife died years ago, and since then, I've had little to think about but work, and my nation's place in history. Under Valeri Volodin, Russia is sliding backward to a place the younger generation is not wise enough to fear, and nothing scares me more. I see it as my role to use my intimate knowledge of the darker aspects of our past to ensure we do not repeat it."

Sergey spoke for a moment more about his trip to the United States, but he seemed distracted, and the perspiration on his forehead had only increased since lunch.

After an imploring look from Cathy, Jack Ryan said, "Sergey, I would like you to do me a personal favor."

"Of course, Ivan Emmetovich."

"I want to have someone look you over, just to make sure you are okay."

"Appreciated, but not necessary."

"Look at it from my perspective, Sergey. How will it play in the world media if the former head of SVR comes over here to the States and gets sick on a bad brisket?"

The Secret Service personnel standing around chuckled softly, but Sergey just smiled weakly. Jack noticed this, and he knew his friend to enjoy a good laugh. His inability to go along with the joke only made Ryan more certain he needed Maura, the physician to the President, to look him over.

Ryan was about to press the issue further, but presidential chief of staff Arnie Van Damm leaned in the door from the hallway. Ryan was surprised to see him here; he did not normally leave the West Wing during the day to come over to the residence. Ryan knew, by his presence, something was up. Protocol intervened for a moment, and Ryan had to introduce Golovko to Van Damm. The Russian shook the chief of staff's hand, and then sat back down in his chair across from Cathy.

"Mr. President, can I have a quick word?"

"Okay. Sorry, Sergey, give me just a second, but you're not off the hook."

Sergey just smiled back and nodded.

Ryan followed Arnie into the Center Hall, and then farther, to the West Sitting Hall. There, waiting for him, was Mary Pat Foley. Jack knew whatever was going on, Mary Pat would have only just heard about it, since she had been at lunch ten minutes earlier, and there seemed to be no great emergency then.

"What is it?"

Mary Pat said, "It's Russia. Thirty minutes ago SVR director Stan Biryukov was killed in a bombing in central Moscow, less than a mile from the Kremlin."

Ryan clenched his jaw. "Oh, boy."

"Yeah, we liked him. Sure, he was a Russian spy, but he was as straight a shooter as we could have asked for in that role."

Ryan felt the same about Biryukov. Although he didn't know the man, he did know he had been instrumental in rescuing Ryan's friend, John Clark, from the hands of brutal torturers in Moscow more than a year earlier. Then, even more recently, Biryukov had secretly assisted The Campus in getting Clark into China. As far as Russian intelligence chiefs were concerned, President Ryan thought Stan Biryukov eligible for sainthood. He asked, "Any chance at all this was a random terrorist act and not an assassination?"

Foley said, "I would say no chance at all, except we are talking about Moscow here. There have been, what, five or six bombings since Volodin came to power last year? The restaurant was popular with the *kulturny* — it wouldn't be beyond the realm of possibilities it was targeted for its high-flying Russian clientele, and not specifically because the head of the SVR was in the building."

"But?" asked Ryan. He'd worked with Mary Pat Foley for long enough that he could hear the thoughts behind the inflections in her voice.

"*But* . . . as you know, there are rumors some of the other bombings were false flag attacks perpetrated by FSB. Biryukov was not a Kremlin insider the way FSB director Roman Talanov is. In fact, he and Talanov are seen as bitter rivals." She corrected herself. "*Were* seen as rivals."

Ryan cocked his head in surprise. "Are you suggesting the chief of the FSB had the chief of the

SVR *killed?*"

"Not suggesting it, Mr. President. Just thinking out loud. It's almost too provocative to comprehend, but everything that has happened in Russia since Valeri Volodin came to power has been dramatic, to say the least."

Ryan thought for a moment. "All right. Let's meet in the Oval Office in an hour with the full national security team. Try to get more answers by then."

Mary Pat said, "It's too bad for Golovko. If he had played his cards right and sucked up to Volodin when he came to power, he might have gotten himself a job offer out of this. There is a vacancy at SVR now, after all."

It was dark humor, but Ryan wasn't laughing. "Sergey wouldn't work for Valeri Volodin if there was a gun to his head."

Ryan headed back to the Yellow Oval Room. Normally, he would cut short a get-together like this to deal with something of the magnitude of the possible assassination of a Russian intelligence chief, but he wanted to use this opportunity to get Golovko's take on the event.

But as he entered the room, he immediately saw a commotion. A Secret Service agent standing along the wall rushed forward toward the sitting area. Only then did Jack notice his old friend on the floor, lying next to his chair on his back. Cathy was with him, cradling his head.

Golovko's face was a mask of pain.

Cathy looked up at Jack. "Get Maura up here. And tell the ambulance to come to the South Portico. Let them know they will be going to GWU!"

Ryan spun back out the door. The Secret Service was already on their radios; surely they were doing the First Lady's bidding, but Jack followed his wife's instructions nonetheless.

Sergey Golovko was driven out of the White House's east entrance in the back of an ambulance, while Jack and Cathy stood just inside the doorway.

The ambulance did not use its sirens until it pulled onto Connecticut Avenue, so as not to arouse the interest of the media around the White House.

Cathy wanted to go along with Golovko, but she knew she would be seen upon arrival at George Washington University Hospital and then, within minutes, the White House Briefing Room would be full of screaming press clamoring for information as to what they had missed. Still, Cathy knew Jack's own physician was riding along with Golovko, and she was top-notch.

President Ryan left his wife after a moment and headed into the West Wing, pushing the shock of Golovko's collapse out of his mind so he could concentrate on the upcoming meeting. He'd only just arrived when he was notified that Mary Pat Foley and CIA director Jay Canfield were in the anteroom, waiting to speak with him. He looked down at his watch. The meeting wasn't scheduled to begin for another half-hour.

"Send them in," he said over the intercom, and he sat back on the edge of his desk.

Foley and Canfield entered in a rush. Mary Pat did not waste time. "Mr. President . . . we have a problem."

Jack rose from his desk. "They are piling up, aren't they? Go ahead."

"Russian television is saying police have cornered and killed a man in a Moscow apartment. They say he is the bomber of the restaurant. He is a Croatian national named Dino Kadić."

"Why is that a problem?"

Mary Pat looked to Jay Canfield. Canfield nodded, then looked up at the President. "Kadić . . . is . . . known to us."

"Meaning?"

"He used to be an Agency asset."

Ryan's shoulders slumped, and he sat back on the edge of the desk. "He was CIA?"

"By proxy only. He worked in the Balkans in the nineties. For a short time he was part of a unit on the CIA's payroll. We gave them some training as well. We dumped Kadić when his group . . . went rogue, I guess you could say."

"War crimes?"

"Of the worst kind."

"Jesus. Do the Russians know he used to be on CIA's payroll?"

Mary Pat spoke up: "Kadić has made a career in the underworld by exaggerating his former ties to CIA. The story he's told anyone who will listen makes it sound like he had a corner office on the seventh floor at Langley. Trust me, the Russians know Kadić has Agency ties."

"Great," Jack said. "Volodin owns the media in Russia. Their morning papers will lead with the story of a CIA hit man whacking their foreign intelligence director."

Canfield said, "You've got that right. We will deny it, of course, for whatever good it will do."

Mary Pat changed the subject. "I heard about Golovko. Is he going to be okay?"

Jack shrugged. "No idea. Food poisoning would

be my guess, but I'm not a medical doc, just a history doc. They rushed him to GWU. He was conscious, but weak and disoriented."

"So you didn't get a chance to tell him about Biryukov?"

"No." He thought for a moment. "With Golovko going into the hospital, it will come out that he was here in the White House. We need to get ready for the repercussions of this, as well as the Biryukov killing."

Mary Pat whistled, putting the two events together. "Jack Ryan whacks the head of Russian foreign intelligence and then meets with a top critic of the Kremlin on the same day."

Canfield added, "Who then pukes up his chicken salad."

"Yeah, DEFCON two, at least," Jack muttered.

Just then, Scott Adler, the secretary of state, entered the room. "Scott," Jack said, "we need to get the Russian ambassador in here so I can express my condolences about Biryukov."

Adler did a double take. "I think that might be a bit excessive."

"There are some details you don't know yet. Better get your Maalox out while Jay briefs you on what's going to show up in the Russian papers tomorrow."

Adler sat down slowly on the sofa. "Terrific."

10

A lone figure walked purposefully through the London night, moving silently through the streets of Kensington. He wore a black hooded sweatshirt and black cotton pants, so he disappeared perfectly in the dark between the streetlamps. Even when he reappeared under the lights, his face was still obscured by his beard and mustache.

He walked with his head down, and the pack on his shoulder swung along with his athletic gait. He meant business, but the two middle-aged women heading home from the Tube station didn't know just what business he was in. They saw the man approaching them, and they crossed the quiet street, just to be on the safe side.

Jack Ryan, Jr., watched the women cross the street; he was certain they were doing it to avoid him, and he chuckled. He didn't get any sort of thrill out of scaring innocents, but it showed him how far he had come with his metamorphosis.

His transformation had been dramatic. He wore a full beard and mustache now, and he'd cut his hair shorter than he'd ever worn it in his life.

When he was at work at Castor and Boyle Risk Analytics, Jack dressed in beautifully tailored suits from a shop on Jermyn Street just off Piccadilly, but away from the office he wore jeans and sweat-shirts or workout gear.

He'd studied martial arts for several years, but now he went to a gym on Earl's Court Road every day, usually late in the evening, as tonight, and lifted with an eye to gaining some size. In eight weeks of heavy weights and a high-protein diet he'd put on nearly ten pounds, most of it in his chest, back, shoulders, and arms, and this made him carry himself differently than before. His walk was a little longer, his footsteps a little wider, and he knew enough about surveillance techniques to realize the benefit of the change in his gait.

He hadn't been recognized by any strangers in well over a month, and by now he was sure even most of his friends in the States would walk right past him on the street without any idea who he was.

He liked the feeling of anonymity, despite the jokes he heard from those around the office about his relentless workout schedule and his new facial hair.

In addition to his extracurricular activities, Ryan had been putting in more than fifty hours a week at work. He had been assigned to a case for a client named Malcolm Galbraith, a Scottish billionaire in the oil and gas industry who owned several companies around the world, including a large natural-gas-exploration concern that mined in eastern Siberia. After he and other private investors poured billions into building Galbraith Rossiya Energy up from nothing, taking a decade to explore and drill in the harsh environs of Siberia, they finally began earning a profit.

But within a year of achieving profitability, and with no warning whatsoever, the company was hauled into a courtroom in Vladivostok on charges of tax evasion. Before Galbraith could get on a plane for Russia to try to sort the whole mess out, the entire company was ordered liquidated by the Russian tax office to repay its debts. Remarkably, all the company's holdings and capital equipment were ordered to be sold immediately at ridiculous knockdown prices, completely wiping out the value of the shares owned by Malcolm Galbraith and the other foreign shareholders.

The ultimate recipient of the assets was Gazprom, Russia's quasi-state-owned natural-gas concern and the largest company in Russia. Gazprom paid under ten percent of the actual value, and of course, they did not spend a single ruble during the years of R&D required to make the speculative enterprise profitable.

Gazprom removed "Galbraith" from the name of the natural-gas exploration company, and they had Rossiya Energy running again within days.

The entire affair was blatant theft; the Russian state had unabashedly colluded to renationalize a company after foreign private business had spent billions to achieve profitability.

Malcolm Galbraith had hired Castor and Boyle to dig through the sludge of the murky deal so that, he hoped, he could find evidence of criminal wrongdoing and recoup some of his huge losses in court. Not in a Russian court. All parties knew that would be futile. But Gazprom owned companies and parts of companies all over the world. If Castor and Boyle could somehow tie any of these worldwide assets directly to the missing billions, then a court in the third-party nation just might award the assets to Malcolm Galbraith.

Jack was in the center of this complicated but

fascinating case as well as other more mundane mergers, acquisitions, and market research tasks: other situations where in-depth business intelligence was required.

Jack Ryan, Jr., made it home to his flat on Lexham Gardens, and he peeled out of his workout clothes. He was just about to climb into the shower when his phone rang.

"Hello?"

"Jack, old boy. Sorry to wake you from your beauty sleep."

Ryan recognized the voice as belonging to Sandy Lamont, his manager at Castor and Boyle. "Is everything okay?"

"No chance you've seen the news?"

"What news?"

"Bloody awful stuff, I'm afraid. Tony Haldane was killed tonight."

Jack only knew of Haldane, he'd certainly never met the famous fund manager, though his office building was just a few blocks away from where Jack worked.

"Damn. Killed *how?*"

"Looks like terrorism or something like that. Somebody blew up a restaurant in Moscow. The head of Russia's foreign security agency was there. He's a goner, too. It seems Tony had the misfortune of eating at the same place as someone on a hit list, poor old sod."

Jack knew instantly that Sandy was calling him because of the high-stakes business implications of the death of one of The City's most successful international fund managers — in Russia, no less. But Jack's mind was out of The City at the moment, and back in the D.C. area. He thought of

99

The Campus and the activity the assassination of one of Russia's two intel chiefs would do to the operational tempo for the analysts there. Perhaps there would even be an increase in the OPTEMPO for the operations arm of the organization.

No. Scratch that thought . . . They are all on stand-down, aren't they?

"That's terrible," Jack replied.

"Terrible for Haldane," Sandy agreed. "Not so terrible for us if we look over his client list for prospects. There will be a lot of worried investors without Haldane piloting the ship. They will pull money out of his fund and start looking for new places to stash it, and they'll need a firm like Castor and Boyle to help them vet potential opportunities."

"Wow, Sandy," Jack said. "That's cold."

"It *is* cold. It is also money. It's the real world."

"I get it," Ryan said. "But I'm slammed right now. I've got conference calls all day tomorrow with investigators in Moscow, Cyprus, Liechtenstein, and Grand Cayman."

Lamont just breathed into the phone for a moment. Then he said, "Aren't you the pit bull?"

"I'm trying."

"You know, Jack, the Galbraith case is a particularly tough one, as it is starting to look more and more like well-positioned types in the tax office were involved. From my experience, these types of cases are never resolved to the satisfaction of our clients."

Ryan asked, "Are you suggesting I don't bother?"

"No, no. Nothing like that. Just suggesting that you don't break your back on it. You've hired investigators in five countries, you've pulled a lot of resources from our legal department, our accounting department, our translation department."

"Galbraith's got the money," Jack countered. "It's not like we're paying for it."

"True, but we don't want to get bogged down with one case. We want new cases, new opportunities, because that's where the real money lies."

"What are you saying, Sandy?"

"Just a warning. I was young and hungry once. Wanted to bloody well fix the system by shining a light on all the schemes in Russia, to make a difference. But the system is cracked, man. You can't beat the bloody Kremlin. You are going to get yourself burned out with this work rate, and it will leave you frustrated as hell when it doesn't pan out." He paused; it seemed to Ryan he was struggling for the words. "Don't shoot all your powder on this target. It's a lost cause. Bring some of that killer instinct toward getting new clients. *That's* where the money is."

Jack liked Sandy Lamont. He was intelligent and funny and, even though Jack had worked with him for only a few months, the forty-year-old Englishman had taken Jack under his wing and treated him almost like a kid brother.

It was a cutthroat industry he was in now. Not literally, of course, but figuratively speaking; the well-dressed men and women in The City were always hunting opportunities, and always protecting what they had with vehemence.

Jack could not help thinking that some of their anger and excitement in chasing the next buck or pound or yen or ruble was rather misplaced, considering the life-and-death struggles he himself had been involved in over the past few years.

Jack wished like hell he was back with the guys, sitting on Clark's porch with a beer and brainstorming ways to find out details of what happened this evening in Moscow. The camaraderie he'd experienced in the past few years was something he'd almost taken for granted. Now that he was here, on his own, all he could do was wonder what the rest of the men of The Campus were up to back in the States.

He felt incredibly alone and unimportant here in London tonight, despite the fact that his colleague was on the other end of the phone.

Suck it up, Jack. You signed on to do a job and you will damn well do it.

"You there, mate?"

"Yeah, Sandy. I'm here. I'll be there first thing in the morning. We can start coming up with a plan to pitch to Haldane's clients."

"That's what I like to hear. Killer instinct. See ya." Lamont hung up.

Jack stepped into the shower. *Killer instinct. If you only knew, Sandy.*

11

The White House might have been referred to as the People's House, but for the last decade no family had lived within its walls more than the Ryans.

President Jack Ryan may have been well into the second year of his final term in office, but he still felt like an outsider here. His real home was up in Maryland. The White House was a temporary address for him, and though he had to admit he enjoyed much of the work of being the President of the United States, he would also enjoy retiring back to the shores of the Chesapeake Bay, once and for all.

An hour before heading to bed, Ryan strolled into the main residence of the White House after putting in a full evening of work in the Oval Office. He and Cathy went into Jack's private study, and together they called George Washington University Hospital to check on the condition of Sergey Golovko. They learned nothing new; a barrage of tests were being run and the Russian remained weak, with low blood pressure and a litany of gastrointestinal and endocrinal complaints. He had been moved to the ICU while they diagnosed his condition, but he was conscious and alert, if very uncomfortable.

Jack and Cathy thanked the doctors for their efforts, then Jack forced himself to brighten his mood so he could accompany Cathy on their nightly rounds of tucking in the kids for bed.

Evenings at the White House were not very different from bedtime in most homes with children in America. Just as everywhere, the nightly ordeal of getting the kids to brush their teeth and ready to go to sleep happened more smoothly some nights than others.

They first dropped in to say good night to Kyle Daniel. His room was the West Bedroom, and it looked in many ways like most American boys' bedrooms; there were toy chests brimming with train tracks, action figures, puzzles, and board games, and the bedspread and curtains had a NASA motif, with planets and satellites and astronauts on a sea of black sky and stars.

The room wasn't huge, but it was admittedly larger and statelier than the average eight-year-old boy's room. This had been the bedroom of John F. Kennedy, Jr., when he was a toddler, and Ronald Reagan used the room as a gym.

Kyle's room wasn't terribly neat, which derived chiefly from Cathy and Jack's instructions to both children to pick up after themselves. Jack constantly reminded the kids they wouldn't have attendants at their beck and call for their entire lives, so there was no sense in becoming overly accustomed and dependent on them.

Kyle seemed to be genetically predisposed to removing Legos, trains, Matchbox cars, and other small, sharp objects from his toy box and leaving them all over the floor.

Although the Ryans gave firm instructions to

the residence staff to leave enough of the daily straightening to the kids that they could develop a respect for responsibility, more than once Jack passed Kyle's room and caught one of the Secret Service agents scooping up toys and putting them back on a shelf or in a toy box. Each time, the President would lean in the doorway with a long gaze at the offending agent, and each time, the agent would sheepishly make some excuse, usually saying the cleanup was only for operational reasons, since she might need to cross the room quickly to get to Kyle, and having an eight-inch-long Lego fire truck in the way might somehow compromise her ability to accomplish her mission.

Jack would invariably raise an eyebrow, give a tiny smile, and shake his head before moving on.

Once Kyle was tucked in for the night, Jack and Cathy stepped down the hall to check on Katie. Katie's room was the East Bedroom; it had been Nancy Reagan's study and Caroline Kennedy's bedroom, as well as the bedrooms of "First Kids" Tricia Nixon, Susan Ford, and Amy Carter. It was noticeably neater than Kyle's room, due chiefly to the fact that she was ten years old to Kyle's eight. On the far wall stood a tall detailed playhouse, a replica of the White House itself, and this, along with a canopied bed in lavender, dominated the room. On a table was a photo of a beaming Katie with a smiling Marcella Hilton, a Secret Service agent who died while saving Katie's life during a kidnapping attempt. Katie did not remember her anymore, but both her parents wanted to honor Marcella's memory by keeping her picture in the White House residence, and they hoped future Presidents and First Ladies would reflect on the importance of the work of the Secret Service.

Once the kids were tucked in, Jack and Cathy went back to their bedroom. Here they both climbed into bed and grabbed reading material. She picked up this month's copy of the *American Journal of Ophthalmology*. Jack opened up a new book about the London Naval Conference of 1930.

They read in silence for half an hour before flipping off the lights and kissing good night.

Jack and Cathy had been asleep for no more than a few minutes when Jack awoke to the sound of the bedroom door opening.

Jack sat up quickly; as President of the United States, he had grown so accustomed to these late-night rousings he was no longer surprised to be brought out of a dead sleep by doors opening or men standing over him. Normally he liked to follow the night watch officer back to the West Sitting Hall so they could talk without disturbing Cathy. But as Jack put his feet on the floor and reached for his glasses, the overhead light in the bedroom came on.

This had never happened before.

Surprised and immediately on guard, Jack put on his glasses and saw Secret Service agent Joe O'Hearn moving quickly toward the bed.

"What is it?" Jack asked, no small amount of concern in his voice.

"I'm sorry, Mr. President, there is a situation. We need to move you and your family into the West Wing."

"The West Wing?" That didn't make sense to

Jack, but he was up and moving before he questioned O'Hearn any further about the danger. Jack had enormous respect for the work of the Secret Service, and he knew the last thing they needed was for him to act like a belligerent jackass in a moment of crisis.

He did ask one more question, though. "The kids?"

"We've got them," O'Hearn assured the President.

Jack grabbed his robe and turned to Cathy, who was up and pulling on her own robe, and, though still pushing out the cobwebs from her sleepy brain, she rushed out the door with O'Hearn and her husband.

The kids were in the hallway with their lead agents. Together, the Ryan family and their four protectors moved quickly but calmly enough down the stairs.

O'Hearn spoke into his headset. "Heading down with SWORDSMAN, SURGEON, SPRITE, and SAND-BOX. ETA three minutes."

Ryan's Secret Service code name was SWORDS-MAN; Cathy was code-named SURGEON, quite understandably; and Katie and Kyle went by SANDBOX and SPRITE, respectively.

A minute later, the four members of the Ryan family were ushered outside and through the West Colonnade. The kids walked sleepily with their parents, but Jack knew it would be less than a minute before Katie began a virtual inquisition about what was going on. He hoped he'd get some answers before she started peppering him with interrogatories.

There were six Secret Service agents around them now in a phalanx; Ryan saw no guns out, and no one was shouting or rushing the entourage along, but the entire detail was acting like there was some sort of threat out there from which the President and his family needed to be secured.

O'Hearn conferred with someone through his earpiece as he kept everyone moving quickly. He said to Ryan, "We're going to put you in the Oval Office for a moment."

Jack looked at O'Hearn as they walked. "I don't understand, Joe. What the hell kind of threat is present in the White House bedroom but not twenty-five yards away in the West Wing?"

"I'm not sure, sir, but I am told I need to get you out of the residence."

"What about Sally and Junior?" Ryan, not understanding the nature of the threat, quite reasonably wondered if his other children were in similar danger.

O'Hearn didn't seem to know. He was clearly operating on information just a few seconds removed from what the President was getting from him. He didn't have a clue what was going on; he was merely getting his principals out of the residence as ordered.

As soon as Jack entered the Oval Office he walked straight to his desk and grabbed his phone. He started to dial Arnie Van Damm, but the chief of staff came through the door that led to his office. Jack could tell Arnie had been working late. His tie was off and his sleeves were rolled up.

He motioned for Jack and O'Hearn to follow him back into the corridor, away from the children, and then he said, "Cathy, why don't you come, too?"

This surprised Jack and Cathy both, but Cathy told Kyle and Katie to wait with the Secret Service team, and the three adults left the room.

"What is it?" Jack asked.

Arnie said, "The Secret Service station here in the White House just took a call from GW. Tests came back on Sergey Golovko. He is suffering from radiation exposure."

"Radiation?"

"Yes. They see it as very unlikely that the White House has been seriously compromised by dangerous levels of the material, but just to be on the safe side, they wanted you and your family out."

Jack turned white. "My God! Cathy, you held the man in your arms."

Dr. Cathy Ryan seemed upset about what she had just heard about Sergey but oddly unconcerned about herself. She dismissed her husband's concerns with a quick wave. "It doesn't work like that. They'll have to check me out, I'm sure. But I'll be fine."

"How can you possibly know that?"

"Because this wasn't something he had all over his body. The way he looked this afternoon. It makes sense now. That's not a guy who ate a bad meal. And it's not a guy who absorbed too many X-rays. He was exhibiting the classic signs of ingesting a large amount of a radioactive isotope. He was poisoned."

She turned to Arnie. "Polonium?"

"I . . . I have no idea. The hospital is still running tests."

Cathy seemed certain. "They'll find polonium in him." She looked at Jack. "Sorry, Jack. If it is bad enough to make him as sick as he was today, it's lethal. There is no antidote."

Ryan turned to O'Hearn. "I want *everybody* out of the residence. Every last cook, steward, security man, and janitor."

Joe O'Hearn said, "Under way as we speak, sir."

Cathy added, "No one should be allowed in the White House residence without level-three hazmat gear while they sweep and clean. It's just a precaution. They'll turn up high levels of the isotope, maybe they will have to decontaminate the cutlery he used and the glass he drank from, but nothing more than that." She thought for a moment. "Maybe the bathroom will need to be decontaminated, too."

Jack wasn't so sure, but it was his job to also consider the political ramifications of this. To Arnie he said, "We'll let them do what they have to do in the residence, but this will not affect the work of the Executive Branch. Business as usual here, okay?"

"Jack," Arnie said. "We need to understand what we're dealing with here. Maybe Golovko wasn't the target. Maybe he was the weapon."

"What do you mean?"

"This could have been an assassination attempt on you and your family. An attempt to decapitate the U.S. government."

Cathy said, "I don't think so, Arnie." She turned to Agent O'Hearn. "We need to get Jack checked out just to be sure, but I feel certain anyone who had access to polonium and the ability to poison Sergey will have done their homework. The level of contact Sergey had with Jack was too incidental to be any threat."

She added, "I don't believe for a second that Jack was the target."

President Ryan trusted his wife on this, so he was thinking of the larger picture. "There is no way in hell this can stay under wraps. Especially if

I have to go to the hospital to get tests run. We need to get out in front of this as much as possible."

Van Damm said, "A high-profile Russian dissident getting poisoned, presumably while in the U.S., and exposing the White House to contamination? This isn't going to look good, Jack."

"No shit." Ryan sighed. "Sorry, Arnie. You are doing what you have to do. But we'll deal with it head-on. It's the only way."

Jack walked back with Cathy into the Oval Office, and they spent a few minutes with the children, letting them know that everything was fine. Cathy explained that a visitor had become sick, and they needed to clean up the places he visited very carefully, but there was nothing at all to worry about.

Kyle was sold on the explanation as soon as he learned his father would let him sleep on the couch in his office. Katie was old enough and clever enough to raise her eyebrows in doubt, but Cathy managed to convince her that they were safe after a little more frank explanation.

Within minutes Cathy was seated at the desk in the Oval Office, getting in touch with doctors on the case at George Washington, probing for details about Golovko's condition that could not be relayed by Van Damm, who might have been one hell of a chief of staff, but he was clearly no doctor. She then woke up colleagues at Johns Hopkins, experts in nuclear medicine and radiation sickness, obtained their confidentiality, and asked them for their take on the situation.

Ryan let his wife take charge; he knew he was lucky to have her expertise on hand in the first moments of this crisis so he could focus on what he needed to do. He headed over to Arnie's office and they concentrated on the political fallout, which, he was afraid, would be every bit as radioactive. The two of them called in the national security team, asking them to get in as soon as possible. The West Wing was all but closed for the evening, but they ordered coffee to be sent to the Cabinet Room in advance of the middle-of-the-night meeting.

Jack headed into the dimly lit Cabinet Room, and Cathy met him there moments later. They sat down at the long table. "What did you hear from GW?" he asked.

Cathy said, "He's bad, Jack. They suspect a high dose of polonium-210."

"Why didn't they know this immediately?"

"The hospital didn't check for it when he came in. It's so rare, it's just not part of any normal toxicology screening."

"And how radioactive is he?"

Cathy sighed. Passing on bad news was an unfortunate part of her job; she had a lot of experience with it. There were times when a little sugarcoating was necessary. But this was Jack; she knew he'd want the facts as cut-and-dried as she could possibly make them. She said, "Let me explain it this way. If he is not cremated, after he dies, his bones will be hissing with radioactivity for more than a decade."

"Unbelievable."

"By mass, polonium-210 is a quarter of a million times more deadly than cyanide. A portion the size of a grain of salt, if ingested, is more than enough to kill a full-sized man."

"I thought we had radiation detectors in the

White House?"

"Polonium emits alpha particles. They don't show up as well on radiation detectors. That's also why it is easy to smuggle into the country."

"Terrific," Jack mumbled. "But you are certain you are okay?"

"Yes. The effects are dose-dependent, and I didn't get any dose to speak of. You touched Golovko yourself, when you shook his hand. They will test us, but as long as we didn't ingest the poison, we are fine."

"How the hell do you know more about this than I do?"

Cathy answered with a shrug. "I'm around radiation every day, Jack. You learn to take it seriously. But you also learn to live with it."

"Sergey's really going to die?"

Cathy nodded grimly. "I don't know how much he was poisoned with, but the amount will only determine how long he suffers. For his sake, I hope whoever did this gave him a large dose. I'd guess he has no more than a couple of days. I'm so sorry. I know he was your friend."

"Yeah. We go back a long way."

12

The national security team met in the Cabinet Room at one a.m. Mary Pat Foley was there, as were the heads of NSA, CIA, and Homeland Security, as well as the secretary of state, the secretary of defense, and the chairman of the Joint Chiefs of Staff. Attorney General Dan Murray stood outside the Oval Office conferring with his senior staff both in person and over the phone, and he stepped in with the others only as the meeting was getting started.

Jay Canfield, director of the CIA, set the agenda with his opening comment: "Ladies and gentlemen, I'm just going to go right out and say it. If anyone in this room doubts for a second that the Kremlin is responsible for this, they are hopelessly naive. You have to understand, this material is very uncommon. Only about one hundred grams are produced worldwide each year. Production is highly controlled and storage is highly regulated. We know where *our* polonium is."

President Ryan said, "You don't have to sell me on the concept that this was an assassination attempt by the Kremlin."

"Mr. President. I'm sorry. I know he is your friend. But this was no assassination *attempt.* It was an assassination. Sergey Golovko is not dead yet. But it's just a matter of time."

Jack nodded soberly.

Mary Pat Foley spoke from her seat on Ryan's left. "Golovko was a thorn in Valeri Volodin's side. Of course Volodin killed him. The question is, can we prove it?"

AG Murray said, "We'll have to do some more testing, but the chemical properties will lead us back to a specific nuclear reactor. I'm going to venture to guess that reactor will be somewhere in Russia."

Scott Adler asked, "If this is so easily traceable, why didn't they just kill him some other way?"

Mary Pat Foley took this one. "For the same reason they didn't kill him in London. Look, I see this as payback for Estonia. They kill the President's friend and they blame us at the same time."

Adler didn't buy that line of thinking. "But we will be able to prove the Russians did this."

Now Ryan reentered the conversation. "Prove it to whom? A board of scientists? The average person in Russia or even in the West, for that matter, isn't going to believe our assertions that we can prove the Kremlin did this, nor are they going to read some third-party scientific study that corroborates the claim."

Mary Pat said, "They will say we did it to frame them."

Adler shook his head. "That is ridiculous."

Ryan rubbed his tired eyes. "I'd bet seventy, seventy-five percent of his domestic population will believe Volodin. We've seen this over and over in the past year — he's playing to his own room. Russia, and all the other countries in that part of the world, are under the effects of Russian-dominated informational space. Russian TV, which is more or less state-controlled, like the old days, is broadcast all over the region. Russia has a massive leg up on us as far as giving their perspective on any issue. The outside world to the majority of people in the former Soviet Union is the enemy, even for those who are no big fans of the Kremlin."

Ryan said, "The head of SVR, and the former head of SVR, both targeted the same day. Something big is happening, and it is the job of everyone here to find out what it is."

The meeting broke up a few minutes later, but Dan Murray, Arnie Van Damm, and Mary Pat Foley remained behind. Ryan said, "Dan, while you get started on your investigation, I am going to talk to Sergey myself."

Murray replied, "I looked into getting a statement out of him already. You can't talk to him now. He's in ICU and is being treated. Even if they could wake him, he is on medication to where he could do little more than stare at you."

Jack was undeterred. "It's in the interests of U.S. national security that he is made coherent enough to communicate. Talk to his doctors, make it happen. I hate to do this to him, but trust me, he would understand. He knows the importance of information in a crisis, and both of our nations are at risk."

Arnie Van Damm said, "Look, Jack. Maybe we can set up a CCTV between the West Wing and his room in the ICU, but I don't want you exposed to —"

"I'm going to the hospital. He is my friend. I want to talk to him in person. If I have to be decontaminated after or if I have to wear a fucking rubber suit, I still owe him a face-to-face visit, especially considering the fact I'm ordering his doctors to wake him up and take him off the sedation."

Murray said, "If you are going to push for this, I'd like to get an agent in there to interview him, too. We can see if he knows when and how this happened."

"That's fine," Jack said. "But they go in after I talk to him. We need to catch the assassin, but the larger ramifications of this are even more important. I don't want them to wear him out before I get a chance to talk to him."

Jack sipped his coffee. "I wish I thought finding the culprit in Golovko's poisoning would lead back to Volodin and cut him off at the knees. There are those in the West, those on the margins, who will be swayed, but that's not the point."

Dan Murray, the law-and-order man, said, "The point is to catch an assassin. I've got my best people on it. We will find out when, where, and how. The why is going to have to come from CIA or State, I guess."

Ryan put down his cup and thought about the prospects of catching the assassin. "Whoever did this is probably long gone from the U.S. CIA or State might end up involved in the takedown of the perpetrators. Keep them updated on the investigation."

Murray nodded. "Will do." He shook his head. "Can you believe it's come to this? What the hell has happened to Russia? We'd come so far since the Cold War. A few years ago I was over there, working hand in hand with their Interior Ministry."

Ryan said, "And I supported their short-lived

move to NATO, helped them in their conflict with China. Times change."

Mary Pat said, "The leadership changed, and *that* changed the times."

"All right, everyone, keep me posted." Jack looked to Arnie. Before he could say a word, Arnie spoke.

"I know. You want to be made available for anyone here if they need you."

"You got it."

13

The new U.S. embassy in Kiev, Ukraine, was on
A. I. Sikorsky Street, in a leafy section on the
western side of the city. Deep within the walls of
the sprawling compound, the CIA station occupied a six-room professional suite on the third
floor of the main embassy building. During the
day a small cadre of case officers, administrative
assistants, and secretaries filled the cubicles and
offices, but in the evening the space had a tendency to quiet down. Virtually every weeknight at
nine p.m., however, the lights in the small but
well-appointed break room flicked on, and a
gaggle of mostly middle-aged, mostly white men
pulled whiskey and scotch out of a cupboard and
sat at one of the break room's large round tables.

The chief of Kiev Station was a forty-eight-year-
old New Jerseyan named Keith Bixby. He ran a
sizable staff of case officers here at the embassy,
each of whom was tasked with running agents in
the Ukrainian government, military, and local
businesses, as well as with reaching out to diplomatic personnel from other nations who were
themselves stationed in the city.

For many years Kiev Station was given short
shrift by Langley for the simple reason that the

best and the brightest officers, along with the vast majority of the dollars, went to combating Islamic terrorism, meaning this and other former Soviet republics were relegated to yesterday's news.

But this had changed, slowly, at first — with the end of the wars in Iraq and Afghanistan and the reduction in focus on the Middle East in general — and then more quickly, with the ascendance of Valeri Volodin to power in Moscow and his imperialistic aspirations. The former Soviet republics began receiving more focus from Langley, and nowhere was that renewed focus more important than in Kiev.

Even though the CIA was putting resources into Ukraine again, it remained a tough posting for Keith Bixby and his team. The country was divided between the nationalistic and somewhat pro-Western west side of the nation, and the staunchly pro-Russian eastern side of the country. Russia itself was actively meddling in the nation's affairs, and like a dark cloud, a very real threat of Russian military power being used against the nation hung over everyone's head.

Keith Bixby had started his career as a young case officer in Moscow, but because of his organization's focus on Islamic-based terrorism, he had spent the entire past decade in Saudi Arabia, scrambling to learn the lay of the land in a completely different environment and culture from what he was accustomed to. Only nine months earlier had that phase of his career ended, and he was given the top posting in Kiev.

And Kiev was, as far as he was concerned, ground zero in U.S. dealings with Russia.

Sure, COS Moscow would be a more prominent posting, but the Moscow Station chief's movements were highly controlled and curtailed. Of course, Keith knew there were FSB agents here in Kiev, and they were no doubt monitoring U.S. embassy personnel to the extent they could. But Bixby and his case officers had a lot more mobility around the city and much more access to the cordons of local power than if they had been working in Russia itself, and for this reason he felt Kiev was a better and more important place to serve as COS.

Bixby worked extremely hard at his difficult job, and he'd been getting less than five hours of sleep a night ever since the conflict up north in Estonia, but he rewarded himself every evening by getting together a group of his staff to play Texas-hold-'em poker and drink Jack Daniel's and Cutty Sark.

As much as he wished he could hang out in a local pub and take in the nightlife here in Kiev, his poker games were with his case officers, and they doubled as one more opportunity to talk shop each day. That wouldn't be possible in the city, of course, so the office's boring and antiseptic-smelling break room was the venue for the nightly event.

Some of Bixby's best case officers were women, which came as no surprise to him, because Mary Pat Foley was known in CIA circles as perhaps the best on-the-ground case officer ever employed by the Agency. But every female case officer on Bixby's staff had a family, and juggling their difficult jobs along with a domestic life was tough enough without adding on the additional chore of heading back up to the office each evening to play poker with the boss.

Keith and a half-dozen of his staff had been at their table for more than an hour when Ben Herman, the youngest case officer in the station, entered the break room with a folder in his hand.

One of the men at the table looked up from his cards and said, "Ben, if that folder in your hand is work, then get out of here. If it's full of cash that you're ready to lose, sit down and I'll deal you in the next hand."

The table erupted in laughter; it was funnier after a few shots of Jack, but COS Bixby waved away his subordinate's comment and said, "You've got something you want to show me?"

Ben pulled up a chair. "Nothing earthshaking, but I thought you might be able to help." The young officer opened the folder and pulled out several eight-by-ten black-and-white photographs. Bixby took them and spread them out on the table over the poker chips and cards.

"Where did these come from?"

"I got them from a guy in the Ukrainian Army who got them from a guy in the SSU." The Security Service of Ukraine was the federal law enforcement arm of the nation's judicial system, akin to the FBI in the United States. "These photos came from the corruption and organized-crime division."

The photos were several shots of the same group of six men, all wearing coats and standing in front of a restaurant, smoking cigarettes and talking. They were definitely Slavic in appearance; five of them looked like they were in their late twenties to mid-thirties; one man was much older, perhaps in his late fifties.

Bixby whistled. "Look at these blockheads. OC?" OC was shorthand for organized crime.

Herman reached for a bag of pretzels on the table and grabbed a handful. "Yeah, they think so.

This group was photographed meeting with enforcers for the Shali Wanderers, which is a franchise of a Chechen group active here in Kiev."

Bixby gave Herman a look. "Kid, I didn't just ship in this morning."

"Oh . . . sorry, boss. I count tanks and helicopters. OC isn't my beat. I'd never heard of the Shali Wanderers before today. I guess I'm not all that familiar with the mafia guys running around Kiev." Herman had spent nine years in the Marine Corps, and his area of focus was the Ukrainian military.

"No problem." Bixby looked at the pictures more closely. "Why did SSU send these pictures to the Ukrainian Army?"

"They were running surveillance on the Chechens, and then these guys turned up. They followed them back to the Fairmont Grand Hotel, and realized they had booked the entire top floor for a month. It's obvious they are OC, but they aren't local. One of SSU's crime guys thought these guys looked military, or ex-military, so he sent it over to the Army to see if they recognized any of the faces. They didn't, so a contact of mine in the Ukrainian Army reached out to me."

Ben added, "They do look military, don't they?"

Bixby was still going through the photos. "The younger guys do, that's for sure. The older dude, not so much."

Keith passed the pictures around to the other men at the table. At first no one recognized any of the men, but the last man at the table, a senior case officer named Ostheimer, whistled.

"I'll be damned," he said.

"What do you see?" asked Bixby.

"The older dude. I've got a name for him, sort of."

"Spit it out."

"He's Russian, I think. They call him Scar."

"Charming."

"A couple years ago when I was posted in Saint Petersburg, this guy popped up on the radar. There was a BOLO for him with the local cops, they had a picture and his nickname. As far as OC guys go in this part of the world, he's done a damn fine job of keeping himself off the radar. Nobody knows his real name. Scar's gang was wanted for bank robberies and armored-car heists and contract hits on local government officials and businessmen."

Bixby joked, "I don't even want to know where his scar is."

All the men at the table laughed.

Ben Herman said, "I guess since I'm the low man on the totem pole, it's my job to find out." He muttered, "For *this* I got a master's in international affairs?"

Bixby said, "Fun and games aside, this Scar guy is clearly in charge of these younger men. Look at the pictures. The military dudes are holding doors for him, lighting his cigarette."

"Could be his security team," someone suggested.

"Doesn't look like security to me. Their coats are zipped up, so they aren't packing heat for defensive purposes, and they aren't looking out at the street for threats. No. These are hard-charging frontliners. Looks like a squad of ex-Spetsnaz guys or something."

"And a Russian crime boss is running them?" Ben said with surprise.

"Would be odd," Bixby admitted.

Ostheimer said, "What's even stranger is this allegation they are meeting with Chechen mobsters. Those are some strange bedfellows for ex-Spetsnaz types. OC here in Kiev is so entrenched, there are shootouts in the street anytime one goon tries to operate on another's turf. I don't understand how the hell some Russian guy can just waltz into town like he owns the place without getting his ass tossed into the Dnieper."

Ben said, "I'll send a cable back to Langley to see if anyone knows anything about Scar."

Ostheimer shook his head. "I checked when I was in Saint Pete. His file was thin. Maybe they've got more on him, but I kinda doubt it."

Bixby handed the pictures back to Ben. "With everything else we've got going on, I don't want anyone getting distracted by this. I'll make some calls tomorrow and reach out to some of the older Russian hands at Langley and see if that nickname makes anything click with them. A guy his age would have been early thirties in the Wild West days of the nineties. If he was a player in Moscow who survived that shooting gallery, someone might recognize him."

Bixby drained the rest of his drink and dealt the next hand. He figured he'd go ahead and lose his last fifty bucks quick so he could go home and get some sleep, because he liked to get an early start.

Being COS in Ukraine was a challenging posting, indeed.

14

Jack Ryan, Jr.'s Monday morning started at 8:15 when he arrived bleary-eyed at his office at Castor and Boyle Risk Analytics, dumped his jacket and his bag, and headed down to the little cafeteria on his floor. He ordered an egg sandwich and a coffee — not tea — and brought his breakfast back to his desk.

The egg was fried in butter and nearly the size of a dinner plate; it hung out of the bread and dripped all over his hand. And the coffee was instant and tasted like road tar. But he ate the egg and he drank the coffee because he knew he would need the protein and the caffeine today.

He'd spent virtually the entire weekend conducting research into the complicated auction of his client's company, Galbraith Rossiya Energy, as well as the subsequent sale of the assets to Gazprom. He'd slept little, and now he was running on fumes.

In his two and a half months here at Castor and Boyle, Jack had dug through reams of corporate documents and file cabinets full of accounting ledgers and transcripts of board meetings. As dry as this sounded, Jack was finding the intricate process anything but, because the work he was

126

doing seemed to have more to do with crime than it did with legitimate business.

And the one inescapable truth he had found in his research of the Galbraith Rossiya case was that the beneficiaries of much of this crime seemed to be the men and women who ran the government of Russia.

The phenomenon of criminal takeover of entire businesses in Russia had a name; it was called *reidversto,* or raiding. This wasn't corporate raiding as it is thought of in the West. With *reidversto,* blackmail, fraud, threats of violence, and falsifying of documents were all used, as was the bringing of frivolous lawsuits whereby bribed judges adjudicated on the side of the criminals. Police and government officials were paid off for their help, often with a portion of the stolen venture used as reimbursement.

Official Russian government statistics claimed as many as four hundred companies a year were successfully taken over by raiders, and Ryan knew what this meant for the nation of Russia. This scared off foreign investments, and it damaged the Russian economy in ways difficult to measure.

His company's client, Scottish billionaire Malcolm Galbraith, had fallen victim to an incredibly intricate and organized scheme to strip him of one of his largest holdings in Russia in one fell swoop. And now Jack found that those working on Galbraith's behalf — law firms, investigators, and other associated businesses based in the East — were themselves falling victim to the Kremlin's wrath.

He'd just heard over the weekend that a lawyer hired by Galbraith directly had been arrested in

Saint Petersburg, and an officer of one of Galbraith's pipeline maintenance firms in Moscow had been beaten up by thugs who, he had told the authorities, had freely stated they had been sent to pass a message along to Galbraith to drop the Rossiya Energy investigation.

These two pieces of bad news might have slowed down the zeal of many, but they only encouraged Jack to work harder. He soldiered on, and through his work on the theft of Galbraith's company he discovered that Gazprom had purchased the pieces of the Scottish-owned gas firm from a series of small foreign companies that sprang up out of nowhere to bid in the auction.

To unravel it all, Ryan had a few weapons he could call on. His main tool was SPARK, a corporate investigation database run by Interfax, a Russian NGO news agency that compiled virtually every nugget of information on every company operating in Russia.

Jack didn't speak Russian — C&B had translators on staff to help him with that — but he'd taught himself Cyrillic in a day, and by now he could sound out the words on the SPARK database quickly and confidently. He'd picked up nearly three hundred Russian words, all related to business, taxes, banking, and corporate structuring. He couldn't ask for the bathroom or tell a girl she had pretty eyes in Russian, but he could read a notation on SPARK giving the address and square footage of the headquarters of a new start-up company in Kursk doing business with Russia's nationalized timber industry.

Another tool Jack made use of was IBM i2 Analyst's Notebook. It was a data analysis tool that allowed him to put in all manner of different

data sets, and then generate quick visual represen-
tations via graphs and charts that he could
manipulate to track trends, see relationships
between people in a target network, and allow
himself a more dynamic way of interpreting
whichever environment he was studying.

Pattern analysis had become part and parcel
with intelligence work; Jack had used it at The
Campus with great effect. But when he started
working with Castor and Boyle he immediately
saw the need to use similar tactics in business
intelligence, and Jack knew good data organized
effectively was the most important commodity for
any analyst.

After an hour going over the database this morning, feverishly adding notes to his database as well
as the two legal pads' worth of chicken scratch
he'd created over his weekend marathon work ses-
sion, he looked away from his screen to sip the
dregs of his cold coffee. Just then, Sandy Lamont
leaned into his office. The big blond man had just
made it in to work, and he held his day's first cup
of tea in his hand. "Morning, Jack. How was your
weekend?"

"It was fine." He thought for a moment. "Well,
it was okay. I worked from home."

"Why on earth would you do such a thing?"

"You told me going up against Gazprom itself
was a losing proposition, so I am digging into the
front companies involved in the Galbraith deal,
trying to find who actually owns them."

"That will be tough going, mate. They'll be
owned by trusts and private interest foundations,
all in offshore financial havens, and the only
names you will find attached to them will be the
corporate nominees, not the real ownership."

"You're right about that, but I did find that the registered agent for several of the auction winners was the same company."

Sandy shrugged. "The registered agent is paid to find the nominee to stand in for the real owners on the corporate documents. One register might work with ten thousand companies. Sorry, lad, but you won't get any valuable information from a registered agent."

Ryan essentially mumbled the next sentence to himself: "Someone needs to put a gun to the head of the registered agent. I bet he'd suddenly come up with some valuable information."

Sandy's eyebrows rose. After a moment he stepped into the office and shut the door. After a sip of his tea he said, "I know it's a frustrating slog. How 'bout you let me serve as a sounding board so you can talk over what you're doing?"

"That would be great, thanks."

Sandy looked at his watch. "Well, I've got an appointment in twenty with Hugh Castor, but I'm yours till then. What have you got?"

Jack grabbed a stack of paperwork off his desk and started looking through it while he talked. "Okay. In order to prove the funds stolen in Russia from the auction of Galbraith's company are now somewhere in the West, where Galbraith can have any chance of laying claim to them, I needed to trace these foreign corporate holdings. We know there is involvement by the Russian government in the theft, so we'll never get the cash out of Russia itself."

"Not in a million years."

"The government accused Galbraith's gas-extraction concern of owing twelve billion dollars in back taxes. The annual tax bill exceeded revenues."

Sandy knew the story. "Right. They owed more in taxes than they earned. It was bollocks, but when the crooks own the courts, that's what you get."

"That's correct," Jack said with a nod. "The tax office gave Galbraith twenty-four hours to come up with the money, which was an impossibility, so the government ordered the company's assets to be sold and the money collected by the state. A hastily arranged series of auctions was set up, and at each auction, only one company showed up to bid on the assets."

"How convenient that must have been for them," Sandy said sarcastically.

"I struck out with most of these phantom companies, but I did learn something about one of them. It's called International Finance Corporation, LLC. One week before the auction, IFC was registered in Panama and claimed its total listed capital assets to be valued at three hundred eighty-five dollars. Yet they were somehow able to go to a Russian bank and borrow seven billion dollars to bid in their auction."

"They must have been bloody persuasive," Sandy said. There was no surprise in his voice about any of this; he was a man well versed in the kleptocracy of Russia.

Ryan continued, reading from notes: "The presumed capital value alone of Galbraith's assets in this auction was roughly ten billion dollars. The auction took five minutes, and IFC won with their opening bid of six-point-three billion. Four days later, they sold their interest to Gazprom for seven-point-five."

He looked away from his notes and up at Sandy. "Gazprom makes an easy two and a half billion just in capital acquisition, and the government retains control of the assets, since Gazprom is government-run. The two and a half billion in added value makes Gazprom's stock go up, and this all gets divvied up between the shareholders of Gazprom."

Sandy said, "Who just happen to be the *siloviki*. Fancy that."

"And, don't forget, whoever the hell runs IFC made one-point-two billion for their trouble."

Jack looked back down at his papers. "Since the Galbraith deal, IFC has continued its run of good luck. This little Panamanian-registered firm has branched off into a bunch of different corporate entities, and each one has an uncanny ability to purchase critical infrastructure at knockdown prices, using their newfound wealth to secure bank loans, mostly in Swiss and Russian banks."

He looked up at Sandy and noticed the man looking down into his mug of tea.

"You following me so far?"

Sandy chuckled. "Sadly, old boy, you aren't exactly tripping me up with the complexity of the scheme just yet. I see this sort of thing every day."

Jack looked back down at his papers. "Okay, well, using SPARK, I managed to trace one of these corporate entities through a series of blind P.O. boxes, trusts, and private interest foundations. I finally made my way to a concrete address."

Sandy Lamont's eyebrows rose. "Really? Now, *that's* something. Where?"

"It's a liquor store in Tver, a hundred miles northwest of Moscow. I sent an investigator from

Moscow to go up and poke around. The people at the store seemed to have no idea what the investigator was talking about, but he feels certain the place is, wittingly or otherwise, serving as a drop box for organized crime."

"Which criminal group, specifically?"

"Unknown."

Sandy looked bored again. "Go on."

"Anyway, a month after the Galbraith deal, this tiny little Panamanian-registered company whose only physical location is a small-town Russian liquor store managed to get an unsecured sixty million euro loan from a Swiss bank that regularly does business with shady offshore corps all over the world. It used this loan to purchase a gas pipeline management company in Bulgaria. Then, a month after that, it bought a pipeline management company in Slovenia for ninety million euros, and another in Romania for one hundred and thirty-three million.

"IFC has dozens of legal entities, all new, and each with accounts in one of the offshore financial centers. Cyprus, Caymans, Dubai, British Virgin Islands, Panama. But one thing I've noticed about all these companies" — Ryan flipped through some pages, looking for something specific — "every last one of these companies also has a branch office in Saint John's, Antigua."

"A branch office?"

Jack shrugged. "They are all just drop boxes or business suites. There is nothing physically there that ties them to Antigua. To tell you the truth, I don't understand that part of it at all. Sure, I get it, Antigua is an offshore banking haven, but these companies already reside in other offshore banking havens. Why do they all have to be tied to An-

133

tigua as well?"

Sandy thought it over for a moment. "The quick-and-easy answer is the real owner of this constellation of enterprises has a connection to Antigua."

"What sort of connection?"

"Citizenship would be my guess."

Ryan looked at Lamont as though he'd lost his mind. "Sandy, I hate to be accused of racial profiling, but I can promise you the oligarch, government bigwig, or mob boss who just made one-point-two billion dollars in a Kremlin-backed scheme in Vladivostok was not born in some Third World town in the West Indies."

Sandy shook his head. "No, Ryan. Didn't say he hails from there. Antigua is one of the few nations where you can show up on a plane, hand someone some cash . . . I'd say fifty thousand U.S. dollars would cover it, and then get yourself a brand-new passport. They hand out citizenship for a price."

"Why would you want to do that?"

"A few reasons. Probably the most relevant is that only citizens of a nation can open up banks in that nation."

Jack was thoroughly confused now. "Why would you open your own bank? Even with banking secrecy laws inside a nation, if you want to do business with another bank — and banks pretty much have to do business with other banks — the other bank needs to be able to trust you. Some shady Russian with a suspicious passport isn't going to be transferring cash to Citibank from the Antigua Bank of Ivan or whatever the hell he calls it."

Sandy laughed. "I love your energy, Jack, but you are a babe in these woods, aren't you? You are correct, many offshore banks lack the licenses to trade with the big boys, but there are ways around that. The Antigua Bank of Ivan, as you call it, just needs to find itself an intermediary bank, someone just slightly better positioned in the banking world that is willing to do business with shady characters. A handsome bribe to a bank official should do the trick. That intermediary will transfer Ivan's funds to another intermediary — by now we should have the money upstream to Switzerland or Liechtenstein or Madeira, somewhere still nontransparent but more respected than bloody Antigua. And from here the money can go anywhere — USA, UK, or, as I would venture to guess in the Galbraith Energy case, back to Russia."

"Why would it go back to Russia?"

The Englishman said, "It's a classic money-laundering scheme called round-tripping. Basically, they take money earned from corruption — theft of property, bribes, organized-crime proceeds, whatever — then they send the money to holding companies in one of these offshore financial centers, where the money is moved to another holding company and then back into Russia as clean funds in the form of foreign investments."

"Damn," muttered Ryan. "I still have a lot to learn."

"You do, lad. But you're a quick study." Lamont looked at his watch. "All of this is very interesting, from an academic point of view, but these shell companies pop up and disappear with such ease, if you don't have a handle on the actual ownership structure, meaning names of real people, you'll never get anywhere near the money. We'll never know who is on the board of this IFC company, or any of its entities. They work very, very hard to keep that information secret, and they are bloody good at it. You've seen all the documentation."

Jack's eyes slowly began to relight. "I have. All the documents are designed to hide the owner, but what if we know where his bank is?"

Sandy scratched his head. "What are you on about?"

"All these companies in Antigua I mentioned. They are all registered in the same building."

"Not uncommon at all. There will be a registered agent, a company that can help you get a passport, lawyers to help you set up your tax-haven accounts. They will use a physical address set up just for that purpose. No real affiliation with the ownership."

Jack said, "The bank will be close by, won't it?"

"It won't be a retail location, lad. No cash machine and tellers. It will just exist on paper, with accounts in other transfer banks. There will be a lawyer who set the whole thing up, but these guys don't exactly advertise on the Internet or post on Facebook. They play this game quietly."

Jack said, "I want to look at the registered agent more closely. I mean, see the building for myself."

Sandy shrugged. "Sure. I do that, just for fun. Google Maps will get you a picture of the building."

Jack shook his head. "That's not what I mean. I want to go down there. Poke around a little."

Lamont just stared for a moment. "*Physically?* You want to physically go?"

"Sure."

"Why not hire a local investigator in Antigua to go for you?"

"Sandy, you said yourself I'm still a babe in the woods. I can read the paperwork or study the structure of the shells on SPARK, and I can hire someone to investigate in country, but I'll get a better understanding of it all if I just fly down there on my own. Take a day or two to see the locations, get a feel for these offshore operations. Maybe even learn something about IFC Holdings and the other entities with corporate addresses there."

Sandy didn't like the idea. He tried once more to dissuade Ryan. "What do you plan on doing? Looking through the bloody garbage of the registration agent?"

Jack smiled. "That's a good idea."

Sandy blew out a long sigh. "I don't think you understand what you're dealing with. I've been on-site before. Trust me, mate, these sketchy Third World financial operations centers will be protected by some rough-and-tumble characters. On top of this, there are mob and drug gangs down there who have a vested interest in keeping the prying eyes of foreign investigators away from the companies they use to launder their proceeds. You are the son of the President of the United States. You aren't used to mixing it up with hooligans."

Jack did not answer.

"You might not get the full picture from a spreadsheet or a PowerPoint, but it's a lot safer to sit at your desk and learn what you can."

"Sandy, tourists go down to Antigua and Barbuda all the time. I'm not planning on pushing my luck. Trust me, I'll fit right in."

Sandy leaned his head back in the chair and stared at the ceiling for a long time. Finally he said, "If you do this, I can't let you go alone."

Jack had been thinking the same thing. "Then come with me."

Sandy hesitated some more, but Ryan could tell his English colleague was already thinking about beaches and piña coladas. "All right. We'll fly down and take a look, but at the first sign of trouble we pack it in and run back to the lobby bar of our hotel, understood?"

"Understood, Sandy." He held his hand up for a high five and said, "Road trip!"

Sandy looked at the hand in the air. "I beg your pardon?"

Jack lowered his hand. He'd overestimated the moment. "It will be fun. You better pack some sunscreen, though — you don't look like you'd last long in the Caribbean without it."

Sandy Lamont couldn't help laughing.

15

It was past ten p.m. at the Emmitsburg, Maryland, farm of John Clark. John and his wife, Sandy, had spent the evening watching a rented movie, and they were getting ready for bed when the phone on the nightstand rang.

Clark scooped it up.

"Hello?"

"John Clark, please."

"Speaking."

"Hi, Mr. Clark. Sorry to disturb you so late. This is Keith Bixby, calling from U.S. embassy, Kiev."

Clark ran the name through the massive database of contacts in his mind. It didn't ring a bell, and, as far as he knew, he didn't know anyone working in Kiev at the moment.

Before he could admit he'd drawn a blank, Bixby said, "Jimmy Hardesty suggested I give you a call." Hardesty was CIA, he and Clark went back decades, and Clark trusted Hardesty.

"I see. What do you do at the embassy there, Keith?"

"I'm cultural attaché to the ambassador."

This meant, to Clark, that Bixby was the CIA's chief of station in Ukraine, and it also meant, to

Clark, that Bixby was freely giving him this information. He would know that Clark would know he was COS.

"Got it," said Clark, not missing a beat. "What can I do for you?"

"A name came up in my work over here, and we didn't have much on the guy, so I did some digging. As I'm sure you know, Jimmy is the chief archivist at your former employer, and he's pretty much my go-to guy when I have a question of this nature."

"Understandable."

"Jimmy didn't have any more on this personality I'm looking at than I do, but he suggested I check with you. He says he recollects you *might* have run into him in your . . . travels."

"Who's the personality?"

"A Russian guy, I'd put him about fifty-five to sixty-five years old, an organized-crime big shot from Saint Petersburg, known as Scar."

Clark said, "Haven't heard that name in a while."

"So you know him?"

"I know a little about him . . . but I don't know *you.* Nothing personal, but let me give Hardesty a buzz, and I'll call you back."

Bixby said, "If you'd said anything else, I would have thought you were slipping."

Clark chuckled into the phone. "Only physically, not mentally."

"I doubt that. Let me give you my direct number."

After Clark hung up, he called James Hardesty, established the bona fides of Keith Bixby, and confirmed the man was, in fact, chief of CIA's Kiev Station. Hardesty spoke highly of the man, and Clark knew the CIA's archivist was a hell of a judge of both ability and character.

Five minutes later, John Clark was back on the phone with Keith Bixby.

"Jimmy says you are both legit and a stand-up guy, but I want to make sure I'm talking to the right person. When and where did you last have a beer with Jimmy?"

Bixby did not hesitate. "A year ago last month. Crowne Plaza, McLean. I was in town for some meetings. I had a Shock Top and Jimmy had a Bud Light, if I'm not mistaken."

Clark laughed. "Okay, you pass. Jimmy was surprised I didn't know you already."

"Keeping my ass under the radar has served me in my career to this point," Bixby said. "I've probably slammed into the ceiling already working out in the sticks, but the seventh floor has never called to me like it has some of my colleagues."

"You and me are cut from the same cloth. I'll tell you whatever you want to know, but keep in mind my intel is going to be several years old."

"Fresher than anything I've got. Who is he?"

"I knew him as Gleb the Scar. A mob boss, but you probably know that already."

"I had my suspicions. Can I send you a photo to see if you can ID him?"

"I'm afraid there is no need. I've never seen him."

"Wow. He really is low-profile."

Clark said, "He's camera shy, but I do know something of his CV. He was born in Dzhankoi, in the Crimea, Ukraine, but he's ethnic Russian. He moved to Saint Petersburg in the early nineties after doing a stint in a gulag for some mob murders, and then came out of Siberia tougher

141

than when he went in."

"Don't they all?"

"Pretty much. He is an underboss in Saint Pete, working for one of the largest Slavic crime gangs, the Seven Strong Men: extortion, smuggling, heavy-handed things. I was running Rainbow for NATO several years back when his organization turned up on our radar. A group of armed gunmen busted into the city administration building, they were after some municipal ministers. A typical mob hit. But the police response was uncharacteristically fast, and the gunmen were surrounded. They took hostages. After two days of negotiations, we were called, and we came over from the UK. We monitored calls out of the building, and intercepted comms between the gunmen and their leader, none other than this Gleb the Scar character. He ordered them not to surrender, to stay and fight. It sounded to us like he was sacrificing them so they couldn't implicate him in the hit."

Clark continued, "Rainbow went in, we cleaned them out. We saved all the remaining hostages, but they'd executed three of the state ministers and a half a dozen building security. We took a couple of light casualties of our own on the takedown." Clark paused, thinking back with regret on the incident. "It wasn't as clean as we would have liked it to be. If we had gotten the green light from the Russians a few hours quicker, we could have saved a lot more lives."

"And Gleb was never captured?"

"Negative. He likes to send his people to do all his dirty work. He's a big shot, a hands-off type. Stays as clean as possible while letting the little fish take the risks."

Bixby hesitated for a long moment. "Well, that's interesting, because he's over here in Kiev now, and he seems to be very much an on-scene commander."

"That's odd. From what I remember about him, Kiev wasn't his turf. The Seven Strong Men aren't active there, are they?"

"No, they aren't. They run the show inside of Russia, and they are big in Belarus, but if they are operating here in Ukraine, that is a new development. Gleb was photographed with a crew of young guys who looked like ex-Spetsnaz. They were meeting with Chechen mob guys here in the city."

"That really doesn't track with what I remember about Gleb the Scar. His crew was all Slav. Before Volodin came in and cracked down on the mafia, Georgian and Chechen OC was all over the place in Russia. But the Gleb I remember didn't have any dealings with them."

"Maybe he's become less bigoted as he's gotten older."

Clark chuckled. "My guess is he's taking orders from someone who sent him on this mission. Moving to Kiev, running with ex-mil, working with ethnic OC. It doesn't sound like Seven Strong Men, it sounds like a whole new business plan."

"That's a distressing thought, Clark."

"Yeah, you got problems. You need to find out who he's reporting to — that son of a bitch will be your real troublemaker."

Bixby blew out a long sigh.

Clark thought the man was disappointed in the intel Clark had passed on. "I wish I could be more help."

"No, you've helped a great deal. You've given me some things to think about."

"Hope you can do more than think about them."

Bixby chuffed into the phone. "As I'm sure you can imagine, Kiev has turned into a hotbed of intelligence activity in the past few months, with all the issues brewing between the Kremlin and Ukraine. Gleb the Scar is a person of interest, but really only a curiosity at this point, because I'm short on resources. He is going to have to do something really impressive to make himself a high-value target."

"I understand," said Clark, but he found himself damn curious about what a high-ranking Russian mobster was doing working in Kiev, apparently slumming as an order-taker for someone else.

"Thanks for your help."

"Anytime at all, Bixby. Keep your head down over there. If the news reports are right, you are right in the middle of the next world flash point."

"I wish I could say the media is exaggerating, but things at ground level look pretty bleak."

16

Russian television was not officially state-controlled, as it had been during the time of the Soviet Union, but it was effectively state-controlled, as the largest networks were all owned by Gazprom, which not coincidentally happened to be partly owned by President Volodin and other members of the *siloviki*.

Those stations and newspapers that were not owned by the powers in the Kremlin were subject to constant harassment, scurrilous lawsuits, and absurd tax bills that took years to contest. More ominous than these measures to keep the media outlets in line, physical threats and acts of violence against journalists who broke ranks from the official propaganda were commonplace. Beatings, kidnappings, and even assassinations had greatly stifled the notion of a free press in Russia.

On the rare occasion when someone was arrested for a crime against a journalist, the accused was discovered to be a thug in a pro-Kremlin youth group, or a foreign-born henchman for a low-level mobster. In other words, no crimes against the fourth estate were ever linked back to the FSB or the Kremlin.

The vanguard of the Kremlin's public-relations

posture was Channel Seven, Novaya Rossiya, or New Russia. Broadcast in Russia and around the globe in seventeen languages, it served effectively as the Kremlin's mouthpiece.

This was not to say Novaya Rossiya was always pro-Kremlin in its reporting. To create an air of impartiality, the network ran news pieces that were somewhat critical of the government. But these were mostly trifling matters. "Hit pieces" on corrupt politicians, but only those who'd fallen out of favor with Volodin, or on niggling municipal and state matters, such as garbage collection, union rallies, and other less consequential matters where the network could portray itself as objective.

But when it came to matters of national importance, especially revolving around Valeri Volodin and policies in which he personally intervened, New Russia's prejudices showed through. Almost every night there were long "investigative journalism" reports concerning the conflict in Georgia and the potential for conflict in Ukraine. The Estonian government, which was staunchly pro-Western and a NATO member state, was a near-constant target of the station; seemingly every possible innuendo of financial, criminal, or sexual impropriety had been ascribed to the leadership in Tallinn. A poorly educated but faithful viewer of New Russia's evening broadcast could be forgiven for coming to the conclusion that the Estonians were nothing more than a nation of thieves and deviants.

Although the moniker "Volodin's megaphone" had been given to the network as a pejorative, on occasion this became an especially relevant description, because Volodin himself often appeared live on set during the *Evening News.*

And tonight was one of those evenings. With no hint that it would be coming, the producers of the six p.m. news broadcast received a call from the Kremlin at five-thirty in the afternoon, announcing that President Valeri Volodin was, at that moment, climbing into his car at the Kremlin and would be arriving shortly to conduct an interview live on the *Evening News.* The topic, the producers were informed by the Kremlin, would be the assassination of Stanislav Biryukov by the CIA, and the just-announced alleged polonium poisoning of Sergey Golovko in the United States.

Although this immediately set in motion a frantic chain of events in the Novaya Rossiya building, it was something akin to controlled chaos, because the *Evening News* staff had dealt with nearly two dozen impromptu drop-in interviews in the year Valeri Volodin had been in power, and by now they had their procedures planned like a choreographed dance.

Once they learned the chief of state was on his way to the studio, the first order of business for the producers was to call Volodin's favorite on-air personality and let her know that even though she had the evening off, regardless of where she was and what she was doing at that moment, she would be on the set performing a live interview with the president in roughly half an hour.

Tatiana Molchanova was a thirty-three-year-old reporter and newscaster, and though he had never said it outright, it was clear to everyone that the married Volodin was smitten with the raven-haired, well-educated journalist. The producers learned the hard way that interviews conducted by any newscaster other than Tatiana Molchanova would be met with displeasure by the president.

As much as her beauty surely attracted him, many secretly thought it was the fawning gaze Molchanova bestowed on Volodin while she feigned impartiality. She clearly found Volodin to be the sex symbol that he made himself out to be, and their own on-air chemistry was undeniable, even if it shattered respectable boundaries of journalistic acceptance.

As soon as Molchanova was reached by phone and notified, one of the station's traffic helicopters was dispatched to pick her up at her Leningrad-skaya apartment.

With the chopper on its way, the show's producers got to work writing the questions for the interview, pulling together graphics, and preparing the involved procedure used to make the president's always dramatic arrival appear smooth and seamless for the tens of millions of viewers who would be watching live.

Everyone in the building knew that Volodin did not take direction from anyone, so they had to be ready to go on-air with his interview the instant he arrived. To facilitate this, the halls of Novaya Rossiya were lined with young men and women with walkie-talkies. As soon as Volodin entered the building after bolting out of his limousine, the walkie-talkie brigade began reporting his entourage's progress through the lobby, directing him into an elevator that had been held for him, then up to the sixth-floor studio he had visited more than twenty times since he became president of Russia.

The brigade worked well this evening, and by the time Volodin strode confidently into the sixth-floor studio at 6:17 p.m., the floor director was ready for him. Volodin was a small man, only five-eight, but fit and energetic, like a coiled spring ready to burst through his dark brown suit. He walked past the cameras and right onto the set without hesitation or prompting from the floor staff. Any issue involving catching him in a camera shot or disrupting what was happening on live television was clearly the studio's problem and not the problem of the president.

The producer of the news program stopped a story in the middle of a remote broadcast and went to commercial the instant Valeri Volodin appeared in the wings of the set. Although this would look unprofessional to all those watching, it was the lesser of two evils, because it also meant Volodin's segment would begin in a smooth and uninterrupted fashion.

Tatiana Molchanova had arrived just two minutes before her guest, but she was a pro, especially at this part of her job. She'd done her makeup in the helicopter, had listened to a producer read the questions three times en route to the station so she could be prepared for them, and she went through some practice follow-up questions she would use if President Volodin showed an interest in conducting a real interview.

She had to be prepared for any eventuality.

Sometimes Volodin sat down for his segment, did little more than make a statement, and then took off, leaving the station staff scrambling to fill the time they'd allotted for him. Other times he seemed as though he had no place to be; he would answer all of Molchanova's questions, engage in lengthy discussions about Russian life and culture, and even the weather and hockey scores. The producers didn't dare cut to commercial, nor did they move on with their regularly scheduled program if the "Valeri Volodin Hour" ran past seven o'clock.

They had no idea which of his two extreme moods would strike him tonight, but Tatiana and her producers were ready in either case.

While Volodin greeted Tatiana Molchanova, an audio engineer clipped a microphone to his lapel. He shook his interviewer's hand warmly; he had known Molchanova for several years, there were even rumors of affairs in the subversive blogs of Moscow, but these rumors were derived more from a few photographs of the two of them sharing innocuous hugs at parties and other public events and the impressions given by her dreamy eyes and wide smiles while he spoke.

As soon as Volodin was in his seat, the producer of *Evening News* cut the commercial that was playing, and the cameras were back live on the set.

Molchanova appeared poised and ready; she spoke to her viewers about the bombing death of Stanislav Biryukov, and she asked President Volodin for his reaction.

With his hands on the desk in front of him, and a forlorn expression, Valeri Volodin spoke in his trademark voice: soft but self-assured, vaguely arrogant. "This looks very much like a Western-backed assassination. Stanislav Arkadyevich did not have real enemies in organized crime here in Russia. His work was abroad, he held no great interest to the criminal scum of the Caucasus and the near abroad."

He looked away from the camera and toward Tatiana Molchanova. "Stanislav Arkadyevich worked tirelessly to protect the Motherland from the pervasive threats coming from the West.

Fortunately, thanks to the impressive efforts of our Interior Ministry police, we learn the perpetrator of Stanislav Arkadyevich's assassination was none other than a known agent of the West. A Croatian employee of the CIA. I do not think one must search very hard to determine who is culpable for this heinous crime against the Motherland."

A passport photo of Dino Kadić appeared on the television screen, across which the words "Central Intelligence Agency," in English, were superimposed in red in a font very similar to the rest of the passport's typeface, giving the impression the document was some sort of official CIA identity card. It was a simple trick good for fooling the low end of the station's viewers, of which there were tens of millions.

Molchanova fed Volodin his next talking point. "And now, Mr. President, on the heels of Director Biryukov's assassination comes word from America of the radiation poisoning of Sergey Golovko, Biryukov's predecessor at SVR."

"*Da.* The case of Sergey Golovko is also very interesting. Although I had my differences with the man, I can forgive him for some of the ludicrous things he has said. After all, he is quite old and he comes from an earlier time. Still, I find his proven ties to financial corruption very unpalatable. He is a darling of the Americans, of course, a friend of Jack Ryan's, until which time the Americans poisoned him."

"Why would they do this, Mr. President?"

"To blame Russia, of course. Clearly they intended for him to show the effects of his poisoning only after he returned to the United Kingdom. Their scientist assassins made an error in their

151

math. Perhaps they need new calculators or scales or something like that." Volodin chuckled at himself, and the interviewer smiled right along with him. Laughter could be heard off camera in the studio. Volodin continued, "I don't know if the scientists used too much polonium, or if the assassins poisoned him at the wrong time. Imagine, though, if their plan had worked. He would have returned to the United Kingdom, and he would have become sick there. America would have been held blameless, and Russia would appear to be culpable. *That* was their intention." He waved an angry finger in the air.

"Since the necessary police action we took in Estonia in January, where our small and lightly equipped expeditionary force met a NATO force much larger, and ground them into the dirt, the Americans have seen Russia as an existential threat. They feel that if they can implicate Russia, blaming us for crimes in which we had no culpability, they can marginalize us to the world."

Volodin looked at the camera. "It will not work."

On cue, Tatiana Molchanova asked her next softball question: "What measures will our government take to keep order and security in this time of heightened foreign threats?"

"I have decided, after careful consideration and consultation with key members of the security services, to make some important changes. It has been said that Stanislav Arkadyevich Biryukov was irreplaceable in his post as director of SVR, and I agree with this. It is for this reason that I have decided not to replace him. As evidenced by the domestic terrorism that led to the death of Biryukov, and several completely innocent civilians, as well as the international terroristic nature of the poisoning of Golovko, it is clear to see our nation's threats, from within and from without, are one and the same.

"The threats against our nation are such that we cannot diffuse the two intelligence organizations any longer. We need cohesion in all aspects of our security services, and to this end I have ordered the reintegration between the SVR and the FSB. The organization will retain the name Federalnaya Sluzhba Bezopasnosti, but the FSB will now take over responsibility for all foreign intelligence collection.

"FSB director Roman Talanov will continue in his present duties and assume responsibility for the foreign component as well. He is highly capable, and he has my full confidence."

Even Tatiana Molchanova seemed surprised; she certainly had no follow-up questions prepared in advance that were relevant, but she covered well. "This news will be very interesting to all our viewers, both here in Russia and the near abroad, where Director Talanov has protected Russia from foreign threats, and internationally, where Russian interests have been so ably protected by the late Director Biryukov."

Volodin agreed, of course, and he began a twelve-minute impromptu speech that delved into past conflicts in Georgia, the current disputes with Ukraine, and other nations in what Volodin referred to as Russia's privileged interests.

His speech expanded to rail against NATO, Europe, and the United States. It mentioned commodity prices for natural gas and oil, and there was even a brief Russo-centric history lesson involving Russia saving Western Europe from fascism during the Second World War.

When the president finished, after the lights dimmed and a commercial for Ford began running on the studio monitors, Volodin removed his own microphone and stood up. He shook Molchanova's hand with a smile. She was the same height as the president, and she had the good manners to always wear flats when he came to the studio.

"Thank you so much for your time," she said.

"It is always a pleasure to see you."

He did not immediately let go of her hand, so the thirty-three-year-old newscaster decided to take the opportunity to press her luck. "Mr. President, your news today was very exciting, and I am sure it will be received well. I wonder if it might not be a good idea for Director Talanov to also come on my show sometime. We have not seen him in the news at all to this point. In light of his new promotion, this might be a perfect opportunity for him to introduce himself to the citizenry of Russia."

Volodin's smile did not waver, his deep, lustful look into Tatiana's eyes did not diminish, but his words seemed darker somehow. "My dear lady, Roman Romanovich will not be appearing on television. He is very much a man of the shadows. That is why he does what he does, that is where he works best, and, just between you and me . . . that is where I want to keep him."

Volodin winked.

For virtually the first time in her professional life, Tatiana Molchanova found herself unable to respond. She merely nodded meekly.

17

The Campus had been created by President Jack Ryan during his first term in office, as a small but hard-hitting outfit tasked with furthering the aims of the United States in an off-the-books fashion.

Jack Ryan put Gerry Hendley in charge. Hendley was a former senator from Kentucky who had retired from public life in disgrace in a staged case of financial impropriety, purely for the purpose of getting out of politics to begin the difficult and crucial work of establishing a sub-rosa spy shop.

To ensure the men and women of The Campus were protected in case any of their operations were revealed, before leaving office during his first elected term, President Ryan signed one hundred blank presidential pardons in secret, and he handed them over to Hendley.

With access to the intelligence feeds between the CIA and the NSA, but free of the bureaucracy and oversight of a government intelligence organization, The Campus had considerably more latitude to conduct their operations, and this had given them a power and a reach that had led to incredible successes in the past several years.

When President Ryan established The Campus,

however, he had no way of knowing that one day the operational arm of the organization would be staffed by his longtime friends and associates John Clark and Domingo Chavez; his nephews Dominic and Brian Caruso; and even his own son, Jack Ryan, Jr.

Brian had been killed in action in Libya two years earlier, and he had been replaced by former Army Ranger Sam Driscoll.

Months earlier, Chinese computer hackers had broken into the Hendley Associates network, and a kill team of Chinese operatives had hit the West Odenton headquarters of Hendley Associates in the dead of night in an attempt to wipe out the organization. The Chinese attack had been thwarted, but Hendley and his team knew their operation could not continue in the same location now that the Chinese knew where they were, and perhaps even *what* they were.

Losing the West Odenton location created a bigger nuisance than just having to find a new building. The Campus had obtained much of its actionable intelligence by means of an antenna farm on the roof of the five-story building that intercepted classified intel traveling back and forth between the National Security Agency at Fort Meade, Maryland, and the Central Intelligence Agency in Langley, Virginia.

That method of pulling classified data was lost to them now that the Hendley Associates building was serving the white side only.

But there was hope for The Campus and its future by means of a fifty-five-year-old paunchy and pale computer geek named Gavin Biery. Biery had spent the months since the Chinese attack working on a method to obtain intelligence via the CIA's Intelink-TS, its top-secret network. He had taken the advanced hacking code used by the Chinese against the CIA's computers, and then, after making sure the CIA had patched their vulnerabilities, he began to search for new threat vectors into Intelink-TS.

So far his work held much promise but little payoff.

While Gavin worked the intelligence-collection angle and Gerry Hendley worked on obtaining a new base of operations, the Campus operators, minus Jack Ryan, Jr., had been using John Clark's expansive farm in Emmitsburg, Maryland, as a training ground.

John Clark's rustic farm was perhaps not the most suitable location on earth for a unit of covert paramilitary and clandestine services operators to train, but for the time being, at least, it served its purpose.

Until recently, the operators had trained in secret locations all over the country, but they were vulnerable now, so they retreated to the farm and ran drills to keep themselves sharp. They'd even taken over a guest bedroom and turned it into a small op center and mini-schoolhouse. The men spent an hour a day or more using foreign-language training software on their laptops and reading the latest open-source information about the world's major trouble spots.

And to a man they hoped like hell their training and study would be put to use with the call to return to operational status.

Gerry Hendley took the afternoon off from his tour of the D.C. area's hundreds of available office buildings to drive out to Emmitsburg, Maryland, where he now sat at the kitchen table in John Clark's farmhouse. Around him were assembled the operators of The Campus, as well as Gavin Biery. They had been getting together here once a week, though these meetings had turned out to be non-affairs, really. Each week Gerry talked about his hunt for a suitable location for the organization, Clark and the operations arm discussed the training they had been undergoing, and Biery used highly technical jargon to let everyone know about the work he was doing to get the information stream from the CIA up and running again.

Though the meetings were polite enough, the truth was that everyone was eager to do something other than sit in Clark's kitchen.

Gerry was prepared to start the meeting with a rundown of a couple of properties he'd been looking at near Bethesda, but Clark said he'd like to discuss something else.

"What's up?" Gerry asked.

"A situation has presented itself."

Clark told Hendley and the others about his call with Keith Bixby, CIA chief of station in Kiev, and how the CIA was interested in a Russian crime boss known as Gleb the Scar.

Domingo Chavez had spent the past few days making calls to some friends in both Russia and Ukraine, mostly men he had served with in Rainbow. Through them, he'd learned more about the Scar and his organization. No one knew what he was doing in Ukraine associating with Chechens, and both Chavez and Clark found this very suspicious, especially since it seemed war was on the horizon over there.

Hendley said, "So all you know is this guy is Russian mob, and he's working in Kiev."

Clark said, "I also know CIA doesn't have the manpower to run a surveillance package on him. They are, quite reasonably, focusing on the professional intelligence officers in Kiev, and not organized crime."

"What is it you want to do?"

"Keith Bixby is a good COS who's in a tough situation. I thought we could go over to Kiev and check into this mob connection, just to see what Gleb the Scar is up to."

Hendley looked at the rest of the group. Not surprisingly, they all looked ready to head to the airport right now.

"How big is this guy in their organization? Is he like a Mafia don?"

Chavez had become something of an expert on organized-crime groups in the past year; it was a topic that he'd focused on in his downtime with The Campus.

Ding said, "Russia doesn't really have a mafia in the sense we know it, that's just a convenient name we use to convey the fact it is a criminal organization. In Russia and the other eastern states, the top dogs of the criminal hierarchy are the *vory v zakonye,* which translates to 'thief-in-law,' but means something like a thief who follows the code. Ninety-nine-point-nine percent of the criminals running around with gold chains and ill-fitting suits want you to think they are big shots, but they are not true *vory v zakonye.* Having said that, there might be several *vory* at the top of each organization, and whoever the absolute top dog is will be *vory* for sure."

Chavez added, "Gleb the Scar, we are certain, is the genuine article. He's *vory.*"

Hendley next asked, "How big is the organized-

159

crime problem in Russia these days?"

"Valeri Volodin's Interior Ministry has chased almost all of the largest and most powerful criminal groups out of Russia proper."

"How did they do that?"

"The FSB has a unit called URPO, the Directorate for the Analysis and Suppression of Criminal Organizations. They are basically a hit squad, taking out OC members throughout Moscow and Saint Petersburg. But interestingly, they only seem to target foreign gangsters.

"There is a group of Slavs that started back in the late eighties that is flourishing now because all the Chechens, Georgians, Armenians, and others have been so heavily pursued by the FSB. This group is known as the Seven Strong Men."

Hendley said, "There are only seven of them?"

"No, they were named after an unusual rock formation in the Komi Republic by that name. It's seven massive stone pillars that jut out of a flat field. The group was formed in a gulag there in Komi.

"These days in Russia, the Seven Strong Men controls money lending, kidnapping for ransom, human trafficking, prostitution, car theft, assassination for hire . . . you name it."

"And Gleb is the head of the Seven Strong Men?" Hendley asked.

"Not the head — the leader of the organization is unknown. Not even most of the people in the group seem to know who's running the show. But we do know that Gleb the Scar is the chief of Seven Strong Men's Saint Petersburg operation. He very well might be the second in command."

Caruso spoke up. "And nobody has a clue what he's doing in Kiev associating with Chechen gangsters, right?"

"None whatsoever. He hasn't been known to leave his turf, nor has he been known to be friendly with ethnic minorities."

Hendley said, "Okay, I approve. But how will you get intel on the Seven Strong Men's operation?"

Clark turned to Biery. "Gavin?"

Biery said, "I can't get into Intelink-TS. Not yet, anyway. But I do have access to the SIPRNet. This is the confidential-level network used by the government. Certainly not as good as the TS-level data, but . . . you know how it is with intelligence. There's a shit ton out there in open source, and twice as much is lightly classified."

Clark said, "With Gavin providing confidential-level intel to aid our physical surveillance in Kiev, we should be able to get a good picture of the situation there."

Gavin added, "Additionally, I've hacked into the servers of the Ukrainian SSU — that's their national police. This is where they keep all the goods on organized crime. Should be helpful, but it's not the same as having Intelink-TS access."

Driscoll spoke up now. "We'll just have to supplement it with old-fashioned shoe-leather spy shit."

The others grinned, but Hendley still had questions. "Who will be going over?"

"Obviously Ryan is in the UK, but all the rest of us will head over," Clark replied.

Hendley seemed mildly surprised by this. "I thought you told me you were done with field-work."

"I did. But I speak Russian, and I can read

Ukrainian. I'll need to go back in the field for this one."

"I guess you don't get to hang up your fedora just yet, Mr. C," Dom joked.

Clark gave Dom a hard look. "Screw you, kid. I've never worn a fedora in my life. I'm not that old."

Dom said, "Don't ruin the badass mental image I have of you back in the day, Mr. C."

Chavez said, "Hey, Gavin. You're coming along, too, right?"

Biery looked to Hendley, like he was a child pleading with his mom to go over to a friend's house to play.

Hendley sighed. "I guess since you made it back from Hong Kong in one piece you consider yourself quite the international man of mystery now, don't you, Gav?"

Biery shrugged, but Chavez came to his defense. "He pulled us out of a real jam over there, Gerry. It pains me to say it, but we might not have made it out of there without him."

"All right," Hendley said. "You can go into the field to support the operation." Hendley turned his attention back to Clark. "Surely you can't go over there with weapons."

"No," Clark said. "We'll have to be ready to get picked up and questioned at any time by authorities. We can use a journalist cover. If our credos are good enough, we'll be just fine."

Hendley countered, "Good documents will help if you get picked up by the police, but they won't help you if you get picked up by Seven Strong Men."

John Clark acknowledged this point. "Very true. We'll be careful not to get picked up by the Scar

162

and his boys."

Gerry added, "John, I don't have to remind you that Kiev is going to be absolutely crawling with all manner of shady characters. Official and unofficial."

John looked at the rest of the team. "I read you loud and clear, and we'll do our best to keep our operation under wraps, from the official and unofficial." He smiled. "But just for the record, I've got my own crew of shady characters."

18

The entourage surrounding the President of the United States arrived in the intensive-care unit of George Washington University Hospital shortly before ten p.m. The press had staked out the main entrances, but there was a loading dock on 22nd Street that had been cordoned off, and the President had arrived in a green Chevy Suburban in the middle of several clandestine Secret Service vehicles and pulled right up to the door, ensuring the press completely missed the low-key arrival.

The White House radiation story had been all over the news. There was talk around the White House of keeping a lid on the polonium angle, just releasing the news that Golovko had been poisoned, coincidentally while he was visiting the White House, and not mentioning that the poison had been, in fact, a radioactive isotope. But ultimately, reason prevailed. Any frenzy prevented by keeping this news from the public would last only until the truth came out, and the truth would come out at a time of its own choosing. They decided to reveal the full story about the event immediately, keeping only some details about Golovko's condition under wraps for the sake of his own privacy.

Sergey had no close living relatives; in the ICU waiting room Ryan was introduced to members of Golovko's traveling entourage: a publicist, a travel coordinator, and a British security officer.

Jack looked around for others, but that was it. After Sergey's long life serving the Soviet Union and Russia, most of his home nation seemed to have turned its back on him or forgotten about him.

After conferring with the doctors about the dos and don'ts of visiting a man in Golovko's condition, Ryan and his Secret Service detail continued up the hall toward Sergey's room. Jack's principal protection agent was by his side, and she had reservations about tonight, but she did not air them. Andrea Price-O'Day knew when to speak up to SWORDSMAN, and she knew when to let it go. Although she would very much prefer to be in the room with Ryan and Golovko, she knew Ryan would not allow it. Instead, she went into the hospital room with two other agents, swept the small space quickly and silently while Golovko lay still like a cadaver on the bed, and then stepped back into the hallway. She would keep a line of sight on POTUS through a window, but he would otherwise be alone in the room with the stricken patient.

Jack entered the room alone, and he was immediately taken by both how small the room was and how completely full it was of medical equipment. In the center of all the machines, Sergey seemed small and pale. The Russian was tubed and wired, and his skin was pierced with IVs. A large pillow held his head up; Ryan had been told by the doctors that the man's neck muscles were too weak for him to lift his head.

His eyes were sunken and rimmed with gray, and his hair was noticeably thinner than it had been just the day before. Ryan saw loose hair on the pillow around his head. An EKG machine behind the bed beeped slowly in time with the Russian's resting heart rate.

Jack thought the man was asleep, but his eyes flickered slowly, and then they opened. After a moment to focus, they locked on Ryan. Jack detected a weak smile, but only for a second, and then Golovko's face went blank, almost as if the muscles tired from the effort.

"How are you feeling, Sergey Nikolayevich?"

"Better now, Ivan Emmetovich." His voice was scratchy, but stronger than Ryan had anticipated, considering his terrible condition. He smiled weakly and switched to Russian. *"Na miru i smert' krasna."*

Jack had not practiced his Russian for a long time. He said it softly to himself. Then, "With company, even death loses its sting." Jack did not know how to respond to this.

"This must be an awkward situation for you. *Iz-vinitie.*" Sergey's brow furrowed; slowly he realized he had lapsed into Russian. He translated for himself: "I am sorry."

Jack pulled the one chair in the room up close to the bed, and he sat down. "I'm just sorry this happened to you. Nothing else makes a damn bit of difference right now."

Golovko looked off into space. He said, "Several years back, the Chinese government tried to kill me."

"I remember, of course."

"They failed, only by my good fortune, but they failed nonetheless. It breaks this old Russian's hard heart to know my own government, my own country, has succeeded."

Jack wanted to tell him he wouldn't die, that the doctors here would get him through this. But that would be a lie, and he owed Sergey more than that.

Instead, he said, "We will find out how this happened."

Sergey coughed. "I shook a lot of hands in the past week. I drank a lot of tea, bottles of water. I ate a hot dog in Chicago." He smiled a little, reminiscing. "Somewhere along my journey here in the United States —" He began coughing again. The fit lasted thirty seconds, and by then it seemed he had lost his train of thought.

Jack waited to make sure Sergey was finished, and then he said, "I know you are weak and tired. But there have been two other events. I almost don't want to tell you about them, but you may be able to help me with some advice."

Golovko's eyes seemed to sharpen a little. Jack could tell he was glad for the chance to help in any way.

Ryan said, "Stanislav Biryukov was killed by a bomb in Moscow last night."

Jack was surprised by Golovko's reaction, or the lack of one. He said, "That was just a matter of time. He was a good man. Not a great man. A good man. He wasn't one of Volodin's inner circle. He needed to be replaced."

"But why kill him? Couldn't Volodin simply replace him with the stroke of a pen?"

"His death will benefit the Kremlin more. They will blame Ukraine or U.S. or NATO or one of their enemies."

"They are blaming us. It has already begun."

"And you will be blamed for this." His papery white hand rose a few inches from the bed and made to wave around the room. It dropped back into the sheets almost instantly, but Jack understood. After a pause Sergey said, "You said there were two events."

"Volodin went on New Russia TV and announced that FSB and SVR will form into one organization."

Golovko's eyes closed for a moment. Softly, he said, "Talanov?"

"Roman Talanov is now in charge of everything, yes."

Sergey said, "Roman Talanov appeared from nowhere in the FSB. I have been with the state security services for all my adult life, yet I had never heard of the man until six years ago, when he was a police commissioner in Novosibirsk. I was director of the SVR, and I received word from my staff that this man, this police commissioner, was replacing the FSB director in the city. His promotion did not come through FSB channels. It was an order that came directly from the Kremlin."

"Why?"

"That was my question at the time. I was told he had been GRU, military intelligence, and he was a favorite of the leaders in the Kremlin at the time. I could not understand how this was, seeing how he was just some ex–military intelligence officer no one knew who was chief of police in a town in Siberia.

"I found out later that Valeri Volodin, who was prime minister at the time, forced the FSB director in Novosibirsk out, and put Talanov in his place."

Jack asked, "What did Talanov do at GRU?"

"I tried to find out myself. Just out of professional curiosity. I heard he was in Chechnya during the first war before he became police commissioner in Novosibirsk. But as to the question of what he did in Chechnya, and what he did before that, I received no answers."

Ryan wasn't sure what his own intelligence service had on Roman Talanov, but he was damn sure he would find out as soon as he left Golovko's bedside.

"Why haven't you told anyone about this?"

"It was an internal matter. For all my problems with the administration, there is some laundry that I did not want to air to the West. Nepotism is cancerous in our government. It always has been. We have a term for a benefactor who gives protection to someone as they make their way up the ranks. We call it a *krisha,* a 'roof.' Revealing the fact Talanov was handed a job in FSB he likely did not deserve was not so surprising. He has a *krisha* high in government. Maybe Volodin himself. Still, his lack of a background with GRU is very troubling."

Jack just nodded. Considering all of Ryan's other problems at the moment, the ancient history of the new leader of Russia's combined intelligence service didn't seem like that big a deal, but it clearly *was* important to Sergey Golovko.

The Russian said, "Find out who he is. What he was."

"I will," Jack promised.

Golovko looked impossibly tired now. Jack had planned on asking him if he wouldn't mind talking to the FBI waiting outside, but at that moment he decided this man did not need the added

169

intrusion. Jack was mad at himself for staying as long as he did.

He stood slowly, and Sergey's eyes opened up quickly, like he'd forgotten Ryan was there.

Jack said, "Believe what I am about to say. This thing that has happened to you will make a positive difference. I'll see to it. I can't tell you how right now, but whatever comes out of what they did to you will make our nations stronger. I will use this against Volodin. It might not happen in days or weeks or even months, but you will win."

"Ivan Emmetovich. You and I have been through much over the years."

"Yes. Yes, we have."

"We will not see each other again. I want to say you have done much good for the world. For our two countries."

"As have you, Sergey."

Golovko closed his eyes. "Could you ask the nurse to bring me another blanket? I don't know how I can be both radioactive and cold, but it is so."

"Of course."

Jack stood, leaned over to shake the prostrate man's hand, and realized he was sound asleep. He took Golovko's hand in his and squeezed it gently. He'd been told by the doctors he would need to be decontaminated if he touched Golovko. Jack assumed it was their idea of a polite warning, cajoling him to keep his distance. He didn't give a damn. They could scrub him down, but they weren't going to prevent him from giving his old friend one last gesture of compassion.

19

Jack Ryan, Jr., and Sandy Lamont boarded a British Airways Triple Seven for the eight-hour flight to the West Indies nation of Antigua and Barbuda. As they checked their boarding passes and headed to the front of business class, they saw the flight itself was only half full, but Ryan and Lamont quickly saw their section was packed.

The luxurious leather seats were arranged to face one another at an offset so they could convert into beds for the transatlantic crossing. Ryan faced rearward, so he could not help scanning the other passengers on the flight. Business class was full of Indians, Asians, British, and Germans. There were a large number of Swedes on board as well, which confused Ryan until he heard a flight attendant mention the 777 had started its day in Stockholm before stopping off at Heathrow.

Coach seemed like it was mostly tourists, but up here in business, and presumably in the completely separate first-class cabin, the aircraft would be full of men and women who did their banking, either in whole or in part, in the offshore tax haven of Antigua. Ryan's work of the past two months made him incredibly suspicious of those around him, and he discreetly eyed the passengers one at a time, making guesses as to their identities and the dark secrets they held.

Jack hadn't heard any Russian accents, but he wouldn't have been surprised at all to learn that first class behind him was full of Eurasian oligarchs and organized-crime lords.

After a few minutes of all this speculation he realized he could drive himself crazy being so suspicious of those around him, so shortly after takeoff he forced himself to concentrate on the lunch menu.

Jack decided he'd work through the majority of the long flight. As soon as the china had been removed from his table after his sumptuous lunch, he pulled out his laptop and began looking through interactive maps of Saint John's, their destination. He did his best to memorize major streets and transportation centers, and he scanned the route from his downtown hotel to the registered agent's office just a few blocks away. He jotted down addresses of other buildings that showed up on SPARK as being involved in the offshore banking and commerce realm, because he wasn't certain just what he was looking for on this trip, so he wanted to go to as many locations as possible.

While Jack was engaged in all this, Sandy watched a movie. Jack couldn't see the film from his seat, but it must have been a riot, because Lamont's nearly constant belly laugh bled through Jack's noise-canceling headphones.

After Ryan read up on his destination for more than an hour, he started looking through some business intelligence resources he'd downloaded to his encrypted laptop. It was an Analyst's Notebook database of translated Russian government tenders, and he kept it updated every day, hoping to find new clues to lead him in his Galbraith investigation.

Despite warnings from Sandy that focusing on Gazprom itself was a futile endeavor, Jack was determined to get a clearer picture of how the largest company in Russia conducted business — specifically, with the government. To this end, he scanned through contract offers across a wide spectrum of industries in which Gazprom dealt, searching for any bids by either companies owned by Gazprom or else one of the firms who had made money off Gazprom's auction-payoff scheme.

He'd been at this for nearly two hours when Sandy took off his headphones and climbed out of his seat for a bathroom break. The blond Englishman returned, ready to get back into the comedy he was watching.

Jack said, "Sandy, you won't believe what I've found."

Lamont leaned closer to his colleague so he could speak softly. The lights were off, and many were sleeping around them. "What are you looking at?"

"Russian government contract offers."

"Oh. And I thought the movie *I* was watching was a laugh."

Jack said, "Actually, some of this shit is so outrageous it's almost funny."

Sandy raised his seat and then moved over next to Ryan so he could see his laptop. "Go on, then. What outrageous financial shenanigans have you managed to uncover since takeoff?"

Jack scrolled through the database and clicked

on a link. "Look at these translated documents. They are Russian government tenders." He picked one and highlighted it; it expanded to the size of the screen. "Here's one offering a three-hundred-million-ruble contract for public-relations consulting for a Gazprom subsidiary in Moldova."

Sandy looked it over. "That's ten million U.S. for public relations for a natural-gas company in a tiny nation, a product for which there is zero competition. Looks like a typical inflated government contract tender." He shrugged. "Wish I could say we don't have the same thing in the UK."

Jack said, "I'm sure we have the same sort of crime going on in my country, although my dad would hang anyone by the balls he caught involved with something like this. But this deal is even more brazen than it looks. Check out the posting date, and then look at the application deadline date."

Sandy looked, then looked at the date on his watch. "It was posted today, and all applications must be in by tomorrow. For a ten-million-dollar tender. Bloody hell."

"Yeah," Jack said. "I'm going to go out on a limb and say there is something shady with that contract." He went to another page on the database and highlighted another contract offer. "And it's not just Gazprom, the entire Russian government is doing shit like this. Here's another request for tender for a two-million-ruble bid for a state-run psychiatry institution."

Sandy looked at the translation of the tender, scanning it for information. His eyes went wide. "The psychiatric hospital is buying two million rubles' worth of mink coats and hats?"

174

Ryan said, "Think of how many crooks have to be involved in that to where they can post an open bid for something so obviously inappropriate."

"It's reached a level of shamelessness over there that I thought I'd never see," Sandy admitted. "I'll give you a good example. For the past few years one of the most coveted majors in Russian universities is the program that trains students to be government tax inspectors. They get a lousy salary, but it is a job where corruption is a piece of cake. You look over a company's books, tell them they owe ten million rubles, then 'allow' them to skate for only five million rubles if they slide you a briefcase with one million rubles. It's pretty much a license to steal."

Jack asked, "Why doesn't Volodin stop it?"

"Because he needs satisfied government employees more than he needs government revenue. Each corrupt member of the apparatus is another powerful person in society who has a stake in the status quo. People are making money off of his administration. That is pure job security for the *siloviki*."

Ryan sat in the low light of business class, and he thought over everything he'd learned about Russia in the past two months. He wished he'd been more focused on that region for the past several years, but he'd been led along by events more pressing to the United States at the time.

Jack asked, "Why do you suppose Valeri Volodin was the one wealthy businessman who was able to successfully parlay his financial power into political power, when all the others had either stayed in the shadows or else were destroyed by the Russian government?"

"I don't know, to tell you the truth."

175

"You know more about his history than I do. How did Volodin get all his money in the first place?"

Lamont lowered his seat back a little and yawned. "You'd have to go back to the last days of the Soviet Union. Volodin was the money behind one of the first private banks in Russia. He doled out the cash that the other oligarchs used to buy up property when Russia went on sale and privatized everything. He loaned a million here, a million there, plus he bought up his own piece of the pie. Soon the Soviet Union had been sold off for pennies on the dollar, as you Yanks like to say, and Volodin and his bank's clients owned controlling pieces in virtually every industry."

Jack asked, "But he was KGB at the end of the USSR, right? How the hell did he get the dough to start this bank?"

"No one knows for sure. He claims he had foreign investment, but at the time Russia had no private property laws to speak of, so he didn't have to prove where his money came from."

Jack wanted to know more about Volodin's past, but Sandy looked again at his watch. "Sorry, Jack. I'm going to get a little shut-eye so I can be fresh on landing. You should pry yourself away from those thrilling government tenders and dream of all the island girls we'll meet tonight."

Ryan laughed. He had dramatically different ideas of what the two of them would be doing on the ground in Antigua, but he didn't want to tamper with any pleasant dreams Sandy might have on the flight down, so he just went back to his laptop to do some more reading, and he left Sandy to his nap.

■ ■ ■ ■

They landed at Antigua's V. C. Bird International Airport shortly after two p.m., and they took a short ride in a Jeep taxi across the northern tip of the tiny island into Saint John's, the capital.

It was a warm and sunny afternoon, strikingly different from London, and a strong wind from the east blew across the island. Ryan thought Saint John's to be no more or less developed than most of the other Caribbean capitals he had visited, which was to say it was simple and small. Passing through the business district, he didn't see more than a handful of buildings higher than four or five stories tall.

He had read that the town's population was only 25,000, but when cruise ships were in port the downtown streets could be thick with traffic. As they neared the port, Ryan checked the harbor and saw nothing but fishing boats, sailboats, and small cargo ships, and the ride through the narrow streets of the city was quick and easy.

They checked into two rooms in the Cocos Hotel. Sandy wanted time to freshen up and answer some work e-mails, so Ryan dropped off his luggage and returned downstairs alone.

By four p.m. Ryan was already walking along the sidewalk on Redcliffe Street in front of CCS Corporate Services, the registered office used by IFC Holdings.

He had no plans on entering, at least not yet. Instead, he found a tiny open-front fish shack a block up Redcliffe just past Market Street. He reached into a cooler and grabbed a bottle of Wadadli, a beer he'd never heard of, paid at the counter, and then sat down in a rickety wooden seat, back away from the open entrance. After a few minutes to settle in, he glanced back up the street. There, up half a block and across two lanes of light traffic, was a three-story turquoise-colored cinder-block building. A single man stood just inside a glass doorway, wearing a cheap blue blazer a few sizes too large for him. Jack pegged him as security, but just a lobby guard.

Ryan took in the entire scene. Next to the turquoise building on one side was a small meat market. Lamb shanks and beef cuts hung in the sun from ropes, and people walking by swatted at flies. On the other side of the building was a lazy-looking trinket shop set up for the cruise-ship passengers who happened to wander the five blocks up from the port.

Jack took a long swig of his beer while he continued to scan. Hard to believe, he had to admit, that this place was linked to a corporate entity involved in a multibillion-dollar natural-gas deal on the other side of the world.

The building itself had two dozen signs attached to it, but most of them told Jack nothing of what went on inside. In addition to the vaguely descriptive CCS Corporate Services, Jack saw ABV Services, Caribbean World Partners Ltd, and Saint John's Consulting Group.

There seemed to be more than a dozen law offices in the building. Each one had one or two names and a phone number, and every third had a website or e-mail address listed as well.

Jack couldn't read many of the signs from where he was without help, but of course, he had brought help. He pulled a small monocle from his pocket and held it up to his eye, and with this he

178

could easily make out even the Internet addresses at forty yards.

He also noticed a spaghetti-like weave of wires into and out of the building strung along poles. He presumed the wires delivered electricity, Internet, and telephone to the building, and in addition to them, there were several satellite dishes and antennas on the roof.

While he sat sipping his beer, he used his camera phone to take pictures of every sign he saw. As he was in the middle of doing this, a text message popped up on his phone's screen.

It was Sandy.

"Where are you? Fancy a drink?"

Jack tapped back, "Way ahead of you, boss." And he added his location.

It took Lamont a while to arrive, so Jack spent the time taking clandestine pictures of all of the names, numbers, and e-mail addresses he could see, not only for the building that housed CCS Corporate Services, but also for another building on the northeast corner of Market and Redcliffe. It looked like it was full of the same type of services as the turquoise building, so he figured he'd pull all this data as well and throw it into his database back in the hotel room.

Finally Jack looked up and saw Lamont heading down the street toward him, perspiring heavily from his forehead as he approached.

Jack headed to the cooler, grabbed another beer, and paid for it. He passed it over to Lamont as the Englishman sat down.

Sandy cooled his brow with the bottle. "You can bloody well give me London's fog any day."

He looked across the street at the building and then back to Ryan. He drank from the bottle and

179

said, "Feel like a regular double-oh doing this sort of thing. Being here with the son of the President adds another layer to the intrigue."

Jack just chuckled. He said, "I wonder how many buildings there are like this in town."

"Antigua makes itself available for those who need to establish shells and launder money. Other nations, like Panama, for example, have tightened their controls a little in order to gain more legitimacy. Antigua is more of the Wild West. Yeah, they pay a little lip service here and there to international regs, but if you have the money you can bring it here so that it can begin its journey through the great big laundry service of planet earth's integrated banking system."

"But the criminals, the drug cartels, the Russian OC people, they don't physically have to come here, do they?"

"Might, might not. Lots of people insist on the face-to-face. Some blokes don't trust the help, others feel like getting in front of the government officials they are bribing helps them get their point across. The lawyers down here are used to meeting with some scary people, and then doing exactly what they're told. But before you start weeping for them, remember, they make a lot of money for their trouble."

A large black pickup truck that seemed to Jack to be newer and cleaner than many of the other vehicles driving around on Redcliffe Street pulled into view. Ryan noticed there were two young black men in the front cab, and he saw that the driver was looking toward the fish shack where Ryan sat with Lamont. Jack turned away from them, and the pickup disappeared up the street.

Jack finished his beer. "I don't think there could

be one hundred people who work in that building. One of them, *at least* one of them, knows who owns IFC and where his bank is."

"They at least know which transfer bank IFC uses. My guess is they send funds from here to Panama, but it could be any one of a dozen places."

Jack muttered to himself, "Wish we had a crew to tail everybody who comes and goes."

Lamont laughed. "*Tail* them. You sound like a double-oh yourself."

"I probably watch too many movies."

Sandy Lamont finished his beer, and the two men went exploring the neighborhood. Jack put his Bluetooth earpiece in his ear and hit a record feature on his phone. He didn't want to be seen taking pictures around here, so he softly read aloud every sign they saw in the business district that looked, in any way, interesting, along with reading off license plate numbers of any of the many expensive cars that rolled through traffic. The Bluetooth would record his notes, and he had speech-to-text software that would put it in his database once he got back to his laptop in his room.

They wandered the streets doing this till nearly eight, then they ate dinner in a harborside restaurant. Just after nine they returned to the hotel, but Jack told Sandy he would download all the data he'd collected into IBM i2 Analyst's Notebook and run it with the data points he had on the Galbraith Rossiya Energy deal.

Sandy retired to his room, took a long shower, and then changed for bed. He imagined Ryan would have him up at the crack of dawn for

181

another day of skulking around the steamy streets of Saint John's, and his feet were killing him already.

Just as he kicked his legs into bed, however, there was a knock at his door. He opened it to find Ryan standing there, a laptop under his arm, and dressed in black cotton pants and a black T-shirt.

"It's not bedtime yet."

"It's not?"

"We're going back out."

"Where?"

"Let me come in a second and I'll show you."

"Do I have a bloody choice?" Lamont opened the door, and Ryan made a beeline for the desk at the far corner of the room. He had his computer open a moment later.

"Look at this," Jack said. "I got all the new unstructured data in the system and started comparing it to the information I've compiled on the Galbraith deal." He clicked on some buttons and a box came up. Thousands of data points were represented by little dots on a white screen. Lines grew between the different points, and then different colors of points and lines began to pop up. Jack said, "Disparate data points, several degrees of separation." Then CCS Corporate Services, the Antigua-based registered agent, appeared with both blue and red points over the name.

Seconds later, a name appeared on the chart. Randolph Robinson, attorney-at-law. It had several colored dots on it.

"Who's this bloke, and what's his connection?"

"I saw his shingle today on a building on Redcliffe several blocks north of CCS. I popped it in the system, and he shows up as being a lawyer used by CCS."

Sandy shrugged. "A local company uses a local lawyer. Probably for nominee services. Contracts, and that sort of thing."

"That's nothing in itself, and his name doesn't turn up anywhere else. But I ran him through all social media and business listings, and I found his mobile number. Analyst's Notebook ties it to two other companies involved in the Galbraith deal, as well as a shell set up by a Saint Petersburg restaurant group."

"Okay. But what does that prove? That a Russian company has dealings here in Antigua? We know that already."

"One layer to go," Ryan said with a smile. "His suite address ties him to a P.O. box associated with a trust that serves as a local executor for Shoal Bank Caribe, which is owned by a holding group in Switzerland. This holding group also owns several other companies, mostly inside Russia and Ukraine. One of these companies has a physical mailing address. That address is the liquor store in Tver, Russia. The one IFC Holdings uses as a drop box."

Now Sandy was on board. "Bingo."

Ryan looked at Sandy. "This ties him to the Russian mob."

Sandy agreed. "This bloke is involved with a bank used to wire funds from IFC."

Jack was all smiles, but Sandy asked, "What is it you plan to do now?"

"You said it yourself, Sandy: I'm going looking in his trash. He might shred it, but if he doesn't, then there could be tens of thousands more data points just waiting for me to get my hands on them. I just need you to watch the street for me."

"You really are a regular double-oh, aren't you?"

20

Just days after Gerry Hendley agreed to the reactivation of The Campus, the five operations officers flew to Kiev, Ukraine, on board the Hendley Associates Gulfstream G550. As cover, The Campus used a company created and maintained for the purposes of providing legends to Campus operators in the field. The company, OneWorld Productions, billed itself as a new-media organization based in Vancouver, which reported on world affairs from a left-of-center perspective and distributed its stories to news outlets around the globe via the Internet.

OneWorld Productions had a website, an actual office location with a receptionist in Vancouver, and had even published some pieces of reportage, although very close scrutiny of its online videos would reveal they were actually created by freelance journalists who had no idea all their work was for the purposes of backstopping a private intelligence agency.

In addition to a veteran pilot and copilot, the Hendley Associates Gulfstream operated with help from their director of transportation, a no-nonsense ex–Navy medic named Adara Sherman. When in the air she served as a flight attendant, but she also worked as a team medic in the field, a security officer, and a general facilitator of all things having to do with both the flight and ground transport.

Once Adara cleared the dinner plates out of the way, she helped the men go through some of the equipment they would be using on their mission. Of course they had cameras, iPads, and satellite phones with two-way communications capabilities — all items that any group of journalists wouldn't be caught without — but they also had brought along several other items that would not hold up so well to close scrutiny by Ukrainian customs personnel.

There was a case full of slap-ons, metallic boxes each not much larger than a box of matches, which held mini–GPS receivers. These gadgets were great for tracking vehicles via apps on the men's phones and iPads.

Also with them — and these certainly were not contraband, although they would be damn hard to explain — were several hobby-grade electric-powered radio-controlled cars specially designed as delivery vehicles for the slap-ons.

The team had no firearms with them other than Adara's short-barreled carbine and pistol, and a second of each, all concealed under one of many hidden access panels in the jet, where they would remain. That said, the four operations men of The Campus would have a few other weapons available to them while they were in Kiev. They each carried a multi-tool with a hidden four-inch switchblade. The pens they would carry in their pockets were made of hardened plastic and could easily penetrate clothing and skin, they wore necklaces made out of a covered wire that could be employed as a garrote, and even their satellite phones had an external battery that supplied very little extra juice to the phone, but actually served as a powerful stun gun that could incapacitate someone at contact distance.

With Adara's help, they hid the more clandestine items in the aircraft's access panels just so they could pass through a customs inspection on landing. Then the men spent some more time on their laptops reviewing FalconView, a high-tech map system available to military and intelligence, and also available to The Campus, since Gavin Biery had accessed the files back before he'd lost access to the feed between Fort Meade and Langley. But even though their FalconView had not been updated in a few months, Gavin was certain it would still be a hell of a lot more helpful than Google Maps.

As they raced across the Atlantic at more than four hundred knots, Clark looked at the aircraft's position on the main monitor in the plush cabin. He said, "Touchdown in five and a half hours. Let's try and catch a few hours' sleep. We're going to need to hit the ground running tomorrow."

Jack Ryan, Jr., and Sandy Lamont walked up Red-cliffe Street in Saint John's, Antigua. There were still quite a few people about now at 10:30 p.m., and enough of them were white tourists so that Jack and Sandy didn't stick out too badly, although Jack was worried about staying low-profile around here for long, especially with an untrained partner.

They found the building with the shingle for Randolph Robinson; it was just an open ground-floor covered parking lot large enough for a dozen or so cars, and above it a single story of office suites. There was a gated fence around the property, but Jack quickly saw how he could easily scale the fence at a corner post.

Ryan looked into the darkened empty lot and saw three large garbage containers sitting lined up against the stairwell. The lid was up on one of them, and he could see paper stacked on other trash.

The two men turned a corner and found a food truck with a large group of people sitting around on milk cartons, eating salted fish and drinking coconut water. They each bought a drink, and then they kept walking so they could talk.

Sandy said, "You can't possibly filch all that garbage."

"We don't have to." Jack held up his phone.

"I don't follow you."

"I jump the fence, then I turn on my video camera. I grab a stack of papers and move through them as fast as I can. I just have to get a tenth-of-a-second look at each one. Then I send the video file to an archiving application I have. It will use optical character recognition to look at every frame of the video and archive every last number and word in a way I can search and reference it later."

"That's bloody marvelous. How much time do we need?"

Before Jack could answer, a black pickup truck drove by, and the driver and front-seat passenger eyed him slowly and carefully. Jack was certain it was the same vehicle he had seen earlier in the afternoon.

Sandy hadn't noticed, but Jack didn't mention it, because the last thing he needed right now was a spooked partner. He could have canceled his plans for the evening, but instead he just told himself he'd keep a close watch on the road in case they came back.

His eyes followed the truck till it disappeared around the corner, and then he answered Sandy's question: "Depends on how much paper is in those cans. I'd say fifteen minutes, tops."

"What if somebody catches us?"

Jack shrugged. "Can you run?"

"Not really."

"Then let's not let anyone catch us."

As they neared the building, Lamont asked, "How is it you know all this stuff?"

Jack said, "I'm not an attorney, I'm not a CPA, and I don't have a ton of experience like everyone else at Castor and Boyle." He held up his phone. "Little tricks like this are force multipliers. They help me leverage my strength."

The actual collection of the data in the garbage cans went surprisingly smoothly. Jack climbed the fence when no one was in sight, then dropped down and raced to the cans. Two of the cans had no papers, but the other contained hundreds of documents, envelopes, and other relevant material. He reached deep into the can to hide his light from the street, then began quickly shuffling through the pages, keeping his phone pointed at them.

Sandy walked the street out front. He was connected to Ryan through their phones, and other than his need to remind Ryan every couple of minutes that he should hurry up, he did a fine job as a lookout.

Ryan made it back onto the street in ten minutes flat, and the two men walked west back toward their hotel.

Sandy asked, "So are you covered in fish guts and other garbage?"

"Randolph Robinson keeps a clean office. Some of his stuff was shredded, but like most people, he's too lazy to shred it all. I got hundreds of documents, envelopes, pamphlets, and handwritten notes. Don't know if any of it will do us any good, but it sure as hell won't hurt."

They were halfway back to their hotel when Jack saw the trouble up ahead. The same black pickup truck — he could tell because it appeared to be about five years newer than the average vehicle on the street — sat parked just beyond the intersection. Inside were at least four men. Jack couldn't be certain from this distance the exact number, but he could tell the guys he saw earlier had gone to pick up at least two more buddies.

Jack was pretty sure *that* was bad news.

Ryan knew better than to head back to the hotel. The last thing he wanted was for these guys to know where he was sleeping.

There was a lively two-level bar between Ryan and the truck ahead. Jack said, "How 'bout a nightcap."

Sandy did not have to be persuaded.

21

As Jack Ryan, Jr., and Sandy Lamont crossed the street toward the entrance, Ryan noticed a second truck pass through the intersection just next to the bar. Its taillights immediately lit up, and Jack looked in the glass of a gift shop across the street just in time to see the vehicle turn down the alleyway behind the bar.

"Oh, shit," Ryan said softly. Sandy was ahead of him and did not hear.

Jack realized he and Sandy would be surrounded once they got inside the building. He thought it over, considered just continuing on back to the hotel and calling the police, but for all he knew, the men watching him were the police.

Ultimately, he decided to rely on the cover of the crowd, and he hoped like hell these guys, whoever they were, wouldn't do anything inside the bar with all the witnesses.

The bar was just a dive. There was a DJ on a podium and a little dance floor and then a bar area, and to the left of the bar was a rear exit.

Sandy led the way, and as soon as they made it to the bar in the back of the room, Jack told Sandy to go ahead and order for them both. He turned his back to the bar and kept his eyes on the front door, but he also checked the back entrance every few seconds.

Jack began playing this through in his head. He figured the men were some sort of local heat, hired by the lawyers and corporate services companies generally, but not tied to his situation specifically.

Of course, he had to entertain the possibility he was wrong about this, and these dudes were here because he was the son of the President of the United States, and they had something more dangerous in mind.

But he decided the first scenario was more likely. He and Sandy had been a little lackadaisical in their surveillance. Ryan realized if he were operating with John Clark or Ding Chavez, he would have put all sorts of operational security measures in place that would have avoided just such an event. But he'd come down here thinking this was some dry and drab business intelligence exercise, and he had nothing more to worry about than getting the runaround from a secretary who wouldn't let him take a business card off a desk.

Two men entered and stood at the front door. One had dreads, the other short hair and big muscles. They talked to the bouncer for just a moment, then started looking around. They made eye contact with Ryan seconds later, and they stood their ground by the door.

Jack looked to the back entrance now. There was no one there, but he felt sure that even a third-rate crew of hired Rasta stoners from some shanty island village would know enough to cover the back door to box their quarry in.

Jack gave up on the hope the men wouldn't confront him in the public setting, and he moved on to the hope that they were here only for intimidation. "Sandy, I need to tell you something, and I need you to stay very calm when I do."

Sandy passed Jack a beer, and he brought his piña colada up to his mouth and began drinking it through a straw. The Englishman's mannerisms didn't give Ryan much hope he'd have a hell of a lot of assistance in the next few minutes, since he wasn't aware of many bar fights won by men who ordered piña coladas.

Ryan had to look at Sandy's eyes over the pineapple spear. He said, "There are a couple of guys at the door watching us. They've been following us for a while."

Sandy started to turn his head. Jack said, "No. Don't do that. I just need you to be ready to move toward that back door."

"You're bloody serious?" He turned his head around slowly, a poor attempt to be covert while looking.

"I'm guessing someone saw us in front of CCS's office earlier in the day. Who knows, there might be some other below-board operation in that building who runs this outfit, hires them out to lean on anyone they don't like the look of. I don't expect any real trouble, but they are going to make a show, just to scare us."

Sandy saw them now. Two men at the front door. One had dreadlocks, his shirt was open to the waist, and he had a thick nest of necklaces around his neck. The other wore a soccer jersey; he had short hair and his black jersey barely constrained his thick muscles. "Yeah, well, they are already succeeding. What are we going to do?"

He began sucking on his drink, as if the ounce of rum in it was going to calm his nerves.

"We're going to finish our drinks and head out

the back. I think they will confront us, but let me do the talking. We'll be fine."

"Why do you want to go into a bloody alley?"

Jack had an answer to this. He didn't want anyone seeing what he might have to do. He'd worked hard to have a low-profile life, and he was willing to risk an ass-kicking to maintain it.

"We'll be fine. Trust me." As he said it, he realized he was pushing his luck with this, but he had the confidence in his physical abilities as well as his ability to talk his way out of whatever might arise.

Sandy said, "Jack, have you forgotten who you are? You can pull out your phone, dial some secret number that I know you have memorized and, Bob's your uncle, an aircraft carrier will appear in the harbor and whisk us both off to safety."

Jack would have laughed at Lamont's master plan, except he was getting his mind in gear for what was starting to look like an inevitable confrontation.

"I'm not calling anybody," he said, his voice taking on a grave tone. "You and I are going to walk out the back door, head up the alley, and then go to our hotel."

"And then what?"

"And then I will come up with another awesome plan."

"Right. Of course."

A minute later, Jack and Sandy entered the alley. It wasn't as dark as he had feared it would be; there were a couple of light poles as well as a glow coming from a clapboard-wall casino building that ran the length of the block on the other side of the single-lane alley.

They turned to walk back to the hotel, but had made it only a few feet when two men stepped out of the shadows in front of them.

"Good Lord," Sandy whispered.

These guys were young and fit. Jack pegged them as part of some local gang. They had tattoos on their arms that were obvious because they wore tank tops.

Jack smiled and continued walking toward them. He scanned their hands and their waistbands for weapons, but he saw nothing. "Evening. Something we can do for you gents?"

The taller of the two spoke with a thick West Indies accent. "You want to be telling us just why the fuck you are so interested in the office building you were snapping pictures of earlier today?"

"Don't know what you are talking about. We're tourists."

"Ya ain't no tourists, man. You're down here sticking your noses where they don't belong, and we don't like that."

Sandy spoke up; his voice was cracked with fear. "Look, mate. We aren't here for any trouble."

Another West Indian–accented voice spoke up, this one from behind. "Trouble's here for you."

Sandy spun around in near terror now. Ryan had heard the door open behind them from the bar, so he just turned calmly and checked to confirm it was the two men he'd seen with the bouncer. His mind was switching into a different gear, he was calm, resigned to the fact these men were going to need to be dealt with, but taking some comfort in the fact his opposition seemed to be supremely confident they had the situation well in hand.

Jack knew he could use that confidence against them.

The man with the dreadlocks spoke now: "We're here to make sure you boys go back home to wherever you came from and never return."

"No problem at all," said Sandy.

Dreadlock smiled, his teeth bright white in the lights of the alleyway. "We're not gonna take assurances, white boy. We're gonna put you two in the hospital so you remember your mistake in comin' here."

Dreadlocks was the leader of the group, that was plain to Ryan. He was just out of arm's length now, and while he didn't have any weapons, Jack knew he had to operate as if all four of them could produce some weapon quickly.

Sandy's hands were up in surrender now. "Completely unnecessary, gentlemen, I can assure you, your message has been received loud and —"

Sandy broke into a run. All four men moved toward him reflexively, and this opened up Jack's options. One of the tank-top men crossed right in front of him, so Jack fired out a right jab into the man's jaw, knocking him unconscious and dropping him in the street. The other tank-top man recognized the threat; he was a few steps farther away, so he stopped his pursuit of the blond and spun toward the dark-haired and bearded American. While doing so he reached for a fixed-blade knife in a scabbard in the small of his back and punched out with his other hand.

Jack closed the distance quickly, and he caught a glancing blow on the bridge of his nose. But before the Antiguan could draw his weapon, Jack was on him. He took him by his right forearm, put the man in a tight wristlock, and pushed his arm away at a forty-five-degree angle. As the man in the tank top screamed out, Jack stomped down on the inside of his knee, dropping the man onto his back in writhing agony next to his unconscious partner.

The other two Antiguans turned away from Lamont to aid their colleagues. They approached Ryan with their own blades drawn; they shouted at him as they advanced up the alleyway.

Jack softened his knees and lowered into a crouch. As the short-haired man in the soccer jersey neared and swung his knife, Jack ducked under his swing, spun around, slammed his back into the onrushing attacker, and grabbed the man's downward-arcing arm. He twisted the arm, snapping it at the elbow, and the knife dropped to the ground.

Dreadlocks tried to stab Ryan, but Ryan had put the man in the soccer jersey between himself and this final attacker. He controlled the wounded man by holding his arms high and pushing into him with his back, and this stifled the last armed man's attempts to deliver a blow. Once the man with dreadlocks lowered his knife to switch hands, Jack pulled down on his prisoner's arms, dislocating one of the man's shoulders, and then he thrust backward, sending the man in the jersey into the air and crashing into his leader. This took Dreadlocks even more out of the offense and onto the defense. By the time he got his underling out of his way, the tall American was on top of him, swatting the knife away and blasting him with a three-punch combination to his face.

The Antiguan fell onto his back on the concrete alley, and Jack kept up the attack, kneeling over him and raining several more blows.

When it was clear Dreadlocks was unconscious, Jack looked around. The man in the black jersey was running off into the night, clutching his arm. A third man rolled around, holding his knee and cursing incomprehensible profanities, and the fourth man was facedown and out cold.

Jack looked in the other direction. Sandy Lamont stood there, just twenty-five feet away, staring at the carnage and the man on his knees in the center of it.

Jack stood and began moving up the alley. "Let's get out of here."

They were back in their hotel twenty minutes later. Sandy had pulled a few airplane bottles of rum out of the minibar with a shaking hand, and he poured them into a glass. Jack sat with him in his room. He had a beer in his hand, but he hadn't even taken a sip yet.

Sandy Lamont just stared at Ryan. "Who the hell are you?"

Jack touched his fingers to the bridge of his nose. It was just scraped a little; no blood flowed. His knuckles were scraped and bruised as well.

He'd come up with an answer to Sandy's question on the quiet and uncomfortable walk back to the hotel. He said, "The Secret Service put me through a hell of a lot of training. Been doing it for years, but when I refused their protection, they really stepped it up . . ." Jack shrugged and smiled. "Hell, I guess I'm half a ninja by now."

Sandy said, "That's bloody marvelous. Those bastards were going to kill us."

"No. They were going to knock our heads together, but don't make this bigger than it was. They are used to intimidating people down here.

They probably work for any drug dealer, shady money launderer, or pimp who pays them. They aren't assassins. Just assholes."

Sandy downed the rum. His hands still shook.

Jack was worried about the next part. "Any chance we can keep this between you and me?"

"What do you mean?"

"I mean, I'd rather Hugh Castor didn't know about this."

Sandy just looked out the window at the ocean for a moment. "Yeah. That's probably a good idea. He'd blame me for the entire thing."

"Why?"

Sandy shrugged. "He's pressuring me about you already."

"Pressuring you? What do you mean?"

"Oh. Bloody Gazprom. He makes a right ruckus every time he hears you are digging into them."

Jack thought back to Sandy warning him away from the giant Russian corporation. "So that was Castor talking, not you."

"Sorry, mate. Orders from the boss. I do see his point. We can do good business without going toe-to-toe against the real seat of Russian power."

"Aren't you overstating it a bit? I would think the Kremlin would be the seat of Russian power."

Now that the subject had turned to business, Sandy was back on level ground. He recovered quickly. "Think about it, Jack. Gazprom not only is owned by the Kremlin, but it also is directly tied to the bank accounts of the *siloviki* in the Kremlin. Castor has always been against us doing anything to provoke the Kremlin, and I'd say fucking with their meal ticket applies."

Ryan looked out over the sea. "I think Castor

should let these investigations go where the facts lead."

"If you want to know the truth, Jack, I do, too. Old man Castor has his eyes on the bottom line, so he'll go to bat for any Russian oligarch who's trying to sue some other Russian oligarch, as long as Volodin and his *siloviki* aren't involved."

"But the *siloviki* is involved in a lot of under-handed stuff."

"I think he's just scared of Volodin and his thugs. He'd never admit it, but all of his tenacity just seems to drift away when the facts lead toward the Kremlin."

Jack was frustrated by this, but it was nice to see that Sandy was frustrated as well.

Sandy said, "I won't mention the fisticuffs down here. On one condition."

"Name it."

"I want you to teach me how to do some of that."

"It's a deal," Ryan said.

22

With all the badges, business cards, equipment, and swagger of a group of independent journalists, Clark, Chavez, Driscoll, Caruso, and Biery landed at Kiev's Boryspil International Airport just after nine in the morning. They were met by a man Clark had hired to use as a fixer for the duration of their operation.

Igor Kryvov was a former member of Ukraine's Security Service's Alpha group, a paramilitary Spetsnaz force used for hostage and counterterror scenarios, and he'd also served as an assaulter on Domingo Chavez's team in Rainbow. He was now retired from that life, having picked up a disability during a training accident when his main parachute failed to open and his reserve chute caught high winds that sent him slamming awkwardly into the ground. He'd broken both legs and shattered his pelvis, and he'd nearly bled to death from the compound fractures.

When he learned his injuries would prevent him from returning to active duty with Rainbow, he took a job as a beat cop with the Kiev municipal police, and while doing so, he earned a master's degree in criminal intelligence. For a short time he was an investigator for the Ministry of Internal

Affairs, but he had no interest in the corruption rife within the organization. His insistence on playing by the book soured his relationship with his employers, so now he was in the private sector, freelancing in security work and taking jobs as a fixer — essentially, a glorified tour guide for foreigners doing business in the city of 2.8 million.

As a result of his injuries, Kryvov walked with a slight stoop and a pronounced limp, but despite his surgeries and his long history of professional violence, he always wore a smile on his face.

"Colonel Clark!" he said as he shook John's hand on the tarmac. "Good to see you again."

"Hi, Igor. I really appreciate you agreeing to work with us."

"Are you kidding? I've been so bored driving CNN reporters around from one protest march to the next. Getting to be with you guys for a few days sounds like fun."

When Chavez came down the steps of the Hendley Associates Gulfstream, Kryvov grabbed the smaller Mexican American and yanked him into a bear hug.

"Good to see you, Igor."

"You as well."

The forty-five-year-old was introduced to the others, and within minutes he had all their equipment packed up in the van. Igor knew the men weren't journalists, but Clark had told him only that he was coming over to do some "poking around." The Ukrainian quite reasonably assumed the men were CIA, but operating under nonofficial cover.

Kryvov was known around the city as a man who worked with foreign press, so Clark knew the ex–Rainbow man could help them establish their journalistic covers. This, along with his knowledge of the local criminal element, made him a perfect fit for the Campus team, since they needed to be dialed in to some of the darker sides of the city in order to learn what was going on over here with the Seven Strong Men.

The entourage left the airport and drove to a rented third-floor flat in an old building on the right bank of the Dnieper River. Though the Americans were tired from the flight, they wasted no time before beginning the lengthy process of preparing their safe house. They swept for bugs using tiny devices hidden in their camera equipment, and they chose routes in the building and in the neighborhood so they could escape quickly if necessary.

Gavin Biery set up his operation in the living room. From the very beginning, Clark had stressed to the team the importance of maintaining their cover. Biery set up his workstation with that in mind. Not only were the computers encrypted and password-protected, but the Campus-related applications were hidden on the machines, while digital editing software and several news-related websites ran openly. This way, even if someone got past the security, they would still think they were looking at the work of an editor or cameraman for a traveling news team.

Gavin fired up his two laptops, and from here he gained access to the CIA's SIPRNet and the Ukrainian SSU network. He also set up a computer that functioned as a digital radio receiver, and this he attached to a speaker system. The radio was able to pick up and decrypt transmissions from local police, although only Kryvov spoke Ukrainian fluently.

They got around this limitation to some degree with the use of translation software, so that the data Gavin pulled up from the Ukrainian police network would be instantly and automatically converted to English. It sounded great in theory, but in practice the software was hit-and-miss. Gavin had to read every sentence multiple times to figure out what was being conveyed, and much of it was just gibberish.

While everyone else was getting settled into their new digs, Ding Chavez took Igor Kryvov aside. "Look, Igor, you and I have known each other for a long time, so you know me to be a straight shooter, right?"

"Sure, Ding."

"I've got something to ask you, so I'm just going to ask you. I know you are Ukrainian, but you come from a Russian family. What do you think about all the rumors going on about Russia these days?"

"You mean the rumors that Russia is going to invade?"

"Exactly."

Kryvov said, "I am Ukrainian of Russian origin, true. But that doesn't mean I want to be ruled by Moscow. Volodin won't stop until he destroys the last vestiges of liberty in this hemisphere, so he and his cronies can control everything.

"You have to understand, Ding, there are three types of people in this country. The Ukrainian nationalists are mostly in the west. The Russian nationalists are mostly in the east. And then there are the Ukrainians of Russian descent who want nothing to do with the Kremlin at all. I belong to that category, and we are everywhere. I have seen enough war to know that I don't want to see any more, especially on my doorstep."

"That's good to know," said Ding. The men shook hands. "I'm sure we could all use a primer on the local organized-crime scene as well."

"I'll tell you guys everything I know."

While everyone prepared the apartment for their stay, Kryvov relayed story after story about the security situation here in the city. According to Kryvov, in the past months Kiev had turned into nothing less than a haven for Russian spies and Russian organized crime. Other crime groups — Chechens, Georgians, and Ukrainian Tatars — were also active in the city, but the word on the street was everyone was now working for the Russians.

Organized crime at the street level, a phenomenon that had declined in Russia, seemed to be on the rise here. Many saw the upswing in criminal activity, violent extortions, and assassinations as just an inevitable result of the political strife the nation was experiencing, but to an old hand like Kryvov, it seemed like something much less organic was going on.

"These new Russian guys in town are bribing local officials to vote in ways that benefit Russia. They are paying off other crime organizations to increase their activity, which causes the local police to be overburdened. They have beaten up, threatened, and kidnapped some journalists who were reporting negative stories about the Kremlin as well. What we are seeing, as near as I can tell, is Russian organized crime here in Kiev doing the work of the FSB."

Kryvov told the men of The Campus he had never heard the name Gleb the Scar, but he knew some locals who could provide them with more information.

Clark listened to everything Kryvov said about the situation on the ground here in Kiev, then he said, "When I was with Rainbow, the Russians were some of our best partners in NATO. They worked with us on terrorism issues, nuclear proliferation, regional security matters."

Kryvov said, "There are still good Russian soldiers, needless to say. Good diplomats as well, believe it or not, but that's just because there aren't enough *siloviki* to staff all the embassies with diplomats as well as spies. But Volodin leads everyone by the nose, pays off his supporters by allowing the level of corruption that exists."

Driscoll asked, "Mr. C, what is our first step?"

Clark said, "Tomorrow I am going to reach out to the local chief of station, Keith Bixby."

Chavez was surprised by this. "Reach out to him? Isn't that a little risky? How do you know he won't just make some calls and get you picked up by the local cops for wandering around on his turf?"

"An educated guess. I'll tell him I've come to help, and I'll impress upon him that I am a private citizen and I *know* I'm a private citizen. He seemed like a pragmatic guy. I think he'll be glad to get another set of eyes in this town."

"And if you're wrong?" Biery asked.

Clark shrugged. "If I'm wrong, this could end up being a short trip."

23

After being uprooted by the radiation scare at the White House, Cathy and the kids decided to move back to their home in Maryland for the cleanup. Jack, on the other hand, wanted to continue working in the West Wing, so he moved across Pennsylvania Avenue to Blair House, the official guest residence of the White House.

The cleanup across the street in the White House residence began almost immediately. Most solid surfaces needed a thorough cleaning with Decon 90, a powerful detergent containing a three-percent solution of potassium hydroxide. The surfaces were then revarnished or repainted, and retested for the polonium isotope to ensure there were no lingering traces.

But the bathroom Golovko had visited had to be completely destroyed. The enamel of the toilet and the sink had been penetrated by the material emanating from Golovko's body, and this could not be cleaned by detergent, so the enamel surfaces were removed and smashed into small pieces, and these pieces were stored at a special processing facility in a lead-lined container. The half-life of polonium-210 was a relatively short 138 days, meaning the material could be more safely handled and disposed of only after letting it sit for several months.

While this was taking place, similar decontamination operations began at Golovko's Capitol Hill hotel, on board the aircraft that took him from Kansas to Washington, and in both his hotel in Lawrence and the rooms affected at the University of Kansas.

While jackhammers were tearing the radiated bathroom fixtures out of the White House residence, Jack Ryan was sitting at his desk in the Oval Office when he took the phone call letting him know that Sergey Golovko died in the ICU at George Washington.

He hung up the phone and headed over to the sitting area in front of his desk, where he sat down and relayed the news to Scott Adler, Mary Pat Foley, and Jay Canfield. They were meeting today to discuss Volodin's announcement concerning the expanded powers of the FSB, and the news of Golovko's death, while no surprise, only made the topic of conversation timelier.

Ryan rubbed his eyes under his glasses. "The KGB is back. Call it whatever the hell you want to call it, dress it up in designer suits and give it a Madison Avenue PR department, but it's the same old gang we all know and hate."

Mary Pat Foley said, "You know, one could make the argument that the new FSB is more powerful than the KGB ever was. The KGB did not have real decision-making power within the Soviet Union. Not like many think. Their job was to advise the Communist Party. They didn't call the shots. But now . . . now the intelligence officers both spy *and* run the show." She paused. "It's worse now."

Ryan said, "The question is, how will the promotion of Talanov change things?"

Jay Canfield responded, "We can expect action on all fronts. Talanov's reign at FSB has been characterized by his use of proxies as a force multiplier for his agency. Rebel groups in Georgia, union workers in Ukraine, organized-crime groups working for him in Chechnya and the Baltic."

Foley agreed. "Every intel agency does this. Hell, *we* use proxy forces to some extent, but Talanov is going back to the KGB model by making it the centerpiece of his foreign intelligence strategy. Volodin is trying to pull all the bordering nations into Russia's direct control, so you can be sure Talanov will execute his marching orders with an eye toward destabilizing countries that don't toe the Kremlin line."

Scott Adler said, "Volodin's aim is to institute something like a new Warsaw Pact. Once that happens, in addition to hundreds of millions of people losing their liberty and self-determination, Europe will be completely squeezed."

Ryan said, "When I talked to Golovko he was very concerned about Talanov. He said it was particularly suspicious how he came out of nowhere to lead the FSB."

"I agree with him," Foley said. "When Volodin made this announcement I reached out to other friendly agencies to see if they had anything substantive on Talanov that we didn't. Of course, we've looked into him before, when he was picked to head FSB, for example, but I wanted to make sure no stone was left unturned concerning him."

"What did you learn?"

"Little officially," Foley admitted. "He was the head of the FSB in Novosibirsk, the largest city in

Siberia, before coming to Moscow last year and taking over as head of internal security. We did a full workup on him as a matter of course, but there are a lot of blanks. We found rumors that he was ex-GRU, and he was in Chechnya, but nothing conclusive. He is the most opaque intelligence chief Russia has had since back in the Soviet Union days."

"Sergey confirmed he was GRU," Jack said, and Mary Pat jotted a note down on a pad in her lap. Jack asked, "How has Talanov stayed so low-profile?"

"It's not that surprising, really. Look at Volodin himself. We know he was KGB in the mid to late eighties, then FSB for a short time. When the Soviet Union fell apart, he went into banking, made a few billion, and then dabbled in politics in his home of Saint Petersburg. He's been such a high-profile businessman for so long it's easy to forget he used to be a spy."

Canfield said, "His official biography says he was just a KGB desk jockey in Moscow, and we've never turned up information suggesting differently."

"Volodin is an autocrat, but he has given Talanov incredible power. Why?" Ryan asked.

Adler answered, "Because he respects his abilities, I assume."

Foley added, "Sure, but also because he trusts him."

Jack pressed the issue. "What the hell did a GRU man and a police chief from Siberia do to earn such a high level of trust? Volodin doesn't have anyone as a closer confidant."

"It is an interesting question."

"Posing it is the easy part. Finding out the

answers is the tough part."

Foley nodded. "That's my cue. I'll get to work."

Something occurred to Jack: "Mary Pat, when I asked you what we knew about Talanov, you said we knew little 'officially.' What did you mean by that?"

"Oh, there was the odd rumor thrown around, but nothing substantive."

"Like what?"

Foley waved her hand dismissively. "Oh, just uncorroborated things that don't really check out. The Finns had a report that he was a KGB niner, but none of the niners we know want to claim him."

Jay Canfield said, "I'm sorry. What's a niner?"

Ryan answered for Mary Pat: "Wow, Jay, you are young, but you are old enough to remember the Soviet Union. 'Niner' is what we call their Ninth Chief Directorate. Their bodyguards, protection detail."

Canfield held up his hands. "Sorry. I was a Near East guy. USSR wasn't my beat. I know about Ninth Directorate, just not the nickname. Anyway, I think that's bad intel from the Finns. There is a special school for Ninth Directorate, and we had the ex-chief of that school on our payroll in the nineties. He gave us all the names, and Talanov wasn't one of them."

Mary Pat added, "The Germans had intel that he was GRU, after serving in the Army as a paratrooper in Afghanistan. They said he was involved in the initial invasion in 1979."

Jack thought that one over. "That sounds about right. He would have been in his early twenties then. GRU didn't fall apart the way the KGB did, so we didn't have as much access to their person-

211

nel information."

"That's true."

"Anything else?" Ryan asked.

"Nothing real. The Brits had a crazy rumor they picked up about him, but they stressed it was uncorroborated and highly suspect."

"Which was?"

Foley didn't seem at all convinced about what she was telling the President. "That he was an assassin. Back in the eighties, there were wild rumors about a lone KGB hit man running around both Eastern and Western Europe killing people on Moscow's behalf. No one could ever find him, or even prove he existed."

Jack's eyes widened. "Wait. Are you talking about Zenith?"

"That's right. The rumor at the time was that this KGB über-assassin's code name was Zenith. You *remember* that?"

"Hell, Mary Pat. I was in the UK when that all happened. I knew one of the victims."

"Yes, that's right. Of course. Anyway, years and years after the fact, the Brits had a single source who ID'd Zenith as an ex–GRU man named Talanov who had been a paratrooper in Afghanistan."

Ryan couldn't believe what he was hearing. For the first time in the conversation, he raised his voice. "Are you saying Roman Talanov is Zenith?"

Foley shook her head vigorously. "No, I'm not saying that. I'm saying one guy told that story to British intelligence and it made it into his file. Again, this was single-source intel, and they were never able to get any confirmation. You know how it is, there is a bushel of chaff out there for each grain of wheat. I looked into our file on the Zenith murder investigation, and we came to the conclusion that there was no Soviet hit man killing bankers and intelligence agents in the West."

Ryan said, "The Brits pinned it on German terrorists."

Foley said, "That's right, the Red Army Faction. An apartment in Berlin was raided by police, several terrorists were killed, and evidence was found linking them to the so-called Zenith killings."

It was quiet in the room for a moment. The three people sitting in front of Ryan could all tell he was thinking back to some point in the past, but they patiently waited for him to speak. Finally he said, "I was never convinced they had the right culprits."

Foley said, "But Mr. President, remember, after the fall of the Iron Curtain, hundreds of ex–KGB spies were only too happy to tell us about their exploits. We have a lot of information about KGB operations personnel in that time period. There was never any proof Zenith existed, and no one ever mentioned the name Talanov. The Russians did their own investigation and came up blank."

"It could have been run off-book. Or Zenith might not have been a KGB asset, but something else," Ryan said.

"What else?" Canfield asked.

Ryan shrugged. "I'd like to know what the SIS has on this matter."

Foley tapped her pen on the notepad on her lap for a moment. "Excuse me for saying this, but this isn't like you. You've been at this too long to chase rumors."

"Indulge me, Mary Pat."

She shrugged. "You're the President. But remember, that was thirty years ago. Some of the players aren't going to be around anymore. Others likely have forgotten."

Ryan thought it over. "We could ask SIS for a look at the raw data on the Zenith case."

"Whatever you say. I'll assign someone to it as soon as we get the files."

Jack said, "How 'bout we bring in someone from outside to go over it? Someone who was active back then. Someone who knew the Soviet Union. The players, the bureaucracy. The times."

"You have anyone in mind?"

"What about Ed? Do you think he'd be interested?"

"Are you kidding? He'd jump at the chance."

"Great. We can get him some office space next door in the OEOB." The Old Executive Office Building was maintained by White House Office of Administration, and it contained many offices used by White House personnel. "He can go through the paperwork on the case, see if he can find anything that would either tie Talanov to Zenith or rule him out."

Foley stood to leave. "If you don't mind me saying so, this sounds personal."

"You're right, it is. That event was very personal to me at the time. But this is more than that. We all admit we know so little about the second-most-powerful man in Russia. If he was, in fact, an active KGB assassin thirty years ago, that is damn well germane to the present. And if this turns up nothing at all, then at least we know we gave it a look."

Mary Pat said, "I'll call Ed as soon as I get back to my office."

24

Chief of CIA Station Keith Bixby had spent the morning in meetings in the U.S. embassy, and now, just after lunch, he had begun a surveillance detection run that would take him into the mid-afternoon. He had a meeting at four with an Italian businessman who owned a small trucking company that smuggled contraband back and forth from Russia.

As chief of station, Bixby found it a little unusual to be having clandestine meetings with agents, but this was nothing if not an unusual situation. Every warm body on Bixby's staff was working, either here in Kiev or in other parts of Ukraine. He also had nonofficial cover operatives working in country, but right now most of the NOCs were off near the Russian border and in the Crimean peninsula, trying to get intelligence about the Russians and their intentions.

Kiev Station did not have the number of personnel Bixby needed, but this was not due to the fact it was some far-flung outpost forgotten by the CIA. The problem was, rather, that most every Russian- or Ukrainian-speaking case officer was already employed in Russia or Ukraine, and the CIA could not crank out Ukrainian-speaking case officers fast enough to meet the intense demand.

As the drums of war beat louder and louder, Bixby took on more and more responsibility to help his office keep up with the workload. This meant he had to leave the embassy himself, and travel the streets on long SDRs, and meet the occasional bad person over a bad meal. This Italian smuggler wasn't terribly important, especially considering how the Russians looked like they would be attacking soon enough, but he did provide intel, so Bixby decided he'd meet with him.

The COS was only twenty minutes into his SDR and had just stopped at a bus stop in front of the massive and magnificent Cathedral of Saint Volodymyr when a man approached him and stood close. The man wore a coat with the hood up, and a scarf was wrapped over his mouth.

The CIA station chief looked the hooded man over. Suspicion was an occupational hazard, but it could also prove to be a lifesaver for someone in his position.

The man lowered his scarf. "I'm John Clark. We spoke last week."

Bixby looked over Clark's face, and he recognized him from the one or two pictures he'd seen of the old CIA legend. Still, he remained on guard. "I'm not sure how you could have misconstrued anything in our conversation as an invitation."

Clark chuckled. "No, of course not."

"Then what the hell are you doing here?"

"I just thought I'd pop over for the borscht."

Bixby's eyes flitted left and right. "Why don't you come back to my office so we can talk?"

"Actually," said Clark, "I'd prefer to keep this

between the two of us."

Bixby thought it over for a moment. "All right, then. We'll need to keep moving. Let's go for a walk."

Clark followed Bixby up Taras Shevchenko Boulevard for a few blocks, and then into the Alexander Fomin Botanical Garden, next to the university.

Here the two men walked along a wide path between trees that were not yet showing any life after the long winter. The blustery weather, as well as the fact it was a workday, meant there were very few visitors walking the pathways. Still, Clark wasn't comfortable with the location. He spoke softly. "Not exactly secure here. I assume the local opposition knows your job at the embassy."

Bixby, on the other hand, was relaxed. "We're fine."

Clark looked around. It looked peaceful, but he had no idea who or what was out in the trees. "Directional mikes?"

The younger CIA man said, "No doubt about it."

"Then why are we here?"

"The thing about the FSB is this. They are everywhere, but they aren't superhuman. We've determined it takes them a good ten minutes or so to set up any type of surveillance. Right now there are probably four guys scrambling out of a van up by the metro station ahead, pulling mikes and walkie-talkies out of bags, trying to get into position ahead of us. I always try to get the important parts of our conversations out of the way quickly, so that by the time the listeners are in place we're out of here."

"Okay," Clark said, and he pulled his hood

forward to further hide his face from any cameras that might try to catch him meeting with the local CIA station chief.

Bixby said, "First things first. Tell me why you are in Kiev."

"I'm a concerned citizen who thought he might be able to help out."

"I hesitate to say this, Clark, because you're an American hero and all. But that's a load of horseshit."

Clark chuckled. He liked this guy. "I am worried about Gleb the Scar. When we spoke the other day, I got the impression you didn't have enough to go on to check this guy out the way he needed to be checked out."

"That's true. I've got FSB running all over the place. A new personality from Russian organized crime operating in the city is interesting, but at this point it's not actionable, especially with a war looming."

"I thought perhaps I could help."

"Help *how?*"

"I've got a friend or two over here. I speak Russian. I retain TS clearance, and I follow orders." He shrugged. "This isn't exactly my first time out of the block."

"I can't take responsibility for you, Clark."

"Not asking you to. I'm not asking for classified intel, either. I'm just asking for your blessing, and an open channel so I can get anything important back to you."

"You know, I've heard of walk-in agents, but I've never heard of a walk-in case officer."

Clark wasn't making the headway he'd hoped. He changed the subject. "What's going on down in the Crimea? Is the Ukrainian military ready for a Russian invasion?"

Bixby shrugged. "I can only give you an unclassified answer. I know you retain clearance, but I haven't figured out what the fuck your deal is yet."

"Hey, like I said, I'm not asking for anything sensitive. I'm just an American tourist thinking of going on holiday in Odessa."

Bixby shook his head. "Okay. Well . . . I would suggest you go to Maui, instead. Maybe you could get a senior discount on a hotel room there. Crimea is going to blow up soon. The Russians are ready to invade, just looking for an excuse. The Ukrainians are moving troops into the region to dispel them — that's in the local news, so I'm not giving you anything TS there — and it's as likely as not the Russians will use the Ukrainians' movements as a provocation for them to go in."

"Because of all the Russian nationals living in the Crimea."

"Yep. You probably know those Russian nationals only got their citizenship because Moscow handed out passports to Ukrainians of Russian heritage. It was an FSB op all the way, setting the stage for the invasion. They called it 'passportization.' The Russians began offering passports to civilians in the Crimea with Russian heritage. They are creating a land of Russians in Ukraine, and then they will say, 'We have to come in to protect our citizens.' They did exactly the same thing in Georgia a few years ago. There were two autonomous regions inside Georgia, South Ossetia and Abkhazia. The FSB went in and discreetly distributed passports to a percentage of the population. Then the Russians used the fact there were so many Russians in these regions to justify sending in their army to kick out the

219

Georgian Army."

"And you make it sound like there's nothing that can stop it."

Bixby shrugged. "I believe they will attack, and I believe they will take the Crimea. That is the low-hanging fruit. What I am worried about is the whole country falling. Russia sees the Ukrainian nationalists in power as a clear and present danger to Russian citizens in the country. Volodin might just march his forces all the way to Kiev."

Clark said, "What could I do that might help you out?"

Bixby stopped in the path and looked at the older man. "You aren't alone, are you?"

Clark did not answer at first.

"Look, man. I sure as hell don't have the time, the energy, or the resources to check you out. The only thing I could do would be call someone in Ukrainian border control and get your visa revoked."

"I'd rather you didn't do that," Clark said. "No. I'm not alone. I'm here with Domingo Chavez."

Bixby's eyebrows rose. Chavez was also well known in the Agency. "Are you here on some sort of a commercial contract? You working for one of the oil companies?"

"Nothing like that. Believe me, I'm not getting paid to be here. But I want to help. I've got a couple other hands, and a local guy who worked for me in Rainbow. We are set up to look into Gleb the Scar and his operation here, but I don't want to get in the way of anything you are already doing. We can provide you a little skilled labor. That's all."

They started walking again, and Bixby shrugged while he walked. "Look. I appreciate the effort

220

you made in putting together a crew and coming halfway around the world, but I'm not a trusting guy. This is my turf you are on, and although I don't have the manpower I wish I had, I'm not prepared to cut you in on my operation."

"You're making a mistake," Clark said. He took a card out of his pocket. On it was the number to his satellite phone. "If you change your mind, I'll be around."

Bixby took the card as he walked, and slipped it into his coat pocket.

As they neared the metro station, Bixby started moving away from Clark on the footpath. He was nearly ten feet to Clark's right when he nodded to a spot in the trees on Clark's side of the path. "We've got company. An FSB flunky is getting into position over there."

Clark said, "There's a second guy behind you. They don't have their mikes or cams set up yet."

Bixby did not look. Instead, he kept his eyes on the path in front of him as he said, "See ya around, Clark. Try and stay out of trouble. I've got enough problems."

Clark himself looked at the ground. No one watching them from distance would know they were together. Clark went around the left-hand side of the metro building for the stairs, where he descended belowground to catch a train.

Bixby walked to the road and hailed a taxi to take him back to the embassy. He'd need to start his SDR all over again before meeting with the Italian businessman.

25

President Jack Ryan lay on his bed in Blair House. It was midnight; he knew this because the grandfather clock in the hall outside the master bedroom had just chimed the hour. He was to be awoken at six a.m., barring anything happening in the middle of the night that would need his attention, so he was hoping sleep would come soon.

But he didn't think it was likely. New developments this evening were keeping him up. Jay Canfield at CIA reported that Russia had moved a mechanized battalion into Belarus. This was no invasion; on the contrary, they did it with the full backing of Minsk. Ryan knew Minsk did whatever the hell Moscow wanted. The authoritarian leader of Belarus was completely in Volodin's back pocket.

No, the troop movements weren't troubling because of what might happen in Belarus; rather, they were troubling because Belarus bordered Ukraine to the north.

Jack had asked Jay if the mechanized battalion in Belarus could put Kiev in jeopardy, and Canfield's response was still running through Jack's mind:

"Yes, but frankly, even the Russian troops on

Ukraine's eastern border can jeopardize Kiev. Defense spending in Ukraine hasn't even been enough for the upkeep of the equipment they have. The Russians can take the Ukrainian capital from either direction." It seemed to Jack as if each day brought a potential invasion even closer. Jack had sent Scott Adler, his secretary of state, to Europe to drum up support on the diplomatic front to try and stop a Russian invasion before it began, but so far Adler had received much in the way of private platitudes but little in the way of public diplomacy from the European nations.

Ryan had a meeting planned with Secretary of Defense Bob Burgess in the morning to discuss the military ramifications of a Russian invasion of Ukraine, and he knew he needed to start planning for what was beginning to look more and more inevitable.

With everything on his plate right now, Jack knew his focus should remain on the present. But try as he might, Mary Pat Foley's throwaway comment earlier in the day concerning a rumor of an assassin called Zenith and a spate of killings thirty years earlier had his mind wandering back to those days.

He had not thought of Zenith in a long time. In the four years Jack was out of office, he had worked on his memoirs. This had been a slow process, made slower by the fact that many of the things Ryan had done had been classified, and he therefore could not very well put them in his book.

But the Zenith affair — they called it the "possible Zenith affair" at the time because no one ever proved there was, in fact, a Zenith — was an event that not only was classified but had been all but stricken from the record. Jack had not spoken of Zenith to anyone for thirty years.

And this made it all the more surprising when Mary Pat mentioned it in the context of a current crisis.

There were so few mysteries left from the Cold War. When the Iron Curtain dropped, virtually all the answers poured out like the Curtain had been a floodgate.

But despite the Russian government investigating the matter, the questions surrounding Zenith had never been resolved.

Jack knew Mary Pat had been right; this wasn't like him to chase details on a single piece of intel. Ostensibly, he wanted to see if Talanov was somehow involved in the Zenith murders; if he was, this would be an important piece of the puzzle and part of developing an understanding of his background and his personality. But if Jack was honest with himself, he would have to admit that he had ordered the look into the Zenith case mostly because it had been one of the few remaining question marks of his career, and if Roman Talanov had something to do with it, however unlikely that might have been, Jack damn sure wanted to know.

He closed his eyes and willed himself to fall asleep. Tomorrow he would need to be fully involved in the dangerous present; he didn't have the luxury of lying awake tonight to think about the dangerous past.

Sandy Lamont was worried about his young and high-profile employee for a couple of reasons. Number one, since returning from the West Indies, Jack had been working so hard he was starting to look like a bit of a zombie, and Lamont was concerned that one of the principals of his firm might pass young Ryan in the hall and then pull Lamont into his office to read him the riot act for abusing his employee.

And the other reason Sandy was concerned was that he was getting calls from Moscow, all basically saying the same thing. Some of the work they had been doing on behalf of Jack Junior was starting to earn them unwarranted attention from the local authorities.

Jack was back on Gazprom, it was clear from the calls. In the course of his investigation, the young American had been sending investigators from Castor and Boyle's Moscow office out to tax offices to request records. This was causing trouble at the tax offices, and Sandy knew he needed to gently persuade his highly motivated new employee to take it a little slower for both his own health and the good of C&B Risk Analytics. Sandy knew there would be serious hell to pay once Castor found out Jack was focusing his investigative efforts on the cash cow of the *siloviki*.

Sandy found Jack right where he knew he would be at the end of the day, hunched over his computer keyboard with his phone to his ear. Sandy waited for the young man to get off the phone with one of the in-house translators, and then he knocked on Jack's office door.

"Hey, Sandy."

"Got a minute?"

"Sure. Come on in."

Sandy came into Jack's little office, shut the door, and sat in the one other chair in the room. "What are you working on?" he asked, but Sandy knew the answer.

"A Swiss shell that does business with Gazprom."

Sandy feigned surprise. "Remember, mate, Gazprom was the ultimate beneficiary of the Galbraith theft, true, but they weren't the ones who stole the company."

"I'm not so sure about that."

"Lad, if you buy a piece of property that someone else has stolen, you might be forced to hand it back over if it was acquired illegally, but that doesn't mean you are a criminal yourself. We need to help Galbraith and his lawyers prove culpability of one of the companies that actually pulled off the deal, not Gazprom, the firm that bought up the assets after the deal was done."

Ryan said, "This thing is big, Sandy. It might go all the way up to Gazprom and the big shots who own it. I know Castor has some trepidation, so I'm proceeding as carefully as I possibly can."

Sandy knew he had his work cut out for him trying to get his energetic analyst to take his foot off the gas pedal. He stifled a sigh. "What have you learned?"

Ryan said, "In all the data I found in the paperwork from Randolph Robinson's garbage, I came across one document for Shoal Bank, the bank we think is owned by the people behind IFC. It was an account transfer from a company in Germany to Shoal Bank. I looked into that company, and from shareholder information I just swam upstream, following names, addresses, looking into holding companies it deals with and loan signatories for purchases it's made."

"What sort of company is this?"

"Germany buys natural gas from Gazprom. This Swiss-registered German firm receives the payments from the German government, and then processes the payments for Gazprom."

"*Processes* them?"

Jack chuckled. "Yeah. They are just an intermediary. Germany wires money to the Swiss account of this company, and then they wire it on to Russia, minus their processing charge. Gazprom uses them for no discernible reason."

Sandy said, "Clearly, the reason is to overcharge the Germans for their gas so that someone gets a payoff."

"Yep," Jack said. "But it's even worse than that. I found the Germans, on Gazprom's request, made a ten-million-dollar payment to a consulting company in Geneva, and they used Shoal Bank of Saint John's to do it. There are attempts to obfuscate the owners of the consulting company, I'm still working on that, but I'm sure it is nothing more than a shell, or a shell of a shell. It was a kickback of some kind. As near as I can tell, the only reason this Geneva firm is around is to facilitate below-board payments."

"Makes paying bribes extra-easy," Sandy said. "Companies like that only exist on paper, and they produce nothing but illegal invoices."

"Right," said Jack. "Some German official who okayed the natural-gas contract with Gazprom sets up an untraceable company in Geneva so his own country can pay him off."

Ryan knew Sandy had been at this a lot longer than he had, and he was going to be hard to surprise. He said, "And this is just one payment, for ten million. Over four billion has gone from the Germans to Gazprom via this Swiss intermediary. There is no telling how much has been skimmed and where it all has gone."

Sandy said, "Well done, lad. When old man Castor told me I'd have Jack Ryan, Jr., working under me, I thought you'd be just a pretty face with a powerful name. Now I'm starting to look over my shoulder thinking you might be sitting in my seat before too long."

Ryan appreciated the compliment, but he had the sense he was being buttered up for some reason. He said, "I inherited a lot of curiosity from my dad. I love digging into a good mystery, but to tell you the truth, all I want to do is solve these riddles. I have no ambition of running a department, much less a company."

Sandy replied, "I was a pit bull myself back in the day. This was the late nineties, Russia was a different animal then. Blokes with gold chains shooting each other in the back of the head. Might seem grim now with all the financial shysters about, but nothing like the nineties."

"Well, we *did* get jumped the other day in Antigua."

"You've got a point there. That was all the rough stuff I ever want to see." Lamont prepared himself to start his lecture, but Jack interrupted.

"Anyway, I found something else in the Robinson data. I found a note stating Shoal Bank's board of directors flew to Zug, Switzerland, on March first of this year for a meeting with the bank there. I decided the key to blowing the entire gas deal open is finding out who showed up from the board."

Lamont's eyebrows rose. "Travel records?"

"Yes, but it's tricky."

"I would suspect so. The nearest airport is Zurich, and there must be a hundred flights a day."

Ryan nodded. "I looked at the commercial

flights that arrived from any point in Russia in the seventy-two hours before the meeting. I just checked first class because, well, because these people were involved in a one-point-two-billion-dollar swindle, so I figured if they went commercial, they weren't back in steerage."

"Safe assumption."

"There were CEOs and CFOs flying into Zurich all day long, but nobody with the connections or the juice to be involved in this level of an operation."

Lamont said, "I assume you checked out private jets."

"Of course. I figured from the beginning I'd probably need to investigate private jets. I looked into all the declared flights, but not very hard, because I figured these guys would be coming in on a blocked flight."

"What is that?"

"The FAA of Switzerland is called Skyguide. Skyguide can block a flight so that the public can't find out any trace of it. We have the same thing in the USA. All you have to do is ask nicely and FAA will hide the identity of your private aircraft and its flight path. Businesses need to be able to conduct business without their competitors tracking the movements of the CEO, movie stars want to avoid paparazzi, plus, there are security concerns."

Lamont said, "I'm sure there are lots of other reasons of the more underhanded variety."

Ryan nodded and reached for his coffee. "Undoubtedly. Anyway, I knew I couldn't just look up a record of the tail numbers and trace the jets that way, so I pulled up the audio files of the Zurich airport tower for the seventy-two hours and downloaded them into a speech-to-text app. Even if the flight number is blocked on all written logs, the plane still has to communicate with the tower and use its flight number. Using the speech-to-text, I pulled out every tail number for a private aircraft and researched each plane individually."

Lamont was amazed by the tenacity of Jack Ryan. He said, "I told you you were a right pit bull."

"It wasn't that hard, because I knew I'd be looking for a blocked aircraft, one whose flight track wasn't also available online. I found several, of course — there are lots of shady corporate planes flying into Switzerland. But there was an Airbus A318, tail number NS3385, that landed at nine-thirty a.m. on March first, the day of the meeting. The ACJ318 is a corporate jet with a bedroom, a lounge, a seating area, and even a closed-off boardroom."

"That's a bloody expensive jet."

"I researched the aircraft and found nothing, so I looked into the records of the FBOs on the ramp in Zurich, and saw that one A318 was refueled that morning. That bill was paid by a holding company based right there in Zurich, and this company also paid for fuel for another aircraft a few months before this at the same FBO. This one was owned by a restaurant group in Saint Petersburg."

Sandy's head cocked to the side. "Restaurant group in Saint Petersburg?"

Jack smiled. "That's right. The same one Randolph Robinson works for down in Antigua. He set up the shell corporation, and he also manages Shoal Bank, owned by IFC."

Sandy said, "You have a name associated with

the restaurant company?"

Jack looked at his notes. "I do. Dmitri Nesterov. He owns a chain of restaurants. Other than that, I don't know anything about him. I've searched and searched. He never went to any business school, he's not a member of the Duma or an employee in the Kremlin.

"But he is a principal in a company that has bought up over twelve billion euros' worth of oil and gas infrastructure in the past four months."

"Bloody unbelievable."

"Yes," said Ryan. "We need to find out who Nesterov is, and why the Kremlin set him up to make one-point-two billion dollars in the raiding of Galbraith Rossiya Energy."

Lamont nodded, but slowly and cautiously. He had to admit to himself, the Yank had gotten further with this than anyone else here in the office could have. He knew Castor was against anyone in-house working against Gazprom, but Jack Ryan was onto something, and Sandy Lamont was not going to get in his way.

Ryan asked, "Was there something you wanted to talk about?"

Sandy just shook his head. "Not at all. Carry on."

26

The situation on the ground in Kiev seemed to be deteriorating by the day. What had begun as a series of daily speeches by pro-nationalist Ukrainians in the city's massive Independence Square had, in the span of just a few days, morphed into ten-thousand-strong rallies where speeches, banners, and chants proclaimed the anti-Russian leanings of the attendees.

The division in the nation was on full display when pro-Russian Ukrainians started their own daily rallies on the other side of Independence Square. Any hopes the police might have had that the situation would defuse itself went away when tents started to be erected on both sides, and nationalists and Russian Ukrainians began clashes that turned more and more violent.

Riot police had broken up fights, tear-gas canisters and Molotov cocktails streaked through the air on a daily basis, and arrests and injuries were piling up by the day.

And this was not just happening in Kiev. In Sevastopol, in the Crimea, skinhead gangs of the Russian majority were shattering the shop windows of Ukrainian nationalists and Tatars, starting fires in the streets, and picking out people at random to beat up.

The morning after Clark surprised Keith Bixby with his offer to help him post surveillance on Gleb the Scar, the men of The Campus awoke in their flat to the sound of sirens outside. They were a few miles from the square, but the noise of a chanting crowd made its way up to their third-floor safe house.

Since they were playing the role of journalists, Clark, Chavez, Caruso, and Driscoll quickly dressed, grabbed their cameras and microphones, and headed downstairs. They walked out onto the street into the middle of a protest march that had begun outside of the city, supposedly spontaneously, and was heading directly for Independence Square. From the banners and the vitriol spouted by the marchers, it was clear this was a group of ultra-nationalists from the west of the nation.

It was obvious they hadn't walked across western Ukraine to descend on the capital; clearly, they had been bused to a location during the night and then formed into a "spontaneous" march.

Once the group passed, the four men went back upstairs. Clark's approach to the local CIA station chief had been spurned, so he decided he would have to improvise. Igor Kryvov had been a cop, and he knew quite a few personalities in the local underworld, so Clark decided he would use this access to get his own ear as close to the ground as possible.

Just after breakfast, he announced to the men in the safe house, "Igor, Ding, and I are going to head out for a little recon."

Caruso said, "I get it, you Russian speakers get to hang out together while Sam and I stay back here with the nerd."

Biery was hard at work on one of his laptops. Without stopping what he was doing, he said, "I'm a geek, not a nerd."

Chavez said, "Igor is going to take us around to meet some people who can get us closer to the world we need to penetrate if we're going to learn anything about Gleb the Scar."

Driscoll said, "So you are off to meet drug dealers, pimps, and human traffickers. Have a nice time."

"Will do," Clark said.

Valeri Volodin was back on New Russia's *Evening News* with his favorite interviewer, Tatiana Molchanova. Tonight the topic of conversation was a new trade pact enacted with China, but Molchanova had notes and follow-up questions in preparation for tackling a wide range of topics, depending on Volodin's whims.

Volodin, as usual, spoke directly into the camera, and his "answers" were less in response to her questions and more the talking points that he'd come to the studio to get across to the viewers of the *Evening News.* With a strong jaw and a proud gaze into the lens, he said, "I am announcing a new trade pact with our friends in the People's Republic of China. Our two powerful nations will tighten our energy security relationship. We will double oil shipments to China, securing their energy needs for growth, and securing that our markets are made stronger, despite the West's attempts to rule us by starvation. The land routes have been decided. Our pipelines will begin construction almost immediately. We will build land bridges and high-speed rail between our two countries. We have begun coal exploration in Siberia in a joint agreement.

"We have put our past differences behind us, and together we will create the biggest economic market on earth.

"With America's so-called Asia pivot, and the illegal attack against China's mainland last year, the Chinese know it is in their interests to accept our friendship and our increased economic cooperation."

The raven-haired beauty nodded thoughtfully and asked her next question as if it had just come to her organically as a response to Volodin's last answer, although her questions had been written by her producers beforehand. "Mr. President, how do you feel this development will affect Russia's relationship with the West? Recent conflicts with NATO and the USA have worried some Russians, who wonder if our economic future might be negatively impacted."

Volodin looked directly at Molchanova now. "On the contrary, just the opposite is true. America's domineering role in the world ends in our sphere of influence. They can make a lot of noise, threaten to expand NATO yet again, and they can continue to make threats on the world stage, but the Europeans need our products and services.

"Now that Russia and China have created a new world order, the childish threats of the West will have even less of an effect on us."

"Mr. President. Do you consider Russia to be a world power?"

Volodin smiled. "No one can deny that the greatest powers of the twentieth century were the United States and the Soviet Union. The fall of the Soviet Union was one of the greatest tragedies of the last century. In my role as leader of Russia,

I cannot say more than this without being branded by the West as a communist. This, of course, is a ridiculous accusation, because, frankly, who in modern Russia has had more success in the open markets than me?

"But it is the West that does not understand our history. The economic model was faulty, but the nation was strong. During our drive from command economy to market economy, we hit many patches of ice, but in retrospect, it was the West that was watering the road."

"Are you saying the West now has less influence on Russia?"

Volodin nodded. "I am saying that exactly. Russia will make decisions based on Russia's interests, and Russia's interests alone, but this will be good for our neighbors."

He smiled into the camera. "A strong Russia will create stability in the region, not discord, and I see it as my role to make Russia strong."

27

President Ryan began his workday in the Oval Office just after six a.m. He still wasn't sleeping well at Blair House, so he had developed the habit of getting into work about an hour before normal to make use of the time.

It was eight a.m. now, and Ryan was already dragging. But as difficult as it was to run the highest office in the land with little sleep, Jack did have to admit he was fortunate to fuel himself with some of the best coffee on the planet.

As soon as Mary Pat Foley arrived for their morning meeting, he poured her a cup, along with a second cup of the day for himself, knowing he'd pay a price for the caffeine by the early afternoon.

Just as they were about to get started, the intercom on Ryan's desk beeped, and his secretary came over the speaker. "Mr. President, AG Murray is here."

"Send him in, please."

Attorney General Dan Murray entered the Oval Office with a fast, bouncing gait and excited eyes behind his thick glasses.

Ryan stood up. "You've got that look, Dan."

Murray smiled. "That's because I have good news. We've found the person who poisoned

Sergey Golovko."

"Thank God. Let me hear it."

Murray said, "Unfortunately, or fortunately, depending on your perspective, I don't have a hell of a lot of experience in dealing with polonium-poisoning investigations. It turns out there isn't much out there easier to trace with the right equipment.

"The polonium leaves a trail wherever it goes. It's called 'creeping.' We were able to follow Golovko backward from the White House to his hotel, to the limo he and his group took from Reagan National, then back to Lawrence, Kansas. Every location, every place he sat, everything he touched, all have traces of the isotope on it.

"At the University of Kansas he made a speech and took part in a Q-and-A with students at the Hall Center. His hotel, his rented vehicle, the dais on the stage in the auditorium where he talked, the waiting room, and the bathroom backstage where he got ready — they all have evidence of polonium."

Murray smiled a little. "And then . . . nothing."

Ryan cocked his head. "Nothing?"

"Yep. The place where he had breakfast before going to the university. Clean. The commercial aircraft he flew from Dallas to Lawrence. Clean. His hotel in Dallas. Clean. We went all the way through all his other stops on his trip. Every hotel, car, restaurant, airplane. There are no radiation traces anywhere before he went into a meet-and-greet room with students at KU."

Mary Pat said, "That sounds suspiciously like a dead end."

"You might think so, but we picked up the trail again. We found a glass in the kitchen of the cafeteria on campus that basically glowed in the dark, even though it's been washed since the event. Witnesses said Golovko drank a Sprite while onstage — we think that was his glass.

"We got a list of the people who worked in the cafeteria during that shift, and we were going to start interviewing them one by one, but they have an employee locker room, so we started there, instead. We tested the lockers, and got a hit on one, both inside and out. It belongs to a twenty-one-year-old student, the same person who gave the drink to Golovko before he went onstage."

"The student, don't tell me he is Russian."

"It's a she, and she's not Russian. She's Venezuelan."

"Oh, boy," said Ryan. Venezuela was a close ally with Russia. If they sent an intelligence agent into the United States for an assassination, it would only further hurt U.S.–Venezuelan relations, which were already bad enough.

Murray said, "We were going to put a surveillance package on her, to build an investigation, but we really need to know there isn't any more polonium out there that might expose others to danger. My experts tell me they think she's handled it so extensively and haphazardly she probably only has weeks to live, but if she's got more of it than what she put in Sergey's drink, then we need to find it and throw it in a lead box asap."

Jack sighed. "Pick her up." It really wasn't a tough call to make, though it was frustrating to think they might miss an opportunity to film her meeting with a Russian intelligence agent.

Mary Pat asked, "What do you know about her?"

"Her name is Felicia Rodríguez. She has been

living in Kansas since she was fifteen years old. She's been back to see her grandparents a few times in Caracas, but not for any length of time. She doesn't seem to be an active intelligence agent, or even affiliated with the ruling power in Venezuela."

Jack said, "You can't possibly think she was unwitting in this."

"She obviously knew she was spiking Golovko's beverage, but she might have been duped somehow. My experts tell me there are so many traces of polonium-210 in her locker, they think she had no idea what she was dealing with. Maybe she thought she was slipping him a roofie."

"A roofie?"

"Yeah. You know, to slur his speech, make him look senile and out of it. The Cubans have done this sort of thing to marginalize their adversaries."

"That's true," Mary Pat agreed.

Murray stood up. "If you'll excuse me, I'll make the call to have her arrested. They will get her to the hospital and put her in quarantine." Murray added, "Where she will be well guarded, obviously."

As Murray left the Oval Office, Ryan's secretary announced the arrival of Robert Burgess, secretary of defense, along with the chairman of the Joint Chiefs, Admiral Mark Jorgensen. They were here for the morning meeting, but immediately Ryan could see something even more pressing was on their minds as they entered.

"What's up?"

Burgess said, "Russia's defense minister announced this morning that a series of war games are starting, today, in the Black Sea. Within an hour of his announcement, virtually the entire

Black Sea fleet started mobilizing. Two dozen ships raised anchor and moved out of the port of Sevastopol."

"They are calling this just a run-of-the-mill military exercise?"

"That's right."

"How threatening is it?"

"The fact that it was unannounced is unsettling, to say the least. It looks like it has been in the works, but that's impossible to know. The Russians' agreement with Ukraine states that military exercises with fewer than seven thousand participants do not have to be scheduled in advance."

"Are they operating within those numbers?"

"Doubtful. There are thirty-six warships involved, and that is fewer than seven-K sailors, but there are also an unknown number of land-based aircraft in the exercise. On top of that, they've announced the drills will include members of paratroopers, GRU Spetsnaz, and Marines."

Jorgensen said, "Just eyeballing the announcement, sir, I put the number around twenty-five thousand, minimum."

"And this is on top of the troops they have already moved into Belarus?"

"Yes, and the forces on Russia's western border."

Ryan rubbed the bridge of his nose. "They are going to invade, aren't they?"

Burgess said, "It sure looks like it. Volodin rattles his saber a lot, but this is a level of mobilization we haven't seen. Even his attack of Estonia didn't have these numbers attached to it."

Ryan said, "The Crimea is a bigger prize."

"Indeed it is."

"What are our options?"

"Limited."

"Limited as in strongly-worded-letter limited, or limited in some other way?"

Burgess said, "Militarily, not much we can do. We have a few boats in the Black Sea, but not enough to intimidate or impact their fleet operations. As far as diplomatic options, I guess that's a question for Adler."

Ryan nodded. He would need to confer with Scott Adler as soon as Scott got back to Washington.

He imagined that over in Moscow, Volodin did whatever the hell Volodin wanted. That was the rumor, anyhow. But was it true? Ryan knew there were rampant rumors about Volodin's ties to organized crime. Although no one had really pinned him down on any involvement with criminal activity, Ryan liked to imagine the bastard was up to his eyeballs in dirty deals with mobsters who had him by the balls. Chances were, Jack knew, that the truth was probably exactly the opposite. With control over the nation's military, interior ministry, and intelligence agencies, Volodin almost certainly was the one true power in Russia.

Ryan asked, "And the Ukrainian military is weak, correct?"

Jorgensen answered, "Very weak. Their defense spending is a whopping one percent of their GDP, just a couple billion dollars. It's not enough money for new systems and equipment. They can barely maintain what they have."

"Tactics and doctrine?"

"They will put up a fight on the border, and they have decent air defenses, but that's about it. Through NATO's Partnership for Peace program, we have been able to put about three hundred

U.S. military personnel on the ground there. We have Green Berets training their infantry, Delta Force guys working with the CIA to get intel on the situation in the Crimea. All reports I'm getting on the situation is that the best Ukraine can hope to do is bloody the Russians' noses a bit as they take the Crimea and the eastern regions of the country. If they make it painful enough, *maybe* Volodin won't march his army all the way to Kiev in the west."

"Jesus," Ryan said. "The *best*-case scenario is they only lose a big chunk of their nation."

"I'm afraid so."

Ryan thought it over for a moment. "Our military on the ground. Do they know to get the hell out of the way if the shooting starts?"

"Yes, Mr. President, they aren't going to stick around to fight with the Russians. I've ordered them all to keep a low profile. Things have been getting dicey in Sevastopol and Odessa, the major cities in the Crimea. Pro-Russian protests are kicking up all over and spreading like wildfire. A good portion of the citizenry wants the Russians to invade. Ukraine is using its military to quell some of the rioting, which just makes the nation look like a police state, which just increases the number of citizens who are backing a Russian 'liberation.' "

Ryan groaned. "We don't want any part of that."

"No, sir," agreed Mark Jorgensen.

As they were talking, Ryan's secretary stepped into the doorway. "I'm sorry, sir. AG Murray is on the phone."

Jack was surprised by this. Dan had just left the Oval Office five minutes earlier. "Put him through," Ryan said, but he turned back to Jorgensen and Burgess. "I want to convene a meeting of our full national security staff to look over all options we have to stop Russia's invasion. Let's say seventy-two hours from now. I need your best and your brightest working around the clock, and I want to see all feasible options."

The men left the Oval Office, and Jack went back to his desk to grab the phone. "What's up, Dan?"

"Bad news, I'm afraid. Felicia Rodríguez was hit by a car. She's dead."

"Damn it. I thought you were picking her up."

"I was just making the call when I got word. We had a team watching her, but they weren't close enough to stop it."

"And the car that ran her down?"

"Hit-and-run. It happened in the parking lot of her apartment building, no security cameras. Our surveillance team wasn't mobile. By the time they got into their vehicle, the car was gone. We're chasing down vehicles fitting the description, but I'd bet you a week's pay it was stolen and will turn up burning under an overpass somewhere."

Ryan looked off into space. "Does that sound like a professional job to you?"

"Very much so."

"Russians or Venezuelans?"

"That's the only question. Either way, it's going to create massive headaches internationally."

"And either way, it was definitely the Russians who orchestrated it," said Jack. "But we find the truth, and we get it out there."

"Absolutely. I'm working on it. Sorry about this, Jack. We should have been quicker."

Ryan could hear the frustration in his AG's voice.

"This will make your job harder, Dan. But don't feel too bad for the girl. From what you told me earlier, she was covered with polonium. After having seen Sergey in the hospital the other night, I can say with authority that I would much rather get run over by a goddamned car."

28

Throughout the day, Clark, Chavez, and Kryvov moved from one bar to the next, each more shady than the last, drinking beer and sitting around while Igor called and texted people he knew on the periphery of the Kiev underworld. They steered far away from the chaos of Independence Square, and instead remained in remote working-class neighborhoods outside the city center. At each different location men would show up, scope out the table of journalists from across the room, and then, as often as not, leave.

But half the suspicious characters that came into the bars to eyeball the two foreigners and their local fixer did, in fact, come over and sit down. These men were drug dealers, human traffickers, and a man who said he could get any car off a German street and into the driveway of any Ukrainian — for a price. Through these men with firsthand knowledge of the local underworld, Clark and Chavez learned a great deal about the workings of the organized-crime situation here in the city.

While it was true that there were representatives of Russian organized crime active in Kiev, Clark and Chavez were surprised to hear how many FSB active measures operations seemed to be going on in the area as well.

Another troubling bit of information that came to light involved the clashes going on all over the city. The Nationalist Party had taken the presidency the year before, wrestling it away from a pro-Russian party that had been caught up in a series of corruption scandals. But the nationalists were not without issues of their own.

The rumor Clark and Chavez were picking up on the street, however, was that the current clashes were stoked on both sides by the FSB. It was said the Russians were organizing bus caravans from the pro-Russian east, filling the buses full of paid union workers, and dumping them in Kiev just upstream from the marches. At the same time, they secretly funded media outlets that pushed the pro-nationalist agenda.

If this was all true, it would show the Russians were interested less in winning hearts and minds in Ukraine, and more with causing chaos and civil strife.

By eight p.m. Clark called a halt to the day's recon, and the men returned to the flat. After sitting together in the living room to discuss the day's events, they decided they would go out for a quick dinner on nearby Khreshchatyk Street. They took a few minutes to sanitize and secure the flat, and then they headed out.

It was a breezy thirty-eight degrees outside, but the residents of Kiev considered this a spring evening; there were many pedestrians out in European Square as the six men walked along toward a restaurant recommended by Igor Kryvov.

As they walked through the square to the

restaurant, they were spread out several yards wide, making their way through the crowd. Clark, Kryvov, and Chavez chatted in Russian, and the three non–Russian speakers mostly walked along with their hands in their pockets to keep warm. Gavin Biery was on the far right-hand side of the entourage, and when a group of young men got in front of him on the sidewalk, he moved to get out of the way. As he passed them, however, one of the men stepped into his path and shouldered straight into Biery's side, spinning him around and knocking him to the ground.

The man kept walking with the rest of his small group, barely breaking stride.

Caruso didn't see the impact, but he saw the result. As the obvious culprit walked away, Dom turned and started after the young man.

Sam Driscoll grabbed him by the arm, restraining him. "Let it go."

Chavez helped Gavin back to his feet. "You okay, Gav?"

"Yeah." He brushed himself off, more embarrassed than hurt.

Caruso looked at Kryvov. "What the hell was that about?"

Kryvov had no idea. "I didn't see what happened."

Chavez finished brushing the Campus director of information technology off and patted him on the back. "I'll buy you a beer."

Once inside the restaurant, the men moved to a long table with benches in the back of a dark bar area. Beer was brought to Gavin, Dom, and Sam; Igor Kryvov ordered a bottle of vodka on ice. Ding and Clark had been drinking in the bars where they met with the locals since ten-thirty that morning, so they ordered mineral water, although Igor had the waiter bring shots of vodka for everyone so they could toast.

They kept their conversation centered on topics that fit with their legends as journalists. They talked about the news in other parts of the world, hotels and computers and other technology. There were enough similarities with their actual lives and the lives of their covers that the conversation was in no way stilted or forced.

Just after their food came, three men in dark coats entered the restaurant. The operators of The Campus all noticed them; they were conditioned to keep an eye open for any threats, even while eating dinner. As the hostess greeted the men, they walked past her without responding and went into the bar area.

Gavin Biery was talking about photography now, the differences between the quality of film prints and digital images, but the other five men at the table were silent, and all focused on the three new arrivals. The sullen, darkly dressed individuals walked straight over to the long table where the Campus men sat, and they sat down on opposite sides of the table just feet away. They turned their chairs toward the group and just stared quietly.

Biery stopped talking.

There were a few uncomfortable moments while the Americans waited for Kryvov to introduce the friends he'd obviously neglected to mention he'd invited along for dinner, but very quickly it became obvious Igor didn't know the men, either.

"Who are you?" Kryvov asked in Ukrainian.

The three men just looked back at Kryvov without responding.

The waiter came by to offer menus to the new visitors, but one of the men reached up and pushed him back, sending him on his way.

After another minute of awkward silence, Chavez looked at Driscoll. "Can you pass the bread?"

Sam picked up the bread bowl and sent it on its way down to Ding.

Within seconds everyone was eating again, and although Dom kept his angry staring contest going with one of the men, he still dug into his lamb and potatoes.

When the check came, delivered by a waiter who went out of his way to approach the middle of the table, staying away from the evil-looking men at both ends, Clark paid it, finished the last of his water, and stood up. "Gentlemen. Shall we?"

The rest of the group followed him out the door, but the three men who'd latched on to them during dinner did not follow.

As soon as they were halfway across European Square, Igor Kryvov said, "My friends, I'm sorry about that."

Clark said, "FSB?"

"Yes. I think so."

Dom nodded, "Those guys are the Keystone Kops. The worst surveillance I've ever seen in my life."

Clark shook his head. "Dom, they are *demonstrativnaya slezhka,* demonstrative shadowing. They *want* us to know we are being followed. They will harass us, annoy us, generally make things tough so we can't do whatever it is they think we came here to do."

Driscoll said, "I could understand that in Russia, but this isn't Russia. How can those guys get away with that here in Ukraine?"

"It's certainly brazen," Clark had to admit. "They must be pretty confident we aren't going to go to the local police."

Kryvov said, "Or else they've got connections in the local police. Maybe both."

Clark added, "It's nothing to worry about. It doesn't mean we are in any way compromised. Our cover is solid." He chuckled. "They just don't particularly like our cover."

Sam said, "These knuckleheads would really blow a gasket if they knew what we were really doing."

Caruso said, "I don't like this shit. Mr. C, how about you let Igor find us some guns?"

Clark shook his head. "As long as we're in cover we can't be carrying weapons, not even covertly. Remember, we can get challenged by the local cops at any time. They pull a piece out of one of our jackets, and our story about who we are and what we are doing will go tits up in a hurry. That happens, and we're off to the local jail, and there I can guaran-damn-tee we will be up to our eyeballs with mob goons we don't want to deal with."

"Roger that," said Dom. He wasn't happy rolling unarmed with Russian thugs literally bumping up against them, but Clark had been doing this sort of thing since before Dom was born, so he knew better than to argue.

They made it back to their building around eleven, and climbed the stairs to the third-floor flat. As they arrived at the door to the apartment, Ding slid his key into the lock, started to turn the latch, but he stopped himself before he opened

251

the door.

"Down!" he shouted.

The other five men had no idea what was wrong, but they hit the deck quickly. Biery did not do so on his own power — rather, Driscoll took the IT director down like a linebacker making a tackle in the open field.

There was no explosion. After a few seconds, Clark looked up to find Chavez still standing at the door, his hand on the key in the lock. He said, "The lock has been tampered with . . . It feels gritty. Maybe it was just picked, but it might have a pressure switch attached. If it does, and I let go, then we go boom."

The men climbed up slowly from the floor in the hallway. There was some nervous laughter between some of them, but not from Clark. He moved to the door and took out a penlight. He knelt down, had Chavez move his hand a little so he could see the latch and the key in the lock.

"It could be wired on the other side. No way to know."

While Chavez stood motionless, unsure if moving the door might trigger an explosion, Caruso headed into the stairwell, climbed out a window there, and shimmied along a narrow ledge to the balcony. In moments the men in the hallway could hear him inside the flat, and in seconds more, he was on the far side of the door.

"It's clear," he said.

Chavez breathed a long sigh and let go.

Caruso opened the door from the inside.

The rest of the men entered the flat and, if the evidence of a picked lock did not already tell them, they now knew for certain they had had visitors while they were out.

The room had been oddly rearranged. A sofa was now in the middle of the room, a chair had been stacked on another chair, and the kitchen table was now upside down. The centerpiece that had been on it now sat at the center of the inverted table.

All of Gavin's laptops were encrypted and password-protected, so no one had been able to search them. But that did not stop the FSB — Clark was certain they were the culprits of this — from unplugging them from their power strips and tying the cords together. The laptops were closed and stacked on one another.

At the same moment, both Clark and Chavez each brought a finger to his lips, telling the rest to keep quiet, as they might now be under audio surveillance. They could still talk, but only in character.

Gavin Biery was shaken. "Somebody has been screwing with my computers."

Chavez patted him on the back as he passed, heading down the hallway to check the three bedrooms.

The bedrooms looked much the same as the front room: random items had been moved around, suitcases stood stacked one upon the other, and clothes lay in piles on the floor.

He shook his head in confusion, then shook it again when he saw a small stuffed teddy bear had been left on one of the beds. It had not been in the flat before. Ding checked it for bugs, and saw that it was clean. Instead, it was just some sort of perverse message.

As he checked the last of the three bedrooms, finding the same random signs of activity, Chavez noticed the bathroom light was on. He leaned in to shut it off but stopped when he noticed a foul odor.

He checked. There were feces in the toilet.

"Classy," Ding said to himself.

Dom came rushing into the room. "Some jackass dumped out all my clothes."

He looked over Chavez's shoulder. "That's just nasty. What is it they are trying to prove? I mean, did a bunch of fucking kids break in here?"

The two men returned to the living room, and here Clark turned on the television and a radio full blast; then he opened all the faucets in the attached kitchen so that the sound of water flowing through the pipes added to the noise.

He brought his men into the middle of the large room. Under all the background noise, he said, "Guys, this is just a little psychological intimidation. They want us to leave, but they are using soft measures at this point. They are showing us we can expect really close and really annoying company at all times."

Clark looked around the room and realized the FSB's tactic was having the desired effect. Gavin and Dom looked at once confused and defeated, as if their operation here had been undermined even before it began. Driscoll just looked angry, as if his personal space had been violated.

Clark said, "These assholes are making it known they can and will do what they want, but we're not going to let it get to us. We can still operate here, we just have to be on our toes. We'll find ways to slip around them while staying in cover."

Gavin shook his head, doing his best to put the worry out of his mind. After a moment, he said, "Whatever. I call first in the bathroom."

Chavez and Caruso looked at each other. Dom said, "It's all yours, Gav."

29

The conference room of the White House Situation Room was chosen as the venue for today's presidential briefing on the situation in Ukraine for one key reason. There were more multimedia options in the Situation Room than there were in the Oval Office, and the President's briefers in the FBI, CIA, DIA, DNI, and the Department of State planned on using a number of different means to paint the picture for the President.

As the meeting was getting under way, Mary Pat Foley asked if she could make a quick announcement. "We have learned some distressing news this morning. It was discovered today in Ukraine that the number-two man in the SBU, Ukrainian's security service, has been spying for the Russians. He has fled Kiev, and there is a manhunt across Ukraine for him, although we assume he will turn up in Russia."

"Christ," Ryan said.

Jay Canfield already knew this. He said, "We are in the process of conducting a security review to see just how exposed our local operations are, but it doesn't look good. Our local people will be ratcheting back their operations accordingly."

President Ryan said, "There go another set of

eyes and ears in the region."

"I agree," said Mary Pat. "This one hurts."

"Who do we have as COS Kiev?"

Jay Canfield said, "Keith Bixby. He's a good man. A field spook, not a desk guy."

"Watch it, Jay. *I* was a desk guy," Ryan quipped.

Canfield said, "No, Mr. President. *I* was a desk guy. You were a desk guy that didn't stay at his desk." Jay said it with a smile. "You know what I mean."

"I hear you."

Mary Pat said, "I know Bixby quite well, and we couldn't have a better COS in place."

"Will we need to pull him out?"

"Bixby himself will be best positioned to determine what CIA's exposure will be on this. He will make the call on what operations to shutter, what people to send home, what foreign agents we need to either break ties with or pull out of the country for their own safety. Needless to say, this is a disastrous time for this to happen. We'll rotate in some new blood, but the Russians will see who is suddenly moving into our embassy in Kiev, and that will tell them who the new spooks are."

Ryan groaned, thinking about how much harder this would make things.

He said, "Okay. Let's move to the next topic. Volodin's statement announcing expanding ties with China. Leaving out the economics of it for a moment, what does the China–Russia agreement mean in practical terms, geopolitically?"

Foley said, "The two nations have been taking a lot of similar stances recently. On Syria, on North Korea, on Iran. China and Russia are burying the hatchet on international issues, so this agreement will only strengthen that.

257

"Beijing, Moscow, and Tehran have become what some have called an iron triangle."

"And economically? What's the end result of this?"

Ryan turned to an economic briefer for the State Department. Her name was Helen Glass; she was a Wharton grad and well known at the White House as an expert on Russia.

"It's a win-win. China lacks Russia's scientific know-how and raw materials. Russia lacks China's market and manufacturing prowess. If they can implement the agreement, both nations will benefit."

"How bad is Russia's economy now?" Ryan asked.

Glass said, "Several years ago, Russia thought it had it made. A huge find of both gold ore and oil, both in Siberia, seemed to portend great things for Russia. But the gold find was not as large as early estimates, and the oil has been difficult to extract, especially when Volodin and his predecessor squeezed out Western companies in an attempt to give Gazprom full control of the fields.

"Energy commodities are roughly seventy percent of all Russia's exports. But there is a downside to this. Huge natural resources have a negative effect on a nation's manufacturing sector. They call the phenomenon the Russian disease."

Ryan nodded. He understood the phenomenon. "The money is in the dirt, it just has to be dug up or pumped up. The money isn't in innovation or intellectual property or in manufacturing. After a while, a nation loses its ability to innovate and to think and to build things."

"That's correct, Mr. President. Russia had great

potential when the Soviet Union dissolved, but in the nineties it all went bad for them when the economy collapsed. It was the largest transfer of wealth in the history of the world without a war being fought."

Ryan said, "As much of a disaster as it was, you've got to give the Russian people some credit for just surviving it."

"They did survive it, yes. But they have not flourished. Volodin is taking credit for things because no one has come out to show Russians what wealth they *should* be enjoying. Russia's economy is big, but it's not modern or dynamic. Industry is focused on the extraction of raw materials. The only manufactured goods people want on the world market are Kalashnikovs, caviar, and vodka."

"You are describing a banana republic with a quarter of a billion people and hundreds of ICBMs," Jack said.

"I try not to exaggerate, Mr. President. But . . . insofar as their economy is limited by what they can dig up and sell . . . yes. And that is not their only problem. Russia's main export is fossil fuels. But coming in at a close second is corruption."

"That's harsh."

Helen Glass did not waver. "But true. There has been a heinous redistribution of property to those in power and the expansion of a police state to protect them. The bureaucracy is a protection racket.

"Russia is governed not by formal institutions, it is run by the will of the *siloviki.* The Duma is nothing more than the Ministry of Implementation. It does what it is told to do by the *siloviki.*"

Ryan said, "The cronies who run business and

the country."

"Yes, and nowhere is the connection between business and government more direct than in the case of Gazprom," she said. "Gazprom is officially privatized, but the Kremlin retains forty percent of the shares, and effectively one hundred percent of the decision-making ability. Woe be to the Gazprom private shareholder who goes against the wishes of Volodin. He says his tougher version of capitalism is what has allowed Russia to prosper, but what he is doing is not capitalism, and Russia has not prospered."

Ryan asked, "Is there any economist in the world who correlates Russia's increased authoritarianism with their increased economic growth?"

Helen Glass thought for a moment. "Sure, you can find some who will say just that, but remember, there were economists predicting the fall of capitalism and the rise of world communism, even in the eighties."

Jack laughed. "Good point. You can always find an expert to confirm your belief, no matter how ridiculous."

"Since 2008, over half a trillion dollars has fled Russia. Most of it is pure capital flight. This is billionaire money, squirreled away in offshore financial centers. The top-five foreign investment locations in and out of Russia are tax havens."

Ryan said, "Meaning it's not investment at all."

Glass responded, "Correct. It is money-laundering and tax-avoidance schemes."

"Right," said Ryan. "As long as energy prices are high enough, the Kremlin can gloss over the fact that a third of its economy is sucked up by corruption."

"Correct again, Mr. President. Foreign investors

are fleeing. The Russian stock exchange has lost nearly a trillion in value in the past year. Capital investment has fallen fifty percent.

"Russia has everything it could possibly need to be one of the great economies of the world. Well-educated people, natural resources, access to markets and transportation infrastructure, land. If not for the pervasive corruption, they would be at the top of the list of world nations.

"Russians are worse off today than they were a decade ago. Public safety, health, law, property-rights security. Alcohol consumption has grown, health spending has shrunk, life expectancy has dropped in the past years.

"They have enacted laws barring dual citizens from appearing on state television. They are removing foreign words from the Russian language."

Ryan said, "It feels like they've regressed thirty years over there, doesn't it?"

"It is very much like that, indeed, Mr. President."

Jack Ryan turned away from the economic adviser and toward Mary Pat Foley and Jay Canfield. "And with all this we have the knowledge that Russia wants to invade its sovereign neighbor, and now our intelligence capability in the nation has been crippled."

"It's a mess, Mr. President," Canfield admitted.

30

John Clark walked through the Obolon underground station on the Kiev metro's blue line. It
was four-thirty p.m., not quite rush hour, but the
tunnels, escalators, and trains were quickly filling
up with commuters.

The American made his way through the crowd,
keeping his head down and walking purposefully
to fit in with everyone around him. He headed
toward the trains, but he wasn't sure what he
would do when he got there, as his instructions
were only to go to the Obolon station to meet
with Keith Bixby.

Bixby had called Clark two hours earlier, asking
for an urgent meeting and giving the time and
location, which immediately sent Clark out the
door of the rented flat to begin a series of twists
and turns, a random sequence of cabs, buses,
metros, and hikes through malls, department
stores, and even a gypsy market, where he bought
a knockoff Nike winter coat after tossing his own
three-hundred-dollar one to a homeless man on
the street so Clark could change his appearance
on the fly.

Now he was here at the designated meeting
place, hoping like hell that whatever burning issue

Bixby wanted to talk to him about didn't involve a team of State Department security guys and a coach ticket back to the USA.

As he neared the end of the station hall, he heard a soft voice close behind him. "Get on the train, direction Ipodrom, last car."

The words were English, but it was not Bixby's voice, Clark was certain. Without acknowledging the instructions, he merged across the crowd moving toward him and walked to the opposite side of the station hall, and then he climbed aboard the Ipodrom train that had just stopped at the platform.

The car was almost empty when he boarded, because Obolon was only the third metro station on the line, but Bixby was there, sitting in the last seat in the back. Clark stepped into the car, turning toward Bixby, while all around him the car filled with commuters. Clark moved back into the corner and sat down next to the Kiev station chief.

Bixby did not look at Clark, but he said, "Nice jacket."

There were people standing and sitting ten feet away, but the racket of the train shooting through the tunnel would make it impossible for anyone to hear the conversation.

Clark put his elbows on his knees and leaned over, pretended to look at a paperback he'd pulled from his pocket. His head was less than a foot away from COS Bixby. "What's up?"

"When we talked the other day I thought having you here on my turf was going to be a pain in the ass. Now, I've got to say, I'm seriously reconsidering your value."

"Go on."

He blew out a long sigh. "This morning we

263

discovered that the number-two man in the Ukrainian intelligence service has been spying for the FSB."

Clark showed no reaction. He just said, "You're sure?"

"Pretty sure. A security investigation by the Ukrainians turned up an e-mail account he was using to set up meetings and dead drops." Bixby growled. "I mean, really. Who still uses dead drops in this day and age?"

"Did they arrest him?"

"Nope. He got tipped off somehow, and he disappeared. He's probably in Moscow by now."

"Does he know enough about you to compromise your operation?"

"You might say that," Bixby mumbled. "He was my main liaison with SBU. He didn't know everything, of course. He didn't know about our NOCs, didn't know the majority of our sources, methods, or resources." Bixby sighed. "But still . . . we worked together on some things, so he knew a hell of a lot. I have to operate under the assumption that FSB is aware of the identity of all my case officers at the embassy and many of our safe houses across the country."

"Ouch," Clark said.

"It's a crippling blow at the worst possible time. I'm pulling most of my people off assignments for their own safety, and I'm closing up some installations we have around the country."

"I can understand why," Clark admitted.

The train came to a stop, and the noise of the tracks disappeared. Both men stopped talking while people passed by and new passengers boarded. Bixby looked over faces and judged demeanors, and only when the train left the underground station and the noise of the tracks returned did he start speaking softly again.

"I'm heading down to Sevastopol tonight with a team. We've got a place there that's been compromised."

"A place?"

"Yep. SIGINT safe house we share with Ukrainian spooks. We have a technical team and a shitload of commo gear. There's a small team of security contractors, and a team of CAG dudes there, too."

Clark knew CAG meant Combat Applications Group, which meant Delta Force. It was no great surprise to him that Delta was in Sevastopol. It was the home port of Russia's Black Sea fleet, after all. The United States would naturally do what it could to keep tabs on the area to see what the Russian Navy was up to.

Bixby said, "We've got a lot of equipment to break down and haul off, and a lot of files to shred and burn. I'll be down there for thirty-six to forty-eight hours."

"Sevastopol is a powder keg right now."

"Tell me something I don't know."

Clark said, "I've been fishing around. It looks like the Scar has been behind a lot of the riots and civil unrest here in Kiev."

"I've been hearing the same rumors."

"What can we do up here while you're away?"

For the first time, Bixby broke cover, although just slightly. No one around noticed when he looked to the man on his right. "What can you do? Right now, Clark, I'll take whatever I can get. You are my eyes and ears here in Kiev until Langley sends me fresh blood, and that won't be for a week at least."

Clark turned the page in his paperback. "Six guys. Including me, we are *six* guys. One Ukrainian speaker and three Russian speakers."

"Yeah, well, I didn't ask you to come here in the first place. But since you're here, why not keep an eye on Gleb? He is staying at the Fairmont Grand Hotel. The bastard has the entire top floor to himself. I've heard from a guy who works at the hotel that Gleb meets with a constant stream of characters all day long. Not FSB, at least not known faces." Bixby shoved his hands deeper into his coat and leaned over a little closer. "A couple sets of trained eyeballs on him would give me a tiny bit of comfort knowing somebody was covering that part of the story here in Kiev."

"Consider it done."

"Sorry about being an asshole before."

"You weren't an asshole. You were just doing your best to keep your op buttoned up."

Bixby smiled mirthlessly. "Yeah, well, look how well that worked out."

The train arrived at its next stop. The station chief rose to his feet, and as he did so, he said, "See ya around."

Clark replied, "I'll be in touch."

Bixby disappeared in the crowd leaving at the Tarasa Shevchenka stop. Without looking, Clark placed his left hand on the seat where Bixby had been sitting, and he scooped up a tiny folded scrap of paper. He slipped it into his pocket, having no doubt it would be the number to an encrypted phone where Bixby could be reached.

Clark sat back in the seat, already thinking about moving part of his operation to the Fairmont Grand Hotel.

31

It was near the end of the workday, and Jack Ryan, Jr., had not left his desk except for runs to the cafeteria for coffee and sandwiches and to the bathroom — he found himself unable to call it a "loo" — but he was looking forward to heading straight home and then opening up his computer there for a few hours' more research before bed.

His phone rang and he did not look at the number before answering: "Ryan."

"Sandy here, Jack. Wonder if you could come upstairs when you get a chance."

"Upstairs?"

"Yes. I'm up here with Mr. Castor. No rush at all."

Ryan had been here long enough to know the subtle understatement of British-speak. Lamont was telling him to get his ass up into the director's office on the double.

"Be right there."

"Lovely."

Jack sat down at a coffee table in the ornate office of Hugh Castor, managing director of Castor and Boyle Risk Analytics, and he sipped coffee from a bone-china cup while Castor finished a phone call in French at his desk. Sandy Lamont sat across from him with his legs crossed.

Ryan whispered, "What's going on?"

But Lamont just shrugged as if he had no idea.

The sixty-eight-year-old Englishman finished his call. He strode over to the sitting area and took the wingback chair at the end of the coffee table.

"You have done a remarkable job. We are all incredibly impressed."

Jack liked an affirming compliment as much as anyone, but in this case he sensed a "but" coming.

He raised his eyebrows.

"But," Hugh Castor said, "Jack, we are, quite frankly, nervous."

"Nervous?"

"Locating the nexus between Russian business, Russian government, and Russian criminal enterprise is, frankly, part of our job here at Castor and Boyle. Having said that, your methods might be perceived by some as overly aggressive."

Jack looked at Sandy. At first he thought this was about what had happened in the alley in Antigua. But Sandy's almost imperceptible shake of his head told him this pertained to something else. "Perceived by whom?" Jack asked.

Castor sighed. "A name came up in your investigation the other day."

Jack nodded. "Dmitri Nesterov. What about him?"

Castor examined his fingernails for a moment. In an offhand way, he said, "As it turns out, he happens to be a large shareholder in Gazprom, as well as a high-ranking official in the FSB."

Lamont said, "Double trouble, you might say."

"Quite," agreed Castor.

Jack said nothing for several seconds.

Castor responded to Jack's silence: "You are trying to decide just how to ask me how it is I know this about Nesterov."

Ryan said, "I looked into him. He is a restaurateur in Saint Petersburg. I didn't discover any connection to FSB or even to Gazprom. You must have other means at your disposal."

"In light of your father's profession before he went into politics, I'm sure you know something about the work of the intelligence services."

You might say that, Ryan thought. He just nodded.

"It is mutually beneficial that we here at Castor and Boyle and the good men and women in British secret service communicate from time to time. We might come across a name, as you did, and want to ask them about it. Or they might like to learn something about what we have discovered in our work."

I knew it, thought Jack. C&B had ties to SIS. But again, he didn't say it.

"Makes sense."

"So I inquired about Nesterov, and they came right back to me and said, in their unique way of doing things, that we should be careful with him."

"Okay," Jack said. And then he added, "I'm careful."

Castor paused. "Flying down to Antigua and Barbuda, going through rubbish bins on private property. This is not careful. I can't imagine the negative press Castor and Boyle would have received if our employee, the American President's child, no less, was seriously injured or killed while on some sort of a secret mission on a Third World island in the Caribbean. It's a right dangerous world out there, lad, and you aren't trained to deal with some of the unsavory characters who operate on the fringes of our industry."

Sandy Lamont cleared his throat slightly, but he said nothing.

"You sending investigators to Tver, your applications to the Russian tax office for information, your research into the aircraft Nesterov uses to get around. This is all far above and beyond our normal scope of inquiry. I am concerned FSB might make things difficult for us, same as they do for many of our clients, and I can't have that."

Jack asked, "Is this about the FSB, or is this about the fact I'm the President's son?"

"Frankly, it's both. It is our job to fulfill the wishes of our clients. In this case, you have done a bang-up job, but we are not going to recommend to Galbraith that he pursue his case any further.

"The problem, lad, is that if Nesterov is an owner of IFC, there is zero chance Galbraith will ever see a shilling of his money. We can't pull them into court, not in Russia, and not in any European country, because Russia controls the flow of energy into Europe."

Jack said, "If we reveal the fact that Gazprom colluded with the tax office to raid Galbraith's company, and that this FSB guy earned a one-point-two-billion-dollar payday, then we can put a stop to this sort of thing continuing."

"We are not a police force. We are not an army. Your father might be the leader of the free world, but that carries no weight in this situation. The FSB can make things difficult for us if we hit too close to home in our investigation."

Ryan gritted his teeth. "If you are telling me the

fact I am employed here makes seeking justice more difficult for you, then I will resign."

Castor said, "That's just it, lad. What we do here is not about justice."

Lamont leaned in helpfully. "It's about money, mate. We want to help our client retrieve lost assets. That is possible if we find tangible assets in the West, but if you start naming high-ranking FSB geezers, Galbraith will not receive any recompense, I can assure you of that."

Castor said, "Jack. You, quite simply, have aimed too high on this one."

After a moment of silence, Jack said, "I understand."

He did not, in fact, understand, but he felt like if he sat here for one minute more he was going to put his fist through the wall.

Castor said, "We're going to put you on something else. Something less incendiary. You do very fine work, we just need to direct your efforts to a new task."

"Sure," Ryan said. "Whatever you think is best."

Jack left Castor and Boyle at six-thirty p.m. Sandy invited him out for drinks and dinner in an attempt to make up for the tough meeting with the director, but Jack didn't feel like he would be much company tonight. Instead, he went to a pub on his own, picked at a shepherd's pie, and drank down four pints before leaving for the Tube.

Ryan's foul mood intensified as he walked up Cannon Street in the rain. He'd forgotten his damn umbrella again, and he punished himself by not allowing himself to buy another. No, he would just let himself get soaked; he thought that might help him remember to grab it next time.

He was thinking about stopping off at one more pub on the way home. He would pass by the Hatchet on his way to the Tube; he'd been there before, and he'd liked the place well enough. Another beer would hit the spot, but, he decided, it would only make him more pissed off and sullen.

No. He'd go home and get some sleep instead.

He crossed the street, glancing back quickly over his right shoulder as he did so. Force of habit, nothing more, and as always, there was no one there who looked in any way out of the ordinary. He chastised himself; it was as if he was having a very difficult time switching into this life. He was overzealous in his work, treating shady businessmen as though they were an international terrorist syndicate, because that's what he'd been dealing with in his old life. And he ran mini-SDRs and stayed on the lookout for surveillance, because that's also what he'd been trained to do in his last job.

And, as another nod to his personal security, he treated every female who got within ten yards of him as a potential enemy plant.

Because that's what happened to him in his last job.

Ryan entered the Mansion House Tube station, cold and soaking wet. On the escalator down to the tracks an attractive woman in front of him turned around and looked up at him. She gave him a sympathetic half-smile. Like he was a puppy who'd come in from the rain. Then she turned back, away from the wet guy in the nice suit.

Twenty minutes later he walked out of the Earl's Court station, hands in his pockets and his collar up. He'd dried off a little in the Tube, but even though the rain had stopped, the evening mist was so incredibly thick he was soaked again within minutes.

After he passed a few people standing under umbrellas in front of an Indian restaurant on Hogarth Road he was all alone, walking along the sidewalk in front of a long set of row houses. He crossed the street over to Kenway, and his mind was lost back in his work. He'd just been kicked off the Galbraith case, but he couldn't help himself; he was still trying to get his head around the mazelike structure of the companies, trusts, foundations involved.

He crossed the little street to cut through a footpath between buildings that would take him to Cromwell Road, and he automatically used the opportunity to look over his shoulder, as if checking for any traffic.

A long shadow under the lamplight around the corner behind him was moving when he turned, but whoever was casting the shadow stopped suddenly and then, slowly, began backing away, causing the shadow to slide back along the street.

Jack stopped in the middle of the road, watching the receding shadow for a moment, and then he started walking in that direction. The shadow disappeared quickly. Jack heard hurried footfalls, and then running.

Ryan began running himself, his leather messenger bag bouncing off his hip as he shot toward the corner. He spun around, hoping to catch a glimpse of whoever was running away.

There was no one. Just two-story white townhomes on both sides of the two-lane road, and cars parked along the street. The heavy mist seemed to hang around the streetlamps, adding a particular eeriness to the scene.

Ryan stood in the middle of the little street, his heart pounding.

He turned back in the direction of his flat and started walking again. For a fraction of a second he wondered if it could have been a potential mugger. But Jack had learned enough in the past few years to know there was no such thing as coincidence. And in this case, there was no other explanation. Someone was following him.

His heart thumped even harder now.

His mind filled with an assortment of government agencies, foreign governments, criminal enterprises, and terrorist groups, trying to come to some sort of conclusion about the entity that had him under surveillance, but until he actually spotted something more solid than a shadow, this was unknowable.

As he made his way home, he felt the palpable sense of potential danger, but he could not deny to himself that with this came an unmistakable exhilaration.

32

After a week and a half of cleaning and repairs, the Ryan family returned to the residence of the White House with little fanfare. The President wanted to keep the event low-key, so without notifying the press in advance, Cathy and the kids were helicoptered from their home in Maryland to the South Lawn, and Jack met them at the south entrance. Katie and Kyle immediately ran up to their rooms and found them exactly as they had left them, though one member of the cleaning crew had picked up Kyle's toys so that the carpets could be steamed and shampooed.

That afternoon, Cathy herself had the idea to host a pool reporter from the White House press office through a tour of the residence. As it turned out, it was a senior White House correspondent from ABC, and Cathy took her, along with her cameraman, all over the common areas of the second-floor residence to show America that the People's House bore no physical scars from the unfortunate event.

The correspondent tried to back the First Lady into a corner by asking if, in retrospect, having a known enemy of the government in power in Russia over for lunch might have been a bad idea.

Cathy replied with grace, saying Sergey was a friend of the family's, a friend of America's, and a friend of Russia's.

Jack Ryan was angry to learn that ten days after the incident, Golovko's body was still in the United States and, effectively, stuck in customs. He personally called the director of Immigration and Customs Enforcement to see what the holdup was. The director of ICE found himself in the delicate position of having to explain to the President of the United States that his friend's body had been, in compliance with U.S. law, classified as contaminated waste, and even though he was in a lead-lined coffin, there was an incredible amount of red tape involved in getting him transported to the United Kingdom for burial.

Ryan was both angered and saddened by this news, but he had the empathy to recognize the situation in which he'd just put the head of ICE. He apologized, thanked the man for his hard work and diligence, and let him get back to work.

The family spent their first evening back in the White House together in the theater room, watching a children's movie. Cathy's idea was to get the kids back into a comfortable routine at home, and to a large degree it was successful. At one point, Kyle made a remark about the "man who made the mess" in the bathroom, but otherwise the kids, like most kids, seemed virtually unaffected by the event they did not really understand. Jack realized it wouldn't be long before Katie would piece together more about what happened that strange night when she was ten years old and had to sleep in her father's office before taking a surprise vacation home for spring break.

■ ■ ■ ■

The next morning, Ryan flew to Miami on Air Force One for a lunchtime speech to Cuban American leaders. He had planned on staying the evening to meet with local GOP fundraisers, but he cut his trip short to deal with the situation in Ukraine and returned to Washington just after lunch.

As soon as his helicopter touched down from Andrews Air Force Base, he was told Ed Foley was waiting for him. Jack headed right over to the Oval Office and found Ed in the anteroom.

Foley had spent the past several days looking over raw data from the British secret service pertaining to the Zenith affair, a thirty-year-old set of murders in Europe. Ryan had tasked Foley with the research project without explaining much about its relevance.

Ryan leaned into the Roosevelt Room, where Ed was waiting for him. "Hey, Ed. Sorry to keep you waiting. Come on in."

Foley followed Ryan into the Oval Office. He said, "No problem at all. How was Miami?"

"I wish I could tell you. I was there all of two and a half hours. Least I got a decent Cuban sandwich and a café con leche out of the trip."

"Careful. That gets out and some folks will say you've gone commie."

The President laughed, and the men sat down on the sofas in front of the desk. Ryan said, "I appreciate you digging in to all this old stuff."

"My pleasure. It was fascinating."

"What did you come up with?"

"More questions than answers, I'm afraid. I've

spent five days reading everything sent to me about the events in question from the perspective of three nation's intelligence agencies and police forces. From the British I have files from SIS, MI5, and Scotland Yard, and SIS also sent over reports they got from the Germans at the time — BfV intelligence reports, as well as relevant case files of the Swiss Federal Office of Police."

Ed continued, "All the parties came to the same conclusion. There *was* no Russian assassin called Zenith operating in Europe. This was just a story cooked up by members of the German terrorist group Red Army Faction. These were politically motivated killings, but at that time the RAF was nearly dormant. Some of the terrorists wanted to keep it that way. The killings weren't sanctioned within the organization, and those not involved were not happy to be tied to the killings, so they pushed the story that it was all a KGB plot."

"And how did Roman Talanov's name get tied to Zenith?"

"That came from British intelligence, but years after the fact. In the early nineties a source inside Russia, name redacted, claimed the Zenith assassin was real, and he was an ex-GRU Spetsnaz officer named Talanov who first served as a paratrooper during the invasion of Afghanistan."

"The name of the source was redacted?"

"Yes, and that is very strange. It is the only redacted name in all of the SIS files sent to me. I showed it to Mary Pat, and she made a request through SIS. They claim the redaction is on the 1991 source document itself, and they don't know who the source was."

"That's unusual."

"Very. It was explained to Mary Pat that a

278

determination was made that the information was false and their source not credible. They should have stricken the entire comment about Talanov, but someone screwed up and just redacted the name of the informant, and not the information itself."

Ryan said, "So you are saying it is bad intel, from a bad source. And it is also a dead end, because we don't even know where the intelligence came from."

"I do have one clue, from the Swiss files, however. One of the Swiss reports was from their Zug Canton police; they detained a man at the scene of one of the killings. He was stopped as a witness, but he refused to comply with the cops. He was handcuffed and put in the back of a police cruiser, from which he promptly escaped." Ed shuffled through his papers for a moment, then handed over a page. Ryan looked it over; it was a photocopied page of a document produced by an electric typewriter, and it was all in German.

Ryan did not see anything at first. He just said, *"Ich spreche kein Deutsch."*

Ed chuckled. "I don't speak German, either. But look carefully in the right-hand margin."

Jack lowered his glasses on his nose, and now he saw a faint marking. It appeared that something had been written in pencil and then erased.

He looked closer. "Does that say 'Bedrock'?"

"Yes."

"What's Bedrock?"

Ed shook his head. "No clue. I've never heard of it before, it's certainly not mentioned anywhere else in any of the Zenith case files. I checked with Mary Pat. The SIS has no record of Bedrock as a code name for either a person or an operation."

"And it's right next to the mention of the witness who escaped from police custody?"

Ed replied, "My German is atrocious, but that's what the translator says."

Ryan looked closely at the English word again. "Whose handwriting is that?"

Ed said, "There are other English notes made on the Swiss and German files. Must have been the Brits. My guess is the notes were made by Sir Basil Charleston himself."

"Interesting."

"I thought maybe you could call Basil. It's possible he won't remember — it's been thirty years, after all — but it might be worth a shot."

Ryan thought it over. "I called him last year on his birthday. His mind is sharp as ever, but I'm afraid he's deaf as a post."

Ed said, "If you'd like, I could head over to the UK and talk to him about it."

"I appreciate that, but there's no need. I'll call Jack Junior and ask him to run by Sir Basil's place and ask him. I haven't heard from my boy in a while, and this will give me an excuse to check in without looking too much like a mother hen."

"How's he doing over there?"

"I don't really know, to tell you the truth. He talked to Cathy the other day. Says everything is just fine and dandy. Maybe I'll get something more out of him."

The two men stood. Ed said, "Sorry I couldn't find anything more in the notes. I know you were hoping you could tie Talanov to the murders, but it really does look like these murders were the work of the RAF. The Germans busted a cell in Berlin and found intel that linked them to all the killings."

Ryan patted Ed Foley on the shoulder. "Maybe so, Ed. Maybe so. But I do know there is more to the story than what is in the notes."

Foley asked, "Why do you say that?"

Ryan gave a tired smile. "Because I lived through every damn bit of it."

33

Although they had hoped to operate below the radar in Kiev, John Clark and his Campus operators had changed their plan somewhat, and now they were, essentially, hiding in plain sight. Their run-in with the FSB a few nights earlier had shown them that Russian intelligence had the run of this town and any attempts at keeping a low profile around here were doomed to failure. With this in mind, Clark decided he and his team would, instead, just make it look like they were a somewhat blundering group of journalists who were blissfully unaware that they were operating in the middle of spooks and mafia, and clueless to the fact everything they did and said was under surveillance.

Gavin had tried the patience of the experienced operatives on the team more than once by straying into conversation that veered toward operational talk. Each time this occurred, whoever happened to be the closest man to Biery got in his face, gave him a dirty look, and then changed the subject of conversation quickly. Biery would wince in frustration at his lack of refinement as a real spy, he'd nod sheepishly, and he'd pick up the new conversation.

Even though they had to remain in character with their conversations because they knew they were being eavesdropped on, they were able to communicate by writing notes on their iPads and then erasing the file, and they wrote on paper that they immediately destroyed. They also texted one another because Biery had installed robust security software on all their electronic devices to keep out even the best attempts to decrypt them.

The Fairmont Grand Hotel Kiev is a massive building on the banks of the Dnieper River in the historic Podil district in central Kiev. From the windows and balconies, guests are treated to views of the river to the east and of hills and golden church domes to the west.

A massive construction project to build a flyover was in the works next door to the building, and the noise, dust, and traffic associated with the big project took much away from any charm the neighborhood might normally have, and petty criminals roamed Naberezhno-Khreshchatytska both day and night. At night, hotel guests were warned by bellmen to patronize only those taxis dispatched by the hotel's transportation service, because of rogue cabdrivers' common tactic of either robbing tourists themselves or driving them to a quiet place where they could be robbed by a confederate.

The Russian known as Gleb the Scar was staying in the Royal Suite on the ninth floor, but his entourage had taken over every other room on the eighth and ninth floors as well. In addition to the security the Scar would have around him at the top of the hotel, the ground floor was crawling with his men. Anyone with an eye for such things who looked around the opulent grounds could easily detect several men who were not hotel staff, but nevertheless seemed to be permanent fixtures in the lobby. Men were encamped at the tables, on the plush sofas, or else just milling about doing nothing.

The majority of these fixtures were Seven Strong Men security personnel, but FSB, Ukrainian intelligence, and interior security men, as well as agents for other intelligence agencies, also hung around. Clark had no doubt that CIA would have liked to keep someone here in the hotel 24/7, had they enough personnel to do so. Even if Bixby wasn't so concerned about the Scar just yet to task his men with establishing a twenty-four-hour eye, Clark knew there would be enough POIs in the Fairmont that CIA would want to at least have paid informants on the staff here.

Clark decided to keep his main base of operations at the rented flat, but he did take one room at the Fairmont so they could have someone close to Gleb the Scar. To effect this move and remain in cover at the same time, Clark concocted a ruse that began in the flat, where he started an argument with the other men about his OneWorld media assignment here in Kiev. For the benefit of the listening devices he knew recorded his every word, Clark, the senior reporter in the group, railed at the younger, less experienced journalists about everything from the equipment they had brought along for the job to production ideas for the project. He complained he wasn't getting paid enough and that his per diem did not cover restaurants suitable for his needs, and he expressed outrage he was being forced to share a room with others.

And then, with a flair for the dramatic that had

the other men in the room fighting to keep straight faces, Clark announced he would be moving into a hotel for the duration of their work here in Ukraine.

John Clark, a CIA officer since the Vietnam era, had never in his life been described, by anyone, as a diva, but his cover now had him adopting exactly that role.

An hour later, John Clark and Igor Kryvov arrived at the Fairmont; both of them pulled along large rolling suitcases full of items that any traveler might carry. Clark was careful to keep his luggage as innocuous as possible, because he was near certain the opposition would search his belongings here every chance they got. He checked into the hotel using his credentials showing him to be the senior reporter for OneWorld Productions in Vancouver, then he and Igor took their luggage to his third-floor room. They chatted along the way, Clark pestering the Ukrainian stringer with stories of other trips he'd supposedly taken with One-World and the better working conditions he'd experienced and the more professional crew of producers, photographers, audio men, and technical experts that he'd traveled with on assignments past.

Of course, Clark was certain he was being watched by cameras, mafia men, and enemy intelligence agencies, so this was all part of his cover.

After helping him with his diva-sized luggage, Igor Kryvov left the hotel and returned to the flat, and soon enough, John Clark moved down to the lobby, where he set himself up at a plush sofa by ordering coffee service, hooking a phone headset to his ear, and putting his iPad in his lap.

While Clark established his satellite op at the

hotel, the rest of the team prepared their end of the operation. They split into two-man teams, with Igor and Sam taking one of their rented Toyota Highlanders and Dom and Ding taking the other, while Gavin remained back in the flat, working from there.

There was concern about leaving Gavin alone in an apartment the FSB had already raided once, so Igor arranged for two of his former colleagues in the federal police to stand outside the flat, telling them they were protecting a Canadian audio technician and his equipment.

At ten a.m. the two Highlanders arrived outside the Fairmont and parked in lots facing different directions within sight of the entrance to the massive hotel.

And then the men did that which they were very accustomed to doing in this line of work. They sat in their vehicles and waited.

It was no time at all before John Clark began attracting attention in the lobby of the Fairmont. Hard-faced men stared at him and even sat shoulder to shoulder with him on the sofa, but Clark did not blink, he just talked into his phone's headset and worked on his tablet computer.

This was more of the "demonstration shadowing" FSB tactics that had been used against Clark and his men the other night.

But Clark was prepared for it now, and he wasn't going anywhere. He ignored the men, regardless of their persistent attempts to get under his skin. Even when two of them sat on either side of him on the couch and carried on a conversation, the acrid smell of their bad breath filling his nostrils and their elbows jabbing him in the side as they

286

gesticulated, Clark only continued reading his tablet as if he were alone.

When he talked on the phone, he acted as if he were in communication with someone overseas with his company, but in actuality he was on a secure conference call with his four men just outside the hotel.

In the vehicles outside, the men just listened to Clark drone on in their headsets about his dissatisfaction with his assignment here in Kiev and his refusal to start submitting his reports back to Vancouver until a new camera was sent in along with a new photographer to operate it.

By noon the FSB men had wandered off; perhaps they found the aged reporter as boorish as he found them. They remained in the lobby, mostly harassing other guests and giving the stink-eye to everyone who passed, but Clark could at least sip his coffee without having to keep his elbows pressed tight against his body.

Although Clark was forced to spend the vast majority of his efforts here in the lobby maintaining his cover, he was, in fact, here for a reason. With expert nonchalance, he was able to keep his head on a swivel and monitor the comings and goings to the elevators on the other side of the room, keeping a watchful eye out anytime someone went to the ninth floor.

Just after twelve-thirty, two men whom Clark immediately ID'd as potential Spetsnaz types entered the big hotel lobby and walked over to the elevators. Here they spoke for a moment with two thick ruffians wearing ill-fitting suits. Clark had pegged the two for Seven Strong Men goons, probably down here controlling who got on and off the elevator. After a few moments of conversation, the hard-cut military-looking men stepped into one of the elevators and the doors shut.

Clark adjusted his reading glasses on his nose. They were built with special lenses that gave him distant magnification when he looked through the very top of the glass. Using these, he was able to read the elevator numbers from across the room, and saw that the car traveled up to the ninth floor.

Yep, Clark said to himself, *these guys are here to talk to the boss.*

Twenty minutes later, the two men appeared in the same elevator car and then walked to the front doors of the hotel.

Clark waited until the instant they pushed through the revolving doors, and then he spoke into his phone as if responding to the other party he'd been talking to all along. "I'm glad you said that, Bob."

This was Clark's code to the cars outside to let them know whoever was leaving the hotel was someone of interest. It was now the job of the two car teams to ID the subjects and their vehicle.

Ding was behind the wheel of a black Toyota Highlander a hundred yards up the street, across from the road construction area. Dom sat next to him. They saw the two men exit the hotel and climb into a waiting Land Rover, and the vehicle took off to the north, toward their position.

Dom spoke into his headset, over the voice of Clark, who chatted away in an imaginary conversation: "Vehicle coming this way. We'll take it from here."

Chavez pulled into traffic a few cars behind the SUV when it passed, and then followed it up Naberezhno-Khreshchatytska Street, along the left bank of the Dnieper, and then onto

Naberezhno-Luhova.

While they drove along, Dominic Caruso opened an app on his iPad and prepared himself to input a quick but crucial set of commands as soon as the time was right.

There was a great deal of traffic in both directions, but Ding stayed three cars behind the target vehicle until they hit a red light. The instant both cars stopped moving, Caruso tapped an icon on his tablet.

Under his seat, attached to the underside of the Toyota, a radio-controlled car the size of a brick lost its magnetic connection with the metal oil pan and dropped to the street. On his screen Dom saw the camera view of the little vehicle, and he pushed forward the throttle icon to accelerate the RC car below him, driving it under a truck parked in traffic directly in front of his Highlander, and then under a four-door sedan.

When the RC car arrived below the target SUV, he tapped an icon on the tablet, changing the image to an upward-looking camera. A tiny light automatically turned on, and now Dom drove his little car slowly, moving it left and right by turning the tablet accordingly, looking for just the exact location on the bottom of the vehicle.

He stopped his tiny remote vehicle below the SUV's oil pan, then tapped a few icons, locking the wheels of the device in place. Once this was done, he switched to his deployment screen on the app, and he tapped a graphic that said, simply, "pneumatic deployment."

Below the SUV the slap-on GPS device attached to the top of the RC vehicle popped into the air under the power of a compressed air-powered launcher. The matchbox-sized transmitter hit the metallic surface below the SUV and stuck to it with its powerful magnet, and instantly the transmitter began sending the GPS location of the target vehicle.

On the conference call, Gavin Biery, who was sitting in front of his laptops back at the safe house, said, "Receiving signal."

"Roger that," Dom replied, and as the vehicles in front of him began rolling forward again, he hastily unlocked the RC car's wheels, switched his camera back to the forward view, and turned the little car around and raced it back to his Toyota Highlander.

Chavez drove forward while the RC car rolled back to him. When the two vehicles met, Dom pressed an icon on his screen and the vehicle itself popped into the air on its spring-fired wheels. With a loud and satisfying *thunk,* Ding and Dom knew the electromagnets on the RC car had reattached themselves to the oil pan, and they made the next turn to their left so they could head back to the hotel.

They stopped along the way back, pulling into a gas station on Volos'ka Street, and here they retrieved the RC car and loaded it with another slap-on. It was early afternoon, after all — Gleb the Scar might well have other appointments that would need tracking.

34

It was a frigid spring morning in Moscow, gray, with rain threatening. In Lubyanka Square, some four hundred fifty men and women stood stamping their feet to ward off the cold. All of those in attendance worked in the large neo-baroque building on the northern corner of the square, the main headquarters of the FSB and the former headquarters of the KGB.

Everyone in the crowd had been directed by e-mail and public-address announcements to leave their desks at ten in the morning to come out to the square. Here they chatted, many smoked, and they waited.

It was just past eleven now, but no one complained.

The square had been closed off before rush hour; no reasons why had been given to drivers and pedestrians, who were directed away from it to the overly congested side streets. The headaches it would cause for the simple people of Russia were not a concern for anyone in charge of this event. Even the Lubyanka metro station below the square had been closed. The drivers of the trains had been notified to slow but not stop, and armed guards waited on the edge of the tracks, making sure no one attempted to disembark from the passing cars.

There had been no explanation given as to why everyone was to stand in the cold and what would be going on out here today, although everyone in the square had a good idea, even though many of them could scarcely believe it.

In front of them was a forty-foot-tall object that had not been there in the center of the square the evening before. Although it was covered with a massive green curtain, the FSB employees in the square had little doubt as to what it was.

Under the curtain, all were certain, would be the statue of Felix Dzerzhinsky that had stood in that spot for decades during the Soviet Union before its removal in 1991.

Dzerzhinsky was a hero of the October Revolution that brought Vladimir Lenin to power, and Lenin himself appointed him director of the All-Russian Extraordinary Commission for Combating Counterrevolution and Sabotage. The organization, known as the Cheka for its Russian acronym, was the state security service from the beginning of the Soviet Union until Joseph Stalin replaced it in the 1920s.

Dzerzhinsky was, therefore, the father of the Soviet state security apparatus. He received the nickname "Iron Felix" for his strict belief in harsh punishment, and his infamy grew across the Soviet Union during his decades in power as the founder of the Soviet gulag system.

The removal of the statue in 1991 had been tangible evidence that the old guard was no more. The reappearance of the statue, if that was indeed what was below the draping, would mean to the four hundred fifty FSB employees here to watch the unveiling that the retreat from the past was over and state security's reascendence to the top of the order in Russia was finally complete.

President of the Russian Federation Valeri Volodin appeared a few minutes later. There was a roar in the crowd, due both to the appearance of their popular leader and as an early show of appreciation for what all expected was about to happen. He walked through the crowd, passing down a lane that opened for him compliantly with only some help from his armed security detail. Walking along with him was a tall man in his fifties; his features, like Volodin's, were classically Slavic, but his eyes held none of the sparkle and charm displayed by the president's.

This man was Roman Talanov, the director of the FSB. Many who worked in the building here in Lubyanka Square just on the other side of the forty-foot-high curtain had never even seen a picture of the man, and they could only assume this was Talanov by his placement alongside the president.

A hush came over the crowd as the two men stepped up to the draping. Each man stood to one side of the massive hidden object, facing the crowd.

The president looked to the closest members of the crowd standing around and smiled. With a wink, he said, "There will be no surprises."

Everyone laughed. Everyone knew.

With a nod from the president, the two men pulled off the green curtain, revealing the forty-foot-tall statue of Felix Dzerzhinsky.

The men and women of FSB erupted in cheers that could be heard all the way to the Kremlin, four blocks away.

When the cheers died down, Valeri Volodin took a microphone that was handed to him.

He took a long breath, and then spoke with emotion. "Some of you are too young to remember Iron Felix standing here, keeping guard over our building. Maybe more of you remember the day he was knocked to the ground and dragged away.

"He was reviled by fools and foreigners. But we protectors of order knew the truth. Felix Edmundovich, and those very few men of his time who were like him, were the ones who ensured nearly a century of power."

Now the crowd roared.

Volodin hammered his fist into the air. "This will be our new century of power! May someday brave and strong Russians stand here and talk of those who returned Iron Felix to his position so that a new, strong Russia could spring forth from that very building, from this very square!"

Volodin gestured to Talanov, who stood silently behind him with no hint of the emotion experienced by virtually everyone else in the square.

"Our struggles in the next few months will be great. But the rewards will be far greater. Roman Romanovich will lead you ably, and when you need to be inspired, just look out your window, or come out here, and gaze at this statue." Volodin beamed. "We should all allow Iron Felix to guide us through the struggles ahead."

Fresh cheers erupted and continued until Volodin left the square minutes later with a final wave to the crowd of intelligence personnel.

No one present was surprised by the fact that their director, Roman Talanov, had made no address to the crowd, and as the square began to clear out after the departure of Valeri Volodin, many noticed that Talanov was already gone. Most suspected he had drifted away, back to his office, while Volodin grabbed all the attention for himself.

The Crimea is a peninsula at the southern tip of Ukraine that dips into the Black Sea. Russians have called this area home since the Crimean War, when Turkey was defeated by the forces of Catherine the Great and a Russian citadel was established at Sevastopol. Joseph Stalin further "Russified" the area by deporting native Turkish-speaking Tatars to Central Asia and replacing them with Russians. In many cases, new Slavic inhabitants moved into the houses left behind by the displaced Tatars.

In the 1950s Khrushchev transferred the Crimea to Ukraine, one of the Soviet Republics. Clearly, he had no hint that his decision would ever create controversy, as he had no way of knowing the USSR would one day cease to be and Ukraine would have the freedom of self-determination.

Everyone knew Russia's ambitions extended to the Crimea, but a few years earlier some steam was let out of the kettle when the pro-nationalist Ukrainian president was replaced by a pro-Russian successor. The fate of the Black Sea fleet in the port of Sevastopol seemed secure, and Russia went about its business.

This all changed when a new pro-nationalist administration ascended in Kiev, shortly after Valeri Volodin took power in Moscow. Since then, the entire Crimean peninsula had been a hotbed of unrest, with protests in the streets, political murders and kidnappings, and even rumors of armed gang activity supported by Russia against public officials who did not support Russia's annexing of the peninsula.

It was clear that the hands of the FSB were all over the Crimea, using all means imaginable to foster interethnic discord.

The Crimean city of Sevastopol is the home port of Russia's Black Sea fleet, and twenty-five thousand Russians live and work within the city for the fleet alone. The residents of Sevastopol are not shy about their affinity for the Motherland of Russia. It was one of the few places on earth where statues of Stalin and Lenin had stood unmolested even in the tumultuous nineties, and now, more than two decades after Ukrainian independence, Sevastopol was as Russian a city as Moscow itself.

Statues of Vladimir Lenin still grace the parks of the city of Sevastopol. The Russians here weren't just pro-Russian, but pro-Soviet.

Keith Bixby had arrived in Sevastopol just an hour earlier, after an eleven-hour drive from Kiev. With him were two other case officers, a twenty-seven-year-old ex–Marine officer named Ben Herman, and a forty-eight-year-old Princeton grad named Greg Jones. The three had driven in two big SUVs loaded down with food and emergency equipment, but they carried no weapons with them, because though the men were "covered" intelligence officers, meaning they carried diplomatic credentials with them, their vehicles were not marked as diplomatic.

Their destination here in the Crimean port city was an old Cold War–era radar installation and military barracks repurposed as a functional but ugly residence. There was a high brick wall around the one-acre property, and inside stood a single three-story building with balconies on all sides and all floors, much like a small beachfront hotel.

This nondescript property in front of a drab park was a CIA SMC, or Special Mission Compound, and the facility held the CIA code name "The Lighthouse." It was staffed by four technical experts from the CIA, half a dozen private contractors from a U.S. security company, as well as a four-man Advance Force Operations team from U.S. Joint Special Operations Command's Delta Force. All fourteen of these personnel either carried on their person or had access to a carbine rifle and a handgun, and there were a few small grenade launchers to launch tear-gas grenades locked in the cabinet that served as the armory.

This wasn't much in the way of firepower, but this was only the Lighthouse's internal security. A second cordon protected the building; this was made up of a half-dozen Ukrainian security guards who were stationed at the main gate. Most of these men were off-duty police, and each carried just a pistol and a shotgun, but the Americans had a good relationship with the Ukrainians and knew they would warn of any threats.

The security guards knew only that the location was associated with the Partnership for Peace, a NATO program that fostered relationships with non-NATO nations. That none of the foreigners inside wore NATO uniforms had been noticed by the men, but no one thought this location was anything more than some sort of civilian liaison administrative building for an obscure and mostly irrelevant NATO program.

The CIA compound had been in operation here for years, but it had been difficult to keep covert as the tide of public opinion in the area had turned more violently pro-Russian in the past months, especially since the Russian fight with NATO in Estonia. Despite the difficulties of operating in the volatile environment, however, the place had most definitely paid dividends to the United States' understanding of the Black Sea fleet.

When Russia rearmed the fleet and refurbished equipment and weapons, Delta Force men based at the Lighthouse had photographed key components of the equipment. When the U.S. Navy cruiser *Cowpens* docked in Sevastopol a year earlier, the men of the Lighthouse had monitored the local reaction to gauge the level of support, or lack thereof, for the United States and NATO in the region. And then, just days earlier, when the port went on emergency activation because of Volodin's surprise military drills, the Delta and CIA men had recorded audio and video of the process that could be extremely helpful in case of actual naval war in the region.

Even though the majority of the population in the Crimea was decidedly pro-Russian, Ukraine was on friendly terms with the CIA, and Ukrainian intelligence had been aware of this CIA signals intelligence location.

And this was now a problem. The revelation that one of the top men in Ukrainian security services had been caught passing secrets to the FSB had set off panic buttons all around the CIA. Keith Bixby had, seemingly, a thousand holes in his ship he needed to fill now that much of his operation had been potentially exposed to the opposition, but nothing on this long list was as important as getting everyone, and everything, out of Sevastopol.

If the Russians invaded, they would move troops

directly into the Crimean peninsula, and they would head straight for Sevastopol. Once here, it would not take long before the Russian Army showed up outside the front gate of the Lighthouse, asking if they could come inside and take a look around.

Bixby was a hands-on station chief, and he had spent much of the day with a screwdriver, disassembling racks of electronic gear so that it could be loaded up into an SUV and driven away. At the moment, he was shredding documents in a long room of cubicles on the third floor of the building.

Twenty years earlier, there would have been days' worth of docs to shred here, but he thought he'd have every scrap of paper in the building destroyed in a couple of hours.

While he worked, the other men disassembled computers, removing hard drives, put small bills of local currency into envelopes to pay off local support personnel, and performed other rushed duties involved with decommissioning a secret intelligence installation on the fly.

It would take a full day of this work before they'd be able to load the Delta men, the CIA men, and the security contractors into the SUVs parked in the parking circle in front of the building and start the long drive back to the capital. Most of these men, as well as Bixby himself, would then fly out of Ukraine.

The men of the Lighthouse weren't needed in country now that the Lighthouse was shutting down, but Keith was leaving because it was assumed by all that he had been thoroughly burned to the Russian opposition by the second in command of the SSU.

It was just past nine p.m. now, and Bixby worked alone. A walkie-talkie was on the table in front of him so he could listen to comms among the other sixteen men in the building. As he reached for a manila folder full of radio traffic transcripts, the voice of one of the Lighthouse CIA technical staff members came over his radio: "Keith. Can you come downstairs?"

Keith fed the transcripts through the shredder while he answered with the other hand. "Unless it's a really big deal, I'd rather you came up to me."

There was a brief pause. "Sorry, sir, but I'm afraid this qualifies."

"I'll be down in a second."

Bixby flicked off the switch on the shredder and hurried downstairs.

In the lobby, Bixby found the Delta Force officer in charge of the small detachment. His call sign was Midas, but Bixby knew the man was a lieutenant colonel named Barry Jankowski who'd spent years as a highly decorated U.S. Army Ranger. He couldn't help noticing that Midas had his H&K assault rifle hanging on his shoulder and a helmet on his head.

He hadn't been wearing either the last time Keith had seen him, a half-hour earlier.

Not good.

With him was Rex, the security contractor in charge of the Lighthouse. He, too, was armed, but he always wore his M4 carbine when he was on the job.

"What's going on?" Keith asked, as he left the stairwell.

Rex said, "We've got trouble. One of the Ukrainian security guys was on his way in for his shift, and he got a call from a buddy on the local police force. The cop told him he shouldn't come in to work tonight."

"Did he say why?"

"He said word was spreading this was a NATO facility, and a protest is being organized. The local cops had been told to stay out of it."

"Shit," Bixby said, then looked to Midas. "What do you think?"

Midas answered, "I think we should pack up what we can, demo the rest, and get the fuck out of here. But it's not my call."

Keith thought of all the classified equipment in the building. "We've got a hell of a lot of sensitive equipment left to break down. If we blow or burn the stuff while we're here we'll just draw attention to ourselves and we won't get out of here. We've got antennas on the roof and more gear in the commo room. If we set charges, we can't be sure we got it all, and you can be damn sure the Russians will pick this place apart when they get here.

"We'll keep working on the double, through the night. We won't have time to completely disassemble all the satellite equipment on the roof — we'll have to just unhook everything and cram it in the trucks." He thought for a moment. "We'll need a couple more vehicles to make it all fit."

Rex said, "I can call some locals for that."

Bixby shook his head. "Not if the cops are already talking about us. I don't want anyone in the neighborhood to know we're about to make a run for it."

Bixby mulled it over quickly. Who could he call to help? There were some nonofficial cover operators in the country, but they were all near the border, and they checked in only when it was secure to do so. He couldn't see a way to ask them to come to the Lighthouse without burning more CIA assets.

There were a small number of U.S. forces here in Ukraine, based mostly on Ukrainian military bases. But none were in the Crimean peninsula, and more important, he couldn't just have a few U.S. Army Humvees roll through the gates without attracting the kind of attention that would make driving out of here quietly an impossibility.

Then it came to him. John Clark and Domingo Chavez.

He turned to Midas. "I'll make a call and have a couple more trucks here tomorrow morning."

Midas said, "Good deal. We've got guys on the roof watching for any developments in the streets. The rest of us will keep packing up in the meantime."

John Clark was just climbing into the plush bedding in his deluxe room in the Fairmont Grand Hotel when his sat phone rang.

"Clark."

"Hey, buddy."

Clark recognized Keith Bixby. He had to chuckle. It already sounded like the CIA man was going to ask for another favor. "Hey, pal," he replied.

"I hate to push my luck with you, but I've got a problem and I could really use some quick help."

"Name it."

"It involves an eleven-hour drive through the night into a situation that is going from somewhat shaky to downright dangerous. You up for that?"

Clark replied, "I'll notify my guys. I guess I better call room service and get some coffee up here."

Bixby explained the situation in brief, and within minutes Clark was on the phone with Ding in the safe-house flat across town.

35

Jack Ryan, Jr., had spent the entire day in his office at Castor and Boyle setting up a new IBM i2 Analyst's Notebook database. This file pertained to his new assignment, the theft of funds from a Norwegian freighter company that had purchased some ships from a Russian firm but, upon delivery, realized they had been sold rusty hulks. Not only was the case cut-and-dried and uninteresting, but the total value of the crime was several orders of magnitude less than the Galbraith–Gazprom affair. Jack had found himself bored by noon, and by two p.m. he was already sneaking peeks at a Gazprom affiliate mind map he'd made on Analyst's Notebook the previous week.

His phone rang, and he reached for it automatically.

"Ryan."

"Hey, Jack. Am I interrupting anything?"

Ryan was surprised to hear from his father. "Hey, Dad! Not at all. Just dealing with the Russians."

"You and me both."

Junior said, "Yeah, I heard. Has Dan figured out who poisoned Golovko yet?"

"Yes, but it's one of those things that creates

more questions than answers."

Jack Junior looked up at his mind map; it looked like multicolored spaghetti noodles in a bowl. "I hear you."

"Mom said you called the other night. Sorry I didn't get to talk to you."

"That's okay. I know you have been running around dealing with Sergey and Ukraine. I hope you guys are doing okay."

"We're fine. We're back in the residence, and it's the same as ever. They tore the john out of the living room bathroom. Can you believe that?"

"Unreal. Look, Dad. I'm sorry I haven't checked in. Just real busy at work."

"It's okay, sport. Been pretty busy at work myself."

The younger Ryan chuckled.

"So how's life?"

"It's fine."

"Living in London is great, right?" Jack Junior could hear the excitement in his dad's voice, almost as if he was enjoying himself vicariously through his son's experience, reliving his own time here so long ago.

Junior just muttered out an unenergetic "Yeah."

There was a pause. Jack Senior said, "It *is* great, right?"

"I guess I'm still settling in a little."

"Is something wrong? Is there a problem?"

"No, Dad. Everything is fine."

Jack Senior paused again. "You know you can talk about anything, right?"

"Of course. And I will. It's all good. Work is just frustrating."

"Okay." The father left it alone, though he could hear tension in his son's voice. He asked, "I was wondering if you had time to do me a favor."

Now Jack Junior lightened up. "Name it. It would be good to think about something else for a bit."

"You remember Basil Charleston, don't you?"

"Of course. It's been a long time. He must be well into his eighties by now."

"And that's the problem. I have a couple of questions for him, and I would love to talk to him in person, but I have a funny feeling he's not going to be able to hear me over the phone. The last time I called him it was hit-and-miss."

"Does he still have his place in Belgravia?"

"He does."

"I can swing by, it's not far at all. What do you want me to ask him?"

"About thirty years ago, there was a string of murders in Europe. At the time, some people thought it was a KGB agent called Zenith who was responsible. We've discovered some uncorroborated intelligence tucked away in an old file that suggests Zenith and Roman Talanov were one and the same."

"Holy shit," the younger Ryan said.

"That's basically my thought, but I don't want to get ahead of myself. I need to know more about this. To that end, the code word 'Bedrock' came up in the Zenith murders. We don't know if that relates to a person, a place, or maybe an operation. We'd like to know just what Bedrock is. And if anyone will remember, it would be Sir Basil."

The elder Ryan explained that it looked like Charleston had handwritten a reference to Bedrock in the file, and he said he'd have his secretary e-mail the file to Jack Junior immediately.

"Surely that's going to be classified intelligence.

Why would he talk to me?"

Jack Senior said, "Basil won't have a problem talking to you. He knows you used to work for Gerry."

Jack Junior knew the phone conversation between him and his father was secure, and he knew his father was aware of this fact as well. Nevertheless, his dad was speaking to him with a little code. The fact Charleston knew the younger Ryan had "worked for Gerry" clearly meant he knew about The Campus. This surprised the younger Ryan.

"Really?"

"Absolutely. He knows you were an analyst there, and he knows the sort of work Gerry was involved with."

"Okay. Next question. Did this take place back around the time we were living in the UK?"

"Yes, exactly that time. I remember this episode well, as a matter of fact. You were in diapers."

"No offense, Dad, but that was a long time ago. Do you think there's any chance Basil is going to remember the case, especially since there is no other record of Bedrock at SIS?"

"Jack, you know better than most, not every important operation gets written down for posterity. If Bedrock was important enough to stay off-book, then I think it's likely Basil will know all about it."

"You've got a point. I'll ask him. Do you really think there is any chance this Talanov character was involved?"

"No way of knowing. I've learned not to rely too much on one single tidbit of intelligence. It takes more to convince me."

"But you are curious enough to have me track down Bedrock."

"Right," Jack Senior said, then caught himself. "Track down? Wait. I just said talk to Basil. I don't need you to do anything else."

"Right," the younger Ryan said.

"So tell me, what's going on at work?"

"I am up to my neck in shady Russians over here. They are swindling clients out of fortunes and businesses and intellectual property. They are lying with a straight face and using the court system to steal and intimidate."

"It's that bad?"

"You wouldn't believe." Jack Junior caught himself. "What am I saying? You used to go toe-to-toe with the KGB."

President Ryan said, "Very true. Do you enjoy the work, at least?"

The younger Ryan sighed. "It's frustrating. I've spent the last few years thinking about justice. Chasing down bad guys and stopping them. But here I am chasing down the bad guys, but the most I can hope for is that some court that has no real jurisdiction over the bad guys will order that some assets are seized, and that probably will never happen."

"Justice moves slowly."

"In this case, it doesn't move at all. My boss, Hugh Castor, is apparently afraid to pin any corruption directly on the *siloviki* in the Kremlin. I understand he doesn't want to get bogged down in court over there, or have his people harassed by the authorities, but we are letting the real criminals off too lightly.

"I can't help but think about what I could do to some of these worthless bastards to make them change their ways. If Ding and John and Sam and Dom were here, I wouldn't be reading old ownership transfer agreements, that's for damn sure."

"I understand. There were a couple of times in my analytical career where I felt like I had connected the dots that needed to be connected, but there was not enough follow-through from those above me to make a difference. There is very little more frustrating than that."

Jack Senior said, "I'll e-mail you the document I'd like you to show Basil. That, and what I've already told you, might be enough for you to prod his memory. I won't go into the rest of it, because it's a long story, and I don't even remember all the details myself."

"No problem. I'll talk to Basil and let you know what he says. Sounds like fun."

Jack Senior laughed a little. "I can't promise you any more excitement than spending a few minutes chatting with an octogenarian in his study, but I guess it's something."

"It *is* something, Dad. You know I love stories about the old days."

The President's voice darkened. "Not this one, son. This story did not have a happy ending at all."

36

Thirty years earlier

Jack Ryan woke to the patter of light rain, although he barely noticed it. This was England, after all; the absence of rain this time of year would have been unique. He reached out with a long, slow stretch and found his wife's warm shoulder in the dark. Cathy was sound asleep still, which, at twenty minutes before six in the morning, seemed to Jack to be perfectly reasonable.

Their alarm was set for a quarter till the hour, so Jack took his time waking up. Finally he reached over and turned off the alarm before rolling out of bed. He shuffled into the kitchen to start the coffee and headed out to the front porch to get the paper.

The street was perfectly quiet. The Ryans lived in Chatham, in North Kent, some thirty miles from London. He and Cathy were the only couple on Grizedale Close who had to commute all the way to the capital, so theirs was more often than not the first house on the street with its lights on and movement inside each morning.

The neighbors all knew Cathy was a surgeon at Hammersmith Hospital, and they thought Jack had some boring job at the U.S. embassy. And while that was officially true, the truth would have inspired much more gossip over the hedges on Grizedale Close.

The young American was, in fact, an analyst in the CIA.

Jack noticed the milkman had delivered his usual half-gallon of whole milk. His daughter, Sally, would drink every drop of it before the next delivery. He picked the milk off the porch, and then searched for a moment before finding the newspaper in the bushes near the door. The copy of the *International Herald Tribune* was wrapped in a plastic bag to protect it from the weather, indicating the paperboy had better sense than he had aim.

Ryan went back inside and woke Cathy, then made his way to the kitchen. After pouring himself a cup of coffee, Jack snapped open the paper and took his first sip of the morning.

Below the fold on the front page, a picture grabbed his attention. A body covered in a tarp lay in a street. From the look of the buildings, he guessed it was Italy or perhaps Switzerland.

He read the headline below the photo.

"Swiss Banker Shot Dead, Four Others Wounded."

Jack scanned the details of the article. It seemed the banker's name was Tobias Gabler, and he worked at Ritzmann Privatbankiers, a venerable family-owned bank based in the Swiss canton of Zug. Gabler was killed, and several others were injured, when someone opened fire from the window of a building into a street full of pedestrians.

So far, the police had no one in custody.

Ryan looked up from the paper when Cathy strolled into the kitchen in her pink housecoat. She kissed Jack on the top of the head, and then she shuffled on to the coffeemaker.

"No surgery?" Jack asked. She never drank coffee

when she had any surgery planned for the day.

"Nope," she said, as she poured herself a cup. "Just some follow-up appointments. A jittery hand while I'm fitting someone for glasses won't be the end of the world."

Jack had no idea how his wife could go to work most mornings and slice into eyeballs. *Better her than me,* he told himself.

On the way to the shower, Jack peeked in on his five-year-old daughter, Sally. She was sleeping, but he knew she would be up and wide awake by the time he got out of the bathroom. He liked to get at least one nice, peaceful look at his little girl while she wasn't darting around like a moving target, and first thing in the morning was his only opportunity.

He next peeked in on Jack Junior. His toddler was sound asleep, facedown in his crib on the top of his covers, his diapered butt sticking up in the air. Jack smiled. His little boy would be walking soon, and that little crib wouldn't keep him for much longer.

Jack started the shower and then took a moment to look at himself in the mirror. Ryan was six-one, in fair shape, although he'd let both his diet and his exercise slip in the past few months here in the UK. Two small kids in the house meant keeping a flexible schedule, which got in the way of his workouts, and it also meant there was an abundance of snacks and cereals and treats in the pantry, one or two of which seemed to call to Ryan every day.

As he did most mornings, Ryan poked at the pronounced white scar on his shoulder. A year earlier he had saved the Prince of Wales and his family from an assassination attempt by an offshoot of the Irish Republican Army. Jack earned himself honorary knighthood from the queen for his quick-thinking ac-

312

tions, but he'd also earned himself a gunshot wound from the terrorists for not being quite quick enough.

Ryan had had other run-ins with danger, both with the Irish and in Vatican City, during the assassination attempt on Pope John Paul II. He'd done his best to prevent the attack, but he'd narrowly missed the Bulgarian agent working under orders from Moscow.

Ryan left the mirror and stepped into the shower, and the hot water instantly relieved tight muscles in his back, another remembrance of his past. As a twenty-three-year-old second lieutenant in the Marine Corps, he'd been stationed on an amphibious assault ship during a NATO exercise in Crete. He'd been in the back of a CH-46 when the aft rotor failed, and the chopper full of Marines crashed into the rocks. Ryan broke his back, lost his commission, and endured years of pain after the fact before a successful surgery gave him his life back.

Ryan started his post-military life at Merrill Lynch, where he made a small fortune in the markets. After a few years of this, he decided to go back to school; he earned his doctorate in history, and then, after teaching for a while at the Naval Academy, he'd gone to work for the CIA.

In just thirty-two years Jack Ryan had experienced more than the average man does in a lifetime. As he stood under the hot water he smiled, taking comfort in the certainty that his next thirty-two years wouldn't be nearly as eventful. As far as he was concerned, watching his kids grow up was all the excitement he'd ever need.

By the time Jack and Cathy were ready to leave for work, the nanny had arrived. She was a young South African redhead named Margaret, and she immediately began her workday by wiping jam from

Sally's face with one hand while holding Junior in her other.

The taxi honked out on the street, so Jack and Cathy gave the kids one last hug and kiss, and then they headed out the door into what now had devolved into a heavy mist.

Ten minutes later they were in the train station in Chatham. They climbed aboard the train to London, sat in a first-class cabin, and read most of the way.

They parted in Victoria Station with a good-bye kiss, and by ten till nine Jack was walking along under his umbrella on Westminster Bridge Road.

Although Jack was officially an employee of the U.S. embassy, in truth he almost never set foot in the embassy. Instead, he worked at Century House, 100 Westminster Bridge Road, the offices of the Secret Intelligence Service.

Ryan had been sent over by his boss at the CIA, Director of Intelligence Admiral James Greer, to serve as a liaison between the two friendly services. He was assigned to Simon Harding and his Russian Working Group, and here Ryan pored through any and all intelligence MI6 wanted shared with the CIA relating to the USSR.

Although he knew they had every right to protect their sources and methods, even from the United States, Jack considered the Brits to be somewhat stingy with their information. More than once he found himself wondering if his counterpart SIS analyst working at Langley came across some of the same roadblocks when trying to get information out of the CIA. He had come to the conclusion that his own service was probably even more tightfisted. Still, the arrangement seemed to work well enough for both nations.

■ ■ ■ ■

Just before ten a.m., the phone on Ryan's desk rang. He was engrossed in a report on Russia's Kilo-class submarines stationed in Paldiski, Estonia, so he reached for the handset distractedly.

"This is Ryan."

"Good morning, Jack." It was Sir Basil Charleston himself, director general of the Secret Intelligence Service.

Ryan sat up straighter and put the dot-matrix printout he'd been reading down on the blotter in front of him. "Morning, Basil."

"I was wondering if I could borrow you away from Simon for a few minutes. Would you be so good as to pop round?"

"Now? Sure. I'll be right up."

"Splendid."

Ryan took the executive elevator to Sir Basil's corner office on the top floor. When he walked in, he saw the director of the Secret Intelligence Service standing by a window that overlooked the Thames. He was talking to a blond man about Jack's age who wore an expensive-looking charcoal-gray pin-striped suit.

"Oh, hello, Jack. There you are," said Basil. "I'd like to introduce you to David Penright."

The two men shook hands. Penright's blond hair was slicked back, and his sharp blue eyes stood out on his clean-shaven face.

"Sir John, it's a pleasure."

"Please, call me Jack."

Basil said, "Jack is a little self-conscious about his knighthood."

"*Honorary* knighthood," Ryan hastened to add.

Penright said with a smile, "I see what you mean.

Very well. Jack it is."

The three men sat in chairs around a coffee table, and a tea service was brought in.

Charleston said, "David is an operational officer, based in Zurich, mostly, aren't you, David?"

"Yes, sir."

"Tough post," Ryan joked with a smile. Neither of the two men smiled back.

Oops, Jack thought.

On the coffee table next to the service was that morning's copy of *The Times* of London. Penright picked it up. "Have you had a chance to look over the paper?"

"I get the *International Tribune.* I glanced at it."

"Did you see the article about the dreadful affair in Switzerland yesterday afternoon?"

"In Zug, you mean? Pretty awful. A man was killed, some others were wounded. The paper says it didn't look like robbery, since nothing was taken."

Penright said, "The man's name was Tobias Gabler. He was killed not in Zug, but in a nearby burg called Rotkreuz."

"Right. He was a banker?"

Penright replied, "He was indeed. Are you familiar with his bank, Ritzmann Privatbankiers?"

Ryan said, "No. There are dozens of small, family-owned banks in Switzerland. They've been around forever, so they must be successful, but like most Swiss banks, knowing just how successful they are is difficult."

"And why is that?" Charleston asked.

"The Swiss Banking Act of 1934 essentially codified their bank secrecy procedures. Swiss banks don't have to share any information with any third party, including foreign governments, unless so ordered by a Swiss court."

316

Penright said, "And good luck with that."

"Exactly," agreed Ryan. "The Swiss are tight when it comes to giving up information. They use numbered accounts, which draws dirty money to them like a bee to honey."

Ryan added, "The numbered accounts aren't really as anonymous as many make them out to be, because the bank itself has to fully verify the identity of the person opening the account. That said, they do not have to fix the name to the account itself. And this makes transactions anonymous, because anyone with the correct code can deposit to or withdraw from the account."

The two Englishmen looked at each other, as if deciding whether the conversation was to continue.

After a moment, Sir Basil nodded to David Penright.

The younger man said, "We have reason to believe a certain nefarious enterprise maintains accounts at RPB."

This didn't surprise Ryan in the slightest. "Cartel? Mafia?"

"We think there is a strong possibility that the man who was killed, Tobias Gabler, was managing numbered accounts for the KGB."

This *did* surprise Ryan. "Interesting."

"Is it?" Penright asked. "We were wondering if, perhaps, CIA had come to the same conclusion about the bank."

"I can tell you with some degree of confidence that Langley doesn't know of specific numbered accounts in Switzerland. I mean, sure, we know they exist. Russian intelligence has to stash black funds in the West so their operatives on this side of the Iron Curtain can have a steady stream of cash, but we don't have their accounts pinned down."

"You're quite sure?" Penright asked. He seemed disappointed.

"I am pretty sure, but I can cable Jim Greer, just to double-check. I'd hope that if we had that kind of information, we'd either find a way to shut down the KGB's access to the account or, better yet —"

Penright finished the thought. "Or, better yet, monitor the account, to see who makes withdrawals."

"Right," Jack said. "That could prove to be a treasure trove of intel about KGB ops."

Charleston spoke up. "That was our idea. The interesting thing here, however, is there is one particular account in question that we are curious about, because it is quite large, and it's just sitting there."

"Maybe they are setting it up for some future operation," Ryan suggested.

Sir Basil Charleston said, "I quite hope that is *not* the case."

"Why do you say that?"

Basil leaned toward Ryan. "Because the account we are talking about has a balance in excess of two hundred million dollars. With regular high-dollar deposits coming in monthly."

Jack's eyes went wide. "Two hundred *million*?"

Penright said, "Yes. Two hundred four million, as a matter of fact. And if the money keeps coming in at the same pace, in another year there will be twice that."

"All in *one* account? That's unbelievable."

"Quite," said Charleston.

Ryan said, "Obviously, this isn't being set up for an intelligence operation in the West. That's *way* too much money. I . . . are you *sure* it's KGB money?"

"We are not sure, but we believe so."

That didn't tell Jack much, but he assumed the

318

Brits were holding back to protect their source. He thought for a moment. "I understand if you aren't going to give me information about your source for this intelligence, but I can't think of any possibility other than the fact you have someone in the inside of that bank."

Basil looked at Penright and nodded again. He clearly was giving the younger intelligence officer the okay to share information with the CIA analyst.

Penright said, "We have a source at the bank. Let's just leave it there."

"And the source has reason to suspect the two hundred mil is KGB money?"

"Something like that."

"And now Gabler, the account manager, is dead."

"I'm afraid so," said David Penright.

"You think the KGB found out their moneyman was compromised somehow, so they killed him?"

Basil said, "That is one operating theory, but there is a major hole in it."

Jack said, "Nothing about the assassination of Gabler looks like a KGB hit."

Penright said, "Quite right. We are confused by that bit. The witnesses say he was crossing a two-lane street, on foot, at six p.m., when an assault rifle appeared out a window of a supposedly unoccupied hotel room. An entire thirty-round magazine was fired at him at a range of less than fifty feet. He was hit three times out of thirty, which isn't terribly impressive accuracy."

Penright added, "Sir Basil's house cat could do that."

Basil raised his eyebrows but did not respond to the quip. Instead, he said, "Four other passersby were wounded."

"And no one saw the shooter?"

Penright replied, "No. A van came screeching out of an underground garage, nearly ran down a group of onlookers, but no one got a glance at the driver."

Jack said, "It's not exactly a poison umbrella in the back of the leg." He was referring to the 1978 assassination of Bulgarian dissident Georgi Markov, who was assassinated just a few hundred yards from where Ryan, Penright, and Charleston now sat.

"No," Sir Basil admitted. "Nevertheless, we are very concerned that Herr Gabler was not a victim of a random act of violence. Could he have been assassinated by another intelligence agency that became aware of his association with the Russians? Could he have been killed by other clients of his, for some perceived violation of their trust? We would like to know if your agency has any knowledge of either the nefarious affairs of the bank or of any names on this list."

Penright handed over several sheets of paper folded in half. Ryan opened them and saw literally hundreds of names.

"Who are they?"

"RPB's employees and clients. As you may know, some numbered accounts are set up by shell corporations, so, despite the rules, even the bank itself doesn't know who actually owns the funds. It's another layer of secrecy."

Ryan understood. "You want us to check our files to see if we have anything on any of the names, in the hopes you can find someone else who had a reason to kill Gabler."

Penright added, "That, and also we'd like you to try and weed through the corporate accounts. U.S. banking is not as private as it is in Switzerland. You might find some similar data sets that can link actual names to these shell companies."

Ryan said, "You need to be certain your source in the bank has not been compromised."

"That's it exactly," Charleston agreed.

"Okay. I'll get to work on this immediately. I don't want to cable this list to Langley, it's too sensitive. I'll go over to the embassy right now and send it over in the diplomatic bag. It will take a few days to get answers back to you."

Penright said, "The sooner the better. I'm trying to get in touch with our inside man in Zug. It's a good bet he is going to be shaken up by all this. If we don't hear from him by tomorrow, I'm going to have to start making preparations to go over there to make contact. I'd like to be able to tell him he has nothing to worry about."

Jack started to get up, but he stopped himself. "Sir Basil. You know as well as I do that Langley will ask to be dealt in to this hand. This autonomous asset of yours . . . are you offering to make him bilateral?"

Basil had been expecting the question. "We will share the intelligence we get from this source with our friends in Washington. And we will readily take any advice you might have for us on the operation. But I am afraid, at this juncture, we are not prepared to go bilateral with this relationship."

"I'll let Greer and Moore know," Jack said, and he stood up. "They might want more involvement, but I am certain they will understand that the main focus right now should be on finding out if your agent is in any danger — for his sake, of course, but also for yours. I can't imagine what two hundred million dollars' worth of KGB money is doing sitting in a Western bank, but we need that inside man right where he is so we can keep an eye on it."

Charleston stood and shook Ryan's hand, as did David Penright.

Sir Basil said, "I had no doubt at all that you would see the urgency of this matter."

37

Present day

Jack Ryan, Jr., arrived at the Belgravia town house of Sir Basil Charleston during a midafternoon squall. He'd called first, of course, even though he'd been warned by his dad that the octogenarian might not be able to communicate by phone. Ryan was surprised when a younger-sounding man answered the phone. He introduced himself as Phillip, Charleston's personal assistant, which Ryan assumed meant bodyguard.

Two hours later, Ryan was invited inside Charleston's home by a housekeeper who was herself up in years, and he met Phillip in the hall. Although the man was well into his fifties, Jack could tell right away he was carrying a weapon and he knew how to use it.

Phillip went to the kitchen to help the housekeeper with the tea, and while Jack waited for Sir Basil in the library, he wandered around the room, taking the opportunity to look through shelves of books, photos, and memorabilia.

He saw pictures of children and grandchildren and several prominently displayed photos of an infant who, Jack assumed, must have been a great-grandchild.

Displayed on the shelves was a British Army

helmet from World War One and a set of leather leggings, and a Second World War helmet as well. A German Nazi Luger in pristine condition hung under glass, and various medals, commendations, and letters from the British government adorned the shelves and walls. Ryan marveled at a photo of Sir Basil with Margaret Thatcher, and another picture of Basil with Jack's father. Ryan recognized the era; it was during his dad's first term, when he'd visited the UK.

Prominently displayed on the shelf next to this picture was his father's first book, *Options and Decisions.* He opened the front cover and saw that his dad had signed it.

Just then Sir Basil Charleston stepped into the library. He was tall and thin, and he'd dressed up for his afternoon meeting with the U.S. President's son; he wore a blue blazer with a red ascot and a carnation boutonniere. Basil walked into the library with a cane and a pronounced stoop to his posture, which gave Jack the initial impression that his health had seriously declined since the last time he'd seen him. But this notion was quickly dispelled when the ex–British spymaster crossed the room quickly with a wide smile and a shout.

"My heavens! Look at you, boy. You've grown since I've seen you, or is it just the beard that makes you look so mature?"

"Pleased to see you again, Sir Basil."

Charleston's housekeeper brought tea, and though Jack would have preferred a cup of coffee to give him a kick on this rainy afternoon, he had to admit the tea was quite good.

Charleston and Ryan talked for several minutes,

and the older man kept Ryan in the crosshairs during the conversation. Questions about his work at Castor and Boyle, his family, and the inevitable question of whether there was a special woman in his life. Jack had to lean forward and repeat himself often, but despite his hearing loss, Basil was very much engaged in the conversation.

Finally Sir Basil asked, "What is it I can do for your father?"

Jack said, "He is very interested in Roman Talanov, the new head of the FSB."

Charleston nodded somberly. "As someone who lived the majority of his life going toe-to-toe with the KGB, nothing makes my blood run colder than seeing Russian state security's come-back. It's a bloody shame."

"I agree."

"The bastards will be invading Ukraine, mark my words."

"That's what people are saying," said Ryan.

"Yes, well, people are saying they will just move on the Crimea, but I know these Russians, how they think. They will take Crimea in a couple of days, and then they will see how easy it was, how muted the reaction from the West is, and then they will keep going, all the way to Kiev. Look at Estonia. If your father hadn't pressured NATO to stop them cold, the Russians would have taken Lithuania by now as well."

Sir Basil knew more about this topic than Ryan did. Jack silently chastised himself for having his head so deep in illegal acquisitions and shell-company shenanigans that he was only remotely aware of an impending war.

Charleston continued, "But I can't say I know a thing about Talanov. Most of the upper-level chaps running Russia now were, at least, lower-level chaps at KGB or FSB back when I was in the service, but Roman Talanov was not someone we knew about when I was at Century House."

Jack said, "My father says there is one old reference to Talanov in your files that connected him with Zenith."

"With what?" Charleston put his hand up to his ear to help him hear.

Jack all but shouted, "Zenith."

"Zenith?" Charleston leaned back in surprise. "Oh, dear. The mysterious KGB hit man? In the eighties?"

"Yes, sir. There was just one note in his file, one piece of intelligence, no follow-up or corroboration."

Charleston frowned. "I am surprised there was no follow-up to the record. We ran a tight ship with our files. Obviously, nothing was electronic then. I doubt the youngsters today could keep up with the file clerks we had back then." He waved a hand in the air. "Anyway, any reference to Talanov on that case must be some sort of a mistake. Zenith turned out to be a ploy used by Germany's Red Army Faction terrorist group. I remember your father expressed his doubt of the official findings quite vociferously, but our investigations never were able to prove Zenith ever existed."

"Well, my dad also says there is a handwritten note in the margins of one of the files that he would like more information about."

"Handwritten note? Handwritten by me, I take it? Is that why you're here?"

"Yes, sir."

"And what did it say?"

"Just one word. 'Bedrock.' "

Sir Basil fell silent; the hollow ticking of the grandfather clock echoed in the library.

Jack sensed a pall of concern cast over the old man. He was suddenly not as bright and cheery as his home and his red ascot made him out to be.

"Might I presume you brought the document with you?"

Jack reached into his coat and retrieved the Swiss police record that had been e-mailed over from the White House. Basil took it, pulled a small pair of eyeglasses out of a side pocket in his blue blazer, and put them on.

For a full minute Basil looked at the page, at the handwritten marking, and brought it closer to his eyes. Ryan assumed the man must have been able to read German, as the one English word would not have taken so long to read, even though it had been partially erased. While he sat there, Jack heard the footfalls of Phillip on the wooden floor of the hallway, slowly pacing back and forth.

Charleston looked up at Ryan, then took off his glasses and handed him the page of the file back. He said, "Suddenly, thirty years ago seems like just yesterday."

"Why do you say that?"

He did not answer the question directly. Instead, he said, " 'Bedrock' was the code name for an operative."

Jack cocked his head. "Mary Pat checked with British intelligence, and they said Bedrock meant nothing to them."

Charleston thought that over for a moment. "Yes, well, I certainly do not want to ruffle any feathers."

"Sir Basil, I am sorry, but my father says this is

extraordinarily important. It very well might make an impact on the problems going on between the U.S. and Russia today."

Charleston said nothing; he seemed lost in the distance.

"Are you able to tell me *anything?*"

Charleston looked out the window for a long time, seemingly lost in thought. Jack almost thought the old man was about to tell him to get out of his house, but instead Basil turned back to him and spoke, softer than before.

"In any intelligence organization, even a well-meaning one, even one in the right, with history and honor on its side . . . mistakes are made. Projects that look good on paper, projects born out of desperate times, have a tendency to make it off the paper and into the real world, where, in hindsight, they don't seem quite so perfect."

"Of course," Jack urged him on. "Mistakes happen."

Sir Basil Charleston's lips pursed as he thought about something. "Quite so, lad." His eyes cleared with resolve, and Jack knew Basil was about to talk. "If Mary Pat went to MI6 and asked about Bedrock, they very well might have looked into the matter and come up with nothing. As you said, it was a while ago. But if she went to our partners at MI5, British counterintelligence, and they told her they'd never heard of Bedrock . . ." He made a face of distaste. "Then that would be inaccurate."

"A lie, you mean?"

"Well. Perhaps the MI5 of today does not know about the actions of the MI5 back then."

Jack thought Charleston was dissembling, but he let it go. "So Bedrock was MI5?"

"That is correct. He was . . ." The old man chose his words carefully. Then his face cleared a little. "He was an operations man. Victor Oxley was his name."

"He was English?"

"Yes. Oxley was Twenty-second SAS Regiment, a member of Pagoda Troop. Quite an elite unit. They are a Special Forces group, quite like your Delta Force."

Ryan, of course, knew this.

"MI5 wanted an operator to work behind the Iron Curtain. To track down leads about spies from KGB and other intelligence services, to break up attacks on our realm before they made it over here to us."

Jack was confused. "Activities behind the Iron Curtain seem like they would have been more the work of your old organization, MI6, not counter-intel, MI5."

Basil acknowledged this with a nod and said, "One would think so, yes."

"There was some interagency rivalry?"

"Something like that. MI5's investigations occasionally led them into denied territory. Oxley bridged the gap in these investigations. He could go to Riga to get pictures of a British turncoat living there, he could go to Sofia to track down reports of a Bulgarian intelligence training evolution that taught their spies how to fit in on the streets of London, he could go to East Berlin and find the name of the bar where Stasi director Erich Mielke liked to take lunch meetings, so if a highly placed British double agent slipped over to be recruited by the DDR's top dog, we knew where to look for him."

The rain on the windows of the library picked

up a little.

"Occasionally, he was tasked with doing more than this. From time to time he was ordered to find counterintelligence threats — I'm speaking of citizens of the Crown who committed treasonous acts and then ran for cover behind the Curtain — and then to liquidate them."

Ryan was impressed. "Liquidate?"

Basil looked at Ryan without blinking. "Kill them, of course."

"That's incredible."

"They say Oxley was quite incredible in his day. MI5 recruited him from the military and trained him up for their needs. He had language — one of his parents was full-on Russian, so he spoke it like a native — and he had the skills and the stones for behind-the-lines work. He was extremely good. He hopped the border better than anyone we had in our service at the time."

Basil added, "I don't suppose you know too much about the history of the British intelligence services, but we've had some traitors in the past, right at the top of our establishment."

"The Cambridge Five," Jack said.

"There was worry that there were more than five. For that reason, it was determined a British asset behind the lines would help keep the men and women in British intelligence honest. If some bloke passed official secrets to KGB and then ran off to Moscow to receive their Order of Lenin and a rent-free flat, chaps at the top of MI5 thought it would have a salutary effect on other UK intelligence personnel if that bloke turned up garroted in a public loo in Gorky Park."

"Holy shit," Ryan said. This story was much more than he'd bargained for when he popped over to a luxury town house to talk to an old man about a penciled note on an old file.

"My colleagues at MI5 played him close to the vest. He was run outside the normal chain of command, so very few knew Bedrock existed." Charleston gave a half-smile. "There was a rumor Five had a hit man cleaning up intelligence messes, and the spread of the rumor was intentional, but almost no one knew if there was any truth to it. His control officer let Bedrock act as he saw fit, to work without a net, as it were."

Jack was more fascinated by this than he let on. "This man had a license to kill?"

"He had no license at all. He knew he would be disavowed if he were ever caught."

"Do you remember Bedrock's relationship to the victims of the Zenith murders?"

Charleston shook his head. With his reticence in talking about Bedrock, Jack had started to look for any clues of deception. As far as he could tell, the old man was being truthful. His hesitations seemed to simply be born out of not thinking of this topic for a long time, and perhaps not being proud of whatever happened with Bedrock.

Charleston said, "As I said before, there was no Zenith."

"But you wrote Bedrock was picked up at the scene of one of the Zenith murders."

"No, lad. I didn't write that."

Jack raised his eyebrows.

"How can I be so certain? Because I knew nothing of Bedrock at the time, and I would never write Bedrock's name down. I don't know who wrote that. Obviously, these files have been around for thirty years. Someone, at some point, looked it over and made that notation. They also removed

331

it, although not successfully. I assume it was someone at MI5 read in on the program, but I cannot be certain." Basil looked at it again. "I don't know anything about Bedrock being in Switzerland on this date. As far as I knew, he never worked west of the Iron Curtain."

"Did Oxley know my father?"

Charleston barked out a quick laugh. "Heavens, no. Certainly not. They would have run in quite different circles. Even if Bedrock was in London for some reason, and I have no recollection that he was, he would not have bumped into your father at Century House. No, Oxley would have had no connection with Westminster Bridge."

"You said you didn't know about him at the time. When did you learn about him?"

"When MI5 came to me for help finding him. He disappeared behind the lines. I do recall that happened to be during the so-called Zenith affair."

"Was he ever found?"

"I don't know. Certainly not by MI6."

"You don't know if he is alive?"

"No, but I also don't know that he's not, and my bodyguard out there — you met Phillip — operates under the assumption that he is."

"What does your bodyguard have to do with Oxley?"

"Phillip has orders to keep Victor Oxley away from me." Charleston gazed out to the rain again. "One must be on the watch for anyone who might hold a grudge against those who directed British intelligence. Again, we looked for him . . . but we did not find him. There are chaps that might think we didn't look hard enough."

Ryan was wondering the same thing. Did they

look hard enough for this missing man? He couldn't imagine anyone finding fault with the polite urbane man sitting across the table from him. He tried to picture Charleston younger and in control of one of the world's toughest intelligence agencies, but he couldn't get the image right in his mind.

Jack asked, "Do you know how I can find out if he ever returned from the East? Does someone keep records on former MI5 members?"

"On MI5 members, yes, but remember, Bedrock was run black, outside their service." Charleston thought. "He was SAS, though, and they have a fraternal organization." Charleston sipped his tea. "Although I can't imagine him taking part in meetings or attending banquets. I'd wager he dropped off their radar long ago, if he is even still alive."

"Do you remember anyone he worked with? Someone I might be able to talk to?"

There was an extra-long pause now. But Charleston's response was more revealing than anything else he had said in the entire conversation. "I am afraid I won't be much help there."

Jack noted Charleston's word choice. He did know associates, but he either could not or would not put Jack in touch with them.

Jack said, "I'll start with SAS, see if anyone knows where he is now."

Charleston picked at the lint on his blazer. "Your father sent you round to my house to talk to me about Bedrock. It was a nice gesture to send family over. I don't believe for a moment, however, that your father had any intention of you running around yourself looking for worn-out old ghosts."

Jack asked, "What are you saying?"

Sir Basil smiled, a fatherly look. "Report back to your dad what I told you, he'll have his people make inquiries through Scotland Yard. Don't do anything yourself."

"Do you mean to suggest Victor Oxley is somehow dangerous?"

"Presuming for a moment he is alive, and you do find him, then yes, I do. Blokes like Bedrock do not like authority, nor do they respect it. You popping round for a spot of tea and an interrogation about old operations . . . that will *not* go the way you hope it might."

"What you are talking about happened a long time ago, Sir Basil. He's probably over it."

"Men like Oxley don't change. Trust me, boy, if he's still alive, he's still filled with hate." Basil sighed, and his shoulders slumped a little. "God knows he's got every right."

Jack didn't know what Basil meant by that, but he knew better than to ask. Basil had said all he was going to say on the subject.

38

Thirty years earlier

After a full day of work at Century House, CIA liaison officer Jack Ryan was just getting his desk straightened up to leave. As he rolled his swivel chair around to pick his briefcase up off the floor, he looked up to see David Penright standing above him. "Hullo, Jack."

Ryan lurched back in surprise. "Oh, Penright. You snuck up on me."

Penright smiled. "Bad habit. Comes with the job."

"Right. I haven't heard back on the RPB list I had delivered to Langley yesterday. I expect I'll have something by tomorrow."

"Actually, that's not why I popped in. I was wondering if you had time to grab a drink before you shove off for the day."

Jack did not have time. He'd planned on meeting Cathy at the station for the ride home. He wanted to get some quality time with the kids in before their bedtime, and the long commute wouldn't leave much room for that. If he missed the nightly 6:10 train, he'd probably not get home till Sally and Jack Junior were asleep.

But this was his job. Exchanging information with the Brits was why Jim Greer had sent him over here in the first place. He realized he couldn't very well pass up the opportunity to get to know one of MI6's operations officers, especially one working on a mission as potentially important as the one going on in Switzerland.

Ryan said, "Sounds great. Let me call my wife."

Penright gave a slight bow. "Much appreciated, and I'm buying." He put a hand up. "Check that. The Crown is buying. I have an expense account." He winked. "I'll meet you in the lobby."

Jack assumed they would be heading to the pub there in Century House. It was drab, like the rest of the building, but more important, it was vastly more secure than just venturing out to some alehouse on the street. While they still had to be careful what they said and who they said it around in the Century House pub, they had much more freedom there, surrounded by the men and women of SIS.

Instead, when Jack showed up in the lobby, Penright sent him back to his office for his coat and briefcase, telling him they would be taking a taxi over to Penright's members-only club.

Twenty minutes later, Ryan and Penright passed over their coats and briefcases to an attendant in the lobby of Penright's gentlemen's club in Saint James's Square. They were ushered through the foyer of a stately building and into an old-world library, where an immaculately dressed and exceedingly polite steward brought them brandies and cigars. There were a few other club members and their guests around; to Ryan they all looked like bankers and politicians, and although there was the odd chortle and even some laughter among the groups of men, most of the goings-on in the club seemed rather hushed and important.

The place was tight and stuffy for Ryan's tastes, but, he did have to admit, it was exciting to sit in a leather wingback chair and smoke a cigar amid a group of London's movers and shakers.

He may have been an honorary knight, and he and his family might have spent more time in Buckingham Palace than any other American family, but he wasn't so jaded that he couldn't appreciate what a unique experience this was.

They were halfway through their first brandy, and David Penright had talked about nothing but his school days at Eton and his family's home in the Cotswolds. Jack found the English spy somewhat like his members-only club. A little stuffy and somewhat pretentious, but decent enough and unquestionably fascinating.

Finally, however, Penright moved the topic of the chitchat to the subject of Ritzmann Privatbankiers.

Penright said, "I wanted to let you know I'll be shoving off tomorrow for Zug. It might take me a couple of days to survey the landscape and talk to my man in RPB. I'll have to give you the number of my hotel. When you get word back from your service about the names on the list, do give me a call."

"Okay," said Ryan. "But the line won't be secure."

"Certainly not. We'll need to set up a simple protocol. If your friends in Washington find anything in those names, just tell me that you need me to check in at the office in Zurich."

"And you'll go to the embassy in Zurich and call me back?"

David Penright smiled, giving Jack a look as though he was a bit naive. "No, Ryan. I have a secure location right there in Zug. I'll go to our safe house and call you back."

"Okay," said Ryan. "I don't know what you'll find from the CIA list, but you have to know that the fact this Gabler was working with the KGB is going to be the most likely reason for his demise."

Penright smoked his cigar in silence for a moment. "I can't tell you much about our penetration into the bank — Basil can be a bit uptight about that sort of thing — but I can tell you that I do not believe for a second that KGB knows we are aware of their accounts. Gabler was not killed by the opposition to silence him."

"So why do you think he was killed?"

"That's why I wanted to talk to you." He leaned forward, and Ryan did the same. "Basil isn't totally on board with filling you in on all the details."

Jack held up his hand. "Then don't tell me."

"Oh, please," Penright said. "It's gamesmanship, nothing more. You and I both know you have gone to your masters for the RPB client information, and they will look into it, then only agree to provide it if we involve them in the operation. That will take days. Basil is an executive, protective of his programs. But I'm the bloke on the ground, fighting in the trenches, and I don't have time for games."

Jack was concerned. He wasn't going behind Basil on this, but this other guy certainly was. *What the hell,* Jack thought. *I can't stop this guy from talking, and I'm not going to run out of the room with my hands covering my ears.*

Jack just sipped brandy and looked into the fireplace.

Penright said, "It looks to me like the large account Tobias Gabler managed, exactly two hundred four million U.S., is actually money stolen from the KGB."

Jack looked away from the fire. No pretense that he didn't care about what the English spy had to say. "Stolen? Stolen *how*?"

"That I don't know. What I *do* know is this: Last month, RPB had some surprise visitors. A group of men who claimed to be Hungarians showed up unannounced and produced the codes necessary to prove they held accounts with the bank."

"Numbered accounts."

"Yes. These were small accounts, owned by shell companies. We suspect it was KGB money. Nothing much to speak of, but it did get the men in the door."

"Go on."

"They had a lot of questions, but not about their accounts and balances. They were, instead, trying to find out if any other money was following the same route as theirs."

"From Hungary?"

"From any state-owned bank behind the Iron Curtain, and then into Switzerland. They also wanted to know about money leaving RPB in the form of cash, bearer bonds, gold, that sort of thing."

"What response did they get from the bank?"

"They got the polite shove-off." Penright held his snifter up high. "God bless Swiss secrecy."

"And the Hungarians just left?"

"No. These were desperate men. My inside man said the more angry they got, the more Russian they sounded. They were most likely KGB. Just think about the chance these blokes were taking. They just walked into the bank all but waving around their Soviet flag. They threatened to close their accounts and take their money somewhere else. They accused the bank of colluding with someone who was shaving from their accounts in the East. They stamped their feet and then made some veiled threats. And then they made some not-so-veiled threats."

"And your man held his ground?"

"He did. They left, and now another man at the bank, Tobias Gabler, the actual manager of the two-

339

hundred-four-million-dollar account, is lying on a slab in the morgue."

Jack leaned forward in his chair. "If they already knew about Gabler and the two hundred million, why the hell did they go to the bank asking questions?"

"I suspect money isn't their biggest concern. I think they want answers. They want the head of the person who stole it from them. Our man at the bank is bloody petrified by all this, and I don't blame him. But I can't pull him out. I do that and the Russians will close everything up, move their numbered account somewhere else, and we will lose any opportunity to exploit them."

Penright added, "For some reason, the entity that is amassing all this money needs it to be in the West, easily accessible and transferable."

"Why?" Jack asked.

"I don't have a clue, Jack. I was hoping you could figure that out."

Penright checked his watch. "Bloody hell, I'm running late for dinner. Previous engagement, as they say. I don't get to London as much as I'd like, and there's this girl. One in every port, two in London." He laughed. "You understand." He stood up. "Sorry, Ryan, but all guests must leave with the members here."

Jack was still stuck on Penright's last comment. He finished his brandy quickly — it would be a shame to waste it, after all — and he climbed out of the oiled leather chair.

"Wait a second. Why do you need me on this?"

Penright headed into the lobby; Jack trailed behind him. "Just mull it over. Basil says you were a Wall Street whiz kid."

Their coats and briefcases were brought to them.

"I wasn't on Wall Street. I traded through the

340

Baltimore Stock Exchange."

Penright slipped into his coat. "Whatever. I know you were with Merrill Lynch, I know you made some moves in the markets on your own, and I know that even though my tie costs more than that suit you're wearing, you earned enough money in commodity trading to buy this club and throw every old geezer out onto the street on their arse. You have the mind for this sort of thing. Plus, I think our cousins at Langley can be of great help to us on this operation." Penright winked at Jack as he headed out to the street to call himself a cab. "Just think about it."

Jack put his own coat on and followed the English spy to the pavement, arriving just as David Penright climbed into a taxi.

Penright looked up at Ryan before closing the door. "And call me in Switzerland as soon as you hear anything."

Jack stood on the pavement while the black cab rolled off into the traffic moving around Saint James's Square.

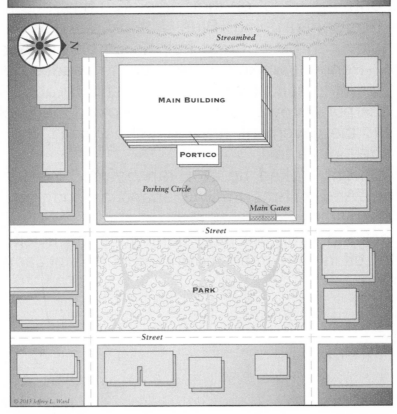

THE LIGHTHOUSE

Streambed

MAIN BUILDING

PORTICO

Parking Circle

Main Gates

Street

PARK

Street

© 2013 Jeffrey L. Ward

39

Present day

John Clark and Ding Chavez each drove a Toyota Highlander through the night, following the Dnieper River for a while before heading southeast toward the Crimean peninsula. Dom Caruso rode along as well, giving them a third driver so that the men could arrive at least somewhat rested.

They knew little about what lay ahead, other than the fact a CIA SIGINT operation had been compromised and they needed a couple of clean vehicles on the fly to help them get some material back up to Kiev and out of the country.

By the time the three Campus men arrived at the front gate of the Lighthouse the next morning, a crowd had formed in the street. Ding estimated there were two hundred people milling about; some had signs saying "CIA Get Out" in English, but most just chanted or yelled or stood in the road.

They parked up the street, within sight of the gate, and Clark called Bixby, who told him to head straight to the entrance.

A moment later, the two Highlanders did just that, honking their horns and approaching at speed. Protesters dove out of the way, and some threw water bottles and cardboard signs at the SUVs as they raced past, but the two vehicles were able to rush through the gates, which opened just before they arrived and were then immediately closed again by armed U.S. security contractors on the inside.

The two Toyotas pulled into a parking circle alongside four other vehicles: two Yukons and two Land Rovers.

As soon as they parked, several armed men — Americans, by their greetings and appearance — approached pushing rolling carts and carrying hardened-plastic cases. The men began loading the Highlanders within seconds.

Clark, Chavez, and Caruso met Bixby in the lobby of the building. Clark could see the worry on the younger man's face.

Bixby shook everyone's hands. "Gentlemen, I can't thank you enough, but when we get out of here, I sure as shit am going to try."

"Not a problem," said Chavez. "What's the situation?"

"We have six vehicles now, which will be just enough to get our guys and gear out."

Dom said, "The question is, is that crowd going to let us out?"

Now Midas, the bearded leader of the Delta Advance Force Operations unit here at the Lighthouse, stepped into the lobby. He said, "We're going to fire tear gas, and then we're going to just try and bust through. We don't expect armed roadblocks or anything like that. Once we get out of this neighborhood, we should be able to make it out of town undetected. Of course, the longer it takes us to get out of here, the harder this shit is going to be."

Bixby offered quick introductions, and Midas shook hands with the three new arrivals, but he seemed a little uncertain. "I thought I knew all the Langley guys here in theater."

Bixby said, "Actually, these men are ex–federal employees. They are good to go."

Midas looked them over again. "No offense, and I appreciate you guys bringing the vehicles, but I don't know you, and I am responsible for keeping this little dump secure. I don't want to see any of you touching a weapon. We clear about that?"

Bixby turned to the Delta man. "Midas, I am COS, and I said I vouched for them."

Midas held his ground. "If you didn't vouch for them, they wouldn't have gotten through the front gate." He pointed at the men. "No guns. Got it?"

Immediately, Clark said, "Not a problem." He turned to Ding and Dom. "Let's see about helping the men load up the vehicles."

Just as he said this, the faint chanting from the crowd at the front gate suddenly grew louder. Over and over, they repeated the same phrase.

Clark listened to it for a moment. "Can you make out what they are saying?"

Midas said, "Been listening to that one for two hours already. 'Yankees go home.' "

"An oldie but a goodie," said Clark, and he, Dom, and Ding headed up the hall to see what they could carry out to the trucks.

Forty minutes after Chavez, Caruso, and Clark arrived at the Lighthouse, the rest of the classified equipment was loaded into the Toyota Highlanders, and Midas broadcast on the walkie-talkies to all personnel, giving everyone a heads-up that they would be leaving in five minutes.

But in the short time since the arrival of the two SUVs from Kiev, the size of the crowd in front of the CIA Special Mission Compound had more than doubled. Local radio stations had announced the location of the CIA safe house — where they and the local police got the information was still unknown — and this had brought protesters and curious bystanders out in droves.

There were union workers in the crowd; Bixby had ID'd them by the slogans on their signs and the men walking around with megaphones telling them where to stand while leading them in chants. He'd also recognized the blue T-shirts of a long-standing pro-Russian youth group, an organized gang of teenagers, mostly, who through the secret backing of the FSB had been turned into roving bands of useful idiots. All over Russia and eastern Ukraine they conducted marches, sit-ins, and any other mass-movement tool as requested by their leadership, who were, in turn, run directly by FSB agents.

When Clark, Chavez, and Caruso arrived, the street in front of the gate was congested with pedestrians, but it was still possible to drive through them, albeit with difficulty. Now the two Delta men on the roof of the Lighthouse reported that the street was nearly impassable and another couple hundred protesters had spilled into the park across the street — essentially, just a concrete pathway around an open block with a few bushes and small trees.

All morning the men at the Lighthouse had been on the phone to the local cops, asking for a police escort out of the area, but so far no one had come. They'd also called a nearby Ukrainian military installation — the Americans were ostensibly a part of the Partnership for Peace, after all — but they were told their request for help was being kicked up the chain of command and, anyway, the Ukrainian Army base had no men or equipment to spare at the moment for a rescue.

Delta AFO leader Midas, the on-site commander of the Lighthouse, had a pair of M79 tear-gas launchers, but using tear-gas grenades was not his first choice. Although gas could be effective at getting people to move away from the front gate, it might also blow back on the Americans as they left the area, and it very well might have the undesired effect of turning the already angry protest into a violent riot.

By noon, the six vehicles were all running in the parking circle in front of the portico at the entrance to the Lighthouse, and six men were ready behind the steering wheels. Caruso and Chavez were tasked with driving the two Highlanders; they would be third and fourth in the convoy, behind the two Delta Yukons and in front of the two CIA Land Rovers.

Midas stood with his radio in his hand just behind the vehicles in the portico at the front of the building, and looked down the driveway at the entrance to the SMC. There, three security contractors, all of whom spoke some Ukrainian, remained inside the locked iron gate, nervously watching the tight group of shouting, chanting, angry protesters. As Midas brought his radio to his mouth, ready to tell the men at the gate to remain in their positions while everyone else loaded into the vehicles, one of the two Delta men on the roof of the Lighthouse transmitted over the net.

"Midas, this is Mutt on the roof. We've got buses off-loading about three blocks up the street."

"Buses?"

"Affirmative. Four full-sized buses. I see people pouring out. Say fifty pax per bus, so two hundred more coming to the gate. Looks mostly male, maybe exclusively male. Civilian dress, but they look like an organized bunch."

"Is it more of the union folks, or more brown shirts from the youth group?"

"Definitely not the youth group. They don't look like union, either. They look like fucking goons. Skinheads. Leather and denim. That kind of thing."

"Weapons?"

"Can't tell from here. Wait. They all have backpacks — not sure what they are carrying."

"Any sign of local law enforcement?"

Mutt replied, "Affirmative. On the far side of the park I see four, maybe five, squad cars, and what looks like some sort of a riot-control armored vehicle. They definitely appear to be standing aside for this."

"Roger that," Midas said, and then he spoke to everyone on the property carrying a radio. "All right, everyone in the trucks except for the two on the roof and the two men on the M79s."

Just as he finished transmitting this order, items began flying over the front wall of the compound. As they crashed to the ground, he identified the projectiles as bottles and bricks, and though they all hit the driveway and the forecourt short of the parking circle where the SUVs were parked, the three security officers just inside the metal gate of the property were definitely in range.

Mutt called over the radio from the roof. "Yo,

Midas? These new fuckers are throwing shit."

More glass bottles came crashing down in the forecourt; this was clearly an orchestrated attack by the new group that had joined the protesters.

Midas brought his radio back to his mouth. "Yep, I see it. Okay, you guys down at the gate, I want you to pull back to the vehicles. We're leaving now."

The rear wall of the Lighthouse compound backed up to a deep concrete ditch with several feet of running water in it, so none of the protesters were hitting them from the back, but people stood on the streets on the opposite sides of the other three walls and threw all types of trash into the compound.

The three security contractors ran back up the twenty-five-yard-long driveway from the gate to the parking circle. The entire way, they were bombarded with debris. One of the men was hit in the back with a piece of board, knocking him down, but he got back up and kept running.

While the three men retreated from the gate, two security contractors wearing gas masks stepped out of the building and into the parking circle next to the Yukons. Each carried an M79 grenade launcher along with a bandolier full of forty-millimeter tear-gas canisters. They knelt next to each other, loaded their launchers, and waited for the order from the on-scene commander.

"How's the wind?" Midas yelled to them.

One of the men looked back over his shoulder. "Wind is good. The gas will push out across the park."

"All right, three cans from each of you into the crowd."

Both men fired, the canisters popped out of the

launcher and arced above the gate, hitting near the center of the massive crowd outside.

More debris flew over the wall now, as if it was a direct response to the tear gas. This salvo came from a position far to the right of the front gate, and two of the projectiles spinning through the air were clearly burning.

These were Molotov cocktails; just the two at first, then more flew into the Lighthouse forecourt from the opposite side of the gate. They streaked through the air over the wall, crashing into the driveway and into a small rock garden in front of the parking circle, exploding in burning fuel and shards of glass.

Black smoke stained the air over the flight path of the Molotovs.

The grenade launchers popped again, this time firing the forty-millimeter shells over the walls near where the Molotovs were thrown.

"Shit," Midas mumbled. With the addition of the homemade bombs, this had suddenly graduated into a lethal attack. The protest had become a riot. He had nineteen men here with him, and most of them were armed with the equipment and the expertise to bring a lot of pain to the attackers, but the Delta Force officer had the responsibility of not making this incident any worse than it already was.

The three security men who had just made it up from the gate all turned around and raised their AK-74 rifles back toward the gate.

Midas yelled at them, "Hold fire!"

They did as ordered, but as the projectiles continued to rain down, and the prospects for getting out of the compound diminished, Midas knew the men's trigger fingers would be twitching.

The men firing the M79 launchers each sent a third gas grenade over the wall. As they reloaded a fourth tear-gas round into their weapons, there was a loud crackle to the west, on the opposite side of the building, far past the rear wall of the compound.

The men outside in the parking circle ducked low or sought cover behind the six vehicles. They all recognized the sound of automatic gunfire when they heard it.

Midas called up to the roof, "Mutt, talk to me."

There was a delay before he answered. "Uhh, wait one, boss." There was another short pause; Midas hoped that meant the two men were moving to cover. Seconds later he heard, "We are receiving small arms from the west. It's either coming from the hills or one of the buildings overlooking our pos, because we're getting bullet strikes up here on the roof. We've repositioned back to a spot between the stairwell and the AC unit. I think we've got cover here for now, but we're not going to be able to get a three-sixty view of the area from right here."

Keith Bixby had moved to the second floor, to an office above the lobby. He looked out a window, past a balcony, and then beyond the front wall of the property. The crowd had thickened to more than one thousand, and there was a chaos to the scene now that a small amount of tear gas had been dropped in the middle of the action. But although rioters ran around in all directions to get away from the gas, the streets were still choked with a thick mass of humanity.

The CIA station chief raised the walkie-talkie to

his mouth. "Midas, we can forget about driving out of here. With that gunfire and all the pax on the road, we're going to need air support and extraction."

Midas spoke calmly into his radio. "I agree. Everyone back inside. We'll have to go to the Ukrainian Air Force for air extract."

Clark, Chavez, and Caruso bailed out of their SUVs along with the others, and everyone ran back to the building. A few cracks of distant rifles could be heard over the near-constant crashing of debris landing all around the property, thrown over three of the four walls by the angry crowd.

Once everyone was back inside the three-story building, Midas sent men to cover the compound from balconies, positioning two or three armed men facing each direction on the higher floors. He then ran up the stairs to the roof to get a firsthand look at the cover his two men were using to stay out of the line of fire.

The Lighthouse had one rifle suitable for long-range shooting, a semiautomatic AR-15 with a nine-power scope and a bipod. It was a Delta weapon, but the best long-range shooter in the building had been determined to be Rex, the head of the six-man security contractor team. Before going into private-sector security, Rex had served first as a scout sniper in the Marine Corps and then as a sniper on SEAL Team Ten. Midas made sure Rex and the scoped rifle were in a good position on the roof, with Mutt staying up to spot for him, and then the Delta officer returned to the ground floor, where he positioned his men with the tear-gas launchers by the front door so they could step out under the portico and fire grenades at the gate if needed. "Anybody tries to come through that gate, you let them have it. I've told the men upstairs not to fire on the crowd unless they ID weapons, so if unarmed rioters climb the fence or smash it in, it's up to you to keep them back."

Bixby appeared from the stairwell and he held his sat phone up. "I'm on the phone to Langley now. Washington is in the process of getting the Ukrainian Air Force to send in an air extraction."

Midas said, "Works for me."

Just as he said that, a call crackled over the walkie-talkie. "Man down! Man down!" One of the security officers, positioned in a two-man team on a second-floor balcony facing toward the gate, had been hit.

Midas raced past Bixby for the stairs to evaluate the status of the injured operator.

40

President Jack Ryan hurried into the conference room of the White House Situation Room at seven a.m., wearing an open collar and a blazer he'd been handed by an aide on his walk over from the residence. He'd been notified a half-hour earlier in the residence that there was a situation involving American military and intelligence personnel in Ukraine, and SecDef Burgess was asking for an urgent Situation Room meeting.

Jack was surprised to find the conference room was empty of senior advisers. Yes, there were some White House military personnel and Situation Room staff in attendance, as well as some senior national security staff, but NSA director Colleen Hurst, DNI Mary Pat Foley, CIA director Jay Canfield, and Secretary of Defense Bob Burgess were all on monitors, speaking from their respective offices. The U.S. ambassador to Ukraine was on a monitor from Kiev, and Secretary of State Scott Adler was on-screen from a secure communications room at the U.S. embassy in Brussels.

Jack sat at the end of the table, then motioned to the men and women sitting along the wall. "Come on, this is ridiculous, fill up the table here with me."

Quickly, several intelligence and military advisers took seats at the table that was normally used just for the President and his senior staff. After all twelve remaining seats were filled, there were just a few junior personnel still seated against the walls.

Jack looked at the bank of monitors displaying his cabinet members, and he found the CIA director on the far left. "All right, what's happening in Ukraine?"

Jay Canfield sat in McLean, Virginia, on the seventh floor of CIA headquarters. He said, "Mr. President, we have a special mission compound, essentially a SIGINT listening post in Sevastopol, Crimea. Its code name is Lighthouse. Like much of our infrastructure in Ukraine, it was compromised in the affair with the SSU earlier in the week, and we were in the process of shutting it down. There were a lot of sensitive electronics that needed to be disassembled and hauled out of there, so it took some time. Unfortunately, the men at the SMC did not vacate before word of the Lighthouse broke to the opposition, and now they appear to be under attack."

"What do you mean 'appear to be'?"

"There was a protest for a couple of hours, it got bigger, rougher, but in the past half-hour a riot has broken out and the Lighthouse has come under small-arms fire from the nearby hills and buildings. We have reports of some injuries to our personnel, though no fatalities as of yet."

"Who is there in the facility?"

Canfield replied, "Normally, at the Lighthouse there is just a four-man JSOC team — Delta guys, that is — along with four CIA technical personnel and a half-dozen security officers. Usually, this is supplemented by Ukrainian security and intel personnel as well, but not at present. Unfortunately, the chief of station and two covered case officers from Kiev were there to help close the facility when the attack started."

"This is that Bixby guy you mentioned the other day?"

"Keith Bixby. Yes, Mr. President."

"And they can't drive out of there?"

"No, sir. They say the streets are blocked, the gunfire is steady enough, and the local cops are just watching it all happen from up the street."

"Son of a bitch. Who is doing the shooting?"

Burgess chimed in on this: "There are reports of irregular forces in the area, though at this point we can't be sure."

Ryan said, "We need to talk to the Ukrainian government."

Scott Adler spoke up: "The Ukrainian president is aware of the situation, and he has ordered Ukrainian Air Force helicopters to pick up the Americans. They are en route to a forward staging area now."

"Good," Jack said, but he caught an uncomfortable look on the Ukrainian ambassador's face. "Is there a problem with that, Arlene?"

Ambassador Arlene Black said, "Mr. President, he is asking — I should say he is demanding — that you call him personally to request the extraction." Black shrugged. "You know Kuvchek. He is a showboater."

There were groans in the room from some of the junior advisers.

Ryan just looked back over his shoulder at one of the Situation Room communications staff standing by the door. "Get Kuvchek on the phone.

I'll make the request. He's a jerk, but this is no time to stand on protocol. I'll kiss his ass if that's what it takes to get our people out of there."

Gunfire into the CIA compound known as the Lighthouse was picking up; windows had been shattered on all sides of the building, indicating the fire was coming from all directions, and the roof was pockmarked, revealing the fact that at least some of the shooters were firing from high positions. So far, none of the Americans positioned on the balconies or on the roof had managed to positively ID anyone in the crowd or in the neighboring hills and buildings doing the shooting.

Small fires from the Molotov cocktails thrown over the wall burned around the property. A group of garbage barrels on the south side of the Lighthouse was fully engulfed in flames, and grass along both sides of the driveway smoldered.

One of the Delta men on the second floor had been shot high on the shoulder, snapping his collarbone, and a security contractor had taken a ricochet round into the back of his hand, breaking bones and tearing flesh. Although both men had been taken to the Lighthouse's infirmary, they were being treated with a small trauma kit on the chest rig of one of the Delta operators, because the first-aid boxes had already been loaded into one of the Delta Force Yukons that now sat exposed to fire on the eastern side of the compound.

Rex, the contractor on the roof with the scoped rifle, scanned distant rooftops and balconies through his nine-power optic, searching for snipers. This was a slow process, because he had to

357

low-crawl under an air-conditioning unit to look in different directions. Mutt was there with binoculars, but he, too, seemed to always be facing away from the source of gunfire when it came. They got the distinct impression the sniper fire coming in was coordinated, and done for the purpose of keeping heads down.

A Delta man on an upstairs balcony took a round into the steel plate on his chest. His partner dragged him back into an office and checked him out, then reported in to Midas.

Midas was in the communications room on the second floor with Bixby when he received this news. He looked to the CIA man. "This fire is too damn accurate to be coming from a couple of untrained civilian assholes."

Bixby nodded. "We could be looking at local SWAT or Ukrainian Army deserters or FSB-trained irregulars." He added, "Hell, it could even be Spetsnaz that came over the border from Russia on a destabilizing mission. Make no mistake about this, whoever is out there might very well be looking to overrun this installation."

John Clark, Ding Chavez, and Dom Caruso appeared in the doorway. Clark asked, "What do you guys hear from Langley?"

Midas said, "Expedited helos are on the way. We've got two Ukrainian Air Force Mi-8s inbound to pick us up. ETA twenty minutes."

Caruso said, "Anything you want me to get out of the vehicles before we get out of here?"

Midas shook his head. "We're going to toss C-4 and demo every bit of that as soon as we take off. I don't want anyone going outside until we have some air cover."

■ ■ ■ ■

A few minutes later, Clark, Chavez, and Caruso stood in the small lobby, watching the occasional Molotov cocktail arc over the wall and explode onto the ground into a raging fireball. The gunfire that cracked around the neighborhood still seemed to be coming from all different directions. No one was manning the front gate now; the security contractors were all above on the balconies with the CIA men and the Delta AFO personnel.

A crowd of rioters in civilian dress, virtually all of them appearing to be young males, pressed against the locked iron gate, but so far no one had tried to breach the compound.

The phone in Clark's pocket rang, and he stepped into the stairwell to find a quieter place to talk before answering it.

"Clark."

"Hey, Mr. C. This is Sam."

"What's up?"

"Gavin has been tracking the GPS transmitters we put on the suspicious vehicles yesterday. Two of them left the city about four a.m., but we had no idea where they were heading. Now Gavin thinks he's figured out their destination."

"Where are they going?"

"Sevastopol. They will get there in about an hour."

"Interesting. I had a feeling this attack involves goons from the Seven Strong Men. That pretty much confirms my suspicion."

"You need us on the way? We can head to the airport now, charter something to get us down there on the double."

Clark said, "No. You guys keep doing what you're doing. We're pinned down in here, but air extract is en route. Don't know where the helos will take us, but when we land I'll let you know if we need help getting back to Kiev."

"Roger that. You guys keep your heads low."

As the extraction neared, the armed men in the Lighthouse spent their time scanning for any targets in the surrounding buildings and hills. Without a weapon in their hands, the three Campus operators felt somewhat useless, just standing around waiting to get flown out of danger, but this changed when another call of a "man down" came over the radio. Ding and Dom raced up the stairs to the third floor and found a CIA technical officer who had been in an interior hallway when a lucky round penetrated a balcony window, then an interior wall, and finally lodged itself in the center of his chest. The middle-aged man was unresponsive with his eyes wide open when he was found by a contractor, and Ding and Dom spent several minutes trying to get the man breathing again. But the bullet had shredded his heart, and there was nothing they could do for him. They helped two other CIA techs drag the body downstairs — a slow, difficult, and exhausting task — and then they put him in a body bag, positioning him by the front door so they could get him on the helo quickly when it landed.

The two fat gray Mi-8 helicopters approached from the north just after three p.m. The men on the roof notified Midas, who immediately began pulling operators, contractors, and CIA personnel from their positions on the balconies and ordering them down to the lobby. The two wounded men were helped down the stairs and positioned next to the body of the fallen technician.

Midas spoke directly with the pilots of the helos and warned them about the sporadic incoming fire, and the Ukrainians' Mi-8s flew in with their side doors open and their mounted machine guns scanning for any threats. But as Midas watched them approach, he thought they didn't seem as careful as they could have been, considering the danger. They flew close together, directly over the riot in the park, and made just one slow circle to search for threats before one of the craft began descending toward the Lighthouse.

Midas got the impression the helo pilots thought just their mere presence would discourage anyone from firing while they were in the air above the installation, and Midas radioed a warning to them that they were approaching a hot LZ and needed to act accordingly.

He saw no change in the tactics in the helicopters above.

There was only enough room between the vehicles parked in the parking circle in front of the Lighthouse building and the front wall of the compound to safely land one helo at a time, so the first Ukrainian Air Force Mi-8 descended while the other circled above to provide cover.

For a moment, there was no gunfire; it even seemed the shouts of the crowd softened as the gray helo came in for a landing. In the CIA building, Midas opened the lobby door, and he and Bixby stepped out under the portico so he could talk the helo down.

As the Mi-8 descended below four hundred feet, right before the eyes of Midas and Bixby, a bright speck of light appeared over the eastern wall of the Lighthouse. It raced up from between two apartment buildings on the far side of the park in front of the CIA compound. It shimmied in the air as it climbed into the blue sky toward the helicopter.

Someone on board the Mi-8 either saw it coming or else the pilot had some sort of onboard warning indicator. The helo banked hard to the right. Bixby and Midas both saw the door gunner fly back inside the cabin of the aircraft as it spun away, trying to get out of the line of fire of the ascending rocket.

The rocket raced just past the tail rotor and shot harmlessly skyward.

But not the second one. The second speck of light on the blue sky also appeared from the east; the men in the portico did not see the origin of the launch, but it rose confidently up to the helo and slammed into its body, just aft of the open side door.

The initial explosion wasn't much, but almost immediately there was a secondary explosion that blew out the sides of the Mi-8 and then shredded the rotors to pieces. Centrifugal force fired metal from the rotor blades more than half a mile in all directions; the burning wreckage fell three hundred feet toward the ground and slammed into the center of the park, right into a cluster of rioters.

A fireball billowed up over the walls of the CIA compound, and a pillar of black smoke rose out of it higher into the sky.

The one remaining Mi-8 helicopter never fired a shot. It had been circling at one thousand feet, but seconds after the first helo hit the ground the second turned to the north and raced away.

There were shouts and exclamations and curses all over the Lighthouse, but neither Bixby nor Midas spoke for several seconds. Then the CIA station chief said, "I'll call Langley," and he stepped back inside.

41

President Jack Ryan learned about the Ukrainian helicopter crash at the same time as the rest of the men and women in the Situation Room, just three minutes after it happened. The conference room and the wall monitors in front of Ryan were full of men and women conferring with one another; he saw the pained and frustrated looks of those who were scrambling to come up with a backup plan on the fly. Some of these men and women — military officers, diplomatic personnel, intelligence types — had themselves been in harm's way in their careers, and Jack knew that despite this devastating setback, he did not need to stress that the full force and weight of the United States would be employed to get the Lighthouse evacuated.

Jack Ryan excused the U.S. ambassador to Ukraine from her remote attendance in the meeting so she could get on the phone with the Ukrainians to pressure them to try and get ground forces to the Lighthouse. When Ryan spoke with Ukraine's president a few minutes earlier he had said he'd been informed by the military that all ground forces suitable for a rescue in the area had been moved to the Russian border, so Jack did not hold out much hope for a convoy of armor to come to the aid of the beleaguered CIA installation. Still, he did not want to take any option off the table, so he instructed his ambassador to do whatever she could to try and make this happen.

A digital map on the wall showed the nation of Ukraine and the position of the few U.S. forces there, and everyone in the room had their eyes glued to it while they talked over options. Discussions among those in attendance in the Situation Room turned argumentative quickly, but Ryan brought the focus back to the task at hand.

President Jack Ryan held many titles, but at this moment he was the National Command Authority, the one who had to make the tough calls, and to do that, he damn well needed his experts focused on task and feeding him the best information as quickly and efficiently as possible. Jack was no longer a military officer; he was no longer an intelligence officer. He was an executive, and it was his job to keep the situation organized so the problem at hand could be solved.

As another heated discussion broke out, this one between a White House assistant National Security Council director and a naval adviser to the Joint Chiefs, Ryan silenced the argument by raising his hand. He then looked up at the monitors on the far wall. "I want to hear from Burgess and Canfield only. There must have been some preparations made in case this location was compromised. What contingencies do we have set up to get our guys out of the Lighthouse in case of attack?"

Burgess said, "We do have Delta, Rangers, and Army Special Forces in Ukraine right now, but they are dispersed all over the country in preparation for the Russian attack and are not prepared to operate as a quick-reaction force. We have a couple of Army Black Hawks at a Ukrainian Army base in Bila Tserkva, you can see it on the map there above Sevastopol. It's a few hours' flying time to the north. We could put together a QRF and send them down right now, but those RPGs in the area make landing rotary-wing aircraft in the Lighthouse extremely risky unless and until we can get some sort of standoff defense down there in addition to the helos."

CIA director Canfield had even fewer good operations than SecDef. "Mr. President, since Ukraine is an ally, our contingency plans for getting our men out of there on the fly revolve around local forces providing a QRF."

"Yeah," Ryan said, strumming his fingers on the blotter in front of him and thinking. "That didn't work out so well."

A Marine Corps Pentagon adviser to the White House, a full-bird colonel named Dial, half raised a hand at the end of the table.

Ryan saw the gesture. "Colonel?"

"Mr. President, we have a pair of V-22 Ospreys with a Marine contingent in Lodz, Poland, doing some training with NATO forces. They aren't a QRF, per se, but they *are* Marines. I can get the Ospreys and two dozen riflemen airborne and en route in a half-hour. The flight down would be roughly ninety minutes."

Ryan asked, "What about defending the Ospreys? I remember they have a machine gun on the loading ramp, but that doesn't seem like much against the threat that's being described down there around the SMC."

Dial said, "It's true, the Ospreys aren't the best platform for landing in a hot LZ like this. But these particular V-22s happen to have the IDWS, Interim Defensive Weapon System, it's a belly turret gun attached to a FLIR and a TV camera. It's operated by a gunner inside the aircraft."

"Is that enough firepower?" The last thing Ryan wanted to do was send two flight crews and two dozen Marines into harm's way without a way to defend themselves in the air.

Dial said, "Mr. President, it's a three-barrel, seven-six-two-millimeter mini-gun that rotates three hundred sixty degrees and fires three thousand rounds per minute. That, along with the fifty cals on the back ramp, will bring a lot of American lead to that fight on landing and takeoff. On the ground I'd put twenty-four USMC riflemen up against five hundred armed rioters any day of the week. I'd prefer to have more guns and platforms there, but considering this is an in extremis situation, I think this is the best we can do."

"Bob," Ryan said, looking to Burgess, "make it happen. If we can get the installation evacuated by the Ukrainians before the Ospreys get there we'll wave them off, but for now, get them en route."

Burgess nodded, turned to his staff there at the Pentagon, and just like that, the operation was under way.

But President Ryan was not satisfied. "Ladies and gentlemen, that is our plan for two hours from now, but we are not finished. From these reports it doesn't look like that installation has two hours. I want to know what we can do in the next sixty minutes to keep the Lighthouse from being overrun."

Burgess blew out a sigh and held his hands up.

"Honestly, sir, if we can't get the local forces to help out, I don't know what we can do."

Ryan looked to Colonel Dial, who had no answer, either.

But one of Dial's assistants attached to the White House was a young African American Air Force major. He sat against the wall behind his colonel on Ryan's left, and when Dial failed to come up with anything, the major turned quickly toward the President. He said nothing; instead, he turned back away and looked down at his hands, but Ryan got the impression the officer thought he had something to offer.

Ryan leaned forward to read the man's name tag on his uniform. "Major Adoyo? Something to add?"

"I am sorry, sir." Ryan detected a slight African accent.

"Don't apologize. Scoot up to the table and talk."

Adoyo did as the President asked, moving his chair next to Colonel Dial's. He looked nervous, and Ryan pointed this out.

"Relax, Adoyo. You clearly have more interest in talking than anyone else in the room right now. I want to hear what you have to say."

"Well, sir . . . we have a squadron of F-16s from the 22nd Fighter Squadron over at Incirlik AFB in Turkey right now. That's just on the other side of the Black Sea. I used to be stationed there myself. It's less than a two-hundred-fifty-mile straight shot up to the tip of the Crimea."

The secretary of defense almost yelled at the young major through his monitor. "We're not going to bomb an urban population in a friendly —"

President Ryan held up his hand. Burgess

stopped talking immediately.

"Continue, Major."

"I know we can't engage the people on the ground, but if we happen to have a flight on the runway or in the air over Incirlik with enough fuel, we could have fighters making low passes at near supersonic speeds over that CIA compound thirty or forty minutes from now." He held his palms up on the table. "I mean . . . it's no silver bullet, but that might keep some heads down for a while, anyway." He paused again. "It is standard doctrine. Happened all the time when I was flying A-10s in Iraq. If you needed to provide close air support but couldn't drop ordnance due to the proximity of noncombatants, you do the next best thing. Fly low, fast, and loud. Make noise and rattle fillings."

President Ryan looked to Burgess's monitor. "Bob? Why the hell not? It's *something*."

Burgess didn't like it. "We don't know if it will make the crowd disperse or the armed attackers back down."

"What do we have to lose? Can anyone in that crowd outside the Lighthouse shoot down our F-16s?"

Adoyo muttered, "No fucking way." And then he gasped, recognizing that he'd answered out loud a question that had been posed for SecDef, and, more important, he'd cussed in front of the President of the United States.

President Ryan looked to Colonel Dial. "Major Adoyo says 'No fucking way.' What do you say, Colonel?"

"Well, we only know for sure that the opposition has small arms. A fighter passing overhead pushing Mach 1 isn't going to get shot down with a rifle or an RPG, I can promise you that."

Ryan thought about the diplomatic implications of this for a moment, then said, "Let's do it." He looked up at Scott Adler as soon as he finished the order, because he knew the secretary of state wasn't going to like this one bit.

Adler spoke first. "Mr. President, sending in unarmed or lightly armed transport aircraft for an emergency extraction is one thing, but what you are talking about is flying fighter bombers over the Black Sea fleet. The Russians are going to go nuts."

Ryan replied, "I understand, and it's our job to deal with that. I want to tell the Ukrainians first, then I want you personally on the phone with Russia's foreign minister in the next ten minutes. If you can't get him, get whomever you can. Tell them we will overfly Sevastopol with the blessing of the Ukrainian government. Tell them we understand Crimea is semiautonomous, we understand this is Russia's neighborhood, and we understand this is provocative. But right now our only concern is the safety of our U.S. personnel in danger, who, you'll need to stress, are only there because they are part of the Partnership for Peace program.

"Tell them we want their blessing for this, but we will accept their passive acceptance." Jack held a hand up. "As a matter of fact, you can tell them we won't push back if they raise holy hell about it on TV, or lodge a formal protest to NATO or the UN after the fact. But you tell them that this *is* going to happen, and it *is* going to happen in about a half-hour. Any intervention by the Russians will escalate into something neither party wants."

Adler, America's chief diplomat, was paid to think through the ramifications. He said, "The Kremlin will want something in return."

Ryan was ready to do some horse trading. "That's fine. We'll remove some warships out of the Black Sea or something, but not until our people are out of harm's way. If you need me on the phone to the foreign minister, or even Volodin himself, I'm sitting right here."

"Got it," Adler said. Ryan could tell the secretary of state was not happy. He couldn't have been pleased to know a CIA compound was running under the guise of a NATO operation in the first place, which gave it a diplomatic-mission status. This sort of thing went on all over the world, but the diplomats, of course, hated it when CIA installations operated under the guise of diplomacy, because it jeopardized legitimate diplomatic installations.

Ryan knew once word got out this building had been a CIA front, all over the planet totally innocuous State Department missions would come under intense suspicion and scrutiny by the local population.

But that was a problem for another day. For now, Adler excused himself from the meeting, knowing he had to perform some diplomatic magic to keep the Black Sea fleet from firing on American aircraft.

42

A flight of U.S. Air Force F-16 Falcons flew over central Turkey in a finger-four formation. Around these jets flew three more four-aircraft flights of F-16s, but these weren't wearing markings of the U.S. Air Force, instead their tails were emblazoned with the red and white flag of the Turkish Air Force. Together all sixteen aircraft flew in a squadron formation above a puffy sheet of white clouds.

The American aircraft were members of the U.S. Air Force's 480th Fighter Squadron, the Warhawks, and although they were based in Spangdahlem, Germany, they had spent the week here in Turkey as part of a NATO training evolution with the Turkish Air Force.

The flight lead for the Americans was Air Force Captain Harris "Grungy" Cole, a thirty-year-old New Yorker, and even though all sixteen aircraft now appeared to be flying in near-perfect formation, Cole had experienced his share of difficulties above the clouds in the past few minutes getting everyone together. His problems stemmed chiefly from the constant struggle to understand the thick accents of the Turkish flight leads. But although he had to request several common transmissions be repeated so that he could be certain everyone was on the same page, he gave the Turk pilots a pass, because he didn't know a damn word of Turkish himself except for *"Bir bira, lütfen"* ("A beer, please") so if today's training had hinged on his own command of a foreign tongue, all sixteen of these planes in this tight formation would have already slammed into one another in midair.

Just as Captain Cole began to transmit orders to the Turkish flight leaders ordering them to maintain this pattern while climbing to thirty-five thousand feet, a call came over his radio from Incirlik AFB ordering him to peel his flight away from the Turkish F-16s and begin heading north toward the Black Sea to await further instructions.

He received no other clarification, other than the fact that this was "real world" and not an exercise.

The Black Sea was a hotbed of activity of late, since the Russian Black Sea fleet began a drill that pushed dozens of their warships away from port and into deeper waters, but Cole could not imagine how his four fighter-bombers could be any help in that looming crisis.

Just minutes later, after his Warrior flight had left the Turkish Air Force fighters behind and proceeded north, Grungy received instructions ordering him to divert at best possible speed into Ukrainian airspace over the city of Sevastopol.

Cole's quite reasonable question, whether or not the Ukrainians had cleared his flight to enter their airspace, was not immediately answered.

He knew he'd need that clearance quickly. To stress the urgency of the situation, he told the controller who'd sent him on this mission, "Be advised, ETA twenty-one minutes."

The terse reply came back. "Understood. We are tracking."

"Uh. Also . . . we might want to think about letting the Russians know what we're doing. They've got their own air defenses over their fleet parked right there in Sevastopol. How copy?"

"Good copy, and we're working on that. General Nathansan will speak with you directly in a moment with more information."

Cole was already surprised by this strange event, but hearing that the commanding officer of the 52nd Operations Group, the fighter component of the 52nd Fighter Wing, would be directly entering his headset to tell him about his flight's mission made the hair on the back of his neck stand up.

Something was up, it was big, and Grungy hoped like hell he'd get the clearance to fly over Sevastopol before he was shot down by the Russians. He also hoped someone was expediting a tanker to the area to get involved in all this, because he and his flight would need fuel if they were going to fly up to Sevastopol and do anything more than fly right back home.

Warrior flight was well over the Black Sea before they had more context for their mission. As promised, General Nathansan himself came on a radio channel to speak directly to Captain Cole. He talked in a rapid and frank manner, informing the captain about the situation on the ground in Sevastopol, passing along the GPS coordinates for the Lighthouse, and ordering Cole to overfly the area for as long as he had fuel to do so and get back to Turkish airspace, where a KC-135 Stratotanker would gas them up for the return the rest of the way back to base at Incirlik.

Cole computed his fuel quickly while Nathansan

talked. The four aircraft in his flight would have enough gas for no more than four passes each over the city. From the way the general explained the situation, all parties involved were hoping four aircraft making a few fly-bys would somehow buy the Americans under attack on the ground the hour to hour and a half necessary to wait for air extraction by Marine V-22s.

Nathansan told Grungy they had the overflight cleared with the Ukrainians, and they were working with the Russians. Cole knew Russia had air defenses all over Sevastopol to protect the port, and immediately decided he'd have his flight approach from an easterly direction, the opposite direction of the port of Sevastopol, so that he would not fly directly over any Russian ships in port.

Before Grungy opened his channel to explain the situation to the rest of his flight, he brainstormed the problem for a moment, trying to think of ways to maximize the impact of their attempt at "shock and awe." He came up with a quick plan, and then relayed instructions to the three other pilots.

"Warrior Oh One to Warrior flight. Here's the sitrep. We're going to put on an air show over the Black Sea fleet."

He explained that an American installation — even though their transmissions were encrypted, Nathansan had not uttered "CIA" — was under attack by unknown forces, and there was concern rioters would attempt to penetrate the walls. He told his fellow pilots that U.S. personnel had already been killed and wounded, and they would need to fly low and hot enough to make a serious impact on events on the ground.

His wingman, Captain James "Scrabble" Le Blanc, asked, "Are we going to be cleared hot for the Vulcan?"

Although these aircraft did not have air-to-ground munitions on their wings, an M61 "Vulcan" twenty-millimeter Gatling gun protruded from each fuselage. The guns were loaded with explosive shells, and could fire more than six hundred rounds per minute.

But Grungy threw water on the prospects for any gun runs today. "Negative. There are going to be too many noncombatants in too small an area for the Vulcans."

Pablo, Warrior Three, next asked, "So we're supposed to just fly around and look scary?"

Grungy replied, "We aren't going to *look* scary. We're going to *be* scary." And then he explained the rest of his rushed plan to his pilots.

The helicopter crash in the open park in front of the Lighthouse seemed to have dispersed the crowd near the front gate to some degree. Chavez, Midas, and Bixby stood just inside the lobby doors and looked across the parking circle, down the drive, and through the metal bars. For the first time in the past half-hour, the large group of young men that had been standing there throwing bottles and bricks and incendiary devices onto the property was gone.

Word had filtered down to those trapped in the Lighthouse that a pair of V-22 Ospreys were en route, and in order for the big tiltrotor airplane-helo hybrids to be able to land within the walls of the Lighthouse, the men inside knew they would have to move everything out of the front of the property. This would create a landing pad about forty yards square, giving one Osprey just enough room to put down.

Midas used the thinning of the crowd to get several men outside so they could move the vehicles and police the area of debris that could be blown around in the prop blast. Clark, Ding, and Dom volunteered, as they were not manning weapons on the higher floors of the Lighthouse, and they, along with Keith Bixby, one of Bixby's men, and Midas himself, each took a set of keys and ran out to the vehicles.

The two Highlanders and one of the Land Rovers were moved quickly and without incident to a gravel area on the side of the building. The second Land Rover would not start, but Caruso used a fire extinguisher to put out a fire on the grass nearby, then he put the truck in gear and, with the help of the CIA men, pushed the fully loaded vehicle to the wall of the Lighthouse and out of the way.

Both of the Delta Force Yukons had been badly damaged by gunfire, and their wheels were all flattened, so the decision had been made to use one of the Highlanders to push the trucks out of the way. Dom got behind the wheel while Chavez directed him into position.

While the men were out on the parking circle and on the drive, Rex, the American sharpshooter on the roof, lay prone and facing the east. He scanned intently for any snipers, while his spotter, the Delta man called Mutt, did the same through his binos. Mutt saw movement on the roof of a four-story building on Suvorov Street, a few blocks away, and directed the contractor with the AR-15 to the location.

Rex identified two men through his scope crawling along the roof of the building. Each man carried an AK-47 rifle. The two men stopped and aimed at the Americans on the driveway of the Lighthouse, so Rex took a shallow breath, then he blew it out halfway. He brought his finger to the trigger of his AR-15 and shot the man on the right. His semiautomatic sniper rifle might not have been terribly powerful, but it was capable of quick follow on shots. He fired again a second later, hitting the man on the left.

Both gunmen on the roof in the distance rolled around in agony for a moment before disappearing from view. Rex did not know if he'd killed either one, but he was reasonably certain they were now out of the fight.

Dominic Caruso had successfully pushed the first Yukon out of the open area in front of the portico with the Highlander, and now he was driving around to line up with the rear bumper of the last remaining vehicle. Midas, Bixby, and four other men worked to put out small fires from the Molotovs and to clear some pieces of debris off the parking lot in advance of the arrival of the Ospreys. They grabbed rocks, bricks, and pieces of metal and broken glass and threw everything to the walls so that the rubble could not be blown around by the huge twin rotors of the V-22 when it landed.

Every twenty seconds or so a crack from a distant rifle filled the air, and occasionally the American men manning rifles, either on the roof or on the balconies, would themselves return fire at targets in the distance.

When this happened, the men on the driveway

ducked lower, but they had no choice but to continue to expose themselves to the nearby buildings while they prepped the Lighthouse grounds for the inbound V-22s.

They were only halfway finished with this task when a new sound came over the shouting of the crowds. Chavez was directing Caruso in the Highlander when the whistling noise came; he dove to the concrete of the parking circle, as did two of the CIA technicians. But the two CIA case officers from Kiev as well as Bixby did not hit the deck; instead, they just looked up for the origin of the noise.

Midas was near Bixby, and he tackled the station chief to the ground; they both crashed on the cold asphalt of the driveway, and Midas rolled on top of Bixby as an explosion ripped through the air twenty-five yards behind them. The whistling sound of supersonic shrapnel passed just over their heads.

Almost instantly, another streaking whistle filled the air and another explosion erupted, this one on the south side of the building. Windows in the Lighthouse building shattered and glass rained down into the parking circle.

"Eighty-twos!" Midas shouted into Bixby's ear.

"Eighty-two *what?*"

Midas rose to his knees. "Eighty-two-millimeter mortars! Get into the Lighthouse!" He pulled Bixby all the way up to his feet, and together with the CIA officers they started to run.

Chavez and Caruso finished moving the last Yukon, then ran for the entrance to the building. Another round crashed into the parking circle just after they returned to the relative safety of the lobby, and shrapnel shattered glass in the lobby windows.

As soon as Midas made it inside, he shouted into his radio, "Mutt, you guys get off the fucking roof! I want all other security personnel repositioned back from the windows with the best line of sight you can get on the compound walls and the streets beyond. If you see any armed target, that includes individuals armed with Molotovs, bricks, rocks, whatever, you are clear to engage. We might get overrun, but we are *not* going down with cold guns."

"Roger that. Engaging," one of the security officers transmitted, and within seconds the sound of rifle fire erupted as a target in the street was identified and engaged.

Just then a crash shook the entire building, and the sound of broken glass could be heard on the floors above. It sounded to the Delta commander as if a mortar round had hit the roof where his two men had been positioned.

"Mutt? You boys all right?"

There was no response.

"Mutt? How copy?"

The radio remained silent.

43

Mutt and Rex were both dead.

Just as the two men had left cover to run to the stairwell, an eighty-two-millimeter mortar round slammed onto the top corner of the building, and hot shrapnel ripped through their bodies, killing them instantly.

They were found a minute later by the two remaining operational Delta sergeants, and their bodies were dragged to cover just an instant before another shell slammed down on the roof of the Lighthouse.

Clark, Chavez, and Caruso helped Midas get the bodies down two flights of stairs and into body bags. It was backbreaking work, and mortar fire continued to rain down on the Lighthouse grounds the entire time.

As soon as the two bagged bodies were dragged to the front door, Midas turned to the Campus men.

"Forget what I said before. You boys better get yourselves some guns. Same ROEs as everybody else. Armed targets only. Got it?"

"Got it," they all said, and they headed up the stairs to get weapons. They were happy to field the new Heckler & Koch 416s. As extensive as their firearms options were with The Campus, this was the first time any of them had fired the staple weapon of Delta Force.

Midas himself went up to the second floor and entered the large office area with a window that gave him a view of the front gate of the building, the park with the downed helicopter, and the neighborhood beyond. He scanned the distance with his rifle, hoping he'd get lucky and spot the mortar position.

Bixby was with him now, speaking into his sat phone to Langley. "We've got inbound mortar fire. Effective RPG and small-arms fire as well. We have multiple KIA and WIA. It looks like we are being engaged by trained irregular forces and possibly Russian military."

Chavez knelt in an office on the second floor of the Lighthouse; his eyes peered through the holographic sight of his HK416 rifle. A red dot was superimposed on the glass lens of the sight, and even though the sight was not magnified, he was able to make out individuals running around on the streets in front of the front gate.

He saw his first weapons in the crowd within seconds. Two men with AK-47 assault rifles low by their sides pushed through the thick crowd of angry rioters.

On Chavez's right, Dom Caruso was scanning a different sector of the crowd. Dom said, "I've got a dude with a rifle. Fifteen yards to the right of the helo crash. He's right in the thick of all the noncombatants there." Dom growled in frustration. "No shot."

Ding said, "I've got two guys with guns. They are mixed in with the crowd in the street to the north of the park. These guys are using the civvies to get right up to the gate."

Dom said, "They're going to try to bust through, aren't they?"

Chavez said, "Bust through. Climb over. Whatever. Yeah. They are coming in."

"What's this all about?" Dom asked.

Clark entered the room with Bixby. They knelt down behind a desk to stay out of the line of fire of any snipers. Clark said, "I've got a theory."

Bixby said, "I want to hear it."

"The Russians want to overrun this place and bust a CIA operation in the Crimea. They are going to use it to justify an invasion."

Bixby said, "The existence of this place isn't enough to justify an invasion, not even for Volodin."

Clark peered through the sight of his rifle. "Maybe not yet, but if Talanov does another one of his false flag attacks, like he did with Biryukov or Golovko, then he can blame the American interlopers for it." Clark added, "If we can get out of here and demo our stuff, we won't make it so easy for them to frame the CIA in their scheme."

Bixby said, "So what you're saying is, as long as they have us and our equipment to use as proof, we are just as good to them dead or alive."

"That's about the size of it."

A school bus pulled into view on the far side of the park. Both Ding and Dom tracked it with their weapons as it came up the road, past the burning helicopter wreckage. It began picking up speed; the driver seemed to have no concern about the men and women protesting in the street. The rioters dove out of the way of the accelerating vehicle.

It was quiet in the second-floor office as the men

watched it approach. Finally, Caruso spoke in a deadpan voice. "Right on, this guy is coming to save us." It was an attempt at gallows humor. He knew this wasn't a rescue — this bus only signaled the beginning of the next phase of the attack.

The bus slammed into the iron gate of the Lighthouse, smashing it in, even tearing some of the stone wall away as it broke through. It tried to keep going up the driveway, but Ding, Dom, and several other rifles in the three-story building all began firing into the driver's side of the windshield, and the bus veered sharply to the right and crashed against the inside wall of the compound.

Almost instantly, a pair of eighty-two-millimeter mortar rounds slammed on the roof of the Lighthouse and the lights in the building went dark.

Midas was somewhere upstairs; his voice came over the radios in the office: "Deploy gas over the wall. Everything you've got. Anyone with a rifle, I want you to put a bullet into every motherfucker that comes onto the property."

Ding reloaded his rifle, and while doing so he noticed men climbing onto the top of the north wall, near where the school bus crashed inside the property.

"Dom! Ten o'clock!"

"Got 'em," Caruso said, and he fired at the men as they dropped down, killing one, wounding one more, and sending a third falling back over the wall as he tried to get out of the line of fire.

More men mounted the wall on the southern side now, gunfire into the compound picked up, and, just when Caruso stepped onto the balcony to get a line of sight on the south side, several incoming rounds whizzed by his head, making a high-pitched snapping sound.

384

Dom dropped down on his chest, but behind him he heard a loud grunt.

Chavez and Clark spun around and looked back over their shoulders.

Keith Bixby was behind them at the entrance to the office. They saw him stumble back out of the office and into the hallway, where he collapsed facedown.

"Bixby?"

Clark crawled over to Bixby on his hands and knees, keeping out of the line of sight from the doors out to the balcony. He rolled the CIA station chief on his back and found his eyes unfixed and a bullet wound to the side of his head.

Clark knew instantly there was nothing that could be done.

Two CIA men appeared in the hall a moment later with a trauma kit from one of the security officers in their hands.

Clark got out of their way, returning to his rifle in the office. Dom and Ding were prone next to him.

"The chief of station is dead," Clark said somberly.

More men came over the walls now; first they moved in ones and twos. To the men of The Campus, the attackers did not look like a military force. Clark was more certain than ever that these guys were Seven Strong Men muscle. They'd been trained to shoot their weapons and they had been ordered to take the CIA compound, but the real skill facing the Americans in the compound were the snipers surrounding them and the mortar squads pounding them from a distance. Those would be Russian forces, perhaps FSB Spetsnaz troops, here with orders to take the Lighthouse before the men and materiel inside could be extracted.

The Americans in the Lighthouse would have been able to hold these attackers back with no great difficulty if not for the accurate and persistent sniper and mortar fire that kept their heads down, kept men crouched behind desks and couches and interior walls, prevented the men from getting a wide field of view on the entire scene. The three American Campus operators, the two Delta men still in the fight, and the other men with rifles had to make do with narrow views from positions around the building that were so far back away from the windows and so obstructed it was a rarity when a gun sight found a target coming over the wall without the gunner having to rise up and expose himself to withering fire.

Still, a few minutes after the plainclothes attackers started coming over the wall, the driveway, the grass on either side of it, and the top of the wall were littered with dead bodies.

A pair of trucks with canvas-covered beds appeared now, and they raced along the road that ran right in front of the Lighthouse, driving right through a low gray cloud of tear gas. At the gate the vehicles braked suddenly, and armed men began pouring out of the back of them. Some of the men ran the wrong way, disoriented by the gas, but most fought through the coughing and hacking and the tearing eyes, and they stormed the Lighthouse.

The ten rifles in the Lighthouse building barked. Semiautomatic rounds rained down on the new group of attackers, who themselves fired automatic Kalashnikovs at the building as they began running up the driveway.

Four more men scaled the wall to the north, ran across the open ground of the parking circle, and made it to the portico in front of the lobby — without being seen, because of the activity at the front gate. The four men raced for the entrance to the building, but the two guards who had been firing the gas grenades from the front portico drew their pistols and opened fire on them.

Two of the attackers were killed, and the other two sought cover behind a concrete planter at the edge of the portico.

While the gunfight was taking place in the portico, an RPG raced parallel across the ground over the park, heading directly toward the Light-house. The American defenders on the two upper floors who saw it all pressed themselves tight to the ground, but the rocket slammed into the northeast corner of the third floor, striking the glass door to the balcony of a room where two CIA men were hunkered down, watching the north for any breaches of the compound there. The shell detonated upon hitting the door, sending glass and shrapnel along with a shock wave through the small room. Both men were killed instantly, and a third security contractor on the floor below was injured when the ceiling caved in on him.

Midas ran for the stairwell to support the men in the lobby from the attack, and Clark ran up the hall to help anyone caught in the RPG blast.

Chavez heard the shooting downstairs, and he felt the rumble of the explosion above him and to his left. As he reloaded his rifle again, he spoke with a calm that belied the situation. "There are too many of them. It's going to get hand-to-hand here in a minute."

Caruso fired at a man racing up the driveway, catching him in the forehead and dumping him to the ground.

He shouted back over the sound of his weapon. "I'd rather fight them in the stairwell than sit here and wait for the next mortar round!"

Another truck full of attackers appeared in the distance, on the far side of the park; it was heading toward the Lighthouse, making its way through the throngs of rioters on the streets.

Three miles due east of the Lighthouse, Harris "Grungy" Cole flew the first aircraft in a trail formation; each plane was lined up, one after the other, a few hundred yards apart. He gave a command, and the three aircraft behind him broke off from the formation; Warrior Two went right, Warrior Three went left, and Warrior Four followed Two to the right. Grungy kept his nose on the blur of black smoke dead ahead, and he pushed the throttle past full military power.

Cole's plan was for each jet to fly directly over the Lighthouse at nearly seven hundred miles per hour; each member of Warrior flight would come from a slightly different direction, and he had it timed so they would arrive, one after the other, about fifteen seconds apart. This would create a constant wall of sound, and they would then each make a turn and then return for a second pass, and then a third and a fourth.

If it all worked according to plan, the attackers on the ground would have no idea how many aircraft were overhead, nor would they have any idea what the jets' intentions were.

He'd designed it to be about four minutes of chaos, confusion, terror, and pounding headaches for the rioters and attackers.

The war birds were only three hundred feet above the ground, racing at nearly Mach 1, their engines roaring and flaming exhaust drawing faint smoke trails in the wake of each single-engine aircraft.

Grungy said, "All right, let's break some windows."

At the speed he was traveling, there was no way Grungy could tell what was going on in and around the Lighthouse. He only had his waypoint set in the computer, and he kept his nose lined up on a tick mark on his heads-up display, keeping much of his focus on his warning systems and the hills around the city so that he could fly as low as possible without impacting terrain.

Grungy saw the haze of dark get closer and closer to his windscreen; even here at three hundred feet it had not diffused completely, and within seconds he raced through the smoke and instantly broke through to clear sky to the west.

He knew he'd flown over the action because his waypoint indicator said so, so he pulled back on the throttle, putting his aircraft into a bank that caused the lower portion of his G-suit to fill, forcing oxygenated blood to remain in his upper body.

44

In the Lighthouse, Chavez and Caruso climbed back up off the floor and onto their knees. When the first jet appeared in the sky in front of them they'd dropped flat on the deck, not knowing if it was friend or foe. The obscene noise of its roaring, fire-belching engine rattled the already broken glass out of the windows in front of them and assaulted their ears, which were already ringing loudly from the gunfire in the enclosed office.

They had caught a glimpse of the jet as it passed, just a dark blur on the blue sky, and then a second jet raced overhead going south to north. By the third high-speed overflight, this one from north to south, the men in the Lighthouse had a good idea these aircraft had come to try and keep the enemies' heads down, and Ding and Dom decided to take advantage of the confusion that was reigning outside.

They opened fire on men inside the walls of the SMC who'd dived for cover or stopped to aim their weapons at the sky. Above and below them, many of the other Americans still in the fight also took the opportunity to thin the herd of armed aggressors.

When the fourth jet appeared in the sky, two

rocket-propelled grenades were launched from rooftops far to the east.

The RPGs didn't have a prayer of hitting a target that was traveling a mile every seven seconds; all the launches did was reveal the RPG locations to the American rifles in the Lighthouse. Two positions were targeted immediately by Delta shooters on the third floor, sending both of the RPG operators to cover.

Jets continued to tear through the sky directly overhead. Ding couldn't tell if he was seeing the same planes over and over, but the noise and vibration and the very sight of the lightning-fast fighters were doing what they had set out to do. The attack on the Lighthouse had all but fizzled out while people on the ground in a several-block radius were running for their lives, desperately seeking any cover they could find.

Clark shouldered up to Ding and Dom. "The guys who stick around through this are the ones who are operating under orders. Find some guy standing his ground and I bet you'll find a weapon."

"Roger that," both men said, and they scanned the area in front of the Lighthouse, searching for more targets.

"We should be charging for this air show," Grungy said, as he began his third pass.

Pablo's voice came over the headset in Warrior Three: "I just hope we're going fast enough so those fuckers down there can't see we don't have any damn ATG ordnance."

Before Grungy could key his mike, Scrabble replied, "You know those ground pounders will see our air-to-air weapons and think we're carrying napalm." He laughed over the net. "There are a lot of Russians shitting their britches down below."

Grungy answered back, "We're going to get a little less scary each time we pass without doing anything." He checked his position. "All right, I'm going to give them one more thrill."

Grungy finished his fourth pass a moment later, pulled up to flight level two thousand, and began heading back to the east, taking a wayward route that would keep him from passing over the port.

Dom Caruso reloaded his rifle and, while doing so, took a moment to get a quick view of the entire area. "Look at 'em run," he said.

Ding took his eye out of his gun sight for a moment and took in the scene himself. There was a mad scramble of rioters; they scurried away in all directions. Men with lit Molotovs dropped them on the ground and ran; a woman who had been rendering first aid to a bystander injured in the helo crash left the victim on the pavement in the park and darted across the street, disappearing into an alley.

There were over a dozen men in civilian clothing lying dead or wounded inside the outer walls of the Lighthouse; the closest had made it all the way to the door under the portico. Another fifteen or more attackers had retreated back out the gate to cover.

Outside the gate, fully seventy-five percent of the rioters and attackers who had been in front of the building three minutes ago had now either fled into buildings, jumped into vehicles and driven away, or otherwise vacated the area.

The men in the Special Mission Compound had

no doubt in their minds that if not for the arrival of the F-16s, which had scattered most of the rioters outside the gate, the three-story building would have been breached. And the men still alive in the building would have been overrun in moments.

But the earthshaking roar of the jet engines subsided almost as quickly as it had started, and an uncomfortable still came over the neighborhood.

Midas entered the room where the Campus men were positioned. He said, "You guys need to be ready. That was it for the air support until the extract gets here. This isn't over yet."

Clark said, "I can guarantee we *will* get hit again. It might take them a minute to regroup and to talk themselves into it, but they'll see that the gun runs were just a bluff, and they will be back, pushing even harder to finish us."

"You sound like a man who's been through this sort of thing."

Clark just shrugged without answering.

Midas got on his radio now. "Everybody reload and do what you can to improve your defensive positions. We've got forty-five minutes more before extract arrives. This shit is *not* over."

Grungy was over the sea less than two minutes after leaving Sevastopol, and here he banked to a southerly heading and slowed his speed down to conserve his rapidly diminishing fuel.

The three other aircraft in the flight all checked in as soon as they were feet wet, and Grungy started to relax a little.

But not for long.

The flight's air controller came over the radio

soon after Grungy settled into his new heading to the KC-135 over the Turkish coast. "Warrior One, be advised, Russian Flankers, flight of four, inbound on intercept course. Heading zero five zero, angels five and climbing."

Cole muttered, "Su-27s. Shit."

Incirlik came back on the net a moment later. "Warrior One, be advised. Flankers expressed their intentions. They are going to converge with your flight and escort you back over the Black Sea to Turkish airspace."

Scrabble heard the transmission and said, "Just to say they did."

Cole responded: "Right. This shit will be on TV in Russia. They'll be talking about how they repelled the Yankee hordes."

Pablo added, "We don't have enough gas for a dogfight. If they want to fly along nice and straight with us, that's not really the worst thing that could happen."

"That's a good point," Grungy admitted.

Cole braced himself for a tense half-hour flight of fuel worries while being babysat by a flight of angry Russian pilots who were looking to flex their muscle. He told his pilots not to worry about the Flankers, and he told himself to make sure he didn't do anything provocative. The excitement of the overflight of the imperiled CIA base was behind him, and now was the time to fly straight, slow, and boring.

He just hoped he'd managed to buy those guys back there in Sevastopol a little time.

The mortar attacks on the Lighthouse started up again fifteen minutes after the jets departed. Clark made the observation that it seemed clear the mortar squads — from the rate and cadence of the incoming shells, the men of the Lighthouse had decided there were two teams at work — had broken down their weapons and sought shelter during the low-level F-16 runs, and had only now reestablished their positions.

The defenders of the CIA station were hunkered down in survival mode now.

Midas ordered everyone to move downstairs to the lobby and other rooms at ground level, because the sniper fire hitting the second and third floors, along with mortar and rocket attacks, had rendered the top two stories too dangerous. There were only nine able-bodied men now, and Midas decided it would be better to consolidate at ground level, so he moved men to all sides of the building, positioning Chavez and Caruso at the front door.

Here at ground level the men were safer from the distant shooters, but as a result of the decision to vacate the upper floors, they'd lost the majority of their visual coverage over the neighborhood.

The mortar rounds had been hitting steadily, two crashing explosions every minute, but then they stopped suddenly. Soon after, a truck raced up to the entrance of the property, made the turn into the smashed gate, and began streaking up the driveway.

Caruso, Chavez, and Midas were all at the front door under the portico, and they flipped the selector switches on their weapons to the full automatic setting.

A pair of RPG rounds impacted the building high above them while they dumped round after round on the truck. They blew out the windscreen, killing the driver, and fired into the gas tanks of the vehicle until they ignited. The truck veered off the driveway, rolled over the grass on the south side of the property, and crashed into the wall.

As soon as it came to rest, armed men leapt from the rear of the burning vehicle. Ding and Dom and Midas fired on them, but the vehicle erupted into a ball of flames that engulfed several attackers before they'd even begun their attack on the Lighthouse.

Burning men ran from the wreck, rolled on the ground, and flailed to extinguish their burning clothing.

As the men in the portico reloaded their weapons, the mortar attack resumed. They ran back inside and took shelter.

Midas said, "Soon enough they are going to figure out that all they have to do is keep those mortars raining down until they are at the front gate. We'll be in here holding our helmets instead of watching for them, and we won't be able to get a bead on the next vehicle till it's on top of us."

A faint crackle came over Midas's radio, and he brought it to his ear.

"Say again last transmission?"

"Lighthouse, Lighthouse. This is Steadfast Four One, inbound on your pos, ETA two mikes. How copy?"

Midas looked up to the low tile ceiling of the lobby and thanked God.

"Good fuckin' copy, Marine!"

Dom and Ding exchanged a high five, but a man posted at one of the windows in the lobby shouted that attackers were once again coming over the northern wall of the SMC, so the celebration was short-lived.

45

V-22 Osprey pilots like to say they can fly twice as fast and five times as far as a helicopter, and though the aircraft is difficult to fly, those who pilot them are uniquely proud of their state-of-the-art platform.

The two aircraft arriving over Sevastopol were designated Steadfast Four One and Steadfast Four Two; they were members of Tiltrotor Squadron VMM-263 of the 2nd Marine Aircraft Wing. The squadron had been given the colorful nickname "Thunder Chickens" when it was a helicopter transport squadron in the Korean War era, and the moniker remained with them through the years as they made the transition from airframe to airframe. The Thunder Chickens transitioned to a tiltrotor squadron in 2006, and since then they had carried troops and equipment into and out of combat environments all over Iraq and Afghanistan.

On this in extremis mission over the Crimean peninsula, Steadfast Four One carried eighteen Marine riflemen, as well as a flight crew consisting of two pilots, two gunners, and a crew chief. Steadfast Four Two carried six Marine riflemen as well as a five-man crew.

The average age of the riflemen in the back of the two aircraft was only twenty-one years old and, as was often the case in the military, no one told the Marines in the back of the Ospreys that they would be evacuating a secret CIA base. No one told the Marines in the back of the Ospreys much of anything other than the fact they would be sweeping into a fluid combat situation, landing in some sort of a U.S. diplomatic compound, and extracting fifteen to twenty Americans who were taking fire from all compass points.

And they knew one other thing. They'd been informed on the way down that they were weapons-free at the target location, which meant they would get to shoot, which was nice, considering they'd already been informed they were going to be shot at.

The first passes made by the two fat aircraft were done in airplane mode; the big rotors on the wings of the V-22s were pointed forward so they could operate as massive propellers. Four One and Four Two raced over the city at one thousand feet with a ground speed of more than three hundred fifteen miles per hour. The attackers on the deck did little more than turn their heads toward the thundering planes with the massive props. Most hesitated; they had never seen an Osprey, and they had a feeling they were looking at enemy aircraft. That said, the last flight of enemy had done nothing more than fly around the sky before departing, so most of the attackers were undaunted by the arrival of these new, strange planes.

The turret gun on the bellies of both aircraft spun as the gunners inside scanned through their FLIR monitor, hunting for targets, using the coordinates given to them by the man on the other end of the radio.

The turret gun was called the Interim Defensive Weapon System; it was a late addition to the Osprey design, giving the big transport aircraft 360 degrees of covering fire. Before the installation of the IDWS, the V-22s had to rely on support helicopters and the single fifty-caliber machine gun fired from the open rear ramp, which greatly limited the survivability of the aircraft in combat operations.

The ramp gunner was on his knees behind his big weapon, and his headset kept him in radio contact with the turret gunner, and both of them were in comms with the gunners in the other Osprey, as well as the man called Midas on the ground at the diplomatic compound via a VHF channel. Midas had spent the last sixty seconds talking all four gunners through where he thought the mortar fire was coming from, and as the aircraft raced overhead, all four of the gunners were hunting for these targets.

The gunners knew they had to take out the mortar positions before landing. An Osprey landing is a big, fat, and slow-moving creature, and an Osprey on the ground is damn near helpless, especially when a mortar crew has had hours to range their weapon to drop shells exactly where the Osprey was parked, so these birds would not land until the gunners could tell the pilots they had destroyed the mortars.

In order to drive the turret gun below him, the gunner in Steadfast Four One used a handheld controller that looked like it had been taken from a video-game console. His FLIR camera was slaved to the weapon's sight, so when he turned the weapon left and right and up and down with the controller, he saw the aim point of his three-barreled weapon represented as crosshairs in the center of his small monitor. He searched an area Midas had suspected as being one of the mortar locations, and almost immediately his screen revealed a two-man team on a building to the east of the Mi-8 crash site in the middle of the park.

The men showed up as black-hot signatures on the green screen. The gunner also saw the hot mortar tube between them. Within moments of spotting the mortar, a black-hot flash showed the gunner that the eighty-two crew was firing a shell toward the diplomatic compound.

Steadfast Four One's turret gunner pressed the fire button on his weapon an instant later.

Below him, hanging out of the bottom hatch of the Osprey, the big Gatling gun roared, smoke and fire shot out with the fifty-round burst, and hot ejected shells poured from the side of the weapon like liquid from a faucet.

On the roof of the building the two mortar men were blasted into the creosote tiles, their bodies shredded into an almost unrecognizable state.

While this was going on, the fifty-caliber ramp gunner in Four Two saw a man with an RPG launcher on a street on the western side of the compound, and he opened fire, raking the street and the side of the building around where the man stood. Dust and dirt and bits of the building filled the air, covering the entire area, but when it settled, the RPG launcher was lying in the street and the man was lying facedown next to it, his legs several feet from the rest of his body.

The two Ospreys flew an opposing racetrack pattern around the entire area, and the four gunners found individual targets and eliminated them. The fifty-caliber machine guns mounted on the rear ramp buzzed as they fired; spent brass went through a long rubber tube like a drainpipe that hung loose, whipping off the end of the ramp, and then the brass tumbled out of the end, falling through the sky.

After the second lap of the pattern, most all guns and gunmen on the ground had sought cover, but the second mortar position had not been found. The pilots of the two aircraft discussed going ahead with the extraction without finding the mortar, but they decided to continue their race-track pattern, giving their gunners more time.

The turret gunner sitting inside Steadfast Four Two ID'd the second mortar position on the fourth pass over the neighborhood. The mortar was in a small parking lot next to a steel waste receptacle, and several crates were stacked next to it, although no obvious personnel were around. The IDWS fired on the area, pulverizing the mortar tube, the receptacle, and several cars parked nearby.

Steadfast Four One's pilot throttled back on the next pass over the Lighthouse. The V-22 slowed as it banked back around again; its airspeed dropped quickly as the wings went from vertical to horizontal and the tiltrotors began transitioning to helicopter mode. While Four Two flew cover above, Four One came to a hover over the Lighthouse. The crew chief on the ramp of the aircraft leaned out and looked down; next to him, the fifty-cal gunner spun his weapon left and right, ready to respond to any threats, and the chief spoke through his headset to the pilot, directing him to just the right spot to put his big fat bird on the ground.

While this was going on, the second Osprey continued its tight circular pattern overhead, its turret gunner searching every doorway, rooftop, balcony, and cluster of cars in the parking lots, desperate to find any dangers quickly enough to neutralize them before they killed either his airship or the one on the ground.

Steadfast Four One touched down, but there was no perceptible change in its two big engines. It wasn't going to spool down here and relax. All eighteen Marines in the back of the aircraft raced down the ramp, their weapons out in front of them, though they could see nothing in the dust being kicked up. Half went to the left, the other half to the right, and they ran on until they reached the front gate and the walls of the compound. The men at the gate trained their guns into the park area, and the men at the walls climbed up on wrecked vehicles and other items so they could get a line of sight on the buildings and terrain outside the walls.

To the young Marines new to the scene, the neighborhood around this compound looked like a postapocalyptic ghost town. Bodies lay in the street, automobiles smoldered and burned, hundreds of windows in buildings all around had been shattered. Car alarms raged. The wreckage of the Mi-8 that had crashed in the center of the park was little more than a pile of ash now, but black smoke still billowed from it.

The Marines knew there were still enemy forces in the area. The crack of a sniper rifle fired from a distance caused rifles in the Lighthouse to return fire, keeping enemy heads down.

The Osprey above identified the sniper position

on the balcony of a hotel, and the pilot turned away from the location so the ramp gunner could get a line of fire on the area. He fired several short bursts from his fifty, killing the sniper and causing the other armed men in the area to stand down.

When the Marine riflemen were in position in a cordon around the Osprey, the men still alive in the Lighthouse came out. Every able-bodied man was either wielding a gun or tending to the wounded or dead.

Ding and Dom carried the bagged body of CIA station chief Keith Bixby, and John Clark steadied the civilian contractor who had taken a ricochet through the back of the hand hours earlier. Clark passed the man off to the crew chief of the Osprey and then stopped at the bottom of the ramp.

In his nearly half-century of military and intelligence service to the United States and NATO, John Clark had climbed aboard most every aircraft, from propeller-driven airplanes, to turboprops, to jets, and he'd ridden aboard more helicopters than he cared to count.

But Clark approached the rear ramp of the Osprey with a tightness in his stomach.

Tiltrotor aircraft made sense, but there was something about that moment of transition from helo to airplane that seemed aerodynamically unsound to John Clark.

Nevertheless, as bad as the prospect of crashing into the ground in a craft with all the flight characteristics of a double-wide trailer sounded, the very certainty of getting sawed in half by a Russian mafia goon with a Kalashnikov if he stuck around helped him find the wherewithal to put one boot in front of the other and board the Osprey.

Thirty-eight-year-old Lieutenant Colonel Barry Jankowski, call sign Midas, was the last of the Lighthouse survivors to board the aircraft. While a third of the Marines had boarded, he and another Delta man quickly set charges on the vehicles next to the building. Midas covered the Delta sergeant holding the remote trigger as he boarded Steadfast Four One, and then ran up the ramp, turned back around, and took a knee with his H&K rifle pointed out in front of him. The fifty-caliber machine-gunner next to him reached out with a tether line and hooked it to his body armor, and then the crew chief called over the intercom to the pilot. "All aboard and clear! Go!"

The massive engines roared even louder, and the aircraft pulled itself up into the sky.

Steadfast Four One slowly transitioned to airplane mode, then began circling the area to provide cover while Steadfast Four Two landed to pick up the rest of the Marines. Once the second Osprey was clear of the scene, the Delta sergeant pushed a button on the remote detonator in his hand, and the six SUVs went up in a fireball that morphed into a mushroom cloud.

The two Thunder Chickens turned to the north and raced away.

The entire extraction, from the arrival of the Ospreys to the relative quiet that enveloped the Lighthouse after the last vestiges of rotor noise left the neighborhood, took only five and a half minutes.

46

Thirty years earlier

CIA analyst Jack Ryan was at his desk in the upstairs den of his home in Chatham, spending the evening coloring sailboats with crayons. In truth, he was doing very little of the coloring himself; his five-year-old daughter sat in his lap, Sally's little head and shoulders hunched over her coloring book, attacking her art with more intensity than Jack himself could muster for his own work at this time of the evening. Jack had tried putting her on the floor more than once, but each time she protested, insisting on sitting at the desk with her daddy. Jack knew he had to pick his battles, and this was a battle Sally would win. The truth was he enjoyed her being up here with him, although he did try to sneak a few glances at a manuscript he was working on on his computer.

This was another battle he was destined to lose. She seemed to be able to sense the moment her daddy took his attention away from her masterpiece-in-the-making.

"Watch me," she said, and Jack did so with a smile.

While Sally colored her sailboats and while Jack tried and failed to get a few paragraphs written, he also turned his attention time and again to his phone. He had an STU, a Secure Telephone Unit, compliments of the CIA, and the telephone-looking part of the big contraption sat on his desk next to his prized possession, his Apple IIe computer. He was expecting a call at any time from Langley regarding the list of names of employees and clients of the Swiss bank that the British had given him the other day, and as much as he enjoyed playing with his daughter right before her bedtime, he could not help being stressed about the fact there was a man out in the field anxiously awaiting this crucial intelligence.

Mercifully, Cathy soon came into Jack's office, with a tired smile. "Give Daddy a good-night kiss, Sally."

"No!" Sally squealed. She was fighting sleep already; getting her in her room now was going to involve a little screaming and crying, but both Jack and Cathy knew things would only get much, much worse if she didn't go to bed right this minute. Cathy persevered, scooped Sally up after she fussed a moment more in her father's lap, and then took her off to bed.

Her little fit was mercifully short-lived; Jack heard her chatting away happily with her mommy when she was still in the hallway.

Jack put his fingers on the keyboard of his Apple, ready to work for a few minutes on his latest book, a biography of Admiral William F. Halsey. Jack's new Apple computer was still a marvel to him. The move from the electric typewriter hadn't been an easy one — there was something of an annoying plastic, springy feel to the keys instead of the satisfying crack of the electric typewriter — but knowing he could make large or universal changes to the text of his manuscript with just a few clicks and store the equivalent of a hundred or more pages of his writing on a single 5.25-inch floppy disk made the odd feel of the keyboard much less annoying.

He'd typed only a few paragraphs when the STU trilled.

Jack slipped his plastic key in the keyhole in the front of the unit and answered the phone.

A computerized voice repeated the phrase "STAND BY, SYNCHRONIZING THE LINE" over and over while Ryan waited patiently.

After fifteen seconds and the words "LINE IS SECURE," Ryan answered.

"Hello?"

"Hi, Jack." It was Admiral James Greer, director of intelligence for the CIA.

"Good evening, Admiral. Sorry, I guess I should say good afternoon."

"Good evening to you. I've got some preliminary information back from the analysts on the employee and client lists for RPB."

"Terrific. I have to say, though, I didn't expect you would be the one to call. Did they find something so earth-shattering that the DDI himself had to pick up the phone to deliver the news, or am I being too hopeful?"

"Very much the latter, I'm afraid. The intel came to my desk, so I thought I'd give you a call. There's nothing here that's going to blow anybody's skirt up over there. The employee list is a big zero. Those Swiss bankers are about as exciting as . . . Swiss bankers."

"That's what I expected."

"I'm sure the Brits already know this, but Tobias Gabler, the man who was killed the other day, lived a monk's existence. He wasn't killed for anything going on in his personal life."

"What about the bank's clients? Any red flags there?"

"The client list isn't as shady as what you might

407

expect. As I said, this is all still prelim, but as far as the individual accounts set up with the actual account holders' names, mostly it looks like regular rich people stashing their money in Switzerland because they want a tax haven, not because they are necessarily hiding criminal proceeds. The clients are old money, mostly. Italian, Swiss, German, English, American."

"American?"

"Afraid so. Of course, we haven't had time to run down all the details on all the names, but we don't see anything alarming. Mostly we think they are just doctors shielding their money from malpractice claims or ex-husbands hiding it from ex-wives, that sort of thing. Unethical, but no major criminality."

"Any East Bloc account holders?"

"None, although you know how it is. The KGB wouldn't be so obvious. Just because the Swiss verify the account holders' identity doesn't mean they know who the account holders actually are. They just check documents. The KGB has some terrific forgers."

"How are we doing searching the corporate accounts?"

"It's slow going, to tell you the truth. As you know, anyone who really wants to hide their affiliation with a bank account will hire a nominee, someone who will sign their name to the account. The nominee gets paid to provide the service, and they don't know or care who is paying them. This can make tracking the actual account owner nearly impossible, but we do have some means at our disposal. We've determined one of the accounts belongs to a casino group, another to a popular hotel chain, and there's an account for a diamond merchant. Also, a law firm in Singapore has an —"

"Wait. Did you say 'diamonds'?"

"Yes. Argens Diamantaire. Based in Antwerp. It's owned by Philippe Argens. His corporate account is with RPB. Does that mean something?"

"Penright, the operations officer, said the KGB was asking about people who might be moving hard assets out of the bank."

"Argens Diamantaire is one of the largest precious gemstone operations in Europe. Mostly South African mines, but they buy and sell stones all over the world."

"Are they aboveboard?"

"In general terms, yes. Precious gems is a business with a dirty underbelly, but as far as anyone knows, Philippe Argens runs a legitimate operation."

Ryan thought about it for a moment. The KGB men asked about hard assets, cash, gold, and the like. Diamonds were most definitely a hard asset. He'd run it by Penright, but it didn't sound especially promising.

Jack said, "Thanks for the information. If Penright was hoping some other bad actor involved with the bank killed Tobias Gabler, I think he will be disappointed."

Greer said, "No Cosa Nostra or Five Families or Medellín cartel linkage here. I'm afraid the Brits will have to entertain the notion that a KGB banker getting murdered in the middle of the street might have something to do with the KGB."

"Right."

"One more thing, Jack. Judge Moore and I had a conversation this morning. We'd like the Brits to involve us in this asset."

"I talked to Sir Basil about that the other day. He made it clear that they will share any product they get from this asset of theirs at the bank, but they

409

have no intention of truly going bilateral."

"That's all well and good, but I am concerned this source of theirs comes with an expiration date. If the KGB is onto him, either they will move their money or they will remove him. We might not have much of a time window here. Better we pool our resources so we can save this operation."

"That's a fair point," Ryan admitted.

"What do we know about the asset?"

"Not much, really. Penright gave up a little more information outside of Charleston's presence. He made it clear the asset met directly with the KGB men who claimed to be Hungarian account holders, so the asset is likely some sort of bank exec. Penright is over in Switzerland now, setting up a meeting with him. Figures he needs to calm the guy down after the Gabler murder. The fact we weren't able to ID any other potential culprits from the client list makes me think Penright has his work cut out for him."

Greer said, "A source in a family-owned Swiss bank has incredible potential. Arthur and I will call Basil tomorrow morning and press him a little."

"Well, okay. Obviously, that's your call, but we are going to need to find something to offer the Brits in exchange. I don't think us looking over the client list is enough for them to warrant their sharing operational control over their asset."

Greer said, "I agree. We'll find something they want, and we'll make a fair trade for access."

As soon as Ryan got off the phone with Greer, he called Penright's hotel in Zug. He gave the code they had set up between them, which sent the MI6 man to a secure phone somewhere else in the city.

It took Penright thirty minutes to call Ryan back.

"Good evening," Ryan said.

"Evening. What's the latest from the cousins?"

"We ran a check on the employee list. Came up with nothing."

"I expected that."

"As to the client list, the preliminary report shows no ties to any criminal organization."

"Nothing?"

"I'm afraid not. We did find that one of the accounts is in the name of a front company owned by a large diamond merchant who has an account at RPB." Ryan passed on the name of the Belgian company, though Penright didn't seem terribly impressed with that information.

"Okay, Ryan. I have a meeting with my agent tomorrow. My main objective is to allay any fears he has, but I will also try to get a little more out of him. He might be able to provide us with internal documents about the holder of the two-hundred-four-million-dollar account."

Ryan said, "I can guarantee the account will be held by a shell corporation. It's going to be tough to dig into it."

"Have any ideas on something that might prove helpful?" Penright asked.

"Yes. If he can provide you information about how the money was transferred into the bank, that might be more helpful than him giving us the account-holder information."

"Really? How so?"

"Because different countries have different banking secrecy laws. If the money was transferred in from another Western bank, we might have more luck ID'ing the owner by looking into the account there."

"That's a good idea."

Jack added, "Obviously, I don't know anything

about your asset. It might be the case that he wouldn't have access to account-transfer data. If he snoops around too much, it might be dangerous for him."

Penright said, "Understood, old boy. I'll make sure he proceeds with caution."

"Is there anything else I can do?" Jack asked.

"Just keep thinking. We men of action can always do with a more sedate brain behind us."

Ryan thought this to be some sort of an unintentional slight, but he let it go.

47

Present day

Clark, Chavez, and Caruso had returned from the action in the Crimea to a capital city rife with protest marches and riots. Political infighting dominated the news, and criminal gangs shot it out with local police in the streets of Kiev.

After reuniting with the rest of their team at the safe-house flat, Igor Kryvov drove Clark to the Fairmont Grand Hotel, where he expected to slip right back into his cover as a disaffected journalist who had decided to put the deluxe room at a five-star hotel on his expense account.

But as soon as he arrived at the front door of the hotel, Clark realized there had been some changes made during his two-day absence.

His first indication that all was not as before came when he was stopped outside the door to the lobby by a uniformed officer from Kiev's Ministry of Internal Affairs and asked for his passport. Clark handed over his cover credos, and while the stern-faced officer looked at them Clark helpfully mentioned that he was a guest at the Fairmont.

The officer passed back the passport and said, "Not anymore. The hotel is closed."

Before Clark could respond, a hotel employee

appeared, took Clark's name and room number, and with profuse, embarrassed apologies explained that his luggage would be brought down, but Clark would have to find other arrangements in the city.

Clark responded with confusion and insolence, but only because it fit his cover to do so. In truth, he'd had a look inside the lobby when the employee came out, and he could tell exactly what was going on now. The Seven Strong Men had taken over the entire hotel, and local police and even Ministry of Internal Affairs men were now protecting the building, keeping out anyone who did not belong.

This was an interesting development. To Clark it meant that some portion of the Ukrainian government, at both the local and the state level, was blatantly supporting the actions of Gleb the Scar and the Seven Strong Men.

Clark wondered if an actual coup would be the next step, or if all the supporters of the Russian criminals here in the city planned on just sitting tight and waiting for the Russians to invade and take over the country.

Clark retrieved his luggage from the hotel and then returned to the safe house. He knew he would need to find a new safe house closer to the hotel so they could monitor the comings and goings. It was beginning to look like the Fairmont was ground zero for some sort of an insurrection here in Ukraine, and Clark wanted to be close enough to the action to understand the players and the game.

They spent the evening tracking down potential places to move in the city center. While checking into this, the men dug into a dinner of steaks and salads picked up by Igor at a nearby restaurant. As always, the TV was on Ukraine's ICTV channel and the volume was up disturbingly high to render any listening devices useless. The six men in the flat had spent the evening tuning out the sounds, but a news story at the top of the eleven p.m. news turned the head of Igor Kryvov first, and then, seconds later, John and Ding, because they understood Russian well enough to decipher the Ukrainian on TV.

Igor translated for the others: "There's going to be a speech in an hour in front of the Verkhovna Rada building, that's the parliament building in Constitution Square. The press is going to cover it live. Oksana Zueva will be there."

"Who's that?" Driscoll asked.

"She's the head of the pro-Russian bloc in our parliament. If the nationalists get thrown out of power, she is a lock to become the next prime minister."

Chavez asked, "She's that popular?"

Igor shrugged. "Valeri Volodin supports her, so her party gets money and backing in secret from the Russians."

While they were talking, Gavin, who had been sitting at his desk tracking the GPS transmitters throughout the city, looked up. "Did you say something about Constitution Square?"

Igor said, "Yeah. I was saying that's where the speech is about to take place."

Gavin grabbed a notepad off the table and jotted something down, then passed it to Driscoll. He read it, then passed it on to the next man in the room.

When it came to Ding, he read it. "The first vehicle we tagged the other day — designated

Target Vehicle Number One — is in Constitution Square right now and stationary. Appears to be parked."

Ding looked at Dom. Aloud, and for the benefit of any mikes that could pick up his voice over the television, he said, "You know, we really ought to take a camera down to that speech and get some footage."

Dom quickly cut off a huge bite of his steak. Before he stuck it in his mouth, he said, "Let's do it. I'll grab the gear."

Forty-five minutes later, Chavez and Caruso pulled up to the Verkhovna Rada building, where the national parliament of Ukraine met. It took a while to find a place to park on Constitution Square; the space was by no means packed, but several hundred people were milling about near a riser and a dais in front of the huge neoclassical building, listening to speeches and waiting for the main event.

Dozens of media groups were represented in the crowd, pressed together in a gaggle directly in front of the riser. Ding and Dom took their video camera, checked to make sure their press credentials were hanging around their necks, and headed toward the pack.

They had their Bluetooth earpieces in so they could stay in constant communication with Gavin Biery back in the safe house. Gavin spoke softly when he spoke at all; usually, he did his best to obfuscate his comments in case anyone was able to hear him through the FSB listening devices that were certainly in the safe house.

As they walked toward the riser across the square, Gavin directed the two men to the parking lot where the target vehicle was parked. When they arrived, however, they found the lot was behind a locked gate inside the Verkhovna Rada building itself.

This was interesting, in that even though they couldn't get close enough to the SUV to learn anything about its owners, it showed them that the guys who had met with Gleb the Scar the other day somehow had the juice to park their ride on Ukrainian government property.

They headed over to the riser and barged through the crowd toward the front as if they were members of an actual media outlet.

There were several politicians present at the made-for-TV rally; some had already spoken, but the headline act was just about to get under way.

The lone female on the riser was Oksana Zueva, and every reporter in attendance was here because of her. Zueva was the leader of the Ukrainian Regional Unity Party, the leading pro-Russian party in the country, and she had not been shy about her interest in running for prime minister in the next election.

Today's speech was expected to be little more than a list of grievances against the pro-nationalist One Ukraine Party. This declaration against the party in power would bring Oksana even closer to pro-Russians in the east, it would endear her to Moscow, and it would put her well on the way to earning the complete backing of Moscow in the next election, a crucial component to victory.

Although Zueva and her husband had been accused of all sorts of corruption in her time as a powerful parliamentarian, the One Ukraine Party had failed in its attempts to marginalize her or pin any sort of corruption directly on her, and her intelligence as well as her ease in front of the cameras had gone a long way to softening her image, even though the votes she had cast in the building behind her were among the most hardline in the Ukrainian parliament.

Regardless of one's politics, though, one had to admit Oksana was a beautiful and striking woman. A fifty-year-old blonde, she usually kept her hair braided in a traditional Ukrainian style, and she wore chic designer clothes that had subtle but unmistakable influences of Ukrainian traditional dress.

While Ding and Dom watched and recorded the event, they had their eyes open for the two men they photographed at the Fairmont getting into the vehicle designated Target One. They scanned the crowd here in the square, but there were a lot of faces in poor light, so they knew that chances were slim they would get lucky and make a positive ID.

While they looked around, Zueva was introduced by one of her party leaders. She rose from her chair and, with a practiced wave and a smile that even managed to charm the two Americans firmly on the side of the opposition to her pro-Russian cause, she began walking to the microphone.

She never made it.

There was a loud crack; many press outlets in attendance would later report it sounded like a car's backfire, but Dom and Ding knew instantly it was the sound of a high-powered rifle.

Oksana Zueva rocked back on her feet onto the heels of her stilettos, her smile disappeared and a look of confusion was caught in all the cameras, and then she crumpled softly to the carpeted riser,

418

ending up on her back.

Blood appeared on her breasts.

The bouncing echoes of the gunshot across the neoclassical façade of the Verkhovna Rada building made determining the location of the gunshot all but impossible. Security men spun around with their weapons in the air while the dozens of journalists ducked to the ground. The crowd began screaming and shouting and running in all directions.

Ding and Dom dove down on the ground like all the journalists and spectators around them, but their eyes scanned the area, and they tried to determine the direction from which the gunshot had come by the location of the wound on the woman's chest.

They focused on the park to the west on the other side of Grushevsky Street.

They leapt to their feet and ran toward their car across the square, but by the time they began driving in the direction of the park, traffic had ground to a halt as police began setting up roadblocks.

Chavez slammed his hand onto the steering wheel in frustration.

Caruso spoke into his headset: "Gavin. Target One. Is the vehicle moving?"

There was a pause. "Yes. It's heading west through the park."

Chavez looked at the roadblock ahead. The SUV with the slap-on was already on the other side, and it would be long gone by the time they got through.

"Shit. They are gone."

Dom said, "I don't get it. Gleb the Scar is here working on behalf of the Russians, right?"

"It sure as hell seems that way. He's working as

a proxy for the FSB."

"But that woman who just got assassinated was Russia's favorite politician in Ukraine. Why the hell would Russia be involved with her death?"

Ding would have answered the question, had Dom not answered it himself.

Dom said, "Of course, if the head of the pro-Russian party gets whacked, all the blame is going to go on the pro-nationalists."

"Yep," Chavez said. "It's going to increase the fighting between the two sides. And who the fuck do you think is going to come in and restore order?"

Caruso whistled softly. "Shit, Ding. If the Kremlin killed their own politician in Kiev, that's pretty cold-blooded."

They peeled out of the line of cars and turned in the opposite direction. There was no point in trying to track the tagged vehicle now; they could pick up surveillance on it at any time.

48

Thirty years earlier

CIA analyst Jack Ryan found himself once again in the plush office of the director general of MI6, Sir Basil Charleston. It was late afternoon, the day after Jack called David Penright in Zug to let him know the CIA was unable to find any alternative motive for the murder of Tobias Gabler. Ryan assumed Basil would have spoken directly to CIA director Judge Arthur Moore today, because Greer had mentioned CIA was going to formally ask SIS to make the source in the Swiss bank bilateral.

Now Jack was up here in Basil's office, and since Jack was the CIA liaison, he assumed he was about to find out just how involved the United States was going to be with the asset in Ritzmann Privatbankiers.

"Well, now," Charleston said. "I have spoken to your directors in Langley, and they are quite insistent that they be more involved in the situation developing in Switzerland. I have agreed to this."

Before Ryan could respond, Basil said, "Our agent in Ritzmann Privatbankiers is code-named Morningstar. He is an executive with the bank, and, therefore, he has access to a wide range of information about both the accounts and the clients."

Well, Ryan thought. This day was gearing up to be

an interesting one.

Basil went on to tell Ryan much of the same information that Ryan had heard from Penright a few evenings earlier: that it looked much like the KGB was somewhat recklessly hunting for a large amount of stolen money stashed in a numbered account at RPB.

After listening to Basil outline the situation, Jack said, "I assume CIA offered something in return for this prize."

Charleston raised an eyebrow. "They did not tell you?"

Jack cocked his head. "Tell me what?"

"They offered you."

"Me?"

"Yes. We will be sending you to Switzerland straightaway."

Ryan sat up straighter. "To do *what,* exactly?"

"We'd like you to go to Zug and to support Penright in the field. He will be getting more account information out of our source in the bank: account numbers, wire-transfer information, information about the trusts and public foundations used to set up the shell corporation involved with the large account. Obviously, this intelligence will need to be quite carefully researched, but I've agreed to have a representative of the CIA there, and on-site, in order to send anything of interest back to Langley as soon as we get it. CIA will, in return, provide support to exploit the intelligence."

Jack said, "This is happening very fast."

"Indeed. This is a very fluid situation."

"Fluid in the sense that your source might not last long in his position?"

"Sadly, yes, although David's job is to keep the man safe."

"How long have you been running Morningstar?"

"He came to us the day after those KGB men sat down in his office and threatened him."

"He was a walk-in?"

"Yes. He doesn't like his bank working with the Russians, and the personal threats were enough to send him over to the other side, as it were."

"So he's so new, you really haven't exploited him as an asset yet."

"We have received nothing from him other than the client and employee list we've already shared with you. As I said, he will be delivering more records of the account. It is our hope that we can somehow shield him from whatever is going on, so we can exploit his intel in the future. But for now, he needs our help."

Basil put his hand on Jack's knee. "Will you go?"

Jack did not answer immediately. Instead, he looked out the window at the Thames for a moment.

Charleston noted the hesitation. "I know you aren't a banker."

"It's not that I'm not a banker, it's that I'm not a field operative."

"Jack, you were brilliant in Rome, and you were beyond brilliant last year dealing with the Northern Irish terrorists. You may be an analyst, but you are more than capable. Besides, you will be based in our safe house there. I haven't seen it myself, but I am certain it is quite secure and quite comfortable."

Jack knew he was going to say yes. He always said yes when asked.

"When do I leave?"

Charleston said, "I'd like to have a driver run you home and pack a bag right now."

"But . . . Cathy. I need to talk to Cathy."

Sir Basil winced. "Yes, of course. My apologies. I

am accustomed to directing field men like Penright. They can go anywhere with a snap of the fingers."

"That's not me, Basil. I'm a team player, but I've got a team at home, too."

Charleston nodded. "Of course you do. Let's send you off tomorrow. Talk to Lady Caroline this evening and come in with a bag in the morning."

Jack realized that if he was being instructed to show up with bags packed tomorrow, he would not be *asking* Cathy anything tonight.

Mr. and Mrs. Ryan met in Victoria Station and took the 6:10 train back to Chatham. Jack did not mention his impending trip to Switzerland, even when Cathy asked him about his day, and he wondered if he would catch hell for that when he got home. But he knew a public train was no place to tell his wife MI6 and CIA were jointly sending him on a secret mission.

On the way home from the train station, Jack suggested they stop at a Chinese restaurant for carry-out. Cathy loved the idea; she had spent several hours in surgery today, and the thought of going home and sitting down to an already prepared meal put her in a great mood.

This, of course, was Jack's plan.

They ate dinner and played with the kids, and then, only when Sally and Jack Junior were sound asleep, did Jack ask Cathy to sit down on the sofa in the living room.

Cathy saw the two glasses of red wine on the coffee table in front of the couch, and she tensed up instantly.

"Where are you going, and for how long?"

"Well . . ."

"You can't tell me where. I get it. But for how long?"

424

"Honey, I don't know. A few days, at least."

Cathy sat down, and Jack saw a change come over her. She could be playful, she could be loving, she could be matronly. But when things got serious, Cathy had a tendency to flip a switch and go very businesslike, almost dispassionate. Jack was certain it came from her work as a surgeon. She was able to distance herself from a problem in order to, if not solve it, at least deal with it.

"When are you leaving?" she asked.

"It's sort of an emergency. I wish I could tell you more details, but —"

"You are leaving *tomorrow*? Just like that?"

Sometimes Jack wondered if he only needed to think something for Cathy to know it. She was intuitive like no one he'd ever met.

"Yes. I'm being sent by Greer and Charleston."

She raised her eyebrows. "Both the CIA and SIS. Is it going to be dangerous?"

"No. Not at all."

Cathy said, "Last time you went away for a couple of days, you told me the same thing. When you came back you admitted you got more than you bargained for. Have you forgotten, have Greer and Charleston forgotten, that your job description describes you as an analyst?"

"I am an analyst. I will be going to a house in a friendly Western nation, and there I will be looking over reports."

"But you can't do that from Century House?"

Jack shrugged, not sure what he could say. After a moment, he said, "There is an urgency to this. We need someone on the ground there to look over the information, to evaluate it, and to send it on to Langley and London."

"Why the rush?"

Jack could see it in Cathy's eyes. She'd already gotten more information out of him than he'd wanted to provide, and now she was hunting for more.

His wife would have been one hell of a spy.

He said, "Everything will be okay. I have to go, but I promise you I won't be away one minute longer than I have to be."

He kissed her, and soon she kissed him back.

Jack apologized profusely, but he had to go upstairs to the den and make a call to Switzerland on the STU. He kissed her again, and left her sitting there on the couch.

Cathy sat with her wine. She wasn't happy. Although her husband had proven that he was able to handle himself in dangerous situations, he had never gone through the Farm, the CIA training facility for operations personnel.

She knew he would do his best, and he would do all he could to come home to his family, but there were dangers out there that he could not seem to turn away from.

And more than anything else, Cathy Ryan simply did not understand why Jack — a husband, a father, a historian, and a desk analyst — had somehow turned into a spy.

49

Present day

Valeri Volodin had a habit of walking at a pace that made others struggle to keep up with him, but this morning he moved even faster than usual. As he stormed out of the elevator and began rushing up the hall on the twenty-second floor of Gazprom's Moscow corporate headquarters, only the fittest security officers in his entourage were able to stay abreast. Gazprom officials, personal secretaries, and public-relations staff all trailed far behind as he headed toward the building's state-of-the-art command-and-control center.

Employees of the massive gas giant watched through the glass walls of their offices or peered over cubicles as the president of Russia passed by in a blur. More than five thousand of the nearly half-million Gazprom employees worked here in the corporate HQ, and these employees were well accustomed to big-shot government types skulking in their halls, since Gazprom was partially state-owned, and the part that was not officially owned by the state was more or less secretly owned by the leaders of the state.

Still, Volodin had been here only once before, the day he cut off the gas lines to Estonia.

And everyone who saw him on the twenty-second floor today, especially those who both took note of his intense demeanor and knew anything about what was going on in the world, knew exactly why he was here.

Volodin passed into the command-and-control room, and then he stopped suddenly. Though he was a single-minded and purposeful individual, perhaps to a pathological degree, he still could not help being impressed by the image in front of him. Fifty or so employees were hard at work at their desks, and beyond them at the front wall of the room, a digital map one hundred feet long by twenty-five feet high displayed a lighted maze of pipes intertwined in different colors. This was a graphic representation of Gazprom's pipeline network, some 175,000 kilometers long, stretching east to Siberia and west to the Atlantic, north to the Arctic and south to the Caspian Sea.

Here, in this nerve center, a few commands into a computer terminal could shut off much of the power across Europe, plunging tens of millions into darkness and cold, and crippling industry and transportation.

And that was the plan.

Volodin had a speech planned; there was a cameraman along with his PR people, and they hustled into the room and began filming.

But Volodin changed his mind on the speech. He decided the less he said, the more impactful his actions would be. He walked to the front of the room, turned around, and faced the controllers. Every man and every woman sat wide-eyed, waiting for the instructions they knew would come.

The president of Russia said, "Ladies and gentlemen, all lines heading to and through

Ukraine will be shut down. Immediately."

Those controlling the flow of the lines to Ukraine had been given a heads-up before Volodin arrived. But no one had said anything about lines flowing *through* Ukraine and into Western Europe.

The director of transfer pipelines sat in the second row. He would comply, of course, but he did not want to make a mistake. With great reluctance, he stood from his desk.

"Mr. President. Just so there is no misunderstanding. Shutting all lines that cross Ukrainian soil will reduce Western Europe's gas supply by seventy-five percent."

The pipeline director wondered if his career would end today for questioning the president, but Volodin seemed pleased to be given the opportunity to expand on his declaration.

The president responded, "The current political authority in Ukraine has shown itself to be unreliable as a steward of the resources desperately needed by the people of Western Europe. Natural gas is our resource, and it is in jeopardy as long as Ukraine continues as an unstable state. We here in Russia call on the world community to put pressure on Kiev to do a better job. It is springtime, Europe will not feel the most drastic effects of this action for months, and I am certain Europe will help us alleviate this crisis long before the cold becomes an issue. I am not concerned about Europe's energy needs as much as I am concerned about Russia's citizenry both here and in the near abroad. With this decision to cut export pipelines, I expect to see a sense of urgency."

There was no smile on Volodin's face. No evil laugh. He delivered the edict that had the power to devastate millions of people as if it were nothing more than a dry administrative decision cooked up by a junior technocrat.

The process to shut the pipeline flows was surprisingly swift and straightforward. Volodin stood there with his hands on his hips and watched the first lines on the massive graphic map change from green to yellow and then to red, signifying a stop in flow.

He did not wait for the entire shutdown process; there were a lot of lines, after all. Instead, he told everyone to keep up the good work, and he stormed out of the command-and-control center just as quickly as he'd rushed in.

Volodin was downstairs and back in his armored limousine in minutes, and as it raced away, shooting north toward the city through a lane reserved for government vehicles, the president looked across the backseat to his chief of staff. "Get Talanov on the line."

While he waited, he thumbed through some papers in his lap and sipped tea from a filigreed holder.

Soon a mobile phone was passed to him by his chief of staff. Volodin took it. "Roman Romanovich?"

"Da, Valeri." Talanov would never have called Volodin by his first name in public, but Talanov was never in public, so this was a nonissue.

Volodin asked, "Has the site exploitation of the CIA compound in Sevastopol taken place?"

"Da. The results were not what we had hoped. The CIA group there vacated with most of their equipment and destroyed the rest. They inflicted heavy losses on our Spetsnaz troops, as well as

Seven Strong Men irregulars."

"And we've got nothing to show for it?" Before Talanov replied, Volodin said, "Bodies? What about bodies of dead Americans?"

"There was a lot of blood in the compound's main building. I am told there was enough blood to say with confidence the Americans lost several personnel. But all bodies were retrieved when the American Marines rescued the CIA men."

"Damn it."

"*Nyet problem.* It will be fine, Valeri. We will salvage a diplomatic coup."

"How?"

"We are recording interviews with Ukrainians who worked in the compound. They will say whatever we want them to say. Plus, we have film of American aircraft overhead. The Americans will say they were NATO-flagged aircraft rescuing their Partnership for Peace troops, but you will make the statement that the CIA has been working in the Crimea to destabilize the area."

"I wanted hard proof."

"Sorry, Valeri, but if you wanted bodies, you should have given the Black Sea fleet permission to blow the American planes out of the sky. But that's not my department."

"No, Roman, it's not. I did not want to provoke a war with America over Sevastopol. I wanted evidence of CIA provocation in Sevastopol to use against the Americans when the time is right."

"I understand. But if you —"

"I need more from you on this, Roman. I need an act that can be positively attributed to the CIA in the region."

There was a short pause on the line. The pause would have been much longer if Roman Talanov and Valeri Volodin did not know each other as well as they did.

Talanov said, "I understand you, Valeri. I will create something, and I will use the evidence we do have from the Sevastopol compound to show incontrovertible proof."

"Quickly. *Very* quickly. I just stopped gas flow to and through Ukraine."

"I will get to work, then. *Paka.*" Good-bye.

50

Thirty years earlier

CIA analyst Jack Ryan arrived at Century House with his bags packed for his trip to Switzerland. He had to be at Heathrow at noon, so he figured he would put in an hour and a half of work before carrying his suitcase back downstairs and climbing into a cab.

His first task of the day was to call David Penright in Zug, to see if he'd received the documents from Morningstar and to check for any final instructions from the English spy in the field.

He had just returned to his desk with his first cup of coffee of the morning, ready to fire up his STU for the call, when the director of the Russian Working Group, Simon Harding, hurried into his office. "Charleston needs you in his office, straightaway."

Jack could see consternation on Harding's face.

"What is it?"

"Just go, mate."

Minutes later, Jack stepped out of the elevator into the director's corner office. On the ride up, he ran a dozen possible scenarios through his head, but he admitted to himself he couldn't imagine what had Harding so agitated.

Charleston stood at his desk with a half-dozen

other men around him, none of whom Ryan recognized. As soon as he turned around and saw Ryan, Basil said, "Sit down, Jack."

Jack moved to the sofa, and Basil sat in front of him. No introductions had been made of the other men.

"What's wrong?"

"Terrible news, I'm afraid. David Penright . . . is dead."

Jack felt a hot stab to his stomach as acid churned. "Oh my God."

"We just learned of it."

A wave of confusion washed over Ryan. "What the hell happened?"

"Hit by a bloody bus."

"A bus?"

One of the other men came forward and sat down across from Ryan. He said, "They are going to find that he'd been drinking. Like most traveling officers, he tipped the bottle more than he should have."

"I . . . I talked to him last night. He was fine."

The man said, "He left the safe house in Zug at nine p.m. Immediately after talking to you, from what I gather. Then he met with Morningstar. After that, he hit the local bars."

"Who are you?" Jack asked.

Basil cleared his throat. "Jack Ryan, Nick Eastling. Counterintelligence Division."

The men shook hands, though Ryan was still in a state of shock.

Eastling nodded to the other men by the window. "That's the rest of my team over there."

The five men by the window just looked Jack's way.

Jack turned to Basil for clarification, and Basil said, "Nick and his team will be investigating David's

434

death. The Swiss are well on their way to determining this was an accident, but our Zurich station will reach out to them to make sure their investigation ends quickly and quietly, so that ours can begin in earnest."

Eastling said, "We'll find the same thing. There were witnesses to the fact Penright came out of a beer hall about half past midnight, walked out into the street to flag a taxi, and then stumbled out of the empty lane and right in front of oncoming traffic. He was run over by a public transport bus. The bus driver is cooperating, to the extent he could. The Swiss say he was horrified by the experience."

Jack was as incredulous as this Eastling fellow was certain. "You actually believe that story?"

Eastling said, "It wasn't an assassination. Obviously, when we get the body back we will do a toxicology test on him, but my feeling is they will find he'd had enough gin to where the only mystery in his death will be how the hell he managed to climb off his bar stool and make it out the front door." The man winced a little, as though he did not want to speak ill of the dead, but then he said, "David had a problem."

Ryan turned away from the counterintel man and asked Charleston, "Does Morningstar know Penright is dead?"

"No. Penright was carrying false identity papers, in the name Nathan Michaels. This sort of death will make the news over there, but the newspapers will identify him as the alias he was traveling under. Morningstar won't recognize it."

"You've got to let Morningstar know."

Basil said, "That has not been decided. We don't want to alarm him unnecessarily."

"*Unnecessarily?* People are dying all around him."

Eastling cleared his throat. "There have been two deaths. Neither of which we have been able to link to any compromise of Morningstar."

Basil added, "These gentlemen will be heading over to launch an investigation. I've spoken to James Greer and Arthur Moore at Langley. We would like you to go along with them."

The thought of not going to Switzerland had not occurred to him. "Yes. Yes, of course."

Eastling appeared decidedly unhappy with this decision, but he did not say anything.

Charleston said, "Excellent. We will make a determination as to how Morningstar will be run as soon as the investigation into David's death is concluded. For now, at least, we will not go near Morningstar, so there is no potential for compromise."

Ryan just nodded. This was a lot to take in.

Eastling stood. "All right, Ryan. Off you go. I'll meet you in the lobby in an hour. I have some more to discuss with Sir Basil."

And with that, Nick Eastling all but shoved Jack Ryan out of the office.

51

Present day

It had taken Jack Ryan, Jr., days to track down Victor Oxley, the ex–MI5 spy known as Bedrock. He first called James Buck, his hand-to-hand combat trainer back in Maryland. James was a friend of The Campus's, and was himself an ex-member of SAS, and he happily promised to make some discreet inquiries on Ryan's behalf.

Jack knew he could have just told his dad about his conversation with Basil, and that would have been the end of it. But the younger Ryan found himself intrigued with the old story. He'd sent an e-mail to his father after his meeting in Belgravia with the ex-head of MI6, and told him simply that he'd learned a few details, but he'd like to look into it a little more.

After Buck did some extensive digging, he told Jack that as far as anyone in the SAS knew, Vick Oxley was still alive. They had no address for him, but by checking some old records, Buck was able to give Ryan his date of birth. This told Ryan that Oxley was fifty-nine. Ryan pulled up UK tax records, a perk of working for a company like Castor and Boyle, and he found exactly one fifty-nine-year-old Victor Oxley on the books. As it happened, the man lived in Corby, two hours north of London. Ryan called the phone number listed and found it out of service, but it was a Friday, and Ryan had banked a few hours of vacation time, so he told Sandy Lamont he'd be leaving after lunch to get an early start on his weekend.

The trip north was uneventful other than the fact Ryan had done very little driving on the left side of the road. More than once he'd winced as he'd passed oncoming traffic passing him by on the right, but after an hour or so his brain started to settle down and get used to this odd sensation.

He arrived in Corby and found the address just after four p.m. Oxley lived in a ramshackle two-story apartment building with a front garden smaller than the living room in Jack's Earl's Court apartment.

Ryan walked through the trash-strewn grass to the entryway and took a staircase up to Oxley's flat.

He knocked, waited, then knocked again.

Frustrated, Ryan headed back to his car, but when he got down to the street, he noticed a pub on the corner, and figured it wouldn't hurt to check in there in case someone knew the man he was looking for.

The pub was called the Bowl in Hand. Ryan found the place to be a little dark and dingy compared with the watering holes he'd been frequenting in The City. Even the locals seemed to agree that it wasn't much of a hangout; it was four-fifteen on a Friday afternoon and Ryan counted fewer than ten patrons in the entire pub, all gray-haired men.

Ryan sat at the bar and ordered a pint of John Courage. When the bartender brought him his beer, Ryan put down a ten-pound note and said,

"I was wondering if you knew a regular here."

The burly man said, "I know when someone's *not* a regular."

Jack Ryan smiled. He expected this; the bartender didn't look like he'd gotten his job for his chipper demeanor. Jack reached into his wallet and put down another ten-pound note. He didn't have a clue what the going rate was for this sort of thing, but he wasn't going to fan off any more money than he had to.

The bartender took the money. "The name of this chap?"

"Oxley. Victor Oxley."

The bartender made a surprised face that Jack couldn't read.

"You know him, then?"

"Aye," he said, and now Jack saw that any suspicions the man carried before were replaced by a sense of mild curiosity. He got the idea there *were* some shady individuals who frequented this pub that the publican wanted to protect, but Victor Oxley wasn't one of them.

Still, the man said, "Leave your number. I'll pass it to him next time he's in, and if he's interested in speaking with you . . . he'll let you know."

Jack shrugged. It wasn't how he'd planned it, but it was Friday; he could get a room in a hotel in town and wait a night, because he didn't have to be in the office in the morning. He pulled his Castor and Boyle business card out of his wallet and handed it to the bartender. Then he said, "There's another twenty for you when I talk to him."

The bartender raised his bushy eyebrows and put the card into his breast pocket without looking at it.

439

Jack turned his attention to his beer and started thumbing through his phone, looking for the closest inn that looked decent enough for one night.

As he did this, the bartender began talking with an old-timer at the end of the bar. Jack paid little attention to them as he concentrated on his phone.

A minute later the bartender returned and dropped Jack's business card next to the glass of John Courage. "Sorry, lad. Vick isn't interested in chatting."

Ryan looked over to the man at the end of the bar, who was lost in his own beer. At first he thought there was no way this man was only fifty-nine. He was wrinkled and heavy; he looked like a slightly thinner version of Santa Claus. But upon closer inspection Ryan thought it possible the man could be younger than he first guessed, and when the man looked up and noticed Ryan looking at him, he gave the bartender a look like he wanted to wring his neck.

This is the guy.

Jack pulled out a twenty-pound note and put it on the bar, then grabbed his beer and headed over.

Oxley shifted his eyes back down to his beer. He had thick, wavy, and slightly long white hair and a full white beard. His bloodshot eyes gave Jack the impression the man had been sitting right here downing pints since whenever this bar opened for business that day.

Jack spoke softly to keep the conversation between the two of them. "Good afternoon, Mr. Oxley. I apologize for coming unannounced, but I would very much appreciate a few moments of your time."

The older man did not look up from his pint. In a voice as low as a locomotive's rumble, he said,

"Bugger off."

Great, Jack thought.

He tried a bribe. It had worked with the bartender, after all. "How about you let me pay your tab, and we go find a booth and talk for a few minutes?"

"I said bugger off."

Basil had said the man might be trouble.

Jack thought he'd try one more avenue. "My name is —"

Now the bearded man looked up from his pint for the first time. "I know who you are." And then, "Your dad's a bloody wanker."

Ryan gritted his teeth. He noticed the bartender had come around from behind the bar and was talking to a couple of men in a booth. They were all looking his way.

Jack wasn't worried, just frustrated. His only real concern was that he would feel bad if he had to beat up a dozen or so old geezers.

He stood up from the bar, looking at Oxley. "It was really a small thing I needed from you. You might have been able to do some good, at no cost to yourself."

"Fuck off."

Jack said, "You were SAS? I find that very hard to believe. You really let yourself go, didn't you?"

Oxley looked back down to his beer. He squeezed it with a meaty hand, and Jack saw the sinewy muscles in the man's hand ripple with the squeeze.

"No response?"

Oxley said nothing.

"I thought Brits were supposed to have manners." Jack Ryan turned and walked out the door without a look back.

52

The rally in the eastern Ukrainian city of Donetsk drew more than ten thousand this weekend, triple the attendance of the week before. Even though it was a cold, rainy Saturday afternoon, Pushkin Boulevard was packed tight with pro-Russian Ukrainians, all out to make their voices heard.

There was nothing spontaneous about this rally. Today's event, like all the others, had the backing of the FSB, who were all over the place here in eastern Ukraine. This was the largest of the weekly rallies this year, and it was no mystery as to why. The assassination of Oksana Zueva and the NATO action in Sevastopol — there were accusations that the CIA had been involved as well — brought the pro-Russian eastern Ukrainians out in droves.

While the men and women in the crowd held their new Russian passports high over their heads and marched behind banners expressing their allegiance to Moscow, and not Ukraine, a van moved slowly behind the last of the stragglers, south on Pushkin. Then it turned onto Hurova Avenue so that it could maneuver to get in front of the action.

Minutes later, the van rolled back onto Pushkin

south of the red banners at the front of the march, and it parked along an open square adjacent to the National Academic Ukrainian Musical and Drama Theater. The square in front of the massive theater served as the midpoint of the march, and here the civilian organizers would make speeches through bullhorns and incite the crowd against the pro-nationalists in power in Kiev, before everyone set off again to march east toward the river.

The two men in the van did not get out when they parked. Instead, they sat there smoking cigarettes with stone faces and watched the crowd in the distance walk up Pushkin in their direction.

The two occupants of the van were members of the Seven Strong Men. They were both Russians by birth, but they had been living in Kiev recently and working under the orders of the FSB.

Behind them, in their van, was a single fifty-five-gallon oil drum under a canvas tarp. The drum had been filled by others the evening before, but the two mafia enforcers knew what was inside.

The explosive was RDX, Research Department Explosive, also known as hexogen. It was not a new or high-tech explosive, it had been around forever, but it was suitable for this operation.

Through the hole in the top of the drum, a shock-tube detonator had been inserted into the granular material, and the detonator was, in turn, attached to a simple timing device. The timer was set for three minutes; it needed only the flip of a switch to start the countdown, so the two men in the front of the van sat in silence, watching the crowd carefully, trying to pick just the right moment to set the bomb in motion.

Local police were out, of course, but they

weren't searching parked cars along the route. They had enough to worry about with trying to stop the protesters from breaking windows of the few known nationalist shopkeepers along the route, as well as dealing with a surprising counterprotest that had materialized a few blocks farther south on Pushkin Boulevard. Though the counterprotest was small, it had the effect of pulling police patrols away from the path of the march.

The pro-nationalists who stood along the road waving Ukrainian flags and yelling at the marchers had been set up by the FSB the evening before, meaning Russian intelligence had a hand in organizing both sides of the conflict here in Donetsk today.

When the red banner was just one block away from the van with the fifty-five-gallon bomb in the back, the two Seven Strong Men operatives opened their doors. Then the passenger flipped the switch on the timer, calmly stepped out, and joined his partner as they walked away to the east.

Two minutes later, they were picked up by a confederate driving a car with stolen license plates.

And a minute after this, when the protest marchers were still forming in the square next to the National Academic Ukrainian Musical and Drama Theater, the shock-tube detonator sent a percussive wave into the RDX, and the entire van exploded in a flash with a blast radius of eighty feet.

A few close by were spared death because the van had been parked in a lot with vehicles on both sides and this stifled some of the bomb's potential carnage, but those in front of and behind the vehicle were torn apart instantly. Those who did not take the full force of the blast but were still within the radius of the major shock wave had their eardrums and internal organs assaulted, and several people in a second ring of victims, just outside the range of the shock wave, were killed by shrapnel from the blast.

The entire rally was pitched into chaos as the dead and maimed littered the ground and thousands ran for their lives, even crushing the fallen in their path.

Within minutes of the attack, a call came in to TRK Ukraina, a local news television station. The caller claimed to be a Ukrainian nationalist, and he took credit for the attack on behalf of the Ukrainian people and their allies in the West. He said any attempts by Russia to take over the Crimea would result in the wholesale slaughter of Russian citizens and anti-nationalists, effectively throwing down the gauntlet and ensuring more unrest between Ukraine's two sides.

The caller was actually an FSB agent phoning from the Fairmont Grand Hotel in Kiev. The FSB had already decided that once the city of Donetsk was retaken by Russian forces, the pro-Russian marchers who died today would have a plaque erected in their name in the square next to the National Academic Ukrainian Musical and Drama Theater.

53

Thirty years earlier

CIA analyst Jack Ryan arrived in Zurich, Switzerland, with the six-man team of MI6 counterintelligence officers late in the day. The men had traveled separately on the same aircraft, and they all had passports declaring themselves to be English businessmen. Ryan sat nervously through the flight. Like many, he was an anxious air passenger, although unlike most, Ryan had an excuse. The helicopter crash he'd narrowly survived a decade earlier came back to haunt him every time he flew through the air, held up by invisible forces he did not completely trust.

But the flight was unremarkable, and by late afternoon they breezed through Swiss customs and walked to the train station.

The train trip to Zug was just over a half-hour in duration; the men sat in different cars, then each made his own way to a large business-class hotel near the *Bahnhof.* Here, three of Eastling's men rented cars, while Nick and the rest of his team turned his top-floor suite into a makeshift command center for the investigation.

Ryan was all but forgotten by the SIS counterintelligence officers for the duration of the afternoon, but he made his way into the command center for a scheduled evening conference.

When everyone was assembled, Eastling addressed his team and, by default, the American tagalong on his operation.

"Right. Tonight Joey will go to the morgue and collect the body. We've straightened it out with the embassy in Zurich. Joey will be presented as the brother of the deceased, he'll get a look at it there in the morgue, just a quick once-over to make sure there's not something obviously queer about the situation."

"Like what?" Ryan asked from the back of the room. He'd decided he was going to be a part of this investigation whether Nick Eastling liked it or not.

Eastling shrugged. "Dunno. Like a suicide note in his pocket. An arrow in the back of his head. Shark bite on his arse. Things that might tip us off there is more to this than a bus accident."

Ryan got the impression Eastling didn't believe this was anything more than an accident, and this entire investigation was just some sort of pro forma Kabuki theater.

Eastling turned back to Joey. "There should be no problem getting it shipped back to the UK straightaway."

"Why do I have to be the sod to blow half his per diem on dry ice?" Joey asked, and this comment elicited a few chuckles in the room.

"Save your receipts, my boy. You'll be compensated for all expenses once we're back in London."

Ryan clenched his jaw. He barely knew David Penright, but these men were so flippant about his death it infuriated him.

Eastling continued, "Next, Bart and Leo will go to the local safe house to start checking it top to bottom. You are to tear the place apart. The rest of us

447

will join you to help as soon as we are finished with our tasks."

"Right, boss," the men said.

"Stuart, you go to Penright's hotel. Talk your way into the room. I checked before we left London, the room is paid for until next week, so they haven't touched a thing. They are waiting on next of kin, so if you can sell that, go ahead and scoop everything up and bring it back here. Eyes out for any corrupting material."

"Right, Nick."

Ryan held up his hand. "I'm sorry. I'm a little confused. I thought Penright was a victim either of an accident or of foul play. You are treating him like he is some sort of a suspect in a crime."

Eastling half rolled his eyes. "Sir John."

"Please call me Jack."

"Right. Jack. From all we've learned about Penright, he was an able enough operations officer. But we've got a little experience in this sort of thing, and his dossier raises certain questions."

"Such as?"

"He was a bleeding drunk," the man named Joey said.

Eastling nodded. "The pattern with these types is always the same. They run risks, not just with their bodies, but with their relationships, and their protocol with secret materials is the first weak link in the chain.

"I expect to find that Morningstar has been compromised by the opposition due to David Penright's actions here in Switzerland. He bedded the wrong girl, he spilled his guts to the wrong bartender, he picked the wrong taxi stand to drop the contents of his briefcase. His death, I am sure we will find, was accidental, but we need to keep a critical eye on the fact the Morningstar operation might have been compromised by the drinking of the officer in charge of the operation."

Ryan said, "I'm really impressed, Eastling. You have been in Switzerland for three hours, you haven't left the hotel, and you've already come to all these conclusions."

Eastling and Ryan stared each other down across the suite. The counterintel man said, "I tell you what, old boy. Why don't you stick with me? First stop tonight will be the tavern where Penright had his last drink. Or, I will hazard to guess, his last ten drinks. We'll poke around and see what we find."

"That sounds fine with me," Jack said. The staring contest continued for a moment, but soon the meeting resumed, and within a half-hour the men began moving out in pursuit of their objectives.

The bar where David Penright drank his last drink was on Vorstadt, right across the street from picturesque Lake Zug. It was nine o'clock in the evening when Eastling and Ryan arrived, which seemed to Ryan to be a lousy time to go poking around, because the establishment was all but packed.

The beer hall was dark and smoke-filled, and the waitresses were young and attractive, dressed in traditional clothing: red tights and puffy white blouses with floral embroidery, although the blouses were cut a little lower than Ryan presumed would be the tradition in a country as cold as Switzerland got in the winter.

Even before they made their way to the bar, Eastling took one look at the waitresses and then leaned over to Ryan. "This looks like our boy's type of place. Care to wager that we'll find his fingerprints on half the rumps in the house?"

449

Ryan ignored the comment.

At the bar, Ryan saw that even though Eastling seemed like a smug prick, he clearly knew his job. The bartender spoke perfect English, and within seconds of ordering a round of plum schnapps for himself and Ryan, the British counterintelligence officer was chatting with the round, bald-headed bartender as though they'd known each other for a long time.

He introduced Jack in passing, then said they worked for the same bank as the man who died the evening before, and they had been sent down from Zurich by his family to collect his things.

"Mein Gott," said the bartender. He leaned close to Ryan and Eastling to talk over the loud music. "He died right out there on the street. The newspaper said his name was Herr Michaels."

Penright had been traveling under the name Nathan Michaels.

"That's right," Eastling said. "Were you working last night?"

The bartender poured a beer from the tap for a customer, then said, "I was here, but I was working the bar. He sat at that table over there." He pointed to a table near the center of the room. Ryan caught Eastling raising an inquisitive eyebrow, perhaps because the spy had chosen such a prominent location in the bar.

"Did he, now?"

"*Ja.* The waitress who served him has been suspended. The police are questioning if she gave him too much alcohol."

Eastling rolled his eyes. "Oh, that's ridiculous. How do you say 'ridiculous' in German?"

"We say *Quatsch.* It's close, anyway."

"Okay, then, that's *Quatsch.* Nathan liked to drink.

450

It's not your waitress's fault."

"*Genau!* Exactly. But this is bad publicity for the bar, of course. She will be fired."

Eastling shook his head — *"Quatsch"* — and ordered another drink for himself and Ryan. Ryan knew he was in the presence of an excellent investigator. He only wished the man's mind didn't already seem made up.

As the second plum schnapps arrived, Jack forced himself to drink down the rest of the first sugary beverage. He thought it was pretty awful, but he was following along with Eastling's friendly and earnest demeanor to try to get information out of the bartender.

"These are delicious," Nick Eastling said, as he held up the glass. "Is this what my friend was drinking?"

"*Nein.* He drank scotch. I remember because he was the only person in the bar drinking scotch at the time."

"Ah," Nick said. "Yes. Nathan enjoyed his scotch."

The bartender nodded as he made drinks a few feet away. As he worked, he said, "He was not drunk. They seemed fine when they left."

Jack cocked his head, but Eastling did not react at all. He just said, " 'They' meaning Nathan and . . ."

"And the girl he was with."

"What girl?" Ryan asked quickly, but Nick Eastling reached under the bar and squeezed his forearm.

"Oh. Didn't I say? He met a girl. They sat together for over an hour. Very beautiful."

"Right," Eastling said. Jack saw just a hint of uncertainty on the man's face. "She was a local girl?"

"She was not Swiss. She spoke with a German accent."

"I see," Eastling said.

Jack leaned forward toward the bartender. "You said he met her. You mean he met her here?"

"Yes. She was at the bar with some other men. Two of them. But they left, and she stayed. When your friend came in, he sat at the bar and started talking to her. They moved to a table."

"And you never saw them before?" Ryan asked.

"*Nein.* Although we get a lot of Germans here."

He poured more beer, but before he served them he held up a finger and said, *"Renate, komm mal her!"* calling out to one of the other bartenders. He spoke to her in German for a moment. Ryan could not understand a word until Renate said, "Berlin." The bartender said something, and she nodded and repeated, "Berlin."

As she walked off, the bartender turned back to Nick and said, "Renate is from Germany. She waited on the girl before the Englishman arrived. I asked her if she could recognize the dialect. You know, the Germans have very specific dialects in different regions."

Eastling nodded. "And she said the girl was from Berlin?"

"*Ja.* She was certain of it."

They left the bar a few minutes later. Ryan had the sickly-sweet flavor of sugarplums in his mouth, and his eyes hurt from the smoke of the bar. He and Eastling walked out into the street, standing more or less where Penright had been hit.

"Not exactly the autobahn," Ryan said. The street was dark and quiet.

"No," replied the Englishman, "but if you fall right in front of a bus, that's pretty much it."

"True enough."

They started walking back to the car. As they did

452

so, Jack said, "So we're looking for a German girl."

Eastling shook his head. "No, Ryan. Penright was looking for a German girl last night, but he found a bus instead." He laughed a little at his own joke.

"Where did the girl go? There was nothing in the police report about a German woman at the scene."

"Maybe they both left the bar and went in different directions. Maybe she wanted to get laid, then decided the dashing Englishman she picked up in a bar lost some of his allure when he died right in front of her."

Jack sighed in frustration.

54

Present day

President Jack Ryan sat at the head of the conference table in the White House Situation Room, a
cup of coffee and a stack of folders in front of
him. He'd been going through this material for
half an hour in preparation for this meeting, and
now, as everyone got situated around him, he
made a few notes on his legal pad: questions to
ask, points to make.

Jack looked up from his papers. He was beginning to see as much of the Situation Room as he
did the Oval Office, and he knew this didn't say
anything good about the current state of peace
and stability in the world.

Around him, key members of his intelligence,
diplomatic, and defense team filed into the room
and sat down. Scott Adler was absent — he was
still shuttling around Europe — but the rest of
the major players were all present and accounted
for.

Today's meeting was to discuss the last seventy-
two hours of activity in Ukraine. Six Americans
had been killed at the Lighthouse Special Mission
Compound, including the CIA chief of station for
the country, and although the international news
organizations covering the action there had

framed it as a violent demonstration outside a NATO compound that led to the death of several NATO personnel, on Russian television they ran breathless stories about American imperialism turned deadly when CIA gunmen opened fire on a crowd of peaceful protesters.

And then, the next day, the assassination of Oksana Zueva. The brazen killing had been characterized by virtually all news outlets on the planet as the work of Ukrainian nationalists, perhaps even ordered by President Kuvchek himself.

Volodin shut off the gas pipelines to Ukraine and Western Europe after the Zueva killing, and then the bombing of the pro-Russian rally in Donetsk came the very next day. Donetsk was presumed to be the work of nationalists, although the Russian Gazprom-owned media was advancing the theory that the CIA outpost in Sevastopol was involved.

At this moment, President Ryan was well beyond the point of outrage. No, after everything the FSB had pulled off in the past few weeks, he'd managed to find a measure of inner calm by telling himself a serious crisis was at hand, and only his level head could bring a quick resolution to the situation.

He brought the meeting to order by addressing Jay Canfield, director of the CIA: "Jay, what are the Russians using as proof the CIA was involved in the Donetsk car bombing?"

Canfield said, "They are showing pictures of the wreckage of the Lighthouse, and they have lists of names of agents we used in country. They claim to have CIA documents that were given to pronationalists that instructed them to make the bomb that was used as well."

"They are claiming they got this from their spy in the Security Service of Ukraine?"

"Correct, sir."

Ryan had read all the reports of the Donetsk bombing. "Why the hell would the CIA use hexogen? That's been around since the Second World War."

Mary Pat Foley answered this one: "The Russians say we used hex because we wanted it to look like local yokels put it together. It's easy enough to come by, and extremely easy to handle and detonate."

Ryan blew out an angry sigh.

"I know. I'm just telling you what they are saying."

Ryan said, "This is like the Golovko poisoning. And the Biryukov bombing. And it's like the assassination of Oksana Zueva."

Foley agreed. "It's pretty much like everything FSB director Roman Talanov has a hand in. He sacrifices people for his needs. His own people. He frames people and organizations he opposes to misplace blame."

Canfield added, "Obviously we were involved in Sevastopol, though we weren't involved in either the Donetsk bombing or the Zueva assassination or the killings of Biryukov or Golovko. Talanov can make all the claims he wants, but there is no proof whatsoever."

Ryan said, "The men who survived the attack in Sevastopol laid responsibility on this Russian criminal organization that has been active in Ukraine. I've been reading up on the Seven Strong Men for the past half-hour."

Foley nodded. "Yes, sir. The Russians have been arming and training the Seven Strong Men as well as pro-Russian Ukrainians in the eastern part of the nation. They have created a fifth column out of the Russian mob and these armed rebels."

Ryan asked, "Is this verifiable?"

Canfield said, "Volodin's enemies have been trying to tie him definitively to organized crime since he left FSB and started his meteoric rise to the top in the nineties. Everyone thinks he had a lot of help along the way. But he's kept his nose clean. That said, he's wiped out and exposed so many gangsters in Russia it's hard to see how anyone known to us would benefit from supporting him, with the sole exception being Seven Strong Men."

"It's an amorphous outfit," Ryan said, looking down at his notes. "No one knows the identity of the leader of the organization." He looked up. "Why can't we figure out who the godfather is?"

Canfield said, "We've identified one of their high-ranking capos, he's working out of a hotel in Kiev. He might even be their number two, but Seven Strong Men's command structure, as you say, is all but unknown to us. We do believe, and recent events make this even more certain, that Seven Strong Men is now working as a proxy force for FSB in Ukraine."

"Why?" Ryan asked. "I mean, what's in it for them?"

"Good question," said Mary Pat. "I have to suspect there is some sort of quid pro quo with the Kremlin. As in, if the Seven Strong Men help Russia take Ukraine, then Russia will turn a blind eye to Seven Strong Men activities there."

Jack rubbed his eyes under his glasses. The Russian military, the Russian intelligence services, the Russian mob. They were all after Ukraine, and he knew that if they took Ukraine, it would only encourage them to push farther to the west.

Secretary of Defense Bob Burgess said, "Mr. President, as far as I'm concerned, the quickening of events means one thing. Russia has done all the blackmailing with pipelines and bullying with threats of violence against Ukraine it can do without actually going forward on its threats. They have upped the ante, even made attempts to marginalize the U.S. and NATO in the region."

Ryan said, "Nothing left for Russia to do but start rolling tanks over the border."

"Correct. JSOC and CIA assets in the east report significant movements of troops on Russia's side of the line. Our imagery analysis confirms all that's needed for the Russians to start rolling is the go order from the Kremlin."

"So . . . what do we do, Bob?"

Burgess had been expecting the question. "Mr. President. Douglas MacArthur said every military disaster can be explained in two words: 'Too late.' If we were going to stop the invasion with military power, I am afraid we are already too late."

Ryan said, "I see no way to stop Russia from taking the Crimea. It's a semiautonomous region already, there are tens of thousands of real Russians and tens of thousands more who were handed out passports in the past year. Volodin can make the case to his people that taking the Crimea is in Russia's national interests. This is going to happen. With Ukraine's weak military, there is no preventing it. But I don't want them moving further west. The more successful Volodin is, the more energetic he will be about aiming for other targets in his region." Ryan thought for a moment. "We have a few hundred military advisers in country. Most of them are special operations troops. How much impact can they make on this?"

"A great deal. The plans have been drawn up to use existing forces there to assist the Ukrainians. We have Delta teams and Green Berets positioned in forward locations, and some British SAS as well. They all have the capability to communicate directly with Ukrainian Air Force assets. The Brits are on board with us on this. If you give the word, we can institute an operation to begin linking our laser targeting equipment to Ukrainian MiG-29 multirole fighters and Mi-24 attack helicopters. We can serve as a significant force multiplier for their Air Force. With luck, this can blunt the Russian attack."

"Covertly?"

Burgess nodded. "Our operational plan is structured with an eye toward covert action. Having said that . . ." Burgess struggled with how to finish the sentence.

President Ryan said, " 'The best-laid schemes o' mice an' men gang aft agley.' "

"That's right, sir."

"Tell me about the readiness of Russian forces."

"It's not good, but it is better than when they attacked Georgia a few years ago. At that time the military was rife with corruption and waste, and it showed on the battlefield. They won the conflict handily, but they did so by virtue of the fact that the Georgian Army was unprepared, and poorly led by civilian leadership.

"When Volodin came into power, it was estimated that twenty percent of Russian military procurement was wasted by corruption, literally stolen by officials. That number is down to next to nothing now. With all the corruption in Russia, it is a significant thing that graft in the military is strictly off-limits."

Ryan asked, "Can I assume he used some harsh measures to effect this improvement?"

Burgess nodded. "Some people got shot. Not many, but enough to make an impression."

"So Russia's military is bad, but they still have numbers."

"More numbers than Ukraine, anyway. And there is one other thing Russia has."

"Nukes," Ryan said.

"Germane to any conversation involving a military conflict with the Russians."

Ryan leaned forward on the conference table. "If we do manage to slow the Russian advance west, what are the chances they will threaten to go nuclear?"

Burgess said, "If you are asking about them using strategic nukes against us, I will be very clear. Admiral Jorgensen and I have been to several meetings about this recently at the Pentagon. Russia no longer has any ability whatsoever to execute a successful debilitating first strike on the United States. Two-thirds of their nuclear weapons are obsolete."

Ryan had read all the reports of the meetings Burgess was talking about, so he knew this assessment by DIA and CIA.

Admiral Jorgensen said, "Can they still launch missiles that would get through any defense we have? Yes. Yes, they can. As you know, Russia has a fleet of strategic bombers permanently airborne, something that stopped with the fall of the Soviet Union but started again when Volodin decided it would make him look tough."

Mary Pat said, "But beyond capability, there is the question of will. These aren't Islamic fundamentalists looking to martyr themselves. Volodin and his inner circle know that any nuclear attack would mean their own deaths within hours, if not minutes."

"And tactically?" Ryan asked.

Burgess said, "Volodin would never use a tactical nuke in Ukraine. It would destroy part of what he considers his home soil. He will fight for it tooth and nail, perhaps, but he's not going to condemn it to nuclear winter."

Ryan drummed his fingers on the table. "Tell me more about the plans in place for active cooperation between our Partnership for Peace forces in Ukraine and the Ukrainian Air Force."

Burgess pulled a file out of a folio and held it up. "Operation Red Coal Carpet. It assumes a conventional air and ground attack by Russia into Ukraine for control of the Crimea and the eastern section of the nation. It provides a blueprint for teams of American special operations forces to operate laser targeting equipment to aid Russian jets and helos, not for the purposes of defeating Russia's invasion force, but rather to keep it occupied as it moves deeper into the interior of the nation. The objective is to stall the attack or slow it enough to where the Russians will suffer debilitating loses while they are still far east of the Dnieper River."

"Do we have enough operators on the ground there?"

Burgess thought over his answer first, then said, "If we go live with Red Coal Carpet, the U.S. Army will move a company of scout helicopters already serving in NATO into Ukraine, again under the auspices of Partnership for Peace. These helos will be used for laser targeting. A small unit

461

of Rangers will also be added for security at the Joint Operations Center. This will bring American and British forces in the country to somewhere in the neighborhood of four hundred fifty troops.

"I do believe it will be enough for this conflict, for one key reason. We are only there to support the Ukrainian Air Force, and the Russians will, to put it bluntly, kill the Ukrainian Air Force. I'm sorry, I don't see any other scenario. Our men with their laser designators will have a target-rich environment, but they won't have enough birds in the sky flying around with air-to-ground ordnance. The Ukrainian helos and strike fighters will be destroyed. I'm afraid putting more men on the ground is not going to help the situation."

Ryan said, "I'm going to have to let key members of Congress know about this. It's not exactly within the scope of Partnership for Peace."

"No, sir, it is not," Burgess agreed.

Ryan looked at the clock on the wall. "Okay, I'm authorizing Operation Red Coal Carpet, so that if the Russian invasion begins, our forces on the ground will have the authorizations in place to begin operations. Bob, come to me with whatever you need, whenever you need it. Mary Pat and Jay will provide DoD with anything they can, as well."

"Yes, sir."

Ryan closed the meeting by saying, "There are four hundred fifty American and British troops in the field who are going to need our support and our prayers in the next few days. Let's see that they get plenty of both."

55

Thirty years earlier

CIA analyst Jack Ryan had spent much of the day on the frigid streets of Zug, Switzerland, following around SIS counterintelligence officer Nick Eastling as he went to each location visited by David Penright in the days before his death. They'd been to his hotel room, the car rental office where he'd picked up his Mercedes, and a pair of restaurants he'd visited.

At each location, Ryan prodded Eastling to ask whether Penright had been seen with anyone else. In most cases, other than the restaurant where he'd met with Morningstar on the night of Penright's death and the bar where he'd apparently tried and failed to pick up the German woman, he'd been alone.

It was evening before they finally arrived at the MI6 safe house where David Penright had worked in Zug. It was a few minutes north of the town proper, set on a hill in a residential neighborhood of two-story half-timbered homes with small gardens in front and large fenced-in backyards. Ryan and Eastling came through the front door and greeted the rest of the counterintelligence team, who'd been working here much of the day.

"Anything, Joey?" Eastling asked the first man in the living room. Ryan saw the home had been all but disassembled. Floorboards had been prized up, wall paneling had been removed, sofa cushions looked as if they had been hacked apart.

"Nothing out in the open. He had some documents locked in the safe."

"What sort of documents?"

"All in German, of course. Look like internal transfers at RPB. A printout from a dot-matrix printer. Numbered accounts, transfer amounts, that sort of thing. Pages and pages of the bloody things."

Eastling said, "He hadn't shared anything with Century House since he arrived. He met with Morningstar the evening he was killed. Might be that he received them from Morningstar, then brought them back here before going out again to the bar."

Joey replied, "Well, if he did, he followed proper protocol. Good job he didn't get caught with RPB documents on his body when the ambulance took him to the morgue."

Eastling acknowledged this with a nod. "Keep looking."

It was a nice enough house, with modern furnishings and a fifty-inch front-projection TV set in the living room. There was a VHS player next to it, with a library of cassettes on a bookshelf alongside the television. One of the counterintelligence officers was systematically going through each video, watching it in fast-forward.

Nick and Jack walked into the kitchen now, and here they found a man pouring cereal out of boxes into bowls, then running his hands through the muesli and corn flakes, searching for any hidden items. A third SIS man crawled on the kitchen floor with a flashlight in his hand, checking the seams in the tile for any sign they had been moved or prized up.

While all this was going on, Ryan asked Eastling, "Why didn't Penright just stay here? Why did he go to a hotel?"

Eastling shrugged. "He wanted to be close to a lobby bar. He wanted a place where he could bring girls home."

"Do you know that, or are you guessing that?"

"As I said, David Penright isn't the first dead officer I've had to investigate. So far, everything I've seen and learned today goes along with my assumptions that this was an accident. Look, Jack. I guess you want this to be some sort of a KGB hit, but the KGB doesn't rub out our officers in the streets of Western Europe."

Before Jack could respond, the phone in the small home office rang. One of Eastling's men took it and then handed it over to his boss.

While Nick Eastling took the call, Ryan wandered out onto the balcony over the backyard. There was a nice view here, looking down across the town and farther on, over Lake Zug itself. Beyond the black water, the far bank of the lake was visible as twinkling streetlights and glowing windows in buildings. The cold, clear air gave Jack the feeling he could reach out across the water and touch the distant shore, although it was surely miles away.

The British counterintelligence officer met Jack outside a few minutes later. In his hands were two bottles of Sonnenbräu beer from the fridge. It was too cold to drink beer outside, Ryan thought, but he took one of the bottles and sipped it as he turned his attention back to the lake below.

Eastling said, "Just got off the phone with London. A medical examiner, one of ours, examined Penright's body this morning in Zurich. No puncture marks, like those made from a hypodermic needle.

We know we'll find alcohol in his blood, but toxicology on anything else will take weeks. From the ME, however, it certainly doesn't look like he had been in any way drugged or poisoned."

Ryan said nothing.

Eastling looked out over the yard. "He got himself drunk enough to trip and fall on the street. Bad show for a man in the field."

"He took his job seriously, you know," Ryan said. "You make him out to be some sort of a clown. I didn't know him well, but he deserves better than this treatment you're giving him."

Eastling said, "He wasn't a clown. He was a man walking on the fine edge for so long he turned to drink and casual encounters to distance himself from the danger. It happens to the best of them, the traveling officers. I am sympathetic to the stresses and strains of what they have to deal with, but at the end of the day, my job is to make sure I have answers."

The two men looked out over Lake Zug and toward the lights on the far side of the bay. It was beautiful; Jack could imagine Penright sitting here just days earlier, planning his next move with Morningstar.

Ryan said, "So that's it, then? We just go home?"

"That's up to London. If Sir Basil is going to send someone else to town to make contact with Morningstar, then we might stick around another day or so to report our findings directly to —"

Ryan's eyes were on the far shore of Lake Zug, and near where he was looking, a brilliant flash of light appeared, casting a glow all the way up to a patch of low clouds hanging over the shore. The light seemed like it was on the land, not over water, but it was hard to tell immediately. Five seconds after the flash, a low rumble reached the balcony where the two men were standing.

466

Eastling had been looking in the same direction. "That's an explosion."

Ryan peered into the distance. "I think I see a fire." He ran back into the flat, asked the men working there if they had seen any binoculars in the safe house. One of the men pulled a decorative but functional brass telescope off a tripod in the office, and the others chuckled as he offered it to Ryan.

The American snatched it and ran back out to the balcony.

He struggled to bring the big telescope up to his eye. Eastling just stood there and watched him.

On the far shore, almost lost in the twinkling of lights from the buildings, he could definitely make out a fire. It was a few blocks from the shoreline, higher on a hill.

"What is that place over there?"

"That's Rotkreuz," Eastling said.

"The same place the banker Tobias Gabler was killed the other day."

"As a matter of fact, yes. It is."

Jack lowered the telescope. "Let's go."

"Go? Over there? Why?"

"*Why?* Are you serious?"

"Ryan, what is it you think just happened?"

"I don't know, but I'm going to get a closer look."

"You are being ridiculous."

"Then why don't you hang out here at the safe house and help your men search through the corn flakes? I'm heading over there." Ryan turned and left the balcony. He scooped up off the table a set of keys belonging to one of the rented cars and then shot out the door of the suite.

As he stuck the key in the lock, he heard someone hurrying down the gravel behind him. It was Eastling. "I'll drive."

467

It took them nearly a half-hour to get around the lake to Rotkreuz. As they entered the little village, there was no mistaking which way to go. A structural fire raged fifty feet in the air. Eastling merely had to keep his car pointed toward the glow and, despite being rerouted by hastily erected roadblocks designed to clear the way for emergency vehicles, he managed to park near enough to the scene so that he and Ryan had to walk only a few blocks.

Jack and Nick worked their way forward through a large crowd of onlookers across the parking lot from the blaze. Jack could feel the heat on his face as he neared the fire.

The building looked like it must have been a beautiful restaurant; there was an open seating area with fire pits to keep the patrons warm on chilly nights, and behind this sat a long structure with floor-to-ceiling windows that afforded the patrons of the restaurant amazing views of Lake Zug. A sign high above the parking lot read "Restaurant Meisser." But now the building was fully engulfed in flames, the windows were broken, and the wrought-iron tables and chairs around the fire pits had all been knocked aside so firefighters and other first responders could pull victims from the carnage.

There were bodies under black plastic sheets in the parking lot. Jack counted at least ten, but it was hard to tell in the wildly flickering firelight and the multicolored strobes of the emergency vehicles.

Dozens of firefighters still worked on the fire, hoses attacked it from a dozen directions, and police kept the crowd back with tape, shouts, and the occasional shove. Someone in the crowd said gas lines were feeding the fire, and then, minutes after Ryan and

Eastling arrived, the entire tapeline was moved back to the opposite side of the street, in fear of a larger explosion.

While Jack and Nick stood there on the edge of the light from the roaring flames, Jack noticed a cluster of Swiss police cars on a street corner on the opposite side of the taped-off parking lot. Two police officers had a bearded man in handcuffs, and they walked him to one of the vehicles and placed him in the back. He looked to be a few years younger than Jack, but from this distance Jack couldn't be sure.

Jack said, "Wonder what that's all about."

Nick started walking that way. "I suppose we could go find out."

By the time they made it around the parking lot, the police car with the man in back had raced out of the parking lot and down the hill, out of view.

Two officers stood by another car at the edge of the police line. Nick Eastling walked up to them and said, *"Entschuldigung. Sprechen Sie Englisch?"*

In German, one of the officers replied, "Yes, but we are busy."

"I understand. I was only wondering why that man was arrested."

"He wasn't arrested. He was detained for questioning. He had been in the building, but he left right before the explosion. He wasn't a patron, he just walked through, then exited through the back. After the explosion, one of the waiters saw him in the crowd and pointed him out."

"I see."

"Were you a witness to the explosion?"

"No, I'm sorry, I didn't see a thing."

Eastling and Ryan turned away and pushed back into the crowd. They left the area a few minutes later, returning to the SIS safe house so Eastling could contact Century House via the STU phone. MI6 would need to pressure the Swiss for information on the crime, the detainment of the bearded young man, and any other information that could be more readily obtained at a higher level.

Eastling dropped Ryan back at the hotel on his way to the safe house. Once again the American CIA analyst felt as though he was being pushed aside by the counterintelligence officer, but he knew he wouldn't have anything meaningful to do at the safe house, so he didn't press the issue.

56

Delta Force officer Barry Jankowski, call sign Midas, had survived the battle for the Lighthouse in Sevastopol, Ukraine, along with two of his operators and eleven other Americans. But unlike most of the security officers and CIA men who'd made it out of the Lighthouse alive, Midas and his boys were still in country.

For the past three days Midas had been in Cherkasy, a mid-sized city in Ukraine's heartland, and the location of a large Ukrainian Army base that was home to the nation's 25th Airborne Brigade.

Midas had lost friends at the Lighthouse, but like most military special operations personnel, he was not given time to grieve for them in the field. Yesterday afternoon, Jankowski had been a lieutenant colonel. But a call from Fort Bragg last night informed him he had been promoted to colonel, and not only was he the highest-ranking member of Joint Special Operations Command here in Ukraine, he was now the senior command authority of all U.S. and British forces in Ukraine for Operation Red Coal Carpet.

Midas had spent seventeen years in the military, first as a Ranger enlistee, then as a Mustang — a term given to an enlisted man who joins the officer ranks. He moved over to Delta six years prior, starting out as an assaulter and then graduating into the elite of the elite, a Delta Force recce troop.

Most U.S. military units used the term "recon" as an abbreviation for reconnaissance, but the founder of Delta Force, "Chargin' " Charlie Beckwith, had served as an exchange officer with the United Kingdom's 22nd SAS Regiment in the 1960s. Beckwith had adopted many traits of the SAS into Delta, and Brits called reconnaissance "recce" — pronounced "wrecky" — so Delta followed suit.

Midas came from a Polish family; he grew up speaking both English and Polish at home, and he'd learned some Russian in college. He'd spent much of the past year here in Ukraine, and with his vast experience and understanding of the landscape, the enemy, and the Ukrainian military, he had been tapped by the Pentagon to lead operations on the ground.

In Sevastopol, Midas had run an Advance Force Operations cell, meaning he had direct control over only three other Delta men. For a lieutenant colonel, this was highly unusual, but given his language skills and his unique knowledge of the region, he had gone where he was needed. Now, just days later, he found himself in control of a force of 429 men. There were sixty operators and support personnel from Delta's B Squadron, along with men from 5th Special Forces Group and 10th Special Forces Group, as well as a unit of British SAS commandos.

He also had a U.S. Army Ranger rifle platoon of forty men here on the base to provide site security.

Besides these assets, he had a few transport and

scout helicopters from the 160th Special Operations Aviation Regiment, three Black Hawks, and six tiny MH-6 Little Birds for transporting his forces around.

And an hour earlier, Midas received delivery of a large addition to his air support. Four CIA Reaper drones flown out of Boryspil International Airport near Kiev were tasked to JSOC, and several Army helos arrived here in Cherkasy from Poland. These helos would be used principally for laser targeting, but Midas had been thinking outside the box on this, and he had sent word that he wanted one flight crew in particular to drop in on his operations center as soon as they settled into their new quarters.

Obviously, the Americans and the Brits were not alone. The Ukrainian military was in place along the border and held in reserve, and they were expecting a fight, but Midas was painfully aware how unprepared for it they were. He had spent the past month receiving reports of the poor state of equipment, training, and, most important, morale in the Ukrainian military. There had been widespread desertions and credible reports of spies and sabotage. More debilitating than this was a general sense from Ukrainian leaders far away from the border that if fighting started, NATO would swoop in and help them out, or at least enact painful sanctions against Russia that would force Volodin to stop his attack.

Midas had been a war fighter long enough to know the suits in Kiev were fooling themselves.

He had spent the morning in secure communications to individual Ukrainian commanders he knew around the region, stressing the fact that the 429 U.S. and UK troops here in country were pretty much all the help Ukraine was going to get.

His most recent conversation, which had ended just a minute earlier, went much like all the others. A Ukrainian artillery colonel told Midas, "If you know the Russians are coming, you need to attack them before they cross the border."

Midas patiently replied that he and his 429 weren't going to be invading Russia in this lifetime.

The colonel replied, "The Russians will attack with a few rusty tanks. They will fly overhead and drop bombs on airports we aren't even using. They will sail their Black Sea fleet around and shell our beaches."

"They will do more than that," Midas replied somberly.

The colonel shouted back at the American, "Then I will die on my feet with a gun in my hand!"

Midas wondered about the last time the artillery colonel had held a firearm in his hand, but he didn't ask.

As a JSOC officer, Barry "Midas" Jankowski had fought in Iraq and Afghanistan, and he had advised militaries in the Philippines and Colombia.

Ukraine was the largest country he had ever operated in, with the biggest GDP and the most educated population.

But he'd never been in a more hopeless situation. His 429 men and women were pitted against somewhere in the neighborhood of 70,000 Russians poised near the border, ready to invade Ukraine. When the Russians invaded, his one and only hope was to use his few troops to assist the Ukrainians to be a force multiplier, not so Ukraine could win. Not so they could beat the Russians back over the border.

No. Their only chance at survival — *his only chance at survival* — hinged on slowing the Russians down, giving them more casualties and headaches than they bargained for in the hopes they would quit the attack.

He'd spent the past day setting up his Joint Operations Center here in Cherkasy with all the communications and intelligence personnel he needed to keep an unblinking eye on eastern Ukraine.

Midas did not control the CIA nonofficial cover assets in Ukraine, they were not part of Joint Special Operations Command, but he did have one more arrow in his quiver. At the Lighthouse he'd run into three men: Clark, Chavez, and Caruso. When he'd learned they weren't CIA, DIA, NSA, or any other official acronym, he'd been ready to kick them back out the gate of his secure location, but all three of the men had proven their abilities and their allegiance in the battle for the CIA compound. After the air evac from Sevastopol, John Clark had told Midas he and his guys would be returning to Kiev, where they were watching over the organized-crime group that had infiltrated the country on behalf of the FSB. Clark also told Midas they were ready to help him, if and when he needed it.

It wasn't exactly by the book — hell, Midas had no authority whatsoever to ask American civilians to assist him in his combat operations. But Midas liked knowing he had a few operators outside the military and intelligence chain of command he could call on if necessary.

Midas had a master's degree in military science

from American Military University. He'd learned much in his higher education that he'd found applicable on the ground, but he'd never found anything in school that more reflected the real world of combat than a quotation he'd picked up studying a nineteenth-century German field marshal named Helmuth von Moltke.

Moltke said, "Strategy is a system of expedients."

Midas himself was from West Virginia, and he preferred plain talk, so his translation of Moltke's quote was "A man's gotta do what a man's gotta do."

When the Russians attacked, Midas expected things would turn unconventional very fast. Moltke's more famous quote, "No battle plan survives contact with the enemy," was another military truism. Once the Russians kicked off this party, Midas expected the meticulously planned Operation Red Coal Carpet to devolve into a situation where he and his team here in the Cherkasy JOC would just start winging it the best they could.

Chief Warrant Officers Two Eric Conway and Andre Page walked across the Ukrainian military base on a bright and cool spring morning. They didn't know their way around and neither of the men could read the Cyrillic signs, but they'd been told to head to the end of the helicopter flight line, turn left, and then keep walking till they saw the gate with the Americans guarding it.

Walking around base without their helmets, the two-man flight crew of the U.S. Army's OH-58D Kiowa Warrior looked very much like two regular Army infantry soldiers. They did not wear flight suits; instead, the men wore tan, gray, and green uniforms under their SAPI (Small Arms Protective Insert) steel plates. They carried U.S. Army-issued Colt M4 rifles on slings around their chests along with Beretta M9 pistols on their hips, and extra rifle magazines hung in ammo racks over their body armor.

They passed a group of Ukrainian helicopter maintenance men who stopped them and shook their hands. None of these guys spoke much English, but they seemed happy to have the American forces here. Dre was black, which was about as rare here as Eric and Dre running into a Ukrainian back at their base in Kentucky, and consequently he drew fascinated stares from the young Ukrainian men.

Eric and Dre were polite, but they broke away from the group as quickly as possible, because their CO had ordered them over to a building on the opposite side of the base.

And they had no idea why.

After fighting in Estonia, Chief Warrant Officers Conway and Page returned to Poland, where they served in European Command. Their unit was part of a NATO detachment that trained with the Poles, and it was as interesting an assignment as either of them needed after the stress of combat in Estonia.

But just yesterday their company received the surprise news that they'd be heading to Ukraine. They assumed it had something to do with the attack on the Partnership for Peace office in Sevastopol that was all over the news, but other than a ton of idle conjecture by themselves and the other men in their company, they didn't have any real idea what they would be doing here.

And they weren't given much time to think about it. For the past twenty-four hours they had been prepping for their mission, and then they and their entire company, helicopters included, flew over from Poland in the back of two C-17s, arriving here in Cherkasy just an hour earlier.

During their walk across the Ukrainian base, Eric and Dre argued playfully about what was in store for them on the other side of the base. Neither thought they were in any trouble, but the fact they'd been separated from the rest of their company, just when everyone else was getting situated in the barracks and bedding down for a little relaxation after twenty-four hours of constant movement, was somewhat annoying.

They found the gate with the Americans, and they entered an area protected by men they recognized to be members of the 75th Ranger Regiment. They were elite soldiers, and Conway and Page normally didn't have much direct contact with them, so Regiment studs were something of a novelty to see.

They next made their way across a row of small barracks with large garage-type doors that were open to let in fresh air. Inside one of the barracks, Conway and Page spied a group of men in camouflage with nonregulation haircuts and beards. They were unboxing some of their equipment, and one look at the haircuts and the gear told the two twenty-six-year-olds that these were Army Special Forces.

Page leaned over to Conway as they passed by. "Eric, first we walked by Regiment dudes, now we're walking by Green Berets. I guess we're working our way up."

Conway just laughed, but he was genuinely curious about just how far into the inner sanctum of the "special" side of the Army they were heading.

Soon they arrived at the last building on the base. It was protected by another group of Rangers, who read Conway's and Page's name tapes and called someone over the radio. A moment later they were led into a hallway and told to knock on the last door on the right.

Nervously, Conway and Page looked at each other, then Conway rapped on the metal door.

"Enter," came a booming voice from inside.

They entered, then found themselves facing a half-dozen men in civilian attire. The average age of these guys looked like it was about ten years older than the Green Berets back in the hangar, and they all wore scruffy beards and different types of adventure-wear clothing. Each one of the men also wore a pistol on his hip, and both Conway and Page noticed that the guns were individual to the men, and this told the young warrant officers that these guys were likely JSOC, Joint Special Operations Command operators. This would mean they were either SEAL Team Six or Delta. Either way, neither Conway nor Page had a clue what they were doing here.

"Come on in, gents. Thanks for dropping by," one of the bearded men said.

In the U.S. Army, one does not "drop by." They had been ordered over here by their CO, but if these guys wanted to be informal about this, Conway and Page were happy to oblige.

The man who clearly was the team leader introduced himself and his men. "I'm Midas, this is Boyd, this is Greyhound, these guys in back are Arctic, Beavis, and Slammer."

Both Page and Conway thought the same thing at the same time. *These dudes are fucking Delta Force!*

Midas said, "It's an honor to meet you guys. I read the AAR about that piece of flying you did up in eastern Estonia. They say you two jokers grabbed a road map and flew into disputed territory so low that Russian radar thought you were driving a taxi. Then you took out a half-dozen T-90s."

Conway knew the after-action review of his operation in Estonia had been classified by the military. Still, it was no surprise these black operators had read it.

Conway beamed with pride but replied, "Thank you, sir. But to be honest, we had some luck."

Page added, "We also had some Apaches."

The entire room burst into laughter.

"I love it," Midas said, and he read Page's name tape. "Mr. Page, what do you say? Is Mr. Conway as good a pilot as that AAR made him out to be?"

Dre Page nodded. "I hate to admit it in front of him, but he's badass, sir."

Midas said, "That's good enough for me. He's the one flying you around, so I figure you are the man to ask about his abilities."

Conway said, "Page does all of the targeting, but he does some flying, too."

Midas pointed to a sofa against the wall, and the two Chief Warrant Officers sat down. Midas walked over to a cooler on a table, opened it, and pulled out some bottles of iced Slavutich beer, a local brand. He popped off the caps on the edge of the table, then walked them over to the two wide-eyed young men.

"Welcome to Ukraine," he said as he handed over the beers. He went back to the cooler and got one for himself. He took a swig, and only then did the helo crew follow suit. Conway thought this was really weird, and he wondered if he was on some new American Forces Network TV version of *Candid Camera.*

Midas sat on top of a wooden table next to his men. The other guys were loading rifle magazines with bullets from ammo cans. Conway and Page noticed the rifles lined up along the wall. They were HK416s, which looked much like their Colt M4s and fired the same caliber bullet, but the Delta Force rifles were far superior.

Midas said, "You're probably wondering why you're here."

Conway was the quieter of the two men, so Dre answered. "Yes, sir."

Midas said, "Some general in Washington has seen fit to give me command authority over this operation in Ukraine. With the arrival of your company, I now have under my command four hundred twenty-nine men." He held a hand up quickly. "Correction. Four hundred eight men and twenty-one women. There are some female intel support, as well as Flight Ops personnel. There is one female pararescue Black Hawk pilot, too, I hear."

"Saw her this morning. She's pretty hot," mumbled the Delta man called Greyhound.

"Anyway, if you hadn't guessed yet, the Russians are coming over the border. Might be today, might be tomorrow, might not be for a week. But they are coming, and when they do, we'll have SOF teams up and down the region, not right at the border, but fifty or so miles inside. They are hooked up with SOFLAM laser designators, and they will mark targets for the Ukrainian Air Force to take out with air-to-ground ordnance. You follow me so far?"

Conway and Page both said, "Yes, sir."

Midas sighed. "Okay, best we get this out of the way. Do me a favor. Cut the 'sir' shit right now."

Conway and Page were regular Army. The idea of calling a man who was clearly a superior officer "Midas" made them both uncomfortable.

"Yes . . . Midas," Conway managed to say.

"We also just got your company of OH-58s. Now, the rest of your company will do the same thing as the SOF troops. That is, use laser designation to find and fix targets for the Ukrainian AF to finish. The other Kiowas will have Stinger missiles to give themselves some air defense capabilities."

"Okay," Conway said, unsure where this was going.

"But I want you guys to do something different. I want to load you boys up with Hellfires, so you can do some of the finishing yourselves."

"Yes, sir," Page said, holding his beer up high in salute.

Midas stared him down for a moment.

"Uh . . . I mean, Midas."

"Good. Our primary mission is to be lasing targets for the Ukrainians, but that's not good enough. I want to have the ability, in an in extremis situation, to operate independently of the Ukrainians."

Conway got it now. "I understand."

"We have Reaper drones from the CIA armed with Hellfires that we can call on targets. But I want my own bird in the air, you guys, to be ready to go places on the fly to attack targets when necessary. Can you do that for me?"

"Absolutely."

"As you might have guessed, I am not conven-

482

tional Army. You guys are in the conventional system, but I need pilots who can think unconventionally in this. From the AAR I read about the stunt you pulled in Estonia, I'm thinking you guys might be perfect as my hired gun up in the sky."

Conway said, "Whatever you need."

"Good to hear it."

Page said, "One question, Midas. Where will we be going?"

"That's going to be classified. Certainly not into the Crimea. Probably not to Donetsk, either. We'll let you know before takeoff, usually, but we just need you ready for a call from us. We'll talk to your CO and get you taken off the regular flight line so you can run your own op."

Eric and Dre finished their beers, shook the hands of the men in the room, and started to leave. Eric turned away from the door. He didn't know if he should push his luck, but he thought he was on a roll. "Um, Midas . . . Ukraine isn't a NATO member. I don't understand. Is our country really going to war for them?"

"Our country is not." He shrugged. "We are. Welcome to the dark side, boys."

57

Thirty years earlier
CIA analyst Jack Ryan awoke to a determined knock at his hotel room door in Zug, Switzerland. He looked at the clock on the bedside table and saw it was just after four a.m. He rolled quickly out of bed and unlatched the door; it was all the way open before it occurred to him that even though he was an analyst and not an operative, he *was* working in the field, and it might have been a good idea to look through the damn peephole before flinging open the door.

C'mon, Jack. Pay attention to what you're doing.

It was Nick Eastling in the hall, and Jack could immediately tell the man had been up for some time.

He could also tell something was wrong.

"What's going on?"

Eastling said, "I need to come in."

"Sure."

Eastling entered, and Jack shut the door behind him. Both men moved to chairs in a comically tiny sitting area.

Jack said, "You just getting back from the safe house?"

"Yeah. Been on the phone with Century House and contacts at the embassy in Zurich."

"What's going on?"

"The explosion tonight at the Restaurant Meisser.

There were fourteen dead."

Jack couldn't read the man's face. He looked simultaneously excited and confused.

Nick added, "One of the victims was Marcus Wetzel."

Jack cocked his head. "And he is . . . who, exactly?"

Eastling gave a long sigh. "You would find out soon enough, anyway. He was our source in the bank. He *was* Morningstar."

Ryan put his head in his hands. "Oh my God."

"Yeah. He was dining with another man, who survived. He identified the body."

Ryan stood. "You still think this was random?"

"I . . . obviously . . . Of course not. I'm no bloody fool, Ryan. Morningstar was murdered. I have to think it was the same actor who killed Tobias Gabler."

"I'm glad you've come around."

"Yeah, well, I've come around to the fact the bankers were murdered, but not David Penright."

"How can you be so certain of that?"

"Because German leftists wouldn't have much interest in David Penright, now, would they?"

"German leftists? What are you talking about?"

"One of the bodies found in the explosion in Rotkreuz was identified as a twenty-five-year-old German woman named Marta Scheuring. The location of her body was curious, it gave the Swiss reason to stop what they were doing and focus on her. She was found in the kitchen, near the gas lines, but she did not work in the restaurant. They are assuming she brought some sort of explosive into the place, but when she tried to set the timer, the bloody thing went off in her face."

Jack assumed there was more. "How do they know

485

she wasn't just looking for the john?"

"You mean the loo, don't you?"

"Yeah."

"Because coincidences like this don't occur. Marta Scheuring was closely affiliated with the Red Army Faction. She has two arrests in Germany for subversive acts. She lives in Berlin. They found her address with her identification in a backpack she'd left in an alley behind the Meisser."

Jack knew all about the RAF. He also knew they did not normally operate in Switzerland. "Why would RAF blow this restaurant up?"

Eastling shrugged. "I don't know. I *do* know I am heading to Berlin. Century House has been in contact with the German police. The Germans will raid her flat, and I will be there when it happens."

"What about the other guy?"

"What other guy?"

"The man the Swiss police picked up at the Meisser restaurant. The man who was taken away in the squad car?"

Eastling said, "Oh, him. He escaped custody. Picked his cuffs and wrestled a gun away from one of the cops. He cuffed the coppers together, back-to-back, around a light pole in the city center near the *Bahnhof.* Looks like he left on the train."

"Surely he was involved, too."

"Might have been. Probably RAF. Maybe I'll find out more in Berlin. As I said, I'm off in a few hours. You are welcome to join me, although I can't speak for the Germans. Might want to get that cleared with your home office."

Jack rubbed his eyes. "Two days ago you heard that a girl from Berlin was drinking with a British agent who was then killed, working on the same case where all these other people have been killed.

486

Now a German woman tied to RAF is also tied to the other deaths.

"Do you really think the death of David Penright was just a coincidence? Why not go back to the bar where Penright died and show them the picture of Marta and ask if it was the same woman?"

"We'll pass it on to the Swiss, who I am quite certain will do just that. But there are German girls all over the place. If Penright had not been chatting up a German, he would have been with an Aussie or a Kiwi or a Frenchie or some Swede. The girl in the bar doesn't matter."

Eastling continued, "We will go to Berlin, look at the RAF evidence there, and if it somehow should lead us back to David Penright's death, we will act accordingly. In the meantime, don't you bloody tell me how to do my job!"

Ryan said, "That's fine. Let's go. But I want to be involved in the exploitation of the intelligence found in the location in Berlin. I don't want to be standing on the sidelines."

"Not for me to say, Jack, old boy. Take it up with the Huns."

58

Present day

Tatiana Molchanova smiled into the camera as New Russia's six p.m. news began. Normally, the evening news here, like every evening news program on earth, began by reporting on the day's events, but Valeri Volodin had shown up right before the start of the newscast, and he'd walked himself onto the set and sat down in what he considered to be his chair.

So the camera faded in with a close-up shot of Molchanova, she stretched an introduction of the president out a little while an audio technician miked Volodin on her left, then she turned and greeted the president with a wide but not overtly unprofessional smile.

Molchanova had no questions for him; his arrival had been a complete surprise, and the producers in her earpiece seemed to be arguing with one another about how to start his interview.

She would have to wing this segment, but she could do it, because she was a pro. Plus, she had a strong suspicion the president wouldn't give her too much opportunity for improvisation.

"Mr. President, there have been some dramatic events within the borders of our largest neighbor to the west. What comments do you have about the attacks in Ukraine that seemed to be so clearly designed to threaten Russian supporters there?"

Volodin was like a coiled spring released. "Not just supporters, Tatiana Vladimirovna. I remind you that millions of Russian citizens live within the borders of Ukraine.

"The attack against my good friend Oksana Zueva and the bombing in Donetsk were both clearly by the hands of pro-nationalist guerrilla forces supported by Western intelligence agencies. Add to this the attack by the American CIA in Sevastopol. These were *provokatsii!*" Provocations! "The enemies of Russia are trying to draw us out into a fight. We have kept our disagreements peaceful and within the diplomatic realm, and they did not know how to handle this level of sophistication, so they resorted to bloodshed."

Molchanova recognized her cue. She asked a vague question about how actions in Ukraine affected the Motherland.

Volodin did not miss a beat. "There are fifty million people in Ukraine, one-sixth of whom are ethnic Russians. And the Crimean peninsula is vital to Russian security interests. That is obvious to even the most basic student of international, economic, and military affairs.

"It is home of the Black Sea fleet. There are oil and gas pipelines to Europe, Russia's vital market, and military highways to the West that are important to our security interests."

Volodin continued, "Ukraine belongs in our sphere of influence. As I see it, there are two threats to our nation. Only two. These are terrorism and the lawless criminality of the West on our borders.

"Our enemies would dismember us, and we

know this, so we keep them outside our borders, but that is not enough. Eastern European countries have become slaves of America and Europe, and we must protect ourselves from them, no matter the cost.

"We have reduced terrorism in Russia to a large degree. Ethnic divisions within, along with the criminal element, most of whom were of ethnic minority, have been controlled to a large measure. We will need to continue our struggle, to promote the strength of our law enforcement and judicial system at home, and increase the scope of our security services abroad. There is no other way to survive.

"But looking into what is going on in Ukraine, I see we not only share interests with our Slavic neighbors, but we also share threats.

"The Ukrainian nationalists in power in Kiev are just such a threat."

Volodin stared into the lens of the camera. Tatiana Molchanova sat meekly to the side. The president had clearly forgotten he was in an interview for the time being. "No rogue regime will be allowed to exist peacefully on our borders. This is just the thing I have been trying to protect the Motherland from.

"The pervasive crime and lawlessness in Ukraine has shown me that the Russian citizens there must be protected, and this protection must be actual, and not some new line drawn on a map, which will not serve anyone's interests."

He paused, so Tatiana Molchanova filled the dead air with her voice: "Can you tell us what steps your government is prepared to take to alleviate the threats along our border?"

"I have ordered our military to prepare a series

of small-scale security actions to protect Russia's interests in the Crimea, and Russia's population who live in eastern Ukraine. I cannot go into any operational details, of course." He smiled. "Not even for you, Tatiana Vladimirovna."

She smiled back.

"But everyone should remember this is nothing more than a mission of *mirotvorsty.*" Peacemaking.

Tatiana said, "Ukraine is not a NATO member state, but they are a member of the Partnership for Peace, which means there is some training and coordination with NATO forces. Do you expect this to cause trouble in any security operation?"

Volodin said, "We were NATO members until a year ago, but I saw the folly of this. How could we continue in NATO, an organization that was set up for the express purpose of defeating us?

"NATO is not so much of a threat. Most European nations are completely reasonable. But America is a concern, and I will give you an example of why. They have an obsession for anti-ballistic missiles. This was started by Ronald Reagan, and it has continued for thirty years. The Americans want these missiles only for one reason. To cloak themselves in safety for an inevitable battle. A battle they plan on starting.

"Now we have been spared President Ryan's hyper-use of force in the past years, only because our leadership was weak and America enjoyed setting all the terms for us. As long as we were compliant, they were kind. A master who pets a lazy cat.

"But we have privileged interests in our region, and America would do well to remember we will protect those privileged interests."

"What do you consider to be Russia's privileged

interests?"

"The neighboring post-Soviet nations where ethnic Russians live. It is my responsibility to guarantee they are protected."

Volodin turned to the camera. "And to NATO, and especially to the Americans. I will remind you this is our backyard." He pointed a finger at the camera. "You have been playing in our backyard, and we let it go. But now I will warn you to stay out of our backyard."

Molchanova struggled to come up with her next question, but she needn't have bothered, because Volodin lowered his pointed finger and continued talking to the camera.

"Ukrainians should understand that we love your country, we are your best neighbors. We don't want to remove your flag or your anthem. I only want to address the question of Ukraine's border. The Crimea is historically Russian — everyone knows this. It will be for the good of both nations for both of us to have the same rights, the same laws, the same bright future."

Tatiana asked the next question with some trepidation. She was not certain if she was being pulled along into the question, but Volodin had made the follow-up so obvious, there was no way she could pass it up. "So, Mr. President, are you saying the Crimea is the objective of the security operation?"

Volodin did not answer at first. He seemed caught off guard. "One thing at a time, Miss Molchanova. We must see how our peacekeeping forces are treated. If the terrorism dies down . . . of course we will leave." He said it with his hands up, as if he was trying to insinuate Molchanova had been the one promoting the takeover of

Ukrainian territory.

The opening attacks of the invasion began as the president spoke on television. The late-afternoon start of the action had the desired effect of surprising the Ukrainian forces near the border. They did expect an attack from the east — but they did not expect one that began at dinnertime.

Long-range missile batteries devastated Ukrainian defensive positions, and fighter bombers flew inland to destroy airfields in the eastern Crimea. Tanks rolled west over the border, much as they had done in Estonia, but here they met more resistance in the form of the Ukrainian T-64s. The older Ukrainian tanks were not nearly the quality of the Russian T-90s, but they were plentiful, and most of them were well dug in or were in hardened bunker positions.

Pitched battles of tanks and Grad multiple rocket launcher system systems on both sides of the line continued for the first hours of the conflict, and as the Russian armor crossed deeper into Ukraine, Ukrainian howitzers were brought to bear. Russian MiGs and Sukhois controlled the skies, however, and they took out the gun emplacements just as fast as they could arrive overhead.

The Ukrainians also had a significant number of self-propelled 152-millimeter artillery vehicles — a Russian-built mobile howitzer named after the Msta River, and these were well hidden and mobile enough to present a problem for the T-90s, but the Ukrainian generals kept the majority of this valuable resource in reserve, all but condemning the forward-deployed Msta units to destruction by Russian Kamov helicopter gunships and MiG-29s.

By nine p.m. the Ukrainian cities of Sverdlovs'k and Krasnodon, both just miles from the Russian border, were taken with barely a shot fired within their city limits, and Mariupol, on the Sea of Azov, fell by ten-fifteen.

At midnight, a flight of six huge Antonov An-70 troop transport aircraft left Russian territory over the Sea of Azov; they crossed into Ukrainian airspace minutes later. On board each aircraft were between two hundred and three hundred troops. Most of them were members of the 217th Guards Airborne Regiment of the 98th Guards Airborne Division, but there were also several hundred GRU Spetsnaz forces in the mix.

The flight of air-transport aircraft was supported by fighter jets and radar-jamming equipment, and when they flew over Sevastopol, Russian ships in the Black Sea also provided defense for their countrymen overhead with their surface-to-air missiles.

The Ukrainians engaged the aircraft with a flight of Su-27s, but all four were shot down over the sea, two by Russian fighters and two more by surface-to-air missiles.

The Russians lost five fighters of their own, but all six An-70s made it to their drop zones.

The paratroopers leapt into the night from the Antonovs and landed all over the southern tip of the Crimean peninsula.

By half past one Russia had 1,435 lightly armed but well-trained troops on the ground in Sevastopol; they attacked two Ukrainian garrisons and destroyed several small anti-air batteries in the center of the city.

If the Ukrainians didn't know why the Russians dropped troops in Sevastopol that evening, they would know soon enough. Across the Black Sea, the small port of Ochamchira in the autonomous nation of Abkhazia had been the makeshift home of a flotilla of Russian ships, on board of which some five thousand Russian marines had been living for several days. As soon as the An-70s took off from their base in Ivanovo, Russia, the flotilla set sail for Sevastopol. They would not arrive till the middle of the following day, but this would give the paratroopers and Spetsnaz forces the time they needed to completely control the neighborhoods around the port.

While the Russian forces spread out from drop zones in the Crimea, tanks and other armor rolled deeper into eastern Ukraine. The Russians had significantly better night-vision equipment than the Ukrainians, and their tanks would use this to press on through the entire night, catching the enemy blind and panicked. Although the invasion itself had been no surprise, the Ukrainian leadership recognized in hours that their generals had misjudged the speed, the tactics, and the utter intensity of the fight that the Russians were bringing over the border.

59

There were a lot of morning joggers in London, not as many as in D.C., but considering how miserable the weather had been here this spring, Jack Ryan, Jr., was surprised just how many men and women he saw lacing up their shoes to get some dawn cardio exercise in the elements.

Usually, however, Jack saw the majority of the runners during the home stretch of his morning cardio. He liked to hit it very early, before the other joggers were out, as this gave him a certain sense of accomplishment that he never felt when he got a late start to his day.

But this morning was different. Yes, he was up early — it was just after six and he'd already run several miles. But he wasn't feeling the normal sense of exuberance that came along with the workout. It was wet and cold, and he was tired, and his head hurt a little from all the ale he drank the night before.

After returning from his wasted trip to Corby to meet a man once called Bedrock, he'd gone to a pub near his flat in Earl's Court. He'd downed two orders of fish-and-chips and several pints of ale. Mercifully, no one noticed him or even talked to him at all in the pub, but on his way back to his place on Lexham Gardens he'd detoured around several blocks, making a winding, backtracking hour-long surveillance-detection run until the early morning, and he was almost certain an unmarked panel truck had passed three different times.

He lay in bed for hours wondering who the hell was tailing him, and now it was half past six and his run was suffering greatly for the poor treatment he'd subjected his body to the evening before.

At mile three he ran through Holland Park, trying to sweat out some of the alcohol and fried food he'd put into his system. He circled a brown soccer pitch enshrouded in mist and then started up the long, steep hill to the Notting Hill neighborhood, following the Holland Walk, a narrow footpath that ran at the edge of the park along a brick garden wall of a long row of townhomes on his right.

He passed a pair of women running downhill with their high-end baby strollers, and they both gave him a smile.

Fifty yards behind them were two more joggers, big and broad men who crested the top of the hill at a leisurely pace and continued down the footpath in his direction.

Jack's mind wandered back to Oxley, the old British spy. Bedrock. Jack had not called his father to tell him he'd struck out in his attempt to get any information from the man. He tried to think of some new tactic to get the geezer to talk, but he hadn't come up with anything so far. He halfway wanted to just forget the entire affair and have his dad sic the CIA or some other organization on the man to try to find out what he knew about a shadowy, perhaps imaginary, assassin called Zenith.

He told himself he'd give himself another day to try to think of a new tactic, and then he would hand over his info on Bedrock.

The war had begun in Ukraine; Jack had seen this on the news this morning as he laced up his shoes. He had no way of knowing the United States had forces in country ready to engage, but he still knew his father would be working diplomatically and in the intelligence field against the Russian government's attack, so he knew finding out any details about Talanov could prove useful in resolving this crisis.

As he ascended the narrow footpath, Jack glanced at the faces and the hands of the two big joggers ahead. He had been trained to identify preassault indicators, small cues of trouble, and he did this automatically now, especially when he saw fit or muscular young men in his proximity.

The two men's hands were empty, and their faces showed no indications of any threat.

Ryan turned his attention back to his run; he forced himself to pick up his knees a little and to relax his shoulders. He still wasn't feeling it, but he decided he would make himself push through the funk and hit five miles, even if it killed him.

When the two approaching joggers were just fifteen yards away, his eyes automatically flicked back to them. He realized he was, once again, scanning them for preassault indicators, and he chastised himself for living his new existence wound up as tight as he had lived his previous life. Despite the situation he had gotten himself and Sandy Lamont into in Antigua, he told himself there was no reason to feel threatened wherever he went. He knew he'd drive himself crazy if he had to rule out every passerby as a potential danger for the rest of his —

What's that? Jack saw some sort of solid object under the pullover of the man running on the right; it pointed through the fabric as his right leg came up. It looked like a stick or some sort of club. Within two strides of noticing the abnormality, Jack saw the man on the right start to reach under his pullover.

Jack's body snapped into alert mode instantly; his muscles tightened and his senses went into overdrive.

The gait of the two men changed at five paces, a slight weight shift, and this was exactly one of the indicators Jack had been trained to recognize. He registered instantly that they were turning their bodies to cross into his path. He carried no weapon, and he knew his only chance was to use the speed and surprise of his own attack to his advantage, along with the momentum of the approaching men.

The man on the right pulled out a foot-long black rod, while the man on the left brought his arms up as though he was planning on simply tackling Jack off his feet.

Jack dove low, below the big onrushing bear hug. He executed a forward roll on the wet pavement, snapping back up to his feet as he spun around, and he charged back at his attackers. Jack's right fist shot out at the man with the club, who was just then spinning back toward him while raising his weapon high as if to strike.

Jack's right jab took the man straight in the nose, snapping his head back and causing him to drop his weapon onto the concrete path, where it made the unmistakable sound of iron clanging on the pavement before bouncing off the path and into the bushes.

The bear-hug man had stumbled, but he pushed himself off the garden wall, and now he charged at Ryan. Ryan didn't see a weapon at first, but the man came at him leading with his right arm outstretched, so Ryan felt certain the attacker must have had some sort of blade. Ryan swept his arm out, blocking the attacker's arm at a forty-five-degree angle, and only then did he see the glint of steel. It was a small hooked knife, no more than three inches in length, but it was deadly nonetheless.

Jack executed his hand-to-hand combat moves with the skill of a man who had trained in the art almost daily for years. He threw his back into the attacker while using both hands to control the weapon hand. He twisted the man's arm hard to the right, and simultaneously slammed his head back hard into the big man's nose, dropping him down to the pavement. The knife fell free, and Jack kicked it off into the grass.

Both of his foes were bleeding from the face, but he could see they were very much still in the fight.

The thug who had dropped his metal club swung a fist at Jack, but the fist missed its target when Jack dropped down onto a knee and then shot up at the man, closing the distance and impacting the man's chest. Both men tumbled to the wet grass between the footpath and the six-foot-high garden wall, and Jack made sure he came to rest on top. He immediately threw a punch into the man's already bloody face, and then he rolled away quickly and shot back up to a standing position because he knew the other thug was on his feet and behind him, where he could easily get an arm around his neck or slam a foot into his rib cage. Jack had chosen his tactic wisely, as the second attacker kicked into the air where Jack had been, and his wild miss caused him to fall on his back.

Jack charged the man on the ground mercilessly and drove his knee hard into the side of the man's head as the thug tried to get up. As soon as he felt the impact, Jack knew the man would be out cold, and his own knee would swell up like a grapefruit.

Now Jack was on his feet and both men were down. One was not moving, and the other was dazed, sitting up with his back against the garden wall.

Jack's adrenaline was through the roof, but he knew he needed answers. What the hell was this all about? Were these the same assholes who had been following him?

They were young, neither older than twenty-five, and they both had short brown hair and big muscles, but Jack could not tell anything else about who they were.

He started over to the man against the wall — he looked like the best bet for conversation at the moment, so he knelt down next to him and brought his fist up high.

A shrill whistle from across the park caused Jack to turn his head.

"You there! What are you doing?" Two police officers, one male and one female, ran across the soccer pitch fifty yards away. One had a whistle in her mouth, and the other shouted again.

"Get off of that man!"

Jack wasn't actually *on* anyone, but he stood up

501

and turned to the police officers.

He'd made it less than five feet in their direction when he felt an impact from behind, between his shoulder blades. The man who'd been sitting on the ground next to the wall had, apparently, leapt to his feet and shoved Ryan with all his might.

Jack was propelled across the path, and he fell face-first into the wet grass. He wasn't hurt, but he was mad at himself for turning his attention away from the men he'd been fighting.

From his hands and knees, he turned and looked back over his shoulder. To his surprise, both men were on their feet now, and they were running away, leaving their weapons behind.

They ran a few yards up the path and then climbed the brick garden wall and disappeared over the side. Jack was astonished that both men were able to stand, much less function well enough to escape. He started to go after them, but both of the police shouted for him to stop where he was.

The cops were still twenty-five yards away, and they didn't have guns; Jack could have easily climbed the stone fence and hopped into the backyard, and there was a good chance he could have run down the two injured men. But the cops had seen him, he lived here in the area, and it wouldn't be terribly difficult for them to find him.

Ryan let the two attackers go, and he put up his hands to show the cops he was no threat. He took a quick look down at his warm-ups and saw them covered with mud and streaked with blood from the gushing noses of the two thugs.

He took long breaths to calm himself down as the police turned him around and had him put his hands on the wall. Later, he was thankful for taking his time before speaking, because in that moment when he paused to control his heartbeat and his breathing, he also realized that if he told the police about the two weapons lying in the bushes, his father would find out that there had most likely been an attempt on his life.

Jack's dad would have the Secret Service rain down on him and form a diamond-shaped barrier of suits and guns all around him, and that would end his time here in England and seriously impede the younger Ryan's future plans.

No, that would not do.

He told the two police that he had been jogging and two men jumped him, demanding money. Muggings weren't uncommon here in London, although a six-thirty a.m. assault of a jogger who wasn't even carrying his wallet was admittedly unique.

Jack was taken to the Notting Hill station by the police after the two patrol officers quickly sorted out the fact the son of the President of the United States had just been attacked before their eyes. He was treated like a celebrity, and the most difficult part of the ordeal for Jack was the fact he had to tell no less than a dozen different people a dozen different times that he neither needed nor wanted to go to a hospital.

His knee was going to be good and sore, but it wasn't hospital sore. He just wanted to go home.

The police lectured him that he was a high-profile person and was entitled to security officers and, if only he would allow this, there would be people around to protect him the next time two muggers in a park chose him as a target.

Ryan thanked them, told them he'd think about it, and a little squad car delivered him back to his

503

flat at eight-thirty a.m. The two officers made him promise to call if he had any other problems, and he thanked them once again for their concern. He climbed the stairs to his flat, went inside, and triple-locked the door.

In the bathroom, he peeled out of his filthy clothes and turned on the shower, then sat down on the edge of his tub. While the bathroom steamed up, he thought about the implications of what had just happened.

He knew he needed to call Sandy and let him know. He'd probably get an "I told you so" from his boss, although Ryan was in no way convinced that what happened this morning had anything to do with his job.

If this *was* about the cases he was working on at Castor and Boyle, if that was the reason he had been followed here in the UK, then what had changed that had made them go from simple surveillance to an attack?

Nothing. Although the Galbraith case involved Gazprom, and some potentially dangerous characters, he'd been on the case for months, and he'd been taken off the case days earlier. If anyone wanted to hurt him for his involvement with Malcolm Galbraith, why the hell would they do it *now*?

Suddenly it occurred to him he had made one change to his routine in the past few days. He'd driven to Corby the previous afternoon in a failed attempt to talk to Victor Oxley.

Jack thought it over. Could that have been the reason he was attacked? It didn't make any sense to him, but nothing else did, either.

There was clearly no relationship between his Castor and Boyle work and the ex–British spy

Victor Oxley. In fact, he knew he had been under surveillance since before he'd ever heard the name Victor Oxley.

But he saw no other explanation. He'd gone to meet with a British spy who might have answers as to the past of the current head of Russian intelligence, and then, the very next day, two guys try to come after him with clubs and knives. Ryan did not believe in coincidence, and though he didn't have any answers, he knew who did.

Either Oxley was somehow behind what happened this morning or, at the very least, he might know why Ryan was attacked. As he climbed into the hot shower, he decided he needed to go back up to Corby and somehow get the surly bastard to talk.

Thirty minutes later, he was showered and changed and behind the wheel of his Mercedes, racing to the north.

60

The direct-action phase of Operation Red Coal Carpet began shortly before four a.m. on the second morning after the Russians crossed the border. Air-to-air battles, mostly between Russian Kamov-52 attack helicopters with sophisticated night-flying technology and Ukrainian Mi-24s that had no night-flying technology but were airborne anyway, had raged over the hilly forests east of Donetsk throughout the night. Below them, a twelve-man A-team from 5th Special Forces Group had positioned themselves on the roof of a press box above an abandoned soccer field in the town of Zuhres. From here, with their sophisticated optics, they could see twenty miles to the east, and range targets with their Special Operations Forces Laser Acquisition Marker at more than twelve miles.

It was a mostly clear night; the Americans watched the helicopters in the distance, pinpricks of light mostly, until fighting started, and flashes and streaks around the pinpricks created a futuristic show. This continued for hours. Occasionally, a fast mover would race overhead, and rarer still, a ground unit of Ukrainian troops would themselves fire artillery to the west, creating two sets of flashes on the horizon.

But shortly before four, the A-team spied a column of vehicles through their FLIR units moving unobstructed up Oblast State's H21 Highway. The American forces ID'd the vehicles as BTR-80 armored personnel carriers, which was armor in use by both Russian and Ukrainian forces. They radioed back to the JOC, letting them know they had possible targets inside the engagement zone, but they could not positively identify the vehicles as enemy, or "red," forces. The JOC tried to get positive confirmation from the Ukrainians, but the Ukrainian Army was fully engaged and in a state of chaos, and even the Air Force was slow to respond.

After fifteen minutes, the BTR-80s had approached to within eight miles of the Special Forces team. Midas ordered one of the patrolling Reaper drones in the area to overfly the column, and it quickly arrived overhead and began transmitting images back to the intelligence personnel at the JSOC facility.

The Reaper showed all vehicles to be wearing the Russian flag. The Reaper itself had two Hellfires on board, but Midas ordered his communications officer to relay the target mission to the Ukrainians again.

This time a pair of MiGs arrived on station quickly. They read the laser designation from the SOFLAM laser designator fired by the Americans, and soon the Ukrainians began raining Kh-25 air-to-ground missiles on the column that was moving up the highway.

The 5th Group A-team on the ground was pleased with the progress of the attack at first, but it soon became clear that the Ukrainian MiGs were dawdling too long over the target area. The team commander relayed his concerns through the JOC, but only half the Russian column had been destroyed when inbound missiles appeared from the horizon in the east. The 5th Group men had not seen the attacking aircraft, but figured them to be fast movers twenty miles or more away.

One of the Ukrainian fighters exploded into a fireball, and the second broke off the attack.

The 5th Group men lased two of the four remaining targets for the Reaper Hellfires to destroy, but two BTR-80s survived.

Operation Red Coal Carpet had begun with a very qualified success. Yes, they had destroyed six pieces of Russian armor well inside Ukraine, but it had come at the cost of one of Ukraine's most powerful air weapons. Midas knew this was an attrition rate that worked to the advantage of the Russians.

President Ryan met with Attorney General Murray in the Oval Office. Both men were tired from overwork, but both men also had the experience and discipline to know how to power through the exhaustion in times of national crisis.

Ryan had spent the morning in conversations with his military advisers, but by necessity he had kept a normal schedule. The Russian attack was getting a lot of attention in the United States, of course, but the White House was busy making statements about sanctions, protesting to the UN Security Council, even threatening to cancel U.S. attendance at the upcoming Winter Olympics in Russia, and other diplomatic "combat" that no one in the Ryan administration thought would do much of anything. But this front of diplomatic hand-wringing was necessary to hide the hard measures America was using to counter the Russian advance, the covert U.S. military action on the ground in eastern Ukraine.

President Ryan didn't have time for many Oval Office visits from cabinet-level staff who weren't in the U.S. military or members of the intelligence community, but he made time for Dan Murray. They sat across from each other and Ryan poured coffee for them both. "Dan," he said, "I really hope you have good news."

Murray could have simply told Ryan what he'd discovered or passed him a two-page brief on the investigation, but he knew his boss liked to get his hands on actual intelligence product, so the AG laid out a set of photographs on the coffee table.

Ryan picked the first one up. It was a color photo of surveillance quality of a young Hispanic-looking woman entering what appeared to be a 7-Eleven-type market.

Jack said, "This is the suspect in the Golovko poisoning?"

"Correct. Felicia Rodríguez."

Jack nodded and looked at the second picture. It appeared to have been taken in the same location, but a different person was passing through the doors. Male, short hair, a fit build, and he wore shorts and a white linen shirt. The photograph was surprisingly clear — it occurred to Jack that the prevalence and quality of CC cameras had been a hell of a boon for counterintelligence and law enforcement work in the past couple of decades.

"Who's he?"

"We don't have a real name yet, but using facial-recognition software we found that he entered the

United States on a private jet from London. His passport is Moldovan, the name on it is Vassily Kalugin, but it doesn't check out. The jet is registered to a shell corporation in Luxembourg. It doesn't check out, either."

Ryan understood the ramifications of all this. "He's a spook."

"Damn right he is."

"A Russian spook?"

"Don't know for sure, but we just put out a BOLO with his face and bogus passport info."

Ryan reached for the next photo.

This was a copy of a passport photo and page of a man named Jaime Calderón. "Another spook?"

"As a matter of fact, yes. He is a Venezuelan intelligence officer. Real name is Esteban Ortega. We've tracked him into the U.S. before, we've watched him, but we've never had anything solid on him."

"I still don't see anything solid here." Ryan held up the last photo. It was an excellent-quality image of a small yellow house with a palm tree in the fenced-in front yard. "Tell me what's going on in this little house."

Dan said, "We know Ortega flew into Miami and rented this house in Lauderdale-by-the-Sea. He was there for two days.

"The mystery Moldovan, whatever the hell his real name is, cleared customs at Fort Lauderdale Executive Airport. Ninety minutes after landing in Fort Lauderdale, he popped into this market, which happens to be ninety-five feet from this little Venezuelan intelligence safe house."

Jack just looked up at Dan. "Ninety-five feet exactly?"

"Exactly. Went down myself yesterday."

Ryan smiled. Dan still liked to use his own shoe leather. "Go on."

"Then, the day after the mystery Moldovan and Ortega arrive, Felicia Rodríguez shows up. She goes in the market, for what it's worth, but more importantly, a GPS track of her mobile phone puts her inside the Venezuelan safe house."

"Hot damn," Jack said in excitement.

Murray added, "She was only there an hour, then she checked into a hotel in the neighborhood. The next morning, she drove back to Kansas."

Ryan looked over all the pictures again quickly, then up at Murray.

The AG said, "Before you ask, we picked up very faint traces of polonium-210 in the house and in Rodríguez's hotel room. However it was stored at that time was much better than how it was stored right before Golovko was poisoned. Clearly, Rodríguez had it in some sort of lead-lined container, but she took it out at the cafeteria at the University of Kansas."

Ryan said, "So let me see if I follow you here. We think the mystery Moldovan is a possible Russian FSB agent who brought the P-210 into the U.S. in the private jet, and then passed it off to the assassin with the help of Venezuelan intelligence officer Ortega."

"That's our theory. It's impossible to say for sure if the Moldovan was in the safe house himself, but again, he was spitting distance away. I know we don't have a real smoking gun here, but —"

Jack cut him off. "We need to find these guys. Ortega and the other guy."

"Actually, we only need the other guy."

511

"Why don't we need the Venezuelan?"

"Because three days after the meeting in Lauderdale-by-the-Sea, the day before the Golovko poisoning, Esteban Ortega was murdered in Mexico City. A drive-by shooting into his taxi. Gunman on the back of a motorcycle, no real description. Only witness was the cabbie, and he was pretty useless."

Ryan leaned back on the sofa. "Covering their tracks." He blew out a frustrated sigh. "They will kill anyone who can pin this on them. Get whatever you need for an international arrest warrant. If we can figure out who the Moldovan is, then we can pick him up."

"Will do."

Ryan looked again at the photo of the young Venezuelan woman. She seemed so young, her entire life ahead of her. "What was her motivation?"

"Not sure we will ever know. She has family back home in Venezuela, there could have been threats against them. We are pretty sure she had no idea what she was handling, so we think the Russian or the Venezuelan tricked her."

"And any clue why the Venezuelans would be involved?"

"Not yet. Again, quite possible Ortega didn't know anything more about what Rodríguez was actually putting in Golovko's Sprite than she did."

"So," Jack said, "Russians get like-minded useful idiots to help them in a plot, and then the Russians screw them over, use them for their own devices."

Murray nodded.

"That sounds like the playbook of Roman Talanov."

"The FSB guy? Really? Sorry to say, I can't say I know too much about his past."

"No one does, for sure," said Ryan. "But I'm working on rectifying that."

61

Jack Ryan, Jr., arrived in Corby at eleven a.m. The sky was even grayer here than it had been in London, and the air felt noticeably colder as he climbed out of his Mercedes on the street in front of Oxley's building.

On the two-hour drive up he'd convinced himself this would be a dead end. He was not letting himself think for a moment that this morning's attack had been a random event, but he could not put together how this old ex-spy would have had anything to do with it. He'd almost turned around in Huntingdon, but he'd pushed on, telling himself that it wouldn't hurt to continue on up to see Oxley — if nothing else, just to annoy the old fart one more time.

Jack decided to tell him about the attack and then gauge his reaction. Jack was confident that if Oxley had been behind it, for whatever the reason, just showing up at his place would cause him to give away his involvement.

Jack took the stairs up to Oxley's first-floor unit, and as he climbed he noticed his knee was aching from his run-in with the two thugs earlier that morning. He should have known to ice the damn thing; sitting still in the car on the ride up would probably ensure he'd be walking with a limp for the next few days.

He pushed this irritating thought out of his brain and focused his attention on the annoying prospect of having to speak with Oxley again. He told himself that if the man made any more disparaging comments about his dad, Ryan would punch him in the jaw.

He would not hit the man, and he knew it, but it made Jack feel good to think about it.

Jack stopped at Oxley's door and brought his hand up to knock, but as he did this, he noticed the door wasn't latched. He looked down at the latch and saw a smeared black boot print right below the lock. Next to it, the doorjamb was broken.

Someone had kicked in the door, recently enough that Jack could see mud in the boot print.

Ryan's blood began pumping hard and fast. Just as had happened this morning during the attack, his threat indicators were redlining. He spun around, looked down the little hallway toward the back stairwell, but there was no one else around.

His first thought was to turn and head down the stairs and back to his car. He could call the cops from there. But he had no idea if Oxley was still alive. If he was, any delay might make the difference between life and death for the old bastard.

As slowly and silently as he could, Ryan put his hand on the latch and pushed the door open.

Instantly, Jack realized Vick Oxley was very much alive. He sat there, on a metal chair at his little kitchen table, just ten feet from the front door of the one-room flat. In front of him was a cup of tea. His hair was askew, and a little sweat shone on his high, wrinkled forehead, but otherwise he appeared to be completely composed. A man in his kitchen, enjoying a morning cup.

On the cold hardwood floor at his feet, however, two men lay on their backs. They were quite clearly dead, and their bodies were unnaturally contorted. Ryan could tell one of the men had had his neck snapped, as his head lay wrenched to the right, opposite from the disposition of his hips.

The other man had bloody contusions on his face, and his eyes were wide open.

Oxley looked up at Ryan, showing some surprise at seeing the young American, although he composed himself quickly and lifted his cup. He waved it and asked, "Just pop round for a cup of tea, did you?".

Ryan raised his hands slowly. He didn't know what the fuck had happened in here, but he was prepared for the big man to launch off his chair and come at Ryan himself.

Instead, the man just calmly took another sip.

Jack lowered his hands. "What . . . what happened?"

"You mean just now?"

Ryan nodded, his eyes wide in disbelief.

"The President of the United States' son just walked into me kitchen."

Oxley had gone from being a complete asshole to being a smart-ass. Ryan wasn't sure that was progress, but at least he had him talking. He entered the flat and shut the door behind him.

"I mean, obviously, before that."

"Oh. Those blokes? They bumped into my brass knuckles, got back up to have another go, bumped into them again, and didn't get up the second time."

Ryan knelt over them, checked them both for

pulses, but found none. Oxley just watched him do it, his face half hidden behind his mug of tea. Slowly he lowered his tea to his lap, and his voice turned dark, almost malevolent. "You brought trouble with you, didn't you, lad?"

"I didn't bring them."

"Well, you show up, then the next day they show up. Either you caused them to come or they caused you to come. Since you were here first, I blame you." He smiled, but it was a patronizing smile. The smile of an annoyed person. "Wet streets don't cause rain, do they?"

Jack pulled up a metal chair and sat down across from the Englishman. He said, "Two men came after me this morning. In London. Not these two."

"What a bleedin' coincidence, that."

"I'm going to go out on a limb and say it was no coincidence." Ryan looked at the heavyset man, then back down at the two bodies. He really couldn't get his head around the obvious fact that Oxley had managed to dispatch these young and fit men. "You killed them?"

"Well, they didn't die of natural causes. You are as thick as your daddy."

Jack gritted his teeth.

Oxley put his mug down on the table. "Despite your parentage, I suppose I have to be a good host and make ya some tea." He climbed up to his feet and moved into the kitchen, grabbed the teakettle and put it back on the gas burner, which he cranked up till the blue gas flames licked up the sides.

Jack said, "Hey! I don't want tea. I want answers. How did this happen? How did you manage to —"

Oxley wasn't listening. He pulled a mug down

517

from the little cabinet, blew into it to clean out the dust, and then he tossed in a tea bag. The kettle began whistling soon after, and the white-haired man filled the mug with hot water. He dropped in two sugar cubes he picked with his fingers out of a cardboard box, then glanced over his shoulder at Ryan.

"Looking at you, I'd say no milk. You aren't that refined, are ya?"

Ryan did not answer. Right now his head was spinning with the implications of this situation. He was the son of the sitting President of the United States, and he was here in a tiny one-room flat with two bodies at his feet. The man who killed them was walking around as if it was no great concern, but nearly every nerve and muscle in Ryan's body was screaming at him to get the hell out of there now.

There was, however, only one thing in this world Ryan wanted now more than getting away from this scene.

Answers.

He sat there, waiting for Oxley to talk.

The big Englishman put the mug of tea down in front of Ryan and sat back in his chair. Only then did he speak. "So, drink up quick, mate, because I'm tossing you out in a moment. Before I decide if I kick you out my door or throw you out my window, why don't you tell me what you know about this?"

Ryan said, "I am not sure, but there is a good chance that this is about you. Your history with the British government."

The Englishman shook his head. Disbelieving.

Jack added, "Or maybe, I should say, this is about Bedrock."

Oxley did not seem surprised at all to hear his old code name. He just gave a half-nod and took a sip from his own mug.

Ryan said, "I came yesterday to ask you a question about some events on the continent thirty years ago."

"Bedrock is dead and buried a long time, lad. And digging him up now is only going to get more people killed." He motioned to the two dead men on his floor. "Not just Russians."

Jack's head spun to the two corpses. *Russians? How do you know they are Russians?*"

The Englishman looked at Jack for a moment, then struggled to get down on the floor on his knees. He moved awkwardly, wincing as he climbed out of the chair, but Jack couldn't determine the exact location of the man's pain. Jack put his mug down and leapt from his own chair, trying to help the old man before he fell on his face.

But Oxley made it down, then reached for the jacket of the first man on the floor. He pulled it off roughly. Jack thought he was going to search the man for identification, but instead he tossed the jacket aside, then reached back down to the body and unbuttoned the man's belt.

"What, in God's name, are you doing?"

Oxley did not answer. He opened the belt and then untucked the dead man's shirt and undershirt. These he pulled up, and he struggled with them, fighting to get them off the man's body.

Ryan was sickened. He shouted, "Oxley! Why the hell are you —"

Ryan stopped shouting when he saw the tattoos.

The man was covered in them, all over his chest and stomach and neck and arms.

519

On his shoulders were tattooed epaulets; there was a Madonna and Child on his left pectoral, an Iron Cross below his Adam's apple, the image of a dagger piercing his neck.

Ryan could not make sense out of any of them, but he could make a guess. "Russian mob?"

"I'd say so," said Oxley. He ran his hand across the man's stomach. A large tattoo that depicted some sort of grouping of stones, seven in all, took up the width of the man's torso.

"He is Seven Strong Men."

He motioned to the other tattoos on the man's body. "The dagger in the neck means he killed in prison, the epaulets on the shoulder means he holds — he *held* — rank in the Seven Strong Men, like a lieutenant. The Iron Cross means he doesn't give a bleeding shit about anyone. The Madonna means he's religious, Russian Orthodox, although he's Russian-assassin religious, which isn't terribly religious, I don't suppose."

Oxley motioned to the other body. "Your turn, lad."

Jack grimaced, then moved over to the other body and pulled the jacket and shirt off. This man was as festooned with ink as the other man, and he had the same Seven Strong Men tattoo on his lower torso.

"Why are these Seven Strong Men after you?" Jack asked.

"The same reason they are after you, I guess."

"Which is?"

"Lad, I don't have a fucking clue. I've had no run-ins with Russian mafia. Ever."

"You think the guys that jumped me today were part of the same group?"

"Did they have little banana knives?"

"One had a small hooked blade. Is that what you mean?"

"Yep. Seven Strong Men."

Jack could not fathom it. "*Here?* In the UK?"

"Of course they are here. London is Londongrad, after all. My God, if you are not as dense as your daddy."

Jack sat back in the chair. "What the hell is wrong with you? Why are you such an asshole?"

Oxley just shrugged and sipped tea.

Jack was still trying to find some sort of connection between his work at Castor and Boyle and the past of Victor Oxley. The fact he had been under surveillance since before his father had mentioned Bedrock meant that the two situations were related somehow, or else it was one hell of a coincidence, and Jack had been at this game long enough that he naturally leaned to the former. One question occurred to him: "How do you know all this about Russian prison tattoos?"

Oxley looked at Ryan. For several seconds there was no sound in the flat except for the ticking of some unseen clock, but with a shrug the white-haired Brit reached to his waist, grabbed hold of his threadbare sweater, and pulled it up.

Jack saw now. Victor Oxley did not have the Seven Strong Men tattoo on his torso, but he wore an incredible amount of ink nonetheless. There were stars and crosses and daggers, and a skull with a teardrop and a dragon, all just on the small portion of the big man's chest and belly he'd exposed to Ryan.

Jack said, "You were in a gulag?"

Oxley lowered his shirt and reached for his mug of tea. "Where the hell you think I learned the bad manners you keep complaining about?"

62

Oxley finished his tea sitting over the dead bodies of the two Russian mafia hit men, then rose from the table and began slowly pacing the little room; each time he arrived at the windows over the road out front, he glanced through the curtains. Jack's mug had cooled somewhat on the table next to him, but he hadn't touched it.

For the past few minutes, Jack had tried questioning Oxley, although the Englishman's answers had remained vague and evasive.

"When did you leave SAS?"

"Eighties."

"And you joined MI5?"

"Don't know where you heard that."

"When were you in the gulag?"

"Long time ago."

"When did you return to the UK?"

"Long time ago."

Jack growled in frustration. He was not nearly as calm as the older man was. "You have a problem being specific, don't you?"

"It's all ancient history."

"It might have been ancient history until the Russian mafia kicked in your door, but these dead guys indicate to me that your past is pretty damn relevant to the present."

A phone started ringing on one of the bodies, but Oxley ignored it. Instead, he said, "Go home. Leave me be."

"I can't just leave. You aren't safe here."

"You going to protect me, are you? Look, as far as I can tell you are the reason these gents came kicking in my door."

"The next crew might have guns, you know."

"Seven Strong Men doesn't use guns. Not in the UK, anyway."

"That's the first good news I've heard today."

"They don't need guns. They favor knives, metal truncheons, that sort of thing. They work in pairs or teams of three or more. They are right brutes."

Jack said, "What are you planning on doing with these bodies?"

Oxley shrugged. "I've got a saw and a bathtub and some garbage bags. I can make this problem go away."

"You can't be serious."

"I am serious. I ain't going to the police. I live a very quiet life, forgotten by my government, and that's the way I like it. The moment the British government learns Russian gangsters are trying to kill me, then I will become interesting to them again."

"What's wrong with that?"

"Everything is wrong with that. The British government are the people who turned on me."

"Turned on you?"

Oxley stopped in the middle of the room. "Turned on me." He walked back to look out the curtains for a moment, then paced across the floor, all the way to the little kitchen. He turned around and walked back in the other direction.

Jack knew the man was trying to figure out what to do. Jack himself was thinking about the dead men, and what this would mean for him. There was no way he could hide this, but revealing this to his father would put an end to Jack's time here in London. He'd be on a plane before nightfall, or else a Secret Service protection detail would be sent over from the embassy to keep him company 24/7.

Shit.

As Ryan considered his own predicament, he noticed Oxley had stopped his pacing. Now he stood at the front window, looking down into the street.

Jack said, "Listen. We've got to come up with a plan here."

Oxley did not reply.

"Why won't you talk to me?"

"I don't like you."

"You don't even know —"

Oxley stepped back from the window, shielding himself behind the wall. "No, lad, I don't know you, but I will sign a truce with you for the time being, because I also don't know the two bastards that just climbed out of a car at the end of my street. I do believe they are on their way here to check on their mates."

"Shit." Jack stood quickly. "More Russians?"

Oxley shrugged. "Dunno. You piss anyone else off of late? These two out front are coming fast. I'd be surprised if they didn't have at least one more heading up the back stairs. Make yourself useful and check it out."

Ryan leapt up, pulled a small knife out of a drawer in the kitchen. Oxley pulled a pair of brass knuckles out of the pocket of his trousers and slipped them on his hand.

Jack raced down the hallway toward the back of Oxley's little building, and here he looked out the window. The back garden had just enough room for a few washing lines and a car park large enough for four vehicles. Jack scanned the tiny car park and the linens hanging over the garden, but he did not see anyone approaching the rear of the building. He checked the other back gardens on the street, looking for any threats, but he saw nothing. Quickly, he turned to run back up the hall to Oxley's place to help him with the two men heading there, but he'd taken only a couple of steps when he heard footfalls on the rear stairwell.

Whoever was coming for Oxley was already in the building. From the sound, Jack determined there were two of them, they were big, and they were ascending the stairs quickly.

Jack flattened his back to the wall in the hallway next to the entrance to the stairwell, and he held the carving knife in his right hand.

A man stepped into view on Jack's right; he was surprisingly big, but his attention had been focused on the flat at the front of the building where Oxley lived. Jack took advantage of this and fired out a left jab just as the man turned in his direction. The blow took the big man in the jaw and snapped his head back; he rocked back into the second man out of the stairwell, but before Jack could execute a second attack, both men were charging forward again.

Jack saw the knives almost instantly. Both Russians swung their short blades at him in the hall; Jack ducked left, went low and raised back up between the attackers, then struck out with his own knife and felt the tip of his blade sweep across the outside of the first man's right shoulder.

The man grabbed at his wound and cried out, but the second attacker moved past him and stabbed at Jack. Jack parried the strike away with his left hand, and realized at the same instant that he needed more room to maneuver. His back was to the door of the flat next to Oxley's, so he donkey-kicked the door as hard as he could when the two Russians both lunged at him again, waving their blades.

The door flew in; Jack fell backward against it and tumbled on his back to the floor, dropping his knife in the process.

The men were above him now, and he kicked the wounded man in the inside of his knee, buckling the joint and sending him crashing to the floor.

Behind him, an elderly woman called out, not screaming in fear — rather, she was yelling in anger at the intrusion. Jack did not look back at her; all his attention was focused on dealing with the two knives sweeping the air toward him. He rolled to his right, just avoiding the curved blade of the second attacker, and as he shot back to his feet, he immediately had to spin away from a whipping blade.

The attacker missed, spun almost all the way around after his wild swing, and Jack stomped down on the back of the man's leg, dropping him to his knees.

The second Russian struggled to climb back up off the floor. Jack could hear the woman shouting, as well as angry screams in Russian from the thug, but he concentrated on the closest armed man, who was now on his knees, facing away from him.

Jack dove onto the man's back, slamming him face-first into the floor. He took the Russian's head in his hands and banged it down again, knocking the young Russian out cold.

The other man was up now, and Jack had his back to him. Jack knew his only defense was to leap back up to his feet and run out of the little flat. He did this, sprinting back into the hallway, and he heard the armed man right on his heels. Jack stopped in the hallway, dropped low, and spun around with a sweeping kick to the running man's legs. The Russian was caught by surprise, and he fell onto Jack just outside the doorway.

Ryan and the Russian rolled around on the hallway floor, both men struggling desperately for the curved knife.

Victor Oxley had met the two men racing up to his flat when they were still in the front stairwell. His swing of the brass knuckles took the first man at the top of the stairs in the jaw and sent him tumbling all the way back down to the ground floor in a crumpled heap.

But the second man leapt to the right so his partner wouldn't take him down in his fall, and then he continued to the top of the stairs, his knife out in front of him, maneuvering for an opening to stab the big fifty-nine-year-old Briton.

"Davay! Davay!" Oxley shouted at the younger Russian mafia assassin. Come on! Come on! The Russian was wary, clearly afraid to commit to a lunging attack with the knife against the bigger man with the bloody brass knuckles on his fist.

But finally he did come on. He stepped onto the landing with the first swing of the knife. He went for Oxley's chest but struck nothing but air. Oxley took the opportunity to strike out himself, but his right hook missed its target as well.

Another jab by the knife caught the loose arm of Oxley's sweater, cutting it through but missing flesh. Oxley threw himself at his attacker, slamming into him, chest to chest, using his left hand to keep the threatening knife from plunging into him. There on the landing between the ground floor and the first floor the two men, one in his early twenties, the other nearly sixty, wrestled in a bear hug. Oxley could not bring the brass knuckles into action because his arm was held up by the Russian, and the Russian could not put his knife to use because his wrist was held down by the Englishman.

Finally, Oxley got the man in the corner of the landing, and then, with brute strength and intense effort, he scooted the man across the three feet of wall to where he was pressed with his back to the plate-glass window overlooking the street from the landing. The attacker looked back over his shoulder quickly, realizing the danger he was in, but all he could do was try to pull his knife arm free of the vise-grip clench of Victor Oxley's left hand.

The two men made brief eye contact. The Russian was afraid, the Englishman, exhausted but resolute.

Victor Oxley slammed his forehead into the face of the Russian assassin, and he kept pressing with it until the window glass shattered behind the Russian's head, his head carried on back out the window, and the jagged glass below his neck cut into him, digging through skin and muscle and stabbing between cervical vertebrae, where the sharp glass then stabbed his spinal cord.

The knife fell from his hand, and Oxley let go, pushed off the man, then stepped back away from him.

The Russian flailed for a moment, eyes wide in terror and in pain, but then he fell off the broken glass and collapsed to the floor in an expanding pool of blood. Bloody broken glass rained down on his dying body as the window shattered completely and fell in.

Oxley reached out and put his hand on the banister to keep from collapsing. His heart felt like it could rip out of his chest with its next powerful beat. He sucked in a deep lungful of air, and only when he held it in did he hear a noise below him on the ground floor. He looked down to the bottom of the stairs and saw the man he'd punched in the face a minute earlier. Remarkably, the man had made it back to his feet, and now he stood there, wobbling a little, and he raised something out away from his body, pointing it at the big Englishman on the landing.

Oxley cocked his head. Slowly he raised his hands when he realized it was a gun.

A *gun?*

Oxley saw the muscles tighten in the neck of the Russian as he began to squeeze the trigger, then Oxley looked up quickly, above the gunman, alerted by sudden movement there.

Jack Ryan, Jr., appeared at the railing on the first-floor landing and launched himself over the banister, dropping ten feet straight down to the gunman below him. He crashed onto the man just as a wild shot rang out. Oxley lurched back; he thought he'd been hit at first, so loud and percussive was the crack of the bullet in the enclosed stairwell.

But he felt himself for blood and holes, and was relieved to find neither.

He looked down at the two men now, both fighting over the small pistol below him. Jack tried to tear it from the other man's hand; instead the Russian slammed Jack to the floor and fell on top of him, the gun between them.

A second shot cracked, and the struggle continued for several seconds. Oxley started down the stairs, trying to get close enough to help, yet by the time he got to the ground floor, there was nothing for him to do but pull the dead body of the Russian off the very alive son of the President of the United States.

Ryan pushed himself up to a sitting position and leaned back against the wall of the stairwell. Oxley, exhausted beyond anything he'd felt in decades, collapsed next to him.

For several seconds the two men just sat there, the sound of their near-hyperventilated breathing filling the small space.

Finally Jack was able to control his breathing just enough to mutter an understandable sentence: "What the fuck was that about these assholes not using guns?"

Oxley took his time responding, needing to catch his breath first. "What can I say? Haven't been keeping up with the habits of the Seven Strong Men. Could be my information is somewhat out-of-date."

"Yeah."

Oxley regarded the dead man on the floor in front of him. Slowly his thick-bearded face tightened into a smile. "I'll be damned, Ryan. You fight like your dad."

Jack looked angrily at Oxley. "Meaning what, exactly?"

"It means I'm impressed. I took you for rich and lazy."

"Again, your information is inaccurate." Ryan was on his feet now. With difficulty, he pulled Oxley up as well. Ryan pointed to the man lying one half-floor above him. "Is he dead?"

"Done and dusted, mate."

"Does that mean dead?"

Oxley said, "It does mean dead. What about the boys in the back?"

"One got away, the other is KO'd."

Oxley looked at Ryan. He controlled his heavy breathing well enough to adopt a patronizing tone. "Well, now, you don't suppose the unconscious bloke might be a bit useful, to us, do you? That is, of course, if you haven't let him get away as well."

Ryan lifted the gun off the floor and headed up the stairs.

A minute later, Jack had dragged the man up the hall into Oxley's flat. He was no longer unconscious, but Jack could see evidence of a severe concussion in his eyes.

Oxley had made it upstairs himself, and here he ignored his elderly neighbor, who stood in the hallway and yelled at him and Ryan.

As the big Englishman entered his apartment, she shouted, "I'm calling the police!"

Oxley said, "I don't give a toss what you do." And with that, he slammed the door.

As soon as it shut, he turned to Ryan. "Don't know 'bout you, mate, but I'm getting the fuck out of here." He retrieved a half-filled duffel bag hanging from a hook by the door, then rushed over to the little dresser by his bed and began pulling out items and throwing them into the bag.

Jack had the gun on the Russian now. "I'll drive you wherever you want to go. Like it or not, we are sort of in this together."

Oxley didn't seem to like it, but he had begun to accept it. With a short nod, he said, "We can take this bloke somewhere and see if he feels like having a conversation with us." Oxley walked over to the man, slapped him across the face. "How about it, Ivan? You up for a chat?"

The man wobbled on his knees, he was still out of it, but Jack steadied him. Looking into the Russian's eyes, he said, "Listen to me. We're going down the stairs and we're getting in my car. Just so you know, if I see any more of your friends I'm going to shoot you in the fucking head."

The man just stared at Jack. Oxley repeated everything Jack said in Russian, and only then did the man nod distractedly.

Jack Ryan and Victor Oxley loaded the bleary-eyed Russian into the trunk of Ryan's Mercedes, then hog-tied him with a length of rubber hose from the garden of Oxley's building. When they were certain their prisoner was secure, Oxley and Ryan shut the trunk, and drove out of Corby just moments before wailing police cars pulled up in front of the ex–SAS officer's apartment building.

Jack had suggested they go to London, and Oxley made no protest. Jack knew he couldn't just be involved in the death of Russian mob goons without one hell of a lot of fallout, but he decided he'd wait till he got back to the capital before calling Sandy, his dad, the police, and anyone else who might be interested in the event. In the meantime, he would have Oxley alone in a car, and he'd hoped to use the time to dig into the man's story.

But it didn't work out that way. Oxley said he needed a few minutes to relax first. Jack was not two miles out of the city before he looked to his left and found Oxley sound asleep. Jack shook him, which woke him, but only long enough to convince Jack the man was not dead. He told Jack to bugger off for a while and let him recover from all the action, and Jack reluctantly obliged.

Ryan drove on, kept company by the nasal snore of the Englishman and the sound of the hog-tied would-be Russian assassin flailing around inside his trunk.

63

Thirty years earlier
West Berlin was populous, prosperous, cosmopolitan, and educated. But it was not a city as much as it was an enclave. Though part of the Federal Republic of Germany, the city was completely surrounded by the socialist nation of the Deutsche Demokratische Republik, a Soviet vassal state, and only seventy miles of double walls, guards, and guns encircling West Berlin separated two armies, two economies, and two belief systems.

In the East, they once claimed the Berlin Wall had been built to keep the citizens of West Berlin from slipping into the paradise of the DDR.

But by the mid-eighties, no reasonable person anywhere on the planet believed such nonsense.

Just five blocks north of the Berlin Wall, an automobile and moped repair shop occupied the entire ground floor of a four-story brick building on the busy corner of Sprengelstrasse and Tegeler Strasse. The building was in Wedding, in the former French sector of West Berlin, and the shop did a huge business with all the BMWs, Mercedeses, Opels, and Fords that passed through the neighborhood every day.

Above the ground-floor repair shop were the offices for the car care center, and above that was a large, mostly open room that served as an artist's shared studio space. Here painters, sculptors, photographers, and woodworkers rented workbenches and floor space, and they worked on their craft throughout the day and into the evening.

Most evenings the last of the artists vacated the building well before midnight, but the building remained occupied. A small narrow staircase in a corner of the second floor led to the attic, and beyond the door at the top of the stairs, six men and women, all between the ages of twenty-one and thirty-three, lived together in a rustic but large three-bedroom flat. One of their number was a painter, and she had managed to obtain the accommodations virtually rent-free from the landlord of the building space, because although he was a wealthy landowner here in decidedly capitalist West Berlin, he had been a radical in the sixties, and he still shared in the ideals of the six young inhabitants of the attic flat.

The residents were members of the Rote Armee Fraktion, the Red Army Faction, a Marxist-Leninist terrorist organization formed here in Germany in 1970. The RAF attacked police, NATO personnel, and wealthy capitalists and their institutions, both here in Germany and in neighboring countries.

The flatmates' security system here above the auto repair shop and the art studio was many-layered, though it was not particularly sophisticated. During the day, when the shop and studio were up and running, employees downstairs kept a lookout for any police or unknown vehicles on the street. At night, a guard dog in the repair shop would alert those sleeping above, although there were multiple false alarms each and every evening.

There were also trip wires set up on the staircases,

attached to air horns, and one member in the flat was tasked to the night shift, essentially ordered to sit on the couch in the common room of the flat, watching TV with an old Walther MPL submachine gun on his or her lap and a pot of coffee on the stove in the kitchen.

For one of the most notorious terrorist organizations active in Europe for most of the past fifteen years, this did not amount to much in the way of security measures, but these six RAF guerrillas were not exactly at the pinnacle of the organization, and the organization was not exactly in its heyday.

The RAF had slipped out of the news in the past few years, and for this reason this cell of the organization had relaxed their guard. These were the days of the Third Generation of the Red Army Faction, and they had not been linked to any attempted lethal attacks since their failed 1981 rocketing of Ramstein Air Base and, before that, their 1979 unsuccessful assassination attempt on NATO commander Alexander Haig. The media characterized the RAF as demoralized, disorganized, and adrift, and the half-dozen young people who lived in the flat here in Wedding certainly appeared to be living down to that description.

It was just past one a.m. on a Friday morning, and cell member Ulrike Reubens was on the couch in the common room, kept awake by coffee and nicotine and a new VHS cassette player connected to the television. She was engrossed in a bootleg tape of Meryl Streep and Cher in *Silkwood,* and as she sat there in the dark watching the grainy video she thumbed the fire mode selector switch up and down on her gun, a small manifestation of her fury at the American government for their criminal use of nuclear power and their lack of concern for the welfare of the proletariat, as portrayed in the movie.

In the two large bedrooms down the hall off the common room, several more men and women slept. Four of them were members of the RAF — a fifth member, Marta Scheuring, had left town suddenly a few days earlier.

Although the symbol of the RAF was a black H&K MP5 submachine gun displayed over a red star, in truth none of the inhabitants of this apartment actually owned an MP5. Instead, they all had older fifties-era machine pistols or revolvers, which were nowhere as state-of-the-art as the MP5 but were, at least, within easy reach where they slept. Four others in the apartment, three women and a man, were bedding down with lovers in the cell, and although all of these hangers-on knew they were in the presence of urban guerrillas, they had no concerns for their personal safety, because this cell of the RAF had been living here a long time with no trouble at all from the police.

Ulrike Reubens finished watching the credits of *Silkwood,* then she climbed off the couch and over to the VCR and hit the rewind button so she could watch it again. While she waited for the movie to restart, she walked into the kitchen to pour herself another cup of coffee, because she was certain she was going to be in for a long, boring night.

CIA analyst Jack Ryan stood in a makeshift command center set up in a dormant concert hall on Ostender Strasse, six blocks away from the RAF safe house. Although he was here with Nick Eastling and his team of MI6 counterintelligence men, and although there were easily fifty German police officers and detectives around him, as well as some characters he was certain were West German intelligence officials, he felt much as he had felt in Switzerland: alone and forgotten by those around him.

Eastling stood with his men on the other side of the big room. The German authorities conferred with the Brits, but other than some initial greetings and introductions, Ryan was mostly ignored by the Germans. He sat to the side on the edge of the stage and waited for something to happen.

It had been a long day. They'd flown out of Zurich at eight a.m., arriving in Frankfurt, Germany, just ninety minutes later, and there they'd caught a shuttle to Bonn, the West German capital. At the British embassy, Ryan had been given a small office with a secure line with which he could contact Langley, while Eastling and his men went into nearly a full day of meetings with officials from the Bundesamt für Verfassungsschutz, West Germany's domestic security services, and the Bundesgrenzschutz, the West German federal border guard, which served as the national police force.

By four p.m. the diplomatic part of the operation was complete, and it had been a success. The British had successfully talked the Germans into raiding the RAF safe house in Berlin. It would be a German mission, all the way, but once the takedown of the property was complete, Eastling and his fellow British intelligence officers would be allowed to exploit any intelligence recovered.

While in Bonn, Jack made a secure call to Jim Greer, and the two of them decided to ask Judge Arthur Moore to contact the director of the BfV to formally request the CIA be allowed to tag along as a witness and adviser. Jack had relayed his doubts about the intelligence to Greer, but at this point there

538

was little Jack, or the CIA, for that matter, could do but go along for the ride.

Ryan knew using Langley to go directly to the West Germans would piss Eastling off, but he did not care. Nick Eastling had tried to push Ryan out of the investigation in Switzerland. Ryan was determined Eastling was not going to do the same here in Germany.

By seven p.m. the six SIS men and Ryan were on a Learjet to Berlin, and by ten p.m. they sat in on a planning meeting with the German authorities.

At midnight they were taken to the theater just blocks away from where German police were quietly and carefully beginning a cover cordon operation around the suspected terrorists.

Now Jack sipped awful coffee from a service set up by the German police assisting with the operation. It immediately made his stomach burn; he'd not eaten all day.

As he sat there on the edge of the stage he heard several big vehicles pull up outside. There was a bustle in the lobby soon after, and then the door to the lobby opened.

Jack looked up and saw that the shooters had arrived.

The uniformed police here at the command center treated the tactical team with deference, and the Germans wearing suits — Ryan suspected they were all either BfV intelligence officers or BGS detectives — livened up quite a bit as the hour of the raid drew closer.

The shooters were members of Grenzschutzgruppe 9, Border Guard Group 9, West Germany's most elite unit of paramilitary operators. Ryan counted two dozen, all in black and carrying heavy cases, which they placed around the large main stage of the theater.

GSG 9 was a relatively new organization, formed after the tragedy of the 1972 Munich Olympics massacre, when it became abundantly clear to West Germany that the country did not possess the tactics, equipment, or caliber of personnel necessary to combat the recent phenomenon of international terrorism. When an eight-man cell of Black September terrorists kidnapped members of the Israeli Olympic team in Munich, the German police allowed them to fly on two Huey helicopters to nearby Fürstenfeldbruck Air Base, where they would then — according to their demands, anyway — board a 727 that would fly them to Cairo.

At the airport, with hours to prepare, members of the German police set up to ambush the terrorists as they moved with their hostages from the helicopters to the jet.

And in this task, the Germans proved themselves to be almost comically incompetent. Five policemen were designated as snipers, though none had sniper training, and they were given rifles without scopes and placed around the airport without radios, with instructions to wait for a signal to fire.

Another six police officers were armed and placed inside the 727 with orders to shoot it out with the terrorists, but just as the two helicopters landed, these six cops decided they didn't particularly care for their orders, so they ran away without notifying their command.

The helicopters landed, and the Black September terrorists realized quickly the airplane on the tarmac was cold and dark, and the Germans weren't planning on flying anybody anywhere, so they knew they had walked into a trap. Quickly the eight terrorists shot out the few lights the Germans had pointing at them, and the snipers who were not really snipers found themselves firing blindly in the vicinity of the hostages.

It took hours for the battle to end, and when it did, one policeman and nine hostages lay dead along with most of the terrorists.

After this debacle, the German government ordered the creation of a designated federal anti-terrorist unit, and, within just a few years, GSG 9 became one of the preeminent tier-one units in the world.

Now, more than a decade later, Ryan could not help feeling some worry about tonight's raid, although the reputation of the tactical team around him was certainly comforting, as was their impressive firepower.

Minutes after they arrived, the cases on the stage lay open and empty and the black-clad paramilitaries were geared up and ready for action. Their primary weapon was the nine-millimeter H&K MP5 submachine gun, a state-of-the-art weapon for close-quarters combat. On their hips they carried P7 pistols, also made by the German firm Heckler & Koch, and various fragmentation, smoke, and concussion grenades hung from their vests.

Jack had spent the past fifteen minutes quietly watching GSG 9 get ready for their raid, so he was surprised when Eastling appeared at his shoulder. He was more surprised to see Eastling wearing a bulletproof vest over his shirtsleeves and tie. He winked at Jack and said, "Good news, old boy. We get to be part of the action."

Ryan stood up from the stage. He noticed the Englishman was carrying a second vest in his hand.

Eastling said, "We will go behind the trucks delivering the trigger men, traveling with the detectives. We can wait downstairs while the takedown goes on, and we can enter with the first team of gents from the BfV when it's all over."

"Great," Jack said, though he wasn't sure just how great this actually was.

"No guns for us, I'm afraid." Eastling winked again. Ryan could see the adrenaline of the impending raid was already amping up the Englishman's mannerisms. "Personally, I have no use for the damn things. I know you are a real trick shot, though. How many terrorists did you kill last year?"

Jack said, "It was the one who shot me that reminds me to leave the gunfighting to the professionals."

"Too right, Ryan. We'll just come up the stairs when they give the all-clear."

64

After CIA analyst Jack Ryan donned the bulletproof vest over his shirt and tie, he was given a zip-up jacket with the word POLIZEI in gold on the back, and handed a radio by a Bundesgrenzschutz detective named Wilhelm.

At one a.m. they climbed into Wilhelm's unmarked car and drove to a staging area just two blocks from the target location. Here the GSG 9 men stood by their armored vehicles and smoked, and several ambulances and more police vehicles, including a paddy wagon, were all parked in a darkened underground garage.

After a call through the radios, Wilhelm, Ryan, and Eastling — the other British intelligence officers remained behind in the theater — began walking up the street, passing local police who were now blocking off the streets in the neighborhood. Wilhelm led Ryan and Eastling along behind another group of armed uniformed police officers to yet another staging area, this one just across the street from the target building. Just as they arrived, the GSG 9 men came in their own vehicles, their trucks driving slowly up Sprengelstrasse with the lights extinguished, and the twenty-four commandos leapt out from the back of the trucks and lined up in two teams of twelve. One group unlocked the car repair shop door with a skeleton key, and the other used a portable ladder to gain access to the fire escape, and they began moving slowly up toward the roof. Inside the repair shop, a barking dog was silenced with a tranquilizer gun, and then this team headed up a staircase to the first-floor offices.

Now Wilhelm, Ryan, Eastling, and several uniformed state police officers crossed the street and entered the target building. They climbed the stairs to the offices on the first floor, and here they stood together in a hallway near the stairs up to the second-story artists' studio. Just ahead of them, the GSG 9 team waited a minute at the stairs, and then they began moving up to the second floor, disappearing from view as they ascended into blackness.

Ryan leaned close to Eastling's ear and said, "They know they are here to arrest the terrorists, right? We won't be able to tie the attacks in Switzerland to the RAF if we end up with a room full of bodies."

Eastling whispered back, "You'd be surprised what a room full of bodies can tell you." He winked. "No stress, the shooters know to give the guerrillas every chance to surrender peacefully." He put a hand up. "Of course, if the bad guys decide they want to shoot it out, these German commandos will kill everything that moves. That's just what they do."

The GSG 9 team moved up the stairs to the second floor and into the artists' collective, and they found the space to be mostly open; there were a few partitioned-off areas here and there. Shelves of paint, rolling carts of art supplies, and easels with half-finished paintings were positioned around the room. Large windows on all four walls allowed the moonlight and glow from the streets below to filter in, so the German paramilitaries were able to head toward the narrow staircase to the top floor without using their flashlights. Many of the windows had been left open, so the room was cold and breezy.

When they were halfway across the floor, a transmission came from the leader of the team who had taken the fire escape to the roof. *"Mannschaft Eins, fertig."* Team One, ready.

The team leader in the studio replied with a whisper, *"Verstanden."* Understood.

At the bottom of the stairwell, the team leader looked up into the darkness. The door at the top of the stairs was open, and he saw a flickering dim glow, like that coming from a television screen somewhere in the flat above.

He turned around to face his team to give the hand signal to order them to prepare to assault up the staircase, but just as he raised his arm, the sound of a loud slap echoed in the room, and the team leader spun around to his right and fell, crashing into a rolling cart full of art supplies.

The crashing sound in the huge, nearly empty room sounded like a small bomb going off. Men dropped to their kneepads and scanned the room with the huge flashlights attached to the tops of their guns.

The closest men rushed to their leader and realized he'd been shot. He was facedown at the bottom of the stairs, and they assumed the bullet had come from the flat above, so two men fired their MP5s up into the flat to suppress the threat while others pulled their leader out of the line of fire.

Ulrike Reubens leapt from the couch when she heard something crashing into the rolling cart downstairs. This was *not* one of the rats that occasionally kept her jittery at night. The noise was too loud for that. No one had said anything to her about any of the studio renters staying late this evening.

Ulrike had just made it into the kitchen when the gunfire erupted in the stairwell in front of her. She leapt back in surprise, screamed, and fumbled with the MPL hanging over her shoulder.

An air horn began to blow on the stairs, which meant someone had tripped the wire on the way up. She raised her weapon in front of her just as she was bathed in a brilliant white light.

The first man through the doorway opened fire on the armed subject in front of him, perforating the woman with eight rounds of nine-millimeter NATO ammo. She crumpled to the ground before she fired a single shot from her gun.

Jack Ryan had expected the takedown of the RAF safe house to begin with the muffled sounds of detonating concussion grenades two floors above him. Instead, the stillness in the dark hallway where he waited was broken by multiple automatic weapons firing directly above where he crouched. Instantly, police radios began to crackle, and the shouts of men echoed from the studio through the stairwell.

Ryan and the men around him instinctively ducked lower to the floor. Wilhelm turned to Ryan and Eastling — he looked like he was trying to decide whether he should shepherd them back downstairs, as the fight was closer than he had expected.

Now there were shouts on the stairs ahead, and the gunfire above grew heavier. Men on the radio started yelling. Eastling grabbed Wilhelm. "What's happening?"

The Bundesgrenzschutz officer assigned to Ryan

and Eastling said, "The team leader on the second floor has been shot!"

"*Second* floor?"

Ryan heard the commotion of men shouting in the stairs, and he saw flashes from the big lights mounted on the top of their H&Ks as they came down; then a group of GSG 9 appeared in the hall. At first Ryan thought the entire force was in retreat, but within a few seconds he saw they were moving something heavy, pulling it with difficulty in the tight confines of the narrow hall. Their guns and other equipment were getting caught on one another's gear, and they struggled with whatever they were carrying.

He knew it would be the wounded team leader.

They shouted in German as they passed, and Ryan and Eastling moved out of the way. Ryan caught a glimpse of the tactical officer being dragged by three of his colleagues. He was completely limp and appeared dead.

The men continued up the hall and then into the stairwell down to the ground floor.

There was another loud crash above him; this sounded like a frag grenade — Ryan had heard enough of them in the Marine Corps to recognize the noise. Plaster on the ceiling in the first-floor hallway rained down on Ryan and Eastling and Wilhelm, as well as the uniformed Landespolizei officers with them.

The walkie-talkies all around Jack were alive with crackling shouts and commands; he couldn't make sense of any of it, but his impression was that something had gone drastically wrong and the situation upstairs had descended into utter chaos.

Seconds later, another group of black-clad officers appeared in the stairwell, dragging a wounded man

547

along with them. In the light from flashlights, Ryan could see the wet blood on the man's tunic.

Jack pushed himself tight against the wall to let them pass, but the officers stumbled while carrying the dead weight of the wounded man.

Ryan ran to the group, then reached down and took the wounded man under his arms. He lifted the man and began pulling him up the hall; the commando's boots dragged on the linoleum flooring. Ryan was not encumbered with guns and ammunition as were the German paramilitaries, so he was able to move a little better and quicker than the others, and he yelled at the men, telling them to get back upstairs.

Whether or not they understood the words, they understood the danger their colleagues were in upstairs, so they turned to head back up to the raging fight, reloading their weapons on the way.

"Nick!" Jack shouted. "Help me!"

Eastling came over and took the wounded man by the legs and lifted, and together with Ryan got him to the stairwell. He was still alive, but apparently he had been shot in the face. His MP5 hung from a sling on his neck, and a rig full of magazines and grenades was strapped to his chest.

Nick and Jack wrestled with the weight of the man all the way down into the garage of the car repair shop, and here a team of two paramedics appeared with a stretcher. All four men struggled to get the wounded officer onto the gurney. A paramedic said something to Ryan; he could not understand, but he thought the man was asking him to remove the MP5, so he unfastened the sling and took the gun.

Ryan accompanied the wounded man and the paramedics all the way outside to the ambulance, but Eastling went back up the stairs, passing a third man coming down with a bullet wound in his arm, aided by a uniformed police officer.

The ambulance raced off, and Jack found himself in the street now; above him in the flat, gunfire crackled. More ambulances had pulled up and police stood in the street with their guns drawn, all looking up toward flashes of light in the windows. Jack didn't know whom to hand the submachine gun to, so he just slung it over his shoulder until he could pass it off to Wilhelm.

He saw some uniformed policemen climbing the fire escape on the south side of the building; they had obviously been ordered up to help with the fire-fight that had continued much longer than anyone had expected.

Ryan ran back to the entrance of the garage, but now another team of paramedics had their gurney at the bottom of the stairs there, and they were loading the man with the injured shoulder onto the stretcher. Ryan wanted to get back to his position on the first floor, so he ran around the building to the fire escape, thinking he could just follow the cops up one flight and return to the hallway where he'd been two minutes earlier.

He headed up the fire escape, climbing the ladder to the stairs. As he started toward the window to the first-floor hallway, he heard a high-pitched hiss and he felt a pressure just in front of his face, and then brick exploded off the building two feet in front of him. The noise and pressure caused him to lose his footing and fall flat on the wet metal.

Even before he hit the cold, wet metal he knew he'd been shot at, and he also knew from the sound that this wasn't someone upstairs firing down. He looked to the right; there was a four-story building across the street. Lights were on in some of the rooms, and Jack pressed himself flat into the wet fire escape landing as he scanned them, looking to see where the shot came from.

But another building was next to it, and, as they were on the corner, Jack realized his position was exposed to windows all the way up the street for two blocks.

There were so many damn windows to check, he had no idea where the gunshot had come from.

He stopped scanning. It occurred to him no sniper would fire from a room with its lights on, so he started looking for the dark windows. A half-second later he realized he needed to be looking for an open window, which cut the potential locations down even more.

What about that one?

A flash in a fourth-story corner window, right next to where he was looking, caught his attention. It was at least seventy-five yards away, halfway up the block. He did not hear a bullet pass, which told him the sniper in the window was using a suppressed rifle and, more important to Ryan, he was now shooting at someone else.

Jack fought to get the walkie-talkie out of the pocket of his jacket. He didn't know how many of the police around here spoke English, but right now he didn't care.

"Sniper! Outside, fourth floor of the gray building up the street! Second window from the corner."

He was answered by a shout into the microphone.

"Wer spricht denn?" Who's talking?

Ryan did not understand; he repeated his announcement, and then he crawled to the open window and dove inside. He hadn't heard another round fired at him, but with all the noise coming from upstairs, he could not be sure.

65

In the living room of the three-bedroom flat on the top floor of the building, the GSG 9 operators still in the fight had themselves come to the conclusion that they were taking fire through the windows on the south side. When two of their number went down here, they at first thought the RAF gunmen in the back bedrooms were firing through the plaster walls. Indeed, in the light from their weapons they saw holes open on the wall, and they felt bullets and fragments of plaster as they passed. So GSG 9 fired back, dumping magazine after magazine of fully automatic fire in the direction of the threats in the bedrooms.

It was only when the third man in the living room went down with a gunshot to the back of his right shoulder, and pitched forward over a table in the middle of the room, that it became evident they were taking fire not just from the front, but from behind them on their right as well.

At that moment someone yelled "Sniper!" on the radio, and then he said something in English. "Sniper" was universal for these federal paramilitary officers, everyone knew the term, so although they could not understand the rest of the English, several of the men looked to their right and saw more glass shatter in the window as another bullet flew into the living room.

All the GSG 9 men hit the deck.

Ryan shouted for the uniformed policemen at the other end of the hall to come to his position here by the window, but they could not hear him through the persistent gunfire upstairs. Frustrated, he chanced a look back out the window, caught a glimpse of movement in the darkened room where he'd seen the flash of light.

Without considering the consequences of firing a gun in the vicinity of dozens of armed men, Jack raised the MP5 toward the open window and aimed the iron sights by putting the narrow blade at the front of the barrel in the center of the round ghost ring by his eye in the rear of the gun. Jack had not spent a great deal of time with the MP5 — it wasn't something that he'd used in the Marines, after all — but he'd shot the weapon before, and he knew enough about sub-guns to know it was a lousy weapon with which to take on a sniper at seventy-five yards.

Jack held his breath to steady himself, then pressed the trigger.

Nothing.

Quickly he looked down at the gun, saw the safety was set to *S* for *sicher,* or secure, and he flicked the selector switch to the single-shot indicator.

He aimed again, and then, just as he put his finger back on the trigger, he saw the flash of another shot coming from the room seventy-five yards away. Illuminated in the quarter-second of light, Ryan saw a bed, a man crouched behind it on the far side of the room with a gun pointed at the building. The gun had a scope and a bipod, but Ryan couldn't tell anything else about the shooter or his weapon before the room was once again covered in darkness.

Jack adjusted his aim, concentrated on the spot where he'd seen the man, held his breath again, and pressed the trigger.

The little H&K jerked against his shoulder as he sent a round downrange. He fired again, and then a third time. He had no idea if he was hitting the sniper or not, but he hoped he would at least encourage the gunman to run.

After the third shot, Ryan went flat on the floor below the window. He didn't want to press his luck against a man with a scoped rifle.

Two policemen ran up to Ryan, and he yelled at them to get down. They had the good sense to do what the American said; they hit the deck and then crawled over to his position, yelling at him with their pistols in their hands.

One of the men raised his head to look out the window, but Jack grabbed him by his sleeve and pulled him down hard. He had no idea if the sniper was still in the fight, but if he were, he would undoubtedly be focusing his attention on this window, where the incoming fire had come from.

The look of absolute conviction on the face of the American told the two German Landespolizei that they probably should just go ahead and move to another window before checking outside. They used their radios to direct a group of cops down at ground level to check out the building that the American CIA man had described, and they ordered the cops blocking off the streets to be on the lookout for a sniper trying to make his escape.

Then they disarmed the American. They had no idea where he'd gotten hold of a gun in the first place.

■ ■ ■ ■

The entire gunfight in the West Berlin neighborhood of Wedding lasted only six minutes, but to Ryan it seemed like an eternity. The GSG 9 men upstairs finally pronounced the flat clear, but everyone remained low to the ground for several minutes until the police went to check out the sniper hide up the street and reported that the area was safe.

Jack was still on the floor in the hallway when Wilhelm walked up to him several minutes later. "We found the sniper position across the street."

Jack stood up quickly.

"There is some blood on the carpet, and three holes in the drywall. You hit someone in that room, but they were apparently still able to collect their weapon and make an escape."

Wilhelm reached out and shook Ryan's hand. *"Danke schön, Herr Ryan."*

"No problem," Ryan said, but his mind was still trying to piece this all together. "How did the RAF know to have a sniper there? Did they know we would be hitting the flat?"

"I do not know."

"Is that something they have ever done before?"

"Nein. Nothing like this. Tonight we had two GSG Nine and one Landespolizei officer killed. Three GSG Nine and three Landespolizei were wounded. We have never suffered such losses against the RAF."

It was several minutes more before Eastling and Ryan were allowed up to the third-floor flat. As they crossed the studio space to the stairs, they passed a lightly injured commando still receiving initial treatment from his teammates, and they saw blood, bullet holes, and broken glass all over the room.

554

Upstairs, the Germans used the big flashlights on the tops of their guns to look for a light switch. They found one by the door, but the light above had been shot out or blown up by a grenade in the battle. Eastling himself turned on a lamp in the attached kitchen and pointed it toward the main room, casting long shadows across everything.

Ryan waved his hand through the air to clear smoke still hanging, and he got his first good look at the room.

The first body he came across was that of a young woman. She was ten feet from the entrance to the stairs, lying on her back and disfigured by the bullet wounds over her upper torso and head. In the lamplight diffused by smoke, she looked ghostlike. An automatic weapon was several feet away from her. Jack thought it likely this was her gun and it had been kicked out of her reach as the commandos took the room.

He followed some men with flashlights down a hallway and into the bedrooms, and here he saw a total of eight more bodies. Four had guns still in their hands or near where they lay, and four more did not. The walls of one of the bedrooms were so peppered with holes there were places you could reach through into the living room. It was clear to Ryan much of this battle had taken place without the two warring sides even seeing each other.

Jack looked at Eastling. "No survivors among the RAF?"

Eastling shook his head in disappointment. "None at all."

"Shit."

All the dead were photographed where they lay and then dragged into the living room and lined up on the floor. While this took place, the police were already beginning their investigation.

Jack and Nick started looking around themselves, but after just a few minutes the radio squawked. "Herr Eastling? Herr Ryan? Can you come to the last bedroom down the hall, please?"

Eastling and Ryan walked to the smallest room in the house, the back bedroom. No bodies had been discovered in here, so they had all but ignored it on their first pass, but now, as Ryan stepped into the room and followed the path of flashlights, he realized why he and Eastling and been ushered in. There were two pictures on a small dressing table; they were smashed, and one was pocked with bullet holes now, but they clearly showed a young woman who matched the ID photo of Marta Scheuring.

"Scheuring's room," said one of the BfV men.

A search of the ten-foot-by-ten-foot space was already under way. There wasn't much to look through, just a bed, a few tables, a pile of clothes in a basket in the corner, and a small closet stuffed with coats and other clothing.

It took no time at all for the BfV men to find a hollow space beneath several loose floorboards under the bed. A BfV investigator pulled a silver aluminum briefcase from the compartment. It was secured with a simple three-number combination, but the German put it on the bed and opened the lock with a tiny pick while Ryan and Eastling peered over his shoulder.

Inside the case were several notebooks and files. The detective shone his flashlight on the contents for the benefit of the Englishman and the American.

"Well, hullo," Eastling said, as he looked at it.

Ryan leaned in and directed the detective's flashlight toward a group of photographs.

The first thing Ryan saw was a black-and-white

photograph of Tobias Gabler, the first banker killed in Zug. The image looked as though it had been taken from a distance, but it was unmistakably the same man Ryan had seen in the news reports on Gabler's murder. Under this was a picture of Marcus Wetzel. Ryan had no idea what Morningstar looked like, but the photo was helpfully marked with a white sticker upon which Marcus Wetzel's name had been typed.

Underneath this photo was a map of Zug, Switzerland.

Next in the case was a one-page typewritten message on a sheet of white paper. At the top of the page was an H&K rifle over a red star, above which the letters RAF were displayed in white.

The German said, "It is a communiqué. It looks official, I have seen these before."

"Would you mind translating it?" Eastling asked.

"*Ja.* It says, 'The nature of these attacks speak the language of reaction. We in the Red Army Faction will not allow those who traffic in the illegal monies that lubricate the wars against the people of Central America and Africa to live freely and in peace. We will show our solidarity with the guerrillas of the world and fight against the bankers who profit from the illegitimate wars in the name of the failed capitalist system.' "

When the BfV man finished, he turned to Ryan and Eastling. "It goes on to say Tobias Gabler and Marcus Wetzel were killed because they were high-profile bankers who dealt with the accounts of German industrialists."

Ryan asked, "And this looks real to you?"

The German shrugged. "It *looks* real."

"But?"

"But Herr Wetzel was killed over twenty-four hours

557

ago. Herr Gabler days before that. Normally this would have been distributed already. I don't understand why it hasn't been."

Eastling said, "Maybe Scheuring was supposed to distribute it herself, but since she was burned to a crisp in Switzerland, she never got a chance."

The BfV officer shook his head. "If this was a real RAF operation, someone from their propaganda wing would send this to the media. Not the actual bomber."

The German began discussing the communiqué with some of his colleagues, so Jack and Nick walked out into the hallway.

Ryan said, "All nice and neat in one package."

Eastling clearly was thinking the same thing. He struggled with his words, finally saying, "It does look suspiciously convenient for us, I'll give you that."

Ryan said, "This is a plant if I've ever seen one."

The English counterintelligence officer seemed to recover from his doubt. He stopped in the narrow dark hall and turned to Jack. "*Have* you ever seen one?"

Ryan had to admit that he had not. He did not investigate crime scenes, but he was a hell of an analyst, and he had dealt with all sorts of opposition disinformation campaigns. This "evidence" did not pass Jack Ryan's sniff test.

They went back in the living room and stood over the bodies. The detectives were trying to match faces to booking photos of known RAF members. So far, they'd ID'd five of the dead, but they had no record of the other four. One of the detectives sent his partners into the bedrooms to look for purses and wallets to try to figure out who they were.

As Jack and Nick looked over the corpses lined up on the floor of the living room, Jack said, "These people, along with another guy two blocks up the street, managed to shoot nine cops and commandos? I don't believe that for a second."

Eastling shook his head. "They walked right into some sort of a trap. Might be a leak in German security."

"There is another possibility."

"What's that?"

Jack said, "Think about it. What if it was the Russians? If the RAF was being set up for what happened in Switzerland, the Russians would have to ensure that no one in the cell would be taken into custody to proclaim their innocence. What better way to make sure nobody talks to the police than turning the arrest into a full-on gun battle? All you would need to make that happen is a shooter with a line of sight on the scene. Once the German commandos started dropping, there weren't going to be any RAF survivors to proclaim their innocence."

Eastling sighed, but Ryan saw definite cracks in the certainty that had been on display before the briefcase turned up. "You have nothing but conjecture. We don't know who was in the sniper's hide. Could have been an RAF gunman who heard the shooting and decided to fight back from that location."

Jack just shook his head. He couldn't prove anything, but his gut told him he and Eastling were up against forces much larger than those of a German left-wing terrorist cell.

66

Present day
Jack Ryan, Jr., and Victor Oxley made it back to London just before five p.m. Of course, Ryan knew better than to return to his flat. Instead, he rented a room at a motor lodge on Wellesley Road in Croydon. Oxley had recommended it, explaining that he came to London from time to time and always stayed there, and he assured Ryan it was an out-of-the-way and suitable place for a "no questions asked" encounter, which was, Oxley pointed out, just what the situation called for now.

They had made one stop along the way. After growing tired of Oxley's pestering, Jack pulled into the parking lot of a supermarket and fanned some bills out of his wallet, passing them over to the former spy. Oxley ducked into the market and returned ten minutes later with two shopping bags.

They pulled back onto the road, heading for the lodge, and this was when Jack learned Oxley had bought a fifth of Irish whiskey, a liter of cola, and two large bottles of beer. As for food, he'd picked up some snack cakes and a stick of sausage that looked to Jack as if it might have been as old as Oxley himself.

As Jack suspected when Oxley described the place, the motor lodge was a complete dump. There was peeling paint, and burns on the carpet and mold on the walls, but each room was over its own tiny one-car garage, clearly for the express purpose of hiding the vehicles of whoever was staying inside.

They pulled into their allotted garage and closed the door, then Jack and Victor heaved the Russian mob enforcer out of the trunk of the Mercedes. Victor yanked the man's jacket up over his head so he couldn't see. They then frog-walked him up a flight of stairs out of the garage and into the hotel room.

The bathroom was tiny and filthy, but it was a good place to stash a Russian gang member for a few minutes. There was exposed piping along the walls, and Oxley expertly tied the man in a fashion that kept his hands high behind his back so that he could not maneuver more than a couple inches without causing himself incredible pain in his shoulders. Oxley then took a pillow with a suspicious stain on it from the bed, removed the pillowcase, and hooded the man with it.

They shut the Russian in the bathroom, and then Jack turned up the television in the bedroom. He and the fifty-nine-year-old Brit stepped out onto a tiny balcony that overlooked a busy six-lane road.

Oxley was angry the lodge did not have a single piece of glassware for his use, but he made do by drinking a few long gulps out of the bottle of cola and then filling the bottle back up to the top of the neck with Irish whiskey. They sat on cheap aluminum chairs on the balcony while Jack watched the man drink and eat for a few minutes,

561

using every last vestige of his patience, telling himself that the more satiated and sauced the ex–English spy was, the more he might talk.

Finally Jack said, "All right, Oxley. I want to question that asshole in the bathroom, but first I would like some answers from you. Do you feel like talking?"

The white-bearded Englishman seemed relaxed; Jack was sure it had something to do with all the whiskey in his cola. He shrugged, said, "First, start by calling me Ox. Second, know this. I'd rather not talk to you at all, but I don't fancy armed Russian thugs chasing me till the end of my days, so I'm willing to work with you to get this all sorted. Still, there are things I can say, and there are things I'll take with me to me grave."

Jack opened a bottle of beer and took a sip. "Fair enough. Let's start with something easy. When did you get back from Russia?"

After a moment, Oxley said, "I returned from the Motherland about twenty years ago."

"What have you been doing the past twenty years? Can you talk about that?"

"I've been around. Here and there. Collecting government assistance, mostly."

"Unemployed?"

"On and off the dole, lad. Do what I can." He shrugged. "But not much more."

Now Ox asked a question: "How is it that the son of the bleedin' American President knows about me?"

Jack said, "My father wanted info on Bedrock, and he thought Sir Basil Charleston would know. I was over here anyway, so I went to ask him. Basil told me you were Bedrock. I tracked you from there, using SAS contacts."

"Good ol' Basil."

"He thinks you want him dead."

Oxley cocked his head. "Does he, now?" Oxley shook his head with a chuckle. "No. Charleston wasn't part of the dirty tricks I was involved with. Old Basil didn't do me any favors, but I can't say he's all bad."

"He said you operated behind the Curtain. You fit in like a native."

"My mum was from Omsk, in Siberia. She defected with her parents through Berlin, back before the wall. She met an English Army officer and they moved to the UK. Settled in Portsmouth. Dad became a fisherman, he wasn't home much. My mum became part of the local Russian émigré community, so I grew up speaking more Russian at home than I did English."

Oxley gulped from his bottle. "And why on earth was your father interested in an old story like Bedrock?"

Jack had brought along the photocopied page from the Swiss police report. He pulled it out of his jacket and handed it over to Oxley.

Oxley looked at the page, then reached into his pocket and scrounged around for a moment for a pair of reading glasses. He put them on and looked at the page again.

"It's bloody German."

"Yes. But your code name is on there in pencil that someone erased. Next to a story from the Swiss police of a man who was detained after the bombing of a restaurant in Rotkreuz, Switzerland."

Oxley nodded very slowly, almost imperceptibly.

"So you remember."

Oxley looked off into space, as if recalling a moment in the distant past. "I was ordered to track down a rumor in the East about a killer the KGB called Zenith."

Jack wondered if Basil had been untruthful about Bedrock's lack of involvement with Zenith, or if he'd just forgotten. Ryan said, "Zenith was in Western Europe. Why did you go to the East?"

"The first rumors about Zenith came from the Czechoslovakians. Two of their investigators working on a case in Prague were found floating facedown in the Vltava River. A Russian staying at a hotel in the area disappeared in a hurry without paying his bill. A search of the man's room turned up some luggage. In it was a KGB cipher book with some writing on the inside flap. The Czechs managed to break enough of the code to decipher the word 'Zenith.' Whether or not that was the code name of the owner of the book with the Russians, no one knew, but 'Zenith' stuck nonetheless.

"The Czechoslovakians went to the KGB, but the Russians said they knew nothing about anyone named Zenith, nor did they admit to having any operatives in Prague."

Jack said, "Yeah, well, the KGB lied a lot."

"True," Oxley said, "and I'm sure the Prague police were thinking the same thing, but suddenly the back alleys off Wenceslas Square started to look like a KGB convention. Russian spies rained down on the city, and all of them were hunting for this Zenith character."

"And the UK learned this from a source in Prague?"

"MI5 got wind. Don't ask me how. Before it was all over, he killed twice more in Czechoslovakia, and four men in Hungary."

"All cops?"

"No. In Budapest he killed employees with the State Bank of Hungary, as well as a smuggler."

"A smuggler?" Jack asked.

"Human smuggler. He was a bloke that helped defectors over the border. It was common in Hungary back then," Oxley said. "Anyway, from our intelligence we got the impression Zenith was not KGB. He was some sort of a rogue. The KGB thought he was an ex–GRU man, who was now being run by a Western power. We were worried we would be implicated in his actions."

"Why would the UK be implicated in his actions?"

Oxley's chuckle was low and raspy. "Because we had an asset operating behind the Iron Curtain ourselves, doing a similar type of work."

Jack's eyebrows rose. Things were starting to make sense. "You?"

"Maybe you aren't quite as daft as I took you for." Oxley played with his reading glasses, moving them through his fingers slowly. He said, "Yeah. I was in Prague when Zenith was active there. I was in cover as a Russian, I was there alone, so naturally I was interviewed by the Czechs. I talked my way out of it, but when the killings continued in Hungary, some dim bulb in London thought I might get tied to the crimes. Zenith might hurt relations, right when we were hoping for a thaw. This was at the height of the arms race, but we liked the way things were heading. Poland was well on its way to democracy, Reagan and Thatcher had the Soviet Union by the knackers. There were still many battles to fight, but a new age was dawning. Zenith was upsetting the apple cart."

"So you were sent to kill Zenith so that the KGB couldn't blame the West for a rogue assassin running around whacking everybody?"

"That's it."

"Then what happened?"

"I couldn't bloody find him. Neither could KGB."

"But why did you go to Switzerland?"

"I was following some KGB geezers in Budapest who were themselves hunting Zenith. I was hoping they might lead me to him. I was quite surprised when they traveled to the West, to Zug, to visit a bank."

"And then people started getting killed there, too."

"Yes."

"Zenith killed them?"

Oxley shrugged, a slow, tired gesture on his big frame; a long stream of air escaped through his nose. He watched the cars roll by on the road below the balcony. "Depends on who you believe."

Ryan looked at Oxley. "Call me crazy, but right now, I believe you."

Victor Oxley smiled a little. "Then, yes. Zenith killed the lot of them."

The Englishman looked up from his drink now. "Now it's your time to talk. Why is your father interested in this story now? This was thirty years ago. Hasn't he created enough problems in the world to where this one could be left where it was?"

"I take it you disagree with my dad's politics?"

"Politics? I've got no patience for politics. Don't give a toss about it."

"Then why do you hate my father?"

"It's personal."

"*Personal?* You know my dad?"

"No, and I don't care to." Ox waved his hand away, dismissing the topic. "I asked you the question, lad. Why now? What does your dear old daddy want with me?"

Ryan shrugged. "Your code name was found in the files relating to the Zenith case. Nobody had looked at them in a long time, I guess, but another old note in a dusty old file turned up suggesting that Roman Talanov was Zenith."

Oxley looked at Ryan. "Talanov? Right. That's the name. So? Again, that was ages ago. What the hell does it matter now?"

Jack was surprised. "Wait. You *know* Talanov is Zenith?"

"I suspect I am the one who put that old dusty note in that file. Back in ninety-two, I think it was. After I got out of the gulag. But you haven't explained why anyone cares about the name of a rogue KGB assassin from a quarter-century ago."

Jack thought for a moment. "I didn't see a television in your flat."

"No use for them. No radio, either. Occasionally, there will be a football match on at the pub, but I have no interest in the news."

"That explains it, then."

Ox was confused. "What are you on about, Ryan?"

"This isn't about what happened a quarter-century ago. It's about what's happening now. You have no idea that Roman Talanov is the head of the FSB, do you?"

Oxley stared ahead, watching the traffic race by on Wellesley Road. After a long time he said, "No. I didn't know that." He took a thoughtful pull on his drink and stared off over the city. "Bloody fuckin' hell."

67

Thirty years earlier
CIA analyst Jack Ryan spent the first few hours after the raid on the RAF Sprengelstrasse flat in a musty vacant office at the British consulate in West Berlin.

As soon as he was given the chance to use a secure phone, Ryan called the CIA director of intelligence, Admiral James Greer. He reached Greer at home — it was nine p.m. on the East Coast — and he filled him in on the events of the past few hours. The admiral was astonished by the news of the shootout, especially his own man's part in it.

Ryan stressed to Greer he was skeptical that the RAF had operated alone, and he was certain there were other shadowy forces involved in this entire operation.

Greer doubted Ryan's theory of Russian involvement. "But Jack. What about Rabbit? You know as well as I do we have an asset who was well informed on KGB operations. We've spent months debriefing Rabbit. I find it hard to believe he's going to just scratch his chin and then say, 'Oh, yeah, I forgot to mention there is an assassin operating in Europe.' "

Jack said, "We need to check with him on this. Maybe he'll remember something relevant."

Greer said, "Look, Jack, we'll talk to him again, but you and I both know he wasn't holding out on us. If there were any active measures that in any way fit the description of what you are describing, he would have told us."

"Zaitsev has been out of the KGB communication room for months. This could be something that started after he left."

"Possible, but unlikely, and you know why. These operations take time to field. Assassinating Western European bankers. Coopting and — I guess you are saying — framing West German terrorists. That doesn't sound like an op that was just thrown together in the past few months, does it?"

"No," Ryan conceded. He paused. "I know what this sounds like."

"It sounds like you are grasping at straws. If it were anyone else, I'd dismiss this out of hand. But you aren't anyone else. You are one hell of an analyst, and I owe it to you to tell you to follow your instincts."

"Thanks."

"But whatever you do, I want you to remember this. The Brits are pretty good at this sort of thing. If they say they are done with the investigation, you'll be on your own over there. You can tap into whatever local agency facility you need to help you, of course, but be careful. You've come too close to danger already. I don't want you taking any unnecessary risks."

"That makes two of us."

Twenty minutes later, Ryan met with Eastling and his men in a second-floor office, and here they all went over the material found in the RAF safe house again. The German BfV retained custody of the briefcase and the contents inside, so two BfV investigators loomed over Eastling's and Ryan's shoulders while the Englishman and the American conducted their own review of the items.

Eastling and his men went first. This had begun as an SIS operation, after all. One of Eastling's men had a fingerprint kit, and he dusted the case and the items inside, then Eastling himself took each piece of evidence and read it over, examining watermarks on paper, the techniques used to print the photographs of the bankers, the typewriter characteristics of the letters on the bomb-making guide and the communiqué.

The case itself was examined for a false bottom or any other hidden compartments, but none were found.

Jack was fascinated by Eastling's handling of the evidence for the simple fact that Jack himself had no training in these types of investigative techniques. He wasn't a cop or a detective. His dad had been a detective on the Baltimore PD, and he'd always been interested in police work, but he'd never seen it as his calling.

He was an analyst, however, so when he finally got his chance to look over the material, he went for the documents first. He wore rubber gloves, of course, and had one of the BfV officers standing with him to translate.

Jack tried to get the BfV men to admit they didn't think it was possible the RAF members at the apartment could have possibly put up such a professional fight against GSG 9, but the Germans weren't as certain as Ryan. There were nine dead civilians in the flat on Sprengelstrasse, and so far only five of the bodies had been identified. The BfV officers said they couldn't pass judgment on the skill of the RAF fighters until they figured out the identity of all those lying on slabs in the morgue.

Ryan learned very little from his examination of the

documents. He wasn't a specialist on the RAF by any means, but the communiqué looked like a standard pronouncement from a left-wing terrorist group, and all the material involving the attacks on Gabler and Wetzel — the photos, the maps, and the bomb-making instructions — seemed legitimate.

The only thing doubtful about the entire scene was that in order to take the briefcase and its contents at face value, one had to believe Marta Scheuring possessed some of the absolute worst operational tradecraft in the history of left-wing terror. Even though the RAF routinely took credit for their operations, like most terror groups, the fact the young German woman had brought her ID along with her on her op strained credulity.

Ryan didn't know what to make of it. Scheuring had a couple of arrests under her belt, but she'd certainly never been implicated in a murder. That said, two of the inhabitants of the flat had been wanted for a rocket attack on a NATO installation several years earlier, and while no one had been killed or even seriously injured in the attack, certainly the intention had been to cause loss of life.

Eastling, as usual, was leaning toward wrapping up this investigation. Ryan, on the other hand, thought the spoon-fed nature of this evidence created more suspicions than the evidence itself cleared up.

As the Germans were anxious to leave with their evidence, Ryan and the Brits finished their review of the material in under an hour.

Jack had been up for more than twenty-four hours, so around nine a.m. he was offered a couch in an unused office to catch a couple hours' sleep.

At eleven-thirty a.m. Eastling leaned into the room.

Ryan sat up, rubbing his eyes and pushing a wool blanket off his legs.

Eastling sat down in the chair in front of him. His eyes were bloodshot, and his clothes were wrinkled. Jack wondered if he looked as tired and worn-out as the Englishman did.

"What's going on?" Jack asked.

"We've been through everything multiple times. The documents we found in Marta Scheuring's room at the RAF safe house look legitimate. The Germans have finally identified the other bodies in the flat. They were three girlfriends and one boyfriend of the occupants. None of them are known RAF members, but of course this will be looked into further.

"They also checked into the sniper location across the street. The one-room flat had been rented by Marta Scheuring three nights ago."

Jack was confused. "Marta rented a room two blocks away from where she lived? Why would she do that?"

Eastling shrugged. "Can't answer that one. Her name is on the ledger, but no one could ID her picture. It's a tenement-type lodging, so nobody pays attention to who comes and goes. Guest workers from Turkey, Ireland, and North Africa, mostly. A couple of people on her floor say they saw a man enter the room last night, late evening."

"What did they say about the man?"

"Twenties or thirties. White. Might have been German, might have been something else. No one heard him talk. No one heard any shooting coming from the room, either."

"How the hell is that possible?"

"Sniper rifle with a suppressor. It still makes a bloody loud racket, but considering the fact two blocks away a small-scale war was going on with more than two dozen people blasting each other and tossing bloody grenades, the *pop-pop* of a silenced weapon could quite easily go missed."

Jack sighed, then he had a new thought. "We've got to go back to Zug, show the pictures of Marta Scheuring to the bartenders at the place where Penright met the German woman the night he died."

Eastling was already shaking his head. "It's done, mate. Swiss did it yesterday, used a copy of her license."

"And?"

"Everyone working that night was in agreement. The woman who Eastling tried to pick up in the bar was not Marta Scheuring."

Jack had been so certain. Now he did not know what to say. He just muttered, "What's the next step?"

"That's what I'm here to talk to you about. I know you have concerns of KGB involvement, and I'm certainly not prepared to rule anything out at this moment, but I do believe this RAF cell committed the attack that killed the two Swiss bankers."

"What about Penright?"

Eastling answered with understated sarcasm: "I am sticking with my assertion that the bus that ran him down was not driven by the RAF, nor was it driven by the KGB. Seriously, Ryan, he wasn't pushed. Remember, there were witnesses saying he was drunk. And we do not think he was drugged. His body did not show indications of known poisons, though toxicology results won't be available for a while. If the Reds have some new poison we don't know about, well, Lord help us all. But that's not within the scope of my inquiry."

"So what are you telling me?"

"I'm telling you we are going home. This afternoon."

Jack rubbed his eyes. He found himself wanting to go home himself, to return to his house on Grizedale Close. Sitting on the sofa with Cathy, Sally on the floor coloring, and Jack Junior in his lap — it sounded like heaven right now.

But he pushed the fantasy out of his mind. *Not yet.*

Jack said, "Have a nice trip. I'm staying."

Eastling seemed to expect this. He said, "Am I going to have to force the issue?"

Ryan's eyes narrowed. "You don't have to do anything. I don't work for you."

"Bloody hell, Ryan, we are on the same side here."

"Not as far as I'm concerned. You are on the side of clearing up the Penright death, and I am on the side of finding out what the hell actually happened. There are other forces at work in this operation. Is it possible that David fell in front of a city bus? I suppose so, but I think we are getting played by the other side."

"How can I convince you?"

"You can give me everything you have on Morningstar. All the files leading up to Penright's trip to Switzerland, as well as the paperwork found in the safe at the safe house in Zug. Give me that, let me look it all over, and I'll draw my own conclusions as to what happened."

"I can't —"

"Basil brought me into this investigation because he thought I could help. I have expertise in this world — in a roundabout way, anyhow. If I was read in on what Penright knew, I could talk to Langley and try to get more relevant information on Ritzmann Privatbankiers. Maybe I can help connect whatever dots Penright was working on when he died."

Eastling said, "You're like some sort of a foxhound, aren't you? You think you've found a scent and now you won't stop, no matter what."

Ryan replied, "I *am* on a scent. I *know* I am."

Eastling did not respond to this, so Ryan prompted him.

"What do you think?"

Eastling said, "What do *I* think? I think you are a sanctimonious Yank who does not know how to behave. You shot up some Ulstermen last year and you got your knighthood, and you shot up some RAF sniper this morning and the Krauts will probably make you a bloody Kaiser or something equally as ridiculous, but your good fortune has advanced you further than your ability to work on a team ever will. If I was the one to make the decision, you would be dumped on your arse outside the U.S. consulate and shipped back to America, where you belong, in a steamer trunk." He took a deep breath and blew it out. "But this isn't a call for me to make."

He sighed again. "I'll talk to Basil, and he will make the determination what, if anything, you can see from the Morningstar files."

"That's all I ask."

68

Present day

Victor Oxley and Jack Ryan, Jr., waited an hour before beginning the interrogation of the Seven Strong Men hit man. Ryan had prompted the Englishman several times to get on with it, but Ox kept saying that he wanted to let the young man stew in the bathroom for a little while longer. He was held in an uncomfortable position, with no clear understanding of where he was or what was going on, and, Oxley explained to Ryan, giving him some time to think about his predicament was standard operating procedure for a hostile interrogation.

Jack thought it was just as likely that Ox wanted to sit on his ass and drink his whiskey for as long as possible, so he was stalling with all this talk of SOPs.

Jack himself got up once, declaring that he would get the ball rolling by asking the man some questions, but Oxley persuaded him to wait a little longer.

"Look, lad, we might have to resort to the 'good cop, bad cop' routine, and for that, I want to start with the bad cop, and that's gonna be me."

Oxley put his mixture of cola and whiskey down on the concrete surface of the tiny balcony, stood without a word, and went back in the room. Jack followed him in and he saw the big man pull off his sweater, revealing a wide back with as many tattoos as Jack had seen on his chest. Ox tossed the sweater on the bed and took a few slow breaths, as if trying to return to a place in his mind he had left long ago. Then he walked over to a small wooden table and chair set in the corner. With surprising ease, the fifty-nine-year-old snapped the leg off the chair with a loud crack, then turned back to Ryan.

"We need to know who sent him and why. Anything else?"

"You don't want me in there with you?"

"No, lad, I'll go in alone."

Ryan knew what Oxley was doing. He said, "Look, I appreciate you wanting to keep me clear of anything that might compromise me or my dad, but I can assure you, at this point I'm already in pretty deep."

Oxley stared at Jack for a moment, then said, "Lad, I don't give a flying toss about compromising you or your bloody daddy. That's a tiny loo in there, and if I have to start swinging, there's not going to be room for the both of us."

"Oh. Okay."

"Why don't you be a bright boy and look over his telephone, see if it has any answers I can't beat out of him? And while you're at it, turn up the volume on the telly."

"Okay. But Ox . . . I don't care if you sweat this guy, but don't kill him."

Oxley nodded; his face had taken on a blank expression since the moment he pulled off his sweater and again revealed himself to be a former inmate of a Russian gulag. He said, "I learned

578

something a long time ago, something you'd do well never to learn for yourself. Surviving is much more painful than death. Believe me, I won't do this arsehole the favor of snapping his neck."

Oxley stepped into the bathroom and shut the door behind him.

He stepped back out twenty minutes later. Ryan had spent the time transcribing numbers off the Russian's phone. All the exchanges were foreign, but Ryan hadn't looked them up yet. He hadn't called any of the numbers, either. The contact list was in Cyrillic, but although Ryan could read it easily, it was just a bunch of first names that told him little.

While Ryan had worked on writing the numbers down and looking through the text history on the phone, he'd heard several low wails and two sharp screams from the bathroom.

Victor Oxley's forehead was covered in sweat now. He was a good sixty pounds overweight, but Jack noticed for the first time that his shoulders, arms, and pecs, although covered in a thick layer of fat, retained a good deal of muscular bulk. He seemed to Jack more of an aging boxer who had let himself go than a completely sedentary bar-stool drunk.

"How is he?" Jack asked.

Ox did not respond at first. Instead, he just walked out to the balcony, breathed in a little cool air, and scooped up his bottle. He also picked up a bottle of beer, then went back inside, opened the bathroom door, and rolled the bottle inside.

He shut the door again, walked over to the bed, and slumped heavily onto his back on the mattress.

Finally he answered Ryan. "He's fine. The two of us got on like old chums. Oleg's his name."

"You didn't have to beat him up?"

"Well, just to say hello. After that, he was a right talker."

"And?"

"He is Seven Strong Men. He's been in the UK for only three days, came over on a Ukrainian passport that he got from Seven Strong Men contacts in Kiev."

"Kiev?"

"That's right. He works for a Russian bloke called Gleb the Scar. Gleb is *vory.*"

"That's like a made man in Russia, right?"

"Exactly. Gleb's blokes in Kiev had ordered some other blokes to tail you, they'd been doing it for weeks, says Oleg. He couldn't name 'em or describe them. He said he never saw them." Oxley shrugged and swigged. "And I do believe him. He wasn't holding out. Anyway, he and two others we met today in my flat came over to London with orders to take over for another crew that was following you around. Nothing more than that. But right after they arrived, you surprised them by driving up to Corby. One of the watchers reported that up the chain to Kiev, and then suddenly more Seven Strong Men henchmen were flying over from Kiev with new orders."

"What orders?" Jack asked.

"You were to get a good knockabout, broken jaw, that sort of thing, enough to send you home to America with your tail between your legs. Me, on the other hand, wasn't going to get off that easily. They had orders to kill me."

"Why?"

Oxley chuckled, a low rumble that shook the

580

bedsprings of the cheap mattress. "Let me explain something to you, lad. Oleg isn't in the 'why' loop of things. He gets a photo and an address, and he goes and does his job without asking about the 'why' part."

Jack thought it over. "So they were onto me before I even knew about you."

"Like I suspected. You brought this down on me."

"It must have to do Malcolm Galbraith."

"Who's that?"

"He's a guy who got screwed out of a billion dollars in Russia. I'm working for him. Well, I was until I was reassigned."

Oxley just sipped his drink, lying back on the pillows of the bed.

Jack asked, "You've never heard of Galbraith?"

The Englishman shook his head.

"What about Gleb the Scar?"

"Not till just now."

Jack thought for a moment. "Do you know a man named Dmitri Nesterov?"

He shook his head. "Who might that be?"

"He's the crook who ripped off Malcolm Galbraith. He is supposedly FSB."

Oxley shrugged and took another drink. The big man looked somewhat tipsy, which was to be expected. Jack was no teetotaler, but he realized he would have passed out long ago if he'd downed so much booze.

Jack said, "I need to talk to my dad, and I need to talk to my boss. Maybe we can put more pieces of the puzzle together."

"What's dear old Daddy gonna say about you shooting it out with the Russian mafia?"

Jack had been thinking about little else for the

past few hours. It was a problem, but this had gone way past the point of shielding his father from possible scandal. He said, "He's going to want me to come home to the USA as soon as he hears what's happened." Jack thought for a moment. "I'll wait for now, and call my dad once I know a little more about what's going on."

"He won't be pleased."

Jack just shrugged. He felt bad about continually worrying his parents with the life he led, but he sure as hell wasn't going to talk to this old Brit about his relationship with his family. He changed the subject: "What are we going to do with your pal Oleg in there?"

"We're going to let him go."

"Let him go? Are you crazy?"

"Might be, but when you think about it, what *can* we do with him? We are the two sods who've put four men on ice today, right?"

Jack didn't answer.

Oxley said, "Look, we turn him over to the cops, and this gets a lot more complicated for you. We cut him loose, and you don't have to admit you were there in Corby."

"What about your next-door neighbor? She saw me."

"Blind as a bloody bat, and half deaf to boot. She couldn't identify you as white, black, green, or blue, trust me."

"But if we let Oleg go, how do we know he won't just come back and try to kill us again?"

Ox laughed. "I'd like to see him try it with his two broken arms."

Jack slowly put his head down in his hands. "You broke his arms?"

"I'm not fucking daft, Ryan. He's a dangerous

582

man. He's not walking outta here with all his parts in working order."

"How the hell is he supposed to drink that beer you gave him?"

Victor laughed at this, too. "Not my problem, is it?"

"Okay," Jack said slowly. "I guess Oleg gets a pass. But if this Gleb the Scar character sent a half-dozen men after us, I imagine he can come up with another half-dozen."

Ox nodded. "It's a safe bet this town is crawling with Seven Strong Men killers."

"Why don't you come with me? You'll be safe. I'll talk to Sandy and see if he has any ideas as to who this Gleb the Scar is. Castor, too. It's possible that they've crossed paths in the —"

Victor Oxley sat up straight on the bed. His eyes were full of intensity again; whatever alcohol-fueled impairment Ryan had detected a moment ago was gone. "What did you say?"

"I said I have to talk to Sandy. Sandy Lamont. He's my boss."

"The other bloke."

"Oh . . . Castor. Hugh Castor. He runs Castor and Boyle, the consulting firm where I work."

Oxley climbed off the bed, stood, and walked over to Ryan. He stood above him, his posture menacing.

"What is it?"

"You asked me if I knew a lot of people, you didn't ask me if I knew Hugh Castor."

"Okay. I take it you know Hugh Castor?"

Oxley squeezed the bottle hard. "Tell me again, lad. How do you know about me?"

"I told you. Your code name. I showed you where Bedrock was written in the file."

"Yeah, you did. But how do I know Castor didn't send you?"

"Send me? Why?" The young American could tell that with his mention of Castor's name, the trust Oxley had slowly begun to give him seemed to be in jeopardy. "Who is Castor to you?"

"He was my control officer at Five."

Ryan's eyes went wide. "Oh, shit."

Oxley just stared at Ryan. Jack could see the older man was looking for signs of deception.

"I didn't know that." Jack stood up. "I don't know what happened between the two of you, but he never once mentioned your name. I've been trying to find a connection between my work at C&B and you, and now I guess I found it." He rubbed a hand over his short-cropped hair. "But I don't know what the hell any of it means."

Oxley turned away. "I don't know what it means, either."

Jack could see the man had become emotional. His face reddened, but Jack couldn't tell if it was anger or the whiskey.

"What happened between the two of you, Ox?"

Oxley just shook his head.

Ryan could tell now was not the time to press. "Okay. I understand. But listen to me. I want to unravel what's going on. My dad sent me to find out about you, to see if it could help tie Talanov to the Zenith killings. You've got your theories, your memories of a story you heard, but that's not actionable intelligence. I need to dig deeper in this, and I really need your help."

Ox was back on the bed, drinking again. His eyes were distant, but Ryan suspected it was from the memories now, and not the alcohol. Ox asked, "What help?"

Jack said, "I need to know where you first heard the name Talanov."

Oxley blinked. Again, it was obvious to Ryan that there was an incredible amount of pain in his memories.

He began speaking slowly: "It would have been about 1989, I guess. Time really had no meaning at all. I was in Syktyvkar, a gulag in Komi. No one there knew I was English. Sure as hell, no one knew I was MI5. I was just another *zek*."

"Zek?"

"A prisoner. Anyway, I'd been inside the system several years already, I was long past solitary. As a matter of fact, I was right popular. I knew enough battlefield medicine to keep some of the other *zek*s healthy, and I was fit enough, despite all I'd been through, to be the chap you wanted on your work crew. That goes a long way over there."

"I'm sure."

"I was still on the job, as far as I was concerned. I spent every day trying to pull intelligence out of the men around me. I thought someday I would escape, I really fuckin' believed it, probably because I would have gone mad without havin' a little hope. Anyway, I worked every other prisoner I could get to like they were a source or an agent. Prisoners know things, Ryan. I'd worked out the names and locations of most every secret military installation in the Soviet Union over the years. None of it made a bit of difference in the end, but as I said, as long as I lived like I was operational, even in the gulag, I had life, I had hope."

Ryan nodded thoughtfully. "I understand what you mean."

"One day I was eatin' my supper and listening in on a conversation between a couple of *zek*s.

One bloke starts off with a story about his day. He says he was mopping the floor in the infirmary when a prisoner from another cell block was brought in. The man had classic symptoms of typhoid: bloody nose, fever, delirium. He was a strong chap, still had his strength and fight. There were no tattoos on his body, so he hadn't been in the gulag for too long."

"Go on."

"This bloke tells me the guy started ranting about the KGB."

"What about the KGB?"

"He says he was a bloody KGB officer, starts telling the doctor to make a call to confirm it, he gives his name, which didn't match the name on his chart."

"Did they believe him?"

"Fuck no. I probably told somebody I was in the KGB at one point or another in Syktyvkar. Prisoners lie, Ryan. Once I met a chap in the gulag who said he was Yuri Gagarin. Of course, in his case, it wasn't so much a lie as a fantasy, as I believe he meant it."

"Back to the KGB guy, Ox."

"Right. So this delirious chap says he's KGB, and he's in the gulag on an operation. Everyone just laughed or what have you, then he starts in with how he was a paratrooper who was there when the presidential palace was taken in Kabul on the first day of the Afghanistan war. Claimed he then went into GRU, that's Russian military intelligence, fighting in Afghanistan.

"I was eatin' me soup through all this, listening in to the bloke, of course, but it wasn't until the guy told the doctor to contact a number in Moscow and report that Zenith needs emergency extraction that I knew I'd stumbled into a piece of me own history."

Ryan was transfixed by the story. "What happened to him?"

"Like I said, no one believed him, but he was persuasive enough that one of the nurses picked up the phone. You've got to understand, everyone must have been thinking, 'It's probably just the fever talking, but if there's a one-in-a-thousand chance he's on the up-and-up, then we might as well make the call,' because everyone working in that infirmary would have been shot if his story panned out and they had done nothing."

"Right."

"The nurse calls, the guy on the other end of the line says he doesn't have a fucking clue what she's on about, and he hangs up. Everyone figures that's that. They decide the bloke on the gurney covered in his own puke and blood and shit has a coin toss of a chance to survive, and they roll him into a corner, just like they'd do to any other *zek*."

Ryan realized there was more. His heart was pounding while he waited for Oxley to tell the rest.

"Five minutes later, I was in the kitchen pouring salt into hot water. I drank it down fast, and within a few seconds I was pukin' across the chow hall. They wheeled me into the infirmary."

Ryan was impressed. "What did you see?"

"I didn't see Zenith, unfortunately, I was shackled to my bed. But I did hear what was going on. The trucks came around midnight. It was a regular prisoner transfer, wasn't KGB, it was the Ministry of Prisons. They had the papers to take the other *zek* away. I heard the commotion as they wheeled him out.

"Later that night a bloke with a mop came by my bed. I offered him all the food I'd managed to save up in me cell to tell me what he'd seen and heard that day.

"He told me the *zek* sick with typhoid had called himself Talanov."

"Oh my God," Ryan muttered.

"The prisoner-transfer truck showed up with doctors in the back of the vehicle ready to tend to him. Didn't sound like any prisoner transfer I'd ever heard of." Ox shrugged. "By the time this chap told me the story, the *zek* named Talanov who'd said he was a KGB officer called Zenith was gone from Syktyvkar."

Ryan believed the story, or he at least believed that Ox believed it.

Oxley kept his eyes on Jack now. There was a lack of trust there still, but Jack also got the impression Oxley didn't know what else to do. He couldn't go home. After a moment, he said, "I'll stick around for a wee bit, Ryan. But I'm watching you. You got it?"

"I've got it."

"What's our next move, then?"

"We untie that asshole in the bathroom, leave him here, get back in the car and go someplace else. Don't know where, but we'll wing it. Once we get there I'll call a friend who can tell me everything I'd ever want to know about every phone number on Oleg's phone. That should help."

"Sounds like a bloody handy friend."

"He has his moments."

69

Eric Conway and Andre Page headed out to their helicopter at five a.m. They'd been up for more than an hour already, drinking coffee and going over weather reports in the flight operations center. Conway had spent a little longer than usual at the weather desk in Flight Ops, because a thick fog had settled over Cherkasy, and storms were brewing to the north. It was something they would have to monitor, but this was combat; it would not affect their planned six a.m. departure.

Even though there was a war going on out there somewhere, it seemed quiet and peaceful here. Most of the Ukrainian ground forces at the base had rolled out for the front lines as soon as the fighting broke out, leaving behind the company of American multipurpose scout helos, the Ranger security force, and Midas's Joint Operations Center.

Four of Bravo Company's eight matte-black Kiowas were already up in the air to support Ukrainian Mi-24 attack helicopters fighting against ground units near Chuhuiv Air Base, a half-hour flying time to the east.

Those OH-58s would be used to fire lasers at targets in locations where the Special Forces and

Delta teams were not available. Their work would be no more or less dangerous than today's flight by Conway and Page, except for the fact Eric and Dre would be flying into battle without any air defense missiles.

Black Wolf Two Six wore four Hellfire missiles on its pylons, and that was all. They had considered operating with a pair of Stingers on one pylon and a pair of Hellfires on the other, but Conway decided to trust in the advanced countermeasures of his helicopter as well as its radar, and to give up air-to-air capability to buy himself double the air-to-ground capability.

They finished their preflight workup outside the helo and each man walked to his side of the OH-58. Here, they stood at the crew station doors, put on their helmets, attached their commo sets, and unhooked their M4 rifles from the slings around their necks. It was impossible for them to fly with rifles hanging off their chests, so they stored the weapons on the dashboard above the instrument panels, keeping them within reach at all times so they could grab them and fire out the open sides of the little helicopter if necessary. They kept a few frag grenades and smoke markers Velcroed into position here as well.

A couple of carbines and some frags wasn't much when compared with the four antiarmor missiles on the outboard stores, but the battle rifles had come in handy for the two men before. Two years earlier, in Afghanistan, they'd been on a close air-support mission over a group of Dutch coalition infantry in danger of being overrun by Taliban on a hillside. They launched all of the Kiowa's Hydra seventy-millimeter rockets at an enemy position, wiping out the threat there, but almost immediately after this an RPG streaked past the windscreen of the OH-58. Conway saw the origin of the launch, called out the location to his copilot, then turned the helo ninety degrees. He flew sideways at the threat while Dre aimed his M4 and emptied a full magazine at the RPG crew, killing both men before they'd been able to fire another rocket at either the helicopter or the Dutch troops in the valley.

The two young warrant officers flew back to Jalalabad celebrating with high fives, but Page had been nearly despondent upon returning to the ready room after the fact when it became clear the Kiowa's gun camera hadn't recorded the shooting for posterity because it had been positioned forward, not facing out the side of the helicopter.

Both men knew that the campaign here in Ukraine would bear little resemblance to what they had experienced around J-bad. The Russian military, with its Air Force and long-range missiles, along with its sophisticated attack helos and T-90 tanks, made the Taliban look like amateurs.

While they prepped for takeoff this foggy morning, each of the men worked from a checklist, going through the various systems on the helicopter; Conway focused on testing his Sperry Flight Control System and his avionics, while Page spooled through his cameras, targeting computer, and mast-mounted sight laser designation and backup systems.

Both men tested their comms, and both men felt over their bodies for all SERE equipment.

Shortly before six a.m. their crew chief gave them a thumbs-up on the pad and Conway started the Rolls-Royce engine. There was a ten-second-long high-pitched whine before the main rotor even began to spin, and it took more than a minute for the Allison engine to transfer enough power to the main and tail rotors for takeoff. Another round of checklists was tackled; by now Page was talking on a channel to the crew chief, discussing the possibility of a quick return to the pad to get more Hellfires in the case of heavy action.

The crew chief insisted he'd be ready for them when they came back, whether it was in four hours or four minutes.

At six a.m. Eric Conway keyed his microphone. "Black Wolf Two Six, Cherkasy Ground, over?"

"Cherkasy Ground, Black Wolf Two Six."

"Black Wolf Two Six, ready for takeoff."

The flight control officer cleared the OH-58 for takeoff and a southerly departure out of the base, and the black bird rose slowly into the foggy morning.

They were just a few hundred feet in the air when a transmission came through their headsets from the JOC, which was different from Bravo Company Flight Ops.

"Black Wolf Two Six, Warlock Zero One. How copy?"

Both Conway and Page knew this was Midas transmitting on the net. He ran the JOC, but in typical Army obfuscation his radio call sign was different from his Delta call sign.

"Warlock Zero One, copy. We are outbound to waypoint Alpha. ETA is one-nine mikes, over."

"Roger, Two Six. Proceed to waypoint Golf and advise. At this point I do not have any targets for you, so I'll need you to loiter on station, how copy?"

"Black Wolf Two Six copies all."

Conway pushed the cyclic forward and pulled up the collective; the aircraft climbed up through the fog as it raced toward the Crimea.

"You don't feel like skimming the trees in this soup?" Page asked jokingly.

"You know what they say. 'Speed is life, but altitude is life insurance.' "

Their mission today was flexible. Their primary task was to collect battlefield intelligence for the force commander, but Conway knew at any moment Midas, or Warlock Zero One, or whatever the hell his name was, might order them to support one of the dozen or so U.S. and British special operations teams active in Operation Red Coal Carpet.

As they climbed out of the fog, seeing nothing but blue sky and green pastureland in the distance, a series of crackling transmissions came over their radios. Two of the Kiowas near the Chuhuiv Air Base had located targets moving through a paved road linking two small towns. The Warriors were in the process of lasing targets for a squadron of Mi-24 Hinds, and their transmissions made the two men in Black Wolf Two Six wish they were part of the action.

The bulk of the fighting so far had been in the provinces — called oblasts in Ukraine — of Donetsk and Luhansk, and the American helicopters were ordered to stay outside of this area, although some of the Delta Force teams were operating in Donetsk just to blunt the speed at which the Russians advanced.

More than an hour into its flight, Black Wolf Two Six was flying low along the E50 highway east of the large industrial town of Dnipropetrovs'k. The highway was filled with civilian vehicles leaving Donetsk to the east; many, if not most, looked like they were full of personal belongings and valuables.

Conway spoke through his intercom: "Hey, Dre, I read that over eighty percent of the citizens around here are, to one degree or another, allied with Russia."

"Something like that."

"So why the hell is everybody making a run for it? They should be glad the Russians are coming, right?"

"They might be glad they are coming to liberate them, or whatever, but that doesn't mean they want to be standing right there when it goes down. There's a shit ton of fighting to be done before this thing is settled."

Conway was about to respond when the JOC came over their headsets and directed them to a grid coordinate just fifteen minutes east of their position. Conway acknowledged and picked up speed and altitude, leaving his flyover of the thick traffic behind and heading over rolling forestland.

As they flew, Midas gave them more information.

"Black Wolf Two Six, Warlock Zero One, stand by for sitrep." There was a brief pause, then Midas said, "Team Frito has eyes on two BM-30 emplacements digging in southeast of Mezhova. They have not been able to raise UDF assets to engage, and the red forces will be in range of major population centers within the next hour."

Conway and Page both knew the BM-30 was a massive Russian missile launcher that fired up to a dozen 300-millimeter rockets at a time at a distance of up to fifty miles. Along with each one there would be several smaller support vehicles. It was a powerful and potent weapon, and the fact four of them had been amassed within range of the city of Dnipropetrovs'k did not say much for the future prospects of Ukrainian forces in and around Dnipropetrovs'k. There was a Ukrainian forward helo base as well as the largest military base in the oblast just on the far side of the city, and both of these locations would be perfect targets for the multi-rocket launchers.

Page took over the radio now to get more intel on the targets. "Can you advise other red assets at emplacement location?" Dre wanted to know if they would be up against troops, tanks, helicopters, or other means to shoot down the Kiowa.

"Warlock Zero One. AWACS advises no enemy air in area. Frito advises troop transport vehicles and multiple dismounts, but no confirmation of anti-air."

"Roger that," said Page, and he looked to Conway. "Dude, what are the chances the Russkis are going to set up two big, dumb, slow missile batteries without protecting them from air attack somehow?"

"No chance at all," confirmed Conway. "We will engage from max standoff distance and minimize exposure."

"Sounds like a plan," Dre said, and he began making preps on his multifunction display sighting system for the engagement to come.

Before arriving on station five miles to the west of the BM-30 emplacement, Black Wolf Two Six was put in direct radio contact with Frito Actual, the leader of the 10th Special Forces Group team in the area. Page's targeting computer showed him the location of the friendly, or "blue," forces, and Frito gave him up-to-date intel on the threats in the area.

Page and Conway both looked over the moving map display when they were still twenty miles out, and Page scanned forward with his mast-mounted sight, looking for anything out of the ordinary. There were a few small villages and factories away from the city, but mostly the area was rolling forest. Page said, "I know Frito says we're golden on this, but I think you want to come in low. Sneak in for a peek with the optics. See them before they see us."

Conway said, "Roger that."

Black Wolf Two Six descended to just forty feet above the treetops, and Conway dipped even lower as they crossed clearings and streams. Page's stomach had long since grown accustomed to the vomit-inducing roller-coaster ride of nap-of-the-earth flight, but in the back of his mind every now and then he still thought Conway made some of his maneuvers for the sole purpose of fucking with his internal organs.

They passed a small town built around a large but deserted redbrick factory building. From the look of its three smokestacks on the roof, Conway thought the factory might have been some sort of smelting operation. He lowered to only twenty-five feet above a gravel road just behind the factory, positioning the three-story brick building between his aircraft and the target area, separated by nearly five miles of forests and farms.

Page was on the radio with team Frito, and he flipped back and forth between multiple views of the target area. He said, "I'm not an expert on the

BM-30, but those fuckers look like they are ready to launch."

Conway had been spending his time with his eyes outside the helicopter. There were enough gadgets and gizmos in the Warrior to where pilots ran the risk of pulling into a hover and then spending too much time absorbing information other than the environment around them.

But Conway was too experienced for that. He let Page do the prep for the attack while he watched the fields, roads, buildings, and wood line around them, knowing that hovering still here above this gravel road in a relatively soft-skinned helicopter meant it would take only a couple of Russians in a jeep with a machine gun to ruin this otherwise decent morning.

He glanced down at Page's monitor and saw the Russian missile trucks. He was no expert, either, but they looked like they could start raining missiles down on Ukraine at any time.

Page switched his view to his own camera, located in the mast-mounted sight, the large pod above the main rotor assembly. The MMS was a ball with two prominent glass "eyes" in front, and Dre called the instrument "E.T." The new version of the Warrior was coming online stateside right now, and Conway looked forward to getting his hands on one because of all the new developments in the aircraft. That said, the new model had its laser rangefinder and designator in a pod below the pilot's feet, so the aircraft would have a new look. Eric had flown E.T. around for nearly four years, and he would miss the distinctive look the MMS gave his bird.

Right now they were behind the building, and

Dre couldn't see the target through his own camera.

He said, "All right, Eric. Let's have us a look-see."

Conway pulled the collective on his left, and the helicopter rose slowly in its hover. At fifty feet above the ground, the mast-mounted sight was above the roof of the brick building just forty yards ahead, peeking at the distant target.

When Page saw what he needed to see on his monitor, he said, "Good. Right there."

Conway held the helo stationary.

Page saw the two targets in a pair of fields separated by a small river; a bridge connected them. Along with the two massive trucks, each with missile tubes pointed high in the air, there were another dozen or more trucks and armored personnel carriers.

"Air defense assets?" Conway asked.

Page couldn't see anything definitive at this distance, but he knew there had to be something out there that could kill him.

But Dre Page knew he had a job to do, and the U.S. taxpayer gave him $38,124 a year to put his life on the line in foreign lands, so he put as much worry out of his mind as possible and said, "Looks clear on the ground. Still no red air to worry about?"

"Negative. Closest threats are seventy miles away in Crimea. It's clear, blue, and twenty-two here, bro."

This was helicopter-pilot speak for good flying weather.

"Range to target?" Conway asked.

Page shot the laser rangefinder. "Lasing target. Seven thousand six hundred eighty-one."

"You good with that range?" Conway asked. It was near max distance. He could move the aircraft closer if Dre felt the engagement necessitated it.

Page said, "Dude, the fighter in me wants to be right on top of them. But the survivor in me kinda likes hiding behind this big fucking brick factory."

"I heard that, brother. Let's rock it from here."

Page transmitted in his headset. "Warlock Zero One, this is Two Six. We are requesting clearance for fires for Hellfire."

Midas came over the radio instantly: "Black Wolf Two Six, this is Warlock Zero One. I've got no Ukrainian air assets in the area. You are cleared hot with Hellfires, over."

"Roger, cleared hot."

Conway said, "Let's do it."

Page ignored Conway; he knew that Conway's adrenaline fired him up like this, but Page prided himself on staying cool. "Frito Actual. Black Wolf Two Six. Be advised, we will be weapons release."

"Roger that, Black Wolf. We are well clear. Negative friendlies at target pos. Get those missile trucks and get the fuck out of here before enemy helos come hunting for you."

"Roger that."

Conway slipped his thumb under the guard on the Weapons Fire switch on his cyclic.

He said, "Firing in three, two, one." He pressed the fire button and sent an air-to-ground missile toward the first of the two huge mobile missile launchers.

"Hellfire blazing," Conway said, confirming he could see good propulsion on the missile as it raced to the east.

"That's sixty-five grand, off the rails," Page said calmly. It was his joke, not Conway's, because

Page was the more relaxed of the two men in combat.

Conway did not wait to watch the impact on the MFD. Instead, he selected a second missile, and fired at the same target as the first. He could have switched between the two targets, but stacking up two back-to-back shots at the same target increased the chances the antimissile features of the battery would be defeated.

The first Hellfire was detected by laser warning receivers set up at the emplacement, and countermeasures were fired into the air. The American warhead was knocked down seventy-five yards away from impact by an automatic missile defense battery that neither Page nor Frito had detected.

But the second Hellfire got through, and detonated above the missile launcher, and even though Conway had been in the process of counting down his third Hellfire launch, he stopped when his MFD whited out.

He thought something was wrong with the system at first, and he began adjusting the monitor.

In his headset he heard, "Two Six, Frito Actual. Good hit, good hit. Multiple secondary detonations. Damn, dude, you really nailed it."

Just then Page called out next to him: "Holy smokes."

Conway looked up. Five miles in the distance, a black form was slowly morphing into a mushroom cloud. Several seconds later, a low boom was audible through his headset and the sound of the rotors above him.

It took a moment to get reset, but he fired his third missile to the east.

Just as he did so, a digitized male voice boomed

in his and Page's headsets. "Laser! Laser! Eleven o'clock."

Page said, "Inbound fire!"

"Rapid release!" Conway said, and he fired another missile, this one at the second BM-30.

Just then Conway pulled right on the cyclic and punched down on the left pedal, turning the craft ninety degrees. He put the aircraft in a nose-down attitude, and the helicopter dove at the gravel road behind the brick factory building.

"Countermeasures," Page said, and the Kiowa automatically fired flares as it plummeted.

Just a few feet above the ground Black Wolf Two Six leveled out, and raced over a field.

Less than one hundred fifty yards behind, a missile from a shoulder-fired launcher slammed into one of the factory's three smokestacks, blowing it to bits and sending redbrick shrapnel in all directions.

Conway kept his speed up as a second missile hit the factory behind them. As he looked back over his left shoulder, his ears filled with an excited transmission from Frito team.

"Hell, yeah! Second target destroyed! Another fuckin' neutron bomb!"

"Roger that," Page said calmly. Now he looked out the open door on his side. The warning alarms had ceased, but he and Conway were still on the lookout for threats.

Warlock Zero One came over the net now. "Black Wolf, hell of a job, but they know you're out there. Return to base."

Conway said, "Roger that. RTB."

Both young men's hearts pounded against their body armor as they raced over a larch forest to the northwest. Normally, they did a lot of fist

601

pumping after a successful target engagement, but right now both men were lost in their own thoughts, because they knew they'd just come a hair's breadth away from death.

70

John Clark and his group of operations officers from The Campus had spent every day since their return from Sevastopol photographing people who visited the ninth floor of the Fairmont Grand Hotel.

They had quite an impressive array of characters in their rogues' gallery, and to put names with the faces, Gavin Biery ran the pictures through facial-recognition software, using databases from the CIA SIPRNet, the Ukrainian Security Service files, and other open-source locations.

Still, none of the team had gotten eyes on Gleb the Scar himself. It was clear that this was by design. The team had staked out all the exits of the hotel in the worry that he had some sort of clandestine access to his penthouse, but after spending a day spread around the neighborhood, watching employee entrances, loading docks, and the rooftop heliport, they came to the conclusion that Gleb wasn't coming and going. No, he was apparently just sitting.

Clark had moved his operation to yet another safe house. This was a smaller flat, just two blocks away from the Fairmont, and it was owned by a friend of Igor's. The flat owner had fled the city with his wife and kids when the war started in the east, fearing the Russians would drive all the way to Kiev, and this gave Clark and company a secure safe house with a living room window that afforded them a good view of the Fairmont, and with their photographic equipment they could get decent imagery of those who came and went in the building.

A balcony on the ninth floor was also in view, and on it they could see two armed security officers standing, twenty-four hours a day. The men had scoped Dragunov sniper rifles, as well as binoculars. They looked out over the neighborhood, scanning for any surveillance or threats, but the Campus men had covered all of their apartment windows with black paper, save for a small hole where they could position their cameras.

Clark and his team had swept for bugs here, and found the place to be clean. The FSB didn't have every apartment in the city under surveillance, of course, and Kryvov's friend had not been deemed a security target by either the Ukrainians or the Russians.

As secure as the Campus staff felt in their new digs, they felt more and more insecure on the streets of the city. In the past three days several police officers and government officials, and even an SSU spy, had been killed on the streets of Kiev. A pronational television station's broadcast had been interrupted by the explosion of a bleach bomb that rendered the air in the studios caustic, and a radio station that had spoken out against Russia's attack in the east had been set on fire and knocked off the air.

Just before eight p.m., Gavin sat on the sofa in the safe house. In front of him on the coffee table

604

sat several slap-on GPS transmitters with their battery compartments open. He and Clark were changing out the batteries, a dull but necessary task, made a little harder for Clark because he'd had most of the bones in his right hand shattered more than a year earlier.

As they worked in silence, Gavin's mobile phone rang; he didn't even look at it before he answered. "Yeah?"

"Hey, Gav, it's Jack."

"Ryan! Good to hear from you. How's everything in jolly ol' England?"

"Not as jolly as I'd like, to tell you the truth."

"No? Well, you should see it over here. Riots in the street, assassinations, bombings, spies, mob thugs, you name it."

There was a pause on the line. "Gerry moved Hendley Associates to D.C.?"

Gavin laughed. "I guess you are out of the loop. We're in Kiev."

"Really? I had no idea. What are you doing there?"

"You know. Spy shit."

"Right. Is everybody safe?"

"Yeah. Got dicey for John, Dom, and Ding the other day, but we're fine."

"Well, I need a favor. I have a list of phone numbers, and I was hoping you could trace them."

"Sure. Send them on."

A few seconds later, an e-mail appeared on Gavin's phone. He opened it and thumbed the list of phone numbers up and down.

"Interesting. Most of these are local Kiev numbers. Where did you get them?"

"Off of one of the mob goons in London who tried to kill me today."

Gavin looked at Clark with wide eyes. Clark saw the look, and he reached out for the phone.

Gavin didn't hand it over immediately. "Are you serious?"

" 'Fraid so. I could use that information as soon as you can get it to me."

Gavin said, "Sounds like it. I'll get on this right now. I've been playing around inside the network of the local telecom system. I can get you names and addresses of the owners of the phone, but I can also do another neat trick."

"What's that?"

"I can backtrack the GPS localizer associated with these numbers. That means I can tell you where each one of these phones has been, physically, for the past thirty days. We call it breadcrumbing."

"That would be great."

Clark snapped the fingers of the hand held out for the phone.

Gavin said, "I've got someone here who wants to talk to you."

Ryan mumbled, "I was afraid of that. He's going to chew me out, isn't he?"

Gavin Biery said, "Think of it as tough love, kid."

Clark got on the phone with Ryan, who proceeded to tell him everything about the events of the past day. Clark listened intently, he did not interrupt at all, but once Ryan was finished with his story, the pause on the line told the younger man that the older man was not pleased.

Clark said, "Kid, I swear to God, you manage to get yourself into the shit, don't you?"

"Well . . . this kind of blew up on me."

"The second you had even just that twitchy feeling that you were being tailed you should have picked up the damn phone and called me."

"Well, John, from what Gav just told me, you've been a little tied up yourself."

"That doesn't get you off the hook on this one. You know I could have had guys and guns around you within a couple of hours. Hell, I know enough old SAS guys there in London I could have had security on you in twenty minutes. You can't just run solo like that, for crying out loud. You are the President's son."

"I know. I thought I was just being paranoid. I didn't recognize the threat level until it was too late."

"This Gleb the Scar you mentioned is a personality we are very familiar with over here."

"Really?"

"Yes. He's Seven Strong Men, from Saint Petersburg. We think he might be the number-two guy in their organization."

"Who's number one?"

"No one knows. But Gleb is over here running proxy ops for FSB."

Ryan said, "Interesting. The guys who attacked me work for him, and in my work at Castor and Boyle, I uncovered an illegal scheme to defraud one of our clients, and traced it as a payoff by Gazprom, which is the Russian government, to a man with FSB ties named Dmitri Nesterov."

Clark told Ryan to hold the line while he checked to see if that was a name they had come across in Ukraine. They had not. He then asked his local expert, Igor Kryvov, if he had ever heard the name, but it was new to him as well.

Clark spoke quickly and with complete self-assuredness. "All right, you are obviously in the center of a shit storm over there, so here's what's going to happen: I'm sending Ding, Dom, and Sam to you right now, tonight, on the Gulfstream. They will escort you back to the States. If your new friend there has a passport, they can take him as well. If he doesn't have a passport, we might be able to swing something."

Ryan hesitated for a moment.

Clark sensed the reticence and said, "Jack, you realize you can't stay there. Right?"

"John, I know it looks like I'm running a hell of a risk staying over here, but I am in the middle of something I can't drop. The stakes are too high. I'd appreciate a little muscle to watch my back, only if you can spare it."

"I'll have them moving in a half-hour. Are you at least in a secure location now?"

"I am mobile. I left my car at a mall and we took a taxi to a car rental agency, where I picked up a new ride. It's in my name, so I could be traced, theoretically, but the Seven Strong Men guys on me haven't shown that they are using much high-tech surveillance just yet. Just to be sure, I've done an SDR, and there is no tail."

Clark replied, "I'd feel better if you'd go back to the States, but for now, I'll get the plane and the guys to London. In the meantime, we will call you back when Gavin runs the names on the phone data you sent him."

"Thanks, John."

Ryan and Oxley drove through the countryside north of London while they waited for Gavin to call back. There was no conversation between the two of them. Ox seemed lost in thought, and Ryan was thinking over his next move.

He wanted to talk to Sandy Lamont, but he was not sure he could trust him. It was very possible Lamont had tipped off someone that Ryan was going to Corby. It was possible that Lamont knew about the connection between Castor and Oxley, although why anyone would need to die over it remained a mystery to Ryan.

The more Jack thought about Lamont, the more suspicious he became. He recognized his affable boss had twice warned him against digging deeper into the Gazprom deal, before finally pulling him off the case altogether. Could there have been reasons for this more nefarious than those he'd stated?

Jack knew the only way to find out for sure was to confront him and gauge his reaction.

They stopped at a fast-food restaurant and grabbed takeout, and then parked in the lot behind a busy motor lodge to eat. They had just finished their meal when Jack's phone chirped.

"Hey, Gavin."

It was John Clark who spoke first. "Actually, it's John and Gavin. We've got you on speakerphone."

Gavin spoke next. "Ryan, you've got yourself a situation there."

"Explain."

"There were twenty-four contacts on the phone that were of possible interest, but I whittled it down to six that needed the full track run on them. Two of the six are personalities we've run into over here in Kiev."

"You've got to be kidding."

"Nope," said Clark. "We've spent most of the past week tagging men who've met with Gleb the Scar at the Fairmont Grand. These two guys on your hit man's phone are obviously mob characters. I put them as lieutenants. They've been in regular contact with your man Oleg for at least the past month, and spoke to him within the past twenty-four hours while he was there in the UK."

Gavin picked up from there. "Two more are apparently in the group you put on ice. Their phones stopped moving just after noon today in the town of Corby, and now they are beaming signals in a police station. I backtracked the GPS bread crumbs to several locations, both in the UK and in Ukraine. They aren't so terribly interesting in and of themselves, but their phones were in the same low-rent hotel the day before yesterday as another phone on the list, and that phone is the most fascinating of all."

"And why is that?"

John Clark spoke now: "Because the owner of that phone has spent part of the past month in a house in a Moscow suburb. That house is owned by a man named Pavel Lechkov, and although we know he's Russian, we don't have anything on him. We tried to find a picture of Lechkov but came up blank, which makes me suspect he might be an intelligence agent." Clark added, "There's more, Jack."

"I'm listening."

Gavin said, "I bread-crumbed his phone number and tracked it to a couple of hotels in London. But Friday evening he went to a private residence in Islington."

Jack asked the next question with trepidation. "Friday evening is after I went to Corby to see Ox. Whose place did Lechkov go to in Islington?"

Clark said, "He spent twenty-five minutes at the home of Hugh Castor."

"Is that right?" Jack mumbled.

Clark said, "Yes. Whether or not he met with Castor, of course, we can't say. Nevertheless, I'm afraid your employer in London is starting to look like he might be involved — indirectly, at least — in the attack on you."

Ryan said, "That's two strikes against him. He's involved with the Seven Strong Men, and he knew Oxley from a long time back. It seems like this Lechkov paid Castor a visit after I went and met with Oxley, and then Lechkov met with Oleg and the other Seven Strong Men goons and gave them orders to kill Ox."

Clark said, "Jack, I hope you will agree, this seems like a fine time for you to head back to the U.S."

Ryan did not agree. "I have someone here in London that I need to talk to. After that, I want to meet with Malcolm Galbraith. He might be able to connect some more dots."

Clark went silent.

To bolster his argument, Jack said, "John, I'll be at Stansted when the plane lands, and we'll fly to Edinburgh. It's *Edinburgh*. It's not Kiev or Moscow. Plus I'll have Ding, Sam, and Dom at my side the whole time. Adara will keep watch on the aircraft and Oxley. All I want to do is go have tea with a billionaire and pick his brain — how much trouble can I get into with that?"

Clark sighed. "I guess we're about to find out."

71

Thirty years earlier

After his altercation with MI6 counterintelligence investigator Nick Eastling, CIA analyst Jack Ryan left the British consulate and took a cab to the West Berlin suburb of Zehlendorf. Here, on Clayallee, a large compound of buildings known as Clay Headquarters lay sprawled over several fenced-in blocks. This was the home of Berlin's United States military command, known as the Berlin Brigade, as well as the Office of the United States Commander, and U.S. Mission Berlin.

Mission Berlin was essentially the State Department's toehold in the city, because there was no U.S. embassy here.

The CIA, not surprisingly, had many secret locations in West Berlin, but their facility here behind the offices of Mission Berlin was among the most secure and well equipped.

Ryan had chosen this location so that he could communicate with Langley.

He was searched by the U.S. Army guards at the Clayallee main gate, and some calls were made to establish his identity. Soon he walked alone up a tree-lined street and entered the side entrance to Mission Berlin. He gave his name to a man behind a desk, and he was searched again, and then escorted to a free-standing building behind the State Department's facility.

This was the local CIA station, and it did not take long for Ryan to establish his credentials and obtain his own small office to work from, along with a secure phone.

It took a few minutes to get the phone working, and as soon as he got a dial tone he called Cathy at Hammersmith Hospital. He was disappointed to reach a receptionist who told him his wife was in surgery at the moment, so he left a message saying all was well and he'd try to call that evening.

He then put in a call to Sir Basil Charleston at Century House, but again, he could not reach his intended party. Charleston's secretary told Jack that Sir Basil was on a call to the United States and that he would get back with him at the soonest possible opportunity.

Jack spent an hour of the afternoon sitting in the office waiting. Finally, at four p.m., Sir Basil Charleston called back.

"I've heard it all from Nick," Basil said.

"Eastling and I don't see eye to eye on this. Or on anything, for that matter."

"I gathered as much. You have to understand one thing, Jack. The nature of the work of our counterintelligence staff makes them a tad different than us. I am going to use a football analogy. I do hope you can follow along."

Jack replied, "I assume you mean soccer."

"Yes, you call it soccer over there, don't you? Anyway, we, as intelligence officers, are offensive players. We see the world as our opponent's goal, and we attack it, leaving the role of protecting our goal to others. Counterintelligence, on the other hand, are the defenders, they are trained to protect the goal. They take issue with us running up the field and leaving them to suss out the opposing side on their own. They look at us as a risk.

"A team needs both types, but sometimes we attackers don't appreciate the tactics of the defenders."

Ryan said, "I hope you will let me play some offense. Morningstar may be dead, but there is more to learn about the accounts at Ritzmann Privatbankiers."

"I spoke with Judge Moore and Admiral Greer this afternoon. I have agreed to give you access to the Morningstar dossier and the preliminary files of the Penright investigation on the condition that you share all your findings with us immediately."

A wave of relief washed over Ryan. "Of course I will."

"Will you be coming back to London?"

"I'd like to stay over here in case I turn up anything."

"I thought you might say that. I'm having everything driven over to you from our consulate in Berlin. A courier will stand by while you look it over. He'll explain the protocol to you."

"I'll get right to work on it here, and I'll call you if I find anything."

An hour later, Ryan met the courier from the local MI6 office in the lobby of Mission Berlin. The man called himself Mr. Miles, and after Jack gave him one look he decided the man had been out of the military and working for SIS for all of about ten minutes. He was middle-aged but square-jawed and muscular and he stood with his shoulders ramrod straight. He carried a briefcase in which, Jack assumed, the files were stored. Jack reached out to take it, and Mr. Miles pulled the arm of his coat up a few inches to reveal the case discreetly handcuffed to his wrist.

"Let's you and me have a wee chat before I hand this off to you. Is that all right, sir?"

"Sure," Jack said. It dawned on the American analyst then that being passed secret documents in the field was a different process from having them sent over to one's desk at Century House.

Together, Jack and Miles walked to the cafeteria, and as soon as they sat at a table, the Englishman had Jack sign several sheets of paper saying he wouldn't steal any of the documents he was about to see, nor would he copy anything, destroy anything, or otherwise do anything that would give the British SIS courier a reason to hit him over the head with a chair.

Ryan thought this fellow to be one of the most serious Englishmen he'd met in his time over here in Europe, but, he had to admit, sending Mr. Miles over with the files did have the desired effect. Ryan told himself he'd better not get so much as a smudge on the paperwork, because he did not want this man annoyed with him.

Soon the courier sat at a table in the cafeteria to smoke cigarettes and drink coffee, and Jack went back to his tiny borrowed office so he could dig into the files relating to the Morningstar case.

He saw immediately that much of it was in the form of notes in David Penright's own handwriting, and other documents — these all related to Penright's death — were in the handwriting of Nick Eastling and members of his team.

Of all the documents present, the dot-matrix printout of internal bank account transfers at Ritzmann Privatbankiers was the most curious to Jack.

At first blush it wasn't much to look at. Just columns of numbered accounts next to other columns of numbered accounts alongside a column that showed, as far as Jack could determine, values represented in Swiss francs.

Paper-clipped to the file was an English translation of the few words on the pages.

There was nothing about the printout that seemed obviously crucial to the case. If the KGB or other Russians were using RPB to hold money, the transfers into the bank to the suspected Russian account would be damn important, as would any transfers out of the bank to other banks around the world. These sorts of transactions could help SIS and CIA follow the money trail.

But internal account transfers did not seem terribly useful to Ryan. He knew enough about banking to know that many account holders had multiple accounts and routinely moved their money around within the bank. Some accounts might be tied to an investment portfolio or another account might be used for payables at the account holder's place of business.

This sheaf of papers seemed to Ryan to be more clerical in nature.

Another problem with the printout was that it was indecipherable to him, because although Penright had given him the list of clients of the banks, the client list was not tied to the numbered accounts themselves.

No, there was no reason to find this printout interesting in the least, except for the fact that, as far as anyone could determine, a bank executive had hand-delivered these internal documents to a British spy on the night the British spy was killed, and the bank executive himself was killed two days later.

That alone made this long, folded dot-matrix printout worthy of further investigation.

Ryan began looking at the dates for the transactions listed. The printout was 122 pages long, and from what Ryan could tell, it seemed to contain all in-house transfers for the past thirty days.

Now he thought back. Tobias Gabler had been killed five days earlier. Ryan ran a finger quickly down the date column, flipped through page after page, and finally found the date of Gabler's death.

He started looking at the numbered accounts, and the in-house transfers, and he searched for multiple transfers leaving the same account. There were dozens of cases of this, so soon he began looking at high-value transfers, or cases where the same account had made many transfers into a single second account.

He used a legal pad to calculate how much had been moved out of each account. It was slow, laborious, and boring, but after an hour and a half he began to focus on two particular numbered accounts. Beginning on the day before the death of Tobias Gabler and continuing for three days, there had been several large transfers out of account number 62775.001 and into account number 48235.003.

It took two more hours to finish his work. All in all, since the day before the death of Tobias Gabler, there had been 704 in-house transfers of funds. Twelve of them came from 62775.001, and the total of all twelve transfers was 461 million Swiss francs. Jack checked the exchange rate in a financial newspaper he found on the desk; then he pulled his calculator closer, and keyed in some numbers.

The amount of the transfer was $204 million. Penright had told him the account being investigated by the suspected KGB men contained exactly that amount. Looking over the 704 transactions, Jack saw that no other account had moved a tenth of the money around as had account 62775.001.

Jack felt certain this was the account in question and all its money had been moved out of it and into another account in the same bank. Jack had no way of knowing if this was simply a poor attempt to hide the funds from the first account, or if it represented some sort of payment to another entity who had an account at RPB.

But whatever was going on here, Jack knew it was important, and knew he needed to find out who owned numbered account 48235.003, the receiver of the $204 million.

Jack put the dot-matrix printout to the side and spent the next hour reading everything else available about Morningstar and the Penright death investigation. There was lots and lots of mundane data: meeting places and times for Marcus Wetzel and David Penright, protocols established for setting up a dead drop, makes and models of vehicles seen in the area. Jack did not learn much from any of this.

But he did discover something interesting. In a meeting three days before the death of Tobias Gabler, Penright had pressured Marcus Wetzel to try to get more information about the account holder of the two hundred million. To do this, it appeared from the documentation, Morningstar had spoken directly to Tobias Gabler at a meeting between the two of them in a park near Lake Zug.

Jack wondered if that conversation set in motion the death of all three men. It seemed possible that once Gabler knew Wetzel was fishing around for information about the account, he might have gone to the Russians directly to warn them a bank executive was asking questions.

Then, it was conceivable to Ryan, the Russians might have decided to move their money to safety and to kill both Wetzel, the man asking the questions, and Gabler, the man in possession of the answers. And then, it was a stretch, but it was possible, the Russians killed the British agent managing the operation against them.

Ryan rubbed exhaustion from his eyes.

Just after nine p.m., Jack called Sir Basil at his home in Belgravia, London. "I don't know what I found, but at least I have a place for us to start."

"Where?"

"First things first. Thank you for letting me take a look at the files."

"Of course."

Jack explained that he'd worked through the in-house transfers, and he was near certain that the money Morningstar had flagged as suspicious had all been moved into another account.

Jack said, "We need to dig into the new numbered account. If we can find out who owns this, we can continue to monitor these funds."

Charleston said, "As usual, Jack, you have done impressive work. But I am afraid what you are asking for cannot just be ordered up. Getting information on the new account would involve finding a new inside man at this particular bank. A bloody rare thing, indeed. I'm afraid Morningstar was a one-off."

"We have to go to the bank. Either SIS or Langley. We can pressure them."

"Pressuring a Swiss bank will not succeed without going through the Swiss legal system, and even if we did receive permission to get information on the account it would take months. Whoever controls that account can move the money out in days, if not hours.

"I'm sorry, Jack. We *had* an inside man, we lost him, and now we have lost the access he provided us."

Jack knew Basil was correct. Morningstar had worked as an asset only because he had come willingly to the British. Any attempts to pressure RPB for information on the accounts would take a lot longer to bear fruit than it would take the Russians to move their money from the bank.

Ryan's work of the past several hours had been, if not a waste of time, certainly nothing that would create actionable intelligence anytime in the near future.

Dejected, Ryan told Charleston he would fly back to the UK the next day, and he wished him a good evening. Then he gathered up all the files and left the little office.

The SIS courier named Mr. Miles had been waiting in the cafeteria the entire time Jack had worked, and now he went through every page of every document, checking the physical files with a printout he had with him. Then he put them back in his case, handcuffed it to his wrist, bid Jack good evening, and headed out to his car.

The CIA staff still in the building offered Jack a bed in a portion of the Army barracks used for CIA personnel, but they warned him there would be no hot shower tonight and that the cafeteria had closed for the evening.

Jack wasn't a Marine any longer; he had no interest in austerity and he wanted to clear his head with a meal and a hot shower. He grabbed his suitcase and walked out the front gate of Clay Headquarters, and flagged down a taxi. The driver did not speak much English, but he understood when Jack said he wanted to go to a hotel.

"What hotel?" the driver asked.

It was certainly a reasonable question, but Ryan didn't have an answer. He didn't know Berlin well at all. He thought back to the area he had been in the evening before. He said, "Wedding? Is there a hotel in Wedding?"

The driver looked up in the rearview, shrugged, and said, *"Alles klar."*

Fifteen minutes afterward, Ryan climbed out of the cab on Luxemburger Strasse, in front of a chain hotel that overlooked Leopoldplatz, a concrete square ringed by buildings all erected since the area had been flattened in World War Two. Jack checked in for one night, then went up to his room. He wanted to call Cathy, but he realized he was starving. Without even taking off his coat or his scarf, he headed back down to the lobby, where he took a map from the desk clerk, borrowed an umbrella from the doorman, and then headed out into the cold rain, looking for a beer and a quick bite to eat.

72

Present day

Sandy Lamont lived in the Tower Hill neighborhood of London in a ninth-floor flat that gave him a spectacular view of the Thames as well as the Tower of London. His place was right in the middle of some of the best nightlife in the city, and Sandy, a bachelor, enjoyed spending his evenings in the pubs with his mates. This evening had been no different, and as usual, Sandy hoped to end the night with some female companionship.

Also as on most nights, Sandy thoroughly struck out, so around midnight he walked alone up the steps of his building to his lobby and then stepped into the empty elevator.

A minute later he entered his flat, then tossed his keys on the table in his entryway and put his jacket on the rack by the door. He flipped on the TV, turned to a sports channel, and sat down on the sofa.

Just as he began checking football scores, a light flicked on in the far corner of the living room, causing him to jump a full foot off the sofa.

Sandy saw a man there, sitting by the window over the street in a chair that he'd obviously moved in from the kitchen.

"Bloody hell!" Lamont shouted in surprise.

The Englishman leaned forward, his hand on his pounding heart, and he said, "Ryan?"

Jack Ryan looked out the window for a moment before speaking. Finally he said, "I might be making a mistake."

Lamont needed another moment to get over the shock of the intrusion, then replied, "I guarantee you're making a mistake! What are you doing in my flat?"

"I mean, I might be making a mistake by trusting you."

"*This* is a show of trust? How the fuck did you get in? Did you pick the bloody lock?"

"No. He did." Ryan nodded to the opposite corner of the room. There, in the dark, Sandy could just make out the silhouette of a heavyset man leaning against the wall as if bored.

"Who . . . Who the fuck is *that*?"

Ryan continued as if he hadn't heard him: "I wouldn't trust you at all, except you were there in Saint John's. You had no idea that we were in any danger, I could see it on your face."

"What are you on about?"

"If you knew about the men after me, you wouldn't have reacted like that. And even though you pressured me to drop Gazprom, that was only after you took heat from Castor. You were as gung ho as I was in the beginning, weren't you?"

"You are freaking me out, Jack. Either you tell me what is going on or I call the police."

The big man in the corner spoke in a gravelly voice: "You won't make it anywhere near your phone, mate."

Jack walked over and sat next to Sandy now. "I trust you," Jack said, almost to himself. "I don't believe you are part of what Castor is doing."

"Castor? What's Castor doing?"

"Hugh Castor is working for the Russians."

Sandy laughed. It seemed nervous, Jack recognized, but he did not detect deceit. He saw more confusion. Incomprehension.

"Bollocks."

"Think about everything going on at Castor and Boyle. We are part of the system the Kremlin is using to pummel its enemies. All of our successful cases are against oligarchs who oppose Volodin. All of the cases against holdings of the *siloviki*, like the Galbraith case, are slow-walked or left in limbo."

"That's preposterous. We've won cases against members of the *siloviki.*"

"I researched it on my own. The only *siloviki* cases we've worked on that had a positive resolution for our clients were ones against *siloviki* who've had a falling-out with Volodin and his top men."

Lamont thought about that for a moment. He slowly shook his head. "You've lost your mind." He seemed uncertain.

Jack looked out the window at the blackness of the Thames. "Castor met with a Russian in his home. A man named Lechkov."

"Okay. So? He knows heaps of Russians."

"Do you know Lechkov?"

"No. Who is he?"

"We think he is an agent for the Seven Strong Men. He sent some goons to beat the shit out of me, and to kill this man."

Lamont seemed genuinely stunned. *"Why?"*

"Oxley here used to be MI5. Castor was his handler. I went to meet with Oxley at his home in

624

Corby, and as soon as I did that, everything changed. The Russians who had been passively tailing me attacked me. They attacked Oxley as well."

Lamont looked back and forth at the two of them. "Right. It's on the news. The murders in Corby."

Ryan just said, "It wasn't murder. It was self-defense."

Sandy Lamont leaned forward now; Jack thought he was going to vomit. Eventually he mumbled something, but Jack could not understand.

"What?"

Sandy repeated himself, louder: "Nesterov."

"What about Nesterov?"

"When Hugh found out you'd zeroed in on Dmitri Nesterov, he went bloody mental. He wanted to fire you for continuing the Gazprom investigation when I warned you away twice. He wanted to fire me for not pushing you harder off it."

"Why?"

"I don't know. He told you he found out from SIS that Nesterov was FSB, but that wasn't true — he knew the name immediately, I could tell. I suspected he had some knowledge of the man. There was something off about the way he acted. I knew it at the time but couldn't pin it down."

Ryan said, "So Castor knows Nesterov somehow. The Kremlin passed well over a billion dollars to him. Why?"

Sandy said, "I don't know."

It was quiet in the room for a moment. Then Jack said, "I need to talk to Castor about this."

"Why not just go to the police?"

"I don't need him arrested. I need answers."

Sandy said, "Castor left town this afternoon."

"Where did he go?"

"I haven't got a clue. He's got property all over the world. He could be anywhere."

Shit, Jack thought. If Castor left town after he learned that Jack and Oxley had escaped, it was probably because he was on the run.

Ryan and Oxley left a very shaken Sandy Lamont alone in his flat, and then they drove to Stansted Airport. Here they met the Hendley Associates G550 in its slot at a fixed-base operator. When the door opened and the stairs came down, Adara Sherman looked out onto the tarmac and eyed the two men standing there by the car. Jack saw her hand move behind her back slightly.

Ryan knew she kept a SIG Sauer pistol in a holster there.

He raised his hands. "Adara. It's me. Jack."

She cocked her head, then relaxed. "I'm sorry, Jack. You've changed, haven't you?"

Jack smiled, pleased his efforts to disguise himself had worked.

Ding, Dom, and Sam stepped off the plane, and each man ran their hands over Ryan's short hair, pulled on his beard, and commented on all the bulk he'd put on in the past few months.

Ryan felt a powerful sense of relief when he boarded the aircraft. Being back with some of his colleagues gave him new energy. As he gave Ding, Dom, Sam, and Adara each a hug, he wondered why the hell he'd come to the UK by himself in the first place.

The team introduced themselves to Oxley without knowing much of anything about who he was. For Ox's part, he was more bemused than anything about sitting in a $25 million Gulfstream with a bunch of Yanks who seemed to be a special operations outfit, but he interacted with the son of the President of the United States as if he were some sort of long-lost colleague.

Adara asked Jack where he wanted to go. She helpfully explained that they could head over to France or Belgium without fueling, but if Ryan wanted to travel much farther they'd need to gas up, and if he was ready to go back to the United States they would need to obtain departure clearances.

He told her he wanted to go to Edinburgh. Now that Castor had run, Jack knew he'd have to find answers some other way. He needed to meet with Galbraith.

They were wheels-up in less than fifteen minutes.

73

To judge from enemy losses alone, the first forty-eight hours of Operation Red Coal Carpet had been a success. Twelve American and British special operations teams and eight scout helicopters had been deployed into the combat zone, each equipped with laser markers that could be linked to Ukrainian Air Force assets. These targeting forces, along with the lone armed Kiowa Warrior and the four armed Reaper UAVs, had registered 109 kills of enemy armor and weaponry. Among the destroyed equipment were nearly thirty of Russia's main battle tank, the T-90, and two massive BM-30 MLRVs.

The 109 kills represented nearly fifty percent of all the targets destroyed by the Ukrainians, a remarkable number, considering that the United States was fielding less than one percent of all the forces in the fight.

Even though Russia completely occupied the Crimean peninsula by the second day of the invasion, after taking the border oblasts of Luhansk and Donetsk, their losses had mounted to the west, and by the end of the day they were effectively stalled by bad weather that grounded most Russian helicopters. The cloud cover also caused problems for Russian jets, as the majority of the ordnance used was general-purpose bombs and unguided rockets, both of which required good visibility to be effective.

But the Americans and British had taken significant losses themselves. Four MH-6 Little Bird lift helos used for transporting ground teams had been damaged or shot down, as well as one Black Hawk and one Kiowa Warrior. Five more helos of different types had been destroyed while on the ground.

Nine Americans and two British SAS soldiers had been killed, and another twenty had been wounded.

The JOC at Cherkasy Army Base had operated twenty-four hours a day since the opening hours of the conflict. The base had been bombed, but the Americans were in a hardened bunker that could survive everything short of the largest bunker buster or a nuclear detonation, and the bombs that had hit the base had been far enough away to be no major concern to Midas.

Even though the enemy was stalled tonight, good weather was forecast for the next three days, and everyone involved in the operation realized this meant the Russians would inevitably push west again.

Some had hoped that, after taking the Crimea, the Russians' will to fight would wane, but so far no one in the U.S. defense and intelligence community had seen any real evidence of that.

The Russians were coming, and it looked like they were planning on moving all the way to Kiev.

Midas knew he couldn't keep his operation here for much longer; there was even talk of moving the JOC to the west immediately, but he quashed the talk quickly. All the forward operating units still in the field had fallen back several times over the past two days, yet they were all still dozens of miles east. Midas determined he would move his JOC only if there was some compromise due to an intelligence failure or if there was a real risk his deployed assets might leapfrog past his position as they continued falling back in order to stay just ahead of the Russian advance.

Despite the fact that his op had significantly slowed the Russian attack, Colonel Barry Jankowski didn't feel like things were going well, so he decided to change tactics after dark this evening. They desperately needed to cover more ground before the Russians consolidated after sweeping through the Crimea and pressing the fight in the direction of Kiev, so he made the decision to reduce each unit's size. He turned his twelve teams in the field to eighteen by sending a few reserve Delta recce troops into two new positions up near the Belarussian border, and breaking some of the larger A-teams down into five-, six-, and seven-man units.

It would cost nothing as far as offensive firepower, as the men in the field weren't using their own rifles, grenades, and pistols to engage the enemy. But Midas knew well it would deplete each force's ability to defend itself if attacked.

He'd radioed each unit and told them they would be lighter and faster now, and they needed to use this as an advantage and not see it as a liability.

Midas had allowed himself a forty-five-minute catnap on a bunk near the JOC, and now he was back on duty, standing behind a row of men with computers in front of them. Beyond them, on the wall, was a monitor about the size of the average flat-screen television in an American home, but it suited their needs to give them a single digital map that everyone could point to with the laser pointers all the tactical operations men kept at their workstations.

One of the men in comms with a 5th Special Forces Group observation unit, call sign Cochise, motioned Midas over to his laptop. "Hey, boss, Cochise is reporting a long column of T-90s has made it behind the Ukrainian defense force T-72s in their sector, and they are now bypassing Cochise's pos, moving up an access road off the M50 highway. They say there are no other Ukrainian ground assets that can engage them at this time."

"Show me where they are now."

The operator used his laser pointer to indicate the unit's real-time position on the map.

Midas said, "These tanks are closer to Cherkasy than anybody, aren't they?"

"Yeah, and they are supported by dismounts and dedicated air that's keeping up CAS. They might lose air during the night, especially in this weather, but by tomorrow morning Cochise advises they will be within twenty miles of the JOC."

"What's the strength of the red column?"

"After the engagement with the T-72s, Cochise Actual puts their strength at fifteen T-90s, and another forty-plus APCs, MLRVs, and other support vehicles."

"Cochise lost a couple of guys yesterday." Midas said it to himself, but the controller took it as a question.

"Yes, sir. The captain leading them was KIA, and they had another troop injured in a hard landing in the initial helo insertion. There are four troops in total still out there, led by a first lieutenant."

"But their SOFLAM is operational, right?"

"That's right, but in order to engage the new column, they'll have to break cover and head southwest. It's going to take them away from the M50, and who the hell knows what else might be coming up that highway that they'll miss."

Midas saw the problem. From the Belarussian border down to the Crimea, he had only eighteen teams to cover about thirty-five possible attack vectors the Russians could be using. It was impossible to man them all, and although the Ukrainian Army was out there on the ground, their technology wasn't giving them the punch in this fight they needed, considering their smaller strength and subpar training.

What Midas needed was another team to fire the laser. He looked down at the controller. "You talk to Ukrainian SF? They got anybody who knows how to do this?"

"Negative, sir. Their equipment is their equipment, and they are all deployed."

He'd been told in no uncertain terms not to use the Rangers on base for forward operations. There simply weren't enough men to protect the American helos and the JOC and also task them with operating the SOFLAM.

Midas thought it over. "Okay. Send the Kiowa, Black Wolf Two Six, and any Reapers that are in range."

"That's not going to be enough Hellfires to stop that attack."

"I know. They'll have to do a hit-and-run, try to slow them down tonight to buy some time for the

Ukrainians to get their shit together and rush some tanks over there by morning."

"You got it, boss," said the controller, and he reached for his walkie-talkie.

74

Malcolm Galbraith was not a pleasant man.

Ryan had learned enough about the seventy-year-old Scottish billionaire in the past few months to know that although he'd had the misfortune of losing ten billion U.S. dollars when his company was stolen out from under him in Russia, he retained a personal net worth somewhere north of five billion.

The Galbraith Rossiya scandal hadn't exactly left him homeless, either. His main residence was a restored eighteenth-century castle in the Scottish village of Juniper Green, and he possessed homes all over Europe, as well as yachts, private jets, and two state-of-the-art Eurocopters.

But wealth had not bought him happiness — this was clear to Ryan the moment he met the man face-to-face in Galbraith's private office in his Juniper Green castle.

Ryan was unable to detect anything but sourness and mistrust in his demeanor, and he hadn't even told Galbraith the bad news yet.

Ryan had asked for the surprise meeting this morning and the request had been granted immediately, even though he had requested discretion and that the conversation be between just the two of them. Jack arrived alone — Sam and Dom had driven him in a rental car and dropped him off at the front gate; then they pulled up the street within sight of the gate and kept the car running.

Jack had expected a robust security force here protecting the man — he was, after all, worth more than the GDP of some small nations — but there had been only a couple of uniformed men at the gate and a rent-a-cop driving around in the golf cart that ran him up the driveway, and here inside the building he was shown into Galbraith's study by a well-dressed man who may or may not have been carrying a weapon under his suit.

But that was it. Even the man's dogs were corgis. Not rottweilers or Dobermans or German shepherds.

It occurred to Ryan that a man who was considering legal action against the Russian government might want to take a few more measures to keep his person secure.

There was a lot about Galbraith that Jack found odd. Jack had not been offered coffee or tea when he arrived, which he suspected was a major breach of protocol for a business meeting in a castle. And when Galbraith himself stepped into the room, Jack was surprised to see the man wearing faded blue jeans and a plain white T-shirt that looked like he'd used it to clean axle grease off his hands.

Galbraith walked past Ryan, who had his hand extended, and then sat behind his desk, put his elbows on it, and asked, "So, what are we going to talk about?"

Either the man didn't know Ryan was the President's son, or else he didn't give a damn. It was just as well for Ryan that the man hadn't offered to shake hands. Ryan was not overly meticulous about his appearance, but Galbraith's body odor was extreme.

Ryan sat back down in the chair. "Mr. Galbraith, as I explained to your secretary, I have been working on your case for Castor and Boyle for the past few months."

No response, so Ryan continued. "It's been a difficult maze, and the illegal raiding tactic used by the government against you makes it almost impossible to identify anyone in the private sector who is culpable."

"So Hugh Castor has been telling me for nearly half a year."

"Yes. But I decided to dig a little deeper into other transactions made by some of the same corporate entities that were involved in the auction of your assets, and by doing this, I have identified a company that benefited from the sale of Galbraith Rossiya Energy."

The seventy-year-old let out an annoyed grunt. "So have I. Gazprom. Why the fuck am I paying you to tell me something I already know?"

Jack took a deep breath. "No, sir. Another company. A smaller company that seems like it was only set up to receive a payoff from the proceeds of the sale."

"A shell company?"

"Yes, but I know who is on the board of directors. Are you familiar with a man named Dmitri Nesterov?"

He shook his head. "Who is he?"

"I am told he is affiliated with the FSB."

Galbraith shrugged like that was no surprise. "And how much did he get?"

"As far as I can tell, Mr. Galbraith, he got all of it. One-point-two billion U.S."

Galbraith leaned forward over his heavy desk now. "Hugh Castor hasn't told me a word of this. How is it you have all the answers?"

"It's a complicated scheme, and uncovering it involved some . . . some tactics that Castor and Boyle does not fully support."

"And that is why you are here and not your boss?"

Jack nodded. "I have identified the bank where Nesterov's Antigua-based bank launders money in Europe."

"Where is this bank?"

"It's in Zug, Switzerland."

Galbraith immediately said, "Let me guess. RPB?"

Jack was astonished. There had to have been a dozen banks in Zug. "That's a good guess."

Galbraith waved away the compliment. "Lot of dirty money at RPB. Dirty, old money. Dirty, old Russian money."

Jack cocked his head. "I have to ask. How do you know that?"

With a shrug, the Scotsman said, "There's a bit of old Scot money there as well."

"You have accounts at RPB?"

"Nothing I want to talk about. Not even to some kid who sneaks up here, hiding from his boss, to try to shake me down for a cut."

"A cut? A cut of *what?*"

"I know your type. Seen a hundred like you, I have . . . What did you say your name was?"

So this guy didn't know him. Jack found himself surprised, but pleasantly so. He just said, "Jack."

Galbraith chuckled, but it was an angry sound. "Okay, Jack. Let me have a go at it. Your boss doesn't give me what I want, so here you come, young, hungry, with a story about how you just want what's best for my company and my bottom line, and if I'll cut you in a wee bit we can do a go-around on your boss and your company and you can recover me assets. What's the pitch? Computer hacking? One look at you and I think it's computer hacking. You can steal my money back or work as a go-between in the middle between me and the Russian mob. Only catch is I slip ten percent of the return to you, paid into your account in BVI or Luxembourg or Singapore. Right? How did I do? Nail on the head?" He stood up, ready to end the meeting.

"Look, Malcolm," Jack said, keeping his seat while the lord of the castle stood there. Jack had given up on polite and respectful. "I don't want one pence of your fucking money. Yesterday, a bunch of Russian mafia goons tried to fucking kill me for what I know about your shitty business, so I am trying to get answers."

"Kill you? Is that right?" He did not believe the American.

"You ever watch the news? Corby? A couple hours north of London? Four dead Russians."

Malcolm Galbraith sat back down now.

Jack said, "Yeah. That was all about you."

"What are you on about?"

"I've been digging too deep into your case. I found out this guy Dmitri Nesterov was tied up in this, and then suddenly a group of Seven Strong Men assassins came over from Ukraine to stop me, and to kill one of my contacts."

The Scottish oil services tycoon softened his tone. "You are completely serious."

"I'm afraid I am."

"Why isn't Castor telling me any of this?"

Jack decided to level with him. "Mr. Galbraith, I think it is very possible that Mr. Castor is somehow . . . compromised by Mr. Nesterov."

Malcolm Galbraith stared Jack down for an uncomfortably long time. Jack thought he was about to meet resistance in his theory, but instead, Galbraith said, "Castor's a fucking crook."

Jack raised his hands and began to temper his comment. "I can't say for sure just what —"

The Scotsman said, "I knew he worked with sketchy, powerful Russians. I just didn't know he worked with the sketchy, powerful Russians who took my money. Who is this contact they want dead?"

"He's an old British spy. I don't know how he is connected yet, but I'm hoping you can help out."

"Name?"

"Oxley. Victor Oxley."

"Never heard of him," Galbraith said, disappointed.

"He was involved in a case in Switzerland in the 1980s. That case, believe it or not, involved RPB."

"The bankers killed by Zenith."

"That's the story. Nothing proved."

"Yes. I remember. I was banking at RPB at the time."

"I came to you hoping you could help me connect the dots between the murders there and the theft of your property. Oxley and Castor are connected, but the same Seven Strong Men henchmen who tried to kill Oxley also had been following me while I worked on your case. I don't know why."

"The connection, lad, is the Russians."

"What do you mean?"

Malcolm Galbraith pressed a button on his desk,

and a female voice came over the intercom.

"Sir?"

"Tea for me, coffee for my new friend."

"Right away, sir."

Galbraith and Ryan had moved to a parlor; in front of them was a tea and coffee service, and Ryan was putting it to good use. He'd slept little in the past twenty-four hours, and he didn't know when he'd get another chance to rest.

Galbraith's mood had made a 180-degree change since the moment he learned Jack wasn't up here with a business proposition. The old man even apologized for his appearance, telling Jack he'd been working on one of his classic cars in his garage and had not bothered to change because he expected nothing more than a visit by a shyster junior analyst.

As they sipped their beverages Galbraith got into his story about RPB. Jack wanted to take notes, but he wasn't about to break the flow by asking for paper and a pen, so he just listened very carefully.

Galbraith said, "Shortly before the death of Toby Gabler — he was the first of the two bankers to die — he came to a friend of mine who held some assets at RPB. Gabler said he had a client who wanted to buy out hard assets the man held in safety deposit boxes."

"What kind of hard assets?"

"Gold. Don't know the value but this bloke had gotten out of the markets and put everything in gold bars. The deal fell through, don't remember why, but immediately after — I'm talking like the next day — Toby came to me and tried the same thing. He said he had a client with a problem.

The client had funds in a numbered account, but he didn't trust the system anymore. He had to get the funds out of the bank in a hurry, couldn't transfer them to another bank because of some sort of corporate dispute. Toby hinted the men were East European. Didn't say they were Soviet, that I would have remembered.

"At the time, I had multiple drilling operations going in the North Sea, I'd done quite well for myself when oil prices went up in the seventies, and I had a deal in the works with one of the young Saudi princes to expand my operations into the Middle East. To do this, I had arranged some hard assets."

"What kind?"

He shrugged. "The prince liked gold. Turned out it was a good investment. I thought he was crazy. Anyway, I began amassing it for the deal, and I kept several safe-deposit boxes full of bars at RPB."

"Okay," Ryan said. He realized the man was talking about some sort of a kickback, but there was no shame in his voice. "What did Gabler say?"

"Toby said he operated as an agent for his client. Said he'd pay way beyond top bloody dollar for the lot of my gold. I had over one hundred million, laddie. At what he was offering for it, I would be a fool not to take the deal."

"What happened next?"

Galbraith lifted his teacup and laughed. "I was a fool. I didn't take the deal. I knew the Saudi contract could pay me for decades, so I hung on to the gold, despite the offer. Sadly, the prince was arrested by his brothers and I never made a shilling."

"And then Gabler was killed?"

"Yes. And Wetzel, one of the VPs of the bank. Didn't know him. The Germans were blamed, as you know, and that was the end of it. I didn't learn anything else about the affair till the early nineties, when I got a visit from a group of Russians."

"KGB?"

"No, no. Far from. These chaps were just accountants. At the time Russia was swirling down the toilet, and they were in search of a mysterious black fund of ex-KGB money filched from Soviet coffers. They were quite up-front about it, and they only came to me because I had mentioned the affair with the RPB gold offer a few times at cocktail parties and the like. That got back to these accountants." He laughed. "I remember thinking that the new Russia didn't stand a chance because the KGB had been replaced with these friendly accountants asking friendly questions. Little did I know the KGB would eat blokes like that for lunch soon enough and take charge once again."

"Did you learn anything from them about this black fund?"

He leaned forward. "No. Nothing to speak of, other than the obvious fact they didn't think the RAF killed Swiss bankers in the eighties. Instead, it was clear to me, someone in the KGB stole the money, had it in a numbered account at RPB, and somehow KGB found out where the money was."

"Any idea how?"

"No, but I can guess. I'd wager KGB was already inside RPB. Whoever stole the money and parked it there either didn't know this or else they thought they were cleverer than they were. Word got to KGB that other Russians were moving large sums of money into the West. The KGB came looking for answers. When this happened the account holder made Gabler run around looking for someone inside the bank who had hard assets so they could physically take the money and run."

Jack said, "But we don't know if they found anyone to do the deal with."

"We don't," Galbraith said with a smile. "But I have a suspicion who does."

"Who?"

"Hugh Castor. Hugh and I knew each other from Eton. We weren't chums, but I knew enough to know he was in the security services. When the Russian accountants met with me and asked me all the questions, I passed on all the information to him. He was quite excited by the prospect of missing KGB riches. He even had me introduce him to the president of RPB.

"I found out later Castor himself became a client of the bank. He grew quite wealthy over the next few years — this was the nineties. He was connected in the new Russia, left MI5 and went into private-sector intelligence. I knew he was trading in information, and that's why, when I lost my company there last year, I went straight to him. I thought he'd be able to clear the matter up with his inside connections."

Galbraith looked at Ryan and sighed. "The bastard protected his friends in power at my expense, didn't he?"

Ryan nodded. "It's beginning to look like that's exactly what he did."

Galbraith said, "The sod even bought a house in Zug, just to be near his money, I guess."

"Castor has a place in Zug?"

"He does. A chalet right on the lake. I've had dinner with him there a few times." Ryan could see the muscles in Malcolm Galbraith's jaws flex in anger. "And then he swindles me on behalf of bloody Gazprom. What do you suppose they are paying him?"

Ryan admitted he had no idea.

Jack said, "Mr. Galbraith, I'm going to be perfectly honest with you. I am not sure what is going to happen, but I don't really expect the FSB to write you a check for one-point-two billion dollars when this is all said and done."

Galbraith replied, "I can't remember the last time I used this phrase, but at this point, this isn't about the money."

Ryan was glad to see Galbraith understood.

Galbraith said, "You are a brave young man for an analyst."

Jack smiled, thought of his dad for a moment, then said, "I have some men with me."

"What kind of men?"

"Men to watch my back if the Russians come after me again."

"These chaps, they aren't employees of Castor's, are they?" Galbraith asked.

"No. Why?"

The Scottish billionaire shifted in his seat uncomfortably now. "Because I'm afraid there is a complication."

Ryan cocked his head. "What complication?"

"I called Hugh this morning, asking him what his junior analyst was doing flying up to Edinburgh demanding a meeting."

Jack groaned. "When I asked for this meeting to be discreet, and just between the two of us, Castor is exactly who I was worried about."

Galbraith held up his hands. "That's clear now, isn't it? Wasn't clear then."

Jack wondered what this meant, but at the very least he knew it meant he needed to get the hell out of here now.

He said, "Just one more question. What phone number did you reach him on?"

The Scotsman pulled his mobile phone out of his pocket. He scrolled through some numbers for a moment, then passed it over to Ryan. "Thinking about giving him a call?"

"No. I have a buddy who just might be able to find him through his phone." Jack looked at Malcolm Galbraith. "At this point in the game, I'd much prefer a face-to-face meeting with Hugh Castor."

75

Thirty years earlier

After venturing out in the rain from his Berlin hotel, CIA analyst Jack Ryan found a small restaurant still open at eleven p.m., and he bought a meal consisting of bratwurst and french fries along with a large glass of pilsner. He sat at the front window and enjoyed his meal while looking out at the dreary weather. After a few minutes, he opened his map to orient himself, and he realized he was only a few blocks away from where the shootout took place on Sprengelstrasse very early that morning.

Though it was after eleven-thirty in the evening when he left the restaurant, he decided to walk the five blocks just to pass by the RAF flat.

It took him less than ten minutes to find the corner, and he was immediately surprised by how dead the area seemed now. The evening before, he had assumed the police cordon was keeping any traffic clear of the intersection, but tonight, with no police cordon whatsoever, the activity level in the neighborhood was virtually the same. Other than the occasional slow-moving taxi and one or two pensioners under umbrellas taking their dogs for late-night strolls, Ryan did not see anyone out on Sprengelstrasse.

The cold rain picked up as he neared the intersection, and he noticed a police car parked in front of the building, facing in the opposite direction. He couldn't see anyone inside the vehicle, but the engine was running, so he suspected the police had posted a guard to keep any curious people away from the crime scene.

Jack stepped back into a darkened doorway on the northeastern corner of Sprengelstrasse and Tegeler Strasse, and from here he could take in the entire scene.

The bay doors of the auto repair shop were closed, which came as no surprise to Jack. There was no light coming from the big brick building at all, and the windows on the higher floors that had been shot out during the gunfight nearly twenty-four hours earlier were now covered with a shiny black material.

As he stood there, it occurred to him that he'd love to get another look inside that flat. Even though he was certain the BfV would have pulled anything of obvious intelligence value, Jack wondered if there was some way they might have missed some small thing, some tiny item that could possibly connect Marta Scheuring, the girl who died in Switzerland, with the Russians.

Ryan wondered what that might be. He wasn't a cop like his dad, crime scene investigation was not his forte, so he recognized the fact he'd need to find something as obvious as a photo of Marta on Red Square to know he had the smoking gun he was looking for.

No chance of that, he told himself.

While Jack stood there, another police car pulled up close to the one parked in the street. Both drivers rolled down their windows and started talking. From a hundred feet away, Jack could hear muffled voices, and he saw the flash and glow as one of the cops lit a cigarette.

Jack stepped out of the doorway and crossed Tegeler Strasse, and began walking along the side of the building. Here he was surprised to see that the fire escape ladder he had climbed the evening before had not been reset all the way. He realized that if he were so inclined, he would be able to reach it and pull it down with the hook of his umbrella.

He was certain the patrol cars around the corner could not see him where he was, and he also knew the cops were distracted by their conversation, so, with no advance plan whatsoever, Jack decided to climb the fire escape and slip inside the building. He knew the police might wander around the corner here at some point, but he seriously doubted that they would be getting out of their warm and dry patrol cars anytime in the next few seconds.

Still, Jack did not reach for the ladder immediately; instead, he kept walking along, his umbrella and his waterproof coat keeping him dry, although he began to sweat as he thought about the prospect of getting another look inside the third-floor flat used as a safe house by the Red Army Faction. Twice he talked himself out of going ahead with his idea, but twice more he reasoned that, in the unlikely event the policemen caught him in the act, he wouldn't be in any serious trouble. He could drop a few names of BfV officers he'd met in the past day, and he'd likely receive an uncomfortable tongue-lashing from the Germans, but the prospect of this paled in comparison with the possibility of having his curiosity satisfied by another look at the flat.

While considering his next move, he'd walked half a block up the street. He stopped, turned, headed back to the fire escape, and looked around at all the buildings, searching for anyone who might be watching what he was doing.

There was no one.

As Ryan arrived again at the fire escape, he used his umbrella to pull down the ladder slowly and relatively quietly, then tossed his umbrella between a couple of nearly bare bushes alongside the building and began climbing.

The window on the first floor had been shattered the night before; this was where Ryan had fired at the sniper two blocks east of here on Sprengelstrasse. Now cardboard wrapped in a black plastic tarp had been fitted in place of the window. Ryan had no trouble pushing in the cardboard and climbing inside the building. He looked back out onto the rain-swept empty street, then pushed the cardboard and plastic back into place.

Just like that, he was in. It was quiet, as he expected, and though this hallway had been dark last night, it had been nothing like this. Now there was not a single source of light.

Fear of the dark is a natural fear, and Jack had no reason to be afraid here, as he was certain the building was both empty and covered by the police, but his heart pounded against his chest as he felt his way to the stairway to the second floor.

Compared with the pitch black of the hall and the stairwell, the second floor was relatively well lit by the large windows on all sides. Several of these windows had been shot out and they, too, had been replaced with the same cardboard and plastic sheeting, but several more were intact, and Jack had no problem finding his way forward through the art collective, toward the stairs up to the third-floor flat.

Jack took a chance in the RAF flat. As in the hallway two floors below him, he could barely see his hands in front of his face. Fortunately, he remembered from the evening before that all the windows in the flat had been destroyed by gunfire or concussion grenades. He presumed that whoever had covered the windows downstairs would have done the same here, so he felt around until he found a small desk lamp on a side table. He pulled the cord and was not surprised to find the lamp was inoperable.

It took several more seconds to find a second cord; this one led to a lamp with a bulb that had not been damaged in the chaotic melee of the evening before.

He took a blanket off a chair against the wall and partially covered the lamp, leaving just enough light for him to take in his surroundings.

The living room felt smaller now that he stood alone in it. A dozen detectives and commandos and British agents had added a sense of expanse to the space, but now it was just a fifteen-foot-by-fifteen-foot room with too much cheap furniture that was mostly shot up and smashed, and walls pockmarked with holes. There was an outline on the floor in the shape of a body lying on its side, with the arms out in one direction and the lower legs in the other, making an S-shape. This was the woman who'd been killed in the front room; Jack had read her name in the report this afternoon. Ulrike something. He remembered seeing her bullet-riddled body the evening before and an automatic weapon lying next to it.

The girl and the gun were gone now, but her outline and a four-foot-wide bloodstain remained.

He stood still in the room for a moment, thinking about the scene last night. He was sure he could still smell the smoke, and he thought he could detect the scent of death.

After a minute, he flipped off the lamp and felt his way forward to the hallway, and then he headed back toward the bedrooms.

Marta Scheuring's little room seemed even darker than the hallway. He felt around on the wall for a moment, hunting for a light switch, but when he found nothing, he dropped to his knees and reached out in all directions. He put his hand on a wire and followed it to some sort of a lamp lying on its side on the floor, and he flipped a switch on it. It was a blue lava lamp; apparently it had been sitting on a folding TV tray that Marta had used as an end table. The tray lay on its side on the floor next to the lamp.

Jack picked up the lamp and used it as a very poor flashlight. He looked around at the smashed furniture and the holes in the wall. He looked at the clothing in the closet and the shattered mirror on a tiny dresser.

It was quiet, the only sound the tinkle of precipitation on the plastic and cardboard covering the windows.

Jack took in his pale blue surroundings. No one had died in this room; there was no blood on the floor or the walls. But it felt like death, because the young woman who lived in this tiny space had been killed two nights earlier several hundred miles south in Switzerland. Her few personal effects were all that remained of her. There was laundry in a hamper in the corner. A threadbare towel, a pair of blue jeans. A black sweater, and a plain tan bra-and-panty set piled on top.

Suddenly it felt wrong to Jack to be here.

Intellectually, he knew the BfV would have searched everything, but Jack had wanted to poke around on his own. But now he did not want to touch her clothing, to look through her drawers or closet.

He realized he'd made a mistake. He'd been at the end of the road in his investigation, and logic had taken a backseat to emotion.

Jack sighed loudly. His mind switched gears, and he started thinking about how his unauthorized late-night visit to this crime scene would look to his peers. Should he even mention his skulking around here tonight to either Sir Basil or Jim Greer? Probably not, he told himself. It might make him look impetuous, undisciplined.

He couldn't tell Cathy, either, but that was probably best for everyone. He told himself he'd just leave now and never mention a word of this to —

Jack heard a noise, the creaking of a floorboard somewhere far away. He leaned out into the hall. The sound continued, and after a moment he realized he was hearing the footsteps of someone coming up the wooden staircase that led up to the flat.

He quickly flipped off the lava lamp, put it down on the floor, and backed into the closet, pressing himself into the clothes hanging from the rack.

Damn it, Jack, he said to himself. He was certain it was the police. He knew he hadn't been seen coming up, and he also knew he hadn't made any noise. He figured the damn lights he had turned on had shone through some bullet hole in the wall and tipped off the cops.

The footfalls approached slowly, moving down the hall now. The closet door was open. Jack did not want to pull it shut, fearing the hinges might squeak, so he very slowly pushed himself backward even deeper into the dresses and coats Marta had left hanging in her closet. He thought he had a chance to remain unseen if the cops just passed by the room and waved their flashlight in, since the closet could not be seen without stepping into the room.

But then it occurred to him. There was no flashlight. Jack would have been able to see any residual light of someone coming up the hall, but he saw nothing at all except complete darkness.

The fact that there was no beam was disconcerting. He had no idea who was in the flat with him now, but he suspected this other person had as little right to be here as he did himself.

The hardwood flooring in the hallway creaked with each step. The drops of pelting rain on the plastic sheeting continued unabated as the steps moved closer.

They stopped in the doorway to Marta Scheuring's room. Jack was six feet away from the other visitor, only partially hidden in the closet.

A figure entered the room in front of him. He could feel the presence more than see anything in the dark. He thought about leaping out, taking the other figure by surprise; his mind raced, and he wondered if this could have been the person who had fired on him and the GSG 9 men twenty-four hours earlier.

He had no weapon at all; his only hope was to stay hidden. He did not move. He held his breath now, and forced his eyes open even wider to take in any ambient light that might give him an advantage.

There was a shuffling sound; Jack recognized the sound of the lava lamp scuffing the floor.

Shit. He poised himself to leap forward as soon as the light came on.

Suddenly the room was awash in dim blue light. A figure in a big black hooded coat knelt on the floor, and then the figure rose back up, facing away. Ryan balled his right fist, he needed to take only two quick steps to be in striking distance, but he quickly realized the figure was moving away from him, toward the bed.

The person knelt down and reached under the bed now. Jack heard the sound of the floorboards moving, and he knew what was going on.

After a few seconds of feeling around, the figure stopped moving, as if giving up, and dropped his head on the bed. Whoever this was, he had obviously been looking for the briefcase, and he'd obviously realized the police had found it.

Jack knew he had to take the initiative now, while the stranger was on his knees with his head down and facing away.

Jack stepped out of the closet and started across the little room. He'd made it only halfway when the floorboards under his feet gave him away.

The stranger launched up and spun around. In the blue light, Jack saw a hand reach into a coat pocket, and then reemerge quickly, wrapped around something small and black. Jack didn't know if it was a gun or a knife, but it didn't matter. He had the momentum, and continued rushing forward with his eyes on the weapon, then balled his fist and reached back.

He saw the pointed steel at the same time he heard the click of the switchblade. The stranger slashed with the knife as Ryan fired out a right jab. His fist slammed into the man's jaw, connecting near perfectly, and the head snapped back.

The knife flew through the air as the body fell backward on the bed and lay there, unconscious.

Jack felt a pain in his forearm, and he realized he'd been cut by the switchblade; he couldn't see how bad it was in the poor light, but he felt through the tear in his jacket, then pulled his hand back and rubbed the wet blood with his fingertips. He didn't think it was too severe, but it stung like hell.

"Son of a bitch!" he shouted, as he pulled off his scarf and wrapped it around the wound.

It took a moment to tie it off, and while he did this he kept his eyes on the figure on the bed in front of him. He couldn't see the face, so he stepped forward, leaning over the unconscious form. He leaned closer still, reaching down and pushing the hood of the coat back, then moving wet hair out of the way so he could see the face.

He stood up quickly, stunned.

This was a woman.

He looked down at his own fist; his knuckles throbbed after the vicious blow he'd delivered to her face. "Oh, Christ."

It took the woman five minutes to come around. In that time Jack tied her hands behind her back with the bra from the laundry basket in the corner and placed her on the floor, sitting her up against the bed. He'd also searched her thoroughly. She had no more weapons, and she carried no identification, only a key chain with a few keys on it and two small wads of currency. Ryan thought it was interesting she was in possession of both West German deutschmarks and East German ostmarks, but this was hardly the most interesting thing about her.

As he sat on the floor in front of her, the lava lamp between the two of them, he studied her face. The lighting was bad, her blond bangs hung low over her eyes with her head slumped forward, and there was a red-and-purple bruise on her jaw from Ryan's fist, so it was difficult to get a great look at her, but he started to suspect he knew who she was.

And when she woke, when her eyes opened and she slowly began looking around the room, Jack was certain.

He said, "I can gag you. If you scream, I will do just that. Do you understand me?"

He could hear her breath quicken. She looked at him, and her eyes widened in fear and tears dripped down her face.

"You speak English, don't you?"

After a moment, she asked, "Who are you?" Her German accent was strong, but Ryan had no trouble understanding her.

In the soft blue lighting, he looked into her eyes. He saw the terror, but he could also see exhaustion. Her wet hair hung on her forehead.

He said, "You can call me John. And how about I call you Marta? Marta Scheuring."

76

Jack had no idea how it was so, but sitting before him was the Red Army Faction member whose body had been identified at the scene of the firebombing in Rotkreuz, Switzerland.

"That is not my name," she said.

Ryan wished that Nick Eastling were here. The counter-intelligence officer had his faults, but he had a knack for getting people to talk.

"There is no use in denying it," Jack said, while looking around the room for any pictures of her. He couldn't find anything, but he wondered if the BfV men might have taken them away as evidence.

"Fucking pig," she said. She turned away, looking at the far wall. "You are American?" she asked.

"Yes."

"FBI? CIA?"

"How about I ask the questions?"

She shook her head. "I don't want to listen to your shit questions. You are a fool. You all are. You think we were in Switzerland, you think we were involved in the attacks there. But it wasn't us. None of us were. You pigs killed everyone here for *nothing*."

Jack shook his head. "Not for nothing. Your friends were killed because you are RAF, and your identification was found at the location where fourteen people were burned to death. When GSG Nine came to raid this place, someone started shooting from your hotel room up the street."

She shook her head. Her wet bangs drooped into her eyes and she blew them back up. *"Was meinst du denn?"* What the hell do you mean? "What hotel room?"

"Did you rent a room in a guest worker hotel two blocks up on Sprengelstrasse?"

"Why would I do that?" Her voice was laced with derision, but there was a definite tone to her words that told Jack she was telling the truth.

Jack figured as much. He said, "I don't know you, Marta, but for your sake, I hope you are smart enough to realize that you have been set up. Your entire organization has been set up."

The German woman cocked her head, and again the bangs drooped. She let them hang. "You believe me? You believe that I didn't kill anyone?"

"I believe you, yes. But right now I am the only one who believes the Red Army Faction is just a pawn in this. As soon as the BfV finds out you are still alive, you will be the most wanted person in Germany."

Jack thought the girl looked like she would start crying again, but instead she just muttered, "Fucking bourgeois pigs. All of you."

"Who was the dead girl in Switzerland with your ID?"

She did not answer.

"Marta, nobody in the world knows I am here right now. If you want, I can go downstairs and tell the cops out front that you're here. Or you can talk to me a little, and then both of us can slip away, safe and sound."

Marta mumbled something.

"What's that?"

"Ingrid Bretz. Her name was Ingrid Bretz."

"Was she Red Army Faction?"

Marta just shook her head. "She was a waitress at a bar in Alexanderplatz, in East Berlin."

"*East Berlin?* She is from the East?"

"*Ja.*"

"What was she doing with your identification?"

"I gave it to her. A week ago, I went over to the East. She said she needed to come to the West for a few days. She needed an *Ausweis,* an identification. We looked enough alike, so I gave her mine."

"You were friends?"

Marta hesitated. "Yes, but she paid me. She paid me to go to the East, to give her my *Ausweis,* and to wait a few days for her to return."

"Who arranged this?"

"No one. It was just an idea she had."

Jack didn't believe her for a second. "If you didn't have any identification, how did you get back into West Berlin?"

Marta shrugged. "There are ways."

"What ways? Like a tunnel?"

"Ha. A tunnel? You are a fool."

Jack didn't press the question. Instead he asked, "Why didn't Ingrid sneak over like you did?"

Marta glared at Ryan. It was a look that a left-wing terrorist might give an employee of the CIA. Full of sanctimony and intellectual superiority. "She was going to Switzerland. There is no tunnel to Switzerland."

Jack realized Marta was saying Ingrid would have needed the identification to get out of East Berlin and into West Germany, and then to get from Germany to Switzerland.

"Do you know why she was going to Switzerland?"

"She told me she had a boyfriend who immigrated there."

"And you believed her?"

"Why not? She showed me a necklace he sent her. It was a big diamond. She didn't even wear it. Not many East German girls wear a diamond necklace around."

"Did she give you the name of her boyfriend?"

"No."

"But you *were* friends?" Jack asked incredulously. He wasn't trained to interrogate. He wondered if his inquisitive nature was pushing things too fast. Before he could think of another, softer line of questioning, Marta spoke on her own.

"Ingrid had never even been to Switzerland. So how is she going to go there, on her own, and start machine-gunning people and blowing up buildings? *Das ist verrückt.*" She translated for herself. "That is crazy."

"They will say she did not do it alone. They will say others in the RAF were working with her. Even you, maybe?"

Marta shook her head. "Ingrid was not RAF. And anyway, what do we care about bankers in Switzerland? There are bankers here. Industrialists here. NATO here." She looked up at Jack, still seated above her on her little bed. "Capitalist spies . . . here."

"How did the briefcase end up under the bed?"

Marta went quiet. This time, Jack answered for her.

He said, "Here's what I think. I don't believe you loaned your identification to this waitress for a few East German marks. I think you were ordered to give it to her by the same people who planted the evidence under your bed."

Her laugh seemed fake, forced. "Ordered by who?"

Jack shrugged. "Stasi, maybe? Or was it KGB? I

don't know. I do know your organization works with both of them. Whoever it was told you they needed to stash something here. You must have told them about the false floor under the bed. Once you found out your place had been raided, you realized you'd been framed."

She shook her head again. "Typical lie of the CIA."

Ryan squeezed the scarf wrapped on his forearm; he felt the wetness from where the blood soaked through. He said, "Listen, Marta, whoever did this used Ingrid because they couldn't get a real RAF member to go to Switzerland and plant the bomb. They got your identification and gave it to her so that your group would be blamed for the killings. Your friends died as a result of it.

"You obviously know you have been set up, because you came back over here, hoping against hope that the evidence was still under the bed and you could get it the hell out of here before you and your group of left-wing losers were implicated even deeper."

"I have nothing more to say to you."

"Don't you want the world to know Red Army Faction had nothing to do with the death of all those innocent people in Switzerland? This is the worst possible thing that could have happened to your organization."

She said nothing. She only shook her head.

"You won't talk, so how about you just listen for a moment? In case you don't know, your friends died because of money. This is all about a bank account. An account with two hundred million dollars in it in a Swiss bank. To hide the money, some people had to die, so the Russians decided they would use you and your friends to take the blame for killing them."

Ryan smiled at her. "It's nothing more than money,

my dear. Your socialist ideals, your struggle for the rights of the worker, none of that bullshit has one goddamned thing to do with any of this. The Russians wanted to keep their money hidden, and the RAF made a useful stooge."

Jack continued, "They are all dead, Marta. All your friends. There is no one to protect except the man who did this to you. If you protect him . . ." Jack motioned to the empty flat around him. "Then you are even more a part of what happened to them all."

She wept openly now, her head hung, tears dripped onto the floor in front of her. But she did not say anything.

"You don't want to talk. That's fine. I respect that. I tell you what. If you can answer one more thing, I'll untie you and let you go."

She looked up. A glimmer of hope in her eyes now. "What?"

"One question only, Marta. I promise."

Her nose ran; she couldn't wipe it with her hands behind her back, so she just snorted loudly. "Okay. What question?"

"Why are you alive?"

She tilted her head slowly to the side. *"Was meinst du?"*

"These people have done an excellent job covering their tracks so far. They killed Ingrid, who was an East German girl and would not be missed over here. And they killed the men who knew about the money the Russians stashed in the bank. I am pretty sure they killed a friend of mine who was trying to expose their operation. And they made sure everyone in this apartment was dead so no one would be left to prove they weren't involved in the attacks."

Jack leaned closer. Not threatening but imploring.

"But *you,* Marta, *you* are the only loose end. You

walking around West Berlin can cause their entire plan to fall to pieces. Do you think they are going to just sit back and let that happen?"

The muscles in her neck tightened. The look on her face melded perfectly with someone who had just lost a key tenet of her belief system.

Jack wanted to feel the schadenfreude of watching a terrorist realize her entire cause was built on a foundation of bullshit and supported by an organization of soulless killers. But instead he found himself feeling sorry for her.

The distant look in her wet eyes made her appear nearly catatonic. She said, "I am not supposed to be here. I was in the East. I came over early this morning when I heard about what happened."

"Came over? How?"

"There *is* a tunnel. It is used by East German intelligence. I know of it because sometimes we help them bring things across."

"No one knows you are here?"

She shook her head again.

He leaned closer, inches from her face, and he took a chance. "Not even your KGB control officer?"

Marta Scheuring shook her head slowly. Tears flowed. "I don't have a control officer. The Russian who connected me to Ingrid was a stranger. I'd never met him before, but he knew others in my organization. They told me I could trust him. I assume he was KGB. I mean . . . how else could he know about us? He told me he would support us if I did what I was told. I could not refuse. We need the support." She looked around, as if just remembering that all her fellow urban guerrillas were dead. "We needed the support."

"What was his name?"

She shook her head. "He didn't give me his name.

663

Only a code name."

"Which was?"

"Zenit."

Jack said, "Zenith?"

"Do you know him?" she asked.

"No. But I think I know his work."

The tears poured now, and mucus dripped from her nose. Her body shook. "He is going to kill me, isn't he?"

Jack said, "If you had stayed in the East like you were supposed to, you would be dead already. This Zenith, and others like him, will be looking for you right now. You have to let us protect you."

"But you are alone, aren't you?"

"Right now I am, but I can take you to Clay Headquarters, and you will be protected by the entire Berlin Brigade. We'll get you out of West Berlin and find someplace safe for you."

"In return for what?"

Ryan realized his concern for the German woman was real. Even though she was misguided at the least, and most likely a dangerous terrorist, his instincts to protect the vulnerable were real enough.

He wasn't thinking about quid pro quo now. He was just thinking about keeping the twenty-five-year-old woman alive.

He wondered if this meant that he wasn't hard and cynical enough for real operational work.

He pushed the thought out of his mind and stood up. "That's not for me to say. First, let's get out of here, and get you some protection. Then we can worry about everything else."

"You are lying. The American government is not going to help me."

"Well, at least we're not going to kill you. Think about it this way, Marta. We are capitalists. You give us something, and we will give you something in trade. You give us information, and we will give you the protection you need. This relationship doesn't have to be any more complicated than that."

"Why should I trust you?"

Jack cracked a half-smile. "Because America works with people it doesn't like all the goddamned time."

That seemed to sink in. Jack could tell that Marta's dire predicament was clear to her. She did not agree verbally, she still seemed to be on the verge of panic, but she nodded.

Ryan untied her. While doing so, he asked, "Why doesn't the RAF release a statement saying they weren't involved in this?"

She said, "I do not lead the RAF. If the KGB tricked us, used me to take responsibility for what happened in Switzerland, the RAF will not come out publicly against the Soviet Union. That would be the final nail in our coffin. We would get no more support from any Communist Party group in the world."

That made sense to Ryan. They were, to some degree, a vassal of Russian intelligence. They might complain internally about the affair, but they couldn't go public and admit they had been used by the KGB.

Ryan helped Marta to her feet. He said, "You go first, I'll walk behind you."

"Why?"

"Because I'm not turning my back on you. You've already stabbed me once."

77

Marta and Jack moved together slowly through the darkened building. On the first floor, Jack turned to go to the fire escape, but Marta said, "No. Follow me."

Jack followed her down another flight of stairs, all the way to the automotive shop on the ground floor of the building. There were a few dim bulbs glowing here, enough for the two of them to easily make their way to a utility room on the northwest side of the building. A narrow wooden staircase led down to the basement. Marta pulled a cord in the center of the room and a bare lightbulb revealed a washer and dryer. Next to these was a metal hatch in the wall.

"What's this?" Jack asked.

"This was a coal chute back before the war. We use it to come and go in case the police are watching the front of the building."

Marta opened the chute; it made a muffled scraping sound, but Jack knew the police on the far side of the building would not have heard a thing. She crawled out first, and Jack followed.

Jack found himself standing in a paved space between two buildings. There was barely room to walk.

Marta said, "Our building survived the war, but this

building on the left came after. They built it so close that on a map it looks like they are connected. The stupid pigs don't even know about this alley."

They made their way through the dark, narrow space for a minute, moving between apartment buildings, and then they came out on a footpath next to Sparrstrasse.

Once they arrived at the street, Jack said, "We need to hail a taxi."

Marta said, "A taxi? You don't have a car?"

"No. I came on foot."

"What kind of a spy are you?"

"I didn't say I was a spy."

Marta looked terrified again. It was clear to Ryan she was afraid of being out on the street. She said, "It's one in the morning. Here in Wedding, at this time, the only chance is on Fennstrasse. That's three or four blocks away."

"Let's go, then."

She hesitated. Ryan saw tremors in her hands. Finally she said, "This way."

Jack held his sore right forearm with his left hand as they walked together past a small empty park. He kept his eyes shifting from the apartment buildings on his right to the woman walking on his left. He saw a pay phone and thought about calling someone at Mission Berlin to come pick them up, but decided against it, figuring they could make it to Clay Headquarters faster by taxi, and he didn't want to wait around out here for a ride.

It was pitch dark in the Sparrplatz, the block-wide green space next to where Jack and Marta walked in the freezing rain, so they could not see the lone man watching them from the trees next to the run-down basketball court. He stood still and silent until they made a right on Lynarstrasse and disappeared from view, then he moved out of the park, passing wide of the glow of a streetlight as he walked on the pavement they had crossed thirty seconds earlier.

He wore a leather bomber jacket, a riding cap, and leather gloves. Anyone watching from the street might note that, even though the rain was heavy enough to warrant one, the man had no umbrella, but he was otherwise unremarkable and impossible to identify.

The man turned on Lynarstrasse just as Jack Ryan and Marta Scheuring made a left on Tegeler Strasse in front of him.

The man picked up the pace and ducked his neck deeper in his bomber jacket to ward off the rain and the chill.

Jack was beginning to worry about Marta. Her nerves were getting the best of her as they walked alone in the rain, as if the darkness between street-lamps was terrorizing her anew. And each time a vehicle passed, she recoiled in terror and looked to Jack for comfort.

They spotted a passing taxi on Fennstrasse, but it drove right past them as they tried to flag it down. A second cab already had a late-night fare, so it rolled by as well. Jack was getting frustrated; he didn't like walking the nearly empty streets, more because of the danger Marta was in than any thoughts of his own safety.

Marta saw the headlights of an approaching vehicle before Jack did, for the simple reason that Jack was too busy watching Marta to have his eyes focused four blocks up the road.

When Jack did look, he could not tell what sort of vehicle it was. "Is that a taxi?" Jack asked, and he

JACK RYAN'S ROUTE THROUGH WEST BERLIN

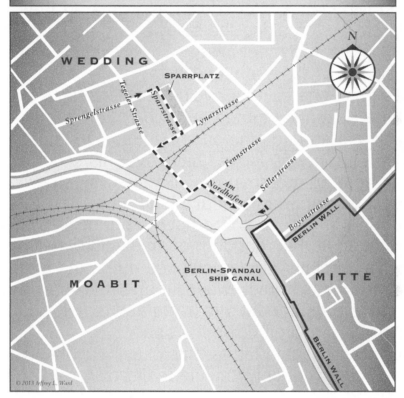

looked back to Marta, and realized she had stopped walking.

"Das weiss ich nicht," she said. Her eyes were locked on the headlights, and they were wide in terror.

"Marta, relax," Jack said, and he stepped to the curb, ready to flag down the car.

But it was not a taxi. It was a large white van.

And it began to slow down as it neared them. It pulled to a stop along the sidewalk in the middle of the block, not fifty feet away.

A side door slid open loudly.

"It's him!" she said, her voice panic-stricken.

Marta Scheuring turned and ran.

Jack started to do the same, but as he started following after her he looked back over his shoulder. A huge stack of newspapers, all lashed together with cord and wrapped in clear plastic, flew out of the open door of the van. The newspapers slammed to the ground at the front door of an all-night market.

A moment later, a man stepped out of the market, gave the van a quick wave, then lifted the newspapers and returned to his warm and dry store.

The van drove off down the street.

Jack called out to Marta: "It's okay!" He blew out a sigh of relief, but only until he realized Marta Scheuring was gone.

He saw the door to an apartment building closing just yards away; he raced for it and tried to follow her through, but the door would not reopen.

Marta had locked the door.

He ran around the outside of the building, looking for some other way in, but when he turned the corner he saw that Marta had left the building through a side door, and now she was running on the other side of the street.

"Marta!" he shouted at her as she raced through the rain, but she did not look back, she only kept running.

Jack chased after her as she disappeared down a darkened street called Am Nordhafen. She had at least fifty yards on him, and he had a feeling he wouldn't catch her before she got where she was going.

The Berlin Wall was just two blocks away.

He shouted for her once more, this time while he raced behind her alongside the Berlin-Spandau Ship Canal, a narrow concrete-lined waterway that ran along Ryan's right as he neared the Berlin Wall.

Marta darted between buildings to her left now, Jack following her in the darkness across a vacant lot, but as he rounded an opening in a metal fence, he slipped in slick mud. It took him a moment to climb back to his feet, and by the time he did so, he'd lost sight of the German woman. Several buildings that ran along the open lot were all dark and vacant, and he saw a dozen blackened windows at ground level that she could have climbed through.

He called out to her, and his voice echoed off the buildings. "Marta? Don't do this. I need you to trust me. We can help you."

There was no response. He ran to a window, looked inside to a darkened room that smelled like sawdust and wet plaster, but he saw no trace of the German woman.

She had talked of using a tunnel to move into and out of East Berlin; he had no idea if it was anywhere near here, but he did know that he didn't have a prayer of finding it in the black night.

He didn't want to admit it at first, but slowly he came to the conclusion that the German woman was gone.

671

Jack stood there in the vacant lot for a full minute, and he noticed his wet hair for the first time, the mud on his pants, and the chill in the air. He walked back to the street, headed down to the corner, and stood there under a streetlight.

The Berlin Wall stood just a block ahead on Boyenstrasse, and beyond the outer wall were the glowing lights illuminating the death strip, a wide-open band between the wall and the backland wall on the eastern side. Inside the strip were automatic machine guns, and men with guns and dogs and searchlights were positioned on the far side of the wall.

Jack stood there, still coming to the realization that he'd lost the proof for his theory concerning the Morningstar case. A car pulled into view on Sellerstrasse, and then, just an instant later, the lights of a second vehicle appeared on Am Nordhafen. A third set of headlights moved across the bridge over the canal to his right.

It wasn't lost on Jack that he had seen only three vehicles in the past ten minutes, yet now suddenly three cars were converging on the street corner where he stood.

He stepped back out of the light and moved up into the vacant lot.

A van raced south on Am Nordhafen, skidded at the intersection, and made a left. A second vehicle, the one crossing the bridge, also raced by the intersection just vacated by Ryan. He got a glimpse inside the sedan as it passed underneath the streetlight, and he saw four men inside. He didn't know who they were, but he had the distinct impression both vehicles were racing into the area to hunt for Marta Scheuring.

Ryan turned to head back up Am Nordhafen, but he saw a figure standing on the sidewalk some seventy-five yards away. The man — Jack assumed he was male because the figure wore a bomber jacket and a riding cap — stood next to a metalworking shop. He was perfectly still and staring in Jack's direction.

Jack crossed the street to the relative seclusion of some trees lining the Nordhafen, a wider area in the Berlin-Spandau canal used for docking and turning around barges. Before he stepped into the trees he looked back and saw that the man was gone. Jack thought he might have gone into the metal shop, although it was certainly closed at this time of night.

Wherever he was, Jack was certain the man had not crossed the street himself.

Jack walked north on the little path between the trees on his right and the waterway on his left. His plan right now was to make it back up to the Fennstrasse, the largest street in the area, and to find a taxi. He'd go directly back to the CIA station at Mission Berlin in Clay Headquarters, and there he would talk to Berlin's CIA chief of station. He hoped the COS could rouse any assets in town to get out into the neighborhood to find Marta before she was found by the Russians, or the East Germans, or whoever the hell was after her now.

Jack began running, knowing time was of the essence.

But he did not get far. Two men in trench coats appeared from the trees in front of him and blocked his way forward.

Ryan stopped in his tracks.

It was dark, but Ryan could see the men were in their thirties; they had short, cropped hair and mustaches. One of the men asked, "Who are you?"

He had a strong German accent, but he'd spoken English, which Ryan found odd, although he knew it was possible they had heard him call out to Marta a minute before.

"Who are *you*?" Jack replied.

"Polizei," one said, but neither was wearing a uniform, and neither pulled out a badge.

"Sure you are." Jack said this as he looked around him. He was alone here, in a secluded area. Behind him was a metal railing, beyond which was a six-foot drop into a frigid canal.

He would not be running away from these guys. He'd have to go through them.

"Show me your identification." It was the same man talking.

What the hell? He was in West Berlin, not East Berlin. Ryan didn't want to show these guys anything, but he reached into his coat pocket as if to comply.

His hand wrapped around the four-inch stiletto, and he clicked it open.

As he started to pull the knife from his coat, both men lunged at him; the first knocked the knife away, and the second got behind him and tried to pin his arms behind his back.

Ryan slammed his elbow back into the man behind, knocking him down, and then he kicked out at the man in front of him. His foot caught nothing but air, but he managed to make a little space for himself, so he turned around and charged at the man there, crashing into him, and the two of them slammed into the iron railing along the water. Jack threw a punch at the German; it grazed his chin without doing much damage, but it did serve to keep the man back for a moment. Jack advanced on him, had him backed up against the railing now, with no room to maneuver. He threw another punch that hit the man in the nose, and the mustached German fell in a heap along the footpath.

Ryan spun around now as fast as he could because he knew he'd left the second attacker somewhere behind him. As soon as he looked up, he saw the man was there on the footpath, ten feet away at most, and he was raising a small black pistol directly at Ryan's head.

Ryan froze as he looked into the German's cold eyes. They told him, without any doubt, that the man was about to shoot him dead.

He thought of his family.

As Jack tightened in anticipation of the shot, he saw movement on the gunman's left — a dark figure appeared from the trees, running across the footpath at an incredible pace. The gunman noticed the movement out of the corner of this eye, and he started to turn his weapon in the direction of the figure, but his speed was no match for the oncoming threat.

The man in the bomber jacket and the racing cap slammed into the German attacker; his gun arm flew to the side and a shot cracked, flashed in the darkness. Jack Ryan leapt back and away from the blast, but he stumbled over the legs of the unconscious man behind him. He fell backward, his lower back hitting the footpath railing, and his momentum flipped him headlong over the side.

Jack cried out as he fell, and he tried to reach out to grab something on his way down, but he hit the water several feet below. As he broke the surface, the cold enveloped him. He flailed in the black water; he had no sense of up and down as the cold shocked his system and disoriented him.

Jack's head came out of the water; he spit out a mouthful of water and sucked cold air. He was ready to dive back down below the water to avoid gunfire, but he looked up and saw no one at the railing.

Then, for just an instant, he saw the man in the bomber jacket. His hat was gone, but all Jack could tell was that he was a white male with a beard and mustache. The man put his foot on the bottom rail, and he looked like he was going to leap over and dive into the water next to Jack.

A second gunshot rang out. The man on the rail stopped in mid-movement, he raised his hands and turned around, and then he disappeared from view.

Ryan felt himself losing feeling in his arms and legs; he kicked ferociously and waved his arms around in an attempt to swim to the edge of the canal. After just a moment he realized the current was pulling him to the south. In the space of just a few seconds he'd already drifted ten yards. He looked down the canal and saw a bridge just another fifty yards on. One of the side spans entering the water near the abutment would be in reach if he just went with the flow, so he concentrated on not drowning and let the water take him.

It took Ryan nearly five minutes to make it back up to street level. By now West German police cars were all over Am Nordhafen, after multiple residents of nearby apartment buildings had reported the gunfire. Most had reasonably assumed someone had been caught in the death strip of the Berlin Wall and shot by East German border guards, but quickly it became clear the noise had come from two blocks within the West German side of the border.

Ryan staggered up to the first patrol car parked by the bridge. Through chattering teeth he told the men he was an American diplomat, and he'd been attacked by two men, one of whom had a pistol.

As far as Jack knew, a Good Samaritan had saved him, but as for what had happened to the man in the bomber jacket, he had no clue.

He was given a blanket and told he'd be taken to the hospital, but Jack insisted they drive him back to the point where it happened instead.

Here they found no trace of either the Good Samaritan or the attackers, and soon the police insisted on taking Ryan to get checked out by medical personnel. He talked them into taking him straight to Clay Headquarters, where he would have access to American medical facilities to get the gash in his forearm treated, but only because he wanted to alert the CIA to everything that had happened in the past hour.

Jack wanted them to do whatever they could to help both Marta and the man who saved his life, because, he feared, they were both now in the hands of the East Germans.

78

Present day

It had been a long day for Jack Ryan, Jr. As soon as he'd left the home of Malcolm Galbraith, he'd returned to the Gulfstream and they'd flown to France. The purpose of their trip was simply to get away from Scotland, because it was clear Hugh Castor knew Jack was there, and there was a chance he would send more Russian assassins after him.

They landed at an airport near Lille, France, and here they waited while Gavin Biery, still in the flat in Kiev, spent hours hacking into the cellular companies in the UK in an attempt to geolocate the telephone used by Hugh Castor in his conversation with Malcolm Galbraith. It became apparent after lengthy research that Castor was using powerful encryption on his phone that hid its connection to mobile phone towers, and Gavin was therefore unable to locate it or bread-crumb past GPS signals.

Just when they were about to admit defeat, however, Ryan got another idea. He called Sandy Lamont, and asked him which of Castor's staff was also out of the office. Sandy seemed reluctant to get involved, but finally he checked into it and told Ryan one of Castor's two security officers, a former MI5 man himself, was also away. Ryan found the man's mobile number by doing a social media search, and soon Biery had located this mobile phone's signal.

It was pinging a tower in Küssnacht, Switzerland, a municipality in the canton of Schwyz. Küssnacht was southwest of Zug; Castor's chalet was on the lake in Baumgarten, a community in Küssnacht.

Ryan discussed it with Ding and the others, and by mid-afternoon the Gulfstream was back in the air, heading southeast over France.

An hour from touchdown in Zurich, Adara Sherman sat directly behind the flight deck, then behind her, Caruso, Chavez, and Driscoll dozed in reclined cabin chairs. Oxley and Ryan were in the very back of the aircraft, and they were the only two awake and in conversation.

Ryan was trying to get information about their destination. He asked, "Did Castor have the place in Zug back when you were there?"

Oxley shook his head. "Not that I knew of. We weren't friends, you understand. He was my handler. He was in London, I was in the field, which usually meant the East. When I went to Zug, Castor never said anything like, 'Why not pop round to my lake house for tea when you've sussed out that Zenith mess?' "

Ryan laughed. Then he said, "One thing Galbraith didn't know was what tipped the KGB off in the first place. When you tailed the men from Hungary to Ritzmann Privatbankiers, did you know anything about the trail they were following?"

"Not a clue. I wasn't inside. I was more engaged

679

in foot-follow surveillance. I had instructions and I carried them out. Tried to, anyway. Your dad would know better than me."

Ryan wasn't sure he heard the last part correctly. "My dad?"

Now the big, silver-bearded Englishman turned to the young American. "Your father. He was there. You knew that, of course."

Jack shook his head. "In Switzerland?"

"And in Berlin."

"Berlin?"

Oxley shook his head in utter disbelief. "Do you two ever talk about anything?"

"Ox, my dad was CIA. I've picked up a lot through the years, mostly through others, but he can't tell me much about what he did back then." Jack said, "You're sure? You're certain he was there when all this was going on?"

"Of course I'm bloody certain."

"How can you be so sure?"

"Because I'll never forget him." Oxley paused before saying the next part. "His was the last face I saw before my world went dark."

It was noon at the White House. President Jack Ryan had spent the first half of the day in and out of meetings related to the situation in Ukraine, and now he was running late to a luncheon here in D.C. He was signing a few documents at his desk when his secretary's voice came over the intercom.

"Mr. President?"

Ryan replied without looking up. "Tell Arnie to hold his horses. I'll be out in one second."

"Sorry, sir. It's Jack Junior on line one."

Ryan put down his pen. "Great, put him

through."

Jack's hand fired out and snatched up the phone. As always, he did his best to keep his voice light to mask his concern for his son. Even now, when he had no reason to think Jack Junior was in any danger, he heard from him seldom enough that his imagination often got the best of him and he could not help worrying.

"Hey, sport. You doing okay?"

"Hey, Dad . . . I have to put you on speakerphone."

Jack Senior was disappointed his son had someone with him. He figured he'd be asked to say hi to some stranger, and though he didn't really mind, he'd rather just hear about Jack Junior's day. He said, "Actually, I might have to call you back. Have to run up to the Washington Hilton for a speech on foreign affairs. As you can imagine, we've been running behind schedule all day."

There was no response for a moment.

"Who do you have there with you, son?"

"A man named Victor Oxley."

Before Ryan Senior could say anything, Junior added, "He's Bedrock, Dad. He's got a hell of a story, and you are in it."

"*I'm* in it?"

A low, gruff English accent came over Jack's phone now. "How cold was that water, Ryan?"

"I beg your pardon?"

"Must have been bloody razor blades. I was there. In Berlin. You were taking a late-night swim. I was just about to join you, when some other gents let me know they'd much rather I came along with them."

President Jack Ryan did not speak.

"Jog your memory, does it?"

Softly, Ryan said, "It does."

Arnie Van Damm walked purposefully into the Oval Office, ready to hurry Jack along to the limo. Jack pointed at the door, and Arnie caught the urgent gesture, the glazed look in his friend's eyes, and he rushed out. In seconds he was on the phone announcing that the President would be a little late to his luncheon appointment.

79

Thirty years earlier

The man in the bomber jacket stood in the trees in the cold rain, watching the drama unfold. Behind him was Am Nordhafen, a darkened street. In front of him was the canal, and in front of that was a footpath. He watched the CIA man get accosted by the two men on the path, and he immediately took them for Stasi goons.

This wasn't going to be pretty. At first he thought they were just going to beat seven shades of shit out of the Yank, but when the men started looking around, making sure the coast was clear, Bedrock realized they were going to try to waylay him, and possibly shanghai him over the border.

Saving the life of some square-jawed CIA suit wasn't Bedrock's mission, so he watched from the trees at first, already thinking about calling this in to Castor, his control officer, after the fact.

He'd spent the evening outside the RAF safe house, staying out of sight, in the hope that the real Marta Scheuring would turn up. He hadn't bought the story about the dead terrorist leaving her ID outside the restaurant before blowing the place up. He knew the ID didn't belong to the body, so he assumed Marta was still alive. If this was true, it stood to reason she would at least come by the flat for a look.

But while waiting for Marta, Bedrock saw the American CIA officer who'd been in Zug with the MI6 team there looking into the death of Penright. He assumed the American had come to Berlin for the takedown the evening before, but Bedrock did not have a clue why he'd come alone in the rain to sneak into the building. At the time Bedrock wondered if the man had much of a plan at all, as he seemed to wander around for several minutes before committing to climbing up the fire escape.

Bedrock took the Yank for a bit of a bumbling idiot at first. He just stood by and watched, looking forward to the spectacle of the local coppers arresting an American spook for breaking and entering.

And then Marta came. He'd seen her up the street when she disappeared between two buildings, and he knew she was slipping into a back entrance.

Bedrock wondered if the CIA man and the RAF woman were going to fight it out up in the flat, and then, when they had been inside the building for what seemed bloody ages, he wondered if they just might be making a baby up there.

Finally they came out, through the back entrance that Bedrock had spotted minutes into his recon of the building. He followed them, in the hope that Zenith himself would turn up looking to punch Marta's ticket.

Bedrock's mission was to find and kill a Russian who called himself Zenith, and the German terrorist was just, as far as he was concerned, nothing more than bait.

Bedrock knew more about the activities in Zug and the actions of a Russian called Zenith than anyone else, because he had been on this operation for more than a month. He had dutifully reported all his actions to Hugh Castor, who, Bedrock only assumed, would have scrupulously held on to this information and not passed a bloody shred of it to MI6.

He was right about that.

After following the unlikely duo through the rain-swept streets of the former French sector of West Berlin, Bedrock watched the German girl do a runner, and he watched the American promptly lose her. It was at this point he noticed two men skulking about the neighborhood, and he watched the handsome American bloke bumble right into them.

He pegged the men for Stasi operators, which meant to him the opposition had a tunnel nearby, which made perfect sense, since Marta Scheuring had just evaporated into thin air.

Bedrock stood in the trees less than twenty-five yards away, while the CIA man fought against the two Stasi officers. The Englishman was surprised to see the American was a goer, and he took down the first Stasi asset with a somewhat adequate right jab to the snout, so when, with his back turned, the other man pulled out a Walther PA-63, Bedrock deemed the man a poor sport, and he decided to intervene.

He violated his mission parameters and broke cover, racing across the footpath in what he thought to be a million-to-one chance of stopping a kidnapping or a murder.

He took the second German down, but the bloody Yank fell into the canal. Bedrock had just picked himself up off the pavement and scanned the windows of the nearby apartment buildings to make sure no one was watching, when four more men came out of the trees.

The neighborhood had gone rotten with East Germans. These would be Stasi as well, which was

685

bad news for Bedrock.

He turned to dive headfirst into the water, his only means of escape.

"Halt!" came a shout from behind. He knew if these blokes came from the tunnel as well, it was likely they would also be carrying Walther PPKs or PA-63s or some other sidearm, since they did not have to go through any sort of control area.

The crack of a gunshot confirmed this, and it stopped him in his tracks. He turned and saw three men with pistols on him, and a fourth man with his gun high in the air, wisps of smoke floating in the rainy night around its muzzle.

Bedrock knew he would never make it into the canal.

A hood was placed on his head, he heard German spoken as he was pushed up the street, and soon he was shoved through the door of one of the buildings a block away from the Boyenstrasse section of the wall.

He was led down a narrow staircase, and then lowered deeper belowground in some sort of a metal basket.

It took fifteen minutes for them to get a hooded and tied man through a hundred-meter-long tunnel. Bedrock moved on his knees with his hands behind his back, and when his knees were so bloody and raw he could no longer stand it, he rolled on his back and kicked his way on, abrading his elbows and head and backside.

When he and the four men made it to the other side of the wall, he was brought back up to the surface and led into a van. As it drove around, the men with him kicked him for a few minutes, just for fun, before the van stopped abruptly.

Twenty-nine-year-old Victor Oxley, code-named

Bedrock, took another boot to the back of his head — it must have been the fifth or sixth, but he'd lost count. This one slammed his face even harder into the metal floor of the van. He felt blood on his lips and running from his nose.

As much as he hurt, he knew this was only the beginning, because he was in the East now, and the opposition could bloody well do with him whatever they bloody well pleased.

The door opened. Bedrock thought he'd reached his destination, but instead someone joined them in the vehicle.

There was a long conversation in German, some arguing, and though Bedrock could not understand the words, he had the impression that it had to do with control of him, the prisoner. It seemed the Germans were getting the upper hand, and for a short moment he thought the men above him might even come to blows, but finally things settled down.

A man leaned right over his face; the Englishman could smell tobacco and sweat. When the man spoke, he spoke in English, but there was no doubt. The man was Russian.

"I do not know who you are, but I think you are one of the people who have been making life very difficult for me and my associates. If I could, I would take you out of here and shoot you right now." He paused. "When Stasi is finished with you, you might wish I had."

And that was all.

The van stopped a moment later, the door opened, and someone climbed out without a word. Bedrock heard footsteps retreating on gravel, and he was surprised to hear from the uneven cadence that whoever was walking away was doing so with a pronounced limp.

They were moving again in moments; the English spy thought it was the Russian who had left, because immediately the German men around him all began talking. Ox did not speak German, but he sensed a wave of relief in the voices of the Stasi men.

The relief did not extend to Oxley himself; the boots just rained down harder.

They drove for more than two hours, but Ox knew enough about Stasi tactics to know they could have just been going in circles, a little theater to keep him guessing about where they were taking him.

When they stopped again, Ox was pulled from the van, and his arms were bound at the wrists and held high up behind him in a stress position, forcing him to lean all the way forward at the waist. There were men on both sides of him, and they pushed him onward, upstairs, downstairs, in elevators that disoriented him to the point he did not know if he was in the bottom of a nuclear silo or at the top of a TV tower.

Finally he was brought into a room, his hood was removed, and his cuffs were attached to a hook at a table.

He had not spoken a word so far, and he made a decision, right there, that would simultaneously save his life but condemn it to unbearable hardship.

He decided to speak Russian.

He had no identification on him, he'd left everything in his hotel, so he could say whatever he wanted without any direct proof he was lying.

As long as he kept his cover up.

For three days he was kept awake with cold water and electric shocks in an attempt to break him, but he spoke only Russian, told the Germans he didn't know what they wanted, and they had no right to do this to a citizen of the Soviet Union.

Ox had heard the stories about how Stasi agents had a particularly nasty way of tracking people they had picked up. The Stasi would sit them down in front of what looked to be some sort of large camera, then tell them to wait while they changed film.

But it was not a camera. It was an X-ray machine, and the entire time the unfortunate subjects sat there they were being bombarded with radioactive particles.

The process would ensure that every time the subjects passed through any of the checkpoints with the West, all of which had radiation detectors, they would be flagged as having been previously picked up by the Stasi.

They might have their lives shortened by decades because of cancer from radiation poisoning, but no matter. The Stasi found the tactic convenient.

But Oxley was not radiated by the Stasi, because Oxley was not heading back out to the West.

No, he was headed east.

The East Germans handed him off to the KGB.

80

Present day
President of the United States Jack Ryan realized he was squeezing the side of his desk with his free hand as he listened to the gravel-voiced Englishman tell a story that had turned out so well for Ryan and so poorly for him.

When the story stopped, Jack knew there must have been much, much more, but he recognized the Englishman was waiting to hear something from Ryan, just to know he was still there.

Jack said, "I don't know what to say."

"Did you call it in? Did you report what happened?"

"Did I call it in? I was with the German police five minutes after the fact, looking for you. An hour later, I had every U.S. intelligence asset in the city on the hunt. By the next day, I was in London in the office of the director of the SIS. Of course I looked for you. I did not know you were a British operative, but I had everyone hunting for you and Marta nonetheless."

Oxley said, "Fair enough, Ryan. I've got reasons to believe you now, thanks to your boy here, but I spent thirty years under the impression you'd kept your mouth shut about the whole bloody affair. I've been holdin' a bit of a grudge, to be honest. I didn't know you from Adam at the time. But years later I was sitting in my pub when your face came up on the telly saying you were the American President."

Jack Junior spoke up now: "Dad, Ox was the man who gave SIS the intel about Talanov being Zenith. He was in a gulag when Talanov was there. He didn't meet him, but he picked up the story."

"Is it credible?"

Oxley said, "Seemed so, but it was a long time ago. My memory is not what it once was."

"I understand, Mr. Oxley."

Jack Junior said, "We have to go. I'm going to get answers for you on Zenith, but I don't have them yet."

"Just tell me you are okay." Jack Junior could hear the emotion in his father's voice. He was lost in the past now, and had no idea what his son was involved in at present.

"I'm with Ding, Dom, and Sam in the Hendley jet."

"The Hendley jet? You aren't in London?"

"We're going to check a lead or two on the continent. I'll call you when I know something. You've got enough on your plate right now dealing with Ukraine."

"It is a difficult situation," Ryan said, "but as long as I know you aren't in the middle of it, I'll feel a little better."

Jack Junior just said, "I'm a long way from Ukraine, Dad."

Ryan, Chavez, Caruso, Oxley, and Driscoll arrived in Zurich in the early evening, rented a pair of Mercedes SUVs, and headed south toward Zug. There was heavy rain and fog, which Ryan hoped

691

would work to their advantage, as they had no idea who was looking for them.

The four Americans were armed now. Before they left the G550, Adara had passed out pistols that had been hidden in an access panel on the flight deck. Jack and Ding both chose the Glock 19, and Driscoll and Caruso took SIG Sauer P229s. The men knew if Castor was protected by any sizable security force they would not be able to initiate any sort of real attack with handguns, but at least with the firearms hidden inside their jackets they would be able to defend themselves from most threats.

They had little information about the physical property of Castor's place, other than some notes Galbraith made for Jack regarding the layout. From this and a careful search of online maps, the men decided their best chance to enter undetected was via the lake at the rear of the property.

They rented a boat and scuba gear in the marina, and by seven p.m. they were a quarter-mile offshore from Castor's lake house, scanning the two-acre grounds through binoculars. They could see some activity inside through the huge floor-to-ceiling windows, as well as plainclothes security men patrolling with submachine guns around the building's exterior and down a hill in the rear of the property at a pier and boathouse on the lake.

The security men looked like a professional group, and it gave Ryan confidence that Castor was, in fact, on the premises.

Ding said, "I see eight to ten guys. We are not getting through them undetected, and we aren't shooting it out with Swiss rent-a-cops."

Ryan agreed. "We'll have to figure out another way in."

The Americans sat on the boat, discussing some way to covertly gain access to Castor without being detected by his security.

Oxley had been silent, sitting alone up on the bow. Finally he said, "Gents, I don't want to tell you your business, but I would like to offer a suggestion."

Ding said, "By all means."

"Why don't we just walk up his bloody driveway and talk to him?"

"Talk to him?" Ryan asked.

"Of course. Castor believes in self-preservation. He believes in playing both sides. He's not a madman. He is not going to kill the President's son when others know you are with him. It is possible things won't go the way we want them to, so maybe your friends can get as close as possible, but my vote is you and I just confront the sod and see what he has to say for himself."

Ryan looked to Chavez. Ding said, "Your call, kid."

Jack shrugged. "I don't have anything better than that."

Sam said, "We can drop you up the coast, then we can anchor a half-mile away and do a covert entry on the back of the grounds with the scuba gear. We might be able to parlay the distraction of your arrival into us getting a little closer to the house than we could otherwise."

Chavez said, "I like it. But remember, Jack. They will search you before you see Castor. You can't take a gun or any communications gear that shows them you brought company."

"I understand."

Jack wanted Oxley to stay on the boat. He knew the fifty-nine-year-old ex-spy had every reason in the world to want to confront Hugh Castor. He sensed there was more to the relationship than Ox had let on, but he'd not mentioned it. Jack saw nothing good coming from Oxley's facing Castor right now. The threat of Oxley's revealing Castor as a Russian spy, Jack reasoned, would be a lot more useful than actually having Oxley enter Castor's grounds, where he would be vulnerable.

But Victor Oxley was having none of it. He made it clear that he would be involved in the meeting, and Jack and his mates would have to tie him to the rigging to keep him from going.

The Russians arrived in Zug in a Russian-built Mi-8, which was not an unusual occurrence at all, as there was a lot of offshore banking still done in Switzerland, and no one did more offshore banking these days than the Russians.

Anyone looking over the men who climbed off the chopper, however, might have noticed that most of their suits were brand-new and off-the-rack, and their average age was only thirty or so, which was young for the average Russian investment banker or white-collar criminal.

These were not Seven Strong Men henchmen. They were Spetsnaz, FSB Special Forces, but their leader straddled the line between both organizations. His name was Pavel Lechkov, he was Seven Strong Men and FSB, and he, like the rest of his unit, carried a small, collapsible, Brügger & Thomet MP9 submachine gun in a shoulder holster under his coat, and a hooked knife in a sheath in the small of his back.

The Russians had a schematic of the lakefront

property of Hugh Castor, and they had gone over it in the helo, and by the time they arrived in Zug and climbed into a van to take them to a property on the west side of the lake, each man in the unit knew his part in the operation to come.

At a small lakeside chalet at the edge of the forest, the men changed clothes, removing the business suits they had worn for cover and putting on dark cotton pants and dark jackets that would help them blend into the night.

Although there were eight of them and they knew they might well be up against a slightly larger force, Pavel Lechkov also knew they would have skill and surprise on their side.

They moved down to the waterline, where an eight-man Zodiac rigid inflatable boat was waiting for them.

Just after eleven p.m. Jack Ryan, Jr., and Victor Oxley walked together up an unpaved winding street. It was almost perfectly quiet, the only noise coming from drips of condensation off the trees on either side of the road and, every few minutes, a passing vehicle, usually a Porsche or BMW or Audi.

They had to walk nearly a mile from the closest place Ding could land the boat, so they had plenty of time to talk about their plan to get Castor to reveal information. Jack knew his best option was to clearly and immediately let the man know that a lot of people knew he was there. He hoped Castor was desperate enough to talk to save himself, but not so desperate that he would just shoot Ryan and Oxley in the head and try to flee to some country with no extradition treaty with either the United States or Great Britain.

This all seemed like a long shot, but Jack was emboldened somewhat by the fact three very able men would be lurking in the darkness outside the lake house.

As they walked, Ryan asked Oxley about what had happened after he was taken out of East Berlin. Oxley said he spent days in a train car under guard, while outside the landscape of East Germany, Poland, and Belarus passed by. He passed into Russia, continued all the way to Moscow's Leningradskaya station, where he was placed in the back of a truck. They drove him around the city, and he was able to see it all through a slit in the wall of the vehicle. Through the slit he saw a sign that made his heart sink. Energeticheskaya Street. He knew then they were taking him to Lefortovo Prison.

Oxley spent weeks in a small cell in Lefortovo with an asphalt floor and a single twenty-five-watt bulb that burned both day and night.

Every day he was taken into interrogations. He claimed he was nothing but a simple defector to the West who walked up on a fight among some plainclothes men, and he got involved. He said he thought one man was being attacked by West German police, and he'd gotten involved only because he was no fan of Western governments.

The KGB did not believe his story, but they'd caught him in no verifiable fabrication, either. After weeks of sleep deprivation, stress positions, torture, and the threat of execution, none of it made him change his simple yet doubtful story.

They were unable to break him.

Normally, the KGB would have made explicit threats involving his family, but this arrow had been removed from their quiver, because the KGB could not pin down any family.

It would have been an easy matter to take the twenty-nine-year-old Russian defector into a field and shoot him, but this was the mid-eighties. The KGB still killed people, the KGB would not execute its last prisoner until the final days of its existence in 1991, but by the eighties a termination required paperwork and signatures and a post-action review.

It was much easier and cleaner to lock him up and let nature take its course.

Ox was placed into the gulag system and shipped in a train into the Ural Mountains in the Komi Republic.

Ryan wanted more; he hadn't yet gotten Oxley to explain how he'd made it home to Great Britain after leaving the gulag, but by now they had almost arrived at Hugh Castor's lake house. They turned to head up the long driveway and made it less than a third of the way to the house before a man stepped out from the darkness and shone a flashlight on them. *"Halt!"*

Jack shielded his eyes from the light. He said, "We are here to see Castor."

"Name?"

"Ryan and Oxley."

"*Ja.* We have been waiting for you."

Ryan had not expected this. He was hoping Castor would be put on his heels with the surprise visit, but clearly that wasn't going to happen.

The security man spoke into his walkie-talkie, and an SUV rolled down the drive. Men climbed out and searched the two visitors thoroughly up against the hood of the vehicle, then they all walked up to the front door as a group.

■ ■ ■ ■

Sam Driscoll rose out of the cold black water of Lake Zug slowly, inch by inch, so the water on his insulated wetsuit would return to the lake without dripping and making noise. He'd already taken off his swim fins and his tank; he pulled them along with one hand as he held his pistol with the other, scanning the darkness to the north of the pier.

Soon Ding Chavez appeared from the black water on the south side of the pier, and he carried his equipment with him as well. He stowed it against a low retaining wall at the edge of the property, making certain it could not be seen from the house, as he did not want any beam cast from a flashlight to reflect off either the tank or the mask.

Dominic Caruso rose from the water under the pier itself, and he tied off his gear and climbed out onto the rocks behind the wooden boathouse.

A two-man security patrol passed the area less than a minute after Dom made it into position. He rolled under the raised boathouse, keeping his body off the sharp rocks by holding himself in a plank position till they passed.

After another minute, the patrol had finished its circuit of the rear of the property and disappeared around the side of the house up the hill. Ding, Dom, and Sam took their Bluetooth headsets out of waterproof boxes and attached them to their ears. They established comms with one another, and all three used binoculars from their packs to search the windows of the house itself to look for Ryan.

■ ■ ■ ■

Hugh Castor stood in front of a roaring fire in the living room of the lake house, and he greeted Ryan and Oxley as they were escorted in by the security officers. The sixty-eight-year-old man wore a black sweater and corduroys, and his eyeglasses and short silver hair shone in the light from the fire.

Oxley and Castor made some eye contact, but Ryan was surprised there were no real words between them. He halfway expected Ox to launch across the room and grab Castor by the throat, but nothing of the sort happened.

Instead, Castor just directed Oxley and Ryan to a sofa, and he sat down on a wingback chair facing them.

Two Swiss security men had been in the living room, but once Ryan and Oxley sat down they stepped into an adjacent kitchen. Ryan could hear them there, just around the corner, and he suspected that was their intention.

Three glasses of red wine had already been poured and sat waiting on the table in front of the men. Castor took his glass and drank a slow sip. Oxley and Ryan did not touch theirs.

Neither Jack nor Ox had been handcuffed or tied, which surprised Jack greatly. So far, none of this was going the way he had imagined it. It was almost as if Castor were happy to have the visitors.

Castor said, "Jack, you might not believe this, but I did not know a thing about what happened in Corby until Sandy told me this morning. I looked it up on the news, and the only conclusion I can come to is that clearly some associates of mine double-crossed me, the same as they did you."

"Sandy told you I went to see him yesterday?"

"He did." Castor shrugged. "No, no. I know what you are thinking. Sandy is not aware of any of this at all. He is just a good company man, and a decent lapdog. He has been a faithful servant for many years. He knows there is more than meets the eye, but he is not so curious about my private dealings with Russia's elite away from Castor and Boyle."

Castor pointed at Ryan with his wineglass. "You, on the other hand, young Ryan. You are the curious one. I must say how terribly impressed I am with everything you have accomplished. Obviously, I underestimated your abilities."

"And I overestimated your character."

Castor's eyebrows rose, and he looked to Oxley. "You've been talking, I see."

Ox said, "*You've* been talking, ya fuck. I owe you not a bleedin' thing."

"I could have left you to rot, you bloody fool! Or I could have let them shoot you!"

"You should have done just that, you old bastard."

"It's not too late, Bedrock. They just might get you yet."

Jack was utterly confused by the back-and-forth.

Castor looked at Ryan, and then back at Oxley. "What does he know?"

"He knows I was shanghaied by the Stasi while trying to help out his father. He knows I was then passed to the Russians. He knows I went in the gulags, and he knows I came out a few years later."

"And clearly he thinks this is somehow my fault."

Ox said nothing.

Castor crossed his legs. To Jack, it appeared an affectation. He wasn't as relaxed as he pretended to be. The short, biting argument with Oxley was evidence of that.

Castor said, "Jack, I had nothing to do with our friend Victor here getting waylaid by the East Germans in Berlin. It was bad luck. That was all. I spent years, literally *years,* trying to find out what happened to him."

Ryan looked to Ox, and Ox conceded Castor's remarks with a half-nod.

Oxley said, "Castor wasn't dirty then. He didn't turn dirty till the Iron Curtain fell down and a bunch of money poured out. That's when he became one of them."

Castor shook his head vigorously. "I wasn't one of them, Jack, old boy, I was an opportunist. I'd spent the years looking into Oxley's disappearance, something of a personal mission, because MI5 had given him up for dead. I made contacts throughout the region in this endeavor. In Hungary. In Czechoslovakia. In Russia. Here in Zug. When the Iron Curtain fell, I was in a position of leverage over some powerful individuals. I used that leverage. Simple as that."

Jack said, "Malcolm Galbraith told you about the stolen KGB money Zenith was involved with."

"He told me bits and pieces, indeed. Others told me other things. But by the time Galbraith told me about the Russian account, the money was long gone from RPB. Zenith got it out via diamonds."

"Diamonds?"

"Yes. Zenith's control officer transferred the entire two hundred four million into another account at the bank, an account owned by a diamond man in Antwerp. Philippe Argens. He met with Zenith here in Zug, passed him two hundred million in uncut diamonds, and Zenith returned to Russia."

"What happened to the diamonds?"

"The Russians in control of the black fund kept them until 1991, and then they sold them back to Argens. Slowly, they liquidated their assets. A few million here, a few million there. It worked for both sides. Argens was able to hide the transactions, so he effectively laundered money for years. And the Russians had the assets they needed to buy up state-run businesses when Russia was nationalizing everything and offering it in rigged auctions for peanuts."

"A quarter-billion dollars buys a lot of peanuts," Ryan admitted. "Who stole the money in the first place?"

Castor smiled. "This is where the bargaining starts, my boy."

"What bargaining?"

"I'll tell you what I want in a moment, but for now, I will whet your appetite." He sipped his wine and then looked into the glass. "It's French, not Swiss, so it's quite good."

Neither Ryan nor Oxley had any interest in the wine.

Castor shrugged and said, "Even before Gorbachev came to power and started liberalizing things, the KGB realized they had a problem. Members of the First Chief Directorate's leadership began meeting in secret, discussing the inevitability that their model could not continue much longer.

"They wanted a fallback plan. They could see

the potential for a complete collapse of the system as far back as the mid-eighties. They began pulling money out of accounts set up to support communist revolutions in Latin America, or to bankroll communist dictators already in power.

"Later, my contact in this group told me ten percent of all the money earmarked by the Kremlin for Cuba and Angola for a two-year period had been skimmed by a single young KGB officer working for the leaders.

"He created this black fund, ready to support them in case they had to run. They studied what the smartest of the Nazis did after the end of the Second World War, and they learned from them, but the KGB had longer to plan and more resources to pull from. The Third Reich had only been around for a decade. By the late eighties, Soviets had been in power for seventy years."

Jack leaned forward in rapt fascination. Castor seemed to be certain of his information, though Jack knew he had his own agenda here.

Ryan asked, "Who was Zenith?"

Castor said, "In order for the KGB graybeards to protect this covert operation, they moved staff out of the intelligence hierarchy, and set them up as their own private organization. A young officer was charged with setting up and protecting the assets in the West, and he brought on board an assassin from military intelligence, a man who had a lot of experience killing from his years in Afghanistan."

Ryan said, "Roman Talanov."

Castor nodded gravely. "*The* Roman Talanov. Of course, I'd never heard of him till Oxley told me when he got out of the gulag."

"How do you know the rest?"

"The young KGB officer charged with protecting the assets realized his control over the man Zenith gave him greater power than the KGB graybeards in charge of the operation, so when the time came for the assets to be distributed to the men who came up with the plan in the first place, the KGB officer sent Talanov to kill them. It was a double cross of a double cross, you might say. There was a two-year period in the early nineties when former KGB and GRU big shots were falling off buildings, stepping in front of buses, turning up in the Moskva River, and committing suicide with guns that were curiously absent from the scene when the police arrived. This was all Talanov and his control officer tying up loose ends."

Castor continued, "One of these men reached out to me in desperation, knowing I was British intelligence and I could protect him. General Mikhail Zolotov, of the GRU, Russian military intelligence. Misha told me about the plan, the black fund, and he told me about the double cross perpetrated by the young officer overseeing the accounts. He told me everything but the names. We were working up to that point when he died in a boating mishap in the Gulf of Finland."

"A boating mishap?"

"Indeed. Apparently, he went to sea and forgot to bring his boat along. He was found floating three kilometers offshore of Saint Petersburg."

"Why didn't you go to MI5 when he told you about this?"

Castor shrugged. "I wanted some of the money. So I went to the Russians."

"Fuckin' cunt," Oxley mumbled. "He knew Talanov's name from me, and he found Talanov in Saint Petersburg. He told him what he knew, told him he'd keep his mouth shut if he could be cut into the deal."

"Why didn't Talanov just kill you?"

"Because I had an ace in the hole and he knew it. I told him about his time in the gulag. You should have seen the look on his face when I told him there was video of him in his typhoid rage talking about Zenith and the KGB."

Ryan stood up. "There's a video?"

Oxley answered for Castor. "There's no bleedin' video. He just told Talanov there was for leverage."

Ryan sat back down. "You told him you made copies, had them hidden here and there, and if something happened to you, they would get out."

"That's right. He paid me off, but then something even better happened. We went into business together. He's been giving me tips for over twenty years, and I've been helping him in his business pursuits."

"What business pursuits?"

Castor did not answer this. Instead, he said, "What is important for you to understand, lad, is this. I committed no treason."

Jack couldn't believe what he was hearing. "How the fuck can you possibly make that claim?"

"Easy. Victor Oxley was not an employee of MI5. He was a civilian. Run completely off the books. When he returned from the gulags and reported in, I merely flew to Moscow and spoke with him, then accurately told MI5 leadership that the man was not an agent of ours, and no further action would be necessary. No official assistance would be forthcoming."

Ryan wanted to kill the old man in front of him. He said, "Even if that were true, you were an MI5 man working with the KGB."

"Wrong again, young Ryan. The men I uncovered in my investigation were working very much against the wishes of the KGB. They may have been former employees, but they were private citizens by this point. They had stolen funds from KGB. They weren't even ideologically connected to them." Castor waved his hand to stress the next point: "I traded no secrets with any foreign intelligence agency, at any time, while I was at Five. When I learned details from Oxley upon his release, I resigned from Five, and then I reached out to Talanov, aka Zenith. I merely entered into an agreement with these men that I would keep their secret in return for payment. I certainly did not tell the Russians that a just-released *zek* had been an MI5 asset. I knew they would kill Victor if they were aware who he was and what he knew about Zenith, but I prevented it by keeping my mouth shut."

Ryan turned to Oxley. "How did you get out of the gulag?"

"They were letting a lot of us political prisoners out at that point. I took a train to Moscow, I almost starved to death on the journey. Didn't have a ruble in my pocket or an onion to eat. Staggered into the British consulate. Just a walk-in off the street. I waited in line nearly all day to see someone.

"I told the woman at the counter I was a British citizen, which caused a bloody ruckus. I was taken into a room, where I was interviewed by an SIS employee. I told him I'd been run off-book by MI5, but I gave him a name."

Ryan looked to Castor, and Castor raised his hand. "I was on the next flight over."

Ox said, "I also told the woman about Zenith, and she had a file faxed over from London. On it was a reference to the explosion at the Meisser restaurant in Rotkreuz. I told her I had been picked up by police there, and she jotted down my code name next to the mention of the incident in the report, intending to research it later."

Jack said, "So when I showed you the file —"

"I knew exactly what it was. I was sitting in front of the woman when she made the note. Funny how you remember the little things."

Oxley continued. "When Castor showed up, he told me I was lucky to be alive. The Americans sold me down the river. The KGB had been hunting me, but they didn't know I was in the gulag. He told me I needed to stay off the radar, forever, because if the off-the-books op from the eighties got out, a lot of people would suffer." Ox shrugged. "Firstly and mostly, me."

Castor picked up the story here. "Oxley just wanted to live out his years in peace. I allowed him that. I said nothing to the Russians that he existed, and I said nothing to MI5 that he had reemerged.

"We had an agreement, the two of us. I sent him money every year, enough to keep him in the manner in which he has become accustomed, and he stayed quiet. He knew there were powerful people in Russia who could have ended him whenever the hell they chose. I kept that from happening."

Ox said, "Now I am learning that no one in Russia knew a goddamned thing about me. It was all a lie."

Castor shook his head. "At least I didn't inform on you, you miserable fuck." He turned to Ryan.

"Victor and I have lived in a state of mutually assured destruction for some twenty years, haven't we?"

Oxley mumbled. "I just wanted to come home and be left alone."

There was one thing Jack didn't understand. He asked Oxley, "Why did you agree to come help me in all this if your only intention was to be left alone?"

"Because once the Seven Strong Men attacked me, I knew the Russians were onto me, and I knew Castor here had reneged on his side of the bargain. It was over. I had to fight back."

Castor looked into the fire. "Which brings me to you, Ryan. The Seven Strong Men had been following you during your Gazprom investigation. I tried to push you away from that affair, gently, through Lamont, and then more forcefully when I had you in my office to order you off the case. But the Seven Strong Men knew you were too close to stop looking. Then, the other night, one of their international operatives came to my house and said you were meeting with a man in Corby. They gave me the address, I realized you and Oxley had gotten together, and I told them who Oxley was. What he knew."

"And at that moment they decided to kill him," Jack said.

"Of course they bloody well did." Castor leaned forward; his eyeglasses caught the firelight and it obscured Ryan's view of his eyes. "Even after all this time, it's not too late for bloody Bedrock here to ruin everything."

81

Thirty years earlier

CIA analyst Jack Ryan returned to London during an afternoon thunderstorm that bounced his Lufthansa 727 all over the sky above Heathrow. Jack tightened his body on the left and the right as if trying to steer the aircraft with the muscles in his back and legs, and he squeezed the armrests, although the burning sting in his bandaged right forearm made this excruciating.

The plane finally pitched and yawed all the way down to the runway, where the wings leveled with the ground effect, and Jack was relieved to find the landing mercifully smooth.

He wanted to go straight home to Chatham and be with his family, but that wasn't an option. He knew he'd need to head to Century House, and he imagined he'd be there until very late in the evening.

He had only enough time to put down his suitcase and slip off his raincoat before Simon Harding stepped into his office. "Welcome back, Jack. How did everything go? Wait a tick! What have you done to your arm?"

Jack had thrown his suit coat away at the CIA station in Berlin. The tear in the arm of the coat wasn't repairable, and the bloodstain wasn't something he wanted to bring home to Cathy after assuring her he'd avoid any danger on this trip.

Without the coat, his cut shirtsleeve was visible, rolled up to his elbow; a thick layer of white gauze was wrapped on his forearm. This wasn't something he'd be able to hide from Cathy, either.

Hell, he hadn't even been able to hide it from Simon.

Jack said, "Had a little accident." It wasn't a great surprise that Harding didn't know about everything that had happened to Jack, but it was still awkward to keep information from an SIS man inside the SIS HQ.

"Let me guess. Flatiron? Every time I venture off without the missus, I am useless when it comes to ironing my own shirts. I've taken to just steaming up the loo and —"

The phone on Jack's desk rang. With an apologetic smile, he snatched it up. "Ryan."

"Oh, good, you've made it in." It was Basil. "Do come up as soon as you're settled."

Jack sat on the sofa in Charleston's office; across from him were Nick Eastling and Sir Basil. He'd been offered tea or coffee, but he'd taken neither. His stomach had tied itself into knots in the skies over London, and this was added to the other stresses he'd endured in the past few days. He didn't want to pour coffee into the acid that churned there.

He spent several minutes going over his actions since Eastling had left him in Berlin. His retelling went smoothly at first; he wanted to make clear to both men that the $204 million in in-house transfers he'd discovered at Ritzmann Privatbankiers needed further scrutiny, although he didn't know how that could possibly be accomplished.

When it came to his decision to return to the

710

Sprengelstrasse flat of the RAF cell, his explanation lost a lot of its detail and emotion. He still wasn't sure what had driven him there, other than some sort of last-ditch effort to learn something actionable in what had been a disastrous trip abroad. Neither Eastling nor Charleston pressed him on the matter; it was more a case of Jack trying to justify his actions to himself.

Then he went into his late-night meeting with Marta Scheuring in her bedroom in the RAF flat. Eastling asked a few pointed questions about how he could be certain this was the real Marta and not, in fact, an imposter. As usual, Eastling's track of thinking annoyed Ryan, but he explained as thoroughly as he could. Eastling wrote down the name of Ingrid Bretz, and promised he'd look into her.

Jack said, "I've checked already with my sources. Langley doesn't have anything on her. Neither does BfV. If she's an Ossi, that's to be expected."

Nick said, "And your Marta, the real Marta. She said nothing about David Penright, correct?"

Jack saw what Nick was doing. His job was to look into the Penright death, and that was it. He saw all the rest of the intrigue as irrelevant. "How the hell would Marta know about Penright, Nick? She wasn't in Switzerland. Ingrid was in Switzerland, using Marta's ID."

"I'm just clarifying, Ryan. No need to be defensive."

Sir Basil turned to Eastling. "Nick, go carefully. Jack's been through quite a lot."

Jack skipped over some details now, and fast-forwarded to the point when he lost Marta in the street. Then he told them about the cars racing into the area, and the two men who had jumped him.

Finally, he told them about the Good Samaritan who'd stepped in and quite literally saved his life.

When he was finished, Charleston mumbled, "Incredible story."

Eastling said, "The BfV found the tunnel this afternoon. They used your statement to go through all the vacant buildings, but it turned out the tunnel was under the floor of an ear doctor's office on Boyenstrasse. About one hundred meters from where the girl slipped away from you. No telling how long it had been up and running, but from what she told you, it was run by the Stasi themselves, with the doctor being their agent on this side."

Ryan just nodded, then said, "Marta was adamant the RAF had nothing to do with the attacks in Switzerland. She said she'd been set up by a Russian who went by the code name Zenith. I didn't tell the BfV about this, but when I got back to CIA station Berlin, I called Jim Greer. He'd never heard the code name, and he checked into it. It's not something that has ever been on our radar. Does that name mean anything to you?"

Nick Eastling shook his head, but Basil turned to Eastling and said, "Nick, can I ask you to excuse us for a few minutes, please?"

Eastling seemed confused. Basil just nodded at him, and slowly the counterintelligence man stood and left the office.

When the door closed behind Nick, Basil said, "There have been some developments late this afternoon. Things we don't need to involve Nick in. Frankly, I'm not cleared to involve you, either, but I think you deserve to know."

"Know what?"

"First things first. West German soldiers manning the border near Göttingen heard a land mine go off in the no-man's-land between East and West Germany this morning. The area is riddled with mines, of course — it's how the East keeps its people in. The West German soldiers arrived at the sight of the incident and saw the body of a young German woman there in the no-man's-land, just as it was being recovered by the East Germans."

Jack put his head in his hands. "Marta. They fucking killed her."

"I think that is what happened, but you know how it will be reported in the news, don't you?"

Jack kept his head down. "They will say East German citizen Ingrid Bretz attempted to flee into the West and was killed by a land mine."

"Yes," said Sir Basil. "And proving otherwise will be impossible."

Jack lifted his head up. "Why couldn't Eastling hear this?"

"That wasn't what I wanted to keep from him. It's Zenith. I first heard the name Zenith today in a meeting I had at Number Ten."

Ten Downing Street was the headquarters of Her Majesty's government.

Charleston said, "The PM wasn't in attendance, but her top staff was, along with Sir Donald Hollis, the director of MI5."

"MI5? Domestic intelligence?"

"Yes. The meeting was to inform me that Five has been running a concurrent operation in Europe. First I've heard of it. It involves the Russian operative called Zenith, who is, at this point, only a rumor."

"What is MI5's interest in Zenith?"

"They have an asset in the field who was trying to track Zenith down. Apparently, their asset is missing, somewhere behind the Curtain but last heard from in Hungary."

"I don't understand. Hungary is MI6's responsibility."

713

"Quite," said Basil. "It might not surprise you to know I gave them a bloody earful about the fact I'm just learning about a program run on our turf. I do not have the particulars as to why this was determined to be in the purview of MI5. Perhaps if we knew about this asset in the first place, had some operational influence over him, then he might well still be up and running and not missing."

"And now they want you to help find him?"

"That's right. MI5 has gone directly to Downing Street, and they have come to us. Maggie Thatcher herself is asking for updates on this case."

"Do you think Zenith might really have been the assassin in Switzerland?"

Charleston said, "Jack, you as well as anyone know that the KGB normally uses proxies for international wet work. Bulgarians, for example."

"That's the model we've seen," Jack acknowledged. "But there is a lot about the last week that has been a deviation from the Soviet playbook."

Basil said, "Admittedly true. That said, despite what Marta Scheuring told you, we think it was likely the KGB ordered the RAF to do the killings in Switzerland. Perhaps it wasn't Marta herself, perhaps it wasn't even her cell, but we believe Ingrid Bretz was working with the RAF nonetheless. There have been a number of cases of collusion between the organizations, expressly for the benefit of the KGB."

"So you don't believe in Zenith?"

"I can only say we have found no evidence there is any sort of KGB assassin running amok in Western Europe. You don't even know it was KGB who did this. Think about it. Why would they kill Tobias Gabler? According to Morningstar, he managed their account. He was their bloke."

"Maybe he was going to talk."

"To whom? Not to Langley. Not to us. Doubtful he was talking to any other Western intelligence service."

"What if Gabler was talking to the KGB?"

Sir Basil blinked in surprise. "If he was talking to the KGB, why would the KGB kill him?"

Jack said, "I have a theory, Basil. But I can't prove it."

Basil replied, "Jack, I want to hear it. I want to know what you make of all of this."

Ryan said, "I've been thinking about it all day. Look at the evidence. Penright's assertion that there were two groups of Russians in play at RPB. All the effort required to kill everyone with knowledge of the two-hundred-four-million-dollar account. The extraordinary measures to shift blame to the RAF cell, and then to wipe out the cell so they couldn't proclaim their innocence."

Jack blew out a long breath. He was almost afraid to say the next part, because, as an analyst, he realized he was reaching into the dangerous land of conjecture.

"I believe the KGB is fighting with itself."

"Why?"

"It's over money. The two hundred four million. That much is clear.

"As far as I can see, if the KGB wanted to kill the Swiss bankers and possibly the British agent, they could have gotten the RAF, or some other left-leaning group, to actually do it. They didn't need to frame them. The fact that they framed them, and then killed them to hide the ruse, makes me think this was not a regular KGB operation.

"That said, the men involved had to have been KGB, because otherwise how would they have all the contacts in place in the Stasi necessary to make this happen?"

Charleston asked, "Why do you think KGB officers have money hidden from the rest of the KGB, and why is it in an account in Western Europe?"

Ryan said, "Isn't it possible that some of them might be working together just to shave funds off other ops for a rainy day? Squirrel away a fortune in a numbered account — in Switzerland, for example — in case they need means for a quick getaway? Look at the Nazis at the end of World War Two. Those that had access to cash had a means of escape."

Charleston said, "That's all speculation, Jack. I don't want to stifle your fertile brain, it's come in quite handy, but look at it from my perspective. Have you brought me anything actionable?"

Ryan let out a long soft sigh.

"No. Nothing at all."

Charleston put up his hands. He'd made a decision. "Eastling wants to close the investigation into the death of David Penright. I am going to deny his request, but without any new information, I suspect it will go dormant. I will also leave the matter of the Zenith operative up to MI5, as they already seem to be working on it without our help. We'll do what we can for them in Central Europe, ask around about their missing man, but I am afraid if they are coming to us with their hat in their hand like this then it is very likely the man is in a great deal of trouble. It's probably too late for him."

Suddenly something occurred to Jack. "How long has this guy been missing? Could he be the man who helped me last night?"

Charleston shook his head. "They tell me he has not checked in for some weeks, and remember, he was an asset behind the lines. In Hungary, they said.

West Berlin was not his turf."

"I don't have a hell of a lot of experience with the operations side of things, but don't these guys go long periods of time without checking in? I mean, if he was operational in the field, he can't exactly jump into a phone booth and call home to London. And don't they do their own thing from time to time? Who's to say he didn't go to West Germany looking for Zenith?"

Charleston thought it over. "I can go back to Hollis and run your concerns by him, but as I said, the missing man is not one of mine, so I can't speak to his methods of operation."

Jack sighed again. "So, what happens now?"

Charleston was sympathetic, but there was only so much he could say. "You go home to your wife and your kids, and you hug them tight. You pushed Eastling when he needed to be pushed in Switzerland, and you saved lives in Berlin, nearly at the expense of your own. Be proud of what you've done. As long as the MI5 operative is missing, however, we must entertain the idea that he is behind the Curtain. It would be best for him — 'crucial' is perhaps the better word — that no rumors make the rounds about a missing British spy."

"You are asking me to keep this from Langley."

"If MI5 wants to ask Langley for official help, allow them to do that. But as a liaison with MI6, I am requesting your complete discretion in the matter. We don't want to get the bloke killed by talking about him."

Jack shook his head. "This operation is nothing but a long list of loose ends."

"Intelligence work is like that sometimes, lad. The opposition has a say in events just the same as we do."

"This feels like losing, Basil."

Sir Basil Charleston put his hand on Jack's shoulder. "We didn't lose, Jack. We just didn't win."

CASTOR'S LAKE HOUSE

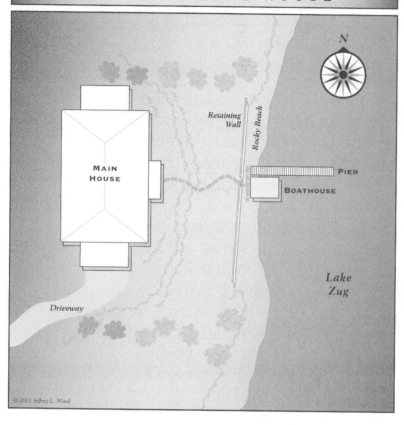

N

MAIN
HOUSE

Retaining
Wall

Rocky Beach

PIER

BOATHOUSE

Lake
Zug

Driveway

© 2013 Jeffrey L. Ward

82

Present day

Driscoll and Chavez had moved forward through the trees on the northern and southern ends of Hugh Castor's lakeside property; they were just twenty-five yards away from the back of the chalet, and they were well hidden. Chavez had a line of sight on Ryan via a large glass window. Through his binos he clearly saw Ryan seated on the sofa with Oxley, and in front of them was an elderly man seated by a fireplace.

A two-man security patrol walked back and forth on the rear deck of the property, so there was no way for Ding and the others to get any closer without risking detection.

He realized that even though he could see Ryan, Ryan was still on his own.

Dom Caruso was closest to the water, hidden between a pair of oil drums and the boathouse near the pier. As he looked through his binoculars at the building up the hill in front of him, he heard a faint rumbling over the water. The engine of some sort of skiff, by the sound of it. He looked out into the darkness and fog and saw no approaching light.

A moment later the faint sound disappeared, as if the engine had been cut.

He whispered into his Bluetooth headset: "This is Dom. I've got some sort of watercraft approaching the pier. It's not using any kind of light, and it's cut its engine."

Chavez said, "Sounds like trouble. I want everyone out of sight. Let me know what we're dealing with as soon as you can, Dom."

"Roger that. Any way we can warn Ryan if this turns into trouble?"

Chavez said, "Yeah, I can start shooting. Short of that, there is not a damn thing I can do to alert Ryan."

While Hugh Castor talked, Jack could not help imagining the sixty-eight-year-old as a young intelligence operative. He was self-assured and intelligent; he seemed to Jack like some sort of long-lost uncle, so comfortable was the conversation, even though the topic involved Castor's deceptions that ultimately led to the attack on Jack.

He realized the man had all but absolved himself of any sort of impropriety. He didn't know if Castor really believed it, or if he was just an incredibly gifted liar. Jack figured it was often like that in the spy world, where nothing was cut-and-dried.

"Everything you do at Castor and Boyle is designed to protect the Russian government," Ryan said, trying to get Castor to admit that he was, if not a traitor, at least a stooge.

Castor shook his head. "No, not at all. Am I remunerated for passing on information to key business leaders from time to time? Yes. Guilty of that, I'm afraid. Industrial espionage."

Ryan said, "The business leaders happen to run

the FSB and the government."

"Do they?" Castor asked, with a sly smile. "I work closely with officials in Gazprom and its affiliates. What they do when they are not at board meetings is none of my concern."

Ryan asked the question in the forefront of his mind now: "What are you trying to accomplish by telling me all this?"

Castor said, "Very soon, key individuals in Russia will get word that the man in Corby you met with was in the same gulag where Roman Talanov had his typhoid attack and made a confession in the medical ward. At that point, they will infer that I misrepresented my leverage over them. They might well determine there never was proof, there was only hearsay. As soon as they decide Oxley and myself exclusively have information that could prove to be their undoing, there will be no reason to allow us to walk the earth any longer."

Ryan translated the man's legalese. "Now that Talanov knows about you and Ox, he'll figure out that you've been bullshitting him about having a videotape. When that happens, he'll send goons to kill you."

"That is my predicament, unfortunately. He isn't the sort of man who will have a good belly laugh at the irony of being tricked. He is usually the one doing the tricking. I can surround myself with guards, but sooner or later Talanov will get to me like he did to Golovko and Zueva and Biryukov and all the KGB and GRU leadership he dispatched twenty years ago."

"What do you want?"

"I am willing to barter certain information I have collected throughout the years in exchange for immunity from prosecution and protection by your government."

"The American government?"

"Yes. I have committed, as I said, some industrial espionage. But I am no spy, I am no traitor. I can more than redeem myself with the information I have. Obviously, your father will not go against the wishes of the United Kingdom, but I feel certain he could encourage the UK to drop any investigation into me that might arise."

"And you will tell my dad what, exactly?"

"I will prove that Dmitri Nesterov, the man who was funneled one-point-two billion U.S. dollars by the Russian government, is none other than a Seven Strong Men capo who operates under the alias Gleb the Scar."

Jack looked at Oxley, then back at Castor.

"You're sure about this?"

"Very sure."

"That's good, but it's not going to be enough."

"That's only the tip of the iceberg, lad. Talanov's control officer is still out there, and he is in play." Castor grinned, he looked like the most confident man in the world. "But that's my trump card. I'll tell your father, face-to-face, when I am safe in the USA."

Jack started to reply, but just as he was about to speak, a security officer ran in from the kitchen. In heavily accented English, he said, "Herr Castor. We have reports of men approaching the chalet from the lake. We have to get you upstairs!"

Caruso watched the men in black leave the boat at the pier, then race past the boathouse, over the small retaining wall, and up the hill toward the back of the house. They fanned out as they advanced, keeping themselves low and moving in two-man fire teams.

Dom presumed the men to be Russian; he couldn't think of any other likely scenario. Whether they were here for Ryan, Oxley, Castor, or perhaps all three, he couldn't say for certain. But he did see they were armed with submachine guns and they moved like a confident and well-trained fighting force.

Dom whispered into his Bluetooth. "They are past my position. If you want, I can open up on them from here."

"Negative," Ding said. "We get in a gunfight with these fuckers out here in the open and the Swiss will just fire down on us all from the chalet. They'll target every muzzle flash in the dark and waste everybody."

Chavez was shielded from the house by a grouping of pine trees. He said, "I'm going to fire one round in the air as an alert to Ryan. Do not engage. Repeat, do not engage."

Chavez raised his weapon to fire, making sure the flash would not be obvious from the chalet. Just as he put his finger on the trigger, the rattle of automatic rifle fire ripped through the night.

It was a single security officer on the driveway at the side of the house, firing down on the attacking force, which was now spread out wide on the hill.

Ding lowered his weapon. "All right. If the Russians make it inside, we go in right behind them and engage any hostiles until we get Ryan out of there. Until then, we hold our positions."

Sam and Dom responded in the affirmative over the radios, but it was difficult for Chavez to hear them now, because a raging gunfight with nearly two dozen automatic weapons had begun.

The security officer ushered Castor, Ryan, and Oxley up a staircase and into a back bedroom. Once they were there, he handed Castor a pistol, then headed back downstairs.

Castor held the pistol by his side, and he looked at Ryan. The Englishman's confidence, so evident a minute ago, seemed to be faltering. "You brought friends?"

Jack replied, "Those guys aren't with me, which makes me think they are probably Russians. Talanov figured out you've been lying to him even more quickly than you thought he would."

The Englishman's face morphed quickly, as he realized young Ryan was correct.

"My men will stop them."

"Sure they will," Ryan said. "Your Swiss security men here are better than an FSB Spetsnaz unit."

Oxley must have known his own life was in danger, but he just laughed at Castor's predicament.

"Help me," said Castor. The terror was obvious.

"Give me the gun," Ryan replied.

"No."

"You don't look like you know how to handle that pistol, so I guess you'll have to talk your way out of this shit."

Castor looked to Oxley now, hoping for any lifeline from the man.

Ox was still smiling. "What he said, ya cunt."

Just then a window overlooking the back of the property shattered. The three men were well out of the line of fire from below, but still Castor spun toward the sound. Ryan started to go for the gun, but the old man recovered quickly and turned it back on the young American.

He said, "Look, Jack. I can tell you anything you want to know. Everything. Call your father. Have him send forces."

"Send forces?" Jack just shook his head. "You think you can bargain for your life when killers are at the fucking door?"

Booming gunfire emanated from the kitchen below them now. Castor jumped and pointed his weapon at the door. Jack started to move toward him again, but once again the jittery weapon turned back to him.

Oxley said, "Hugh. Put down the fuckin' gun before you hurt someone. Pass it to one of us, and we'll get through this, the lot of us."

Castor shook his head. "I'll keep the gun," he said. "If they get through, I'll need it."

Oxley muttered angrily, "You'd do well to put the barrel in your bloody mouth right now."

"If I die, you die, Ox."

Chavez, Driscoll, and Caruso had broken cover and were on the move now. Each man ran toward a different entrance of the chalet. Driscoll arrived at the side door to the driveway; it was open, and a dead Swiss security man lay on his back on the pavement with his automatic weapon by his side. Driscoll hefted the weapon and reloaded it with a fresh magazine from the dead man's chest, and then he entered the building.

Chavez was on the opposite side of the chalet, and he'd followed a two-man Russian fire team along the trees and watched them enter through a sliding glass door to a bedroom. It was dark here outside, no security officers had engaged the Russians as they approached, but there was gunfire throughout the ground floor of the house as soon as the fire team entered.

Ding started toward the sliding glass door, but submachine-gun fire from the front of the property echoed through the night, and instantly he heard the snapping sounds as bullets passed by his head. He raced through the doorway, narrowly avoiding being shot to death by one of the Swiss.

Caruso had the longest to travel before entering the house, but he finally arrived at the back door on the deck. By now the glass had been shot out of the door and the windows around it, so he stepped through the glass, and he instantly encountered two Russians who were moving through the kitchen with their weapons held high.

Dom saw them first; they swiveled to engage him, but he fired twice, shooting them both dead. Just then he heard gunfire in the next room, and then shouts in German. Return fire from a pistol boomed, and masonry dust began bursting from the wall near where Dom stood. He dove to the floor behind a sofa.

Upstairs, Castor stood by the bed. His gun swiveled back and forth between Ryan and Oxley, who were standing eight feet to his right, and the door to the landing, which was dead ahead of him some ten feet away.

Jack saw the terror in the man's eyes and worried his shaking hand might send a round cracking out of the gun.

Castor was still trying to leverage his importance to get himself out of danger. "Your father needs me alive. I have information."

Oxley said, "You've been peddling your bloody

information for your whole life. At the moment it won't do you any good. Shut the fuck up and wait for the Russians to come up the stairs."

But Jack tried to calm him. "Look, Castor. I've got three guys outside who will help us, we just have to hold out till they get the situation under control. I promise you one thing, though. If they come through that doorway and see anybody but me with a pistol in their hands, then they will shoot without hesitation."

Castor replied to this by saying, "It was Volodin. I can prove it was Volodin."

Jack didn't understand. "*What* was Volodin?"

"I can prove that Valeri Volodin was Roman Talanov's case officer. He ran Zenith back in the eighties. He stole the money from the KGB leadership. He had them killed when the Curtain dropped."

Jack shook his head in disbelief. "Bullshit."

"It's *not* bullshit. Get me out of here and I will give you proof."

Ryan looked at Oxley, and Oxley just shrugged. He did not know if the information was true or not.

Castor added, "Volodin knew that when the Soviet Union dissolved, the underworld would take over as the true ruler of the nation. And he knew the organized criminal gangs who populated the gulags, running the prisons with their own hierarchy there, would lead the underworld.

"He and Talanov came up with a plan. He had Talanov thrown into the gulag so he could establish his bona fides with the Russian mob. He was taken to the prison in the Komi Republic near Syktyvkar, and there he caught typhoid. The plan was scrapped for a few months while he recovered, but then he tried again. He was put in another gulag, and he spent four years there growing his power in the Seven Strong Men."

Fully automatic gunfire raged throughout the ground floor of the chalet below them.

"When he was released from prison, he was set up at the top. He was made *vory v zakonye,* he had a small army of men who pledged loyalty to him, and he used this power to help the *siloviki* retake the government. He protected the *siloviki* as he grew his organization.

"They assassinated enemies of Volodin, destabilized politicians in power to grease the way forward for him. Talanov took over as the leader of Seven Strong Men in secret, so he could enter government himself. He became a police commissioner in Novosibirsk, and then, when Volodin came to the Kremlin as PM, he put Talanov in as a regional FSB chief."

Ryan said, "And now Valeri Volodin has Roman Talanov as the head of all Russian intelligence."

Oxley started shaking his head back and forth. He looked at Ryan. "Impossible. The fucker is lying to save his skin. Telling you a fairy tale."

"How do you know he's lying?"

"Talanov would never have been made *vory v zakonye.* You have to understand how the Russian mob works. You can't be a made man in the Russian mafia if you ever worked for the Soviet government. Trust me. It's an organization with heaps of ironclad laws, but that is at the very top of them. You couldn't deliver the fucking mail for the Soviets and be made into *vory,* much less work for the bloody security services."

Jack said, "But if Talanov was put into the gulag as a plant, then maybe he kept knowledge of his former life from them."

Castor nodded wildly. "That's it, lad! That's how it happened!"

Jack said, "Ox, what would happen if the Seven Strong Men found out Talanov used to be KGB and then lied to become leader of their organization?"

Oxley looked at him a long time. Slowly, a sly smile grew on his face. He said, "They'd fucking kill the cunt."

The door in front of them burst in, splinters and door frame flew away from it, and Castor spun toward the commotion. He raised his pistol, but Jack took the opportunity to leap at Castor. He grabbed the pistol in Castor's hand and wrenched it away with a vicious yank. As Jack pulled back hard, he looked into the doorway. A man in dark clothing raised an automatic weapon at him. Jack realized the attacker had a clear shot; he spun and raised the weapon into a firing grip, but he knew he would not be in time to fire first.

Victor Oxley appeared on Ryan's right, falling through the air, putting himself between Ryan and the Russian coming through the door. A burst of automatic fire erupted, and the big Englishman jolted back from multiple impacts, then dropped down toward the floor.

Hugh Castor was unarmed now; as Oxley fell, he brought his own hands up to protect himself, but the Russian shot him through the chest and stomach, sending him tumbling away.

The Russian spun his gun toward the last standing target, and he pressed the trigger, but his hand relaxed and let go of the gun as a single round slammed into his forehead.

Jack had shot the man dead at a range of twelve feet.

Jack Ryan leapt over Ox and ran forward, kicked the gun away from the dead man, and then leaned out into the stairwell. Another Russian was moving up with his gun in front of him.

Ryan opened fire, shooting the man over and over until he fell face-first and slid back down the stairs.

Jack ran back to Oxley. The fifty-nine-year-old had taken three nine-millimeter rounds to the chest. He heaved and his eyes fluttered.

"Fuck!" shouted Ryan. "Hang on, Ox!"

Oxley squeezed Ryan's arm, and blood smeared across the American's shirt. Oxley coughed, and blood wet his lips and beard.

Jack pressed down hard on the man's chest, but the wounds were too severe, the blood flow too heavy. He looked around for something to help him with the pressure. A towel or a coat, or a bedsheet.

There. A comforter was on the end of the bed. He started to reach for it, but Oxley squeezed his arm tighter.

He spoke, but his voice was so soft Jack had to lean into it: "It's all right, mate. It's good like this. You watch yourself, now. Watch yourself."

His grip relaxed, and his eyes fluttered and shut.

Jack did not want to look away, but noise on the staircase forced him to swing his pistol toward the doorway to the landing.

A figure appeared at the top of the stairs.

It was Caruso.

Dom lowered his gun quickly, and Ryan did the same. Dom spoke into his headset: "I've got Jack.

Upstairs. We're clear up here."

Dom rushed to Oxley and dropped to his knees next to Ryan, but he immediately saw that there was nothing that could be done.

83

Bodies lay all over the grounds, both inside the chalet and out on the property. Sam, Dom, and Ding checked the area quickly to make certain there were no more threats, and in so doing they counted eighteen dead.

The chalet was secluded and in a thick forest, but the men knew the gunfire would have carried over the lake itself, so Ding told everyone they needed to exfiltrate before the police arrived. Driscoll hurried through the wreckage, taking pictures of the faces of the dead Russians to send to Biery to run through facial recognition, while Dom pulled mobile phones and pocket litter.

Soon Chavez had Ryan down in the Russian Zodiac boat. Dom and Sam leapt aboard, and they raced away into the fog, just minutes ahead of the first responders.

They were wheels-up at Zurich sixty minutes later. They had filed a flight plan for Paris, which meant there was no customs departure check to deal with, although they had no real sure plan of where they would go.

Ryan was still in a state of despondency over Oxley. He couldn't get past the fact that the man had taken bullets meant for him. He knew he had to call his dad and tell him everything he'd learned from Hugh Castor, although what he had been told was not the same as what he could prove. But he couldn't make himself pull the cabin phone out of the cradle and dial the number. Instead he just lay there with his head down on the table, while the men around him worked, discussed the battle they'd just fought, and occasionally patted him on the back to check on him.

After a phone call to Clark, the decision was made to go to Kiev, although Clark was adamant that Ryan would not even get off the plane. The other men would deplane to head back to the safe house so they could continue the investigation into Gleb the Scar, while Jack would return with the Gulfstream to the United States.

They'd been in the air for less than an hour when Clark called back. Sam flipped on the speaker-phone function in the cabin.

"What's up?"

"I've got big news, guys. You hit the jackpot."

Chavez said, "How so?"

"The dead guys you photographed at the scene. Gavin got zip on seven of them, but number eight came up huge."

"Who is he?"

"We photographed him here in Kiev at the Fairmont meeting with Gleb the Scar last week. At the time Gavin ran his face through all facial-recog sources we had and there was no match. But we ran tonight's picture, just to be sure. It came up with a match. There is a BOLO out for him with the FBI. They have a pic of him loaded, and it's a match."

Ding said, "The dead picture worked better in the software than the live one? That's weird."

"No. The last one didn't work because there was no pic of him uploaded then. The BOLO is brand-spanking-new. He's wanted in connection with the polonium poisoning of Sergey Golovko."

The men in the cabin of the G550 exchanged shocked stares. It was quiet for a moment until Chavez said, "Well, I'll be damned."

Gavin spoke up now: "Yep. And there's more. He was carrying the phone we'd tied to Hugh Castor's villa in Islington. The one owned by Pavel Lechkov. We're assuming that's his name."

Caruso said, "So Lechkov is Seven Strong Men and an associate of Gleb the Scar, and was in on the Golovko assassination."

"Right to all of that, Dom," said Gavin.

Ryan sat up straight now. He said, "And according to Castor, Talanov, the head of the FSB, is also the head of Seven Strong Men. That puts the Golovko murder in the lap of the Kremlin. I'm going to call my dad. At the very least he needs to get a team into Kiev to pick up Nesterov, aka Gleb."

Clark came on the line now. "Sending a team to the Fairmont, even SEAL Team Six, isn't going to be easy. Gleb has a shit ton of security in his suite, and the entire hotel is crawling with armed men loyal to the Russians. More important, the Russian Army is forty miles east of the city and advancing."

Ryan said, "If the U.S. doesn't take down Nesterov right now, they will miss their chance. Once the Russians come, or once he flees to Russia, he'll be unreachable."

Driscoll added, "And now that Lechkov is missing, Nesterov's got to be sweating bullets wondering if his man has been captured and is singing like a canary."

Clark's voice came over the speaker. "You guys hurry back over here. I'll try to ascertain the situation at the hotel so we have good intel in case the U.S. decides to go ahead with a takedown. I'll meet the plane at the airport and give you a lift back to the safe house."

84

The men of the 75th Ranger Regiment had arrived at Boryspil International early in the afternoon in four Chinook helicopters. As soon as they were off the helos they fanned out into the buildings at a far end of the busy airport, checking the security of the site and making sure the fences, gates, and other facilities were in good condition.

Within an hour, the location was secure and more American helos began landing.

The pilots of the helos landed in a grassy field. It wasn't optimal; they were on the grounds of a major international airport, after all, so one might imagine there was a piece of tarmac to be had for the Ranger Chinooks and the Air Force pararescue Black Hawks and the JSOC Little Birds and the Army Kiowa Warriors. But the Ukrainian military here at the airport had explained to the U.S. forces that the northern end of the property was the most secure from any potential sappers, so that is where the new American JOC was to be established.

The four Reaper drones had been flying out of this airport for the entire war. Now that the entire JOC and all the aircraft had arrived, the four Reapers had to share hangar space with troops and equipment, but the CIA crews were glad to be under the protection of U.S. forces now and not Ukrainian Army units whose loyalties had been questioned more than once in the past few days by Ukraine's president.

The relocated JOC was up and running here by eight p.m., and by eight-thirty they were commanding forces on laser targeting missions to the east.

Colonel Barry Jankowski, code name Midas, moved throughout the JOC, talking to intel officers in comms with the teams still lasing for the Ukrainians. The United States and British forces were pulling back, still in an organized manner, but as the Russians continued their advance across eastern Ukraine toward Kiev and the Dnieper River, Midas knew his soft holding action had already turned into a series of less coordinated hit-and-run strikes, and it soon would be little more than small-scale harassment in the midst of a full retreat.

That said, his boys were still out there, they were still killing Russian armor, and had it not been for this small coalition of special operations personnel, Russian tanks would likely already be driving down the streets of Kiev.

As Midas reached for a can of cola from a Styrofoam cooler, a voice came through his headset. "Midas, call from the Pentagon. SecDef."

Midas forgot the cola and headed back to his desk. A moment later, he answered the call from Secretary of Defense Robert Burgess, and ten minutes after he finished that call, he picked up his handheld sat phone and walked out of the JOC. He stepped into a quiet grassy space near the pararescue Black Hawks and made a call of his own.

After several rings he heard: "Clark."

Midas blew out a sigh of relief. "It's Midas here. You still in Kiev?"

"I am. How about you?"

"I'm at Boryspil Airport. We've moved our operation here."

"That's still twenty-five miles east of Kiev. Are you guys safe there?"

"We'd be safer in Idaho, but I couldn't get command to approve the move."

Clark laughed. "I'm impressed by a man who can keep his humor in all this."

"It's about all I have left."

"What can I do for you?"

"I need to know if you still have eyes on the Fairmont."

"We do. Not a perfect location, but we can see the front from our safe house. We can also see the balconies at the top where the POI is holed up. Why?"

"Can you see the roof?"

"Affirmative."

"What's up there?"

"Last time I checked, there were a few goons and a pair of Eurocopters. They are civilian models, but they look pretty robust."

Midas said, "I was afraid of that."

"Can you fill me in on what's going on?"

"Any chance you can come over to Boryspil for a chat?"

Clark said, "I'm ten minutes out. Meeting an aircraft with some of my guys on it. They'll be landing in an hour and heading over to an FBO hangar on the southern side of the airport. Where are you located? I'll drop by."

"Tell you what, Clark. You are a little bit like my crazy aunt in the attic. I'd rather as few people knew about you as possible. I'll meet you at the FBO. Say twenty minutes?"

"Roger that," Clark replied with a chuckle.

Clark sat alone on a bench in the cold night air. There was no one around, although the airport runway a quarter-mile away was in a constant state of activity as planes landed and took off with no more than thirty seconds' separation between them.

Half of the flights were civilian carriers full of people getting the fuck out of town, and the other half were military transport or combat aircraft.

Clark had just started thinking of other civilian airports he had seen in war zones around the world and over time, when Midas appeared around the corner of a metal outbuilding attached to the FBO. He was dressed in jeans and a nylon coat, under which Clark assumed he wore body armor and a gun. He was alone, which Clark found fascinating given that this man was in charge of U.S. combat ops in the entire country.

"Thanks for meeting me," Midas said, as they shook hands.

"Glad to see you are still in one piece," Clark replied. "How can I help you out?"

Midas didn't waste time. "I've been ordered to send a force to the Fairmont Grand to arrest Dmitri Nesterov, aka Gleb the Scar. Apparently he's got something to do with the polonium attack on Golovko."

Clark knew this, but he didn't bother mentioning it. He said, "Why doesn't JSOC send SEALs to do it?"

Midas gave Clark an annoyed look there in the darkness. Clark knew there was a little friction between SEALs and Delta, predominantly of the good-natured variety. Both forces wanted to get in on the big hits, and this was most definitely a big hit. "You were a SEAL, weren't you?"

Clark said, "Guilty as charged. We didn't have a Team Six back then, though."

"Yeah, well, Six won't get here in time. The problem is, they have reason to believe he's about to make a run for it. Maybe even tonight. If we don't grab Nesterov now, he can shoot north to the Belarussian border, or east to get behind the advancing Russians. He does that and the only way SEAL Team Six can take him is to enter denied territory."

"So you need to grab him right now."

Midas looked out into the night as a pair of MiGs took off on the runway. "Like I don't have enough on my plate."

"How many men do you have available for this op?"

"I've got A-teams in goddamned pickups smashing through gridlocked traffic trying to stay in front of the Russian armor. I've got all my ODAs down below half-strength, and if I pull any of them out of the field there will be no way to reinsert them. The Unit guys I have are split up as well. I've got a dozen assaulters and recce men back here in the JOC because their position was overrun this afternoon, but that's it."

"Could you use your Rangers for this?"

"No. I need the Ranger QRF on standby for emergencies to the east, and the rest pulling security here. I'm sure Rangers would get the job

741

done, but shit like this is what the Army pays us Unit guys to do."

"A dozen guys can't take that place," Clark said flatly.

"They don't have to take the place, they only have to take Nesterov."

Clark whistled. "Damn, Midas. I don't know if you are planning on hitting that hotel with a dozen men, but I hope I can dissuade you from that. Delta or no, a dozen shooters is going to mean a dozen dead Americans."

Midas said, "I've got an idea or two. I'm in good with a Ukrainian Army colonel. His battalion has the duty of protecting the government offices of the city, he's a nationalist, and he's culled his unit of everyone who thinks differently than he does. He's worked with the CIA for years, and I've known him since I came over here last year.

"I don't trust him to hit that building to capture Nesterov — he'd probably try to level it with T-72s — but I do trust him to keep quiet about this to the Russians. I'm thinking I can have him send troops to the Fairmont, just park outside like they are going to hit from below, maybe send some armored cars up to the door to engage men in the lobby, just to keep the majority of the Seven Strong Men forces there occupied."

Clark said, "If you do that, Gleb will fly out on a Eurocopter."

"Not if we hit the roof, disable the helos, and cut off his escape. Personally, I'd just have a Little Bird fire rockets onto the roof to blow the Eurocopters to shit, but we run the risk of killing the dude we've been ordered to take alive. His suite is right below the roof, so we can't just blast the helos. We have to do an in extremis takedown and

742

get him out of there before the Russians come."

Clark nodded, and he understood why Midas had come to talk to him. He said, "I've got three tier-one-level shooters. The two you met the other day and another guy, who was a Ranger. You can insert your men to grab Nesterov, and my boys will take care of the helos and be ready to support the Unit teams in the hotel if necessary."

Midas said, "I appreciate it. One question: How are your boys fixed for weaponry?"

Clark answered, "Hey, man. I'll provide the labor. You are the U.S. Army. You can provide the guns and bullets."

"Fair enough. I'll see what I can scare up that might be helpful."

When the Gulfstream landed twenty minutes later, John Clark boarded and explained the situation to his men. Sam, Dom, and Ding were ready to go immediately, of course, but Clark knew he'd have to deal with something else first.

Jack Ryan said, "John, one more gun on that roof might make a difference."

"Sorry, Jack. I can't let you go on this."

"And why is that?"

"You know why. You can't compromise your dad by exposing yourself like this. Even with your beard, you might be recognized by Delta boys. It's one thing to operate for The Campus, but you can't just mix in with military, not even black-side guys like Delta."

Ryan turned to Chavez, looking for a confederate to help him make his case.

But Ding said, "John's right, and on top of that, we've been training the last few months. You've been away from the team. This is going to be an in extremis rush job, and we need to be tight and smooth whatever goes down."

Dom reached over and squeezed Jack's shoulder. "Come back to the States with us when this is over. We'll get you trained in no time."

Ryan nodded. Not satisfied that he'd have to stay back here at the airport while the operation went on in the city, but resigned to the fact.

While Clark met with his men, Midas arrived at the Kiowa Warrior section of the flight line. He found Conway and Page lying on sleeping bags in the corner of a dry-goods storage room next to the cafeteria. Both men were in full combat gear, they even had their boots on, but they were trying to catch an hour of sleep before their next mission.

They were awake now, though, and both young men stood when Midas approached.

Midas said, "Evening, chiefs. Dumb question. Do you guys have the capability to carry troops?"

Conway rubbed his eyes. "Yes. We've got a thing called the Multi-Purpose Light Helicopter kit. We can take off our weapons pylons and attach benches so we can carry up to six guys on the outside of the fuselage."

"Have you ever done that before?"

The two young men looked at each other. Conway shook his head. "Never."

"Well, this will be a new experience for everyone, I imagine. We're going to need you to insert men onto a roof. We don't think the opposition has any real air defense other than assault rifles and maybe RPGs, but we'll have to go in without much of a picture of the terrain."

He then sat down with the men and told them

exactly what he needed. When he was finished, he said, "I can't make you do this, and it's going to be pretty much the definition of dangerous, but that's the deal."

Page and Conway exchanged a look, and Conway spoke for both men, confident he was expressing Dre Page's sentiments as well as his own: "We're good to go, Midas. We'll get the helo outfitted for the op."

Midas shook both men's hands and then hurried back to the JOC. He still had a hell of a lot to do.

85

The grass field helicopter flight line at the JSOC base on the northern end of Kiev's Boryspil International Airport was alive with activity at one a.m.

Two MH-6 Little Birds already had their rotors turning, and Black Wolf Two Six, the Kiowa Warrior operated by Conway and Page, had already gone through its preflight checklist, although the pilots were still in Flight Ops getting last-minute intel.

Both Ding Chavez and Sam Driscoll had sat on the outside of a moving helicopter before. Dominic Caruso, on the other hand, had not, nor had he ever had much of a desire to.

He saw the tiny little bench bolted onto the side of the Kiowa, and he realized this was where he was supposed to sit. Then he saw the small restraining cable that would hook to his body armor to keep him from plummeting to his death, and his first thought was *No fucking way.*

He looked at Ding. "I've got a better idea. How 'bout I take a bus and catch up with you guys?"

Ding patted him on the pack. "Mano, I learned a trick a long time ago. I just strap myself in, then I tell myself I'm watching a really awesome movie on a really awesome big-screen TV with a really awesome audio system."

Caruso looked at him doubtfully. "And that works?"

Chavez shrugged noncommittally. "It did when I was young and dumb." With a wink, he added, "You should give it a try."

As the three men strapped themselves in, two figures in dark uniforms and body armor walked over from the JOC building. From the HK416s on their shoulders, it was obvious they were Delta Force operators.

One of the men looked at the Kiowa. "We drew the short straws, so it looks like we're on the other side of this old piece of shit." He shook Ding's, Dom's, and Sam's gloved hands with a gloved hand of his own, and the other Delta man did the same.

"Who are you guys?" one of the Delta Force men asked Chavez.

Ding smiled. "You are probably more used to people asking *you* that."

"You didn't answer my question."

"Do *you* ever answer that question?"

The man shook his head. "Negative."

"Well, then," Ding said. "There you go."

There was an obvious presumption by the Delta Force operatives that Ding and his men were CIA Special Activities Division officers, which was exactly what Clark and Chavez used to be. Chavez did nothing to dispel this notion, and Clark had even mentioned that Midas was on board with keeping up this ruse with his men.

Before the Delta operators went to the other side of the helo, Conway and Page came out of Flight Ops and introduced themselves to the men they would be flying in to the operation.

Conway said, "We're going to depart to the southwest, away from the city. We'll be right behind the two MH-6s. We'll pick up the Dnieper River and then turn to the north, go low and shoot straight up into Kiev. With the route we're going to take, it will be thirty-one miles to the target. We are going to do everything we can to keep everyone from knowing who we are, where we are going, and what we are up to.

"That means we're going to fly really fucking low and really fucking fast. I just want to let you dudes know, this is going to be a wild ride. You see bridges or power lines in our path, then it's a good bet I see them, too, so don't freak out."

The five men just nodded back at the helo pilot. Dom Caruso's nod was the least sure of them all.

Conway continued, "Like I said, we're going in behind the Little Birds, but I'm not a Night Stalker and this is not a Little Bird, so if they have some capabilities to keep the men on the outside of their aircraft from shitting their pants and puking up their MREs, then the guys on the other helos will be better off than you, because, frankly, I've never done this before."

Caruso was already turning green with the thought of what was to come.

Ding said, "Don't worry about us. We'll be strapped in. As long as you don't slam this into a wall or into the ground, then we'll be okay."

Conway nodded. "When we get there, the guys on the other helos will fast-rope to the roof exits and the Little Birds will get out of the way. I'll land on the roof, and when I do, I want you guys off my helo PDQ. I'll take off and head back over the river, and I'll wait for your comms to come back and pick you up."

Ding said, "That sounds good."

They talked another minute or two about the possibility they might be leaving with a prisoner, and also about the possibility for evacuating wounded after the raid. Ding didn't think it sounded like there were many feasible options to get out of that hotel from the roof with a gunshot wound, and he got the impression from everyone that a downed American might have a better chance at survival just waiting for a Ukrainian ambulance there.

He did his best to put those concerns out of his mind, told himself it would be best if he didn't get shot or let any of his buddies get shot, and then he sat down on the narrow bench.

Five minutes later the Kiowa Warrior was airborne, flying slow and low across the airport grounds. It soon climbed into the night sky, following the MH-6s a few hundred yards ahead.

For Dom, the first couple of minutes weren't nearly as bad as he thought they would be. His earplugs kept the rotor noise to a minimum and the fact he was sandwiched between Sam and Ding meant he wasn't rocking around as much as he'd feared. As they raced over flat farmland, his main issue was the incredible cold brought on by the wind. He was wearing a lot of clothing and gear, as well as a Kevlar helmet and goggles, but his cheeks felt like they would freeze solid.

Just when he decided the flight itself wouldn't be so scary, the Kiowa lurched into the air suddenly and violently. Dom slammed his helmet into Sam, and Ding slammed his helmet into Dom.

They shot just over a set of high-tension wires

across an open field, so close Dom thought his boots would catch a wire.

Then they dropped straight down on the other side, leveling out at less than twenty feet. Dom felt the vertebrae in his back compress, and he also felt the acid in his stomach churning.

He leaned forward and looked ahead, and his heart sank. There were more wires and hills between him and the river.

Fuck.

Now it felt, to Caruso, like he was reliving a horrifying plane crash over and over and over again. The Kiowa Warrior fired up a few hundred feet to climb above wires and buildings and hills, and then it plunged down, nose forward, picking up speed. Although Dom was strapped in to the narrow bench, his body felt weightless, his legs rose in front of him, and he had to squeeze the 416 on his chest tightly to his body to keep his arms down and the gun in place.

Then the weightlessness ceased, and he felt the pull on his straps and the pressure in his low back against the bench as the Warrior bottomed out and raced so low over the ground that, when Dom did open his eyes, he saw the roofs of small houses at eye level and treetops higher than the helicopter he was riding on.

He had no trouble convincing himself that the pilot was insane, and he suspected the pilot was personally trying to give him a heart attack.

The helicopter raced low over some sort of a strip mine in the middle of a forest. There was enough light to see pyramids of gravel all around them.

Without warning the aircraft turned on its y-axis, the tail shot out to the side, and the three men on Dom's side of the aircraft were all pulled to the right. For a hundred yards or so it seemed to Dom as though he was at the front as the Kiowa raced along sideways, slowed, and then began flying forward again.

It was just a sudden change of direction, but the men on the bench had been rocked, pummeled, and spun by it. Dom looked to his right just in time to see Sam Driscoll lean forward slightly, then vomit violently out into the dark sky.

Caruso leaned away from his colleague. Getting Sam's puke on his boots wouldn't be the worst thing Dom had to deal with this evening, he was sure, but he kicked his feet out to avoid the vomit nonetheless.

When Sam was finished with his puking fit, he took a hand off his rifle and wiped his mouth and beard with the back of his arm. He turned to Dom, saw that he had seen the whole thing, and shrugged slightly, as if it was no big deal.

The helicopter plunged again on the far side of the hill, and Dom himself began throwing up.

CW2 Eric Conway raced his helo thirty feet over the cold water of the Dnieper River, his eyes darting between the two birds he was following into the target, the water and the boat traffic on it, and his various sensors that told him how far until his next waypoint and the status of all the aircraft's systems.

The mast of a ship was just ahead, so he pulled on his cyclic to avoid it. He knew he was tossing the men on the outside of the fuselage around like marionettes, but he didn't have the ability to focus on anything as unimportant as the creature comforts of his passengers at the moment.

751

Soon he saw the Fairmont ahead on his left; it was the tallest building along the water on the western side of the Dnieper. The Night Stalker pilot in the lead Little Bird announced "One minute" on the radio, and Page reported that he was getting no warnings of inbound bogeys on the radar.

Conway watched as the two small black helos rose above the water and slowed, then made one quick circle around the roof of the hotel. He saw the flashes of gunfire on the roof, and immediately he saw more flashes coming from the Little Birds.

He began climbing away from the river himself, and pitched up his nose to slow his speed.

Over the radio he heard: "Taking fire from the roof and balcony on southern side."

Conway slowed further as he made it to roof level. Now he could hear the Delta Force guys on his side of the helo firing down at targets near the helicopters. Within seconds all the targets were down, and then, with a command from one of the other helo pilots, both Little Birds descended just above the roof. Conway kept his eyes flitting between his multifunction display and his outside environment, but he caught a glance of men sliding down ropes from the helicopters.

In seconds, ten men were on the deck and moving to the stairwells, and the MH-6s were climbing back into the sky. Conway wasted no time moving into position to drop off his passengers.

There was space on the roof enough for three helicopters. The two big Eurocopters were on helipads, but there was a wide-open area a little lower than the raised pads that was just enough room for him to put down.

He came in as quickly as possible, and while he

watched the rotors during descent Page leaned outside the open door to count down the distance in meters to the deck.

"Five, four, three, two . . . one . . ." They touched down, and Page turned and yelled at the men on his side of the fuselage, "Go! Go! Go!"

Conway turned to do the same, but the Delta men on his side were already running for the stairs, stacking up with the men who fast-roped off the Little Birds.

The men on Page's side got off the bench quickly, and Page told Conway they were clear. The Kiowa rose into the night and turned to the south, careful to avoid the MH-6s already positioning themselves to the north.

86

Ding Chavez led his two men to the first Euro-copter. As he climbed onto the helipad he saw the last of the Delta operators disappear into stairwells leading down to Nesterov's suite, but he didn't focus on the stairwells for long. He was listening in to the comms of the assaulters so he could be ready when they came back up, but for now he would ignore their transmissions so he could pay attention to his portion of the mission. Dom had a small shaped charge given to him by a Delta demolitions man, and he pulled it from his pack. Sam and Ding lifted Dom up onto their shoulders, he balanced himself on the fuselage of the helo, and then he put his boots on their shoulders and stood so he could reach the rotors. He planted the device at the base of the rotor shaft, and then he slid back down.

It took another minute to do the same to the second helo. After Dom slid back down to the heli-pad, all three men ran down the helipad stairs and toward one of the stairwells.

Ding had been advised to speak on the Delta communications net as little as possible, so there wouldn't be any unnecessary cross-talk. But when he and his two mates made it into the safety of the stairwell and Dom had his detonator in his hand, Ding did broadcast: "Assault team, this is Topside. Charges are in position on the roof."

"Roger, Topside. Confirm we are all clear of the roof. Blow them."

"Roger that," Ding said, and Dom turned a dial on his radio detonator.

Above them, a pair of loud booms confirmed the destruction of the rotors of the helos.

Chavez knew his portion of the mission was complete, other than the extraction, but he could hear massive amounts of gunfire two floors below. On the radio he heard the call "Wounded Eagle," which meant one of the Delta assaulters had been injured.

Ding called into the already crowded radio traffic. "This is Topside. We're in stairwell Bravo. We can come down and recover the wounded if you need us, over."

"Topside, do it. Descend to stairwell on the ninth floor. We will meet you there. Do not leave the stairwell. We have a blocking force in the eighth-floor stairwell keeping enemy below us, and all persons in the ninth-floor hallway will be considered hostile and engaged."

"Understood," Ding said, and he, Sam, and Dom rushed down the stairs.

From the sound of the gunfire, Ding could tell the Delta blocking force below him was heavily engaged. No sooner had they arrived at the meeting point for the first wounded operator than a second Wounded Eagle call came, this one just one floor below them on the stairs. Ding sent Sam down to try to help get that man up to the roof, while he and Dom waited for the first injury to arrive from the hallway.

As the radio traffic continued at a calm but rapid clip, Dom leaned over to Ding. "Too many fucking Russians."

"Yep," Ding said.

The hallway door opened, and two Delta men appeared, dragging by his body armor a man with a bloody leg wound. Dom and Ding got the man to his feet and put his arms over their shoulders to support him.

The two Delta men turned to go back into the suite, but Ding said, "It sounds like it's falling apart in the stairwell."

A loud explosion, just below their feet, confirmed this.

One of the Delta operators said, "It's going bad all over. Get him on the roof and then head back to help out down there."

"Roger," Ding said, and then he and Dom struggled to climb the stairs to the roof.

After five minutes of constant gunfire all over the upper floors of the building, Delta announced on the radio that they had Dmitri Nesterov in custody in the suite, but they were pinned down. Sam and two surviving Delta men in the stairwell had retreated up to the ninth floor just before they were overrun by dozens of Seven Strong Men gunmen, but now they were dropping frag and flash grenades down in an attempt to hold the horde of attackers back.

Dom and Ding had been pulled out of the stairwell by the Delta team leader, who told them to get into the hallway to cover the elevator. They arrived to find a dead assaulter lying in an open car, with four dead Seven Strong Men with him.

The second elevator car arrived, and Dom and Ding got their guns up just in time to see a half-dozen armed men inside.

Both Americans dropped to the floor and opened fire, and each of them dumped an entire magazine into the men. When they were all down, Dom ran forward and pulled a body halfway through the door, ensuring it could not close and send the car back downstairs to pick up more enemy.

A door at the end of the hall opened suddenly, and Chavez swung to it, pulling his pistol because his rifle was empty. He saw two Delta operators pushing along a hooded man with his hands zip-tied behind his back.

Everyone with a gun in the hallway, all four men, pointed their weapons at one another. Ding was the first to lower his pistol. Into his radio, he said, "We're friendlies!"

The Delta guys got the message quickly. They lowered their rifles and pushed the prisoner forward. Ding saw one of the assaulters had been shot himself. His right shoulder was covered in blood, and a bloody bandage was wrapped around it.

Dom was already pulling gear off the dead operator. Soon he had him over his shoulder, and he struggled back to the stairwell.

The four men had made it only a few feet toward the stairs when Sam and two Delta men came through the door. Again, everyone swung their guns up at potential targets, but quickly they recognized they were all blue forces.

Sam said, "We're overrun in those stairs. Gotta find another way back up."

The force of men headed back toward the

entrance to the suite. Ding and Sam kept their weapons trained on the door to the stairs, and soon it burst open. The two Americans cut down the Seven Strong Men gunners there, and a Delta man threw a smoke grenade to obscure their retreat up the hall.

In the suite the team leader called over the radio. The rest of the force had managed to keep the rear stairwell clear, so everyone moved to the back of the suite, went back into an employee access area, and linked up with the Delta Force operators there.

It took nearly fifteen minutes to get everyone back to the roof. Delta had two dead and six wounded. Sam Driscoll had cuts on his face and arms from an explosion in the stairs, but Dmitri Nesterov was in hand.

The first Little Bird arrived, and the two most severely wounded were strapped on between the four lightly wounded men. The helo jolted into the air and took off for the relative safety of the river.

The Kiowa was called in next. The Campus men and the Delta operators covered the two stairwells on the roof as they waited for the helo to land.

As Conway lowered toward the roof, Page shouted into the radio, "Come right! Come right!"

Conway didn't know what was going on, but he followed instructions. As he did so, he realized Page was grabbing his rifle off the dash and aiming it out the open door of the helicopter.

Dre Page shouted, "Pivot one-eighty and hold!"

Conway did as instructed. He was only twenty-five feet from touchdown, and by looking out past Dre he saw that a group of men had used a rope to climb onto the roof from the ninth-floor balcony. Obviously, they were doing this so they wouldn't have to exit the stairwells, which would surely be covered.

Dre aimed his M4 rifle and opened fire on the four men. He blasted one man off the roof, and the man fell more than a hundred feet to the street below. Another man fell where he stood, dead on the roof. Two more dove behind the lip of the helipad, but the Delta assaulters on the roof saw what was happening and engaged them.

Conway landed a moment later, and a hooded prisoner was attached to his portside bench. Operators strapped in quickly; a couple of the men looked wounded, but Conway kept most of his focus on his radar and the stairwell exit right in front of the nose of his helo. He knew that at any time it could fly open and armed enemy could pour through.

Someone on the radio said, "We need thirty seconds!"

Conway called back, "*Fuck* thirty seconds! We've got to go, now!"

He looked over his shoulder and saw men firing on the other stairwell entrance. He knew at any moment bullets could start tearing through his aircraft. He grabbed his own rifle while he waited and leaned out, aiming it behind him.

Before he saw any targets, however, Page came over the radio: "We're good my side. Three passengers locked in and ready."

Conway saw two passengers on his side. One was the prisoner. He called to the Delta team leader. "Black Wolf Two Six. Ready to depart with five pax, including prisoner. Confirm that is correct."

"You are correct, Two Six. Get off the fucking roof."

"Roger that."

The helicopter rose into the night. Men on the fuselage opened fire on more attackers coming over the side from the balcony. Conway knew to fly in the opposite direction of the origin of fire, so he flew out over the western wall, then dropped down toward the street like a rock in the hopes any armed men on the balcony would not be able to get a shot off.

Dom Caruso held on to the strap attaching him to the helo and shut his eyes. He was certain they were going to auger into the street, but as every time before, the Kiowa leveled off and his spine paid the price. He didn't open his eyes for nearly half a minute, and when he did, he was happy to see they were out over the water again.

The flight back to Boryspil was as eventful and uncomfortable as the flight in. Multiple times Dom thought they were being chased by other helicopters, because the Kiowa took all sorts of crazy evasive-action maneuvers.

Nesterov himself vomited right next to Dom. The puke seeped out from under the man's hood, and Caruso stuck his gloved hand under the cover to clean off the man's face and nose so he didn't suffocate.

This made Dom want to vomit again, but he had nothing left to offer the forest below him.

87

John Clark stood alone on the flight line when the helicopters arrived. He watched as the critically wounded Delta operators were taken off first and piled into ambulances, then two dead Americans were carried off on litters.

Men who were only lightly wounded were helped over to a place on the flight line where Air Force pararescue men could tend to their wounds.

Finally the bruised and battered and tired left the helos, most walking along with their prize possession, the Russian in the vomit-covered hood.

As this was all going on, Midas found Clark standing by himself. He shook his hand. "Your boys sure as hell came through on this one. Not sure how I can thank you."

Clark did not miss a beat. "I know just the way. We want to talk to Nesterov. Give us five minutes."

Midas cocked his head. "As far as I'm concerned, you can take him out back and beat him with rubber hoses. Why do you want to talk to him?"

Clark explained, briefly, that he and his team had information about Nesterov that could be used to compromise other members of the Russian government. He didn't go into any details, but he finished his semi-explanation by saying, "We see this as a potential way to get Russia to quit Ukraine. It might be a long shot, but it's worth pursuing."

"I'm all for that," Midas said. "What the hell? I've been playing fast and loose with the regs on this op enough as it is. Might as well go all out and pass my prisoner over to a couple of civilians for a chitchat. Five minutes max, though, I've got to get him ready to fly out of here in an hour."

Nesterov was brought into a small office in the back of a warehouse in the JOC property and he was chained to a chair. His filthy hood was kept on except when a pararescue man checked his vital signs and gave him a drink of whiskey.

Two Rangers stood guard outside, and Nesterov thought he was being left alone in an empty room, so he jumped at the sound of a light switch clicking on. Clark and Ryan entered, pulled up chairs in front of the hooded man, and sat down.

It was quiet for a few seconds more. Nesterov looked around left and right, but he couldn't see past his hood.

Clark spoke in Russian: "Dmitri Nesterov. At last we meet."

Nesterov did not react.

Clark said, "I know who you are. I know you are Gleb the Scar, *vory v zakonye* and member of the Seven Strong Men, as well as Dmitri Nesterov, president of Shoal Bank, Antigua and Barbuda, and chairman of the board of IFC Holdings."

Nesterov spoke in a weak and unsure voice: "Untrue, but please continue."

"Pavel Lechkov is in U.S. custody."

"Who is that?"

"He *is* the man who delivered the polonium to the United States last month. He *is* the man who conspired to attack the son of the President of the United States, and he *is* the man who was photographed here in Kiev, meeting with you. He tried to assassinate British businessman Hugh Castor in Switzerland. He failed, and now he and Hugh Castor have given us everything on you."

Clark was hoping these lies based on truths would carry weight with the Russian.

Nesterov said, "I don't know what you are talking about."

Clark said, "You are here working for the FSB, but the tide is going to turn before Russia makes it to Kiev, so that won't help you. We'll have you shipped off to a black site, anyway, so it doesn't really matter what happens here." Clark leaned right into the man's shrouded face. "You belong to us now, Dmitri. You are fucked."

Nesterov did not reply.

Clark leaned back up and changed his tone. It was less grave, more matter-of-fact. "I want to know how it is you can work for Roman Talanov."

"Talanov? I don't understand. A minute ago you said I was in organized crime, and now you say I work for the intelligence services? Can you get your story straight and try this again?"

Clark didn't miss a beat. "Talanov is the leader of the Seven Strong Men. That has been confirmed."

"Confirmed?" Nesterov laughed. "Did you read it on Facebook?"

Clark laughed with him, patted him on the back roughly. Then his voice darkened. "Something else is confirmed, Dmitri. Roman Talanov was in the

763

gulag system — in the late eighties and early nineties. This is where he became Seven Strong Men. He was a charter member."

Nesterov's hood was perfectly still.

"But Roman Talanov was not born in the gulag, Dmitri. He arrived after working for the KGB."

Nesterov laughed again. "Whoever you are, you are operating with so many incorrect assumptions that it is obvious you are just flailing around, trying to find out some information from me."

"Tell me, how I am wrong, Dmitri?"

"The accusation you just made is impossible."

"*How* is it impossible?"

Nesterov just chuckled under the bag.

Clark said, "You think it is impossible because you know that Talanov is *vory v zakonye,* and he was *vory v zakonye* before he went into the FSB. This was allowed by the leadership, because of the times, because of the access this gave Seven Strong Men to the real power in Russia. The Kremlin."

Nesterov said nothing.

Clark said, "But he used you, just like he uses everyone."

After a moment of quiet, Nesterov said, "He didn't use us. He is one of us."

Clark said, "How can he be *vory* if he was a captain in the GRU and then a KGB assassin in the eighties? Did you guys change your entrance requirements?" Very coldly, he added, "He is using you right now. Your organization was just a stepping-stone to power. Becoming *vory* was a KGB operation to them. A very successful one, at that."

Nesterov said, "That is all a lie. And even if it were true, that was a long time ago."

"No, it wasn't. I know how organizations like yours work. You won't forgive him just because a few years have gone by. Each one of those years when he was honored as *vory* was a further insult to the sanctity of your code. He made a mockery of you all."

Clark leaned closer. "And you can't let that stand, can you?"

The pause was long. Finally the voice under the hood asked, "What do you want?"

"The news I just told you is about to go public. Talanov might deny it, but you know how this works. People who knew him will come forward now. Everyone will know the head of the FSB is also head of the Seven Strong Men. This will be troublesome at home. Troublesome for everyone, except perhaps the man directly under him in the hierarchy of the organization."

"What are you saying?"

"When the word gets out that Seven Strong Men was nothing but another shill, another proxy force doing the work of the Kremlin, then your organization will have no alternative but to make some changes.

"You can survive this, Dmitri." Clark leaned forward again, almost into Nesterov's ear. "But Talanov won't." He paused. "Will he?"

88

President of the United States Jack Ryan sat at his desk in the Oval Office. On the blotter in front of him was a legal pad with several bullet points written in his own hand. He looked at the clock quickly, then down at his telephone, and he did his best to control his racing thoughts.

This was one of those crucial moments of statecraft where he knew that everything he did in the next few minutes could determine life and death for thousands, tens of thousands, or perhaps even hundreds of thousands.

He'd spent hours in meetings the night before, with Scott Adler, with Mary Pat Foley and Jay Canfield, with Bob Burgess and Mark Jorgensen and Dan Murray.

They had all talked him through this conversation, but more important than the input of any of these learned professionals was a ninety-minute phone call he'd had with his own son that set the ball rolling.

Jack Junior had started the conversation with the news that Bedrock had been killed by the Russians. His father's first question was about the safety of his own son. Jack Junior convinced his father he was safe only by putting Domingo

Chavez on the line.

Once that was done, and with President Ryan still reeling with the news that the man who'd once saved his life had died saving the life of his son, Jack Junior then bombarded his father with facts and figures and details. Stories about Roman Talanov and Valeri Volodin and the man who poisoned Golovko and his relationship to a mafia boss in Ukraine.

Jack Senior had jotted notes down, asked for clarifications, and then made notes under his notes about things he would be able to double-check on his own.

The news that the account at Ritzmann Privat-bankiers had been liquidated into diamonds owned by another account holder had been especially interesting to him. Ryan vaguely remembered that at the time there had been a question about diamonds, though he could not recall any specifics after thirty years.

When he got off the phone with Jack Junior he called everyone into the Situation Room and he explained everything. Foley and Canfield and Murray hustled out to check what items they could. Adler had advised the President on what he needed to do about all this.

Ryan made the decision to order the immediate arrest of Dmitri Nesterov. Burgess suggested operators in the field in Kiev could handle it, and Ryan signed off on the plan.

Now that Nesterov was in pocket, even though he hadn't said a word yet, the consensus was that President Ryan needed to get on the phone with Volodin and lay everything out. It was little more than a Hail Mary attempt to marginalize the man by threatening to reveal everything they had, or everything they could convince Volodin they had, which was a lot less than what they could actually prove.

The light on the phone blinked, letting Jack know the call had been put through to Moscow. He took one deep breath, situated his paperwork in front of him, and lifted the receiver off the cradle.

Volodin's voice came over the line. He spoke Russian, of course, but Ryan recognized the fast tempo, the self-assuredness. The voice of the translator in the Communication Room was louder than Volodin's, so Ryan could hear the translations easily.

"Mr. President," Volodin said. "We speak at last."

Ryan spoke English, which was handled quickly by Volodin's translator in the Kremlin. Ryan said, "President Volodin, I need to start this conversation by making a suggestion that I hope you will seriously consider."

"A suggestion? Maybe you will suggest that I resign. Is that the idea?" He laughed at his own joke.

Ryan did not laugh. He said, "My suggestion is that you ask your translator to leave the conversation. What I have to say to you is for you alone, and my translator can convey this. If you choose, when I finish, you can bring your man back into the conversation."

"What is this?" Volodin asked. "You do not set the terms for our conversations. This is just some ploy so you can control the dialogue. I will not be bullied by you, President Ryan. That was the last president of Russia, not me."

Jack listened to another few seconds of bluster conveyed through his translator, and then he said,

"This is about Zenith."

This made its way through Volodin's translator, and then all was quiet on the line for a moment.

"I don't know what that is," said Valeri Volodin.

"Well, then," replied Jack Ryan, "I will tell you. I will tell you every last detail. Account numbers, names, dates, victims, consequences. Would you like your translator to step away, or shall I go ahead?"

Jack didn't expect to hear anything on the other end, but Volodin said, "I will indulge you briefly." His voice already sounded on guard.

When there was no one else at the Kremlin on the line, Ryan went in a different direction: "Mr. President, I have direct evidence that connects you to the polonium poisoning of Sergey Golovko."

"I expected to hear this even sooner. I told the world you would have all manner of lies to implicate Russia."

"Pavel Lechkov, an operative of the Seven Strong Men criminal organization, passed the polonium off to the Venezuelans, who in turned poisoned the victim. We have photographs of Lechkov in the United States."

Volodin said, "No one believes photographs. Plus, if this man was a criminal, what does that have to do with me? Your own nation has trouble with crime, does it not? Shall I blame you for the activities of your gangs?"

"Lechkov was also photographed meeting with Dmitri Nesterov, a member of the Seven Strong Men."

"I am putting my translator back on the call. You have nothing that cannot be heard by every citizen of Russia, although it will only show them

769

the foolishness of an old Cold War spy."

Ryan said, "Roman Talanov's relationship to the Seven Strong Men was established by you as an intelligence operation, and he rose to the top of that organization, just as you have risen to the top of the Russian government. But Roman Talanov is now damaged. We have already informed key members of Seven Strong Men that Talanov was KGB before he became a made man, and that is very much a sign of disrespect to their organization."

Ryan added, "I should think this will make life very difficult for him indeed."

Volodin spoke up now, and Jack noted that he had not called for his own translator to return to the line. He said, "These are all lies."

"Mr. President, Hugh Castor has given us evidence. Evidence you know exists. We captured Dmitri Nesterov alive last night. We have shown him the evidence, and he is angry enough to where he is talking quite a bit already. Once we put him on television explaining how he was paid one-point-two billion by the FSB to destabilize Ukraine, to poison Sergey Golovko, and to facilitate illegal business transactions so that the *siloviki* can continue to rape the public holdings of the people of Russia, then your situation will become dire.

"President Volodin, even though Talanov will be destroyed by this, there is a way forward for you, if you so choose. We will reveal our findings of the polonium investigation. They will point to the Seven Strong Men. That, and the fact that Talanov just became as toxic as Golovko was, gives you an opportunity to publicly distance yourself from him before your affiliation destroys you."

Volodin asked, "What is your objective in all this?"

Jack knew what he meant. Volodin was asking what it was that the United States wanted in return for not exposing the Russian government's payment to the Seven Strong Men.

Ryan said, "It is very simple. Your armor stops where it is, and returns to the Crimea. You will have won a small victory, but any victory at all is more than you deserve. If that happens, we will not connect the dots between yourself and Zenith."

"I cannot be blackmailed!"

"But you can be destroyed. Not by me. I don't want war. But you can be destroyed from within. Russia needs to know who is at its helm. No one in Russia will believe me. But there is evidence. Evidence from Nesterov and Castor and other men, and the evidence will speak for itself, and it will get out there."

"If you think I am afraid of your propaganda, you are mistaken."

"President Volodin, the old guard still alive in the KGB will look into the dates. The bankers will look into the account numbers. The bureau of prisons will look into information on Talanov. Several European nations will reinvestigate old crimes. If it is my propaganda that starts the snowball, it will only be for a moment, at the top of the hill. Everything I say will be proven now that everyone knows where to look."

Valeri Volodin hung up the phone.

An aide came on the line a second later. "Mr. President, shall I try to get him back?"

"No, thank you," Ryan said. "I delivered my

771

message. Now we have to wait to see his response to it."

Roman Talanov resigned from the FSB two days after Russia ceased offensive operations in Ukraine and pulled forces back to the Crimea. Typical of his career in government service, Talanov made no announcement himself; instead, Valeri Volodin went before his favorite news presenter, and after accepting high praise for his successes in stamping out terrorism in eastern Ukraine, he said he had a very unfortunate announcement to make.

"I have decided I have lost confidence in Roman Romanovich Talanov. Disturbing facts have come to light about his dealings with organized crime, and as the person responsible for the integrity of all Russian citizens, I recognize Talanov is not the right man for the job."

Volodin appointed a man no one had ever heard of — he himself picked him from a cabal of trusted advisers, though the man had no intelligence experience — and he ordered Talanov's name removed from all official correspondence.

Roman Talanov knew what it meant to be a disgraced *vory*. There was no more dangerous position in all of Russia, because everyone he had surrounded himself with became, in the blink of an eye, the very people most hazardous to him. He retreated to his dacha in Krasnodar Krai, on the Black Sea coast, with a security staff of twenty trusted men, and he armed them all from an armory of weapons stolen from a KGB Spetsnaz unit.

Valeri Volodin sent an emissary — he would not speak with Talanov himself — and assured him he would have government protection and all the proceeds from selling his Gazprom shares, in exchange for making no public announcements.

Talanov agreed. He had been following the orders of Valeri Volodin for more than thirty years; he really didn't know how to do anything else.

It was a member of his own staff who killed him. Six days after Talanov was outed as a KGB officer who misrepresented himself to earn *vory v zakonye* status, one of the junior members of his guard force, a civilian who secretly aspired to great things in the Seven Strong Men, waited for Talanov to step out of his shower and then stabbed him through the heart with a dagger. He took pictures of the body with his cell phone, and posted them on social media to brag of the event.

There was a special irony in the fact that the first image most Russians ever saw of the former intelligence chief was of his bloody naked body lying faceup on a tile floor, his eyes wide in death.

Jack Ryan, Jr., called his father from the back of the Hendley Associates jet when he was over the Atlantic. His dad had been worried about him for the past week for the simple reason that Jack had gone to London to move out of his flat, and even with Dom and Sam to help him, it still took a little time.

Jack didn't want to call his dad while he was still in the UK. Instead, he called his mom and sent e-mails, assuring them both that he'd be home soon.

Dom and Sam loved the UK, and Jack had to admit he was going to miss it greatly. He recognized it was his own melancholy when he arrived that had made his time here tough going at first, long before the Russian mob made the experience even less cheery.

But now he was on his way home, which meant he could talk to his father without having to hear all the concern in his voice that Jack had heard so much of the past few years. He realized he made his dad's tough life even tougher by his choice of profession, but he also realized one other thing.

If there was anyone on earth who understood the need to serve a greater good despite personal danger, it was his own father.

After establishing the fact that his son's next stop would be the United States of America, Jack Senior said, "Son, I haven't had a chance to thank you for passing me all the intel last week. You turned the tide. You damn well saved a lot of lives."

Jack Junior wasn't patting his own back, though. "I don't know, Dad. Volodin is still alive and in power. They are dancing in the streets in the parts of Ukraine where he is now the head honcho. Doesn't quite feel like a victory."

Ryan said, "It's not the ending any of us wanted. But we stopped a war."

"Are you sure you didn't just delay it?"

Jack Senior sighed. "No. I'm not sure at all. In fact, in some ways a weakened Volodin is even more dangerous. He might be like a wounded animal. Ready to lash out at anything. But I've been at this sort of thing for a while, and I feel like we maximized benefit and minimized detriment. A lot of good people lost their lives over this: Sergey, Oxley, men in and out of uniform serving in Eastern Europe. It's okay to wish we got more out of this, but the real world bites back."

"Yeah," Jack Junior said. "It does."

Jack Senior said, "We didn't lose, Jack. We just didn't win."

That sank in after a moment. "Okay."

Ryan asked, "What's your plan now, son?"

"I want to come home. I've talked to Gerry already. He found a new building in Fairfax County, and Gavin has come up with some new technology to help us move forward."

Ryan said, "That's good. I know you miss working with the team. I can't say I don't wish you would live a safer life, though."

Jack Junior said, "You saw what happened when I took a boring job with no chance for danger."

"Yeah, I did. I sent you off after some of that danger, didn't I?"

"You trusted me. I appreciate that. Thanks."

"You bet, sport. Drop by as soon as you can when you get home. I miss you."

"I will, Dad. I miss you, too."

EPILOGUE

Thirty years earlier

CIA analyst Jack Ryan climbed out of the taxi in front of his house on Grizedale Close. He'd borrowed a coat from a colleague at Century House, and he was glad he had, because it was a cold night here in Chatham. The street was empty, and he figured it had to have been after midnight, but he'd taken his watch off in Berlin when the doctor treated his injury, and he'd thrown it in his suitcase after that.

It had occurred to him on the train from Victoria Station that he should have called home from his office. Instead Sir Basil had insisted he get his forearm looked over by their doctor, and then, after that, he'd spent hours reviewing a facsimile of a copy of the contact report he'd written that morning at Mission Berlin. His first draft ran some eleven pages, and while reading it at Century House he'd added another five pages of information, using a map of Berlin and some other reference materials to help him get every detail just right.

He'd been too distracted to call Cathy then, and by the time he thought of it he was already on the train.

He entered through the front door as quietly as he could; he didn't want to wake the kids. He put his luggage down in the foyer and started to take off his shoes so he could step even a little more quietly, but he heard Cathy moving up the hall in the dark.

Cathy all but leapt into his arms. "I missed you," she said.

"I missed you, too."

It was a tender moment, broken only by "Did you get a new coat?"

"Oh. It's borrowed. Long story."

They hugged and kissed all the way to the living room, where Cathy sat on the couch. She looked beautiful to him, even in her housecoat. Jack pulled off his coat, forgetting that his right forearm looked like it had been mummified.

"Oh my God. What did you do?"

Jack shrugged. He couldn't lie to Cathy, because she was his wife, but he also couldn't lie to her because she was a surgeon. She'd take one look at his forearm and know that he'd been slashed by a knife.

Within seconds, she had the bandages unwrapped and held his arm up to the light from the lamp on the end table. She examined it with a practiced eye. "You are lucky, Jack. It's long, but it's not deep at all. It looks like someone did a good job dressing it."

"Yes."

She started rewrapping it. "I'll clean it again and rebandage it in the morning. What happened?"

"I can't say."

She looked at the injury, then up into his eyes with an expression that was one of both concern and hurt. "I knew you were going to say that."

"I *can't*," he repeated himself, imploring her to not dig any deeper.

And this told her most everything she needed to know. "The only reason you wouldn't be able to tell me is that this had something to do with the CIA. Were you attacked?"

You might say that, he thought. *But not just by the German terrorist with the knife. There was also the little matter of the sniper and the unknown goons by the Berlin Wall.* He didn't say any of this, of course. Instead, he just said, "I'm fine, babe. I promise."

She did not believe him. "I've been watching the news. The restaurant in Switzerland. The art gallery in Berlin. Jesus, Jack, which one was it?"

Ryan could have said "Both," or he could have been pedantic and pointed out that it wasn't actually an art gallery. Instead, he said, "You have to believe me, Cathy. I didn't go looking for any trouble."

"You never do. You just can't turn away from it when it presents itself."

Jack looked across the room. He was too tired for a fight, and there wasn't much he could say, anyway. She was right. She didn't marry a soldier or a spy. She married a commodities trader and a historian. He was the one getting himself into situations like Berlin. He had no valid argument that Berlin came looking for *him.*

He said the only thing he could think of, and it was truly the only thing that mattered to him now: "I love you, and I'm glad to be home."

"I love you too, Jack, and I like having you around. Which is why it's so damn difficult when you are gone for days, and then come home with a knife wound. Please tell me you understand that."

"Of course I do."

They hugged. There was nothing about this matter that was resolved, really, but she showed him she was going to let it go for now.

Cathy said, "I'm sorry, but I have surgery at nine."

Jack looked at the time. One a.m. The night before at this time, he'd been sitting with Marta Scheuring, and two nights earlier he'd been minutes away from a gun battle. Three nights earlier he'd stood in Zug, Switzerland, watching a building burn.

Jack kissed his wife, and she headed to the bedroom. He called after her, "I'll be right in after I check on the kids."

Ryan looked in on little Sally. She was sound asleep, with her stuffed bunny clutched tightly. He stepped in silently and kissed her on her forehead.

Next he leaned into little Jack's room, and he was surprised to see his toddler standing up in the crib. Under a shock of black hair were wide blue eyes and a big smile for his daddy.

Ryan laughed softly. "Hey, sport." He picked Jack up and hugged him, then carried his little boy into the living room, where he sat on the sofa with the boy on his lap.

It was quiet in the room even with the ticking of the clock, and as Ryan sat there he felt his son's heartbeat against his own chest.

Suddenly the danger and death of the past few days rushed to the front of his mind. His life had been on the line multiple times, and now his own heart pounded in terror with the knowledge that he could have lost everything he had, everything he held.

And his family could have lost him.

He squeezed Jack tighter, and the little boy squirmed in his arms.

He told himself he had to get away from this life before little Jack and little Sally lost their father.

As he sat there contemplating his own mortality and what he suddenly saw as the irresponsibility of playing fast and loose with his life, he thought not only of the peril he had been in, but also of others. Of David Penright, of the two Swiss bankers he'd never even met, the innocents killed in Switzerland and Germany, and he thought of Ingrid Bretz, of Marta, and of the man who'd come out of the trees to step in to help a stranger, at great danger to himself.

Jack got into this intelligence game to make the world a better place. It was naive, he had the self-awareness to admit this, but at the end of the day, he knew he'd done some good. Maybe not much, but hell, he was just one man, and he was doing his best.

He looked down at Jack Junior again, and was pleased to see he'd fallen asleep, just like that, right there in his arms.

Ryan knew he could not walk away from doing his best. He would do whatever he could to stay safe so that he could live a long life and provide for his family, but he realized now that the more he did himself, the harder he fought to make this world a better place, the greater the chance the world Jack Junior would inherit would be just a little better off, and a little safer for him.

Jack figured his own late father, a Baltimore cop named Emmet Ryan, had probably held him in his arms and thought the same thing. Hell, it was every father's wish, though he wondered how hopeful it might be. For all Ryan knew, little Jack would face dangers Ryan himself could never imagine, but as he stood up and carried his sleeping son back to his room, he realized every father owed it to his children to try.

ABOUT THE AUTHORS

Thirty years ago, **Tom Clancy** was a Maryland insurance broker with a passion for naval history. Years before, he had been an English major at Baltimore's Loyola College and had always dreamed of writing a novel. His first effort, *The Hunt for Red October*, sold briskly as a result of rave reviews, then catapulted onto the *New York Times* bestseller list after President Reagan pronounced it "the perfect yarn." From that day forward, Clancy established himself as an undisputed master at blending exceptional realism and authenticity, intricate plotting, and razor-sharp suspense. He passed away in October 2013.

Mark Greaney has a degree in international relations and political science. He is the author of the Gray Man novels, the most recent of which is *Dead Eye*. In his research for those novels, he has traveled to a dozen countries and trained alongside military and law enforcement in the use of firearms, battlefield medicine, and close-range combat tactics.